The Hills of ESTRELLA ROJA

For my parents, Steve & Alma,
for always encouraging my love of art & stories
(especially the spooky ones).

Clarion Books is an imprint of HarperCollins Publishers.
HarperAlley is an imprint of HarperCollins Publishers.

Copyright © 2023 by Ashley Robin Franklin

Library of Congress Control Number: 2023931288
ISBN 978−0−35−856702−8

Colors by Nakata Whittle
The artist used paper and ink for illustrations. Colors were done in Clip Studio Paint EX.
Letters by Ashley Robin Franklin

23 24 25 26 27 GPS 10 9 8 7 6 5 4 3 2 1

First Edition

The Hills of ESTRELLA ROJA

By Ashley Robin Franklin

Clarion Books
Imprints of HarperCollinsPublishers

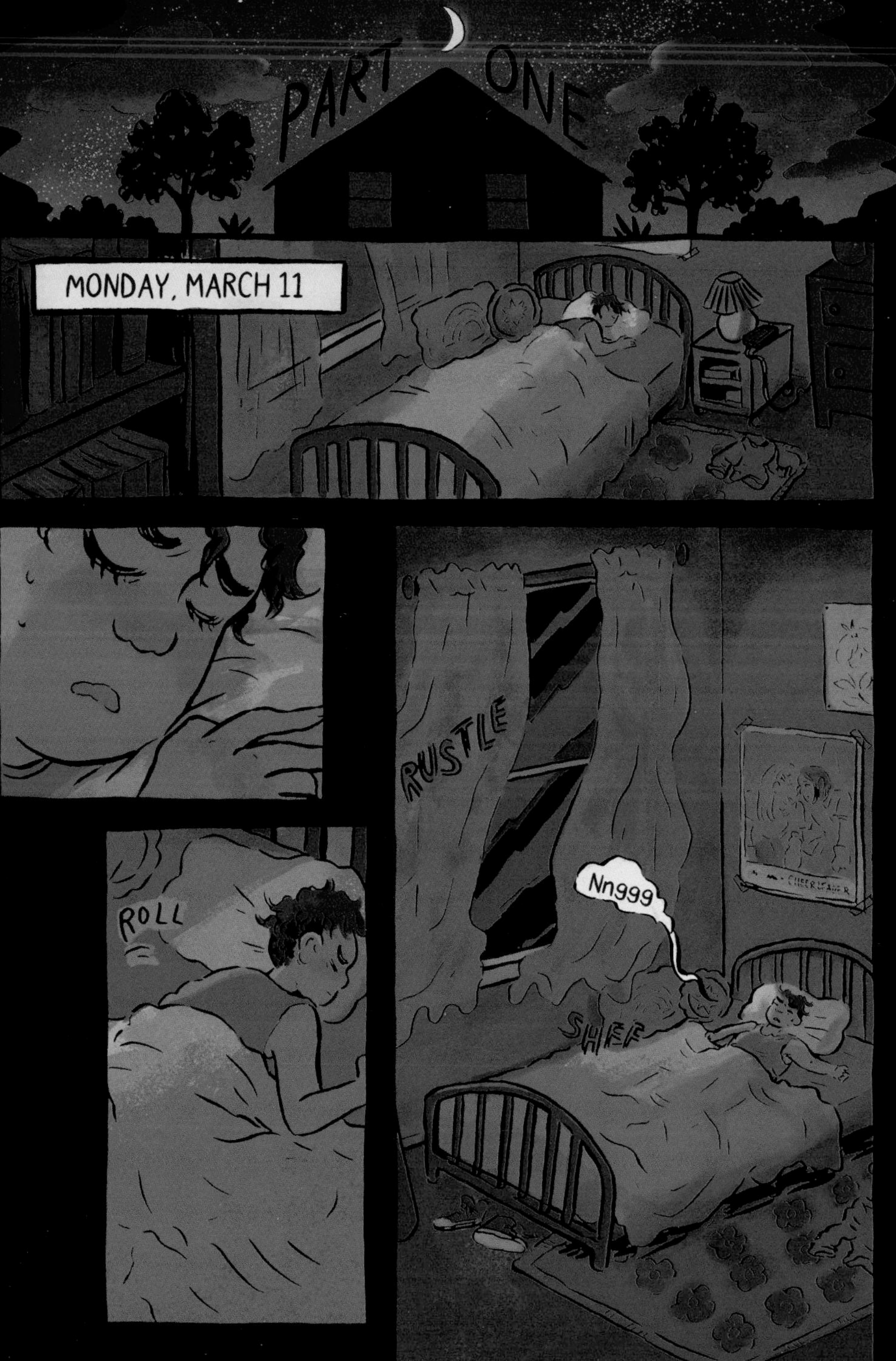
PART ONE
MONDAY, MARCH 11
ROLL
RUSTLE
Nnggg
SHFF

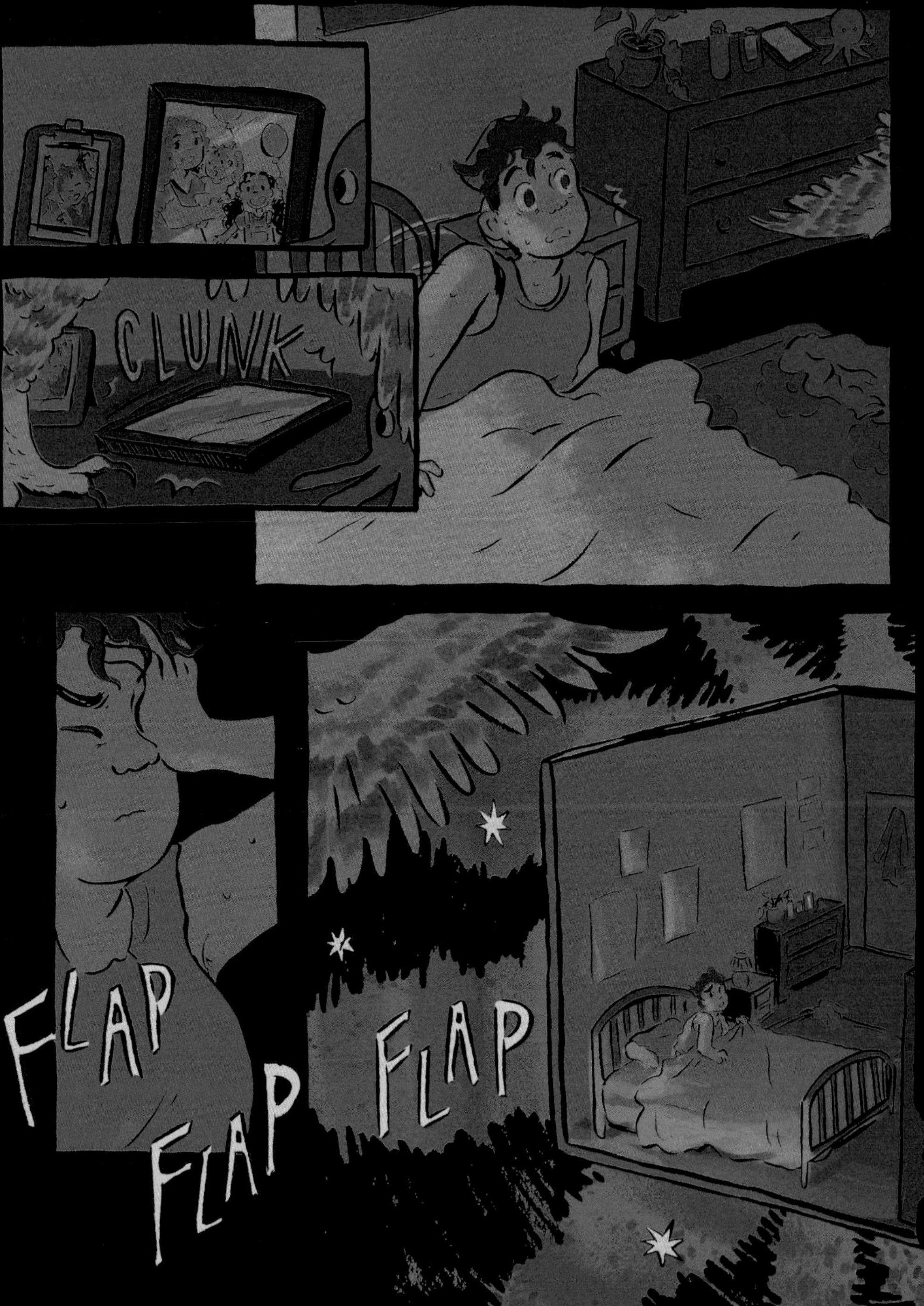
CLUNK
FLAP
FLAP
FLAP

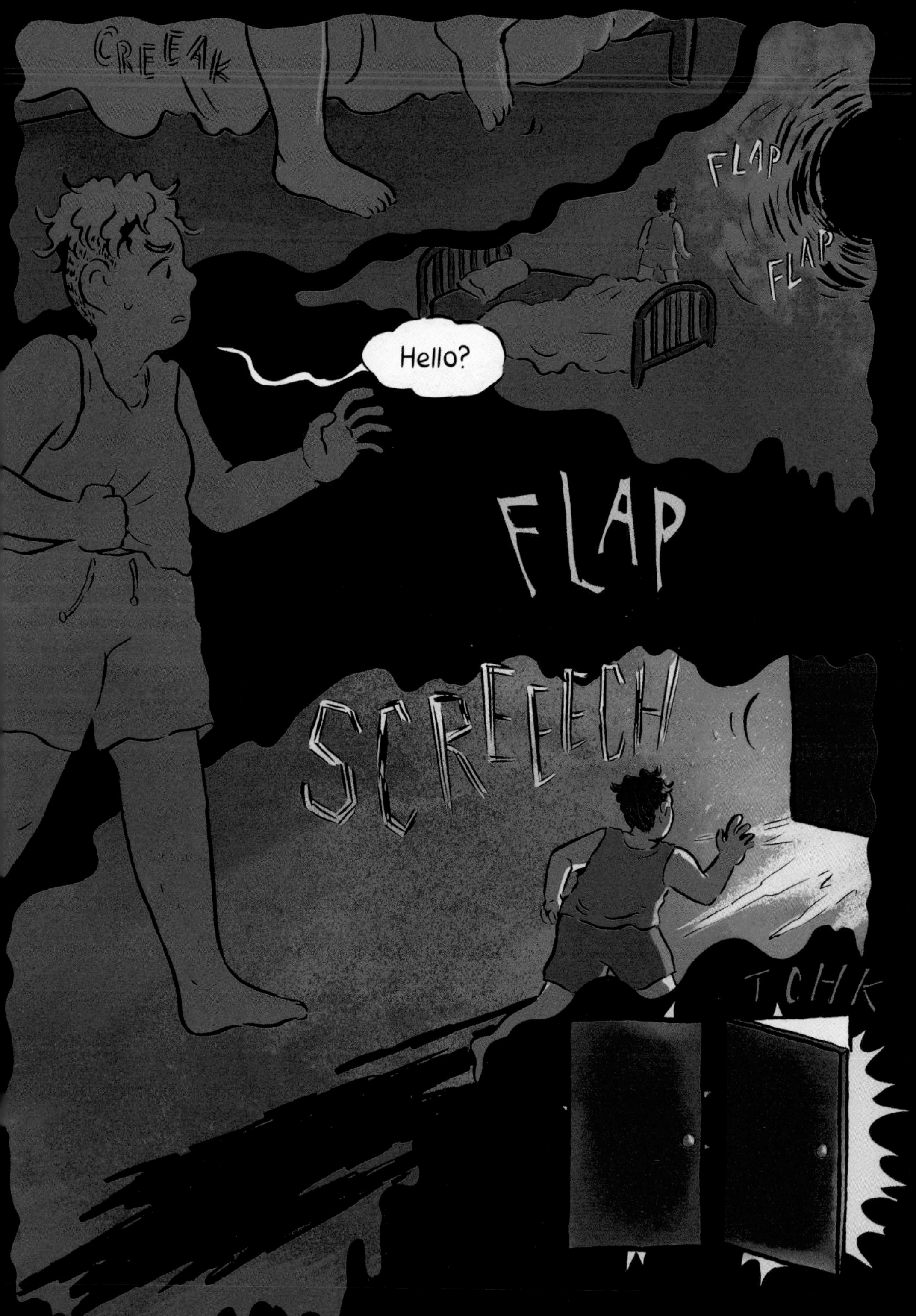
CREEAK
FLAP
FLAP
Hello?
FLAP
SCREEECH
TCHK

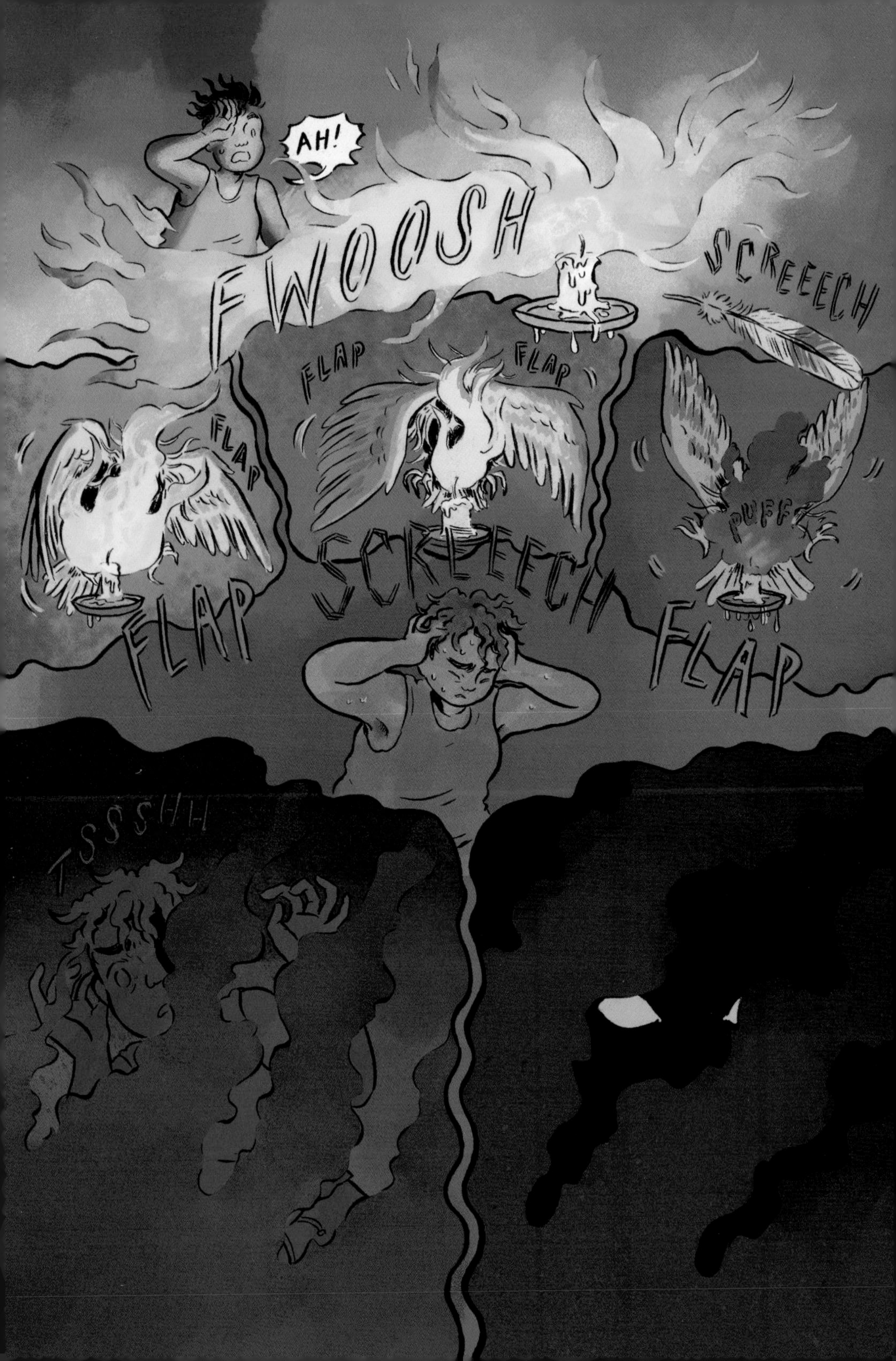
AH!
FWOOSH
SCREEECH
FLAP
FLAP
FLAP
FLAP
SCREEECH
PUFF
FLAP
TSSSHH

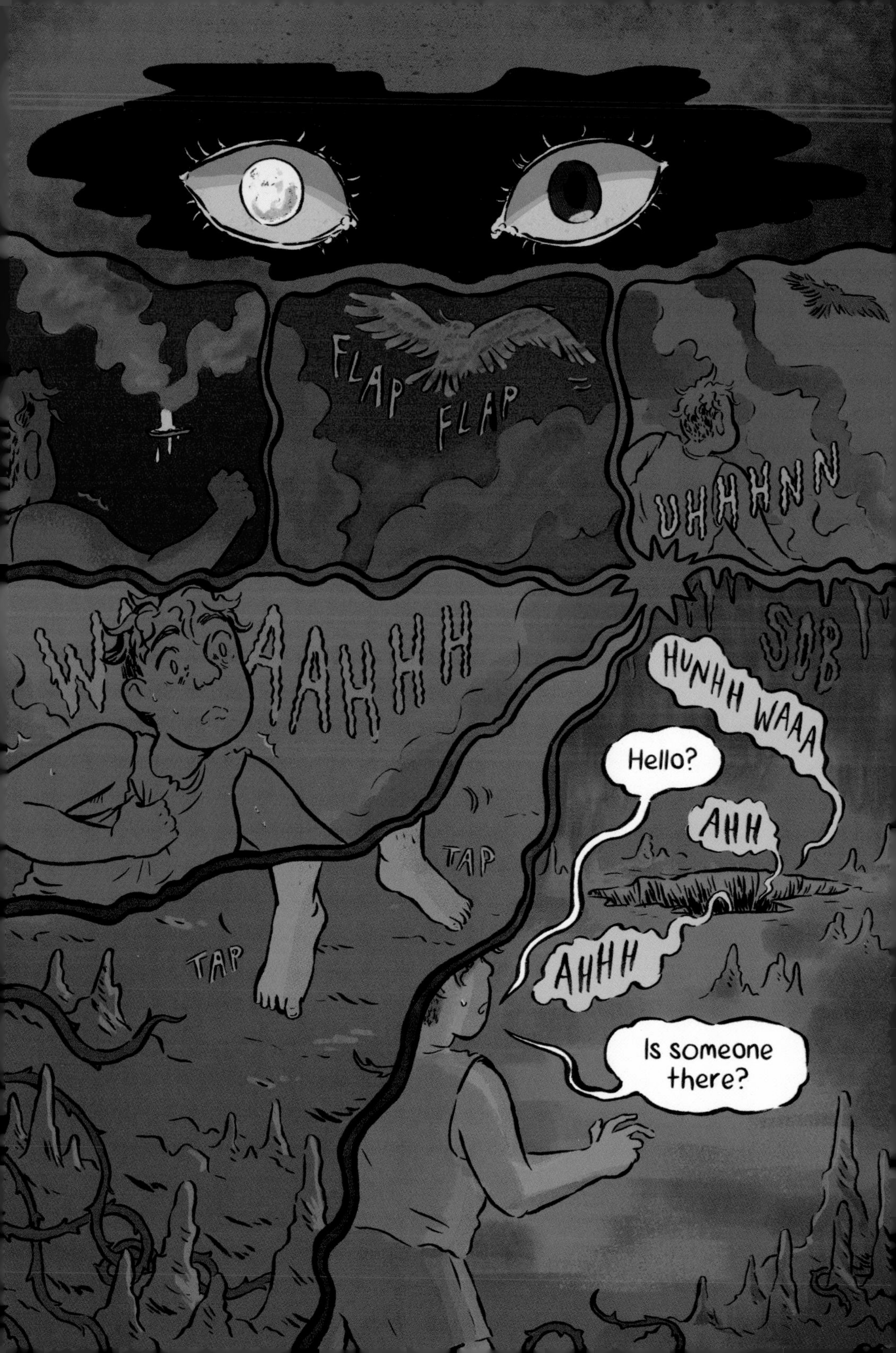
FLAP FLAP
UHHHNN
WAAHHH
SOB
HUNHH WAAA
Hello?
AHH
TAP
TAP
AHHH
Is someone there?

OUT. OUT.
OUT.
MARI,
LET US OUT!
HELP US, MARI!
HUFF HUFF
What a weird dream . . .
CREEAK
tap
tap
tap

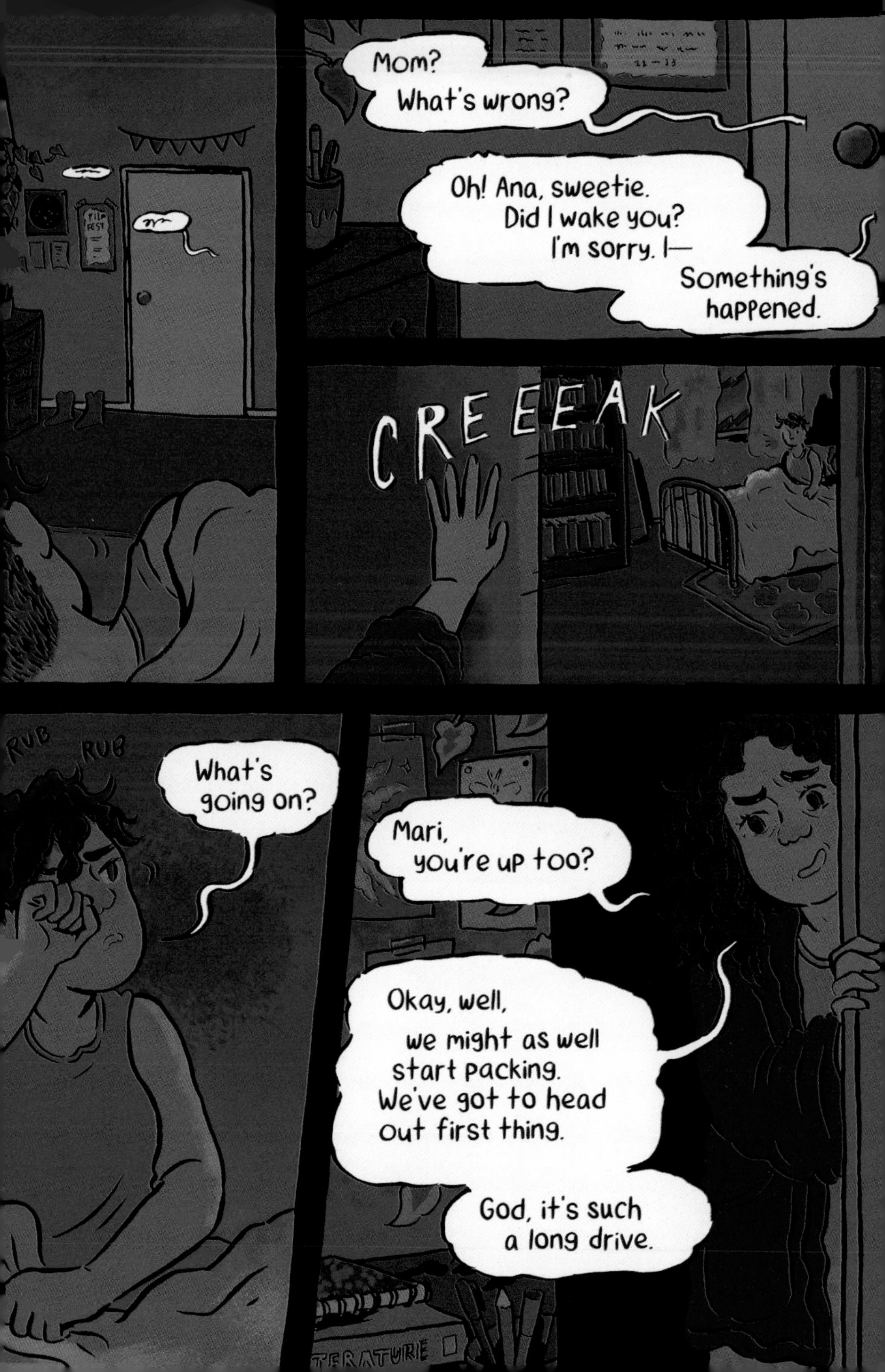
Mom?
What's wrong?
Oh! Ana, sweetie.
Did I wake you?
I'm sorry. I—
Something's happened.
CREEEAK
RUB RUB
What's going on?
Mari, you're up too?
Okay, well,
we might as well start packing.
We've got to head out first thing.
God, it's such a long drive.

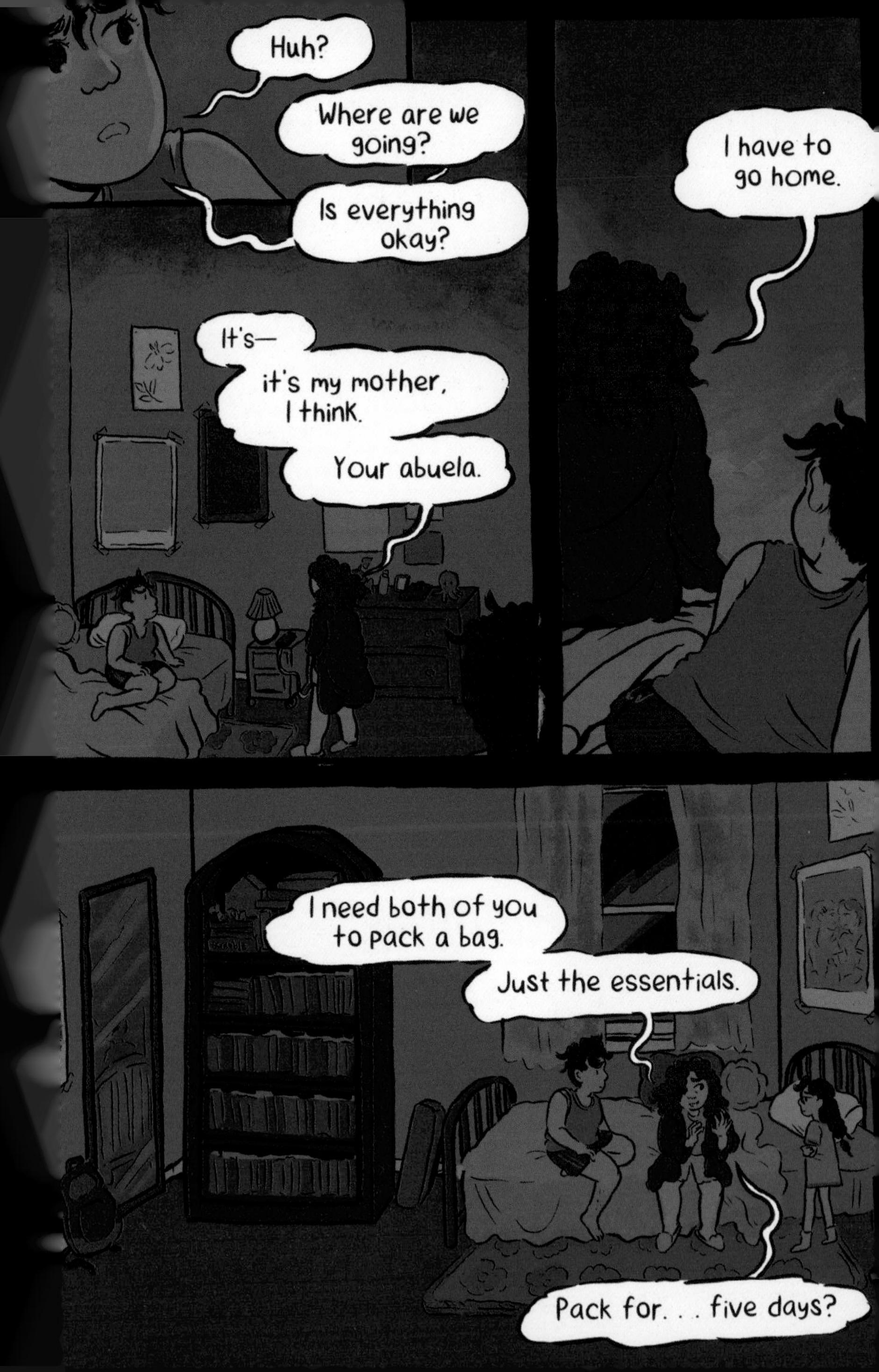
Huh?
Where are we going?
Is everything okay?
I have to go home.
It's—
it's my mother, I think.
Your abuela.
I need both of you to pack a bag.
Just the essentials.
Pack for. . . five days?

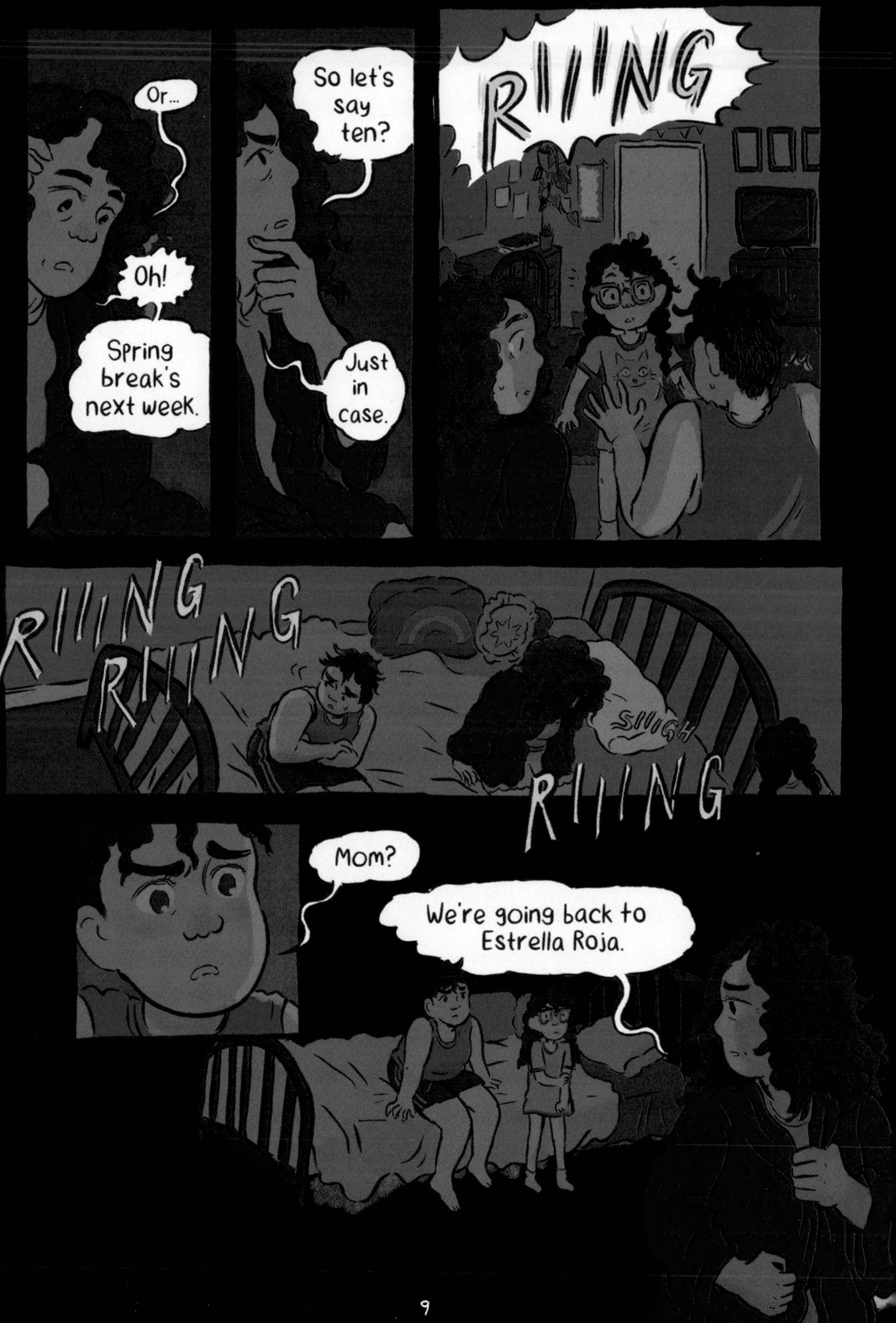
Or...
Oh!
Spring break's next week.
So let's say ten?
Just in case.
RIIING
RIIING
RIIING
SIIIGH
RIIING
Mom?
We're going back to Estrella Roja.

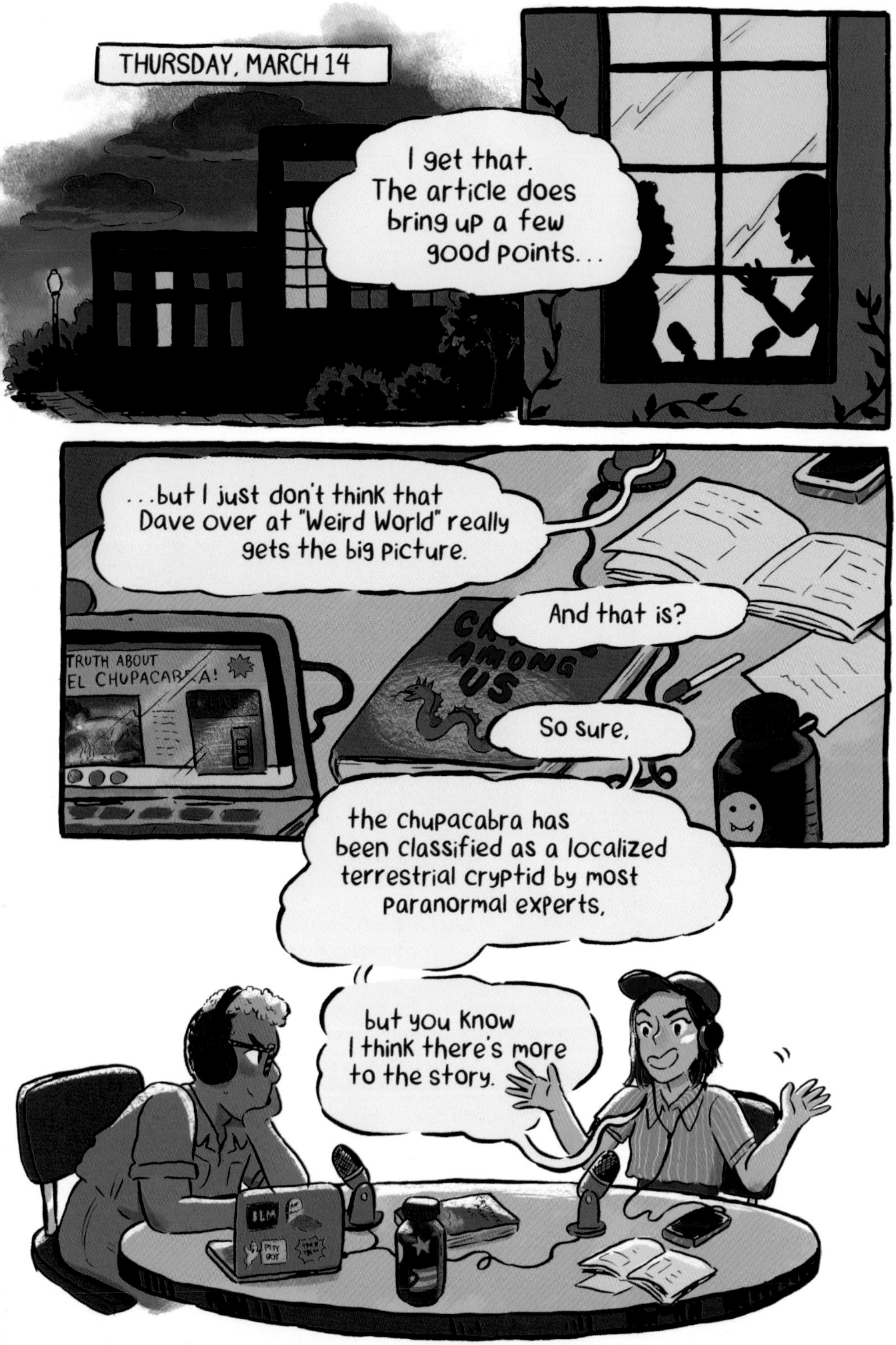
THURSDAY, MARCH 14
I get that. The article does bring up a few good points...
...but I just don't think that Dave over at "Weird World" really gets the big picture.
And that is?
TRUTH ABOUT EL CHUPACABRA!
So sure,
the chupacabra has been classified as a localized terrestrial cryptid by most paranormal experts,
but you know I think there's more to the story.
BLM

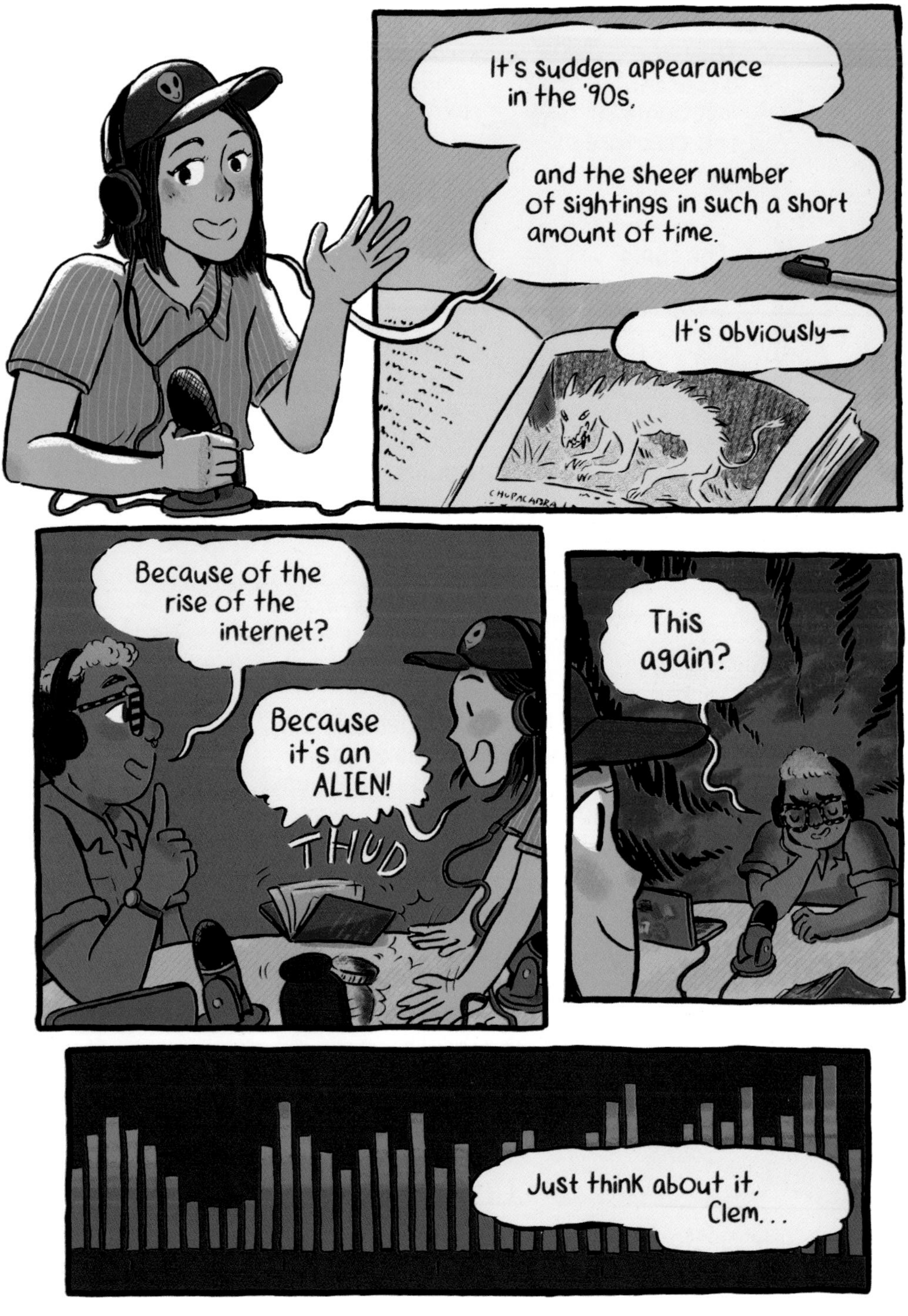
It's sudden appearance in the '90s,
and the sheer number of sightings in such a short amount of time.
It's obviously—
CHUPACABRA
Because of the rise of the internet?
Because it's an ALIEN!
THUD
This again?
Just think about it, Clem...

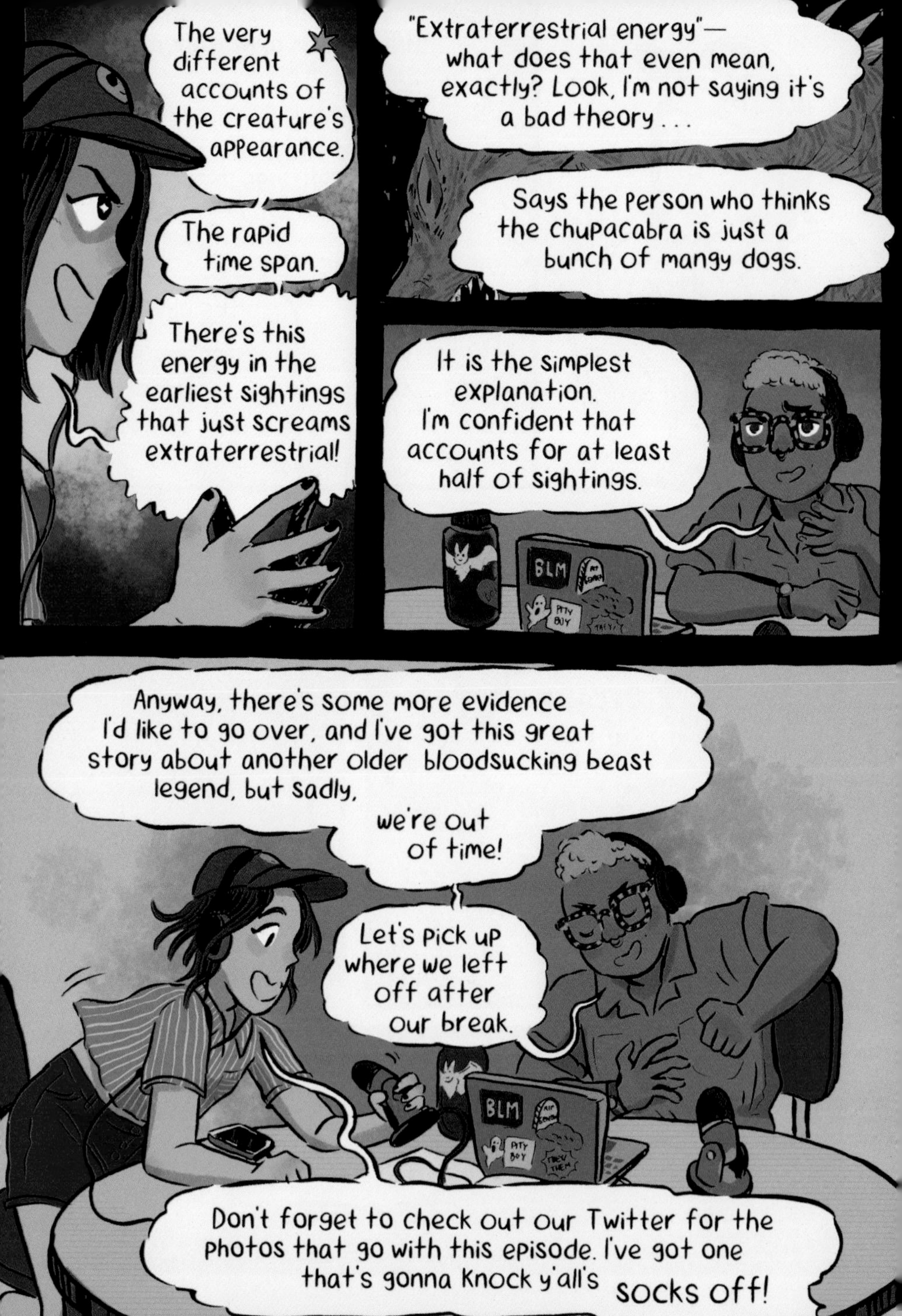
The very different accounts of the creature's appearance.
The rapid time span.
There's this energy in the earliest sightings that just screams extraterrestrial!
"Extraterrestrial energy"— what does that even mean, exactly? Look, I'm not saying it's a bad theory . . .
Says the person who thinks the chupacabra is just a bunch of mangy dogs.
It is the simplest explanation. I'm confident that accounts for at least half of sightings.
BLM
PITY BOY
Anyway, there's some more evidence I'd like to go over, and I've got this great story about another older bloodsucking beast legend, but sadly,
we're out of time!
Let's pick up where we left off after our break.
BLM
PITY BOY
Don't forget to check out our Twitter for the photos that go with this episode. I've got one that's gonna knock y'all's socks off!

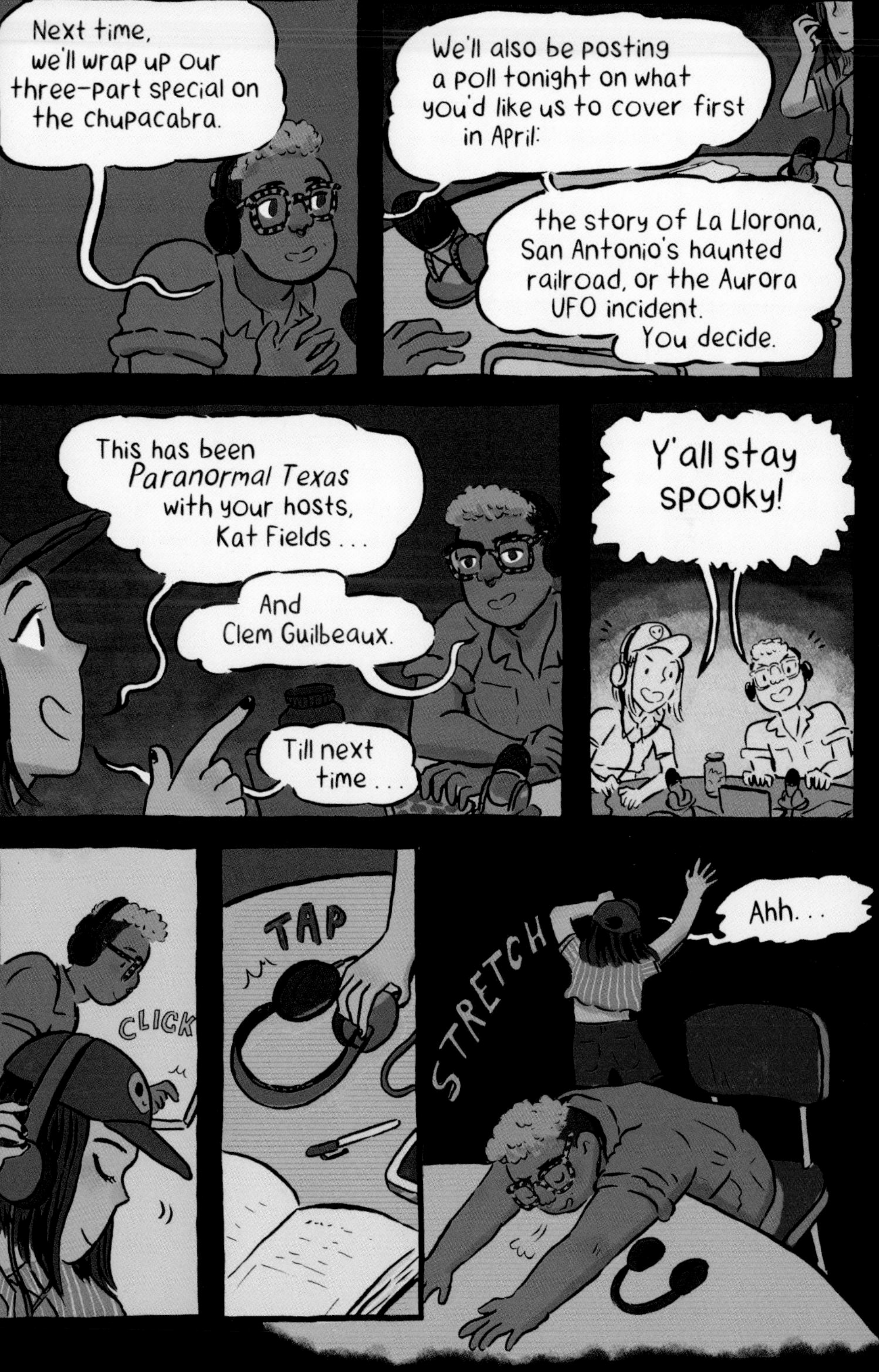
Next time, we'll wrap up our three-part special on the chupacabra.
We'll also be posting a poll tonight on what you'd like us to cover first in April:
the story of La Llorona, San Antonio's haunted railroad, or the Aurora UFO incident. You decide.
This has been *Paranormal Texas* with your hosts, Kat Fields . . .
And Clem Guilbeaux.
Till next time . . .
Y'all stay spooky!
CLICK
TAP
STRETCH
Ahh. . .

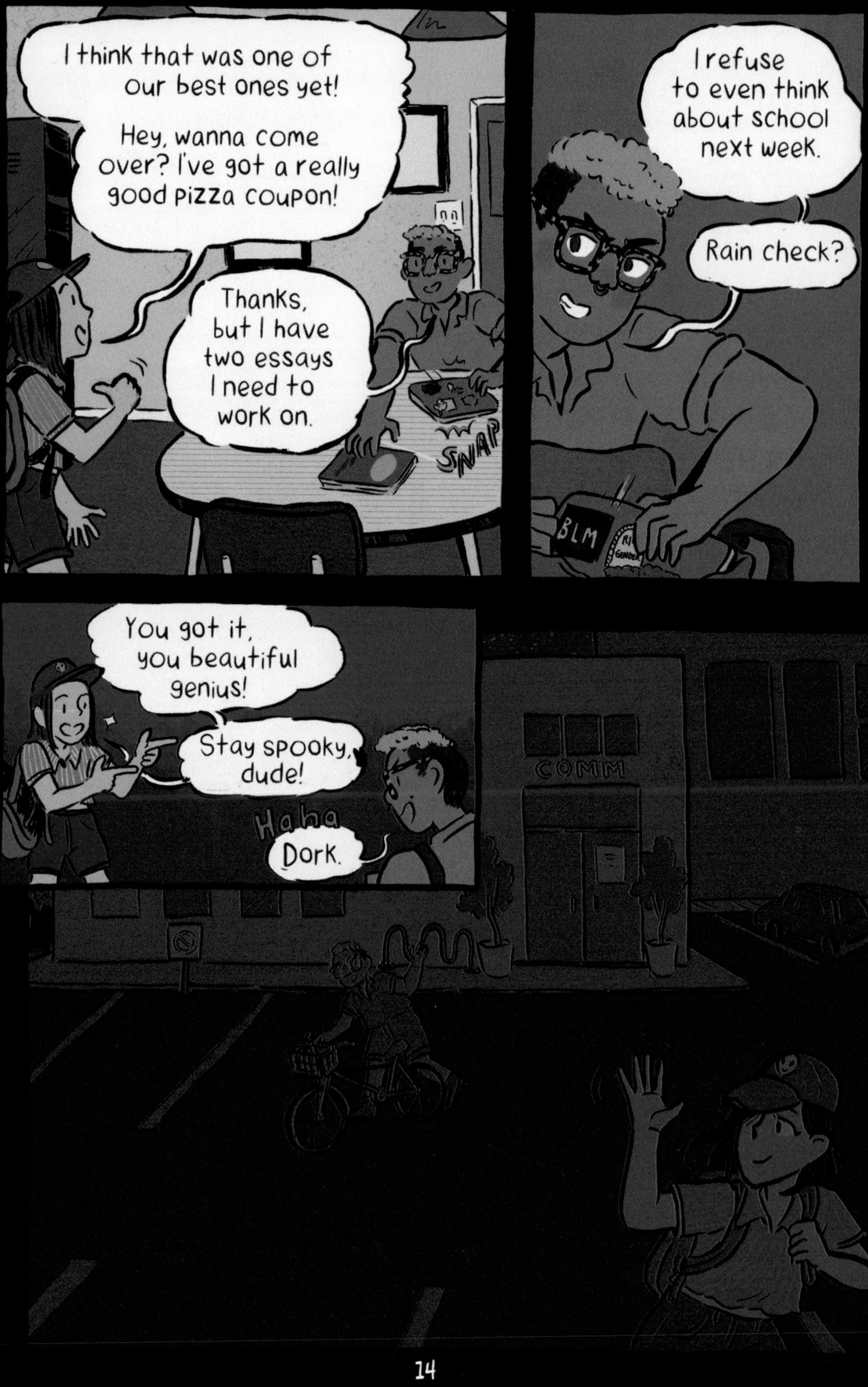
I think that was one of our best ones yet!
Hey, wanna come over? I've got a really good pizza coupon!
Thanks, but I have two essays I need to work on.
SNAP
I refuse to even think about school next week.
Rain check?
BLM
You got it, you beautiful genius!
Stay spooky, dude!
Haha
Dork.
COMM

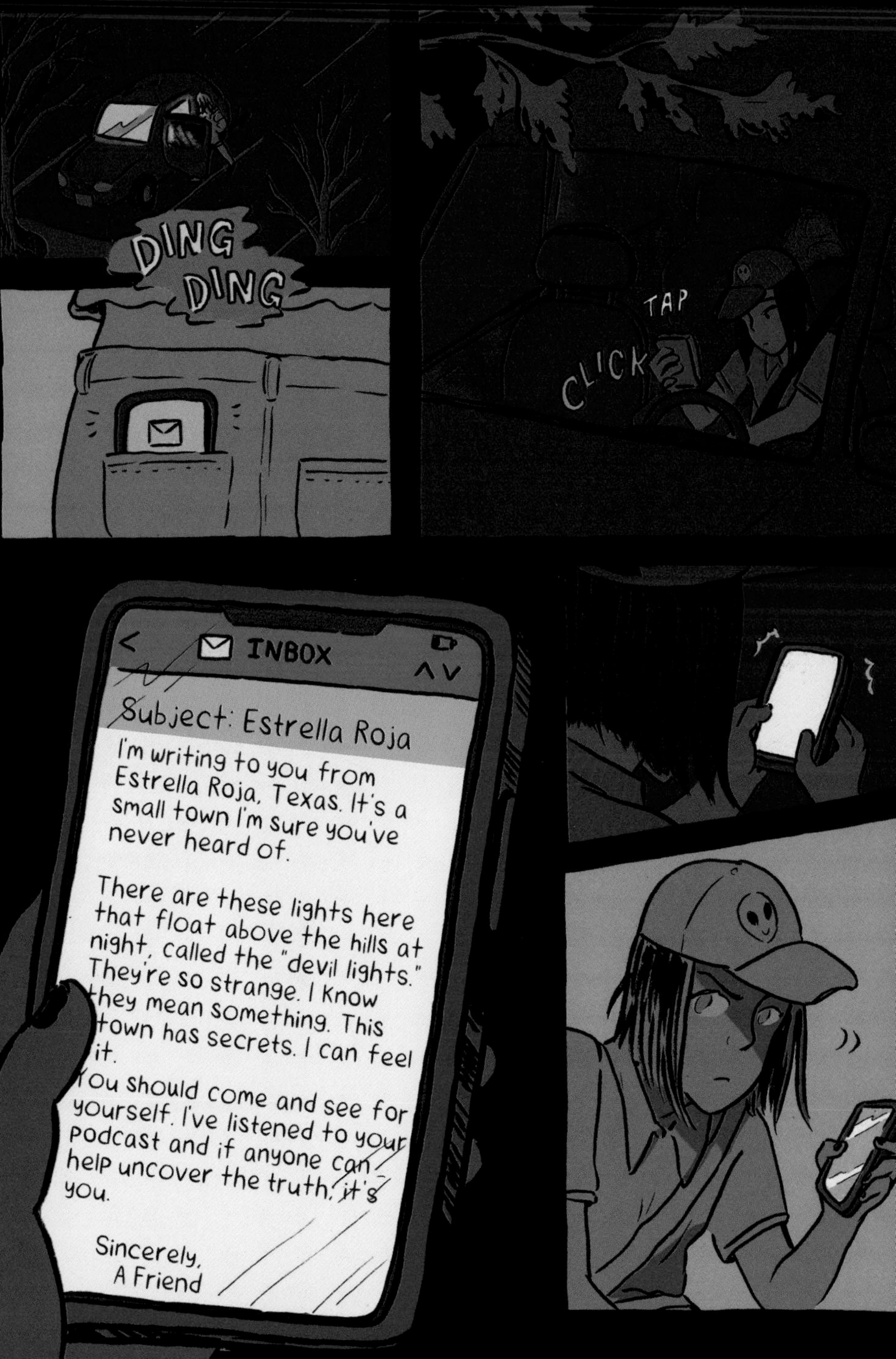
DING DING
TAP
CLICK
INBOX
Subject: Estrella Roja
I'm writing to you from Estrella Roja, Texas. It's a small town I'm sure you've never heard of.
There are these lights here that float above the hills at night, called the "devil lights." They're so strange. I know they mean something. This town has secrets. I can feel it.
You should come and see for yourself. I've listened to your podcast and if anyone can help uncover the truth, it's you.
Sincerely,
A Friend

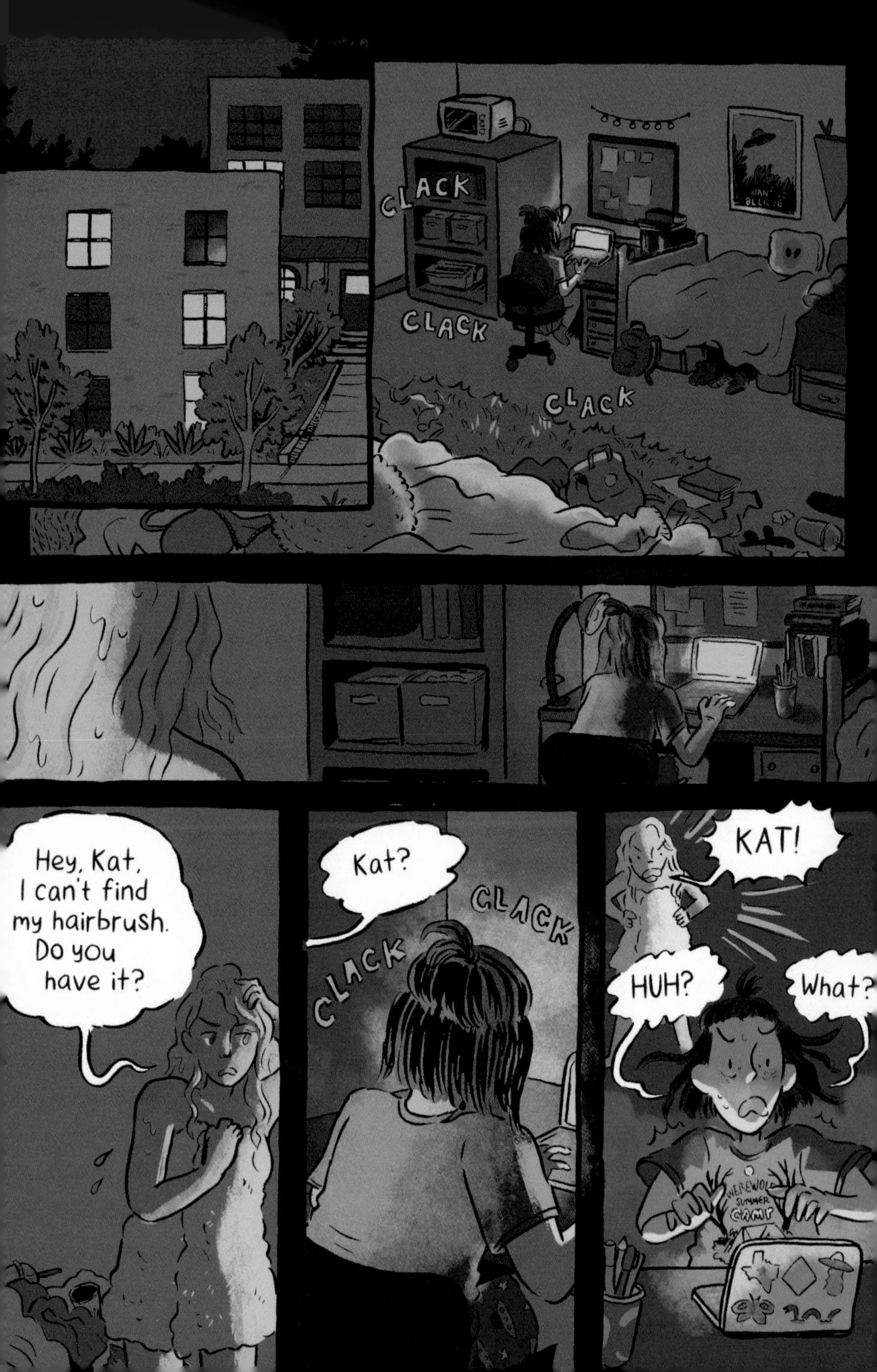
CLACK
CLACK
CLACK
Hey, Kat, I can't find my hairbrush. Do you have it?
Kat?
CLACK
CLACK
KAT!
HUH?
What?
WEREWOLF SUMMER CAMP

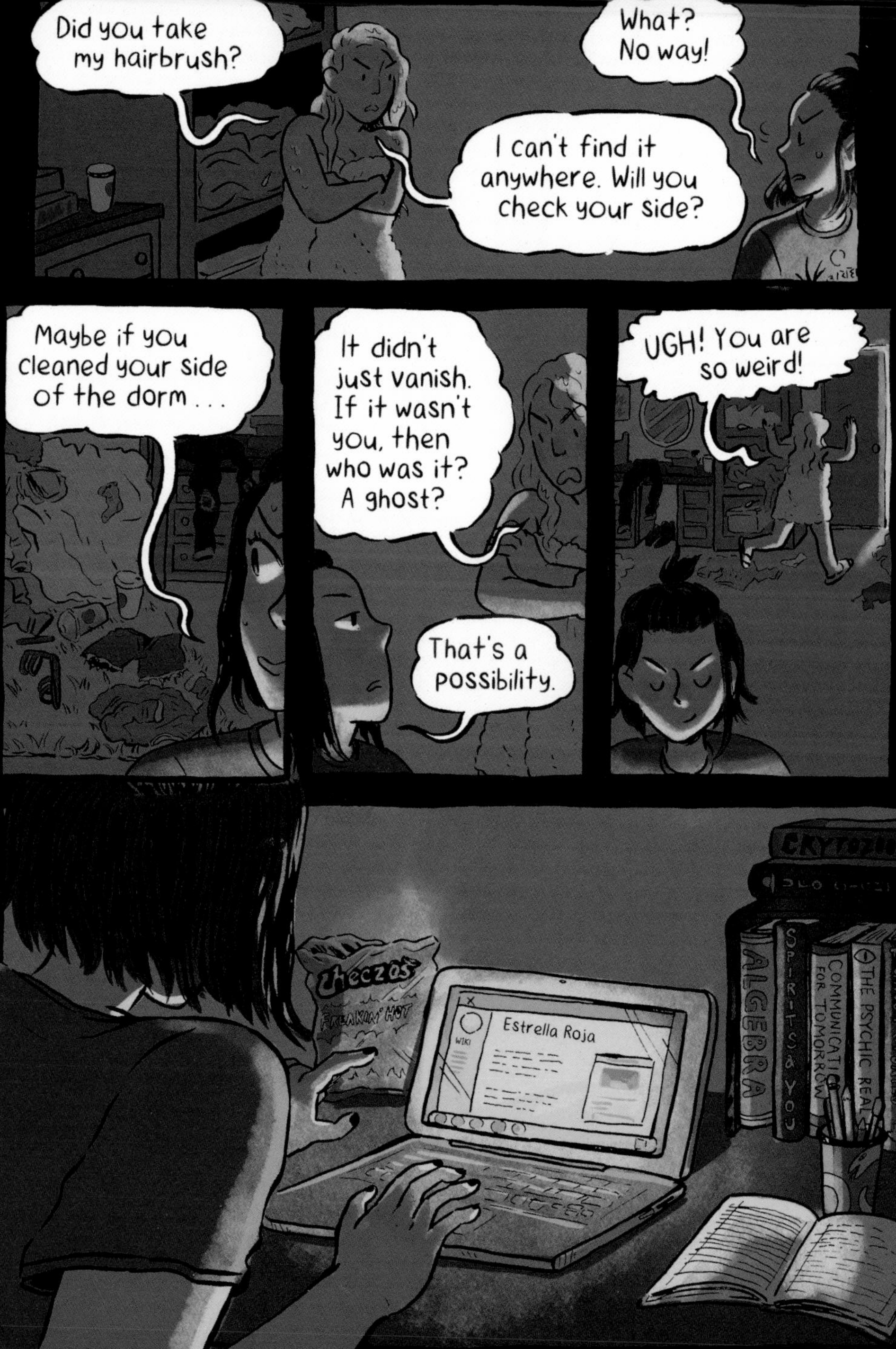
Did you take my hairbrush?
What? No way!
I can't find it anywhere. Will you check your side?
Maybe if you cleaned your side of the dorm . . .
It didn't just vanish. If it wasn't you, then who was it? A ghost?
That's a possibility.
UGH! You are so weird!
Cheezos
FREAKIN' HOT
Estrella Roja
WIKI
ALGEBRA
SPIRITS & YOU
COMMUNICATI FOR TOMORROW
THE PSYCHIC REAL
GHOST STORIES

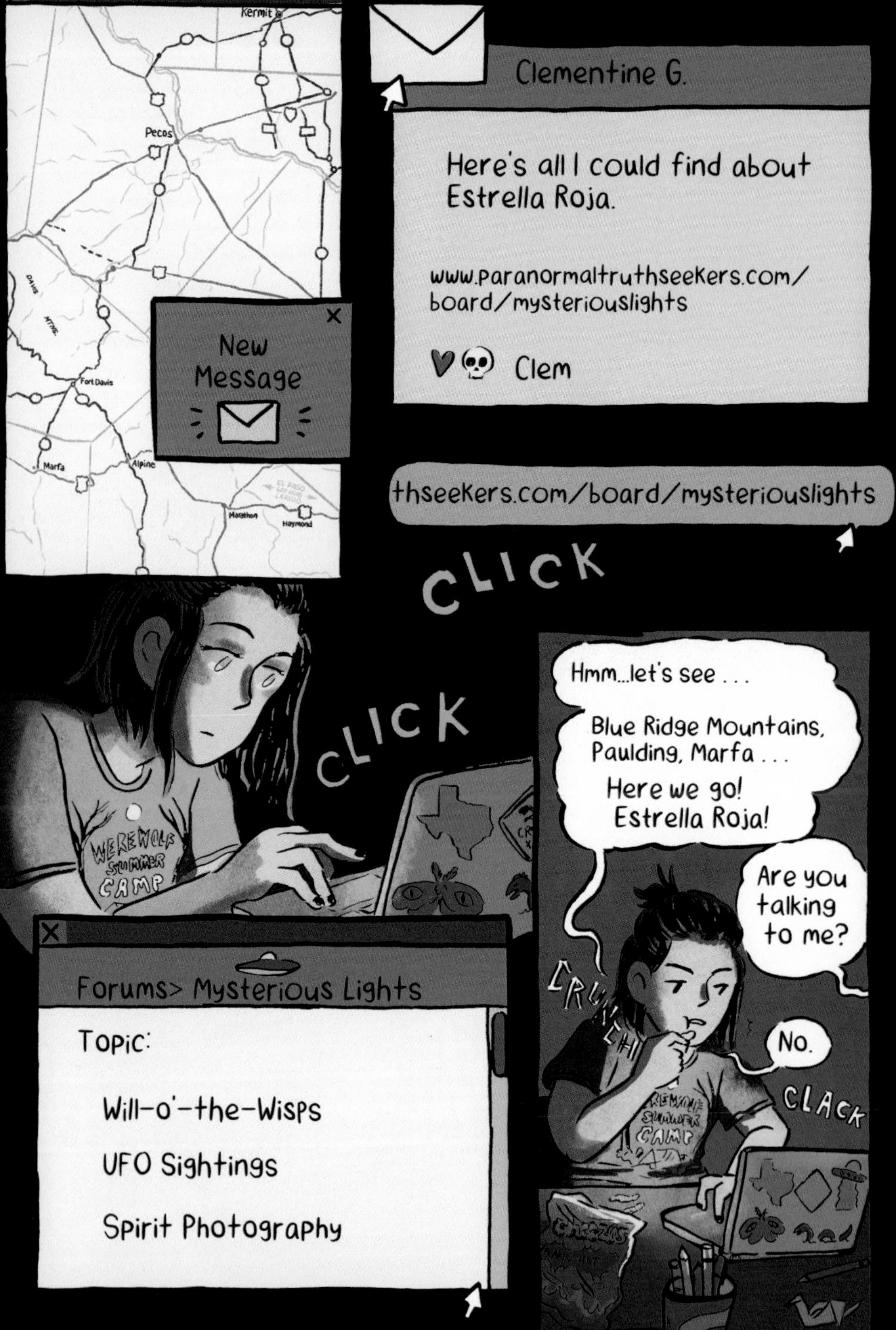
Kermit
Pecos
Fort Davis
Marfa
Alpine
Marathon
Haymond
New Message
Clementine G.
Here's all I could find about Estrella Roja.
www.paranormaltruthseekers.com/board/mysteriouslights
Clem
thseekers.com/board/mysteriouslights
CLICK
CLICK
WEREWOLF SUMMER CAMP
Hmm...let's see . . .
Blue Ridge Mountains, Paulding, Marfa . . .
Here we go! Estrella Roja!
Are you talking to me?
CRUNCH
No.
CLACK
Forums> Mysterious Lights
Topic:
Will-o'-the-Wisps
UFO Sightings
Spirit Photography

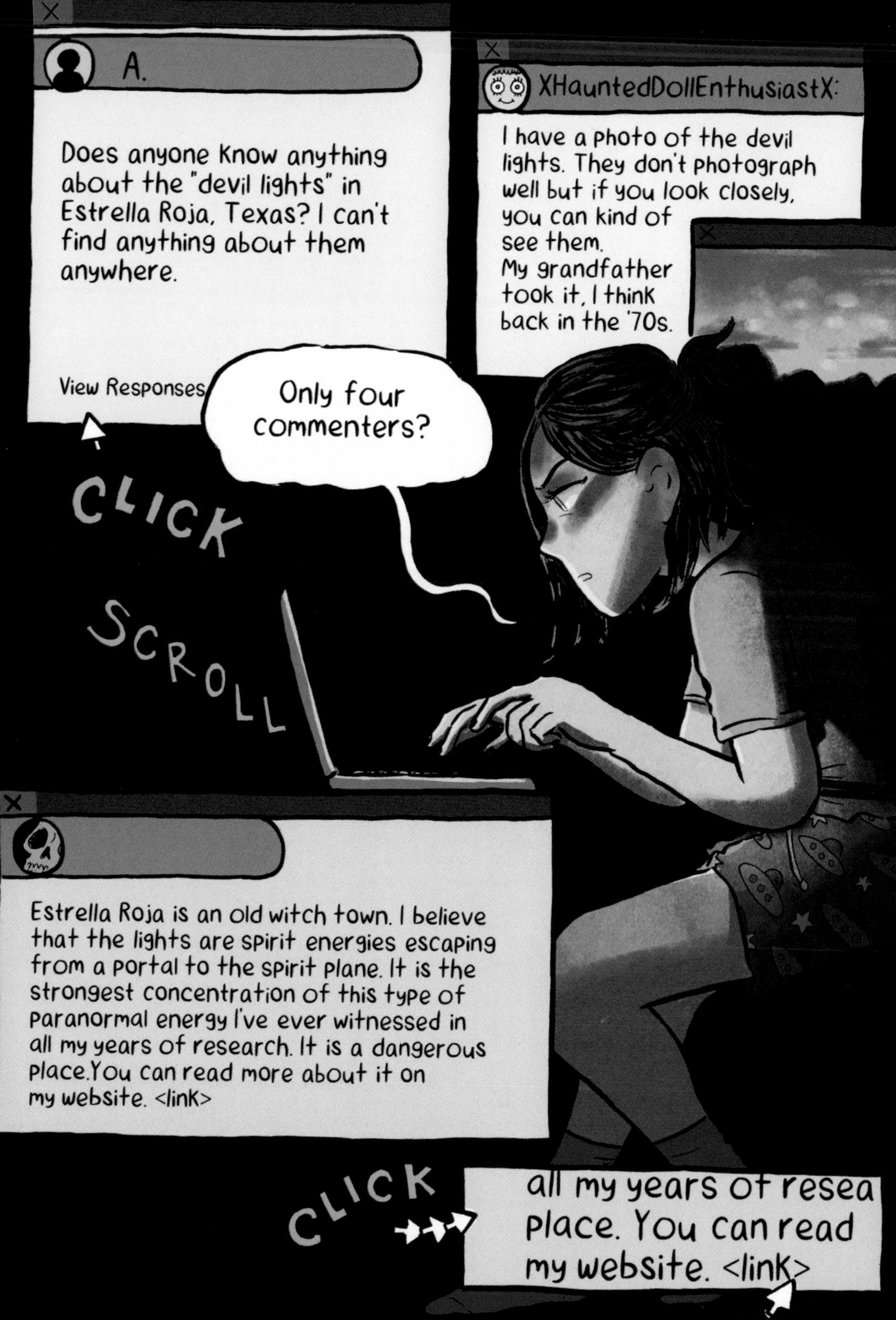
A.
Does anyone know anything about the "devil lights" in Estrella Roja, Texas? I can't find anything about them anywhere.
View Responses
XHauntedDollEnthusiastX:
I have a photo of the devil lights. They don't photograph well but if you look closely, you can kind of see them.
My grandfather took it, I think back in the '70s.
Only four commenters?
CLICK
SCROLL
Estrella Roja is an old witch town. I believe that the lights are spirit energies escaping from a portal to the spirit plane. It is the strongest concentration of this type of paranormal energy I've ever witnessed in all my years of research. It is a dangerous place.You can read more about it on my website. <link>
CLICK
all my years of resea
place. You can read
my website. <link>

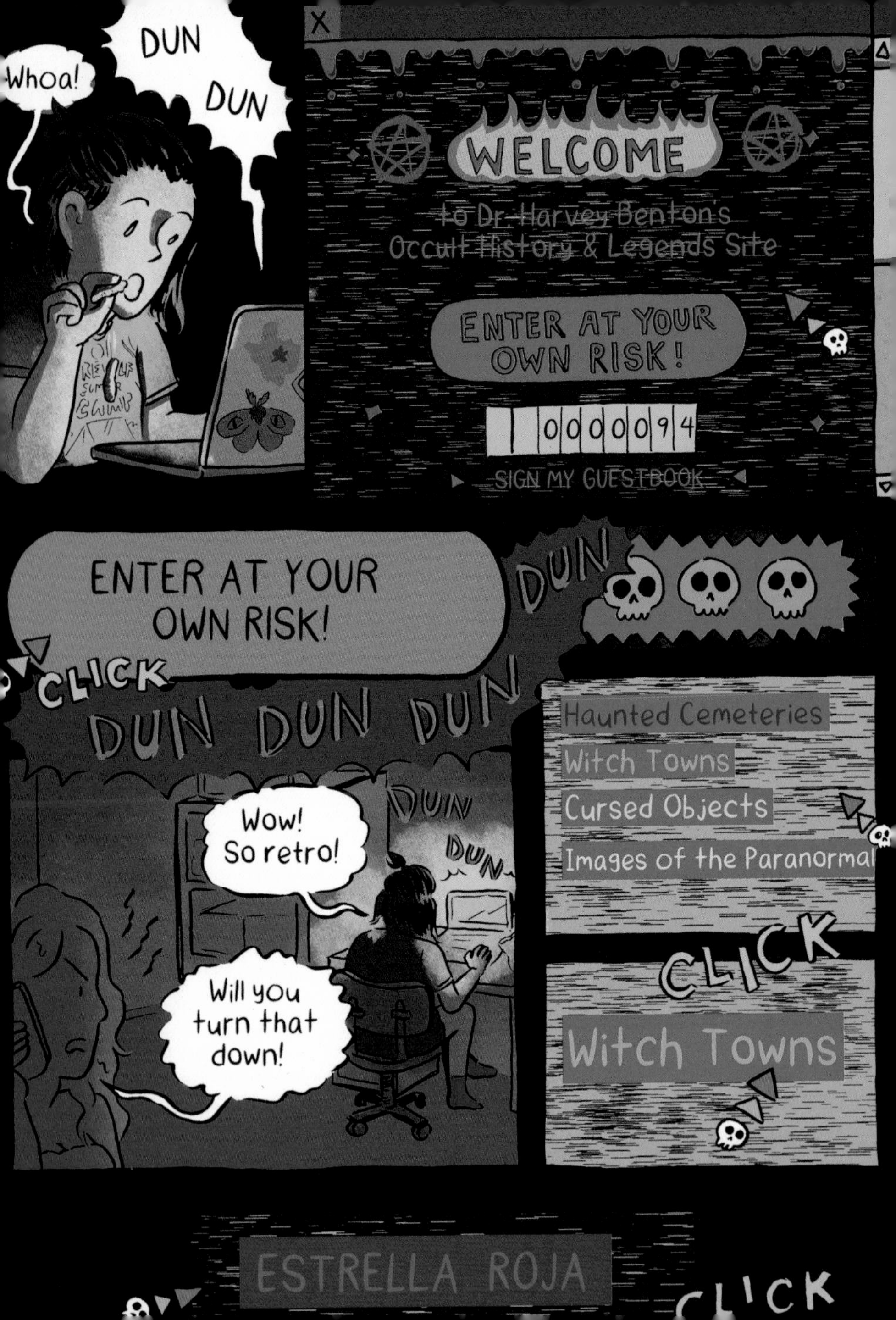

Whoa!
DUN DUN
WELCOME
to Dr. Harvey Benton's
Occult History & Legends Site
ENTER AT YOUR OWN RISK!
0000094
SIGN MY GUESTBOOK
ENTER AT YOUR OWN RISK!
DUN
CLICK
DUN DUN DUN
Wow! So retro!
DUN
DUN
Will you turn that down!
Haunted Cemeteries
Witch Towns
Cursed Objects
Images of the Paranormal
CLICK
Witch Towns
ESTRELLA ROJA
CLICK

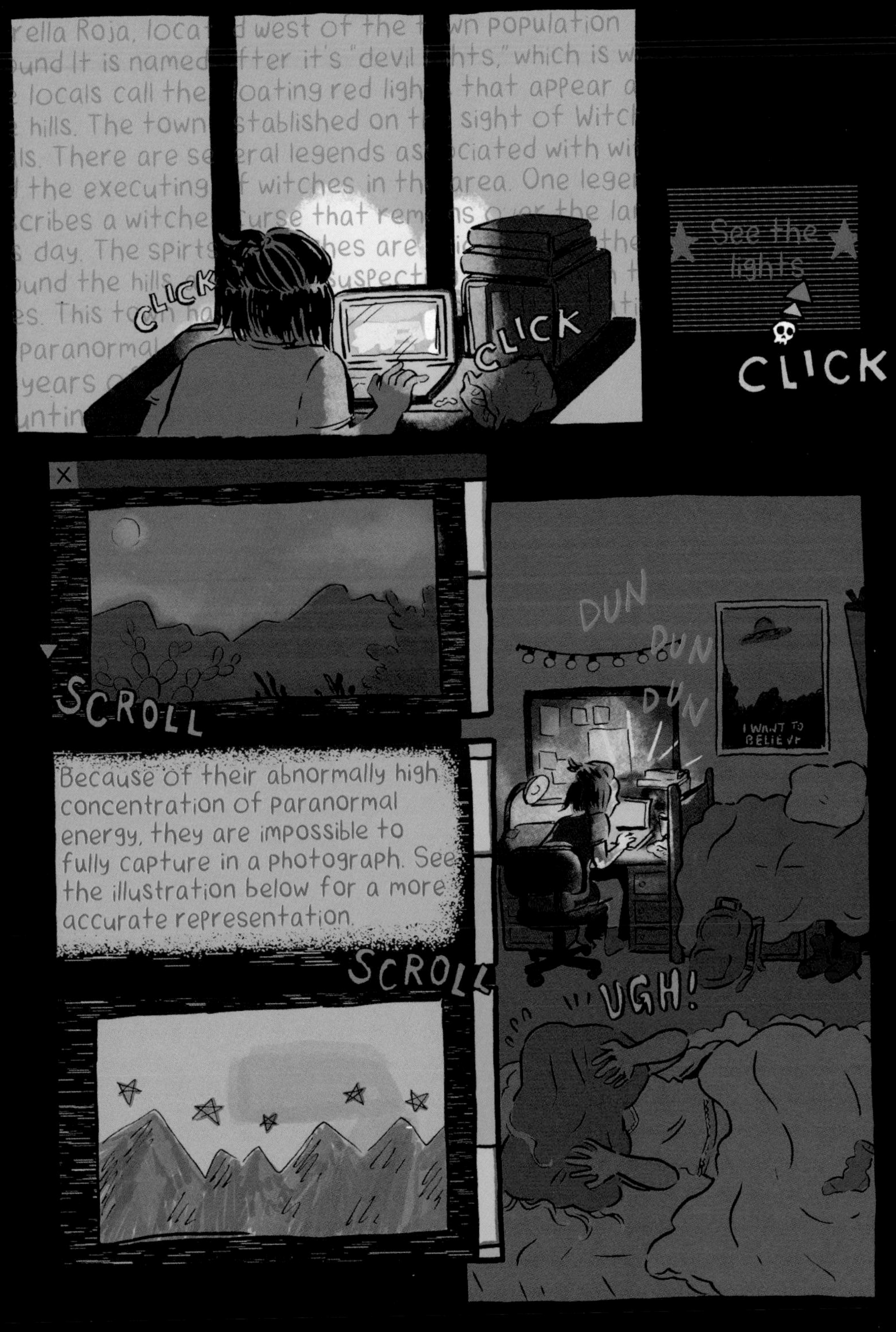

rella Roja, loca d west of the t wn population
und It is named fter it's "devil hts," which is w
locals call the loating red ligh that appear a
hills. The town stablished on t sight of Witc
ls. There are se eral legends as ciated with wi
the executing f witches in th area. One leger
cribes a witche urse that rem
CLICK
CLICK
See the lights
CLICK
SCROLL
Because of their abnormally high concentration of paranormal energy, they are impossible to fully capture in a photograph. See the illustration below for a more accurate representation.
SCROLL
DUN
DUN
DUN
I WANT TO BELIEVE
UGH!

No way.

You really want to drive FIVE hours out to the middle of nowhere because of an email?

It's not just the email. I mean, you know I've been wanting to do more field research. I think it's what the podcast needs... some crunching footsteps, colorful local interviews...

And I've never even heard of this place before! It'll be something totally fresh for our listeners!

It's SPRING BREAK, Kat. It's time to let loose, relax.

Not to get lost on some loco road trip to make content for our ten listeners.

Hey! It's more like thirty... And anyway, it'll be fun. I'll drive. We can make a playlist 'n' eat our weight in snacks—

Can't.

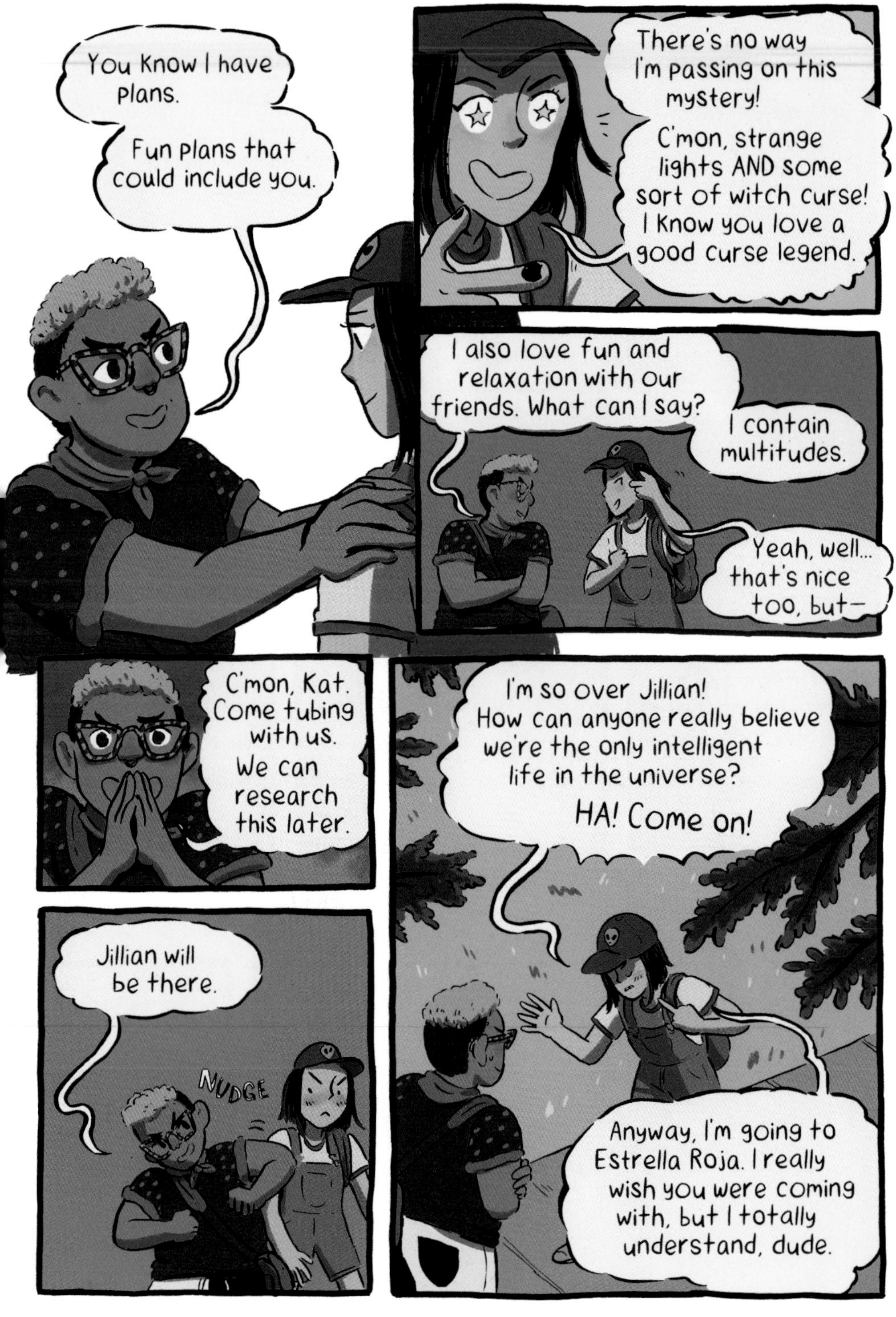
You know I have plans.
Fun plans that could include you.
There's no way I'm passing on this mystery!
C'mon, strange lights AND some sort of witch curse! I know you love a good curse legend.
I also love fun and relaxation with our friends. What can I say?
I contain multitudes.
Yeah, well... that's nice too, but—
C'mon, Kat. Come tubing with us.
We can research this later.
I'm so over Jillian! How can anyone really believe we're the only intelligent life in the universe?
HA! Come on!
Jillian will be there.
NUDGE
Anyway, I'm going to Estrella Roja. I really wish you were coming with, but I totally understand, dude.

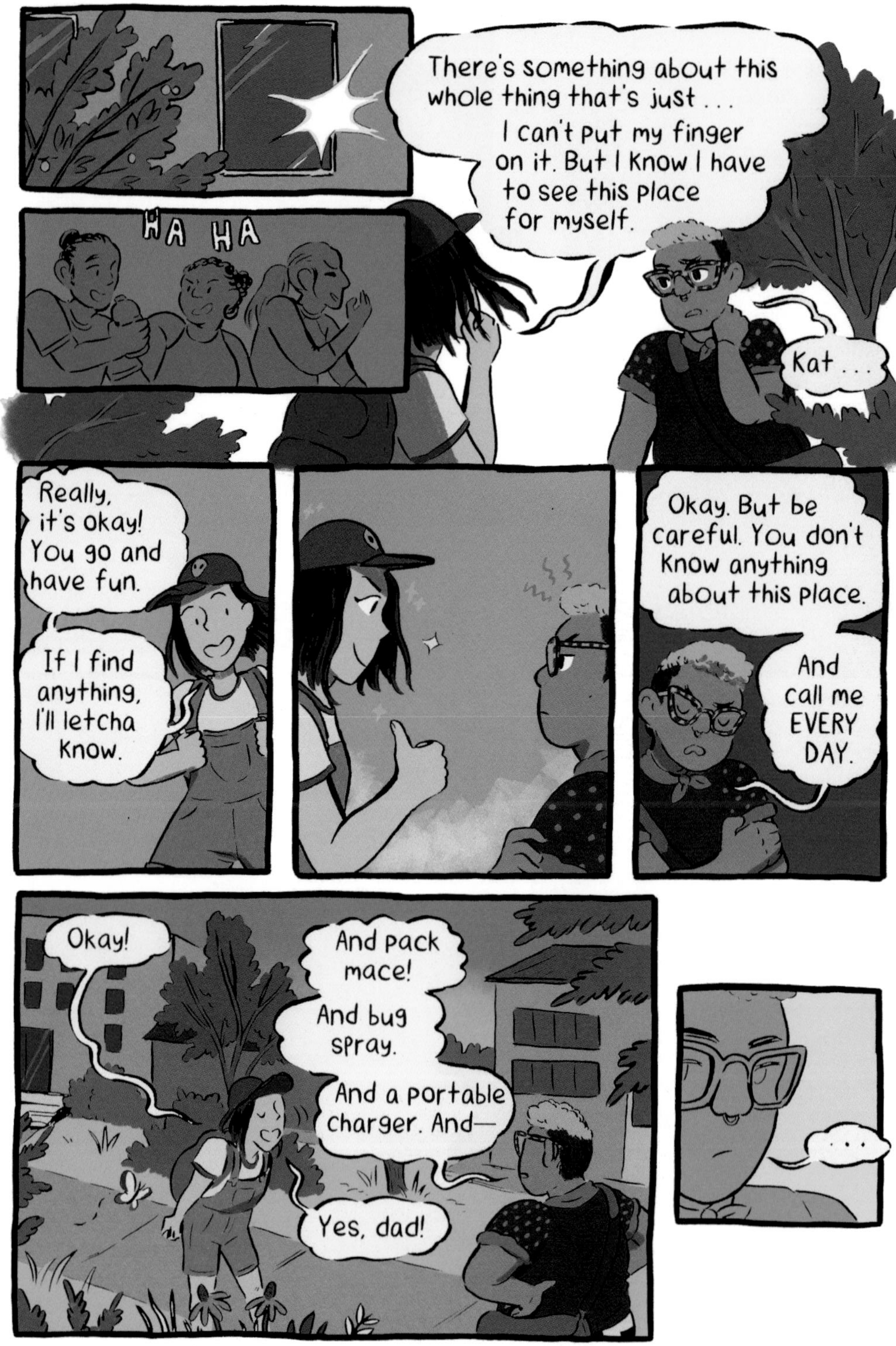
HA HA
There's something about this whole thing that's just . . .
I can't put my finger on it. But I know I have to see this place for myself.
Kat . . .
Really, it's okay! You go and have fun.
If I find anything, I'll letcha know.
Okay. But be careful. You don't know anything about this place.
And call me EVERY DAY.
Okay!
And pack mace!
And bug spray.
And a portable charger. And—
Yes, dad!
. . .

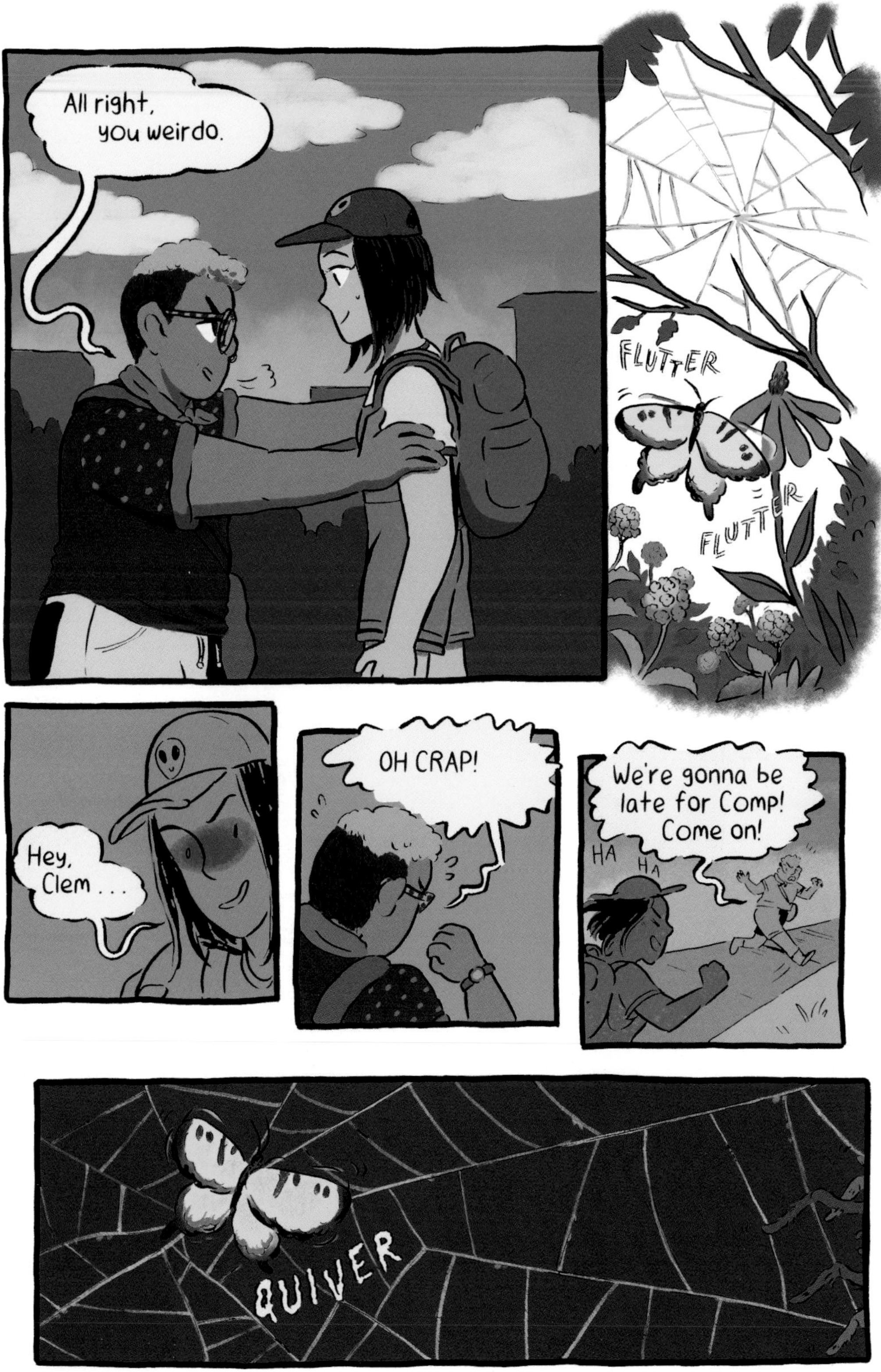
All right, you weirdo.
FLUTTER
FLUTTER
Hey, Clem . . .
OH CRAP!
We're gonna be late for Comp! Come on!
HA
HA
QUIVER

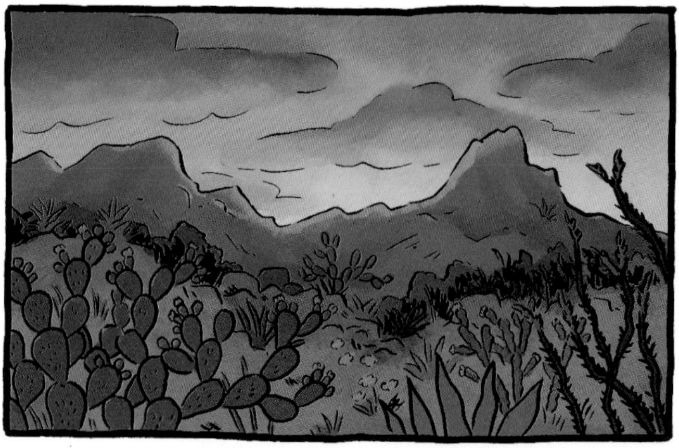

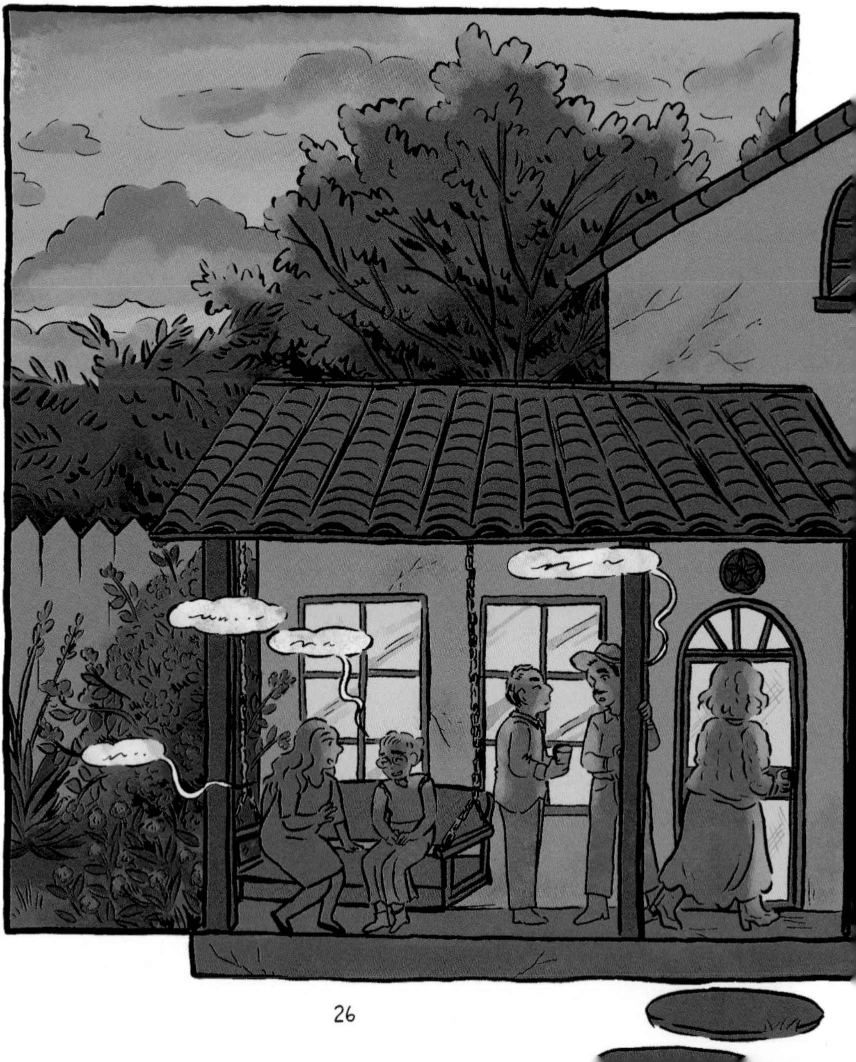

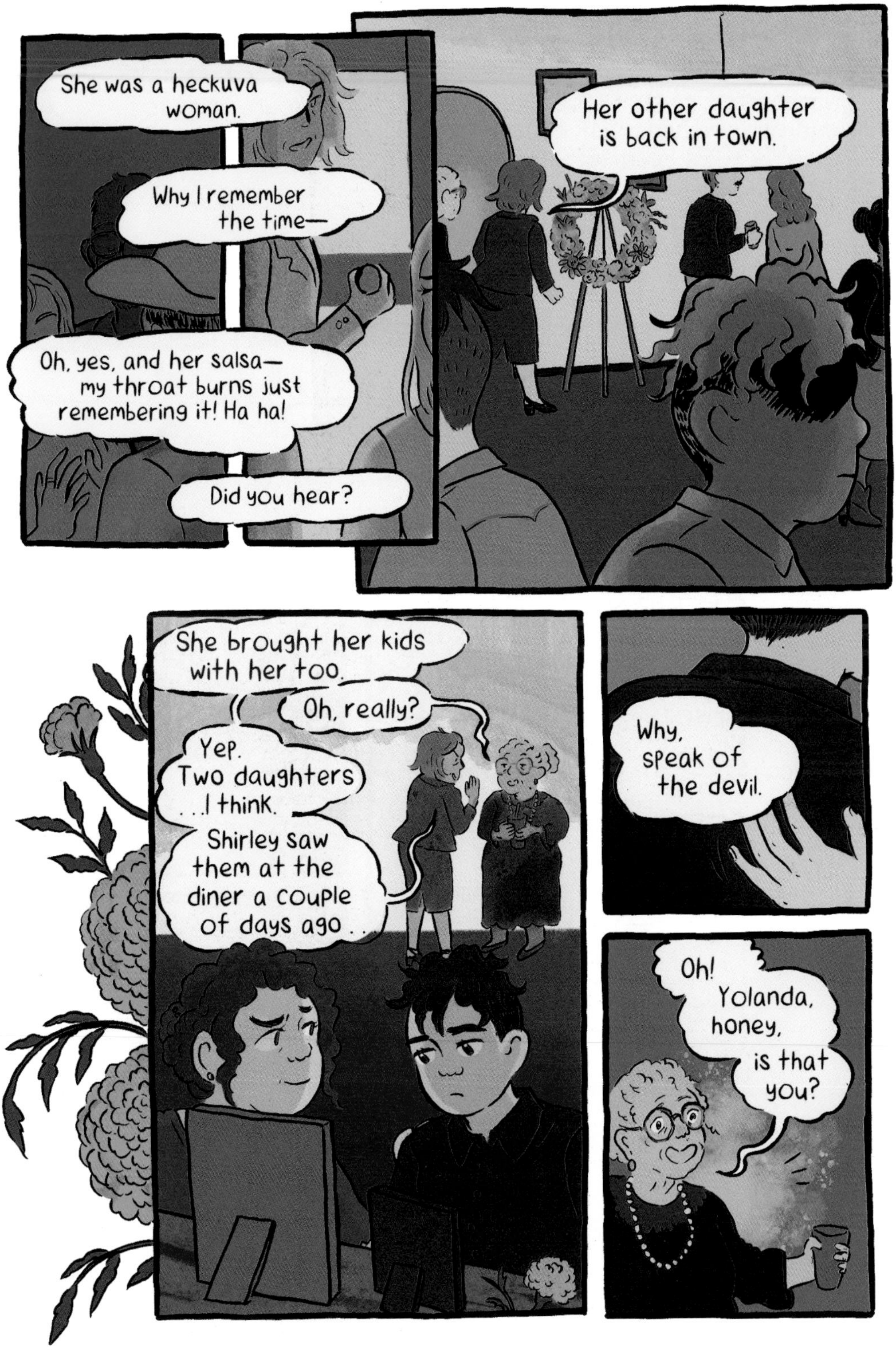
She was a heckuva woman.
Why I remember the time—
Oh, yes, and her salsa— my throat burns just remembering it! Ha ha!
Did you hear?
Her other daughter is back in town.
She brought her kids with her too.
Oh, really?
Yep. Two daughters . . . I think.
Shirley saw them at the diner a couple of days ago . . .
Why, speak of the devil.
Oh! Yolanda, honey, is that you?

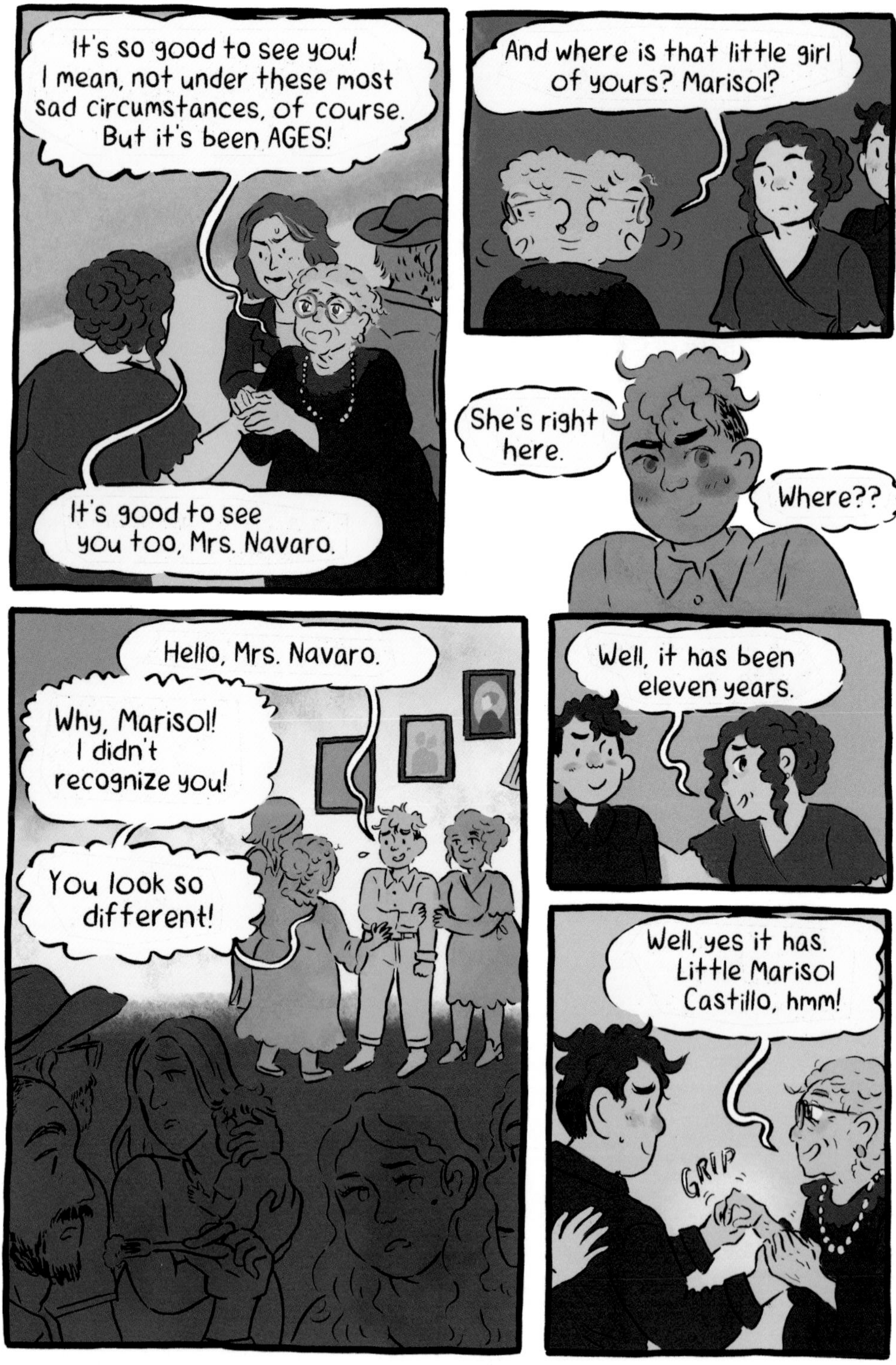
It's so good to see you! I mean, not under these most sad circumstances, of course. But it's been AGES!
It's good to see you too, Mrs. Navaro.
And where is that little girl of yours? Marisol?
She's right here.
Where??
Hello, Mrs. Navaro.
Why, Marisol! I didn't recognize you!
You look so different!
Well, it has been eleven years.
Well, yes it has. Little Marisol Castillo, hmm!
GRIP

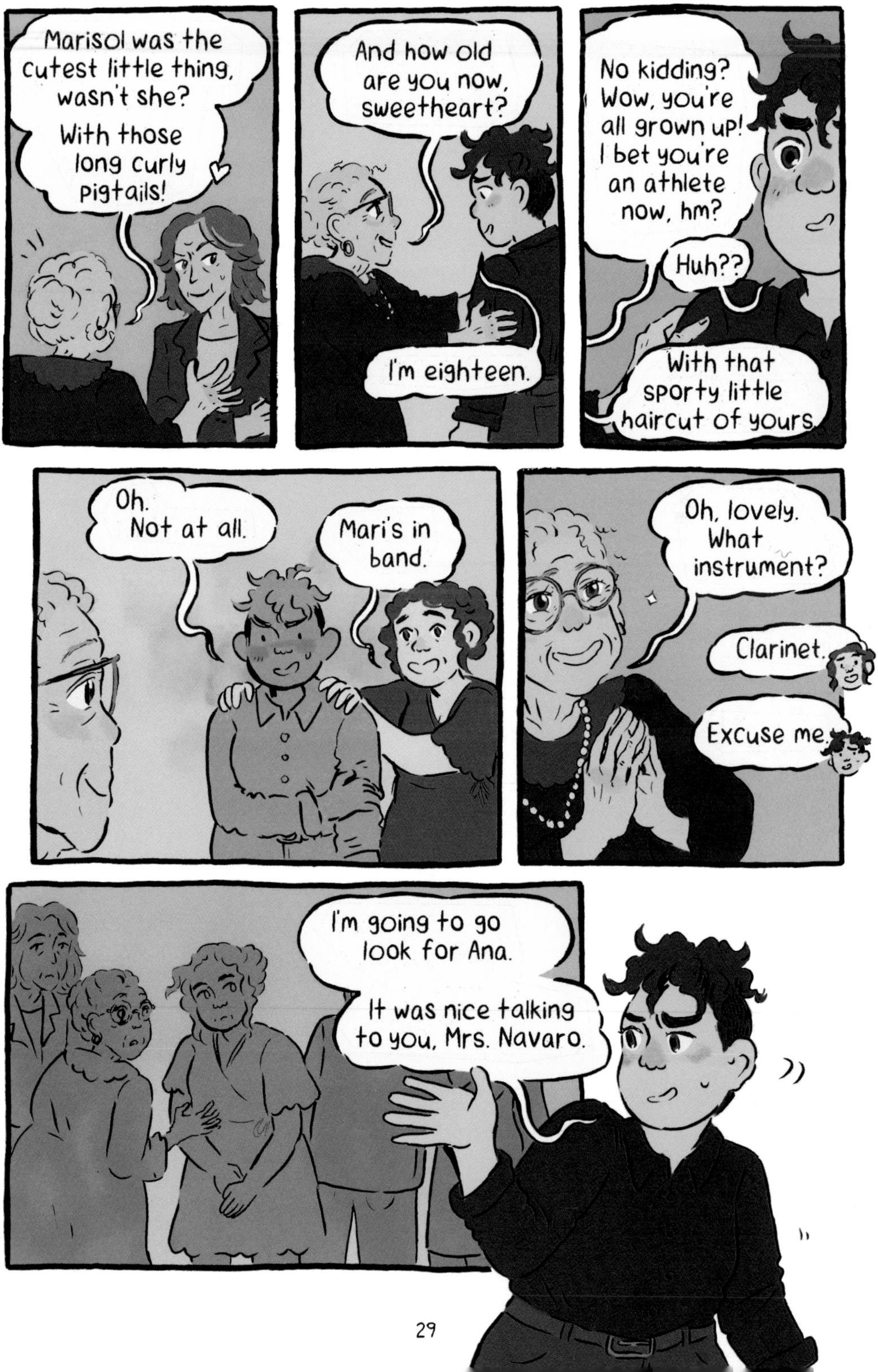
Marisol was the cutest little thing, wasn't she?
With those long curly pigtails!
And how old are you now, sweetheart?
I'm eighteen.
No kidding? Wow, you're all grown up! I bet you're an athlete now, hm?
Huh??
With that sporty little haircut of yours.
Oh. Not at all.
Mari's in band.
Oh, lovely. What instrument?
Clarinet.
Excuse me.
I'm going to go look for Ana.
It was nice talking to you, Mrs. Navaro.

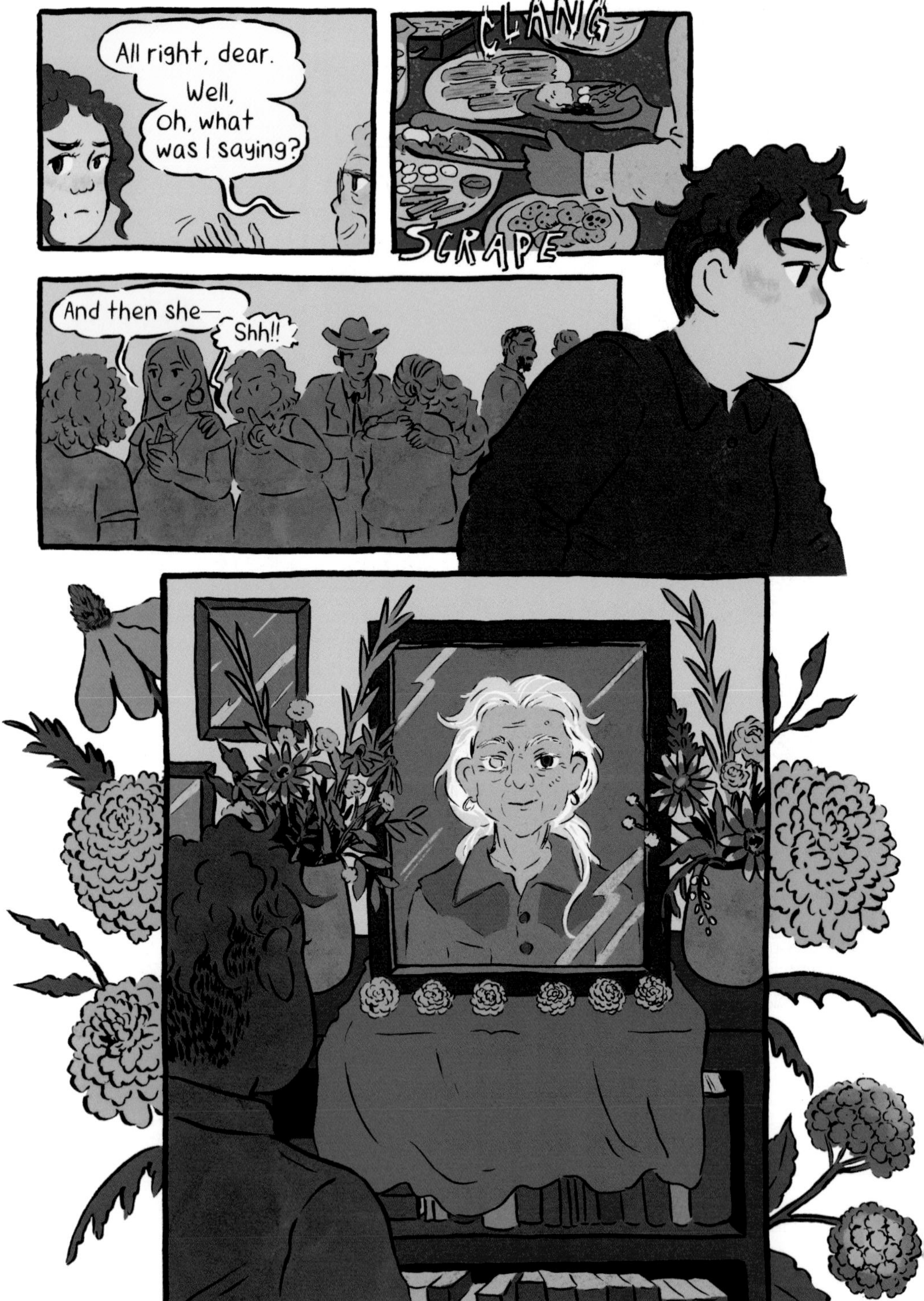
All right, dear.
Well, Oh, what was I saying?
CLANG
SCRAPE
And then she—
Shh!!

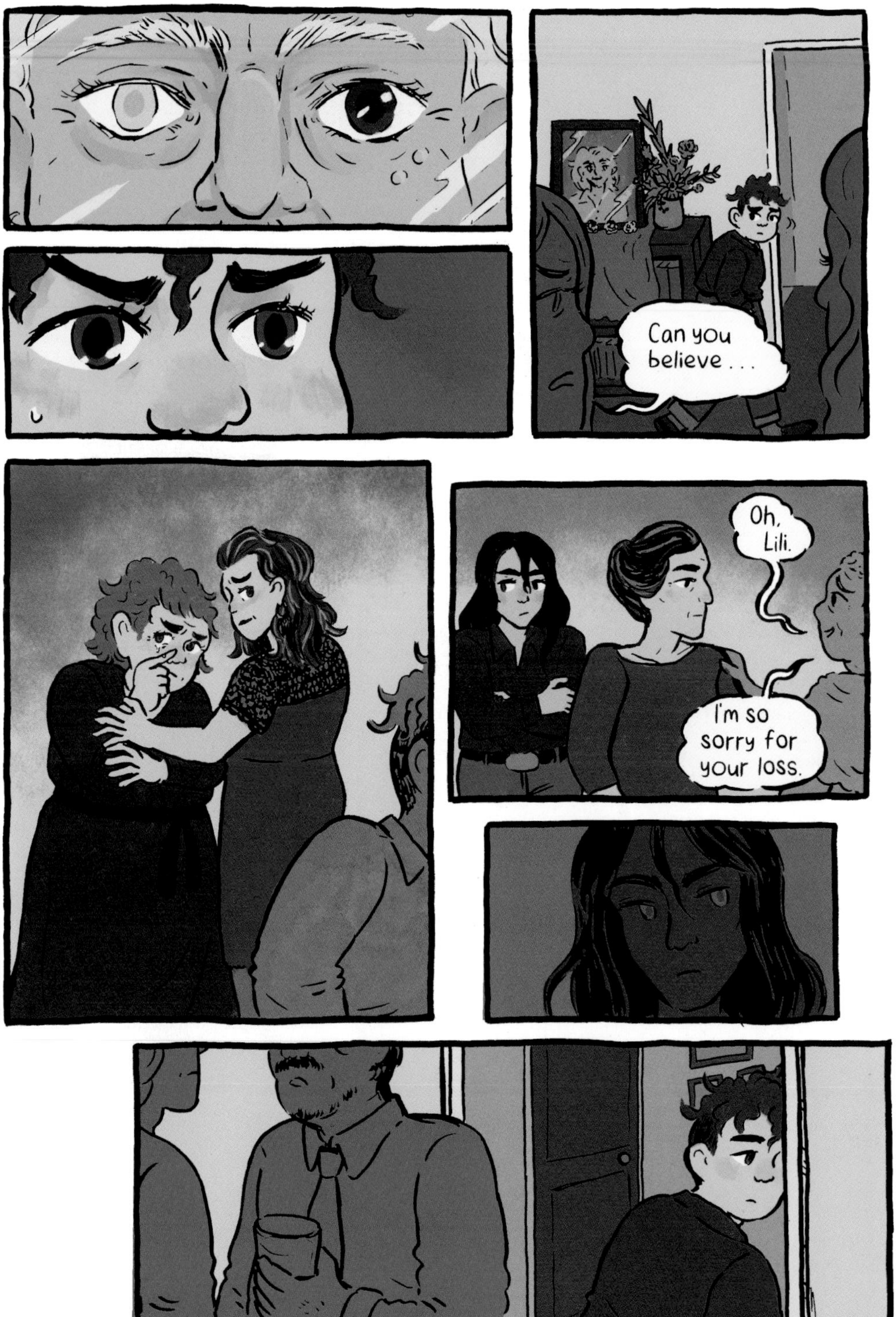
Can you believe . . .
Oh, Lili.
I'm so sorry for your loss.

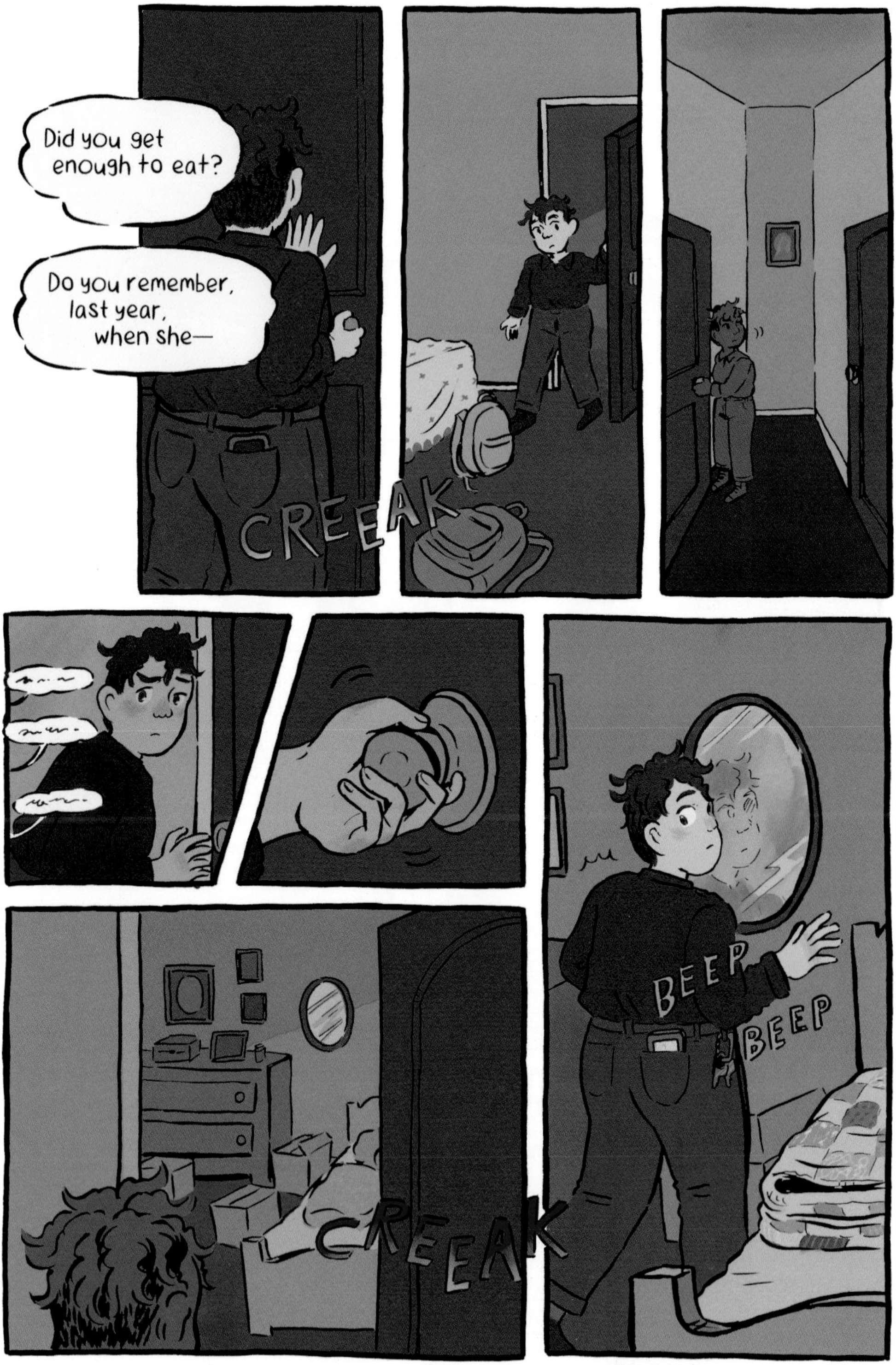
Did you get enough to eat?
Do you remember, last year, when she—
CREEAK
BEEP
BEEP
CREEAK

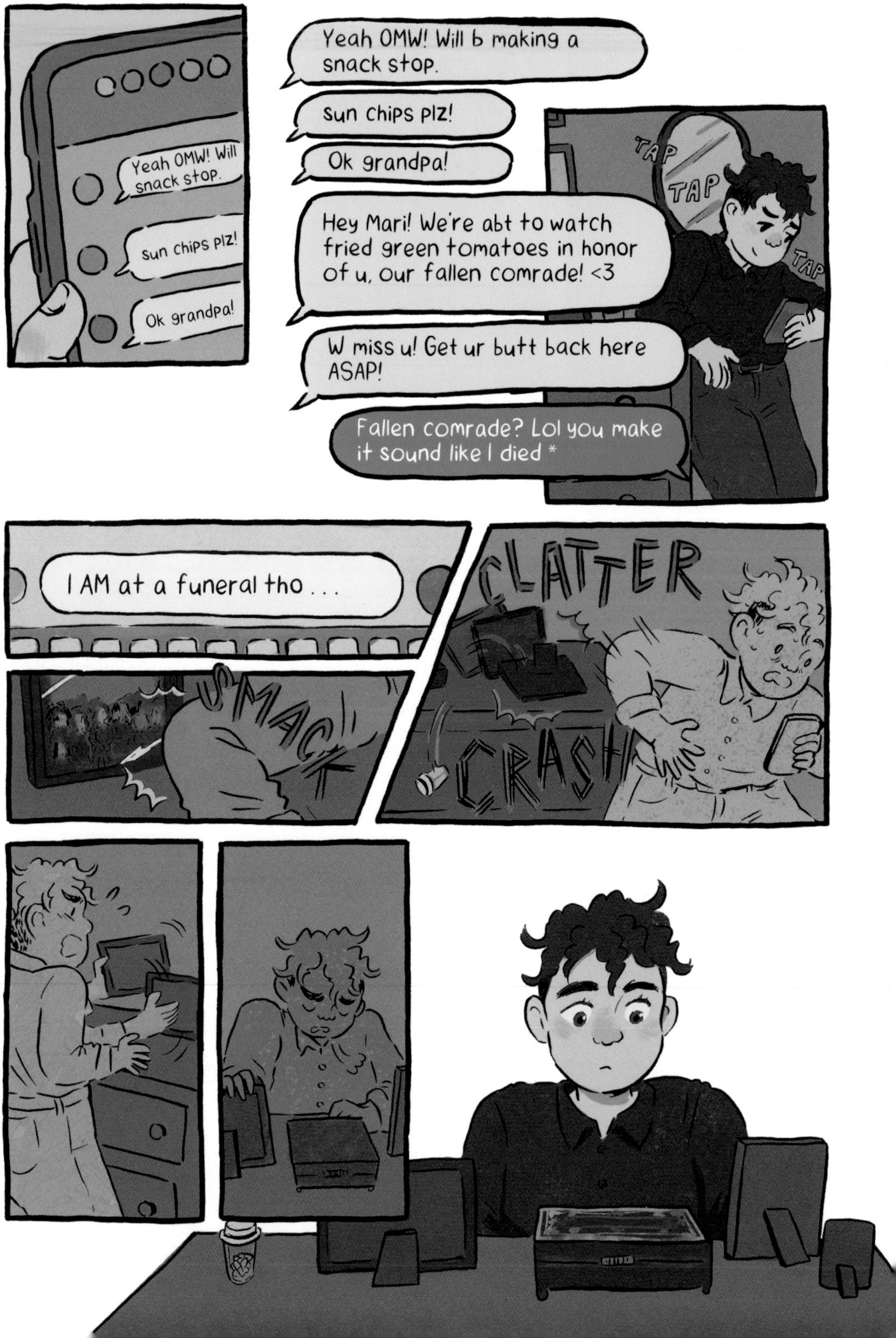
Yeah OMW! Will snack stop.
sun chips plz!
Ok grandpa!
Yeah OMW! Will b making a snack stop.
sun chips plz!
Ok grandpa!
Hey Mari! We're abt to watch fried green tomatoes in honor of u, our fallen comrade! <3
W miss u! Get ur butt back here ASAP!
Fallen comrade? Lol you make it sound like I died *
TAP
TAP
TAP
I AM at a funeral tho . . .
SMACK
CLATTER
CRASH

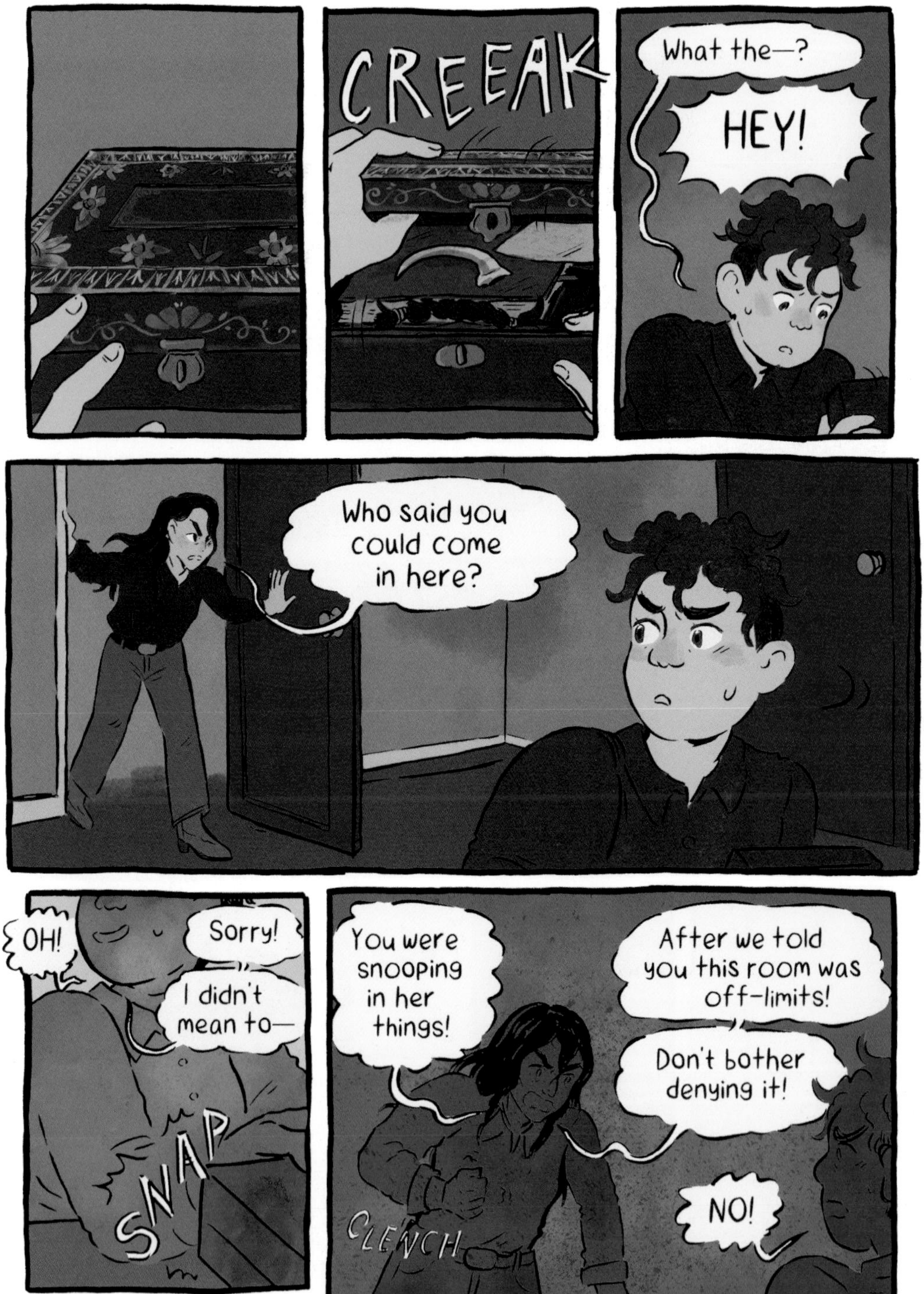
CREEAK
What the—?
HEY!
Who said you could come in here?
OH!
Sorry!
I didn't mean to—
SNAP
You were snooping in her things!
After we told you this room was off-limits!
Don't bother denying it!
NO!
CLENCH

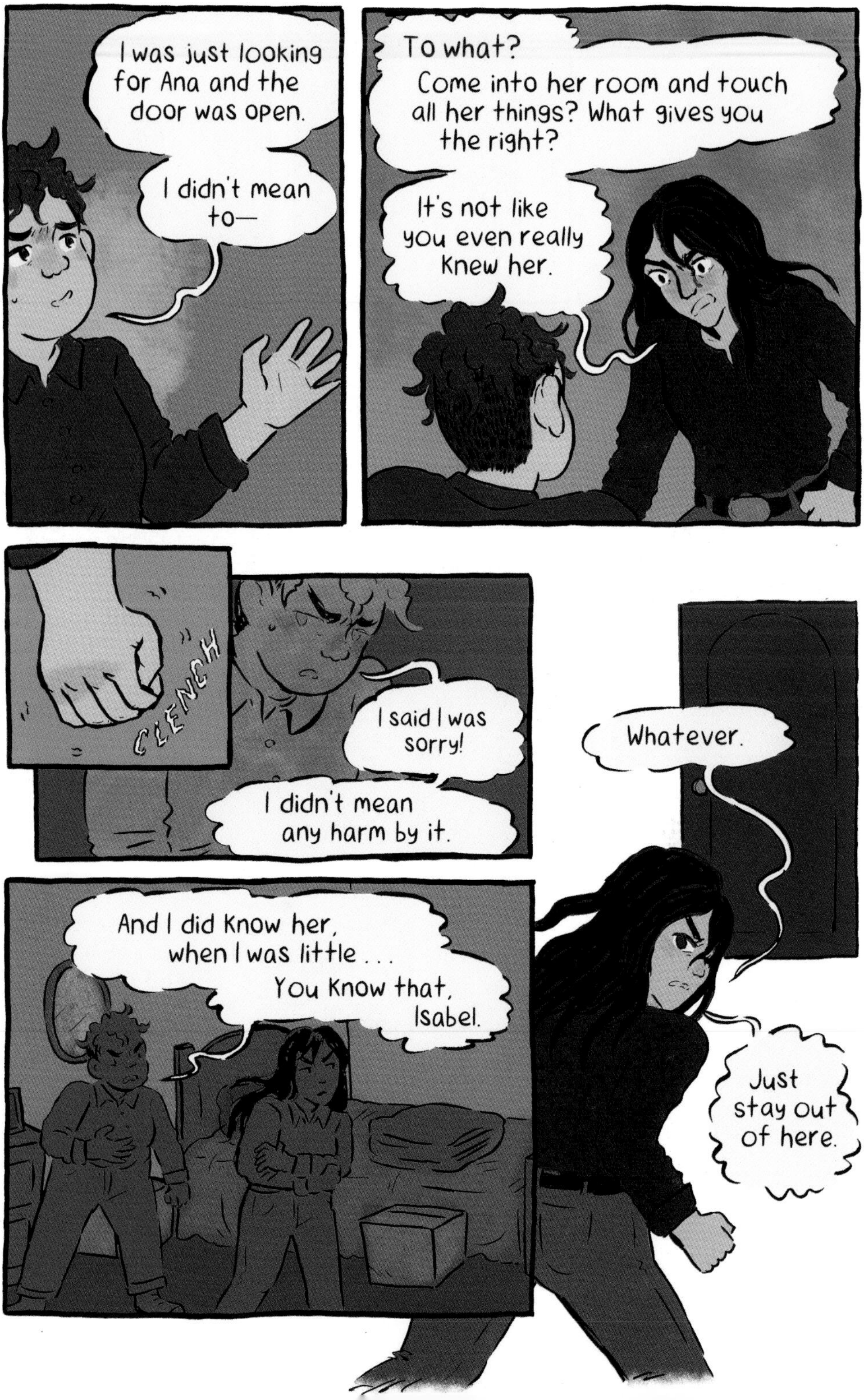
I was just looking for Ana and the door was open.
I didn't mean to—
To what?
Come into her room and touch all her things? What gives you the right?
It's not like you even really knew her.
CLENCH
I said I was sorry!
I didn't mean any harm by it.
Whatever.
And I did know her, when I was little . . .
You know that, Isabel.
Just stay out of here.

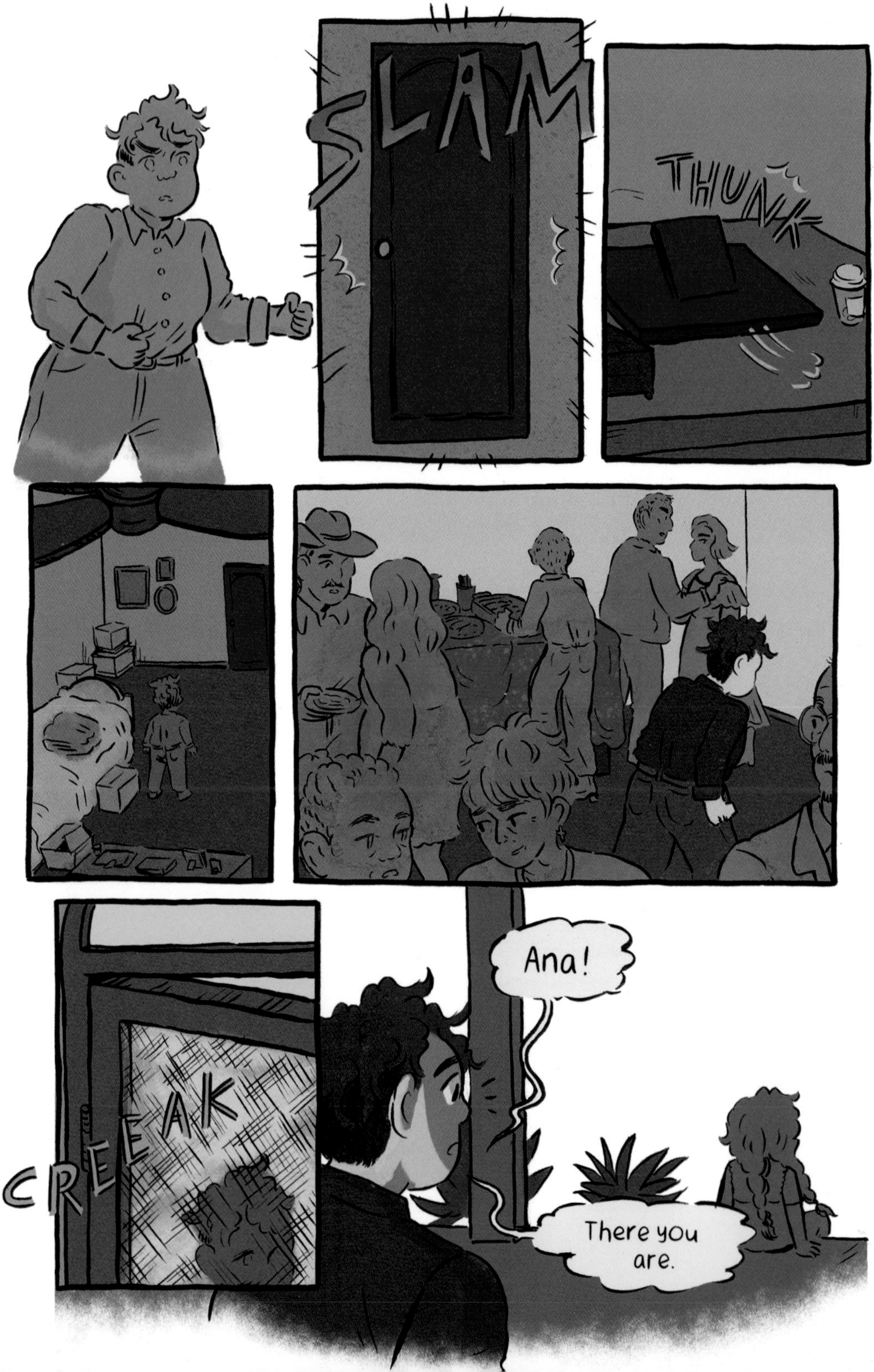
SLAM
THUNK
CREEAK
Ana!
There you are.

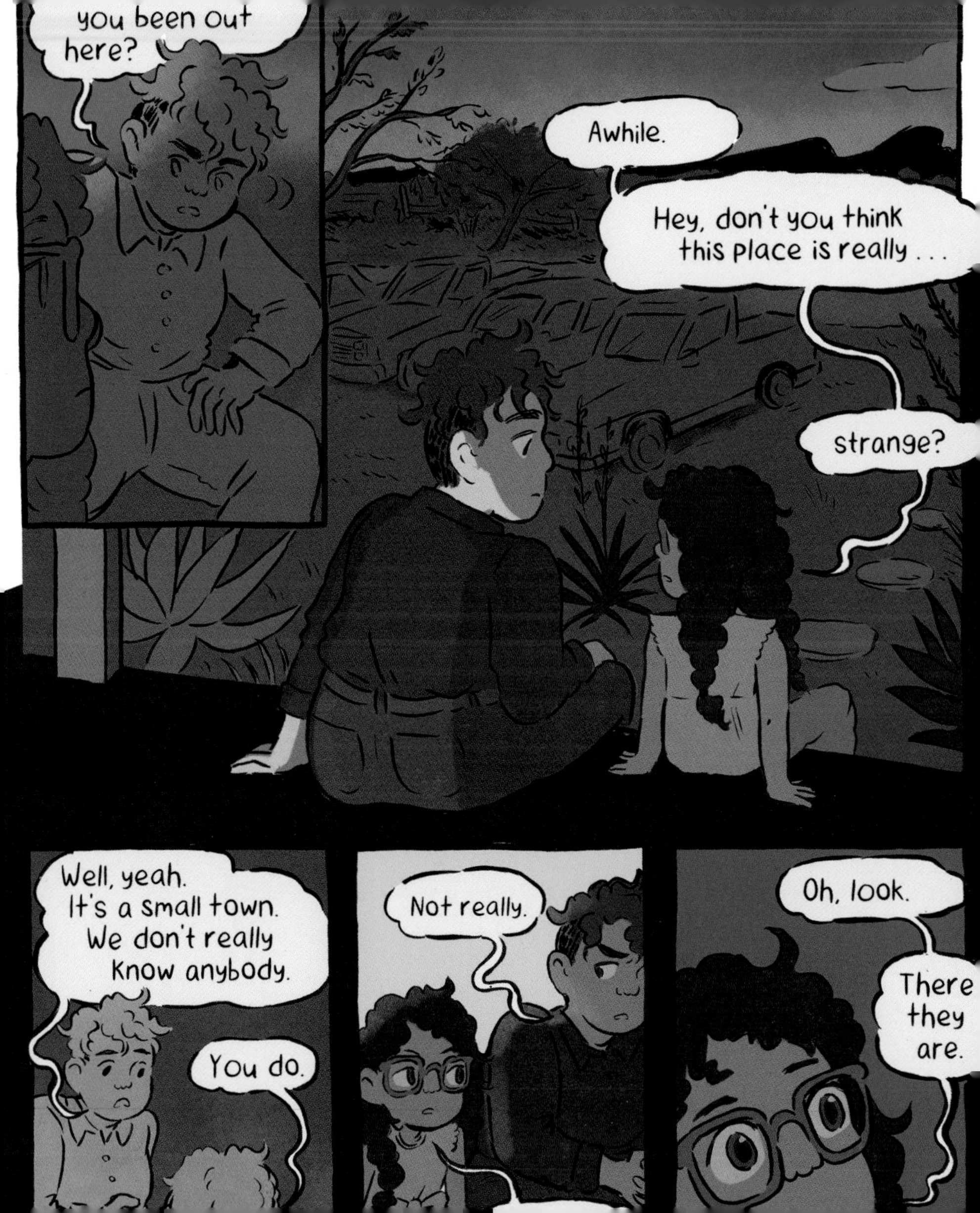
you been out here?
Awhile.
Hey, don't you think this place is really . . .
strange?
Well, yeah. It's a small town. We don't really know anybody.
You do.
Not really.
Oh, look.
There they are.

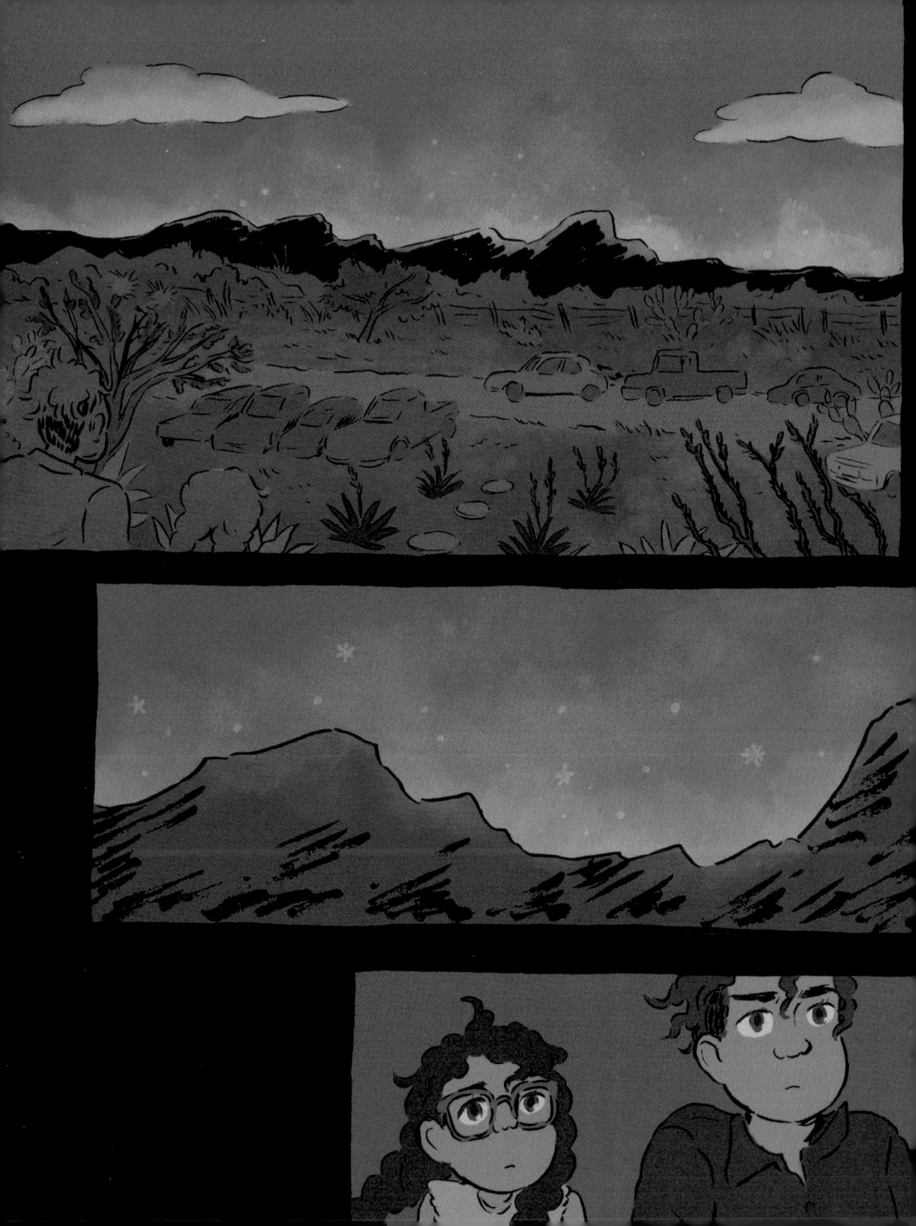

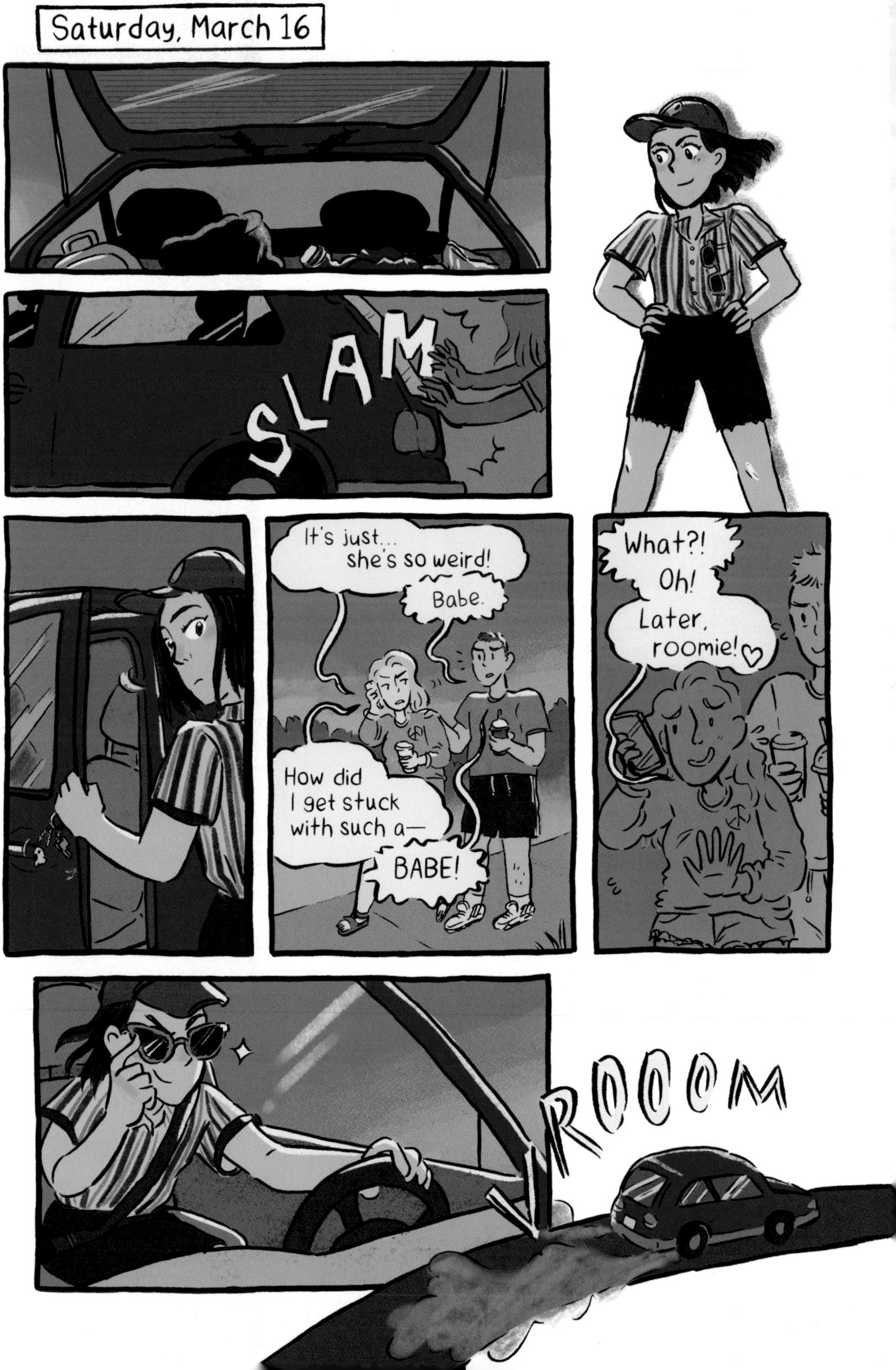
Saturday, March 16
SLAM
It's just... she's so weird!
Babe.
How did I get stuck with such a—
BABE!
What?! Oh! Later, roomie!♡
VROOOM

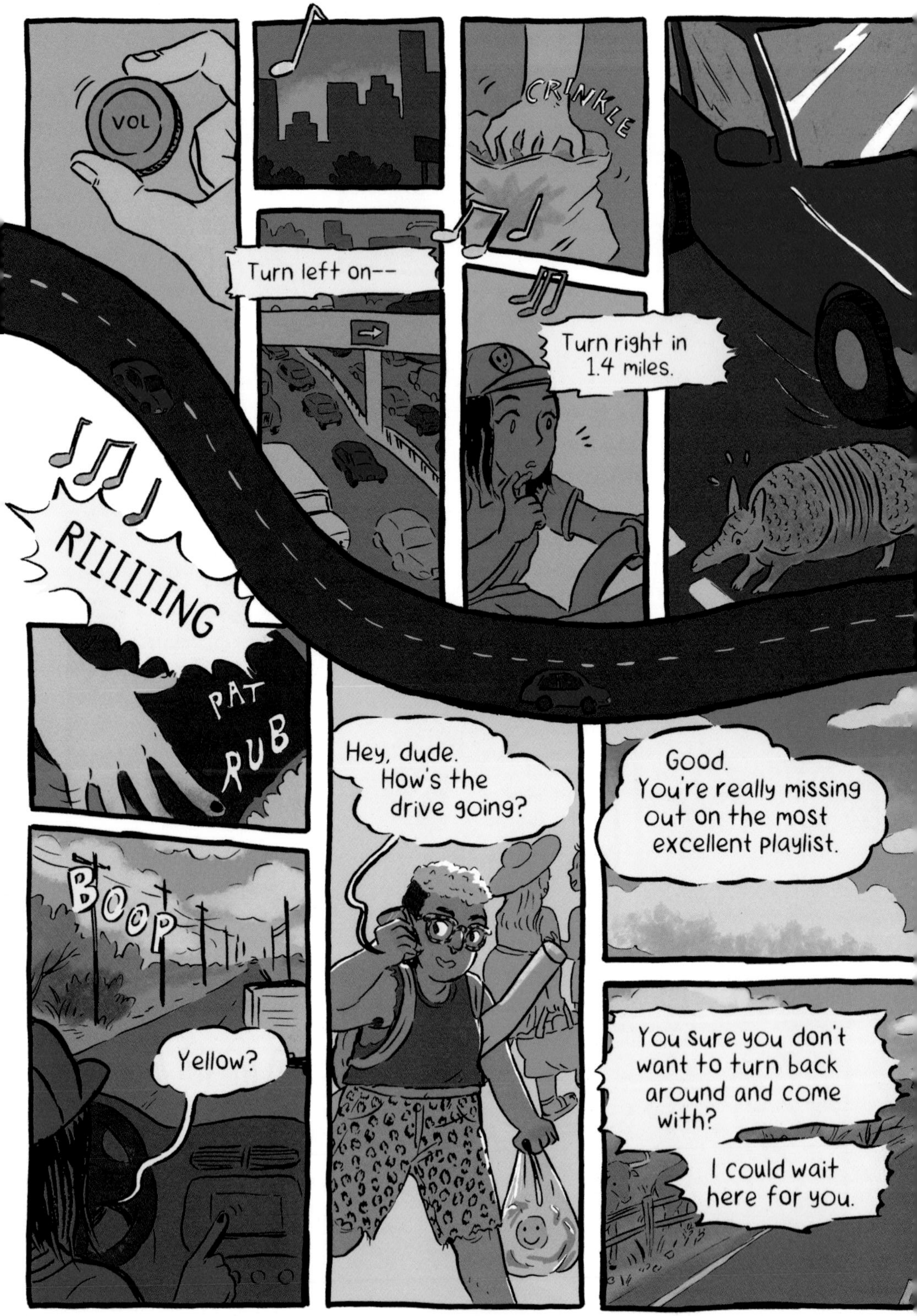
VOL
CRINKLE
Turn left on--
Turn right in 1.4 miles.
RIIIIIING
PAT
RUB
BOOP
Yellow?
Hey, dude. How's the drive going?
Good. You're really missing out on the most excellent playlist.
You sure you don't want to turn back around and come with?
I could wait here for you.

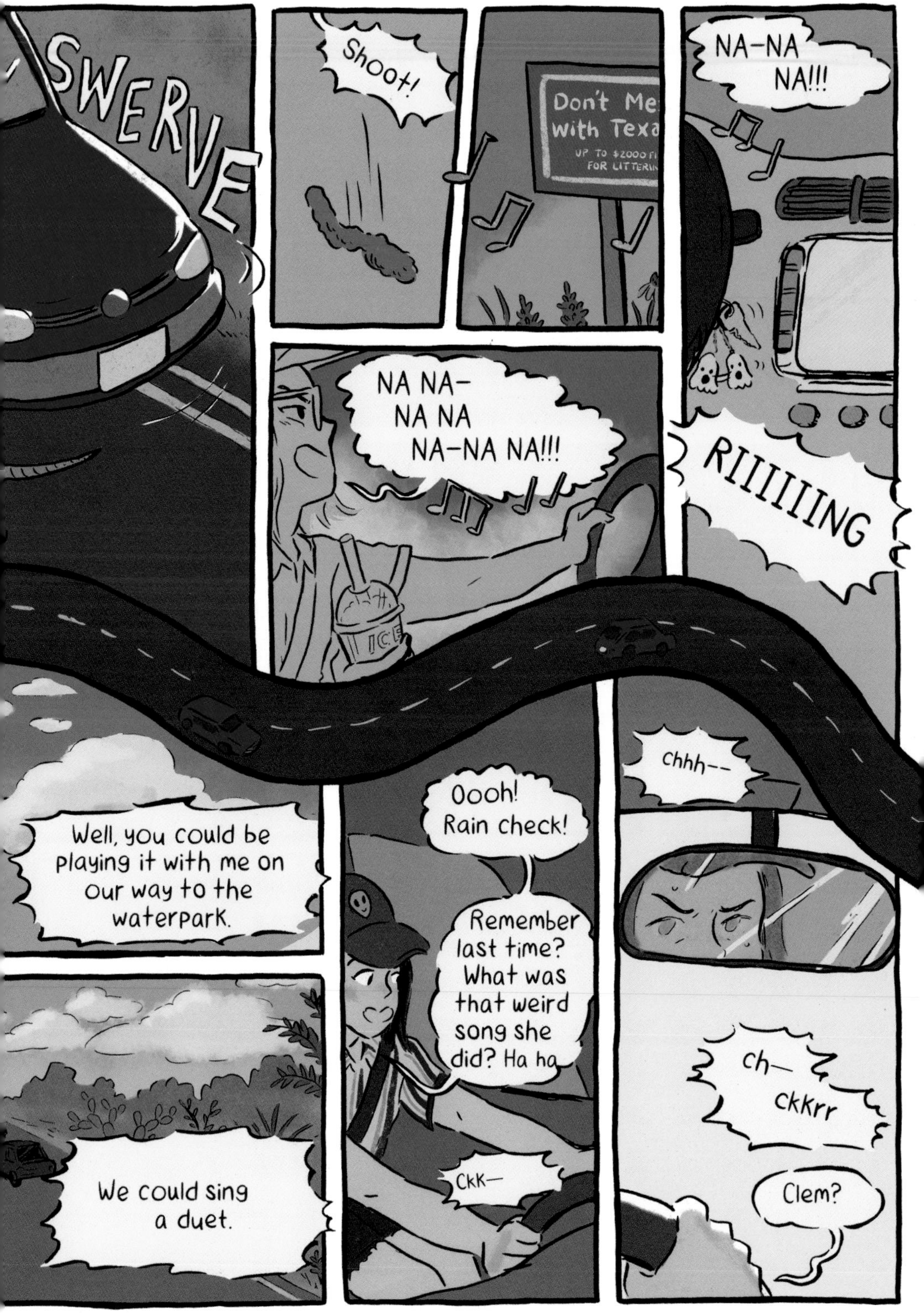
SWERVE
Shoot!
Don't Mess with Texas
UP TO $2000 FINE FOR LITTERING
NA-NA NA!!!
NA NA- NA NA NA-NA NA!!!
RIIIIIING
ICE
Well, you could be playing it with me on our way to the waterpark.
We could sing a duet.
Oooh! Rain check!
Remember last time? What was that weird song she did? Ha ha
Ckk—
Chhh--
Ch— ckkrr
Clem?

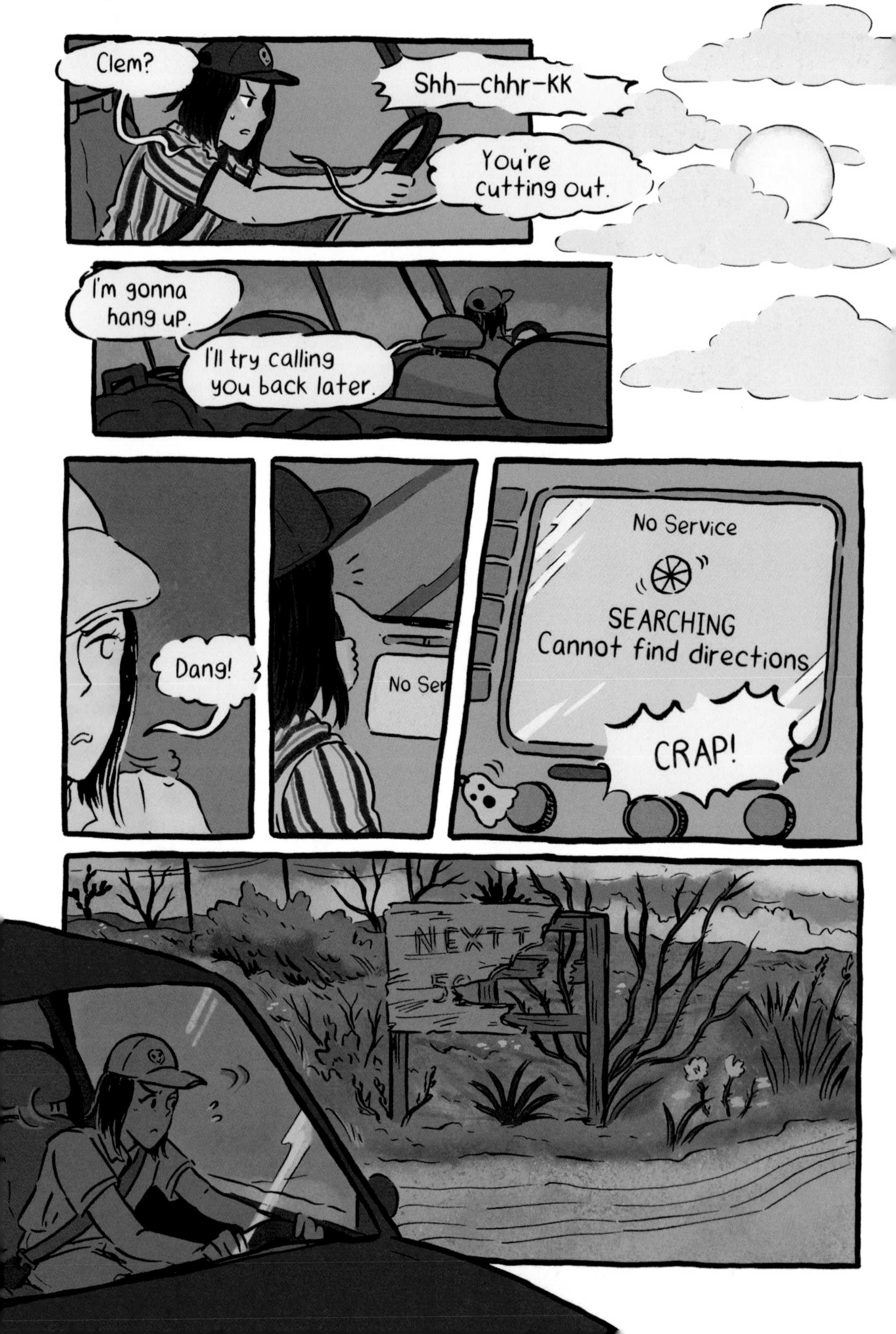
Clem?
Shh—chhr-KK
You're cutting out.
I'm gonna hang up.
I'll try calling you back later.
Dang!
No Ser
No Service
SEARCHING
Cannot find directions
CRAP!
NEXTT

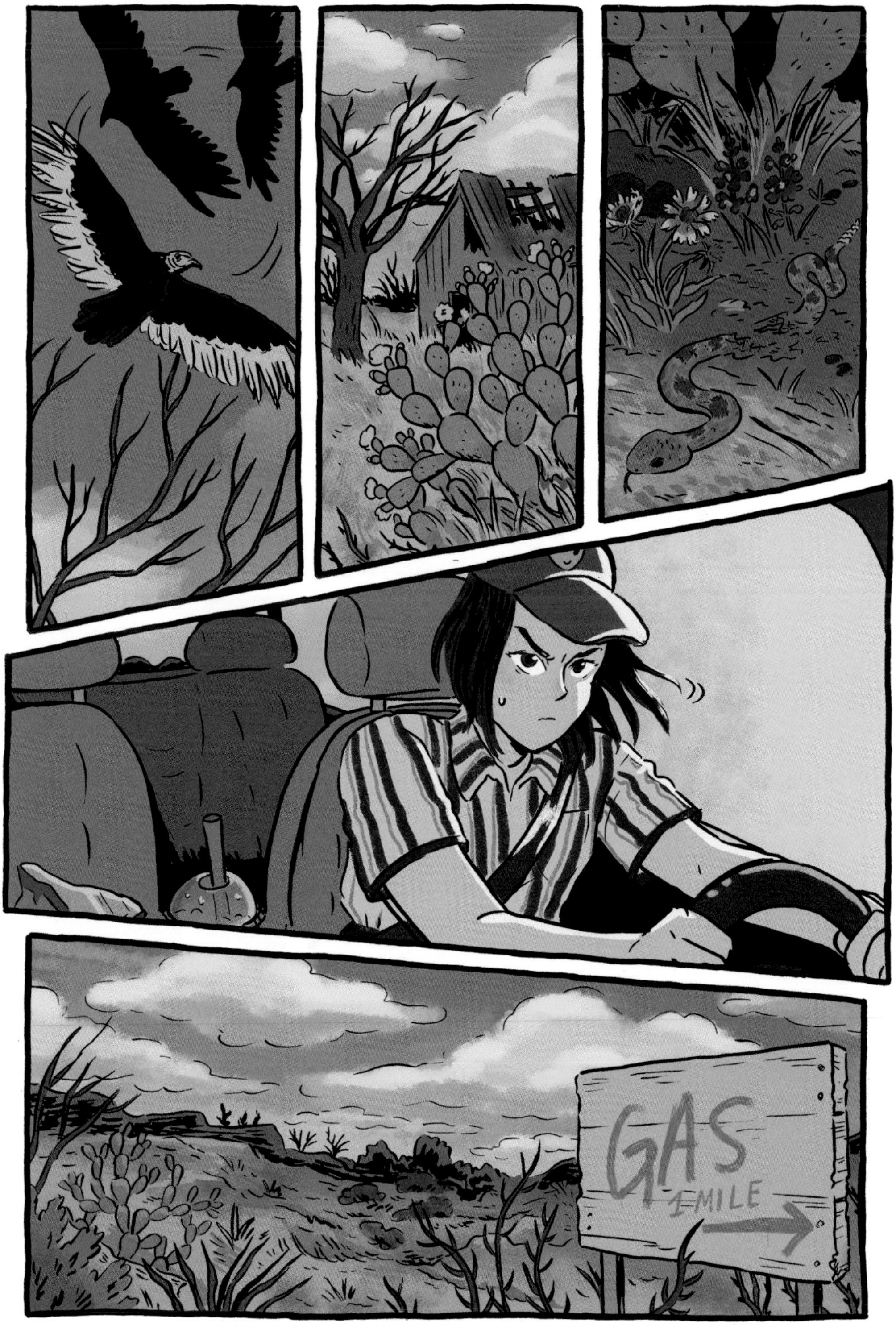
GAS
1 MILE

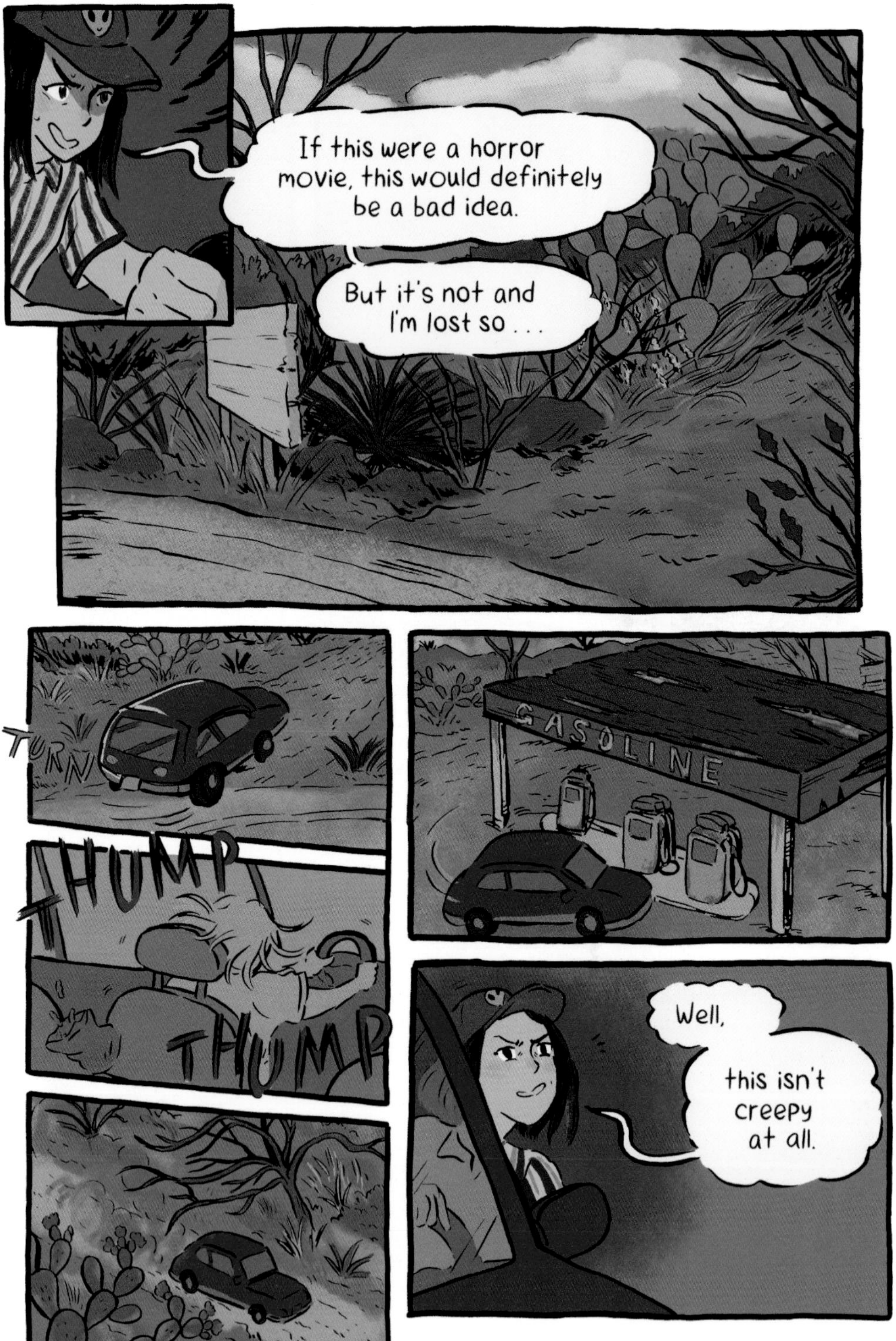
If this were a horror movie, this would definitely be a bad idea.
But it's not and I'm lost so . . .
TURN
GASOLINE
THUMP
THUMP
Well,
this isn't creepy at all.

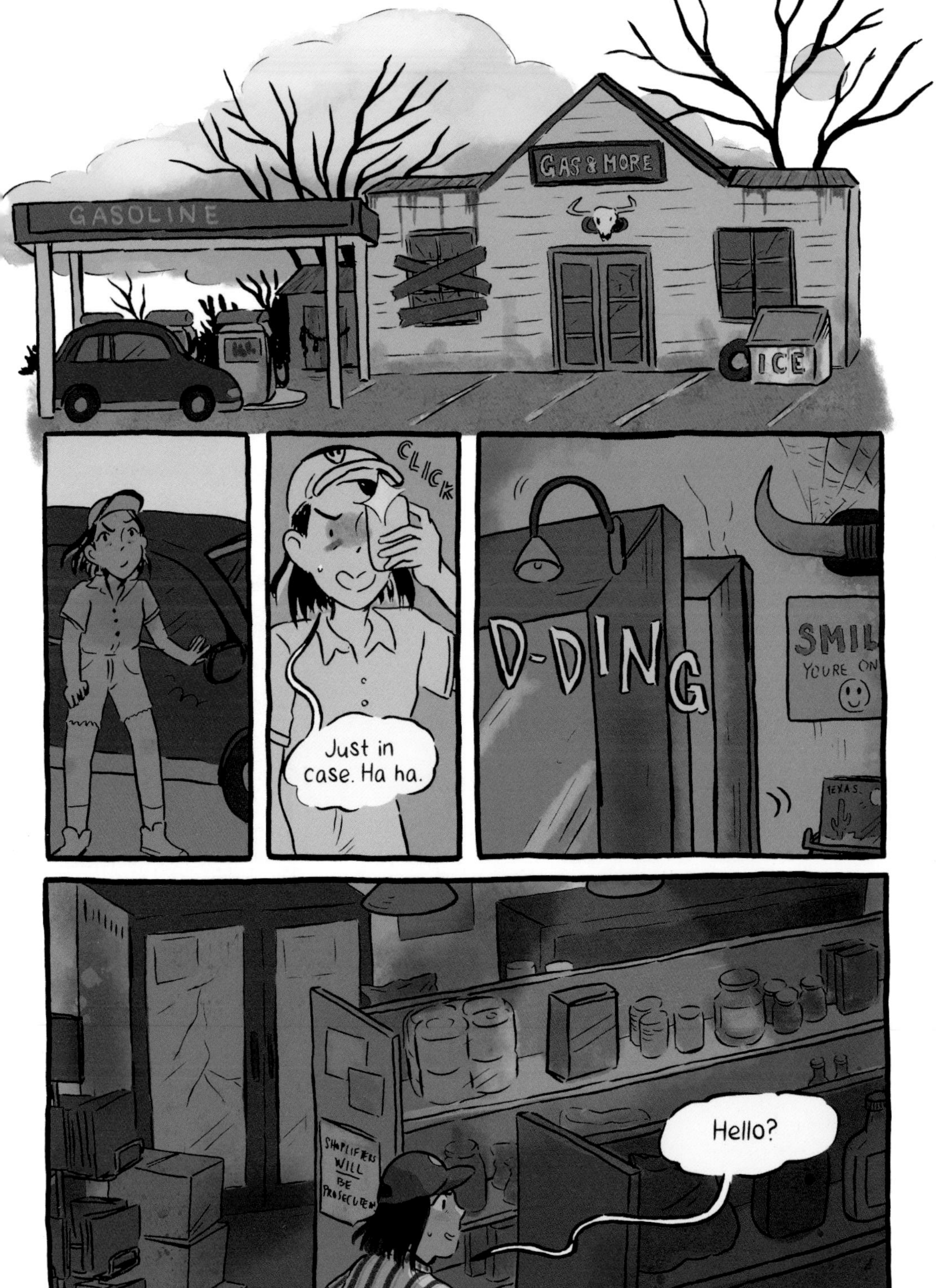
GAS & MORE
GASOLINE
ICE
CLICK
Just in case. Ha ha.
D-DING
SMIL
YOURE ON
TEXAS
SHOPLIFTERS WILL BE PROSECUTED
Hello?

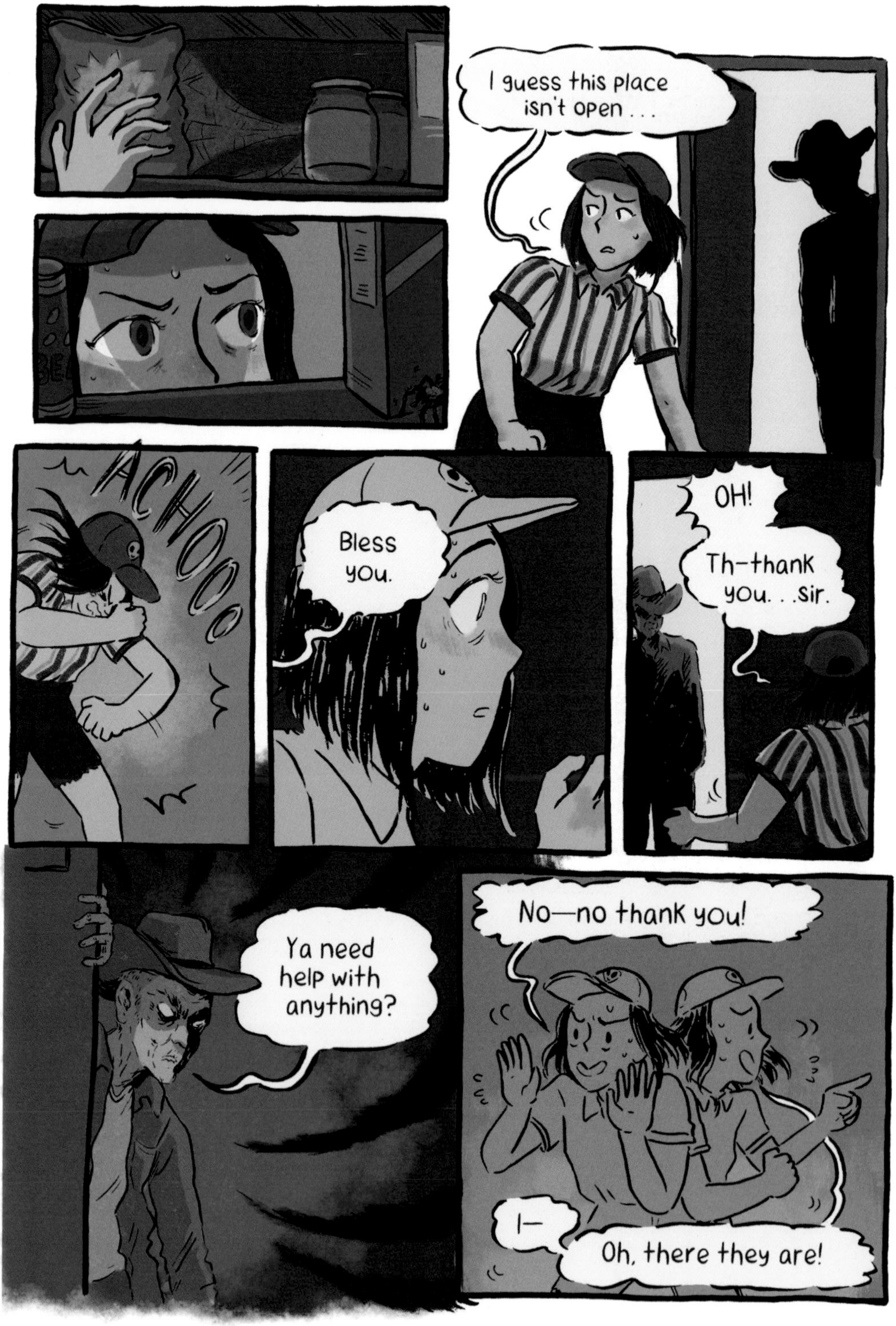
I guess this place isn't open . . .
ACHOOO
Bless you.
OH!
Th-thank you. . .sir.
Ya need help with anything?
No—no thank you!
I—
Oh, there they are!

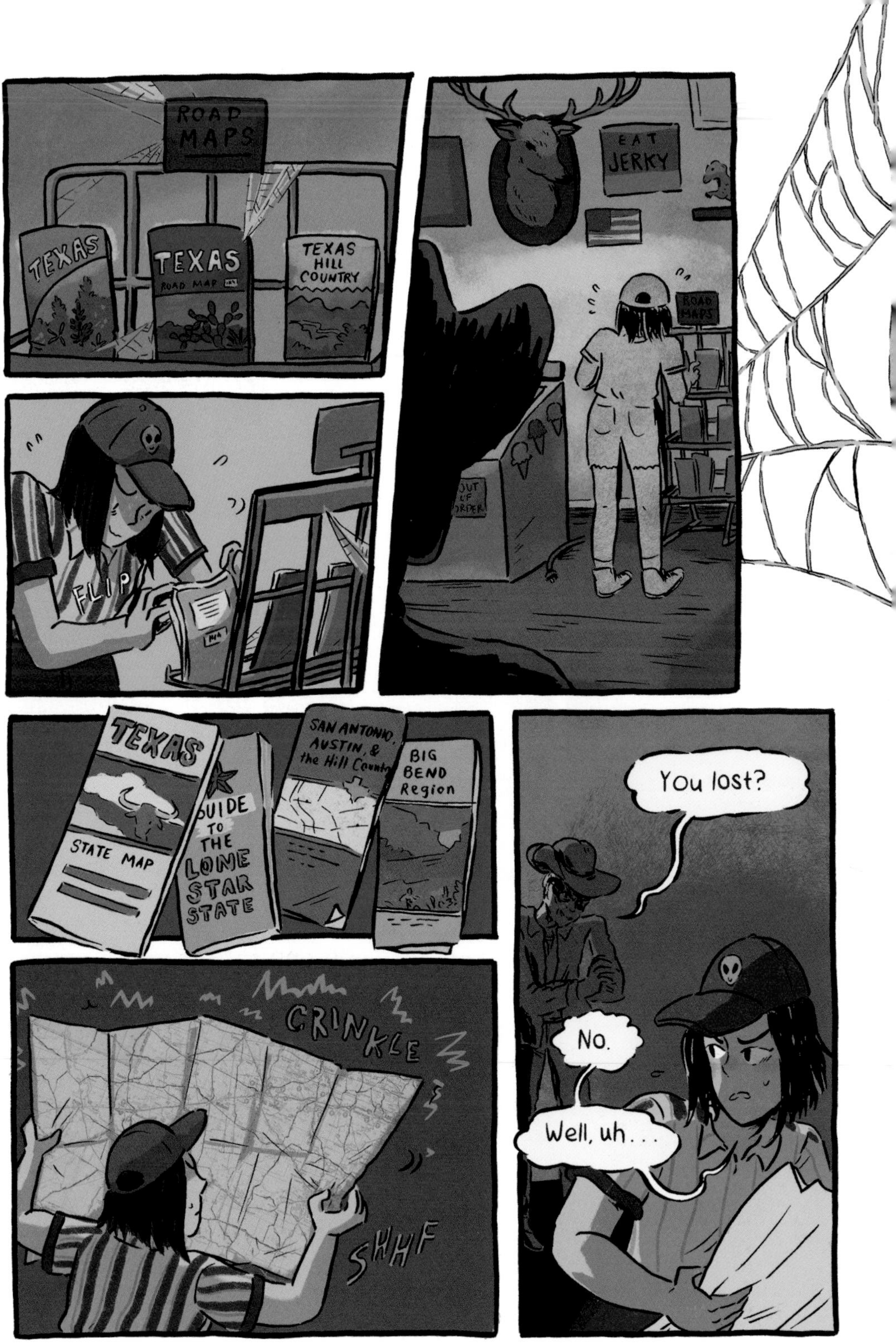
ROAD MAPS
TEXAS
TEXAS
ROAD MAP
TEXAS HILL COUNTRY
EAT JERKY
ROAD MAPS
OUT OF ORDER
FLIP
TEXAS
STATE MAP
GUIDE TO THE LONE STAR STATE
SAN ANTONIO, AUSTIN, & the Hill Country
BIG BEND Region
CRINKLE
SHHF
You lost?
No.
Well, uh...

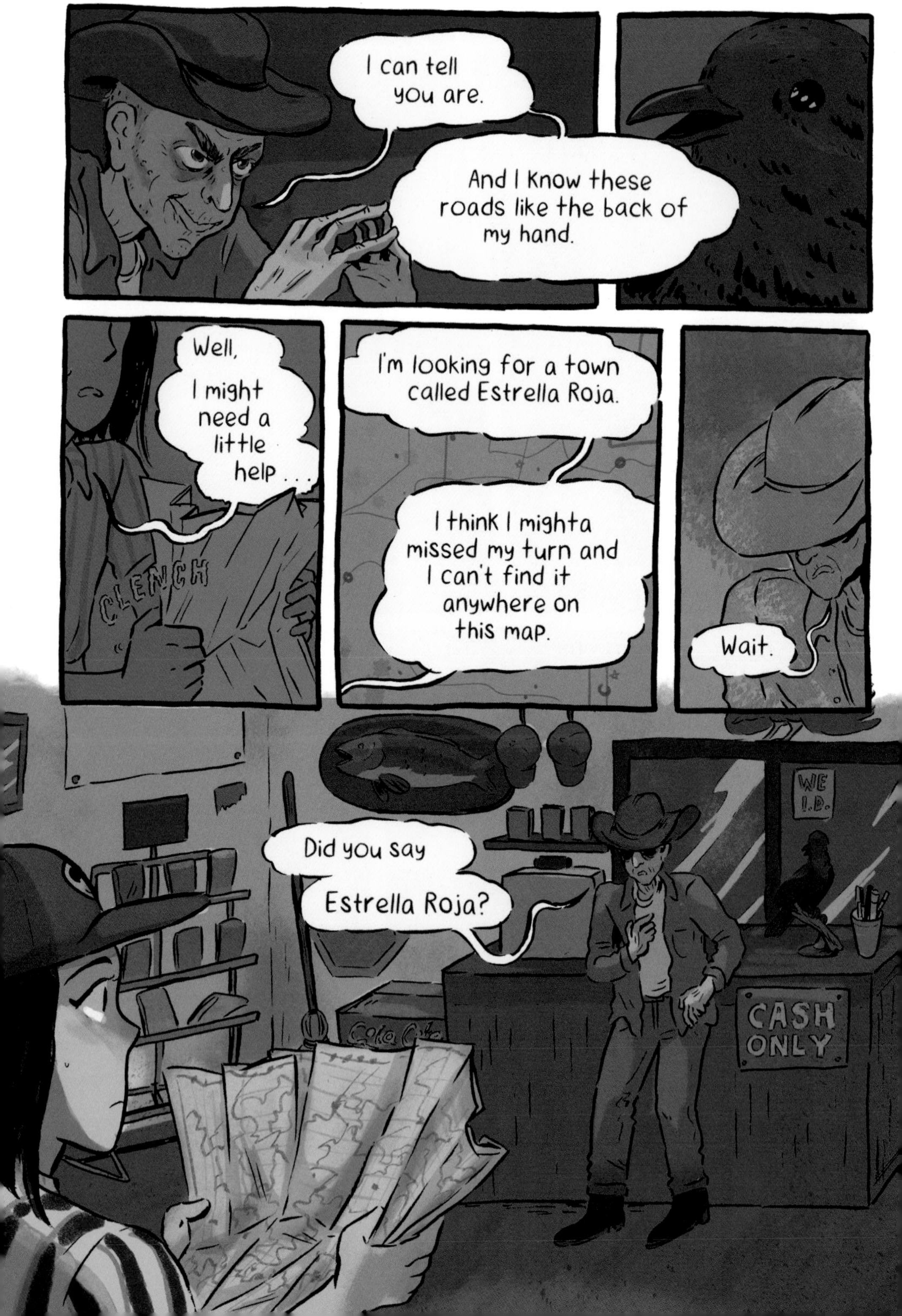
I can tell you are.
And I know these roads like the back of my hand.
Well,
I might need a little help . . .
CLENCH
I'm looking for a town called Estrella Roja.
I think I mighta missed my turn and I can't find it anywhere on this map.
Wait.
WE I.D.
Did you say
Estrella Roja?
CASH ONLY

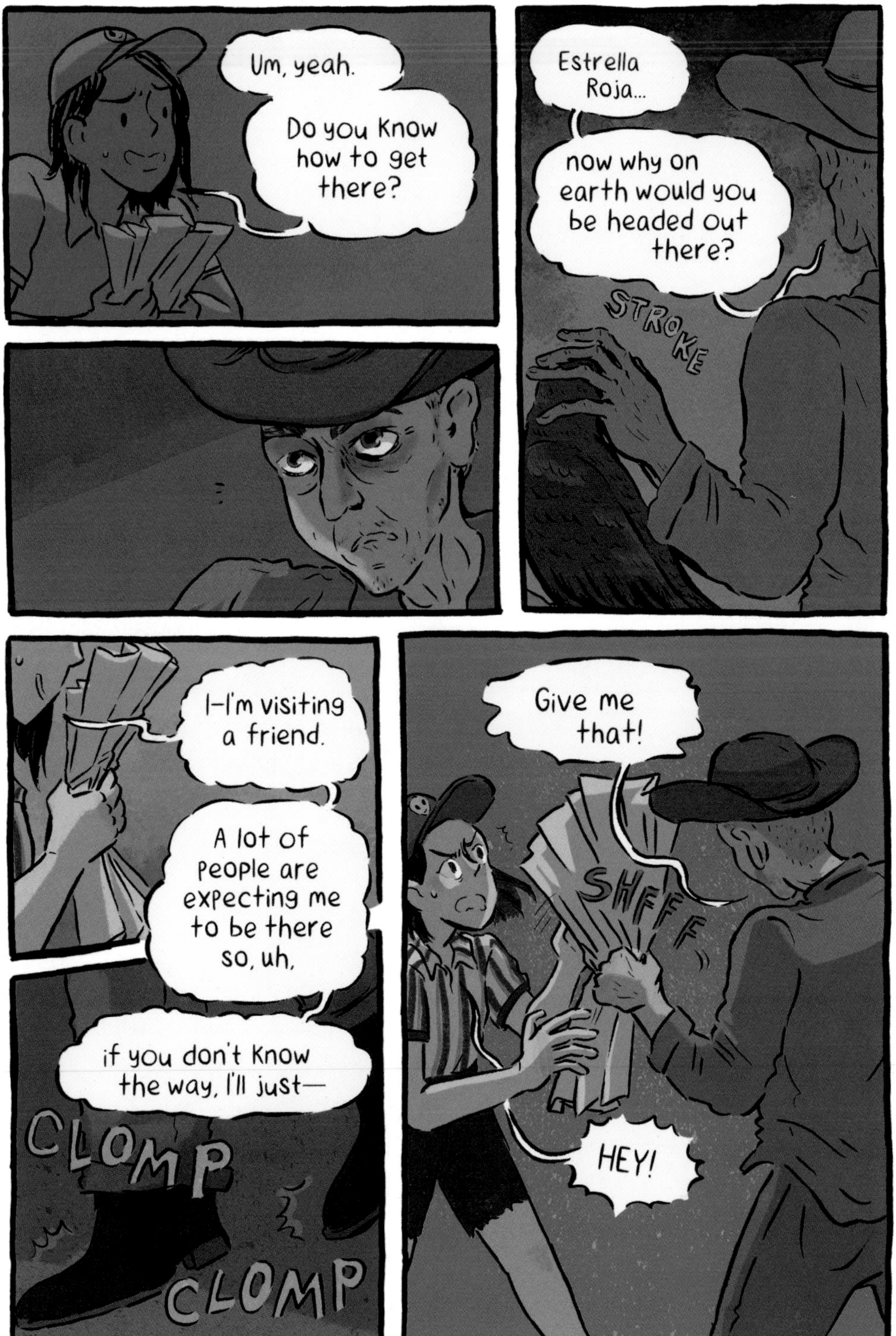
Um, yeah.
Do you know how to get there?
Estrella Roja...
now why on earth would you be headed out there?
STROKE
I-I'm visiting a friend.
A lot of people are expecting me to be there so, uh,
if you don't know the way, I'll just—
CLOMP
CLOMP
Give me that!
SHFFF
HEY!

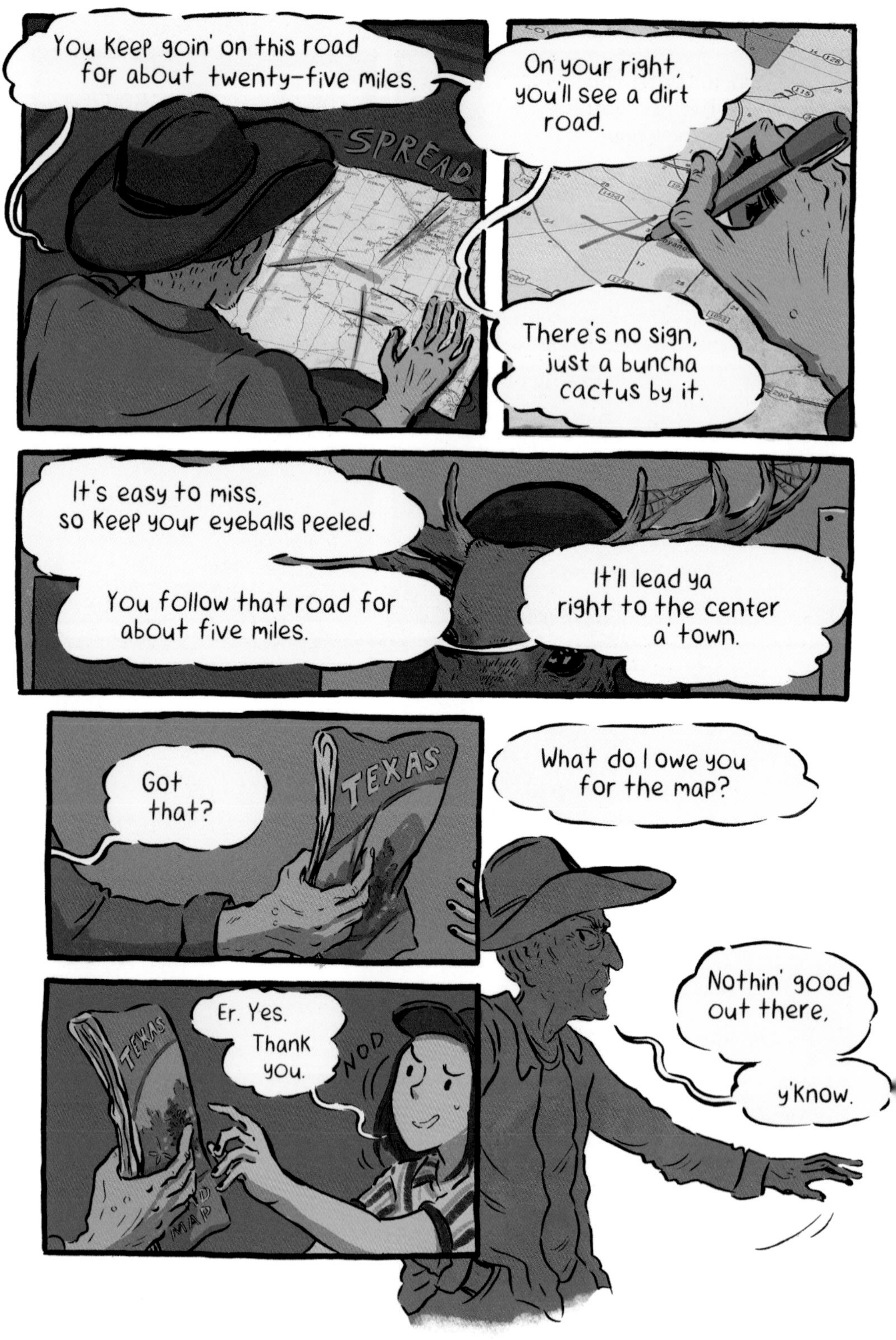
You keep goin' on this road for about twenty-five miles.
SPREAD
On your right, you'll see a dirt road.
There's no sign, just a buncha cactus by it.
It's easy to miss, so keep your eyeballs peeled.
You follow that road for about five miles.
It'll lead ya right to the center a' town.
Got that?
TEXAS
What do I owe you for the map?
Er. Yes. Thank you.
NOD
TEXAS
MAP
Nothin' good out there,
y'know.

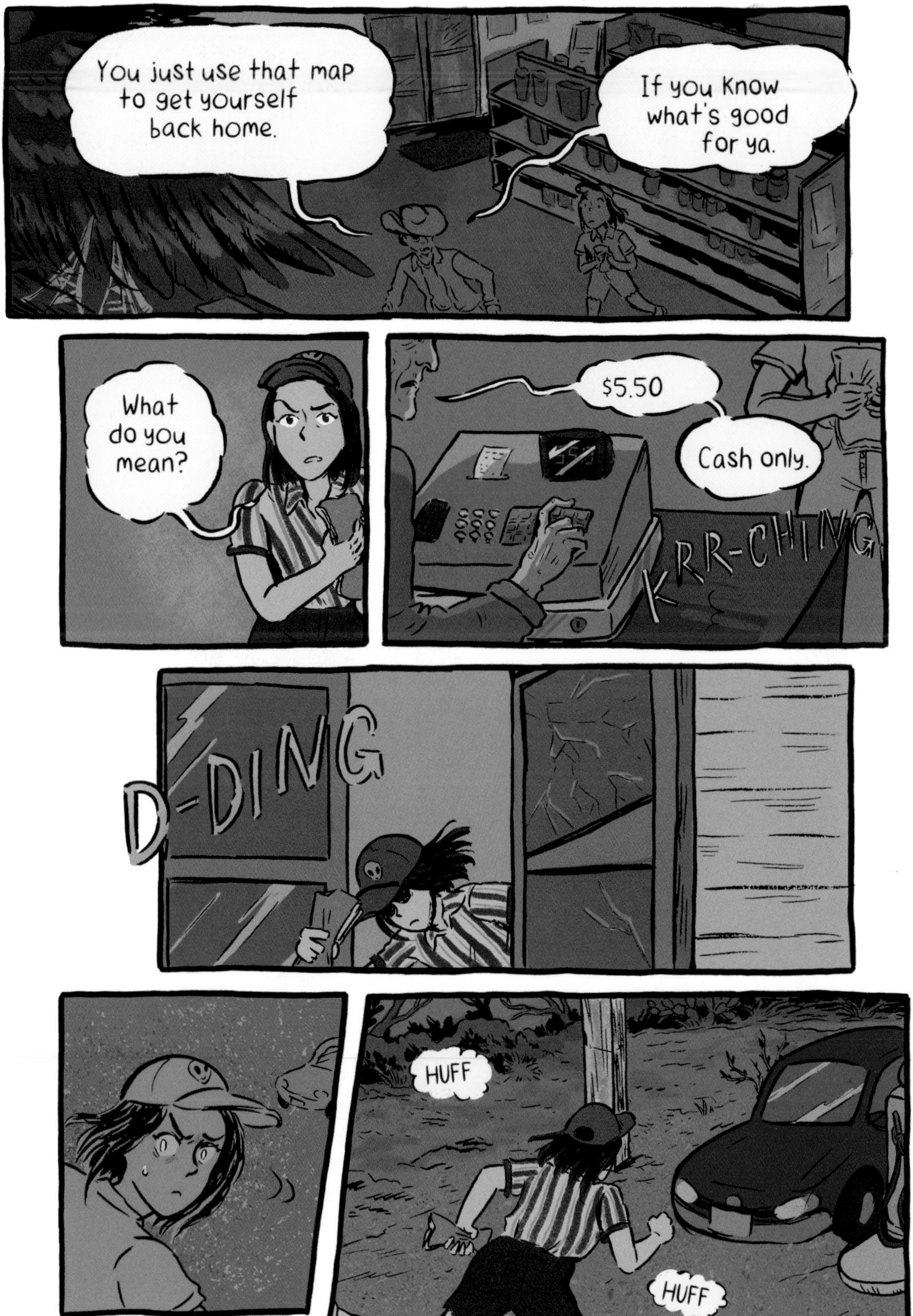
You just use that map to get yourself back home.
If you know what's good for ya.
What do you mean?
$5.50
Cash only.
KRR-CHING
D-DING
HUFF
HUFF

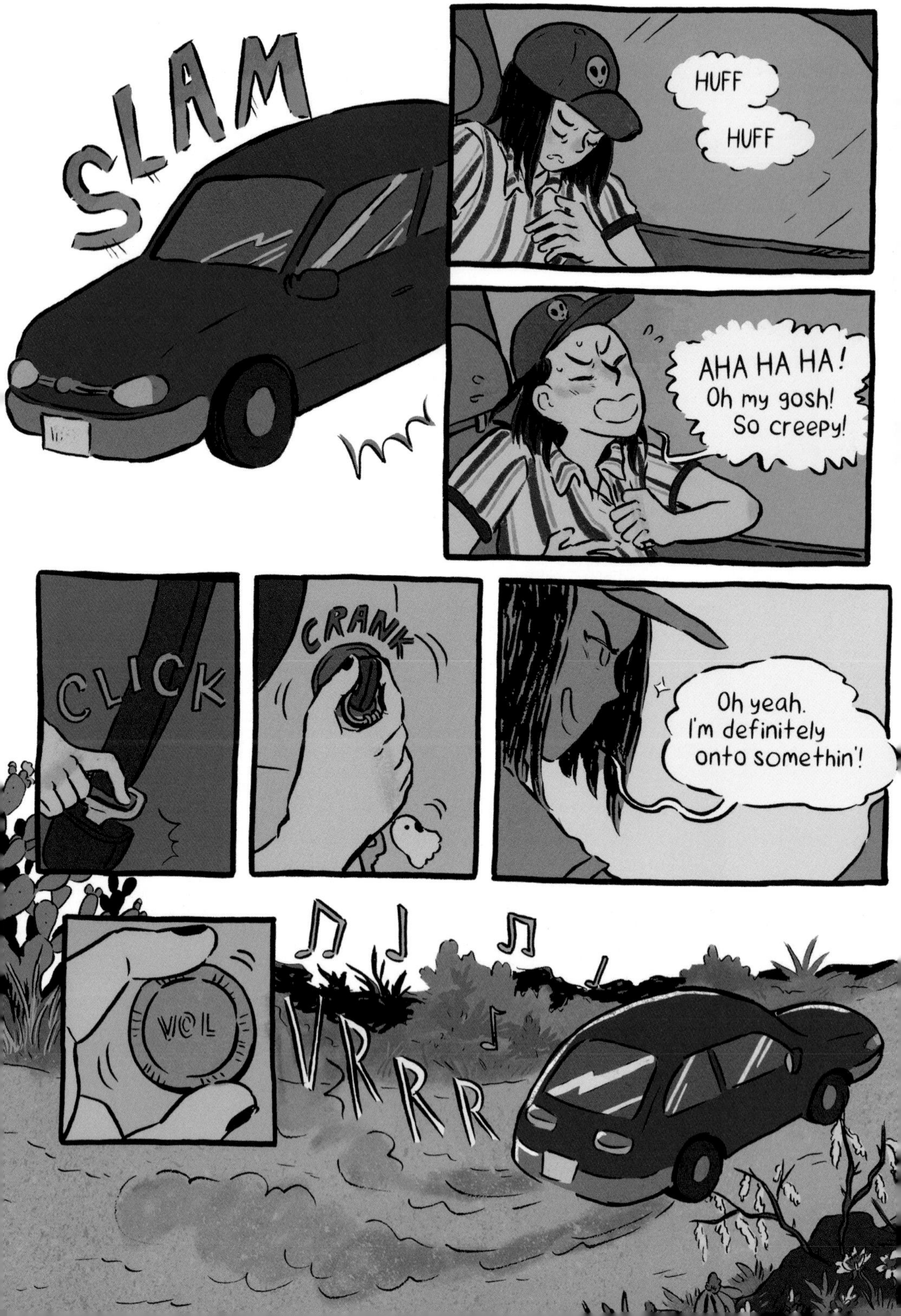
SLAM
HUFF
HUFF
AHA HA HA! Oh my gosh! So creepy!
CLICK
CRANK
Oh yeah. I'm definitely onto somethin'!
VOL
VRRR

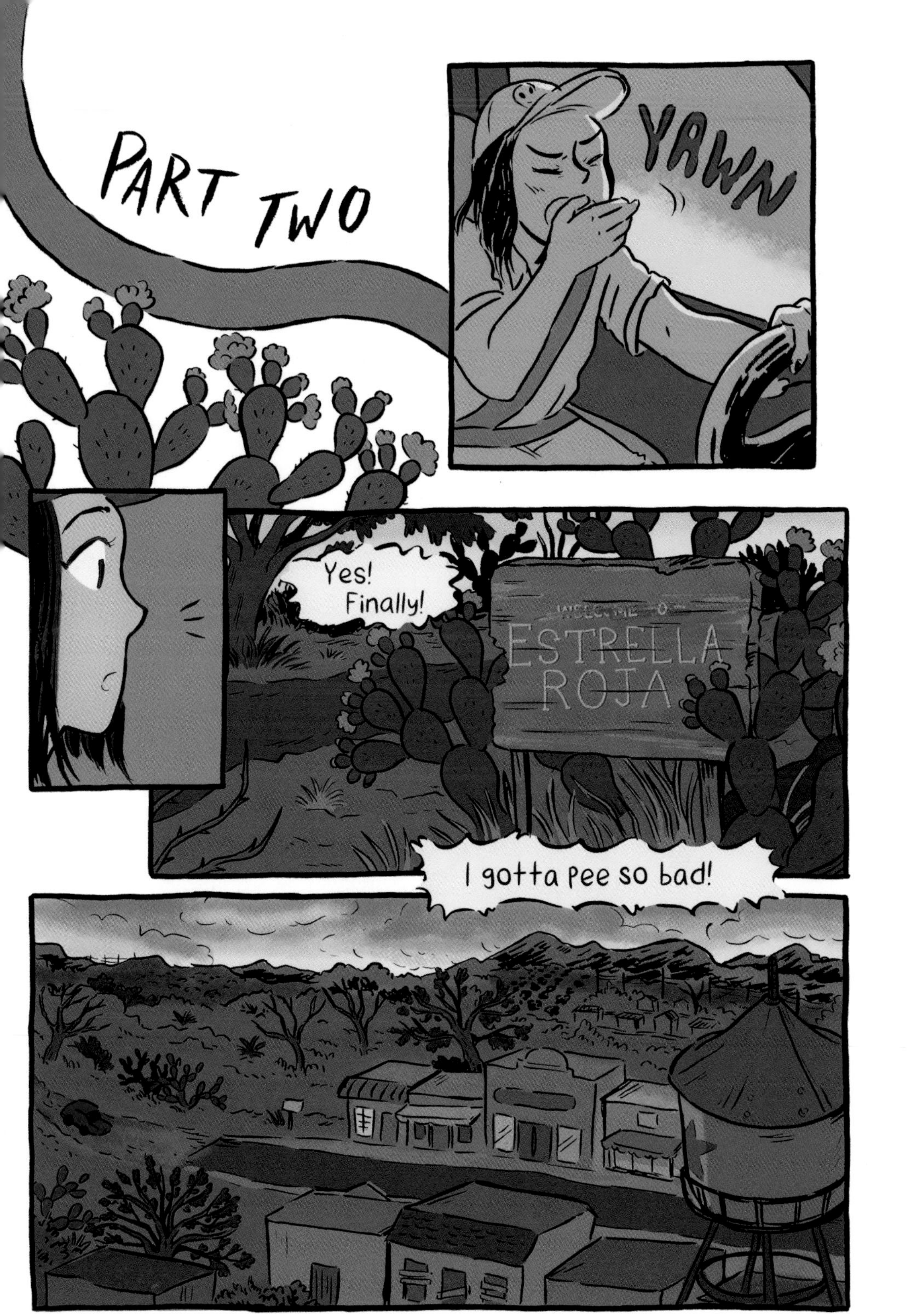
PART TWO
YAWN
Yes! Finally!
ESTRELLA ROJA
I gotta pee so bad!

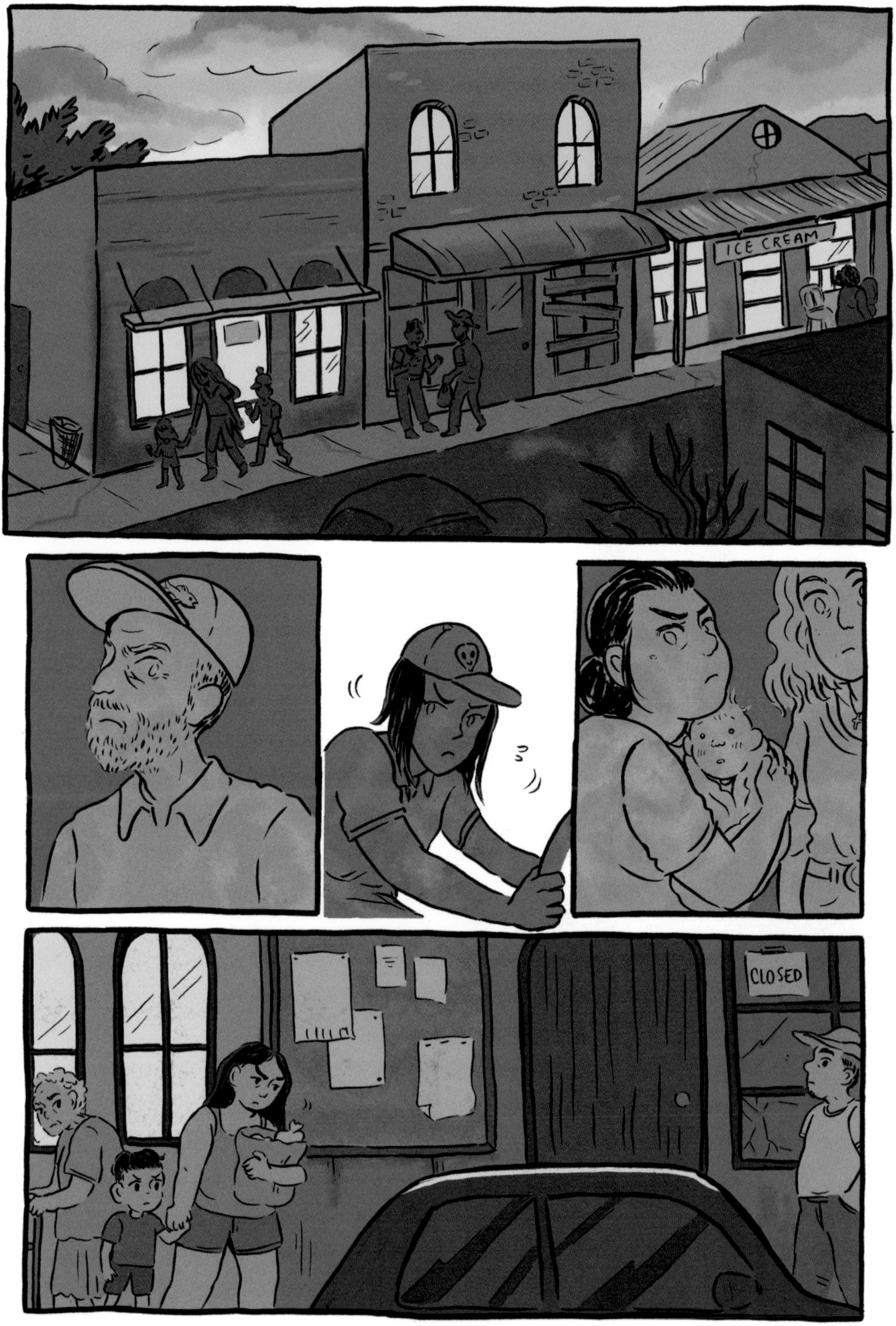
ICE CREAM
CLOSED

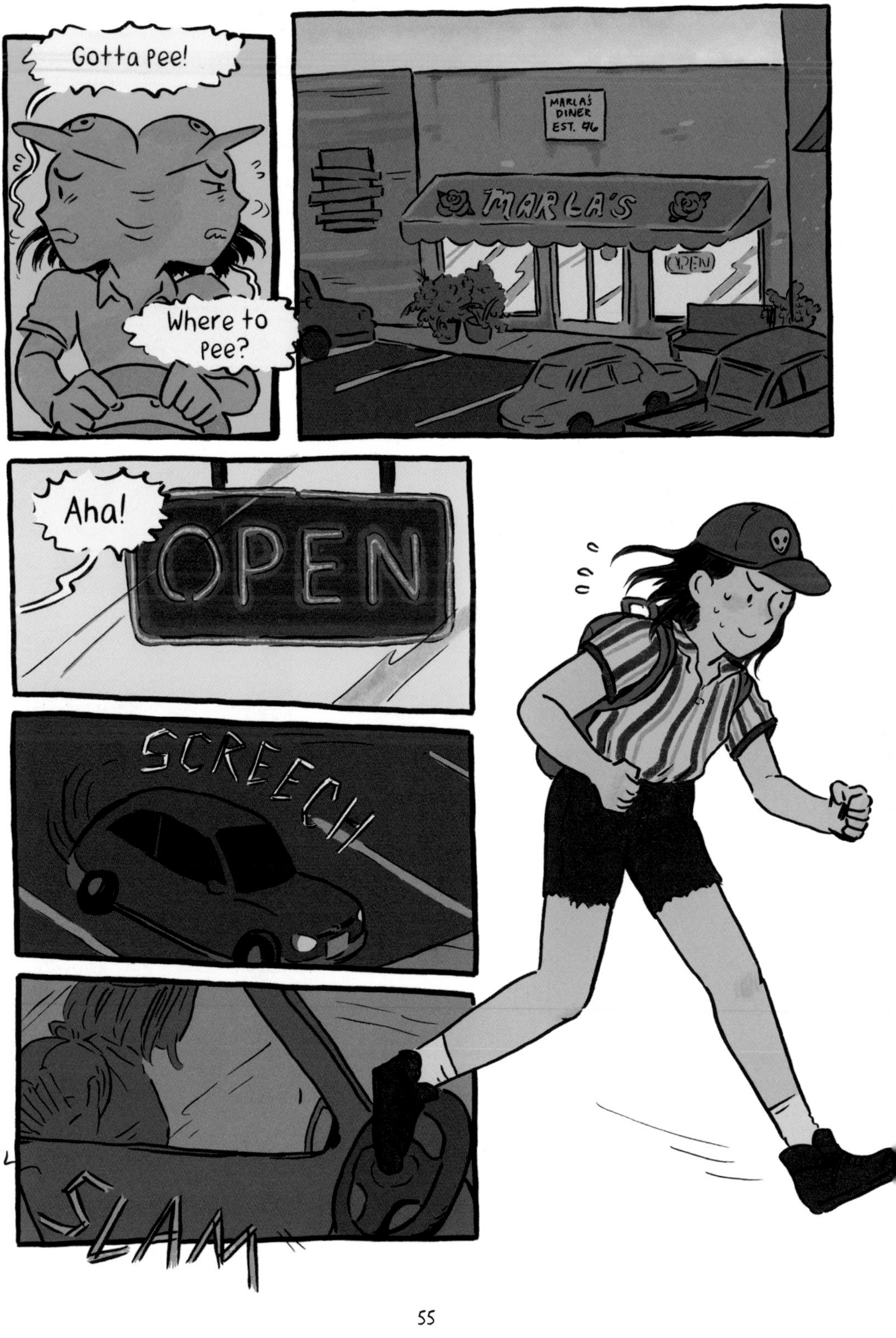
Gotta pee!
Where to pee?
MARLA'S DINER EST. 46
MARLA'S
OPEN
Aha!
OPEN
SCREECH
SLAM

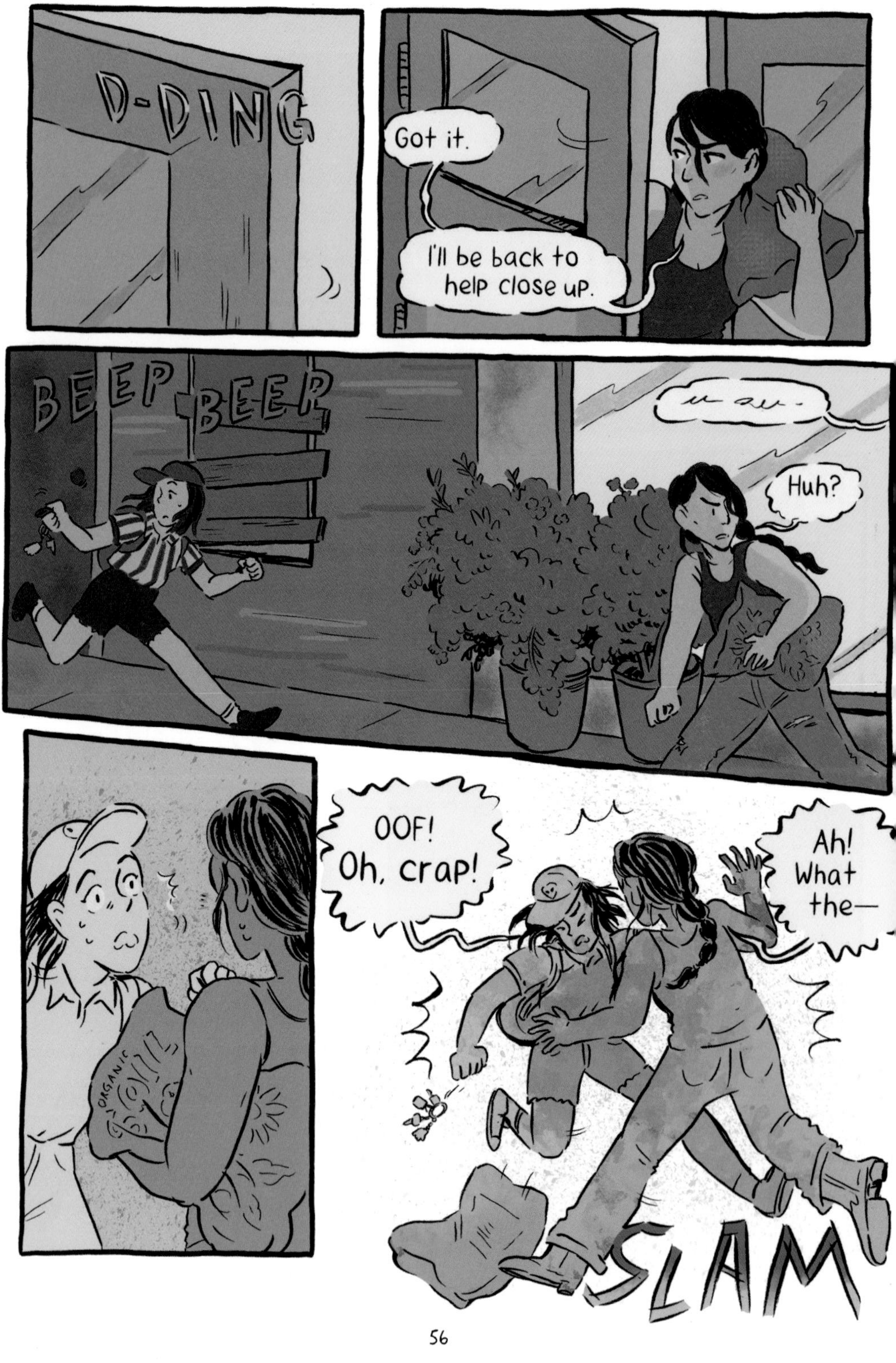
D-DING
Got it.
I'll be back to help close up.
BEEP BEEP
Huh?
OOF! Oh, crap!
Ah! What the—
ORGANIC
SLAM

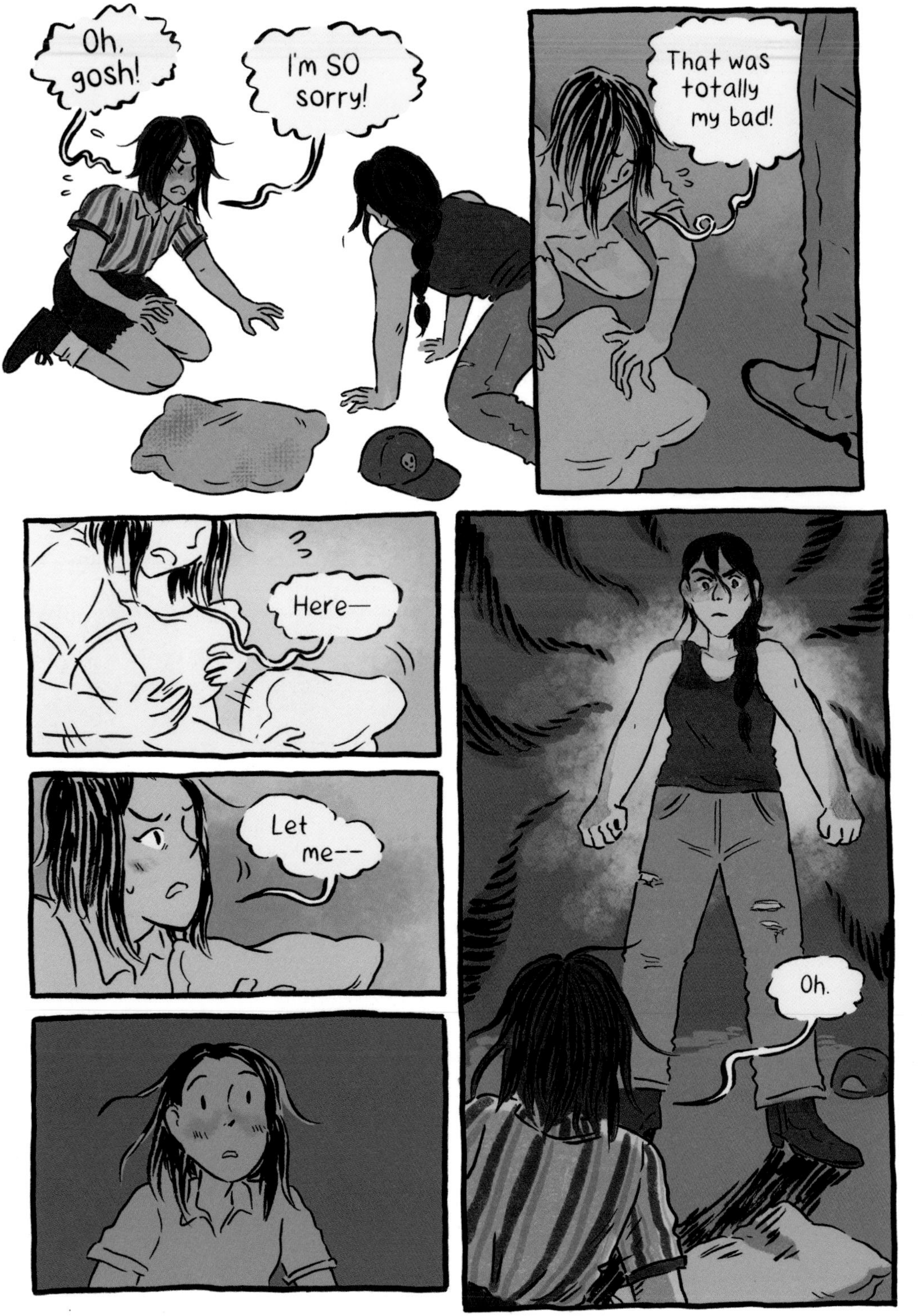
Oh, gosh!
I'm SO sorry!
That was totally my bad!
Here—
Let me--
Oh.

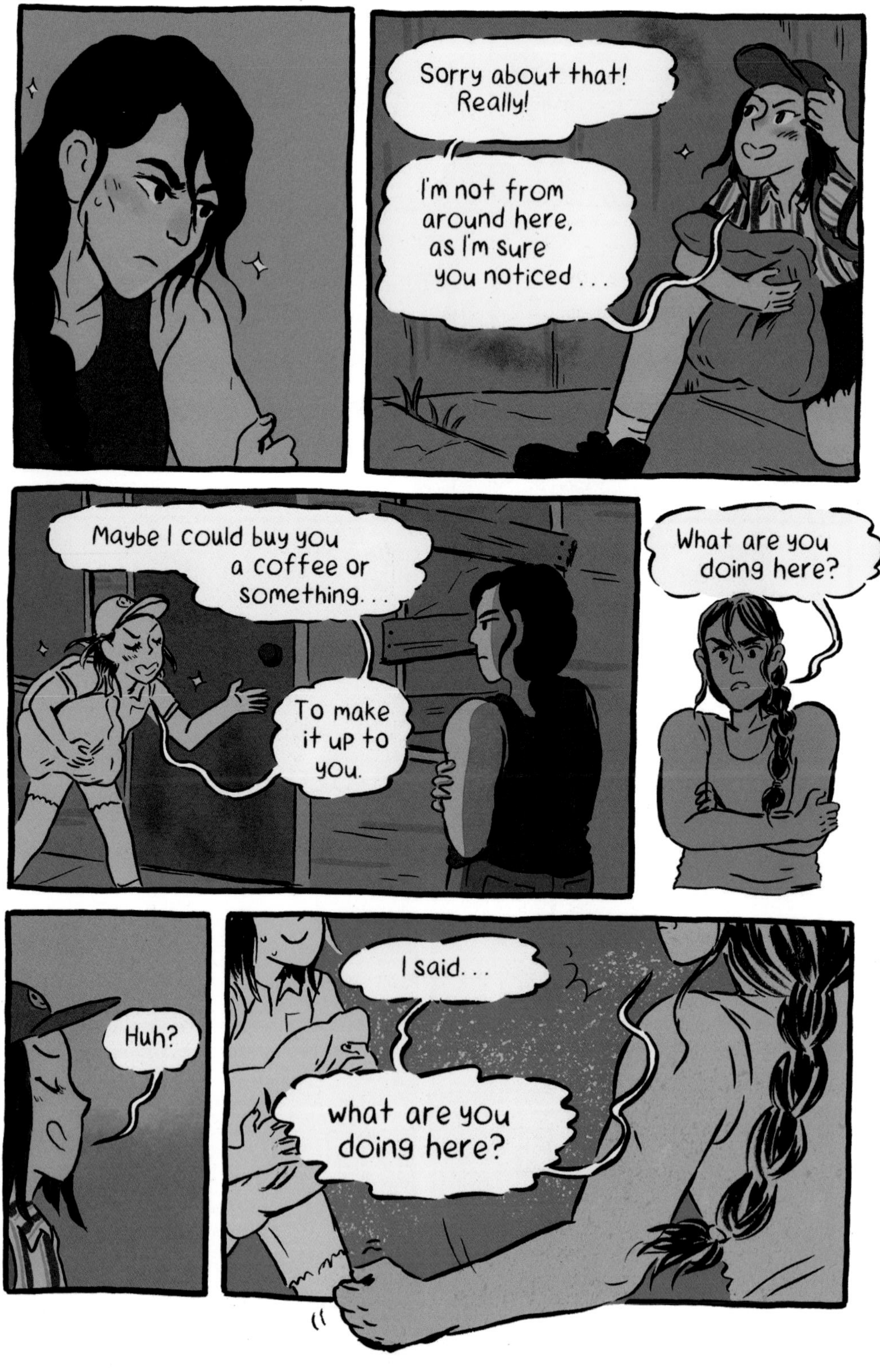
Sorry about that! Really!
I'm not from around here, as I'm sure you noticed . . .
Maybe I could buy you a coffee or something. . .
To make it up to you.
What are you doing here?
Huh?
I said. . .
what are you doing here?

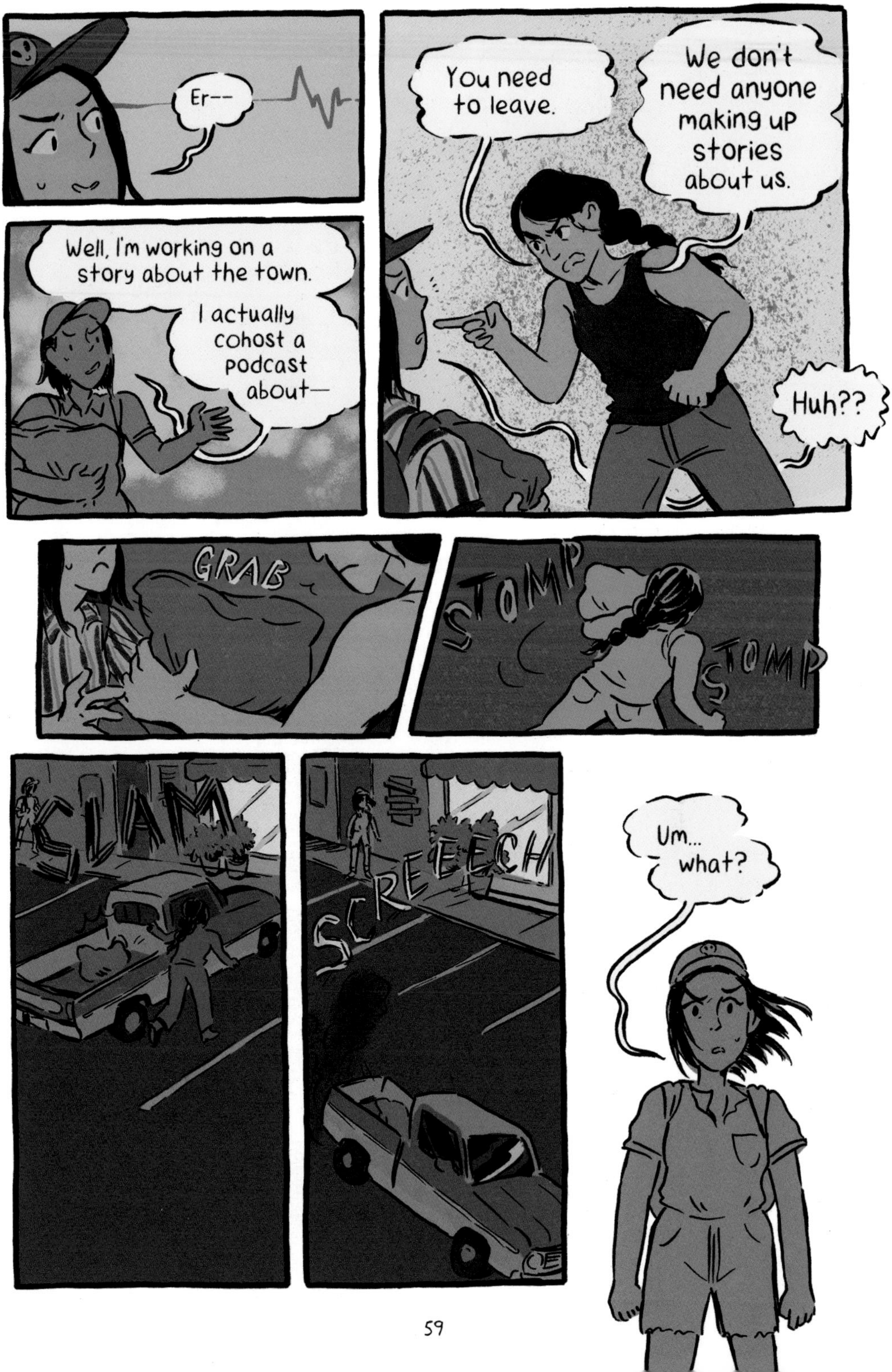

Er--
Well, I'm working on a story about the town.
I actually cohost a podcast about—
You need to leave.
We don't need anyone making up stories about us.
Huh??
GRAB
STOMP
STOMP
SLAM
SCREEECH
Um... what?

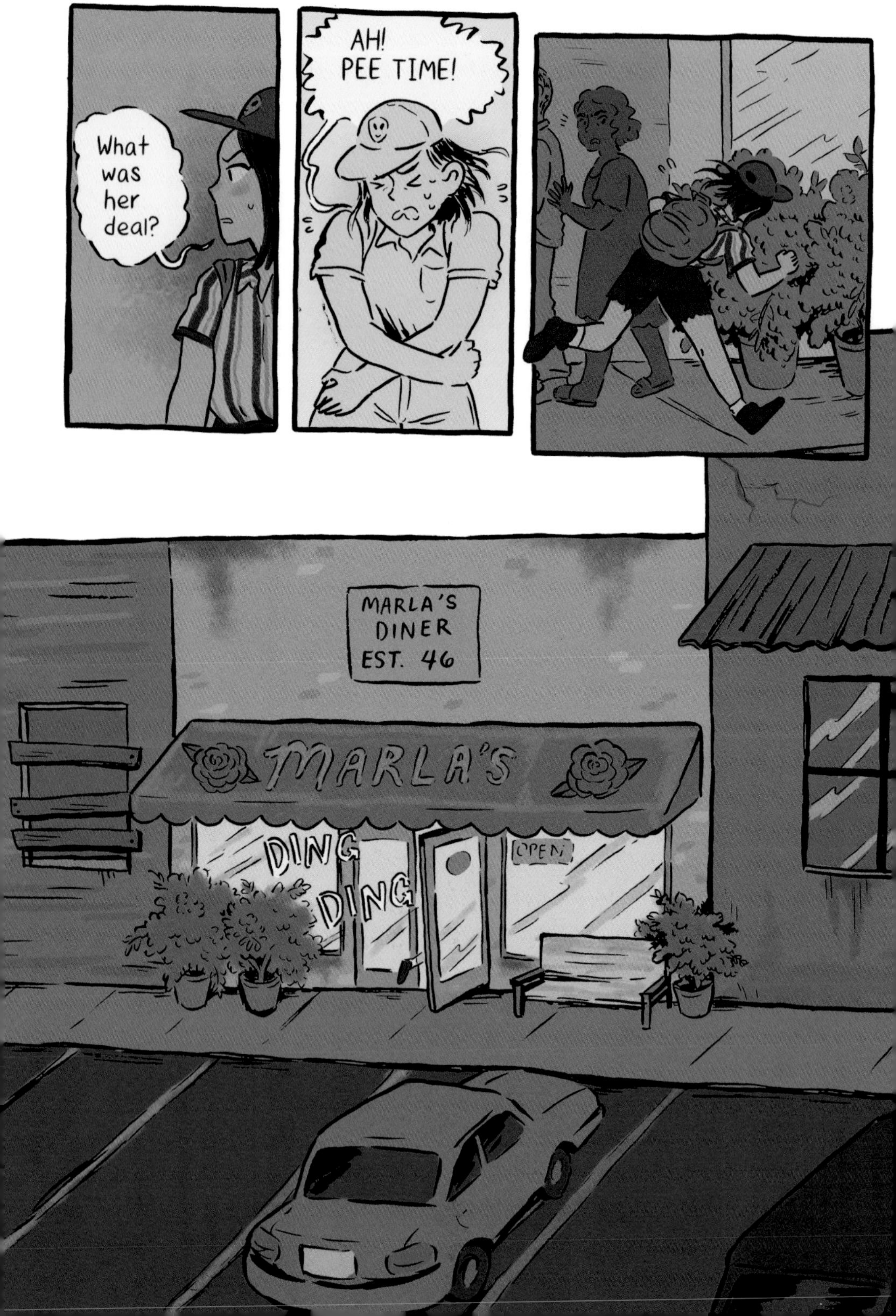
What was her deal?
AH! PEE TIME!
MARLA'S DINER EST. 46
MARLA'S
DING
DING
OPEN

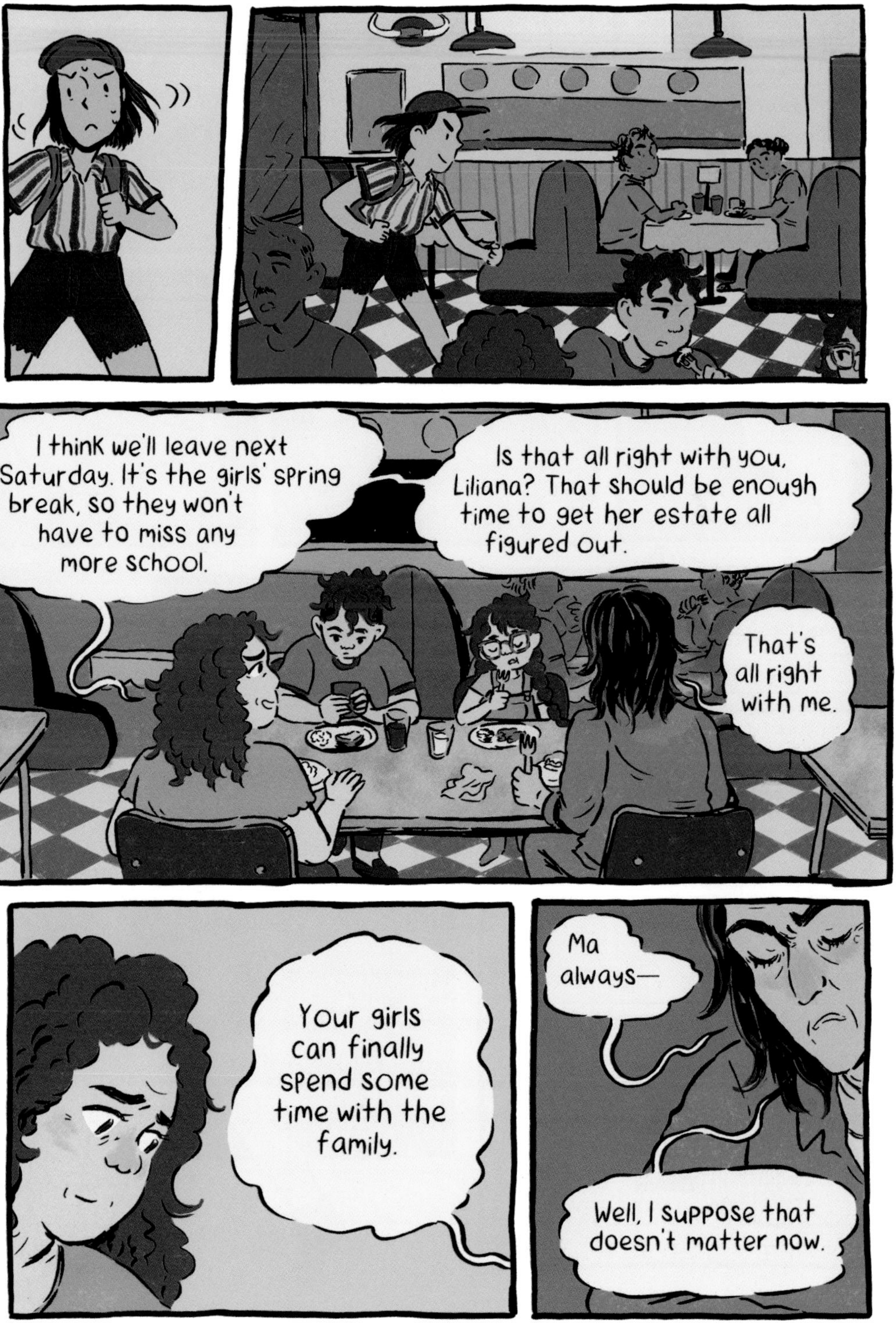
I think we'll leave next Saturday. It's the girls' spring break, so they won't have to miss any more school.
Is that all right with you, Liliana? That should be enough time to get her estate all figured out.
That's all right with me.
Your girls can finally spend some time with the family.
Ma always—
Well, I suppose that doesn't matter now.

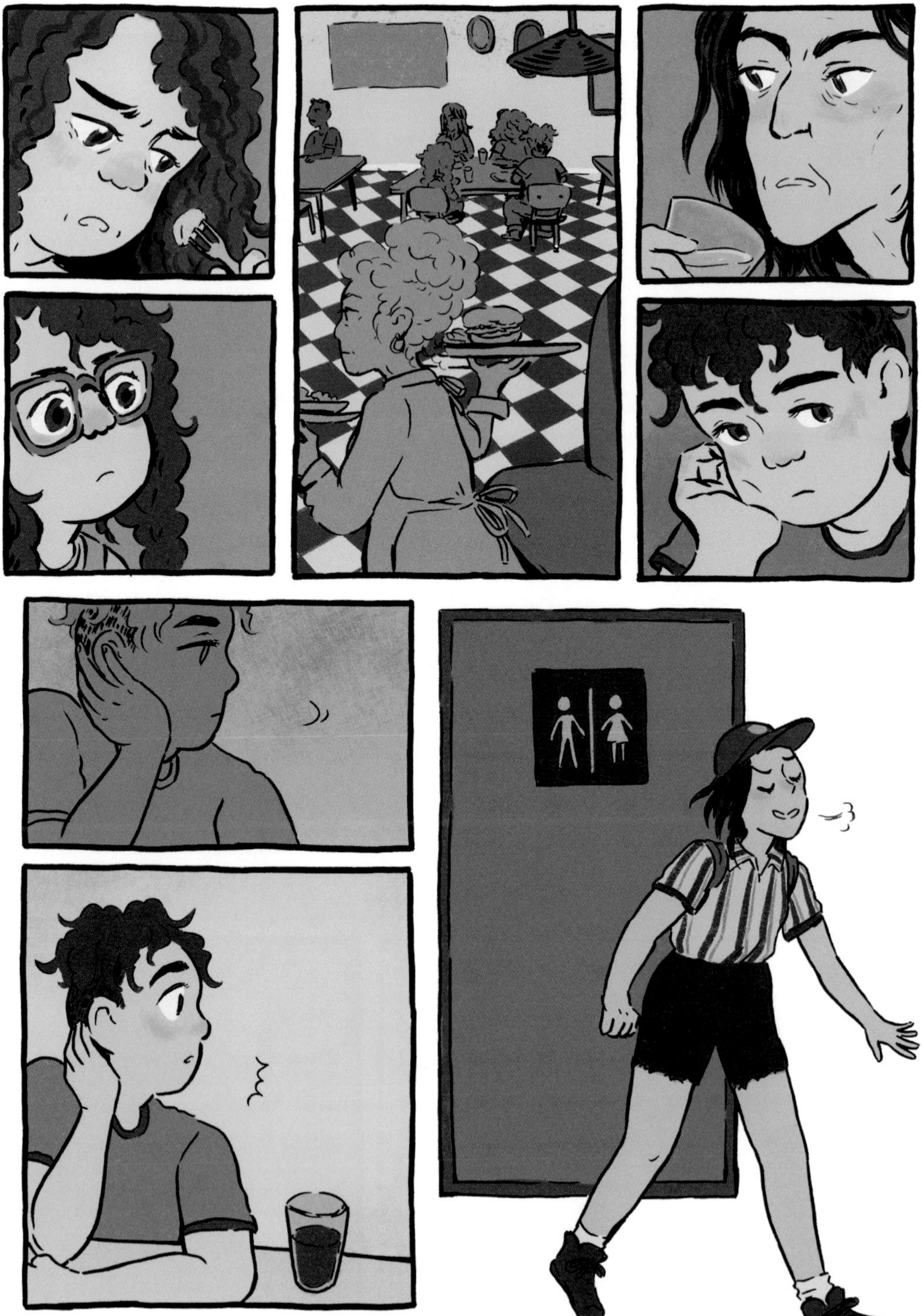

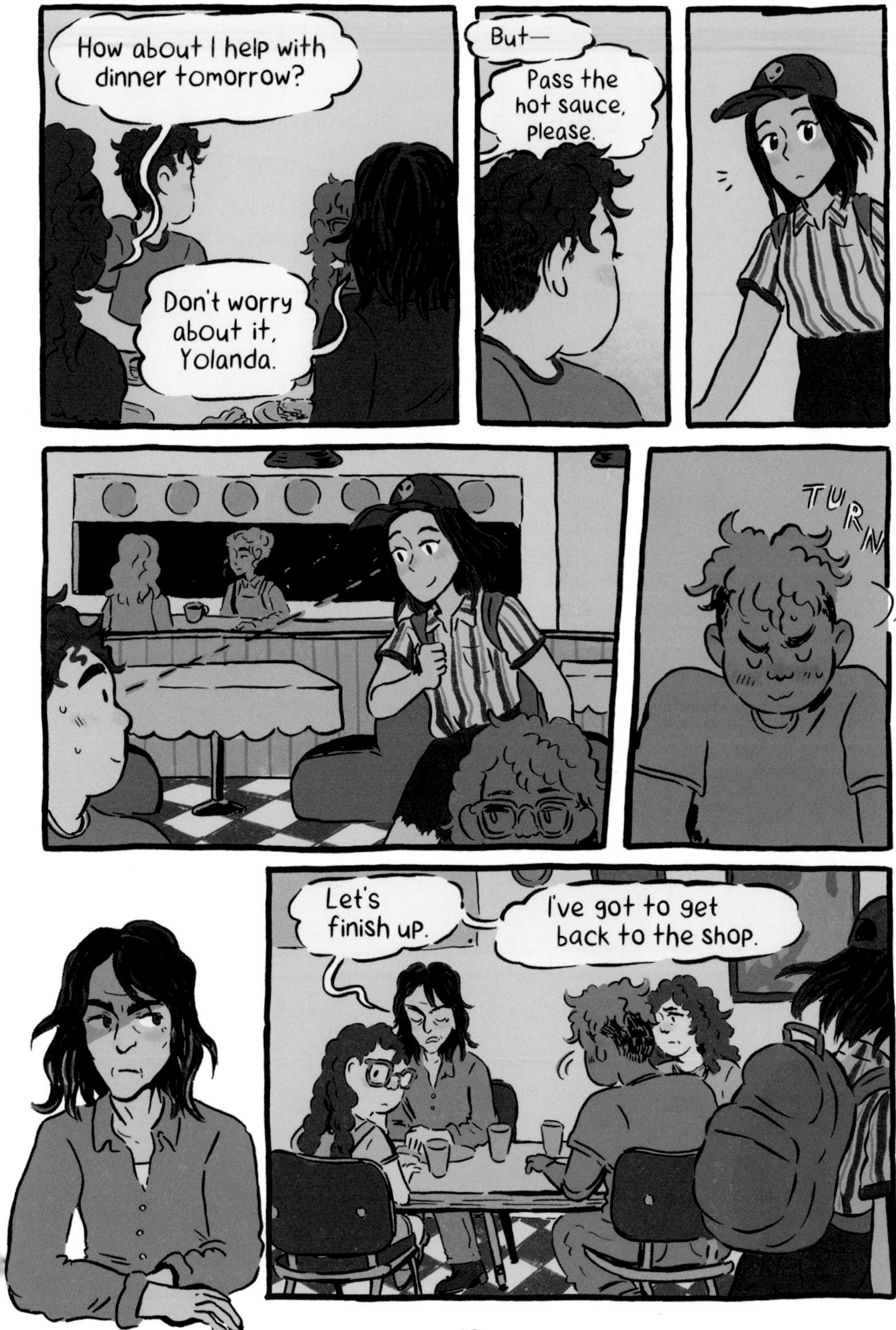
How about I help with dinner tomorrow?
Don't worry about it, Yolanda.
But—
Pass the hot sauce, please.
TURN
Let's finish up.
I've got to get back to the shop.

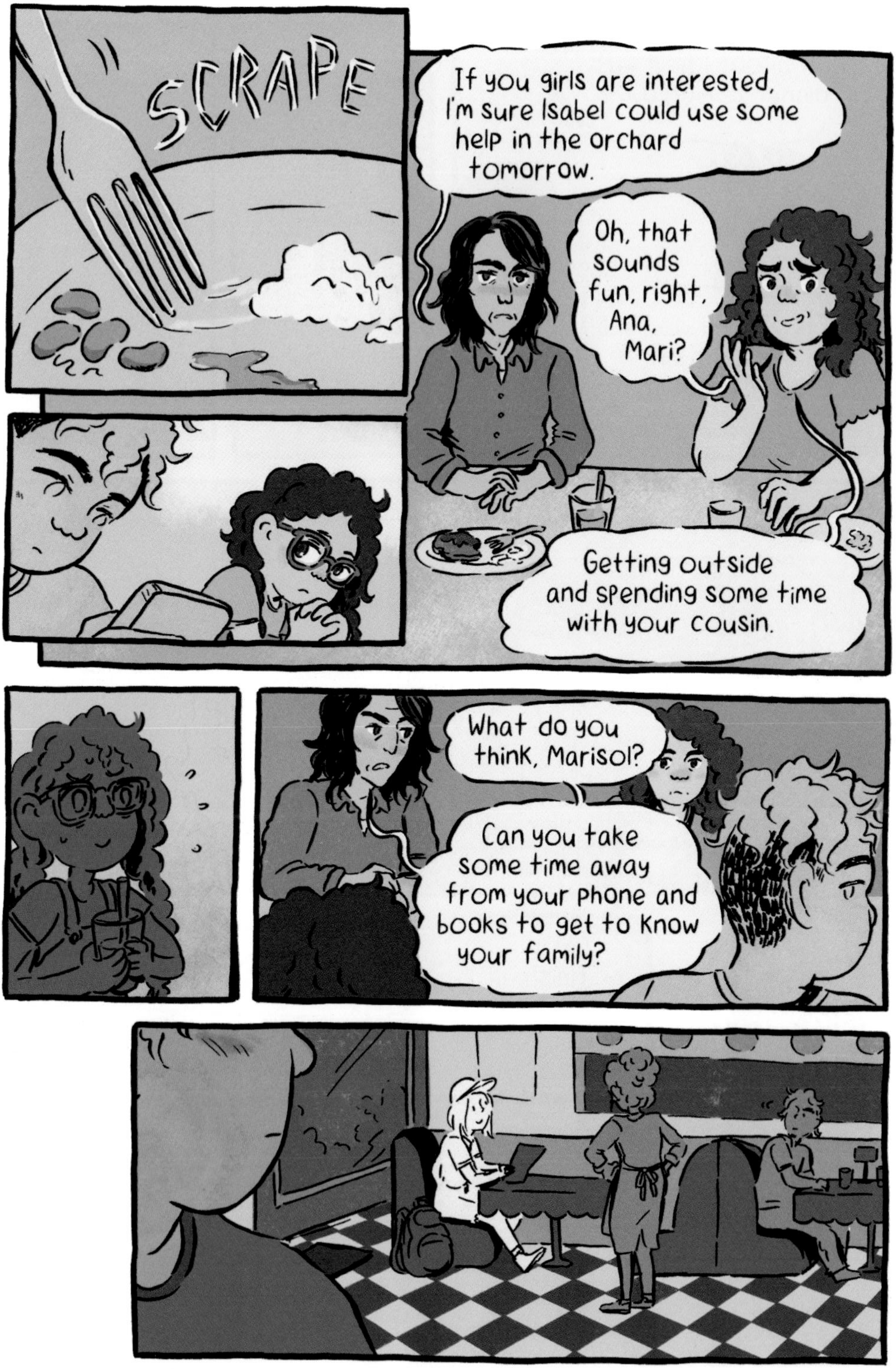
SCRAPE
If you girls are interested, I'm sure Isabel could use some help in the orchard tomorrow.
Oh, that sounds fun, right, Ana, Mari?
Getting outside and spending some time with your cousin.
What do you think, Marisol?
Can you take some time away from your phone and books to get to know your family?

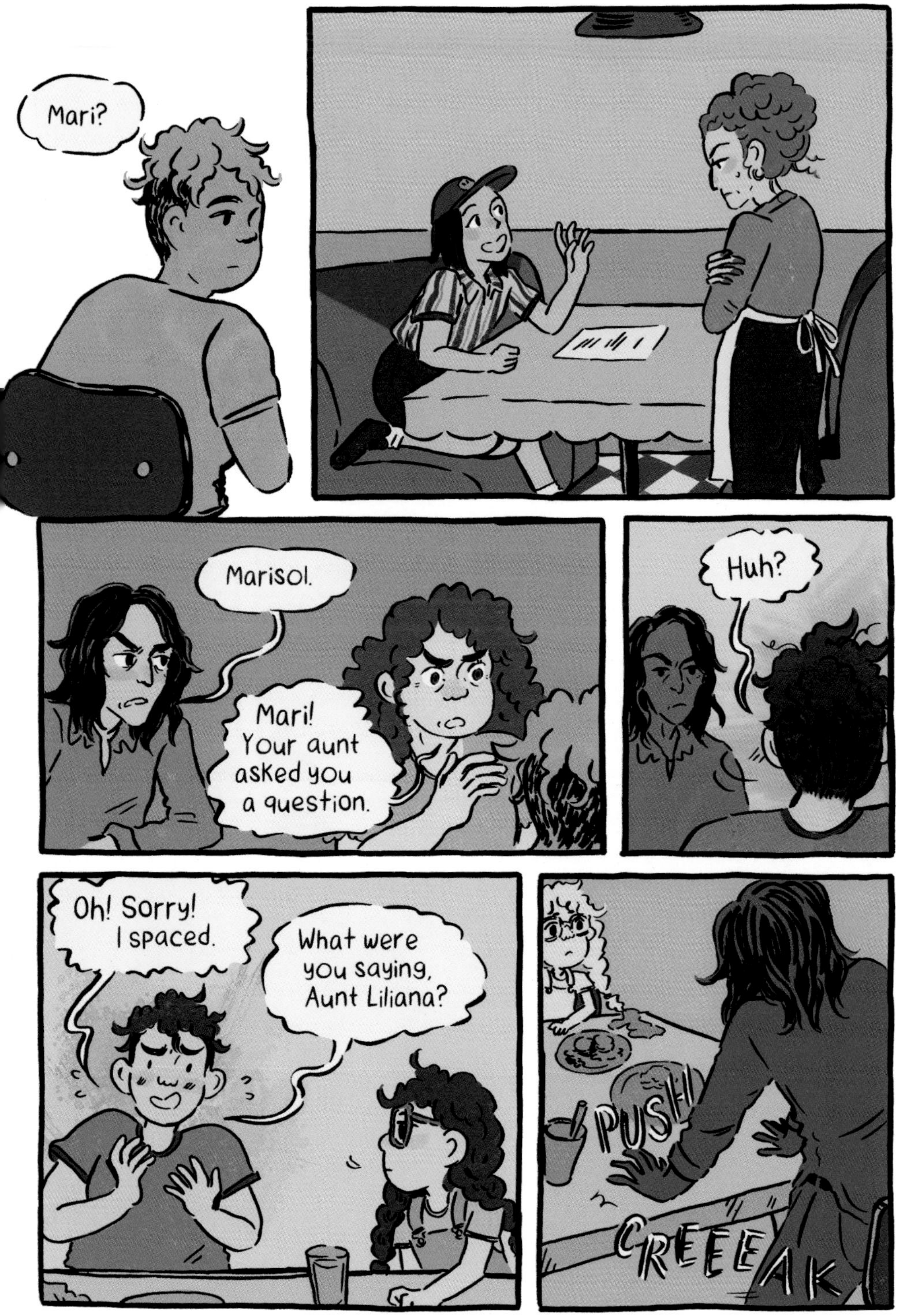

Mari?
Marisol.
Mari! Your aunt asked you a question.
Huh?
Oh! Sorry! I spaced.
What were you saying, Aunt Liliana?
PUSH
CREEEAK

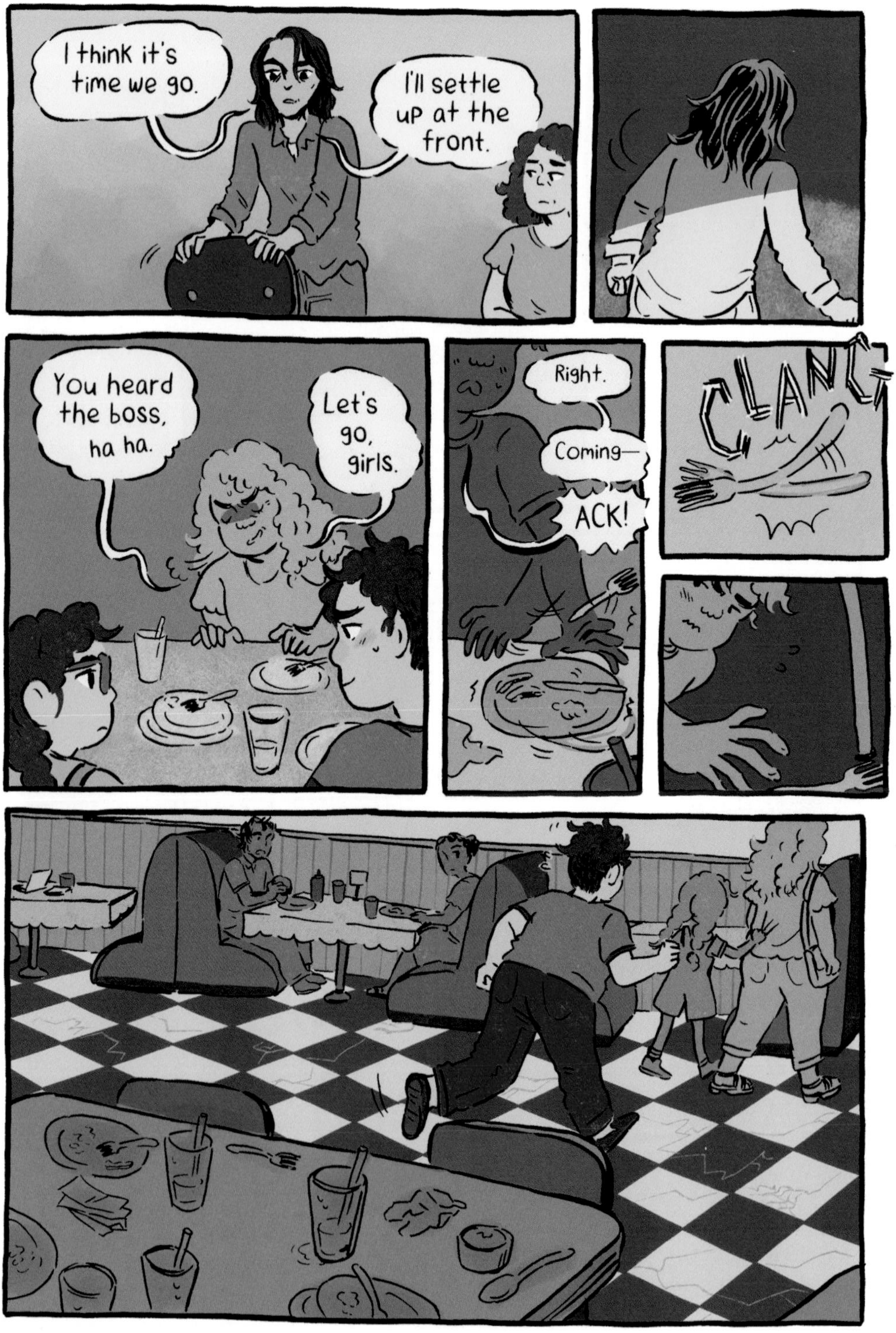
I think it's time we go.
I'll settle up at the front.
You heard the boss, ha ha.
Let's go, girls.
Right.
Coming—
ACK!
CLANG

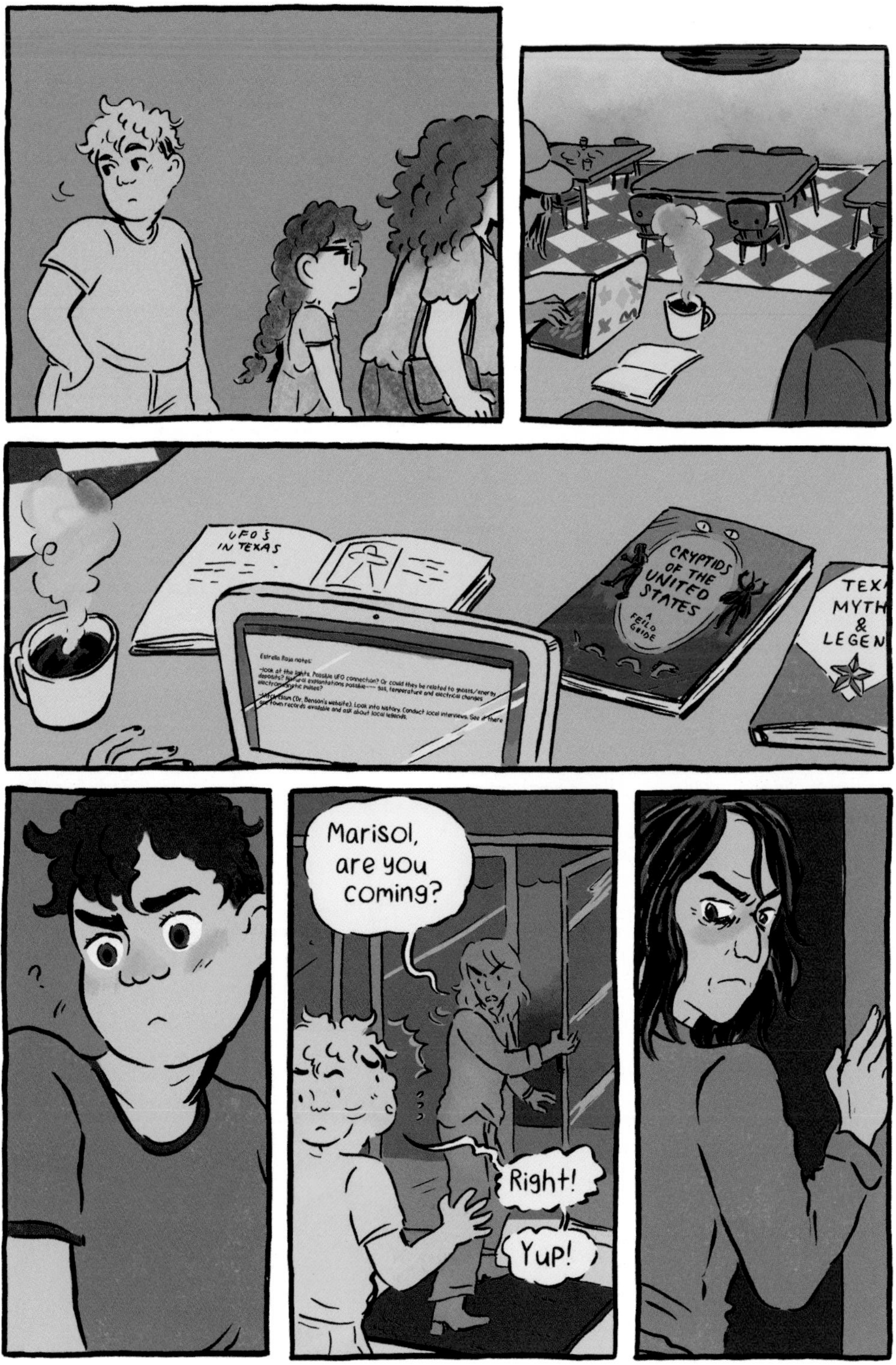
UFO's IN TEXAS
Estrella Roja notes:
Possible UFO connection? Or could they be related to ghosts/energy
explantations possible— gas, temperature and electrical changes
(Dr. Benson's website). Look into history. Conduct local interviews. See if there
town records available and ask about local legends.
CRYPTIDS OF THE UNITED STATES
A FEILD GUIDE
Marisol, are you coming?
Right!
Yup!

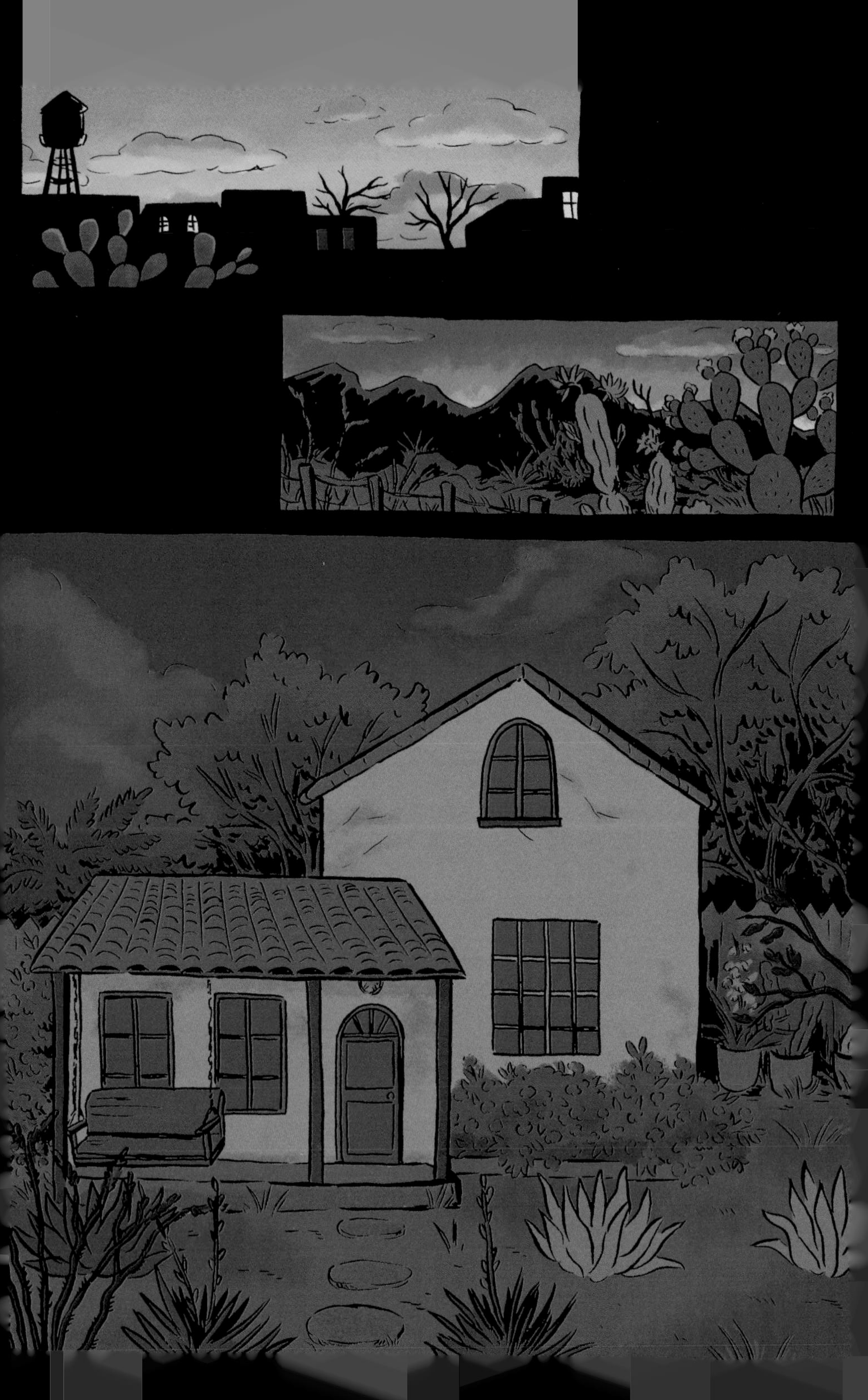

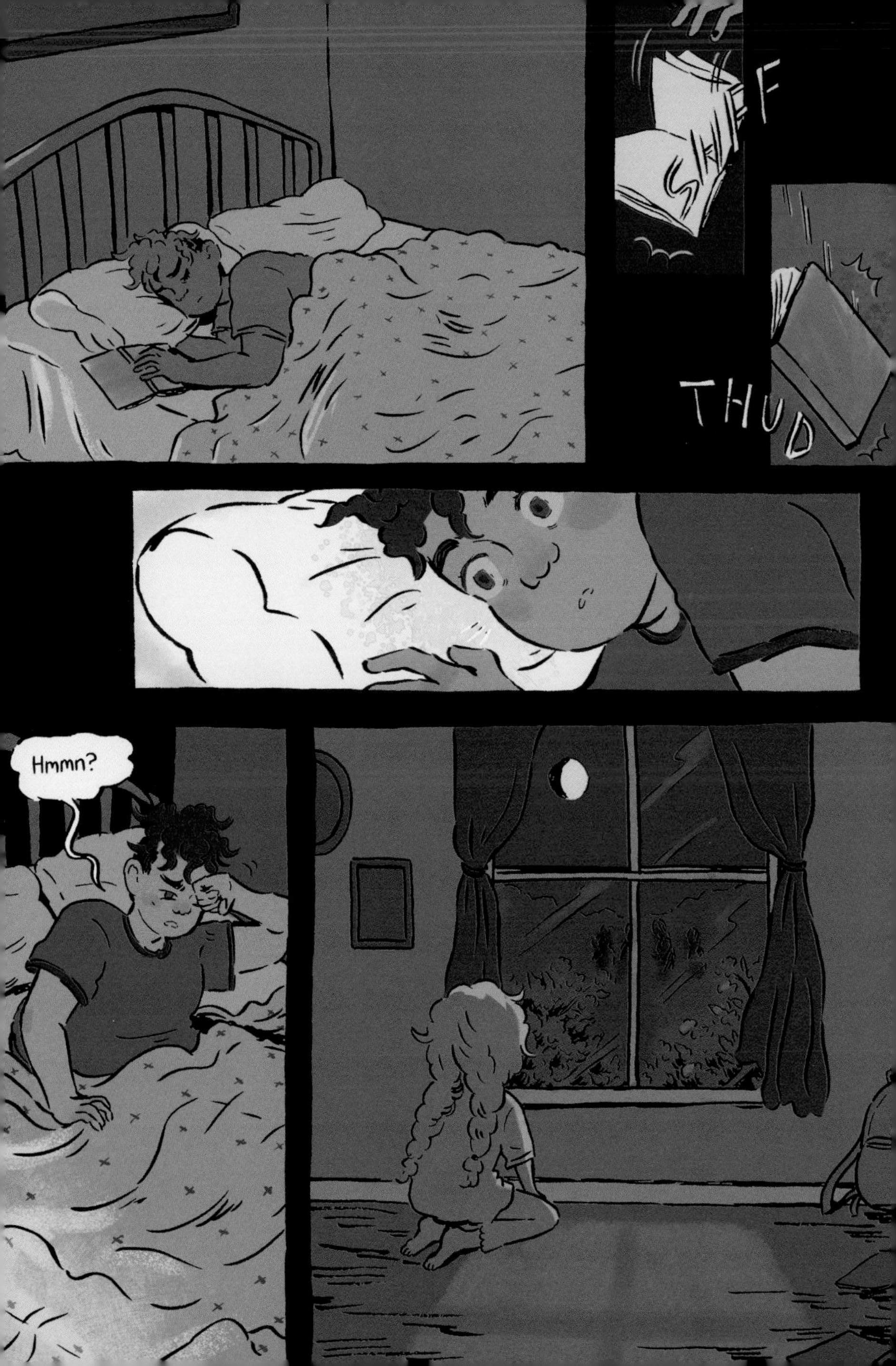
SHFF
THUD
Hmmn?

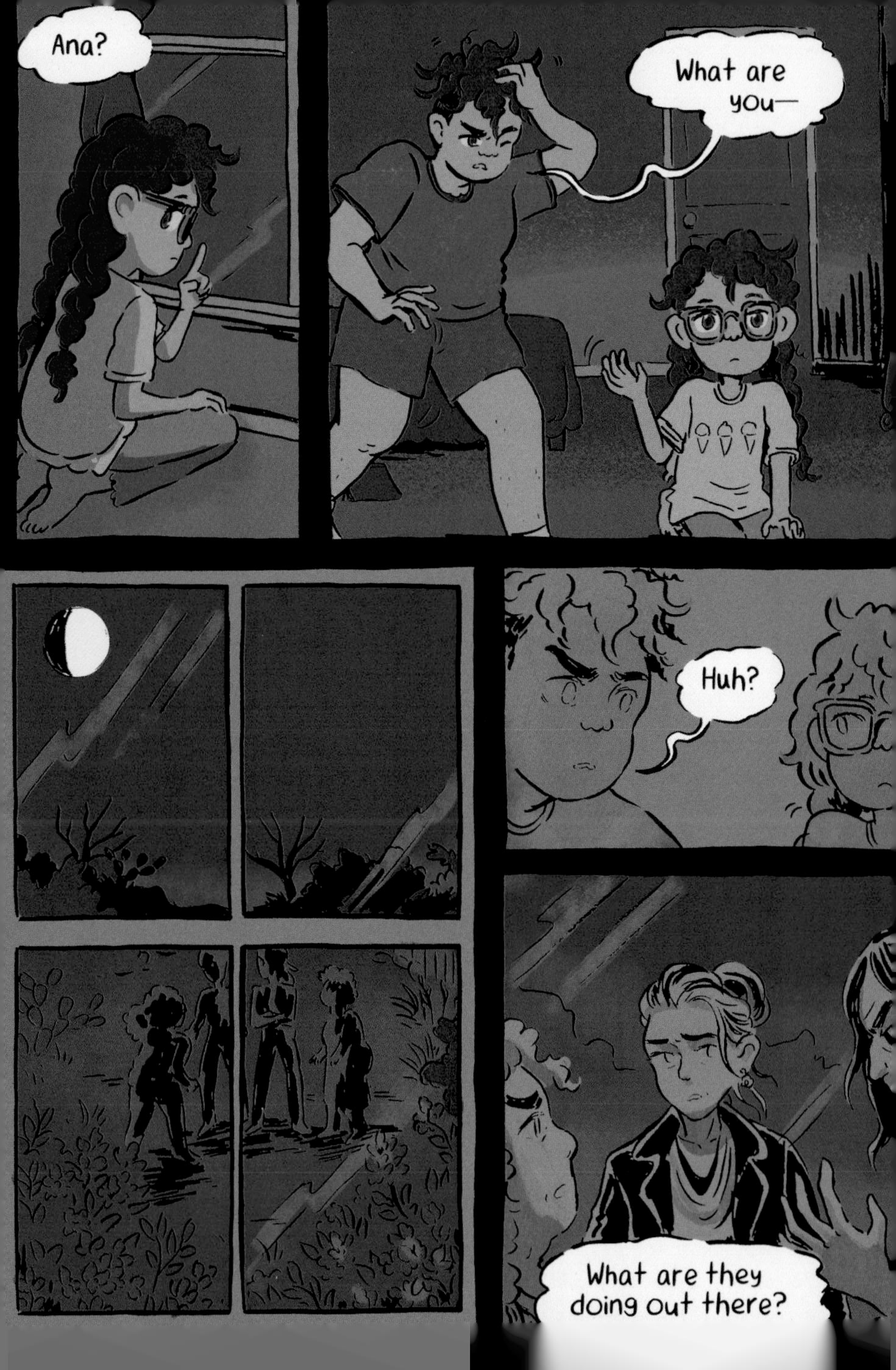
Ana?
What are you—
Huh?
What are they doing out there?

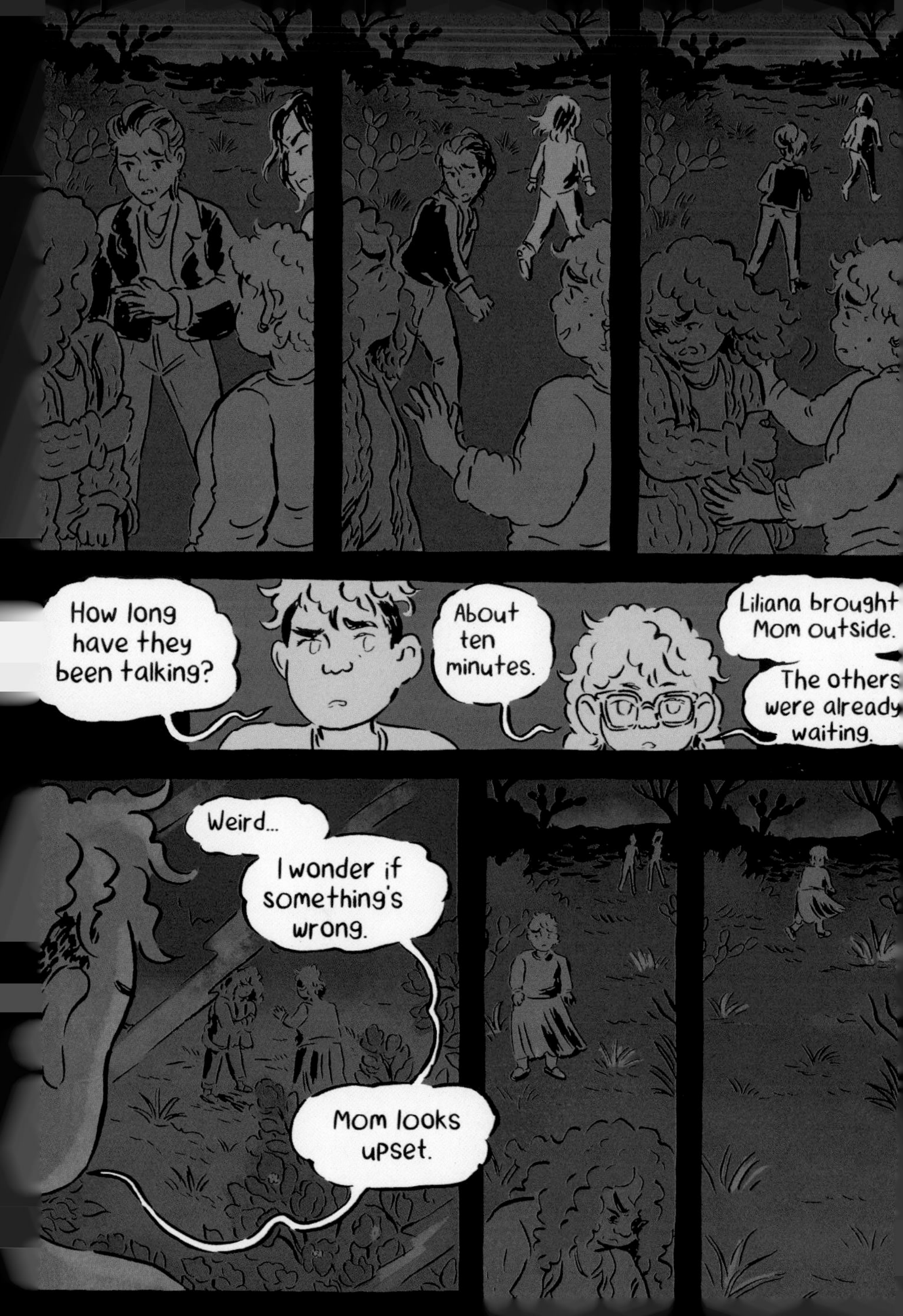
How long have they been talking?
About ten minutes.
Liliana brought Mom outside.
The others were already waiting.
Weird...
I wonder if something's wrong.
Mom looks upset.

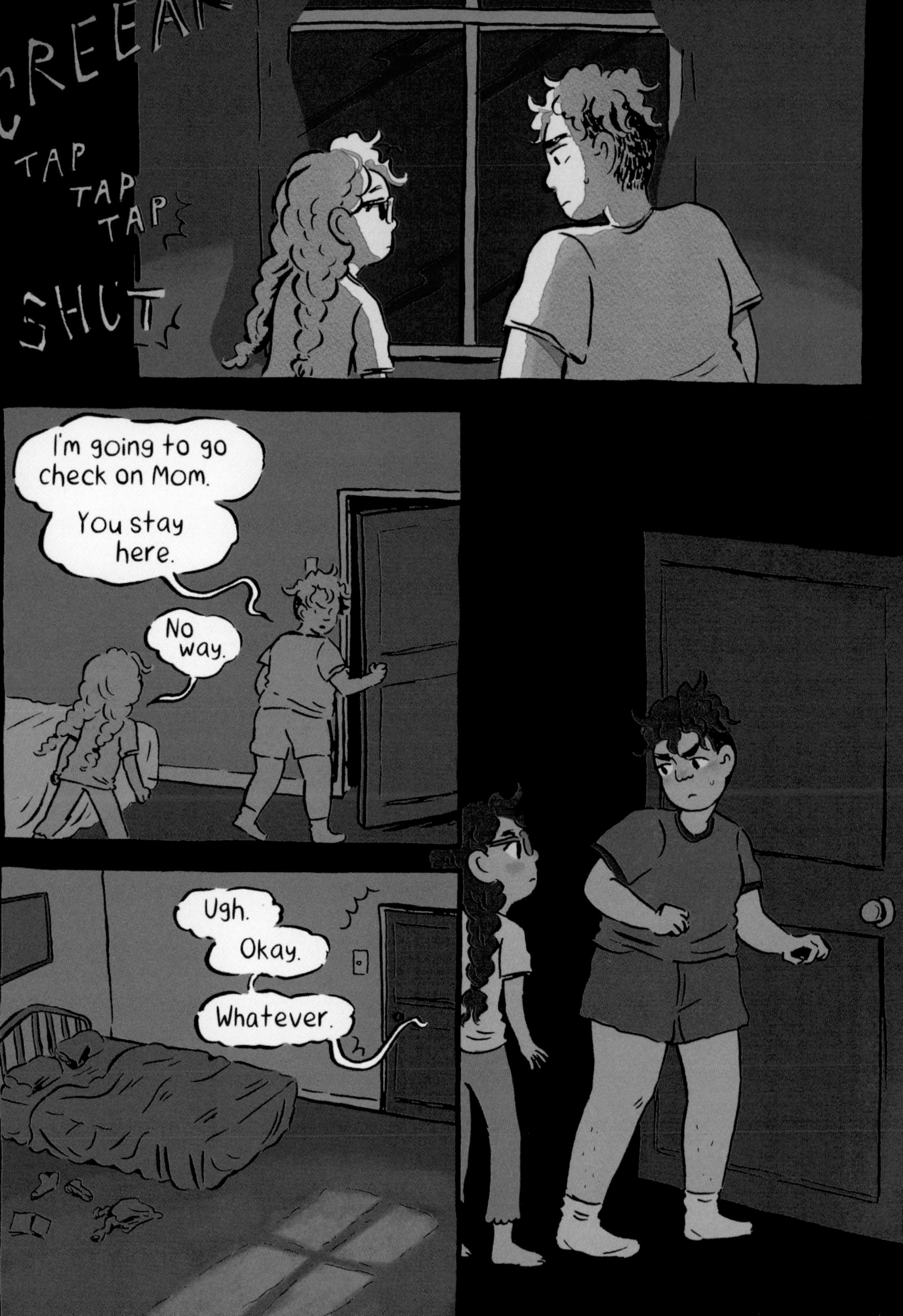
CREEAK
TAP
TAP
TAP
SHUT
I'm going to go check on Mom.
You stay here.
No way.
Ugh.
Okay.
Whatever.

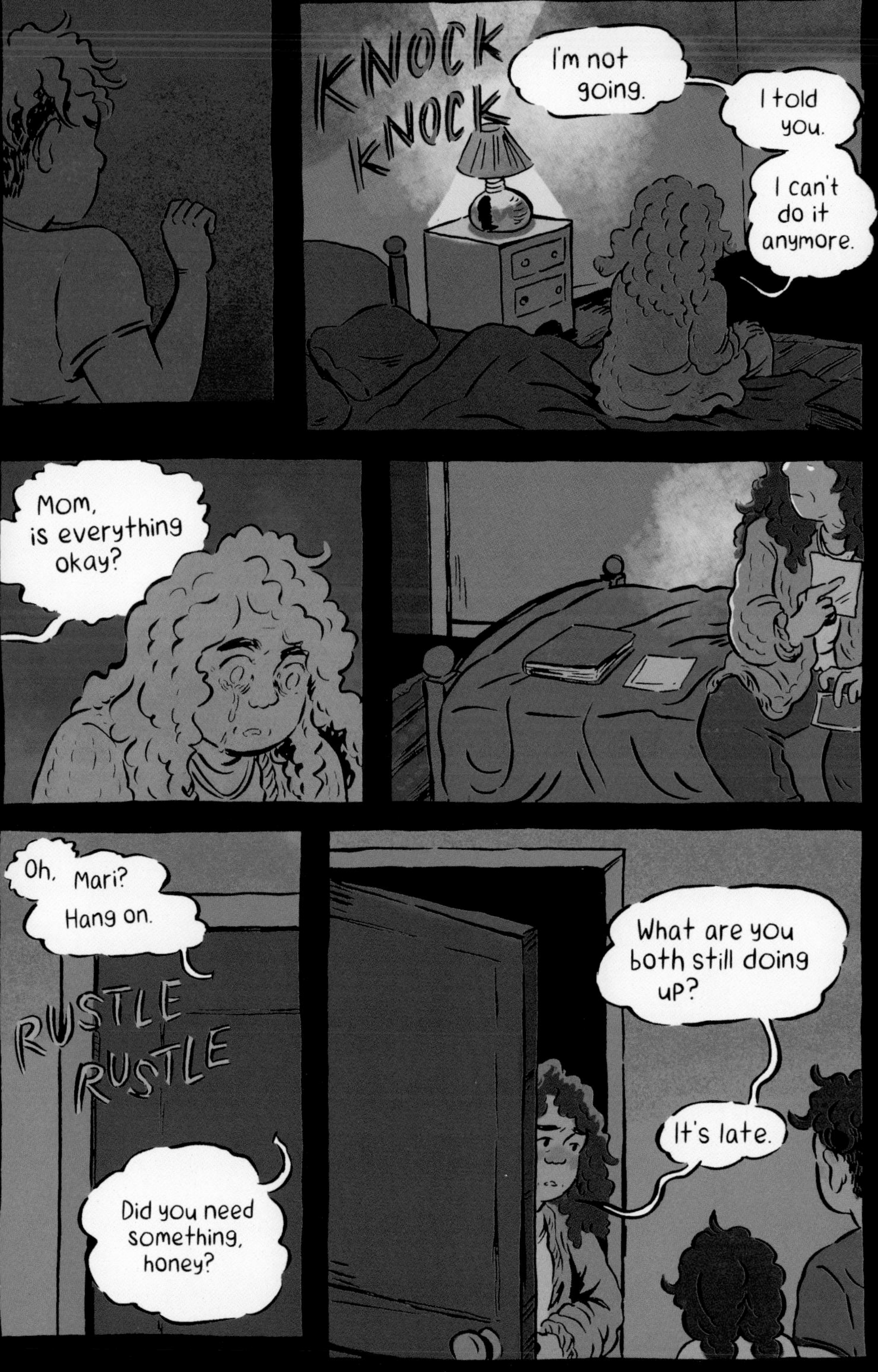
KNOCK KNOCK
I'm not going.
I told you.
I can't do it anymore.
Mom, is everything okay?
Oh, Mari?
Hang on.
RUSTLE RUSTLE
Did you need something, honey?
What are you both still doing up?
It's late.

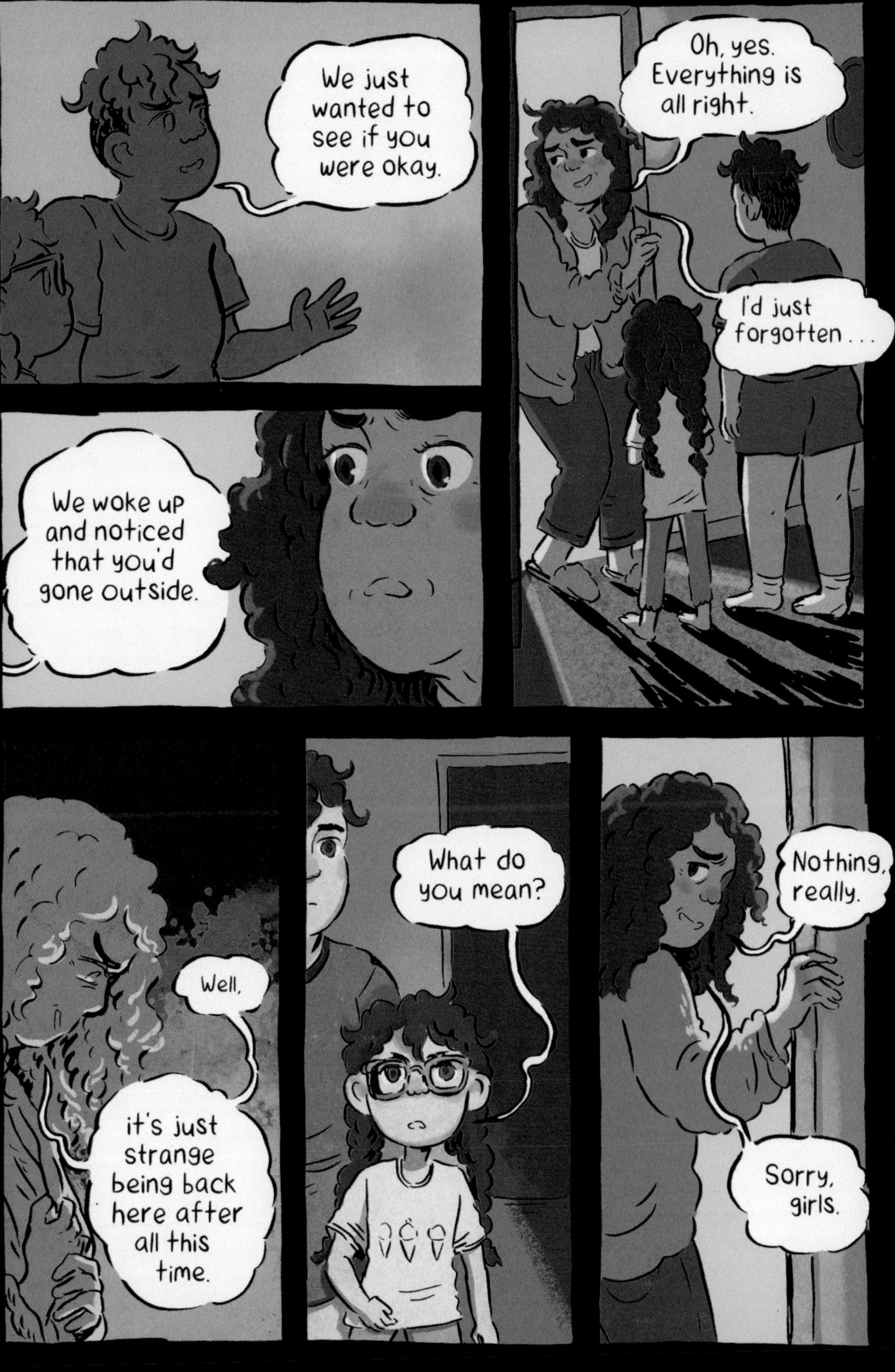
We just wanted to see if you were okay.
We woke up and noticed that you'd gone outside.
Oh, yes. Everything is all right.
I'd just forgotten . . .
Well,
it's just strange being back here after all this time.
What do you mean?
Nothing, really.
Sorry, girls.

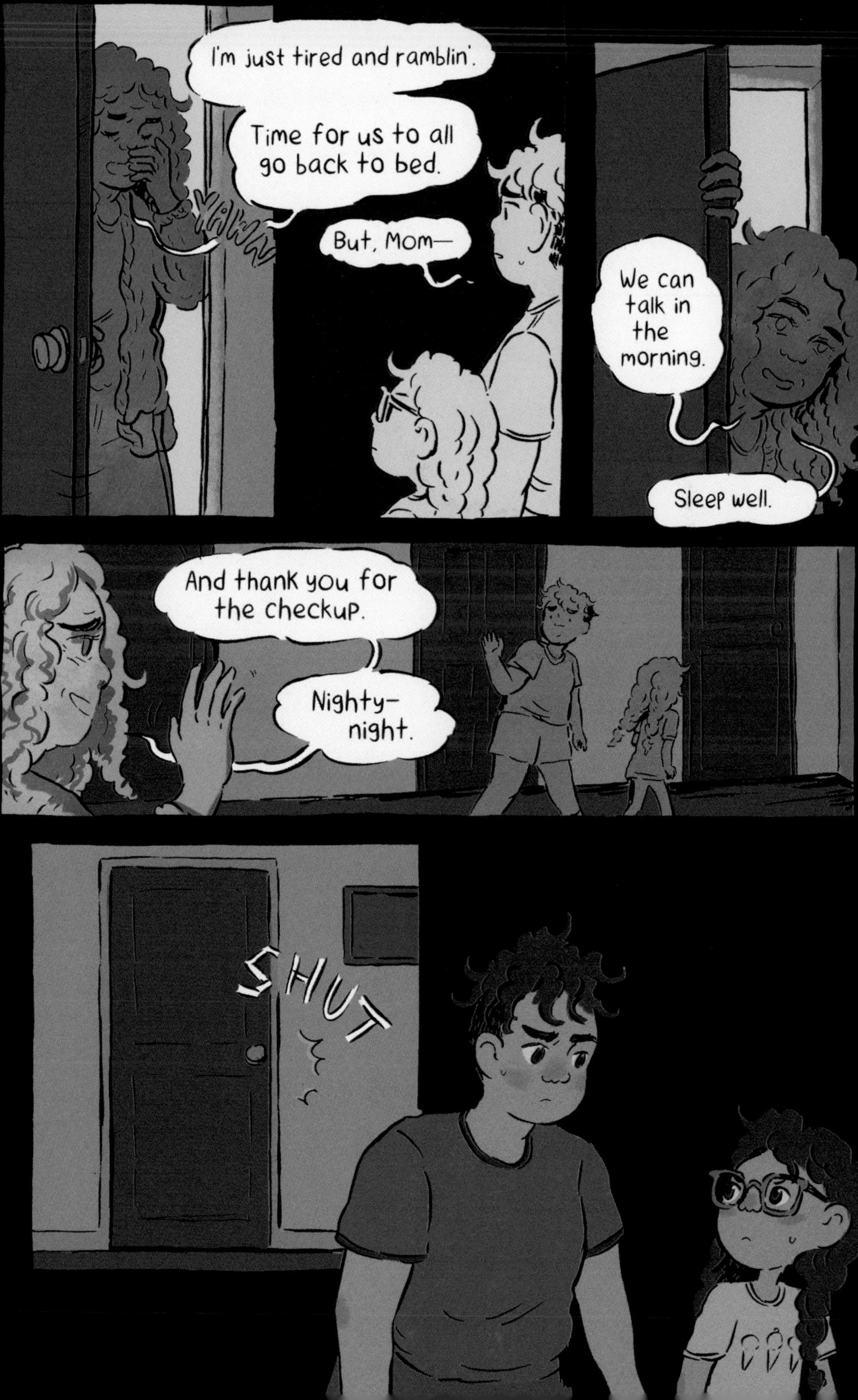

I'm just tired and ramblin'.
Time for us to all go back to bed.
YAWN
But, Mom—
We can talk in the morning.
Sleep well.
And thank you for the checkup.
Nighty-night.
SHUT

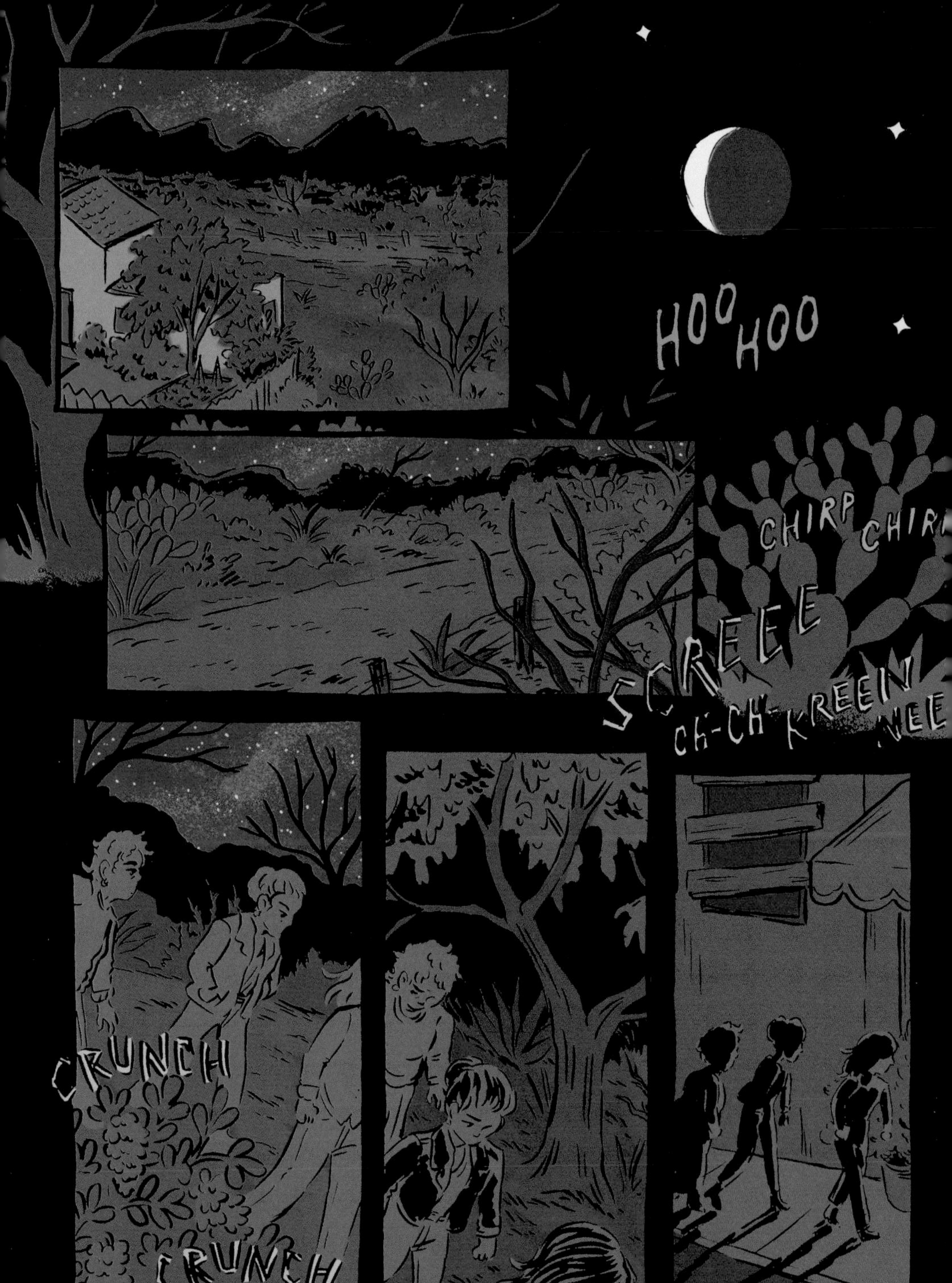
HOO HOO
CHIRP CHIRP
SCREEE
CH-CH-KREEN
NEE
CRUNCH
CRUNCH

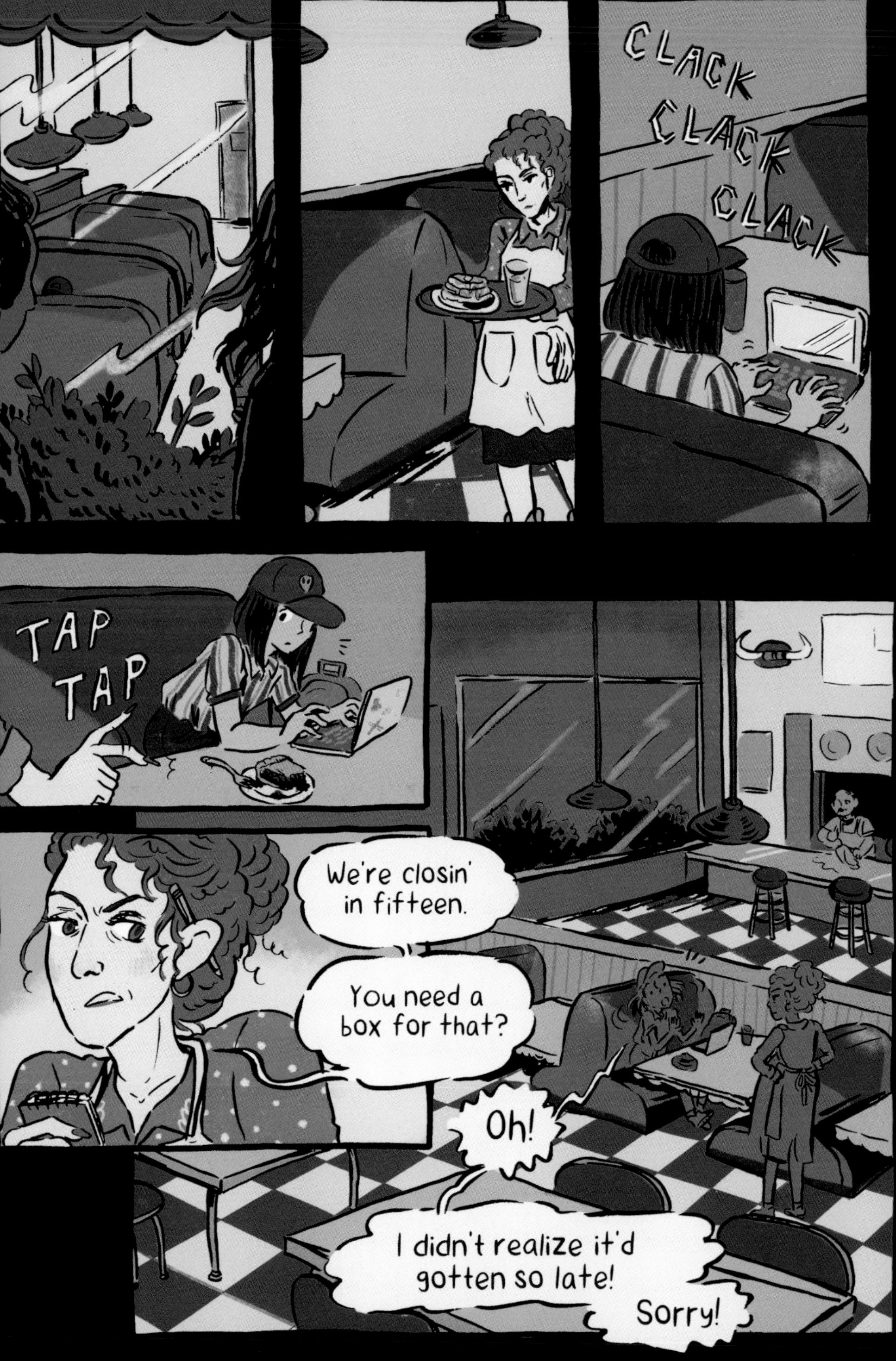
CLACK
CLACK
CLACK
TAP
TAP
We're closin' in fifteen.
You need a box for that?
Oh!
I didn't realize it'd gotten so late!
Sorry!

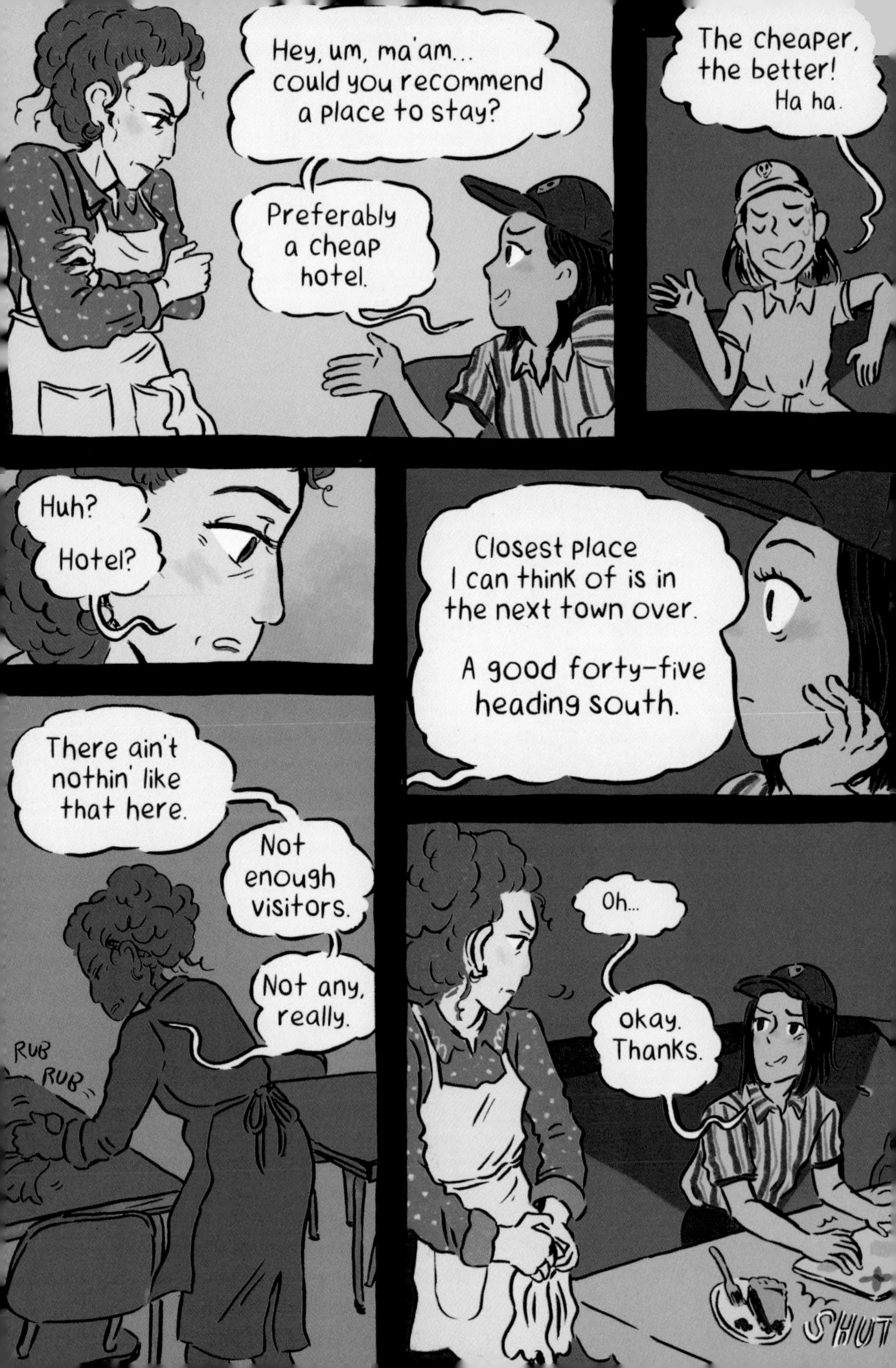
Hey, um, ma'am... could you recommend a place to stay?
Preferably a cheap hotel.
The cheaper, the better! Ha ha.
Huh?
Hotel?
Closest place I can think of is in the next town over.
A good forty-five heading south.
There ain't nothin' like that here.
Not enough visitors.
Not any, really.
RUB RUB
Oh...
okay. Thanks.
SHUT

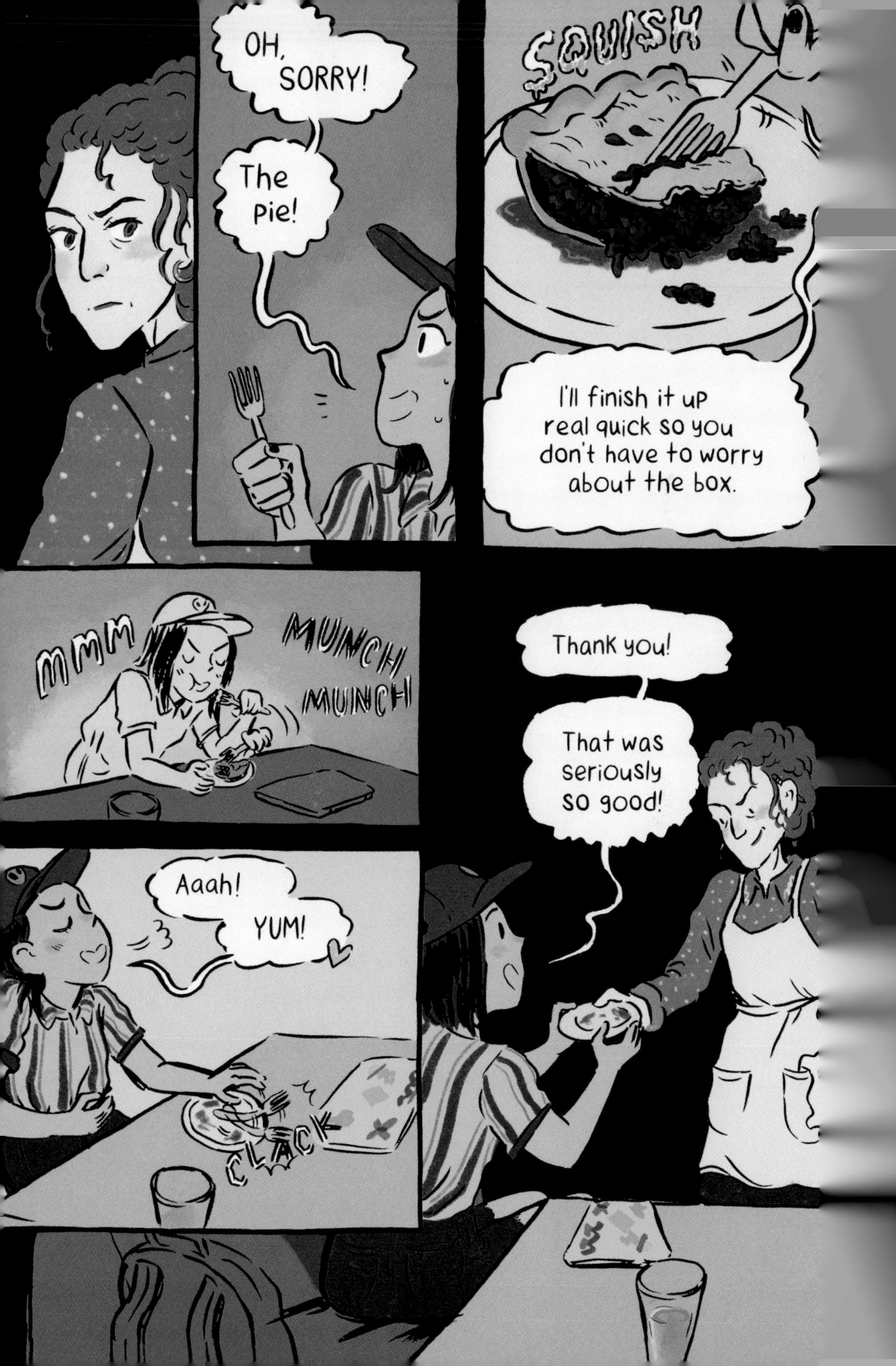
OH, SORRY!
The pie!
SQUISH
I'll finish it up real quick so you don't have to worry about the box.
MMM
MUNCH MUNCH
Thank you!
That was seriously so good!
Aaah!
YUM!
CLACK

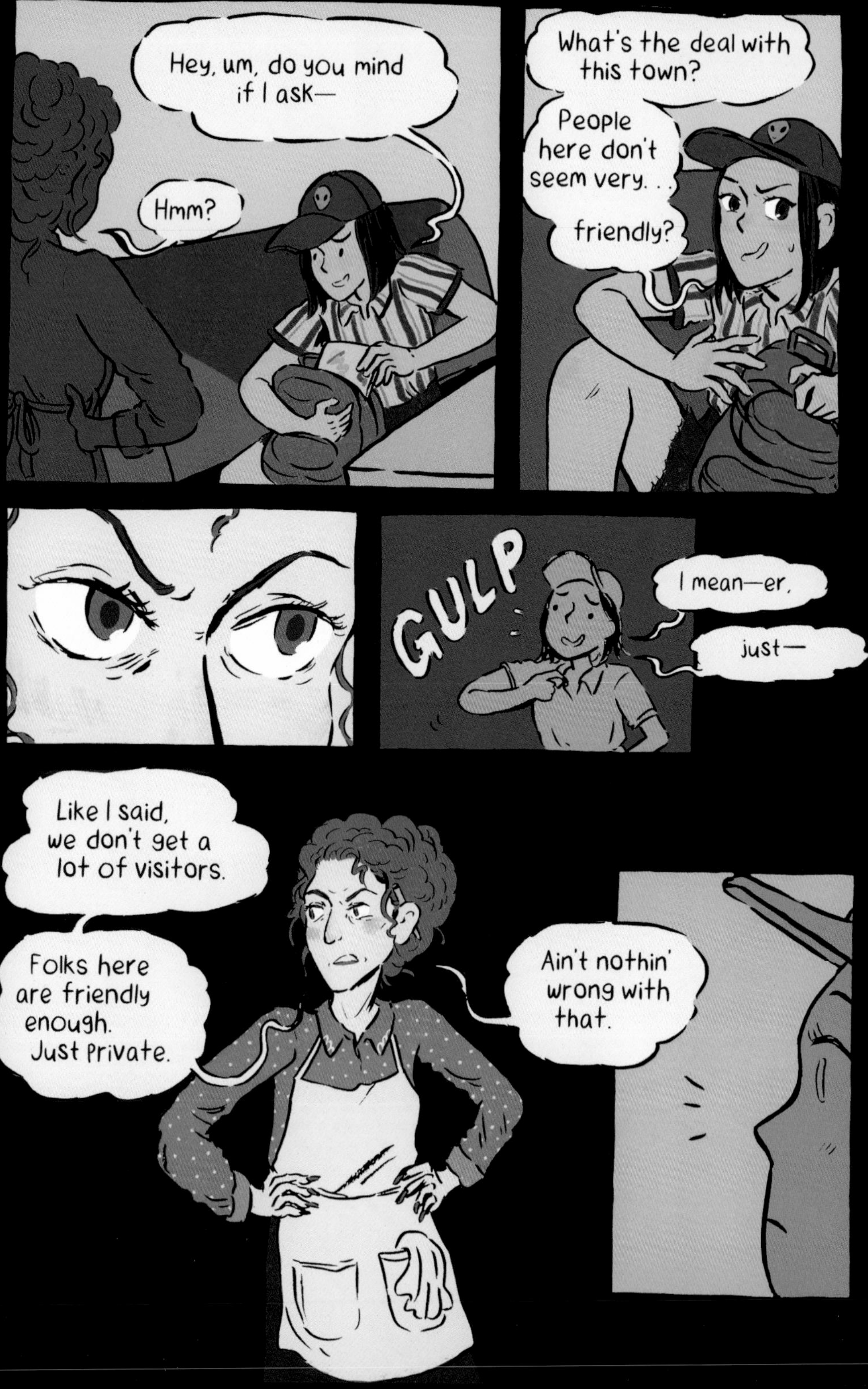
Hey, um, do you mind if I ask—
Hmm?
What's the deal with this town?
People here don't seem very. . .
friendly?
GULP
I mean—er,
just—
Like I said, we don't get a lot of visitors.
Folks here are friendly enough. Just private.
Ain't nothin' wrong with that.

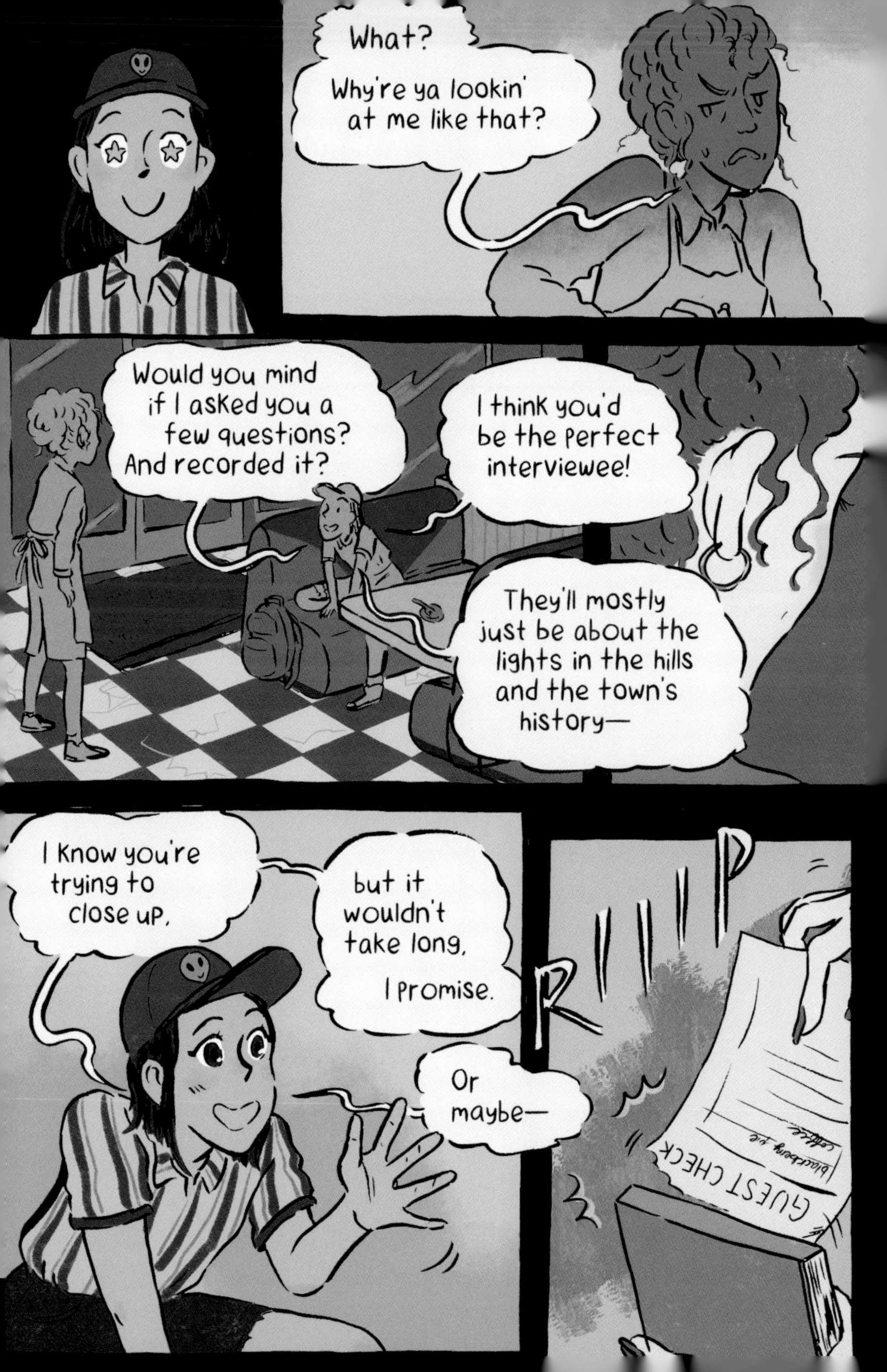
What?
Why're ya lookin' at me like that?
Would you mind if I asked you a few questions? And recorded it?
I think you'd be the perfect interviewee!
They'll mostly just be about the lights in the hills and the town's history—
I know you're trying to close up,
but it wouldn't take long,
I promise.
Or maybe—
RIIIP
GUEST CHECK
blackberry pie
coffee

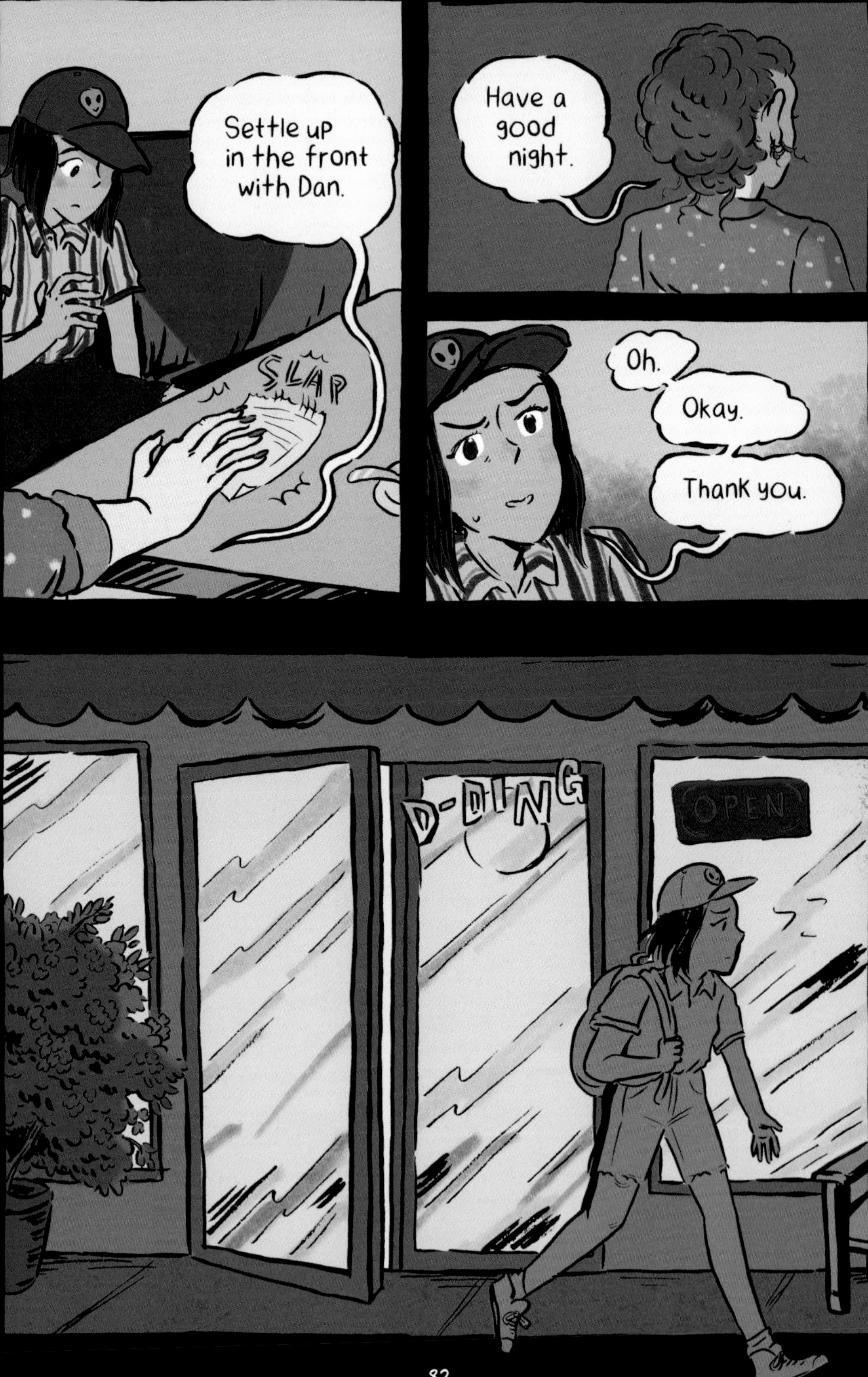
Settle up in the front with Dan.
SLAP
Have a good night.
Oh.
Okay.
Thank you.
D-DING
OPEN

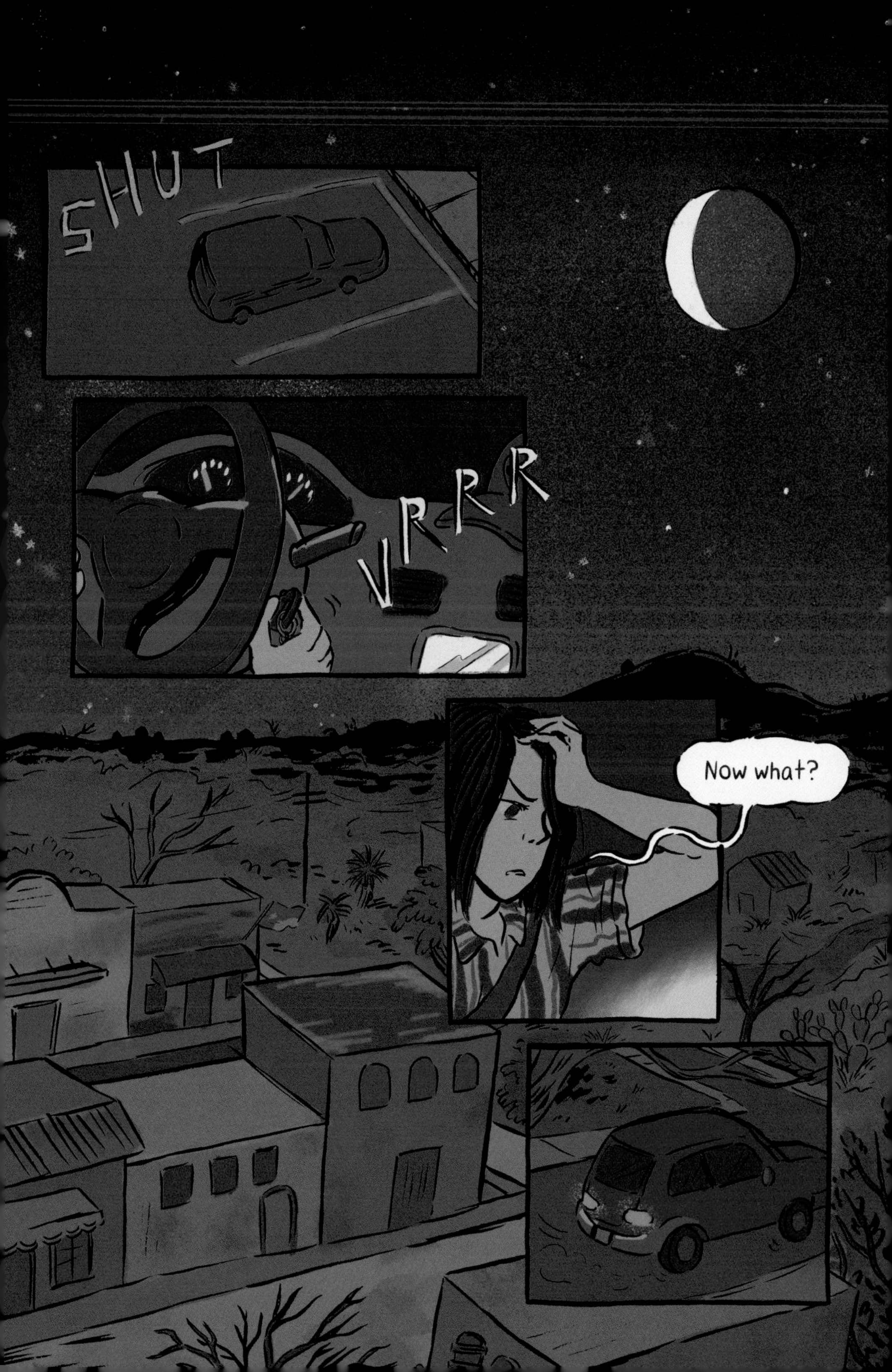
SHUT
VRRR
Now what?

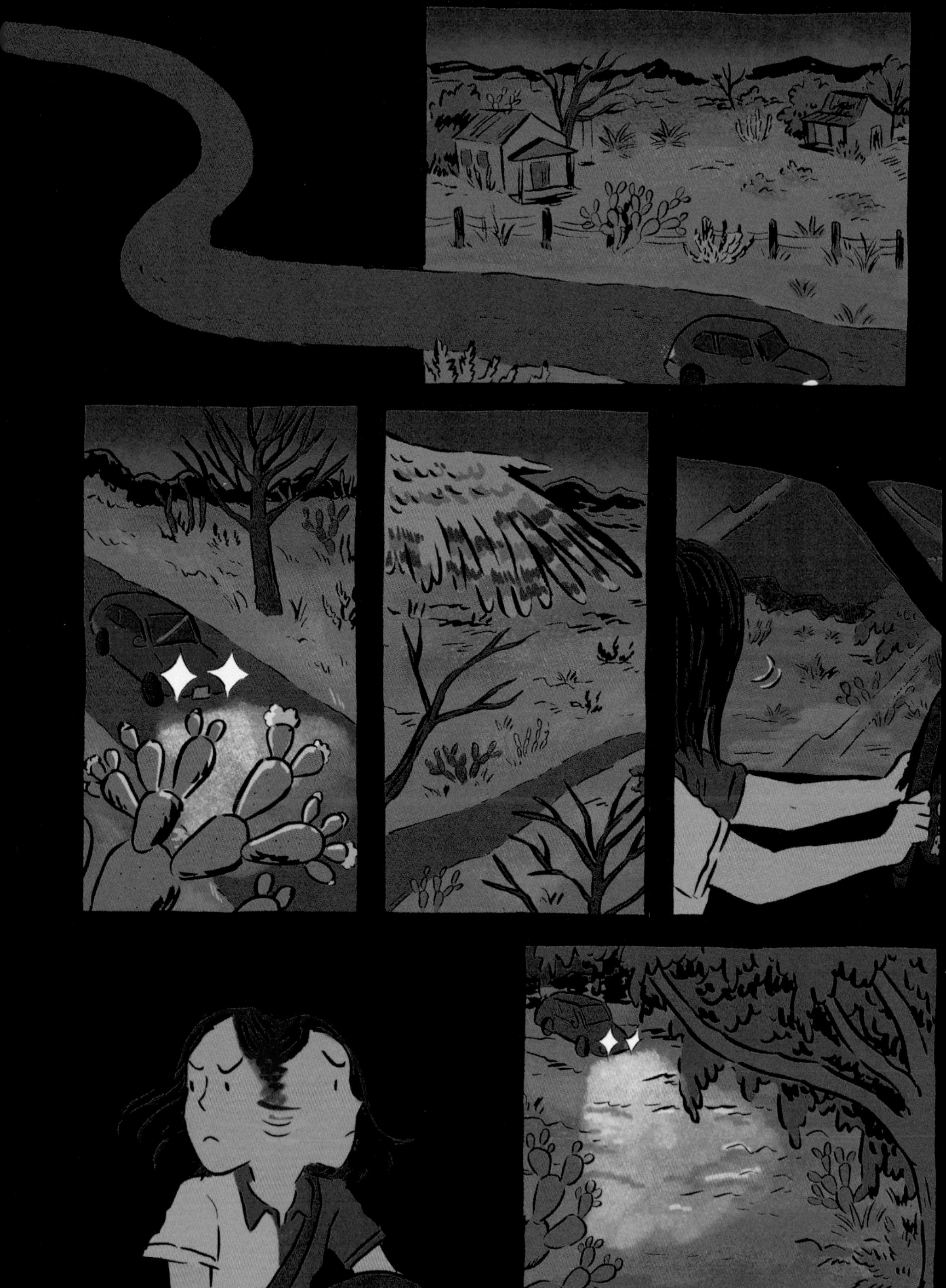

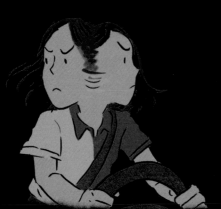

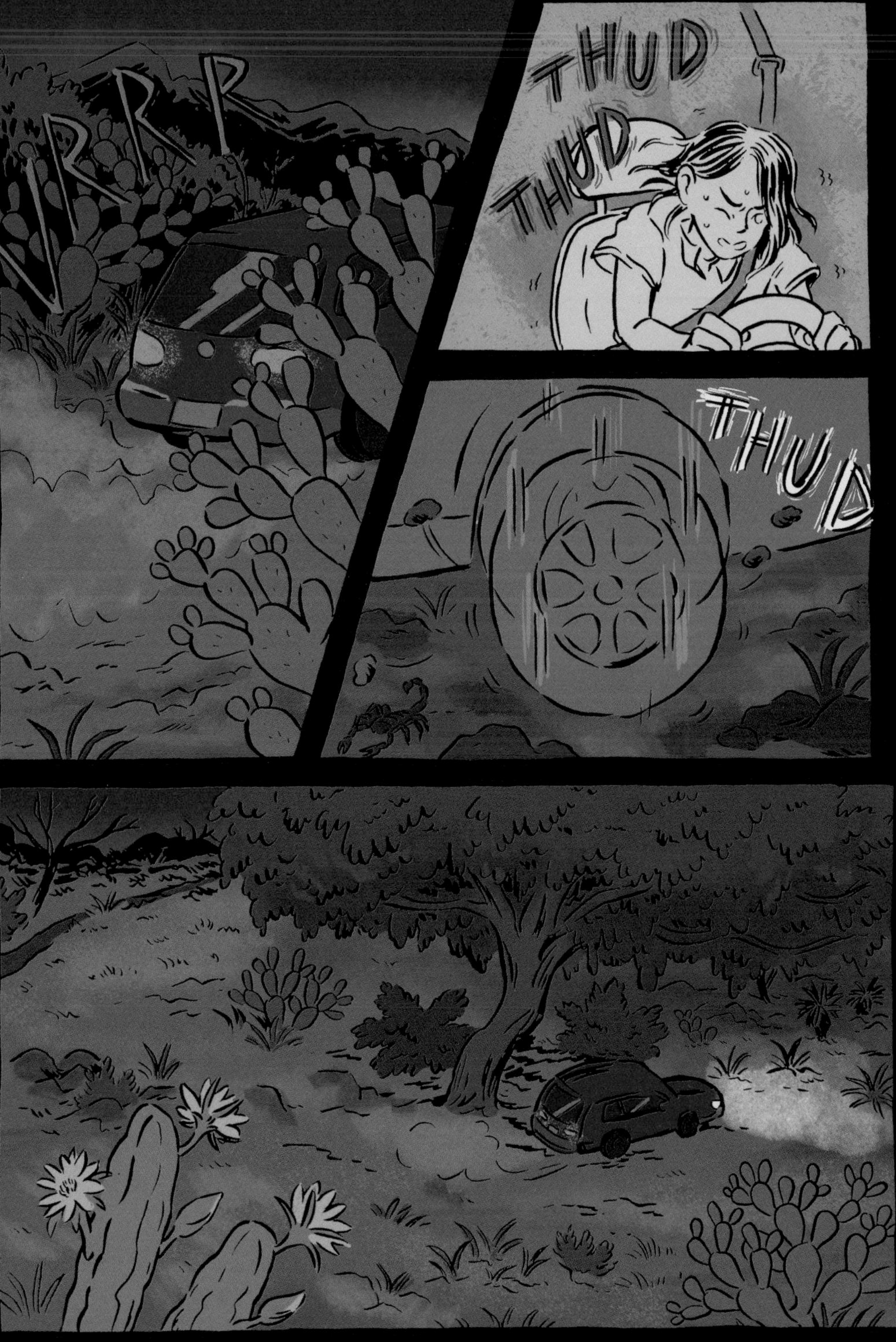
RRRR
THUD
THUD
THUD

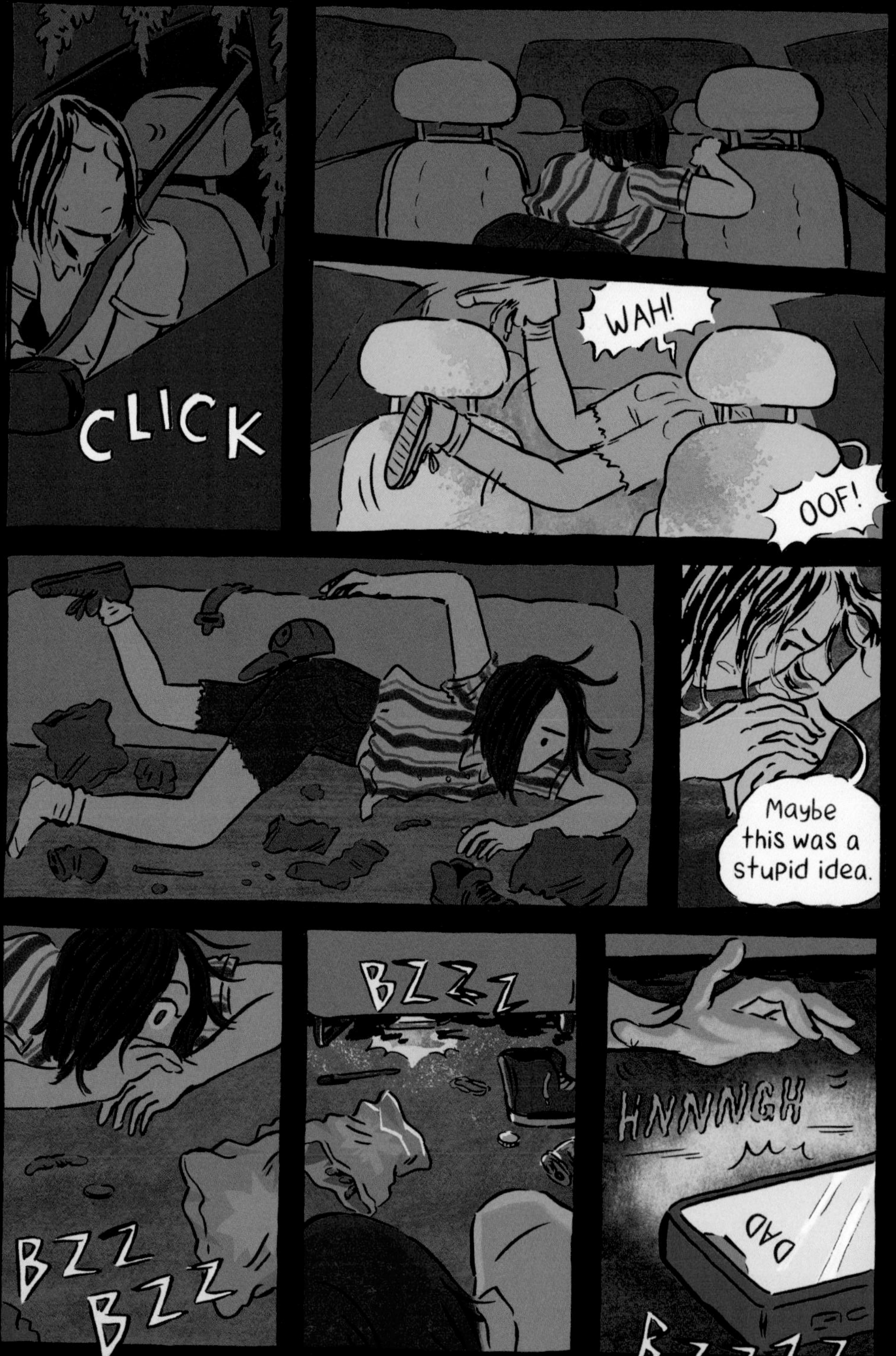
CLICK
WAH!
OOF!
Maybe this was a stupid idea.
BZZZ
BZZ
BZZ
HNNNGH
DAD
BZZZZ

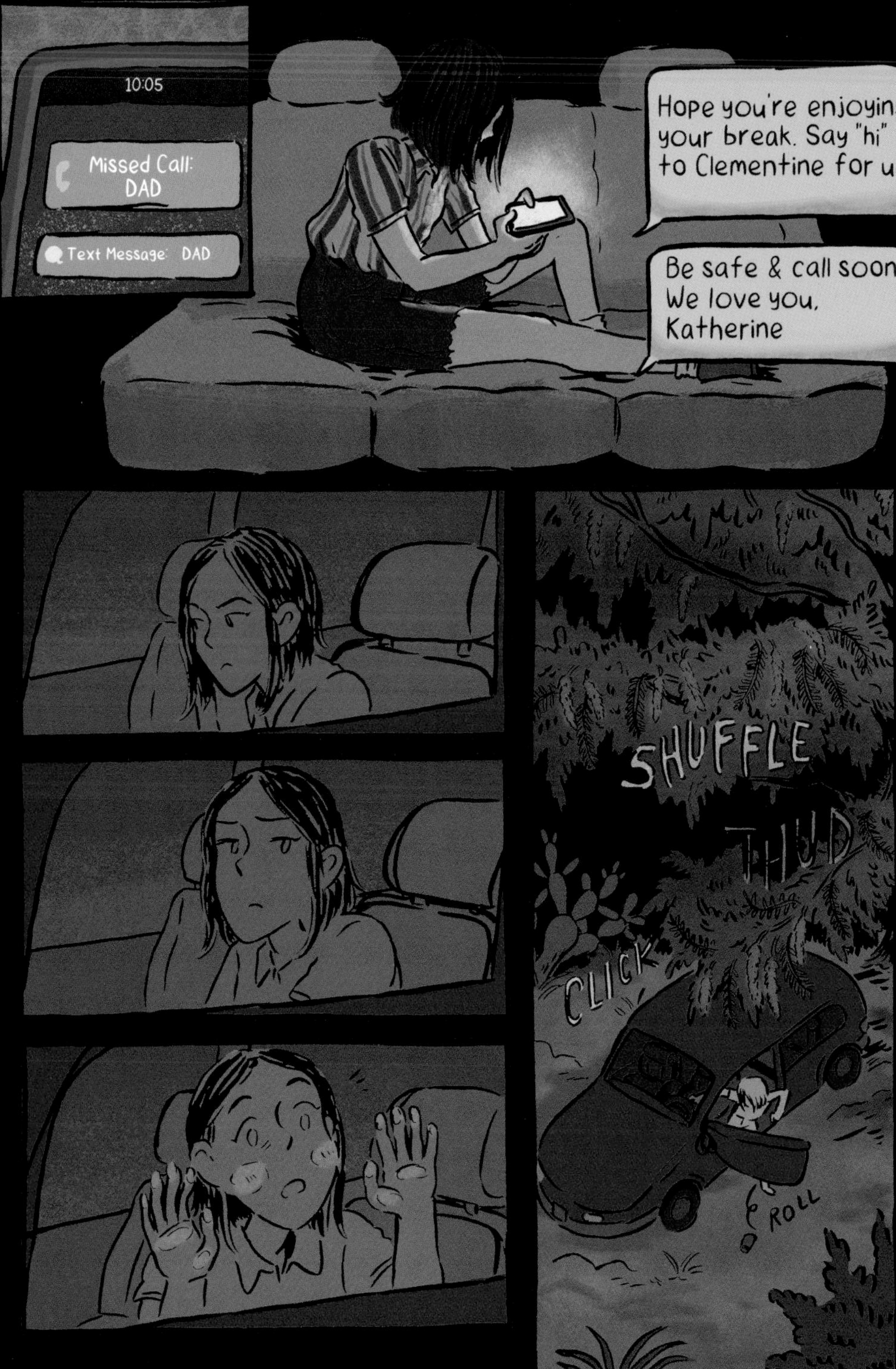
10:05
Missed Call: DAD
Text Message: DAD
Hope you're enjoying your break. Say "hi" to Clementine for us.
Be safe & call soon. We love you, Katherine
SHUFFLE
THUD
CLICK
ROLL

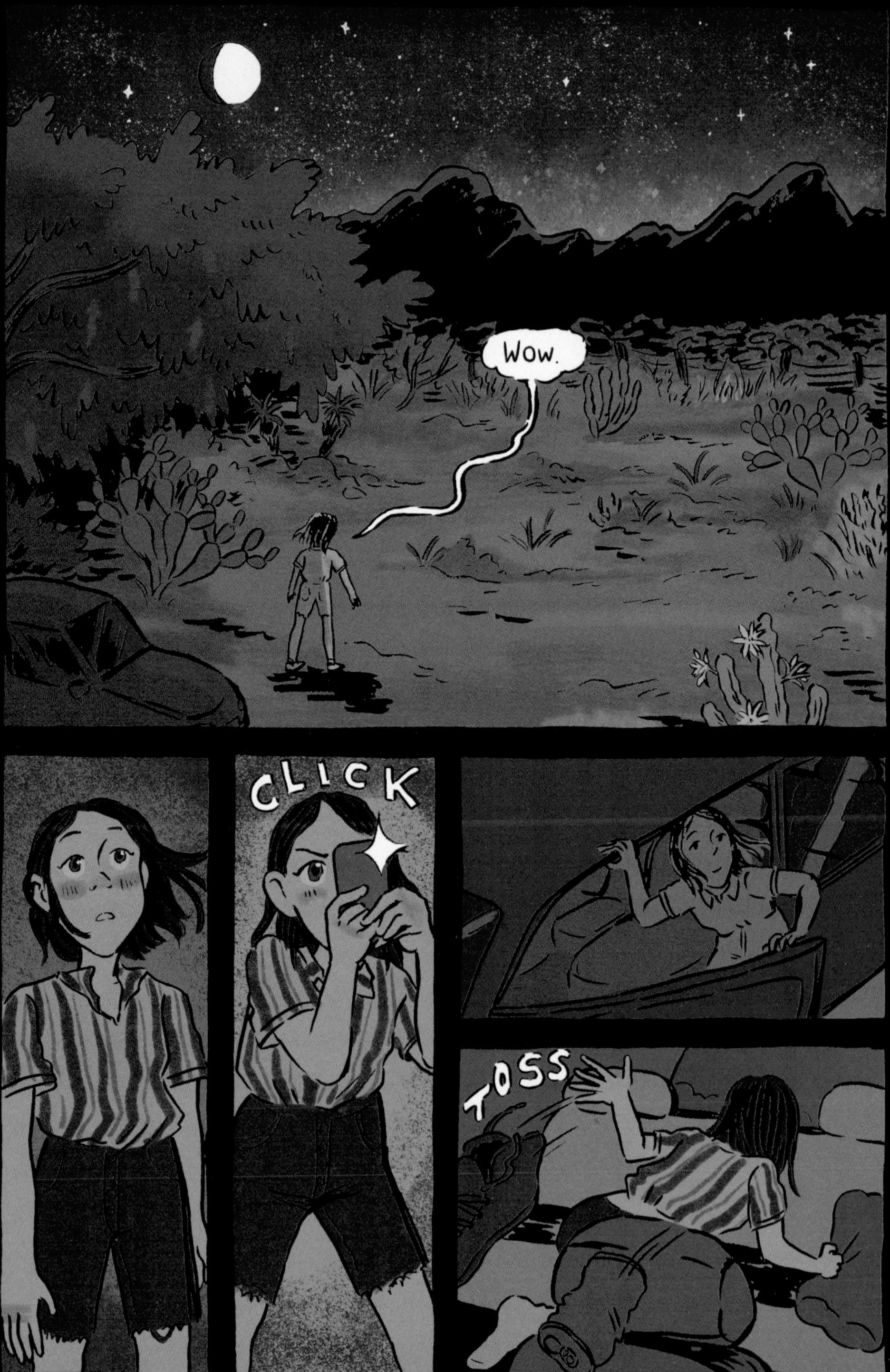
WOW.
CLICK
TOSS

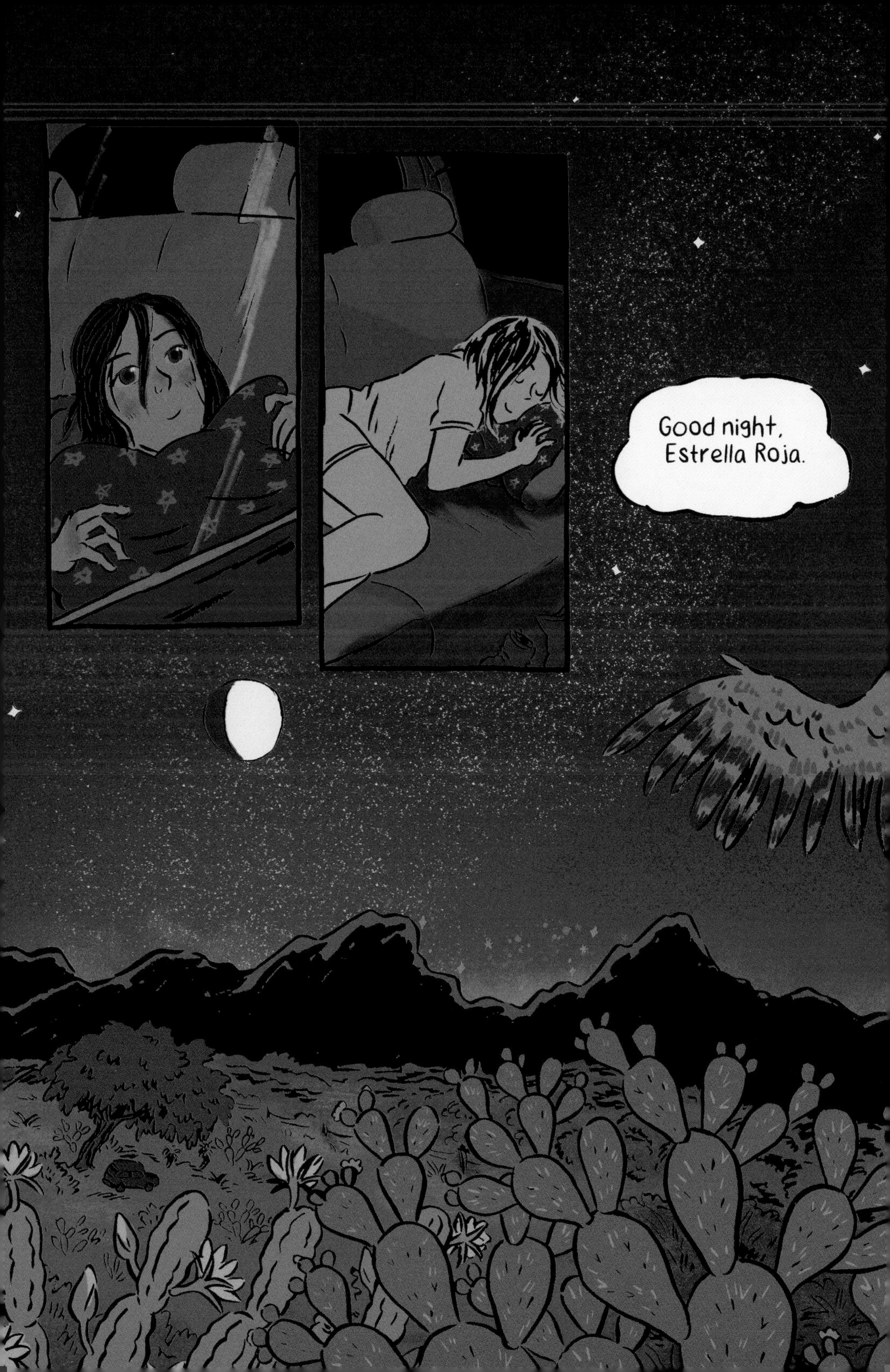
Good night, Estrella Roja.

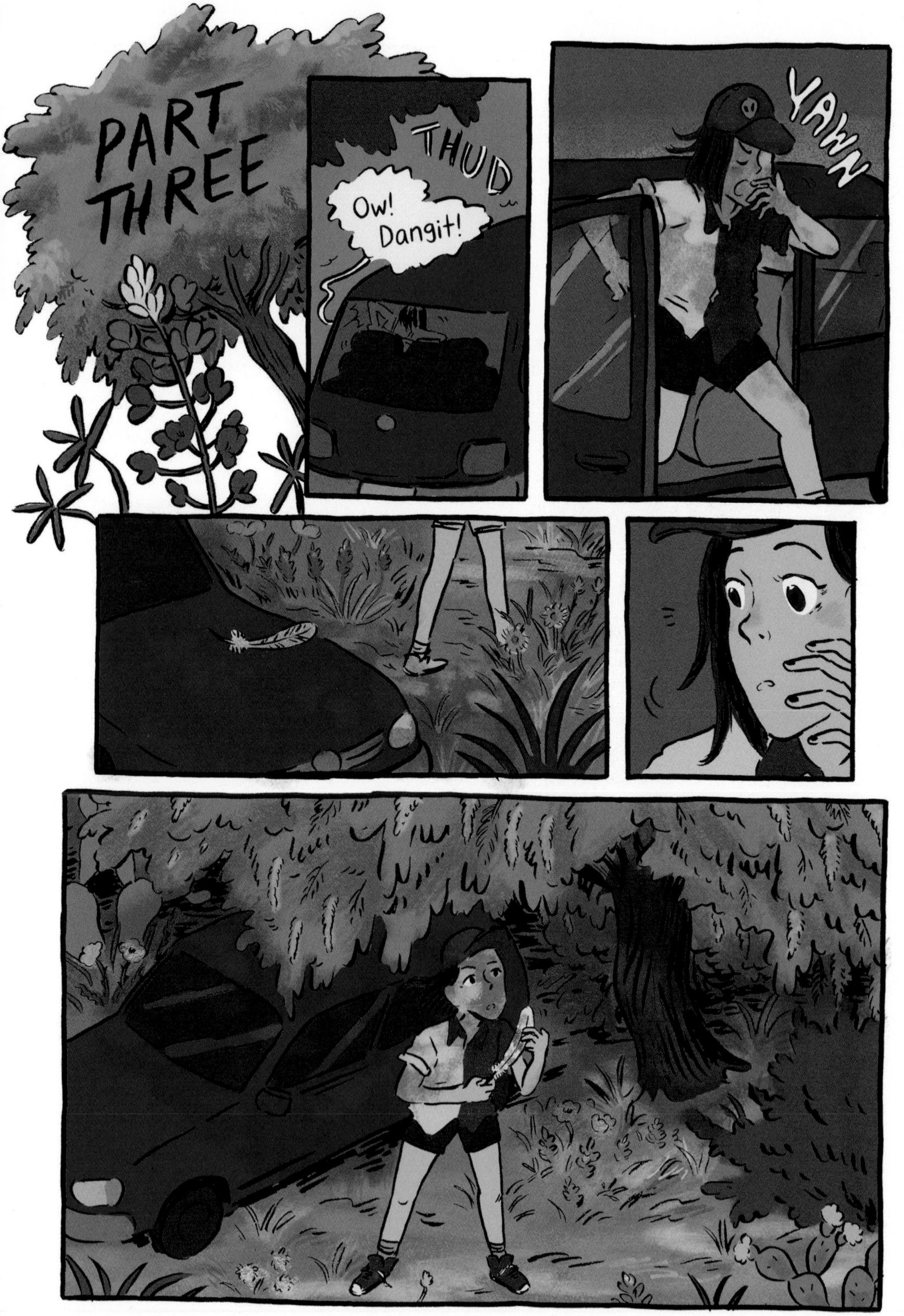
PART THREE
THUD
Ow! Dangit!
YAWN

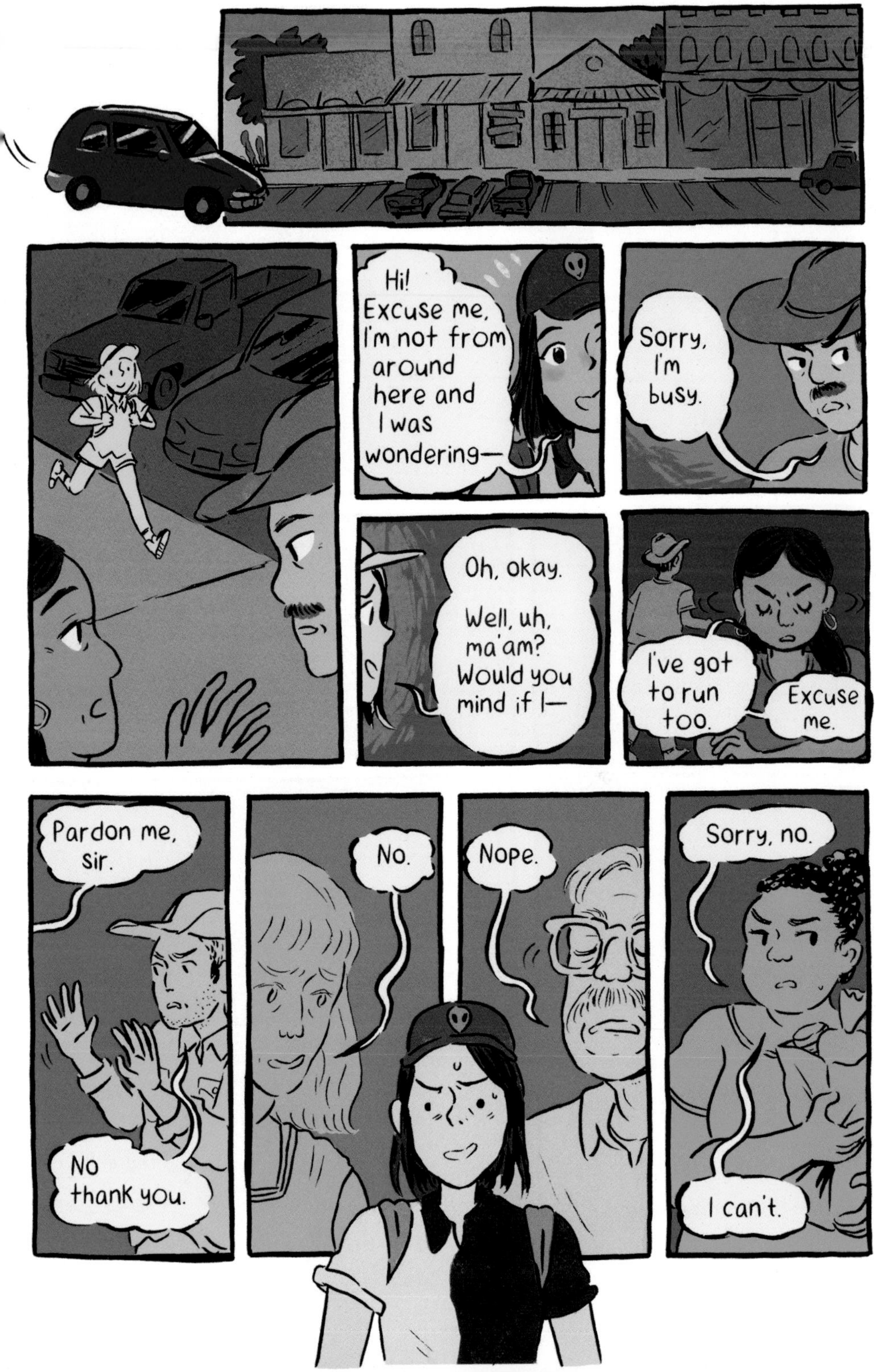
Hi! Excuse me, I'm not from around here and I was wondering—
Sorry, I'm busy.
Oh, okay.
Well, uh, ma'am? Would you mind if I—
I've got to run too.
Excuse me.
Pardon me, sir.
No thank you.
No.
Nope.
Sorry, no.
I can't.

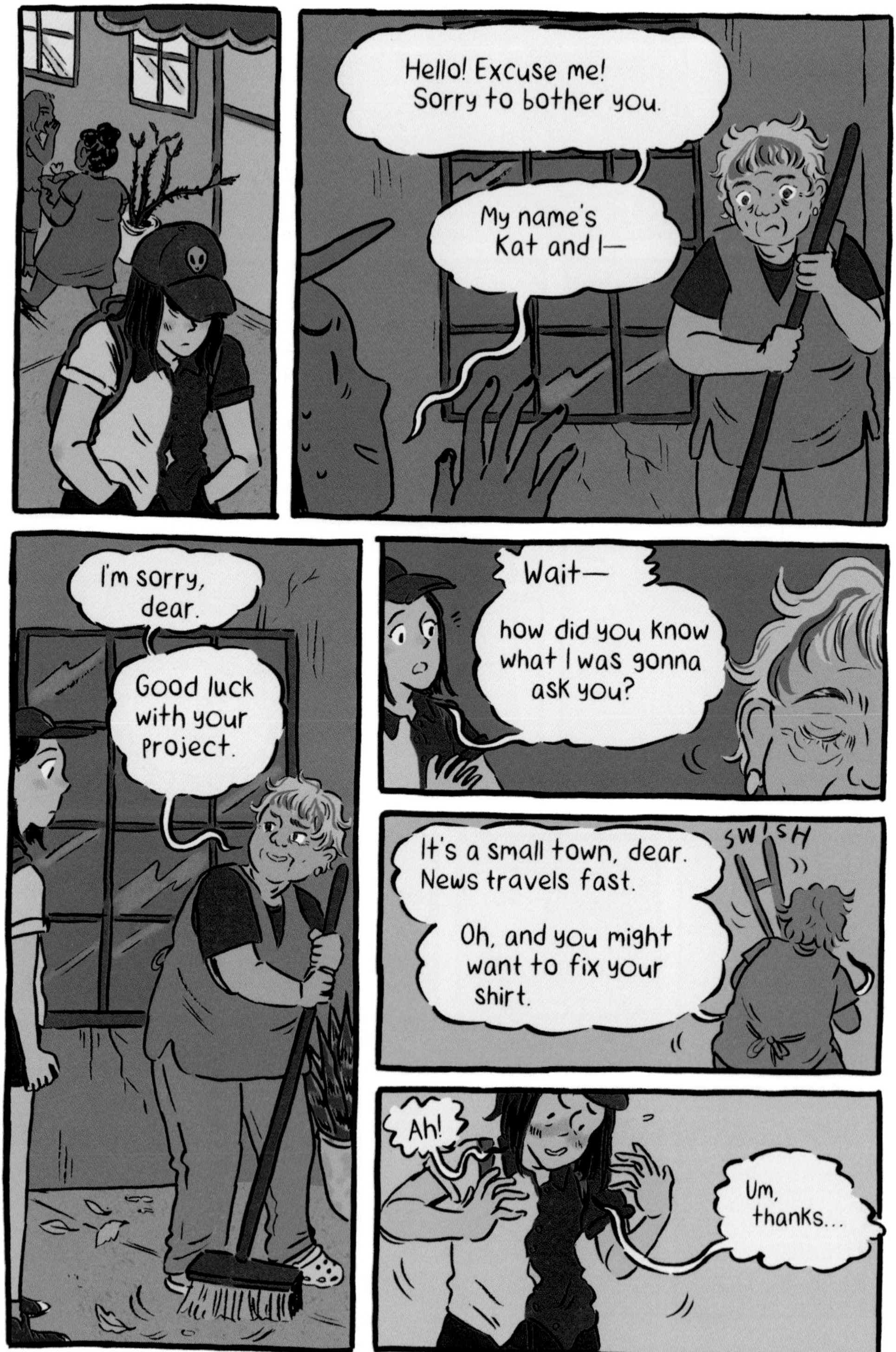
Hello! Excuse me! Sorry to bother you.
My name's Kat and I—
I'm sorry, dear.
Good luck with your project.
Wait—
how did you know what I was gonna ask you?
It's a small town, dear. News travels fast.
Oh, and you might want to fix your shirt.
SWISH
Ah!
Um, thanks...

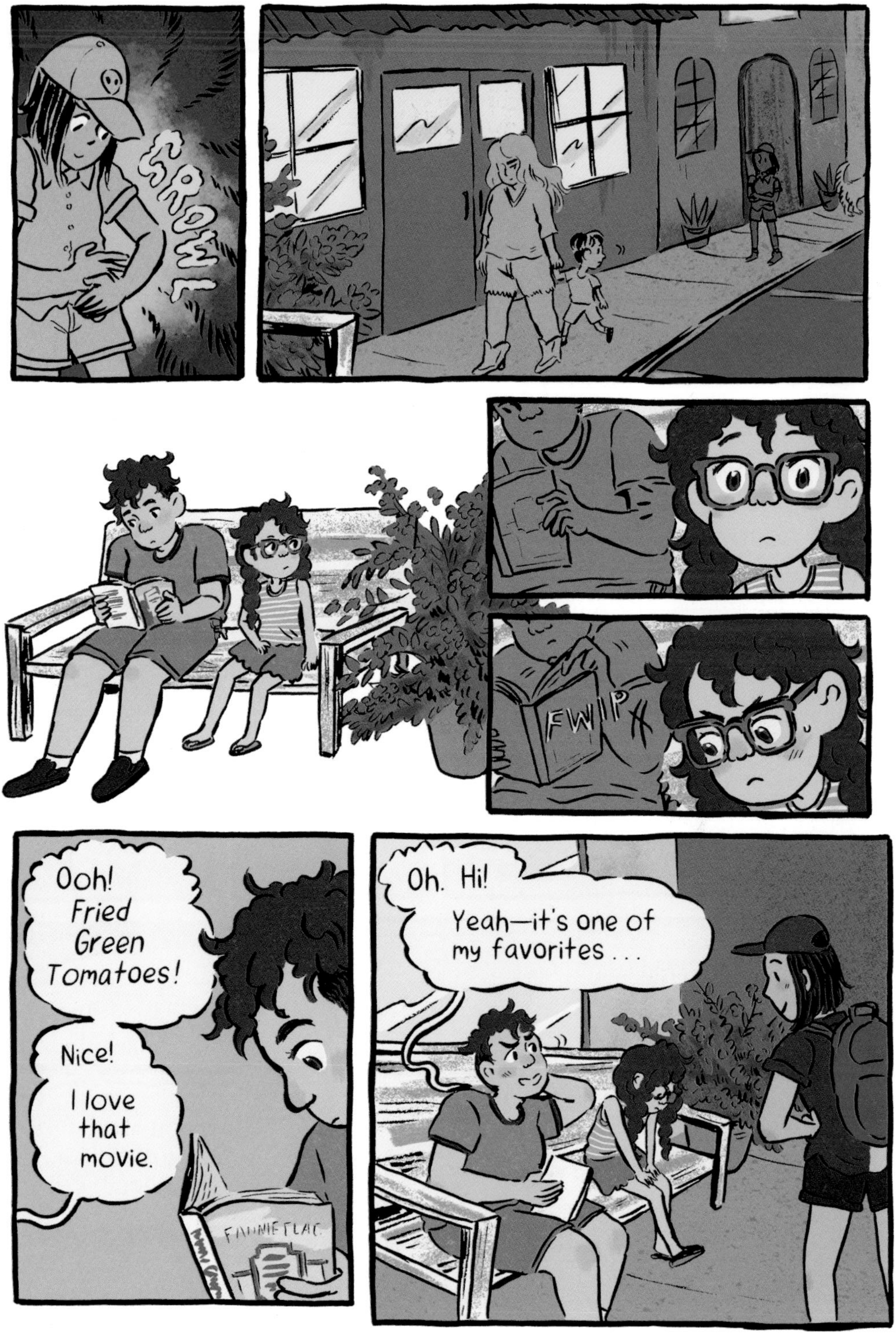
GROWL
FWIP
Ooh! Fried Green Tomatoes!
Nice! I love that movie.
Oh. Hi!
Yeah—it's one of my favorites . . .

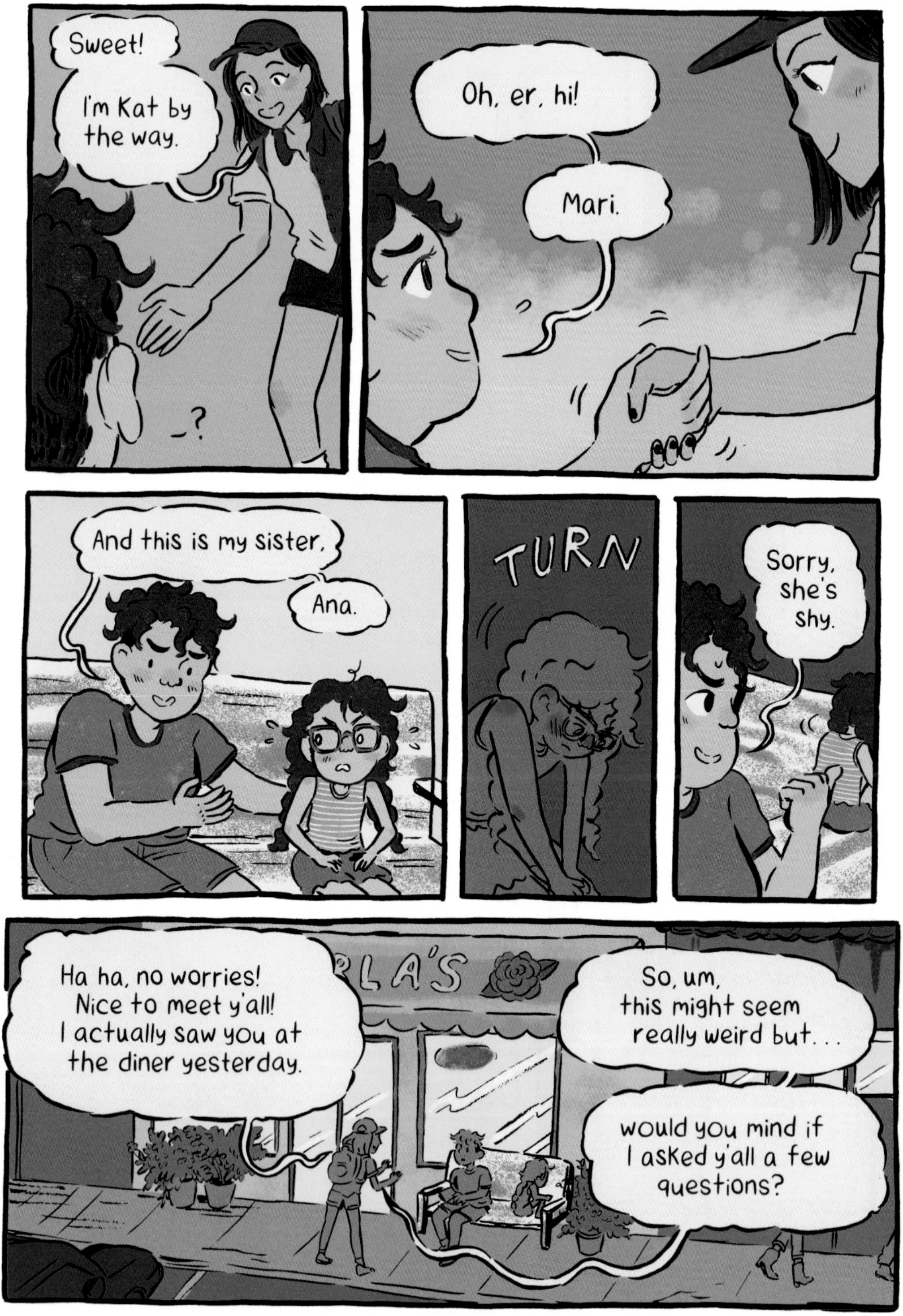
Sweet!
I'm Kat by the way.
_?
Oh, er, hi!
Mari.
And this is my sister,
Ana.
TURN
Sorry, she's shy.
Ha ha, no worries! Nice to meet y'all! I actually saw you at the diner yesterday.
LA'S
So, um, this might seem really weird but. . .
would you mind if I asked y'all a few questions?

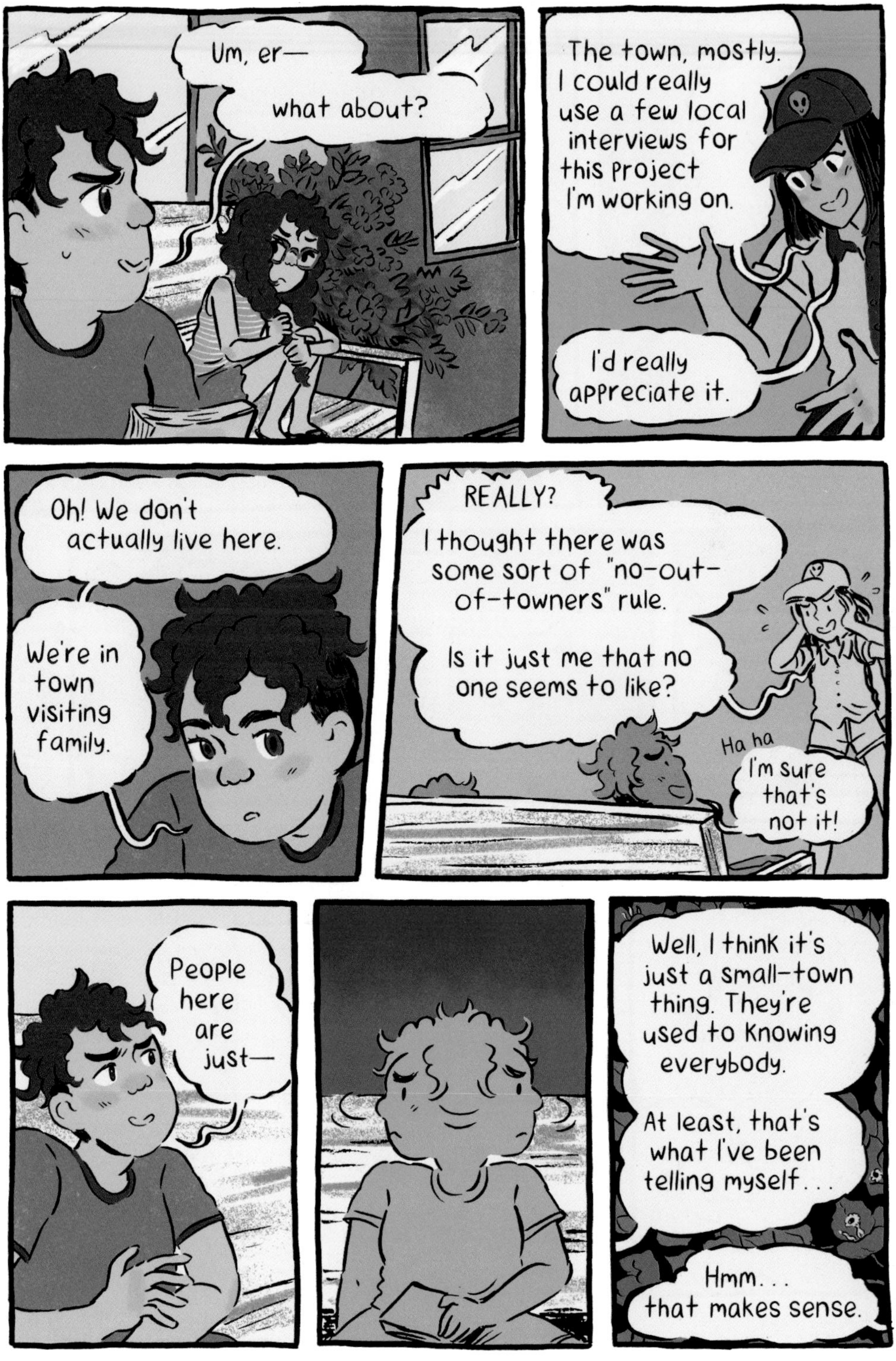
Um, er—
what about?
The town, mostly. I could really use a few local interviews for this project I'm working on.
I'd really appreciate it.
Oh! We don't actually live here.
We're in town visiting family.
REALLY?
I thought there was some sort of "no-out-of-towners" rule.
Is it just me that no one seems to like?
Ha ha
I'm sure that's not it!
People here are just—
Well, I think it's just a small-town thing. They're used to knowing everybody.
At least, that's what I've been telling myself...
Hmm... that makes sense.

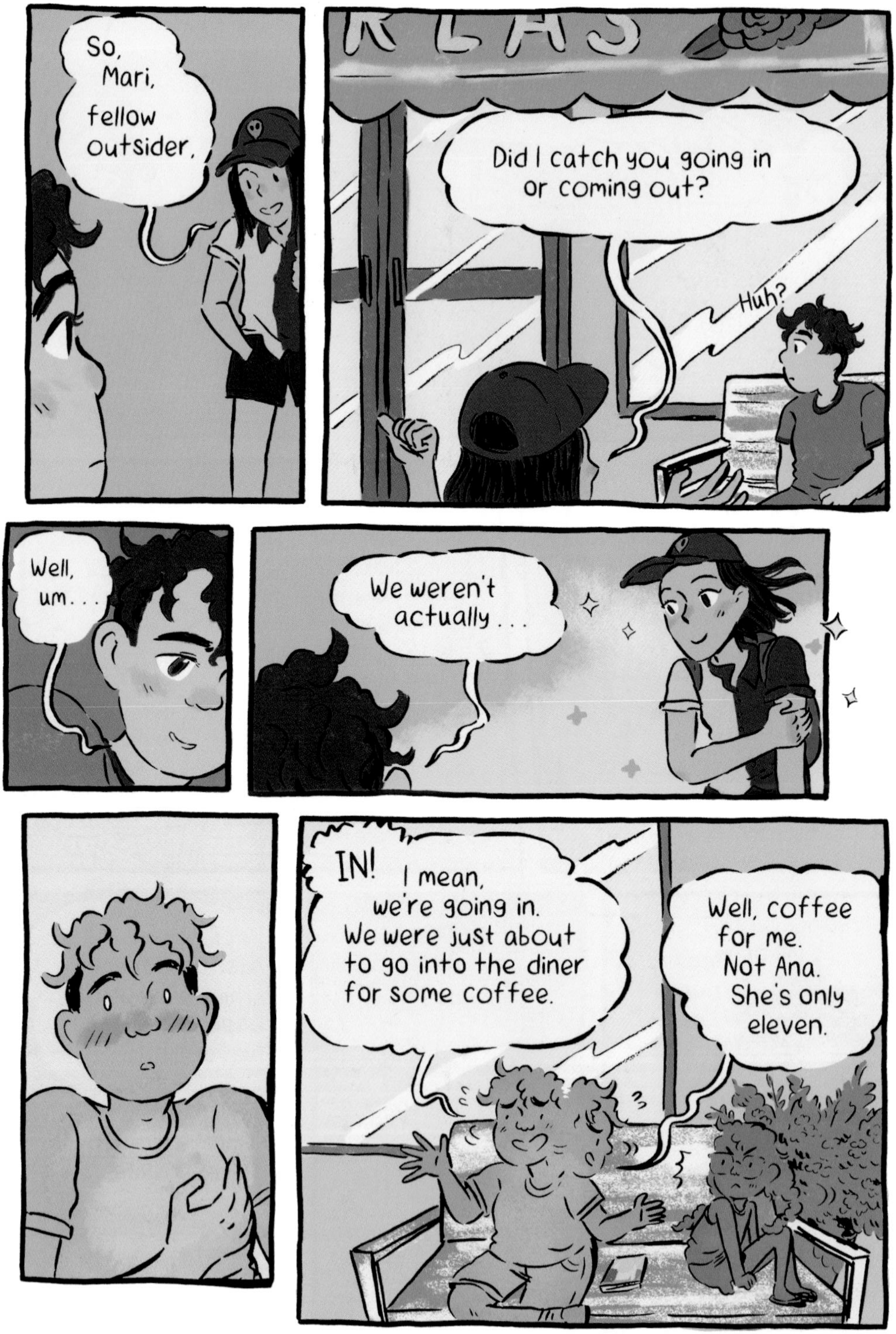

So, Mari, fellow outsider,
Did I catch you going in or coming out?
Huh?
Well, um...
We weren't actually...
IN! I mean, we're going in. We were just about to go into the diner for some coffee.
Well, coffee for me. Not Ana. She's only eleven.

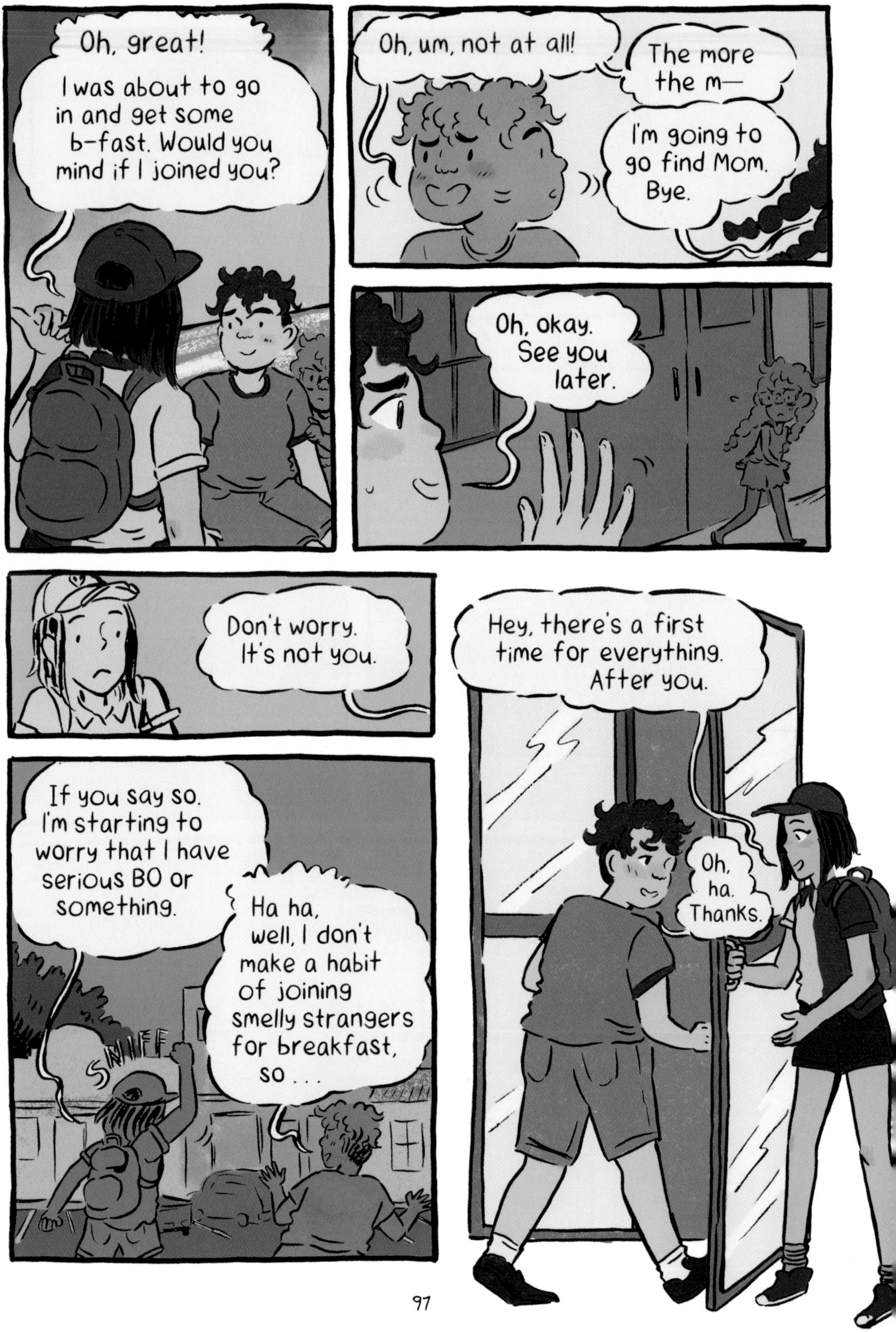
Oh, great!
I was about to go in and get some b-fast. Would you mind if I joined you?
Oh, um, not at all!
The more the m—
I'm going to go find Mom. Bye.
Oh, okay. See you later.
Don't worry. It's not you.
If you say so. I'm starting to worry that I have serious BO or something.
SNIFF
Ha ha, well, I don't make a habit of joining smelly strangers for breakfast, so . . .
Hey, there's a first time for everything. After you.
Oh, ha. Thanks.

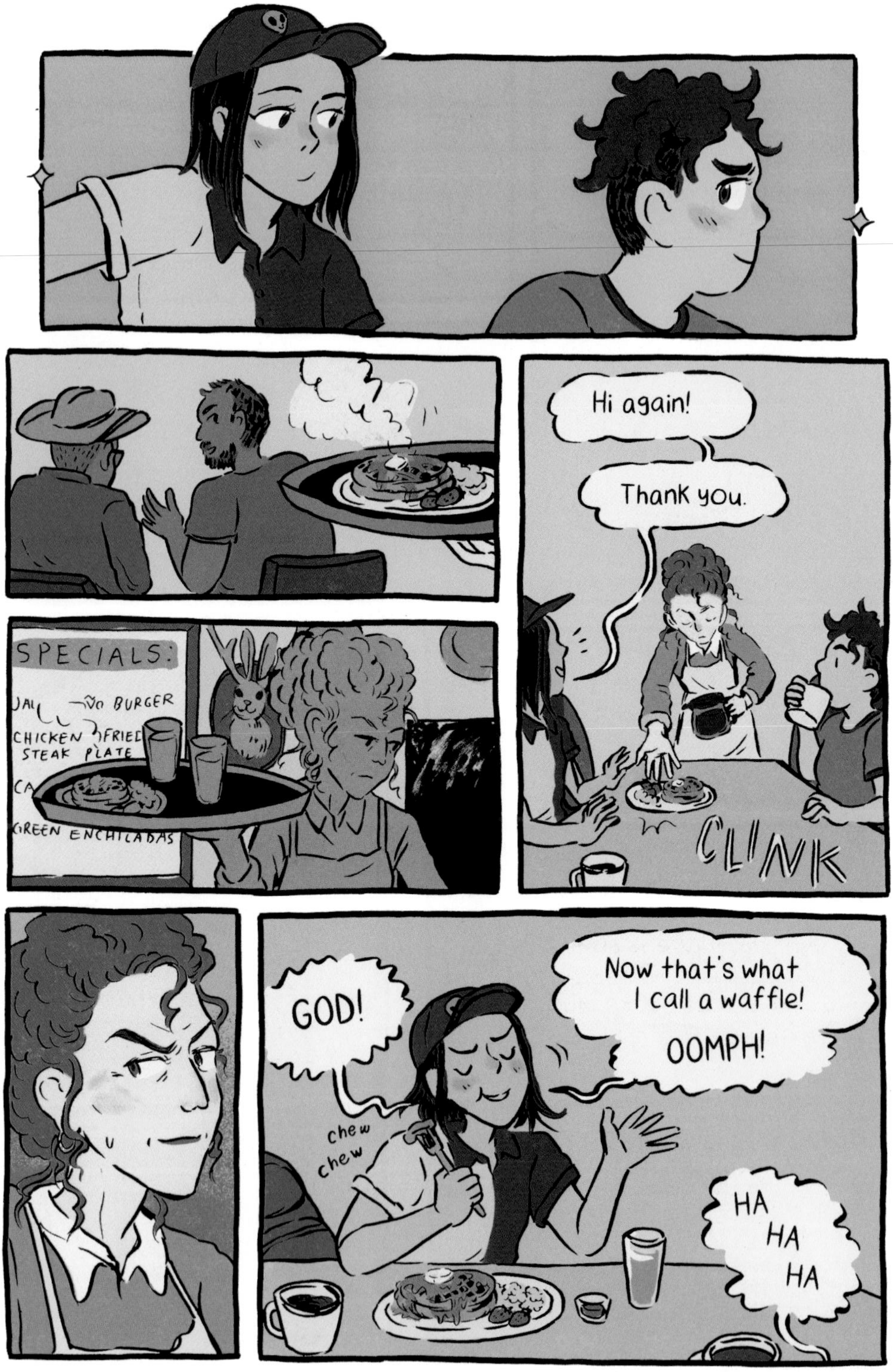
Hi again!
Thank you.
SPECIALS:
CHICKEN FRIED STEAK PLATE
GREEN ENCHILADAS
CLINK
GOD!
Now that's what I call a waffle!
OOMPH!
chew chew
HA HA HA

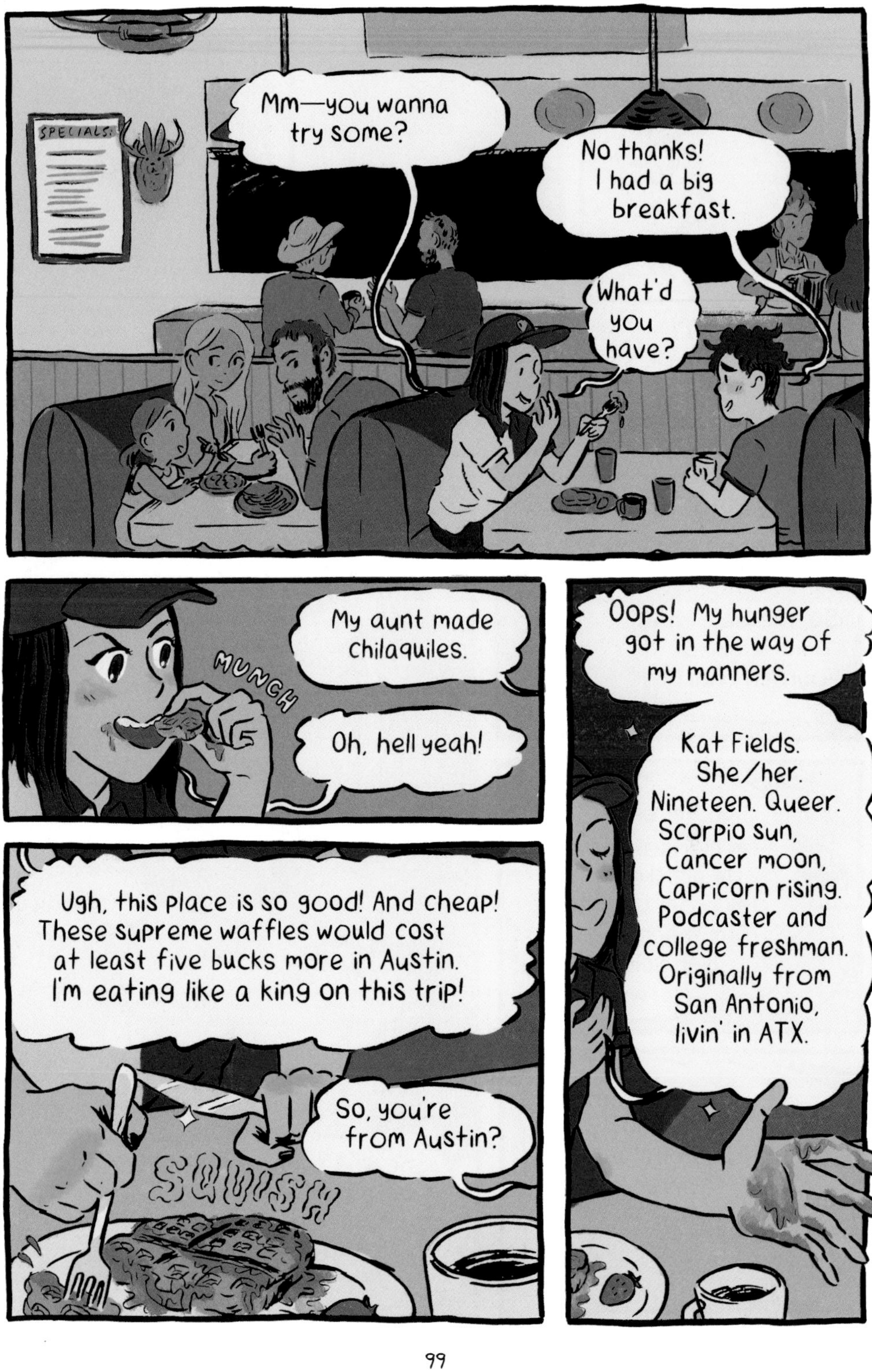
Mm—you wanna try some?
No thanks! I had a big breakfast.
What'd you have?
My aunt made chilaquiles.
MUNCH
Oh, hell yeah!
Ugh, this place is so good! And cheap! These supreme waffles would cost at least five bucks more in Austin. I'm eating like a king on this trip!
SQUISH
So, you're from Austin?
Oops! My hunger got in the way of my manners.
Kat Fields. She/her. Nineteen. Queer. Scorpio sun, Cancer moon, Capricorn rising. Podcaster and college freshman. Originally from San Antonio, livin' in ATX.

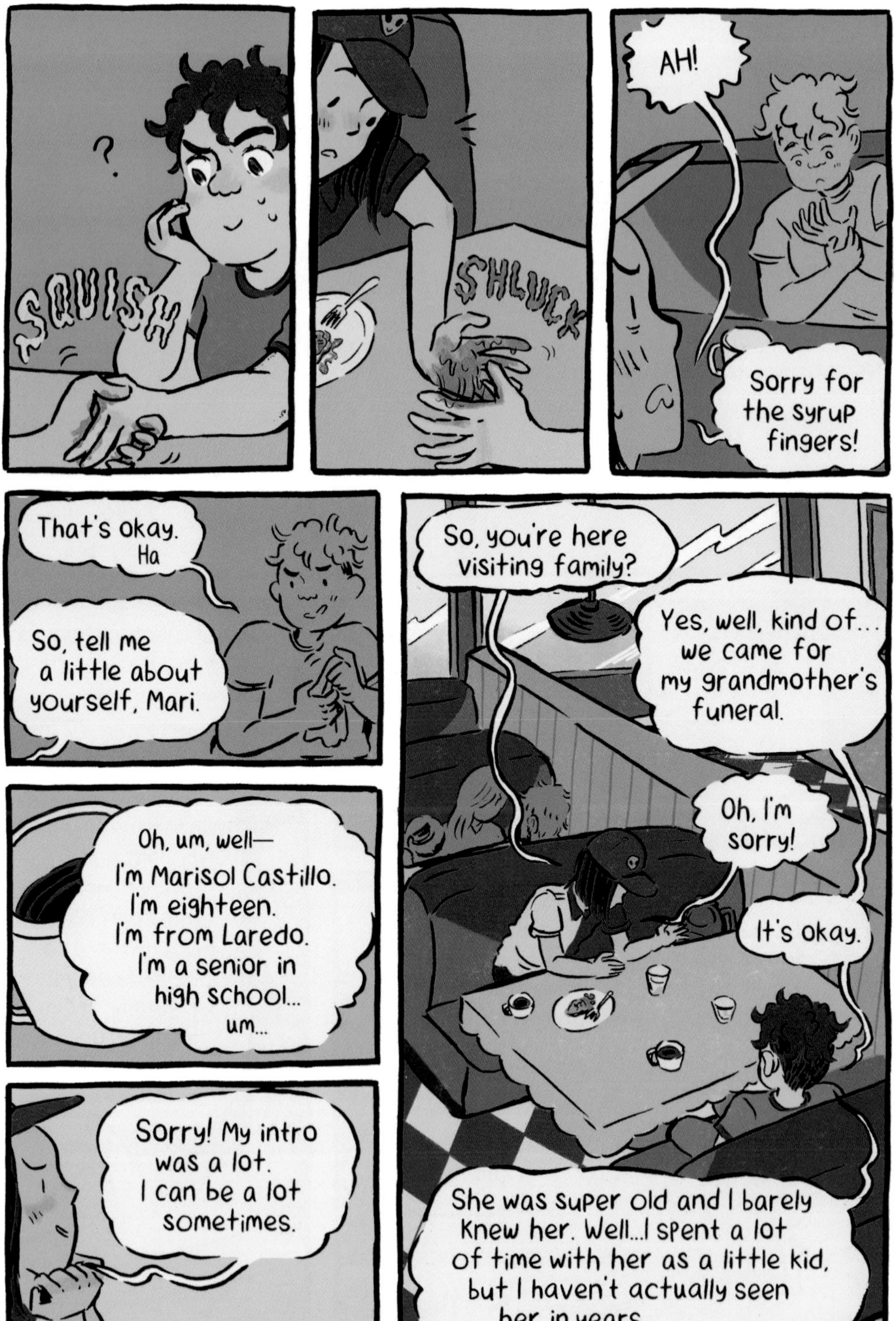
?
SQUISH
SHLUCK
AH!
Sorry for the syrup fingers!
That's okay. Ha
So, tell me a little about yourself, Mari.
Oh, um, well— I'm Marisol Castillo. I'm eighteen. I'm from Laredo. I'm a senior in high school... um...
Sorry! My intro was a lot. I can be a lot sometimes.
So, you're here visiting family?
Yes, well, kind of... we came for my grandmother's funeral.
Oh, I'm sorry!
It's okay.
She was super old and I barely knew her. Well...I spent a lot of time with her as a little kid, but I haven't actually seen her in years.

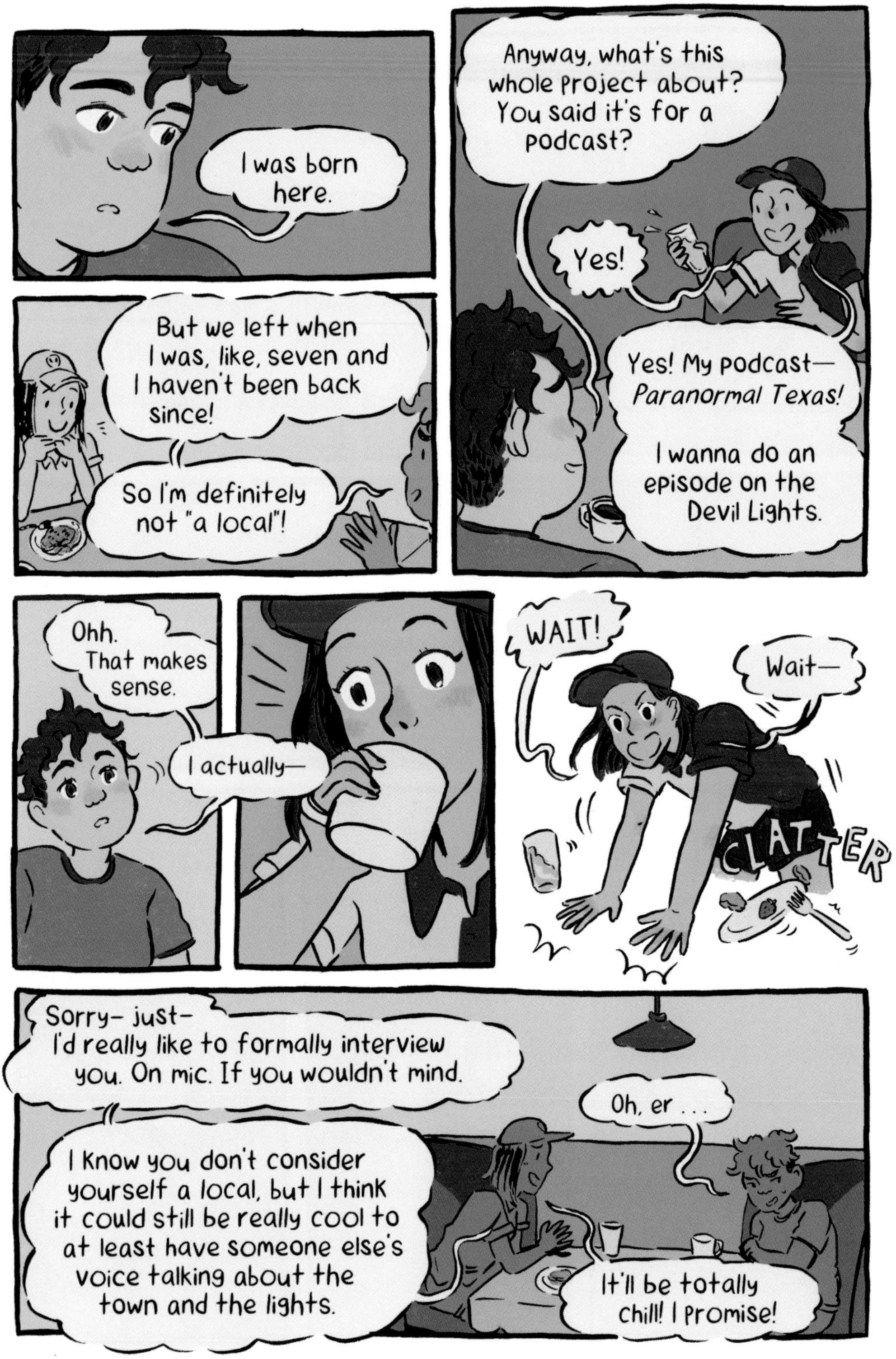
I was born here.
But we left when I was, like, seven and I haven't been back since!
So I'm definitely not "a local"!
Anyway, what's this whole project about? You said it's for a podcast?
Yes!
Yes! My podcast—*Paranormal Texas!*
I wanna do an episode on the Devil Lights.
Ohh. That makes sense.
I actually—
WAIT!
Wait—
CLATTER
Sorry– just– I'd really like to formally interview you. On mic. If you wouldn't mind.
I know you don't consider yourself a local, but I think it could still be really cool to at least have someone else's voice talking about the town and the lights.
Oh, er . . .
It'll be totally chill! I promise!

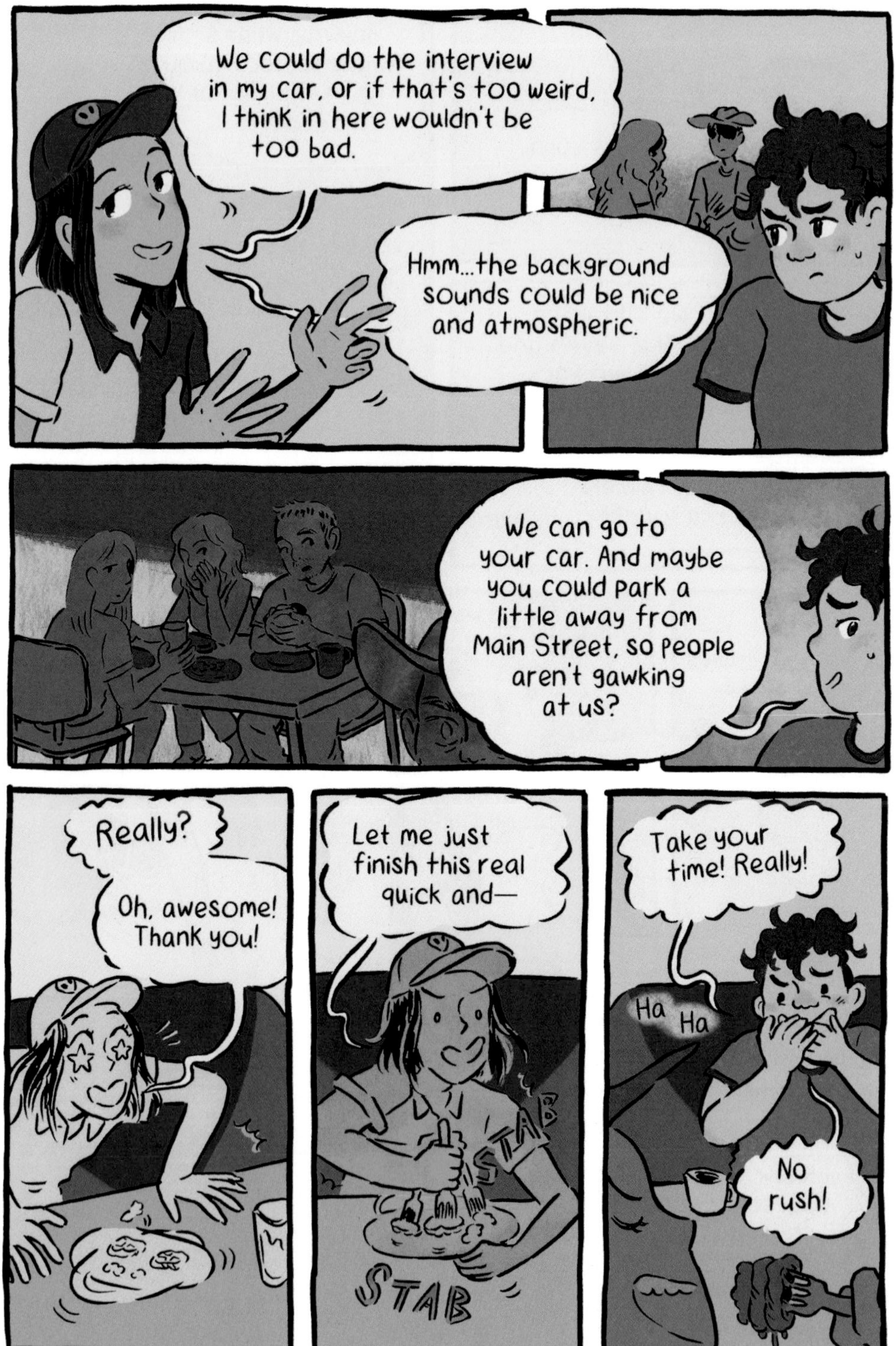
We could do the interview in my car, or if that's too weird, I think in here wouldn't be too bad.
Hmm...the background sounds could be nice and atmospheric.
We can go to your car. And maybe you could park a little away from Main Street, so people aren't gawking at us?
Really?
Oh, awesome! Thank you!
Let me just finish this real quick and—
STAB
STAB
STAB
Take your time! Really!
Ha
Ha
No rush!

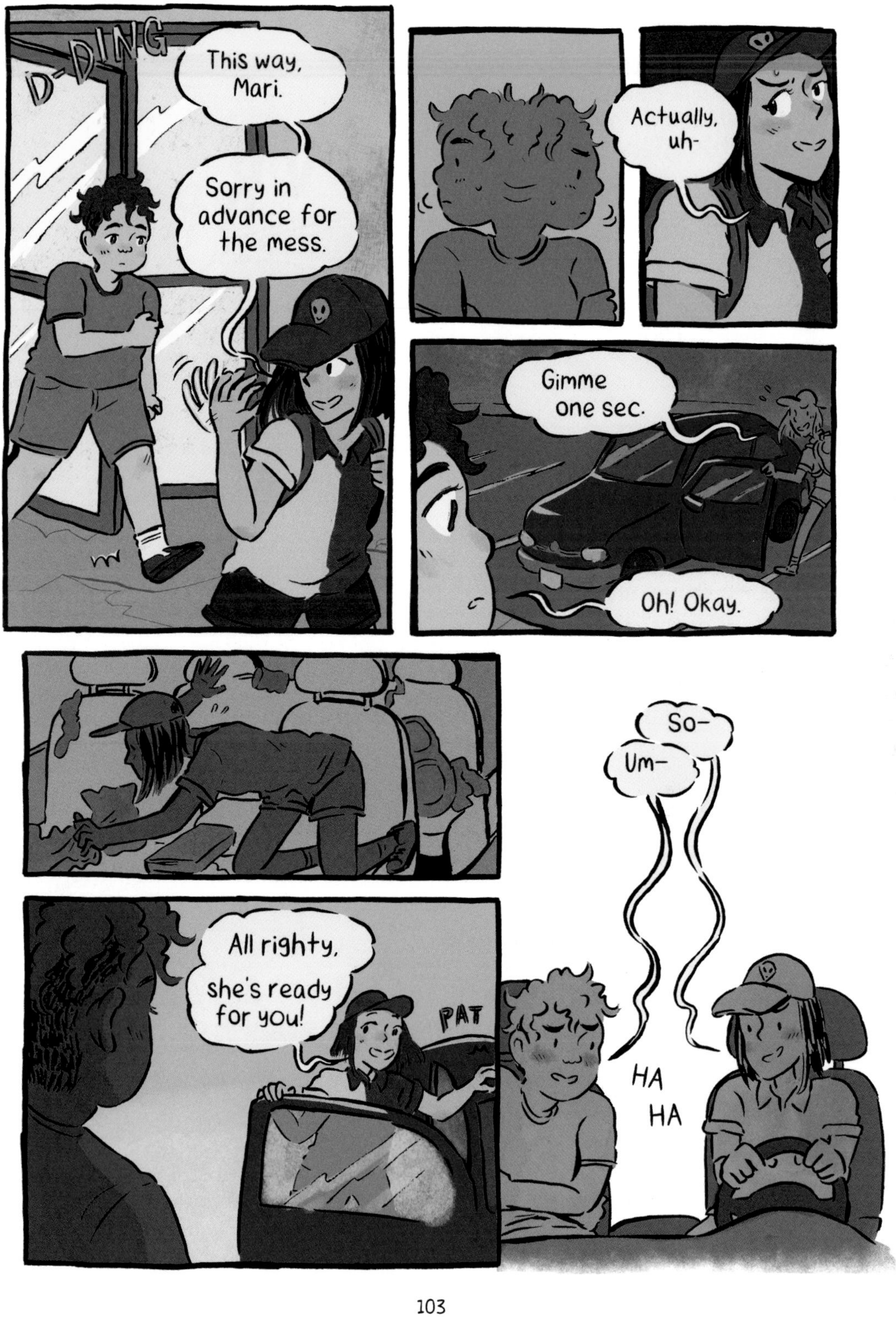
D-DING
This way, Mari.
Sorry in advance for the mess.
Actually, uh-
Gimme one sec.
Oh! Okay.
All righty, she's ready for you!
PAT
So-
Um-
HA HA

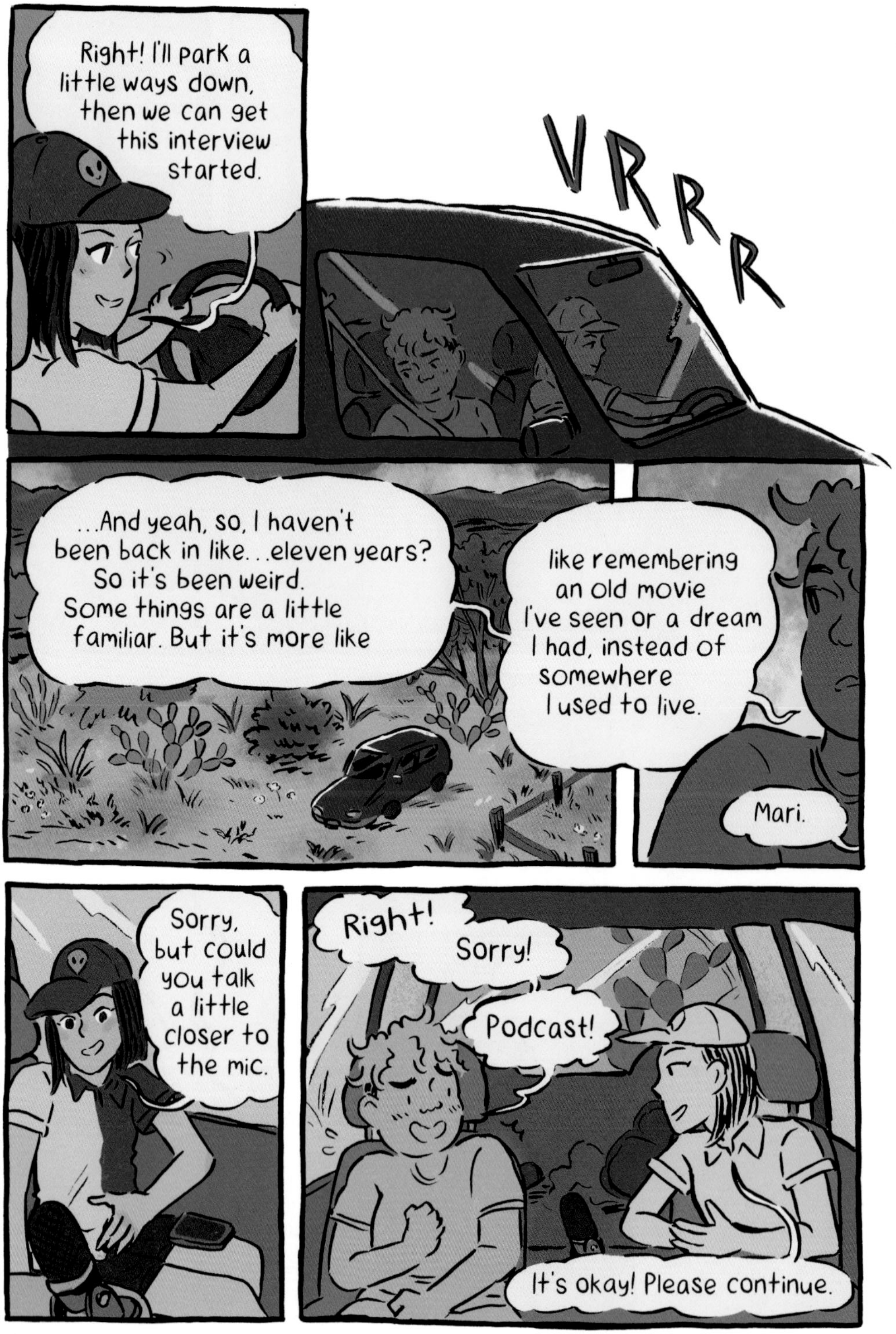
Right! I'll park a little ways down, then we can get this interview started.
VRRRR
...And yeah, so, I haven't been back in like...eleven years? So it's been weird. Some things are a little familiar. But it's more like
like remembering an old movie I've seen or a dream I had, instead of somewhere I used to live.
Mari.
Sorry, but could you talk a little closer to the mic.
Right!
Sorry!
Podcast!
It's okay! Please continue.

That's it, really. I'm practically a stranger to this place too.

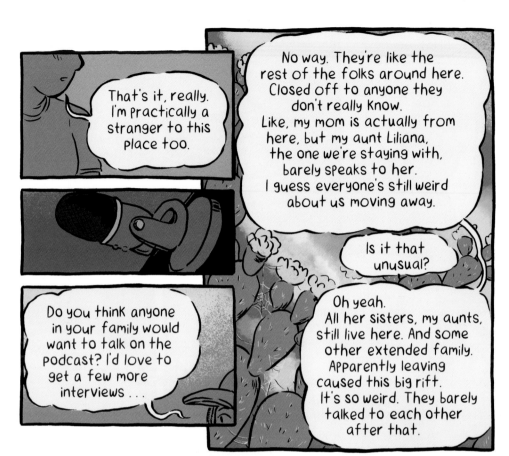

No way. They're like the rest of the folks around here. Closed off to anyone they don't really know.
Like, my mom is actually from here, but my aunt Liliana, the one we're staying with, barely speaks to her.
I guess everyone's still weird about us moving away.

Is it that unusual?

Do you think anyone in your family would want to talk on the podcast? I'd love to get a few more interviews ...

Oh yeah.
All her sisters, my aunts, still live here. And some other extended family.
Apparently leaving caused this big rift.
It's so weird. They barely talked to each other after that.

Just the occasional phone call ...

Sorry—this isn't really relevant.

Um, actually, can you not include that part on your podcast?

Sure. Of course. And it's okay! I asked and it's interesting.

Your podcast is about ghosts though, right?

Well, sometimes. Any kind of paranormal activity really.

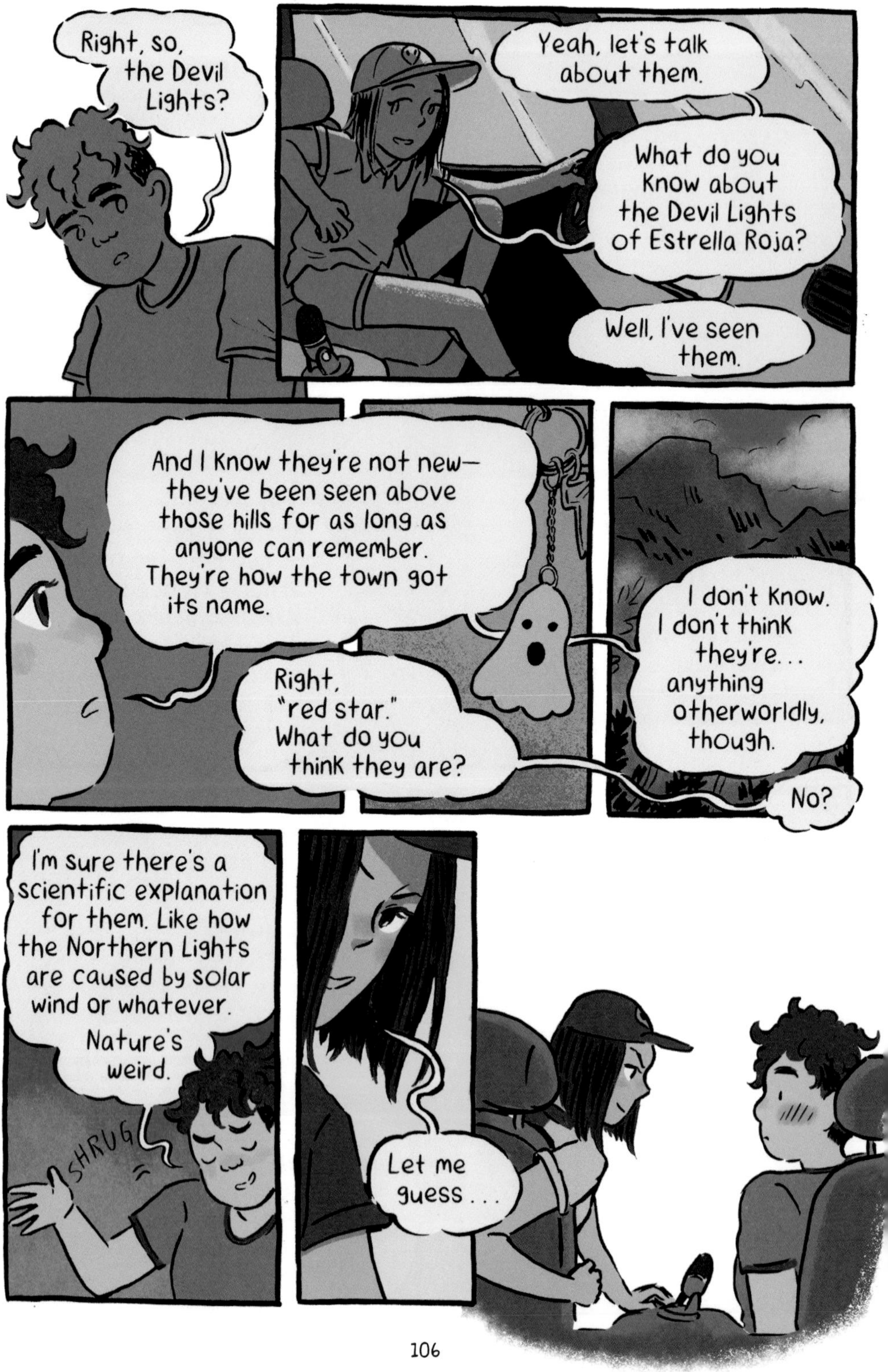
Right, so, the Devil Lights?
Yeah, let's talk about them.
What do you know about the Devil Lights of Estrella Roja?
Well, I've seen them.
And I know they're not new— they've been seen above those hills for as long as anyone can remember. They're how the town got its name.
Right, "red star." What do you think they are?
I don't know. I don't think they're... anything otherworldly, though.
No?
I'm sure there's a scientific explanation for them. Like how the Northern Lights are caused by solar wind or whatever.
Nature's weird.
SHRUG
Let me guess...

You're a skeptic.

I wouldn't say "skeptic." Well, maybe I would.
Ha.

I'm just really not interested in that kind of stuff—
Er—

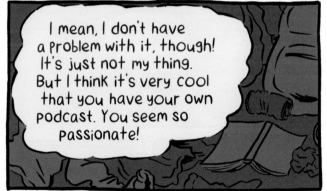
I mean, I don't have a problem with it, though! It's just not my thing. But I think it's very cool that you have your own podcast. You seem so passionate!

Thanks! And that's okay.

I still appreciate you letting me interview you. Skeptic or not.
NUDGE
HA HA

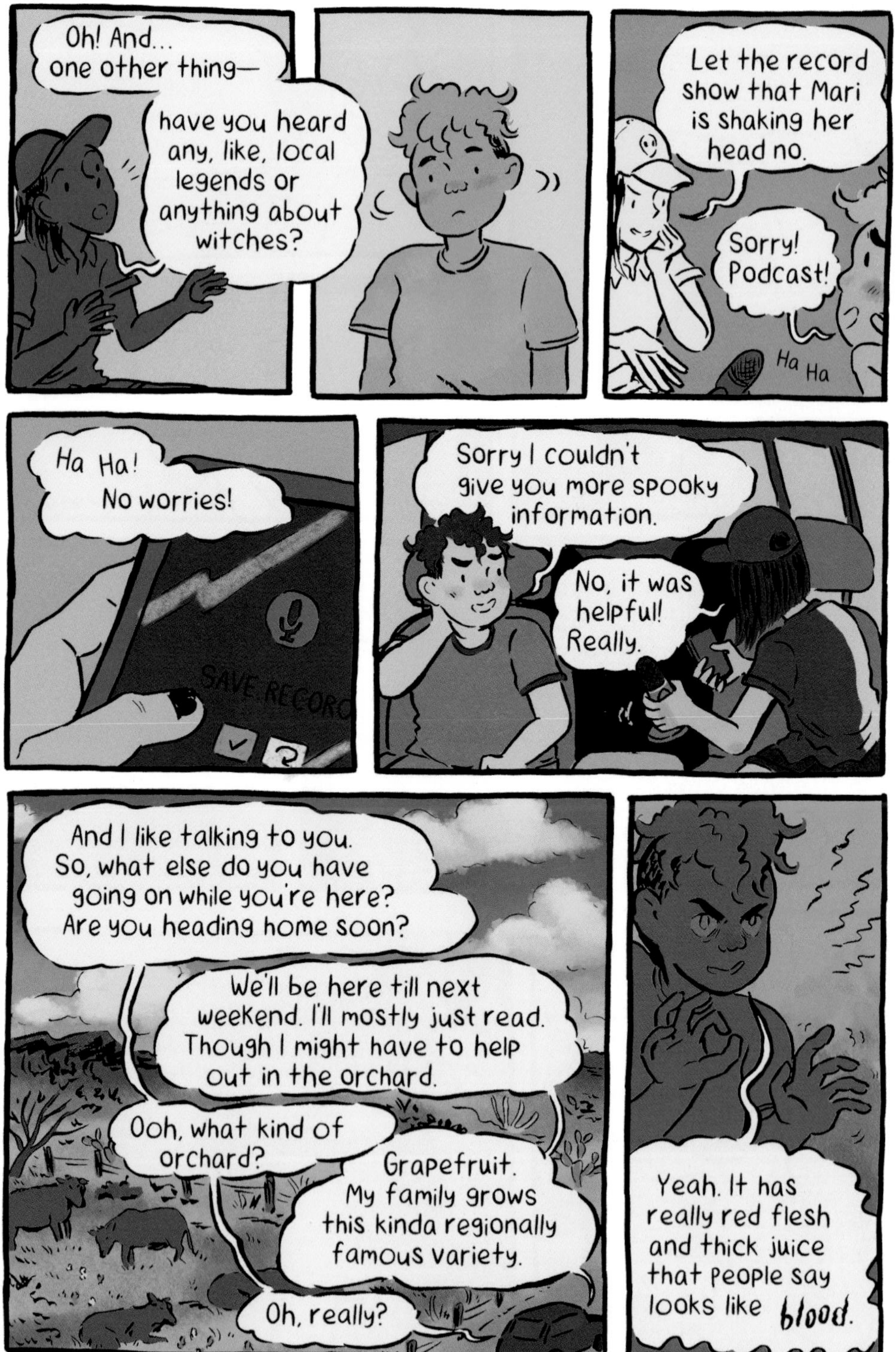
Oh! And... one other thing—
have you heard any, like, local legends or anything about witches?
Let the record show that Mari is shaking her head no.
Sorry! Podcast!
Ha Ha
Ha Ha! No worries!
SAVE RECORD
Sorry I couldn't give you more spooky information.
No, it was helpful! Really.
And I like talking to you. So, what else do you have going on while you're here? Are you heading home soon?
We'll be here till next weekend. I'll mostly just read. Though I might have to help out in the orchard.
Ooh, what kind of orchard?
Grapefruit. My family grows this kinda regionally famous variety.
Oh, really?
Yeah. It has really red flesh and thick juice that people say looks like blood.

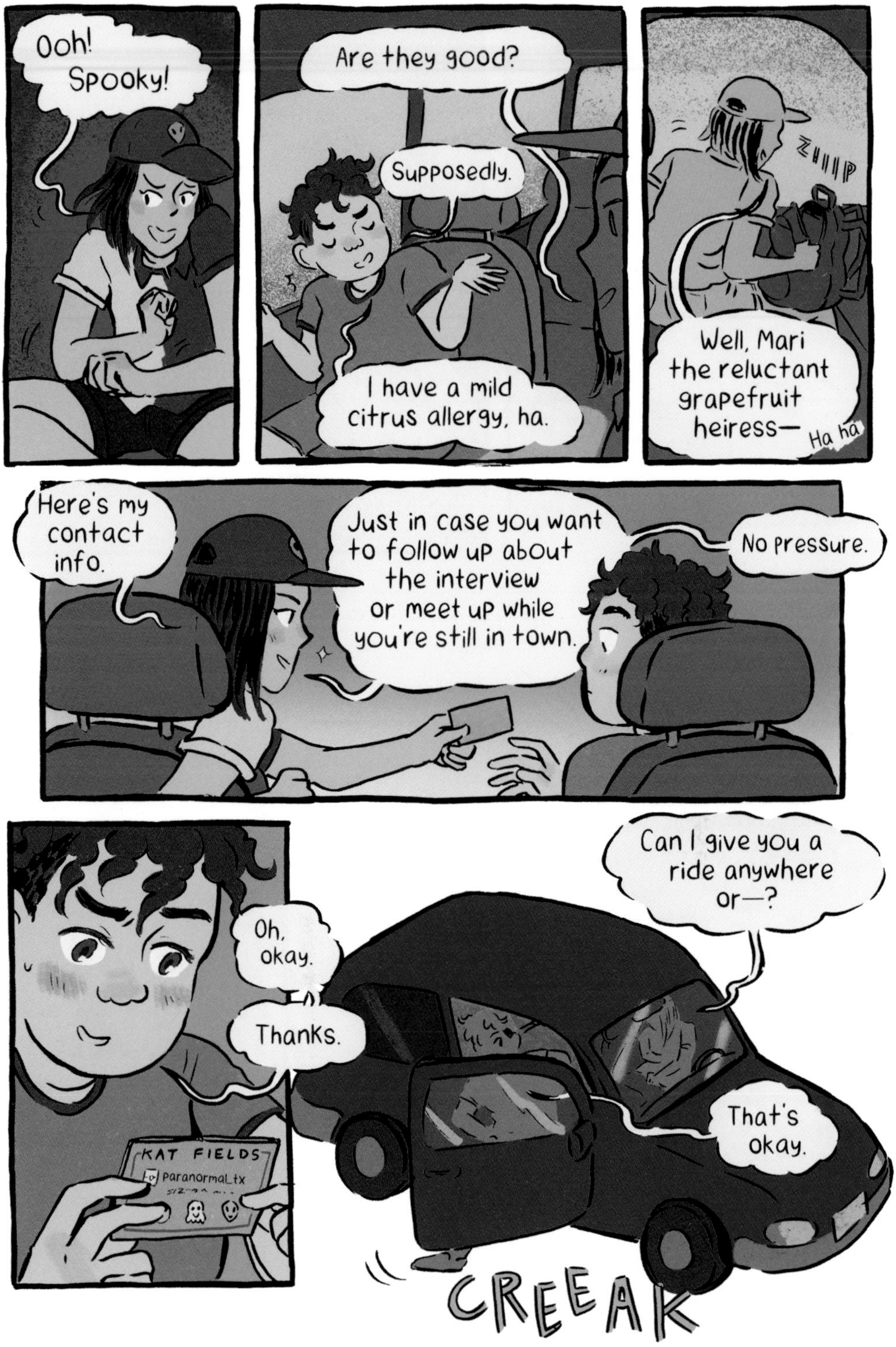
Ooh! Spooky!
Are they good?
Supposedly.
I have a mild citrus allergy, ha.
ZIIIP
Well, Mari the reluctant grapefruit heiress—
Ha ha
Here's my contact info.
Just in case you want to follow up about the interview or meet up while you're still in town.
No pressure.
Can I give you a ride anywhere or—?
Oh, okay.
Thanks.
That's okay.
KAT FIELDS
paranormal_tx
CREEAK

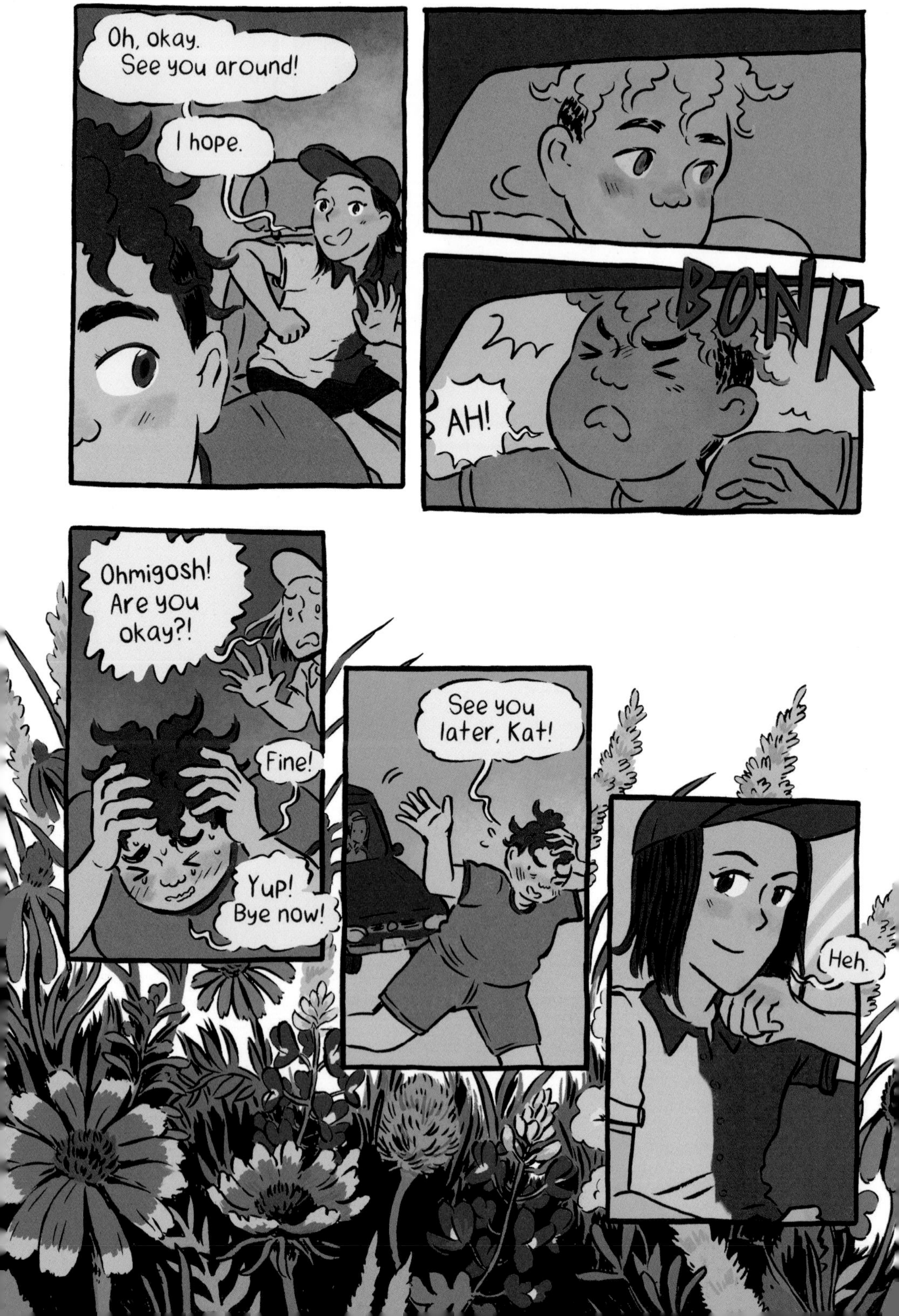
Oh, okay.
See you around!
I hope.
BONK
AH!
Ohmigosh!
Are you
okay?!
Fine!
Yup!
Bye now!
See you
later, Kat!
Heh.

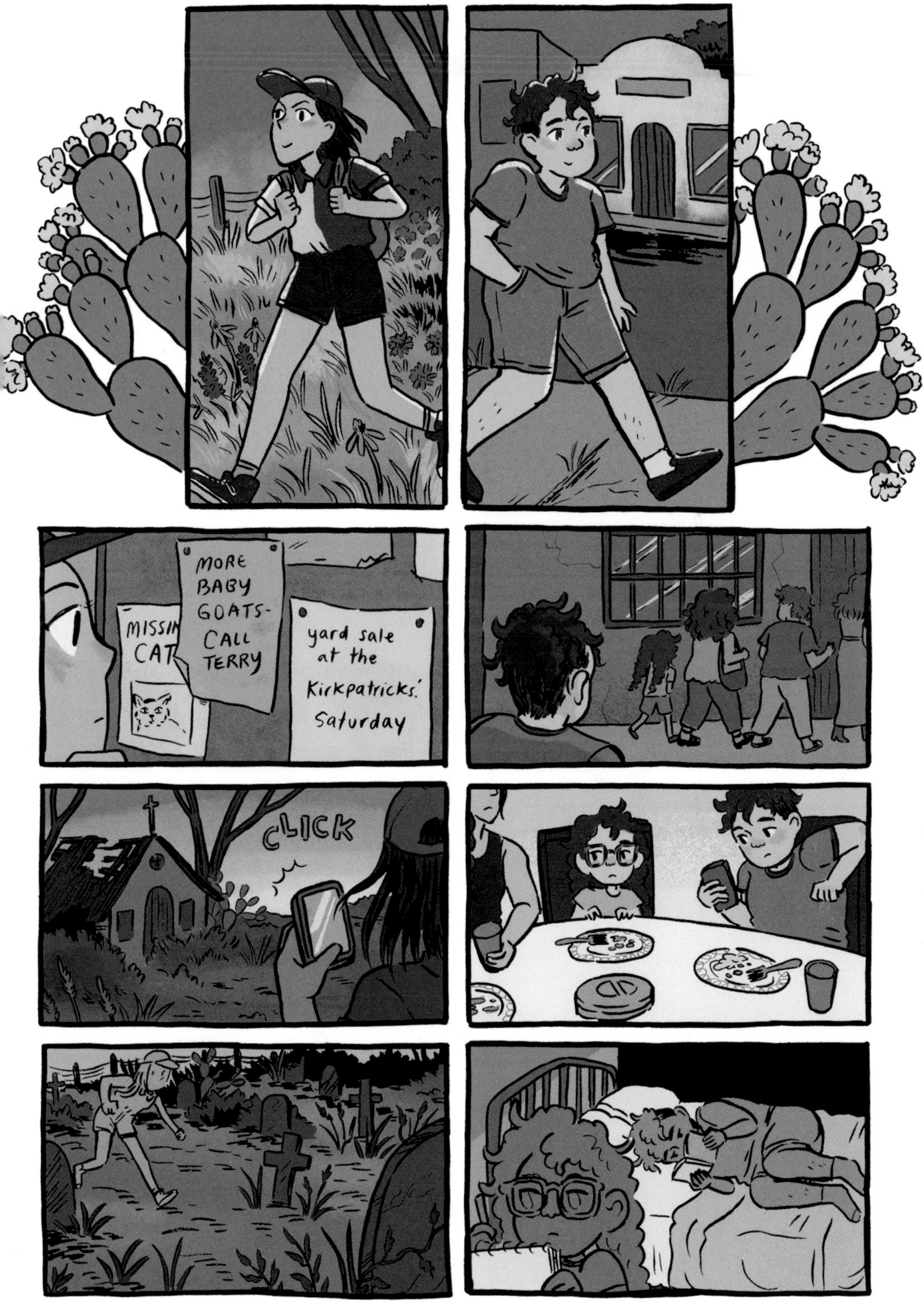
MISSIN
CAT
MORE
BABY
GOATS-
CALL
TERRY
yard sale
at the
Kirkpatricks'
Saturday
CLICK

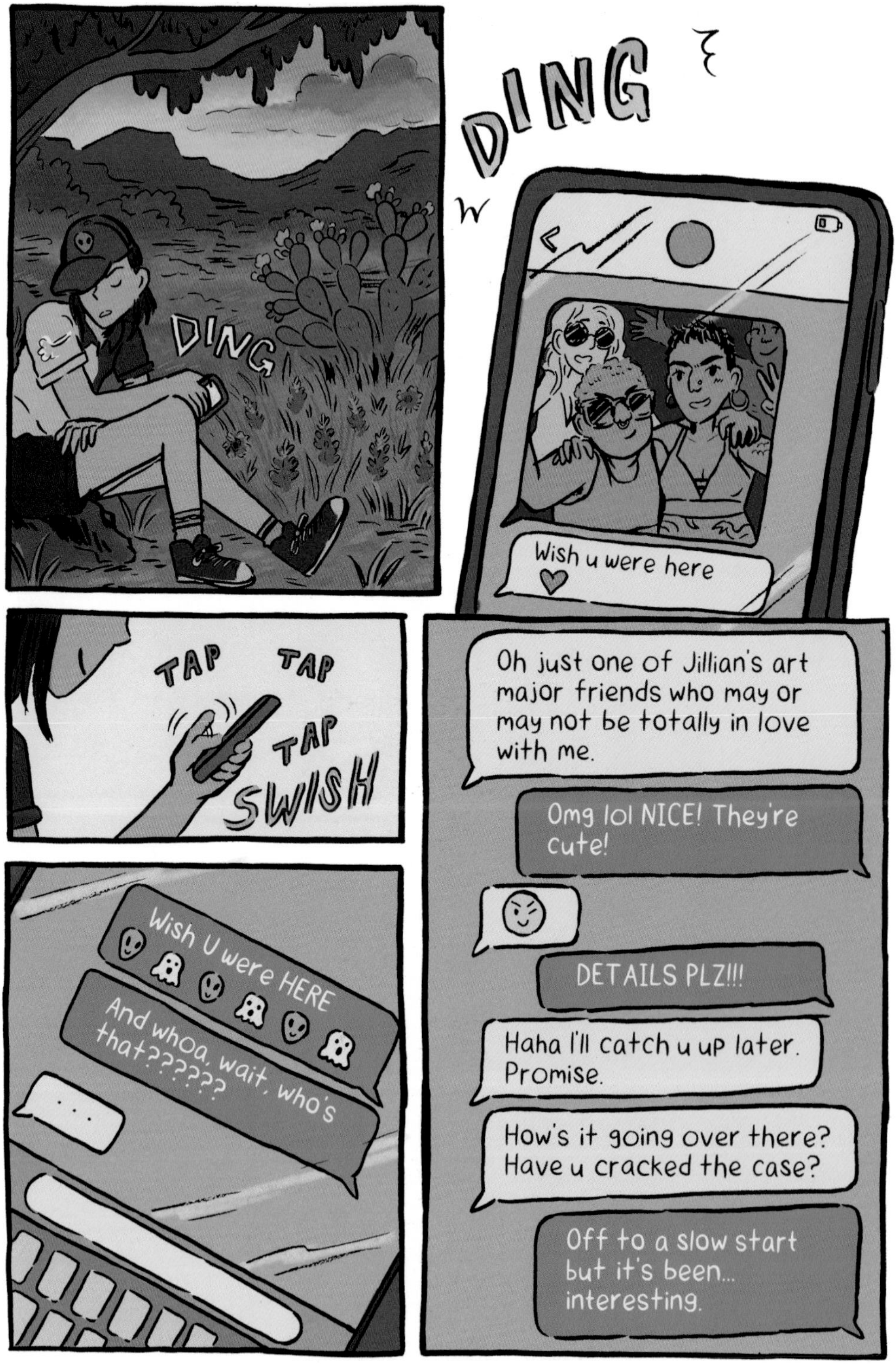
DING
DING
Wish u were here
TAP TAP
TAP
SWISH
Wish U were HERE
And whoa, wait, who's that??????
...
Oh just one of Jillian's art major friends who may or may not be totally in love with me.
Omg lol NICE! They're cute!
DETAILS PLZ!!!
Haha I'll catch u up later. Promise.
How's it going over there? Have u cracked the case?
Off to a slow start but it's been... interesting.

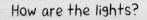
How are the lights?

TAP TAP WOOSH TAP

They're amazing IRL. I just can't seem to get a good picture of them! I'm gonna try to get a closer look tonight.

Hmm...yeah, that doesn't look like anything. Just be careful out there.
Plz don't fall into a pit or get bit by a rattlesnake or anything ridiculous, ok?

I'll try my best. Have fun, Clemmy!

I mean it. Be safe out there, dude!

Thanks u too! Don't get shark-attacked or anything!

Uh yea...we're at a WATERPARK so I'm more likely to get foot fungus or a waterslide injury lmao but thanks dork

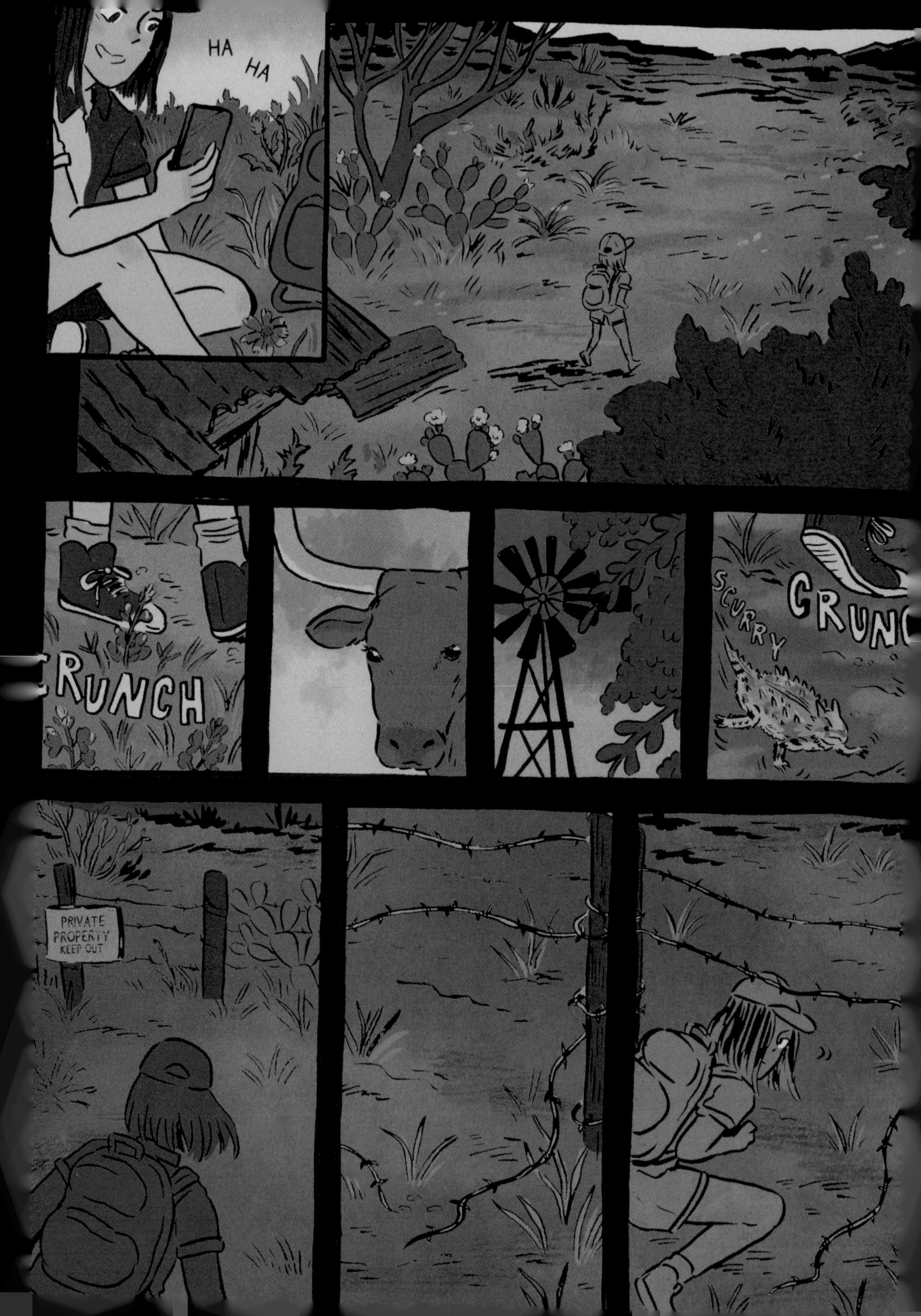
HA
HA
CRUNCH
SCURRY
CRUNC
PRIVATE PROPERTY KEEP OUT

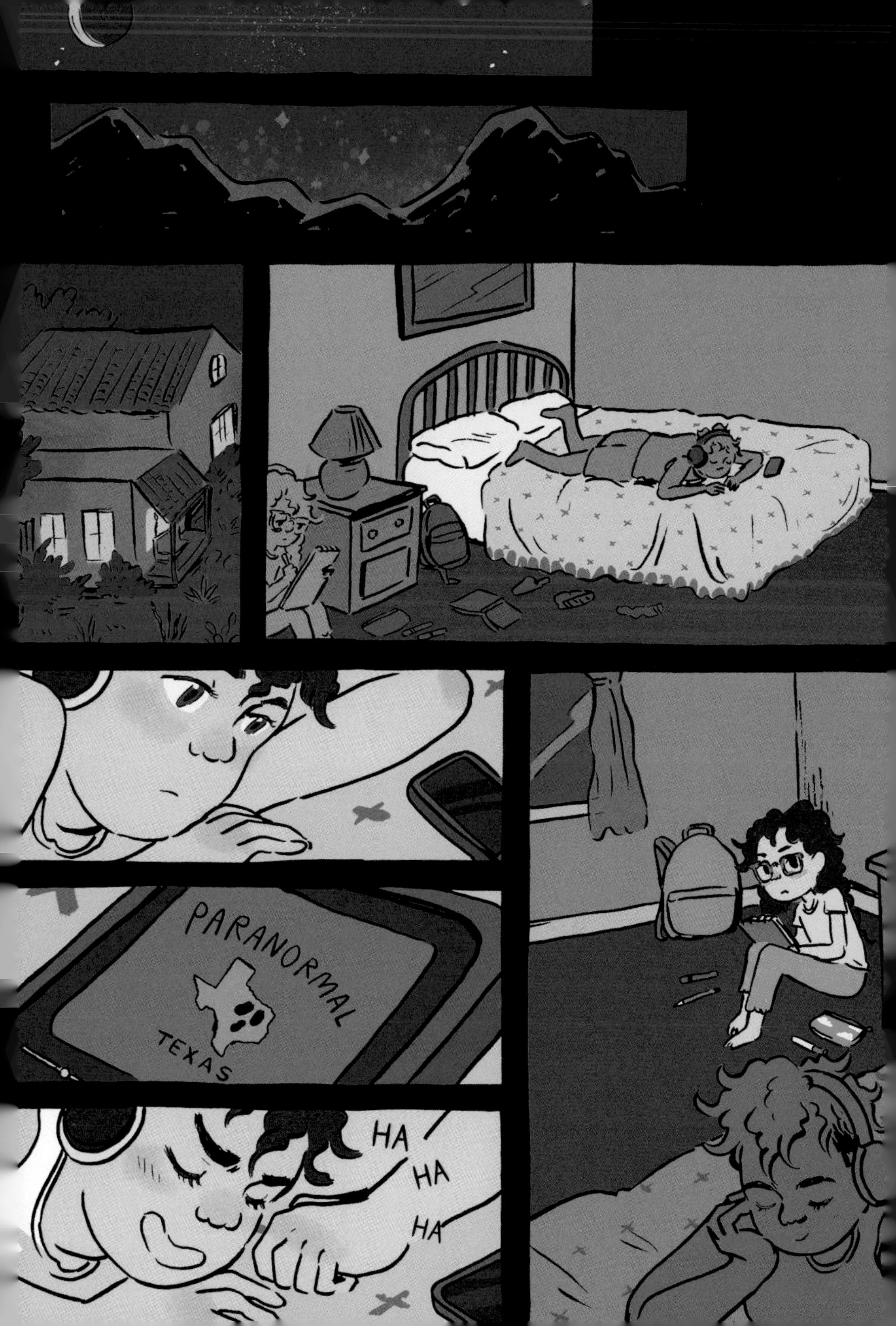
PARANORMAL
TEXAS
HA
HA
HA

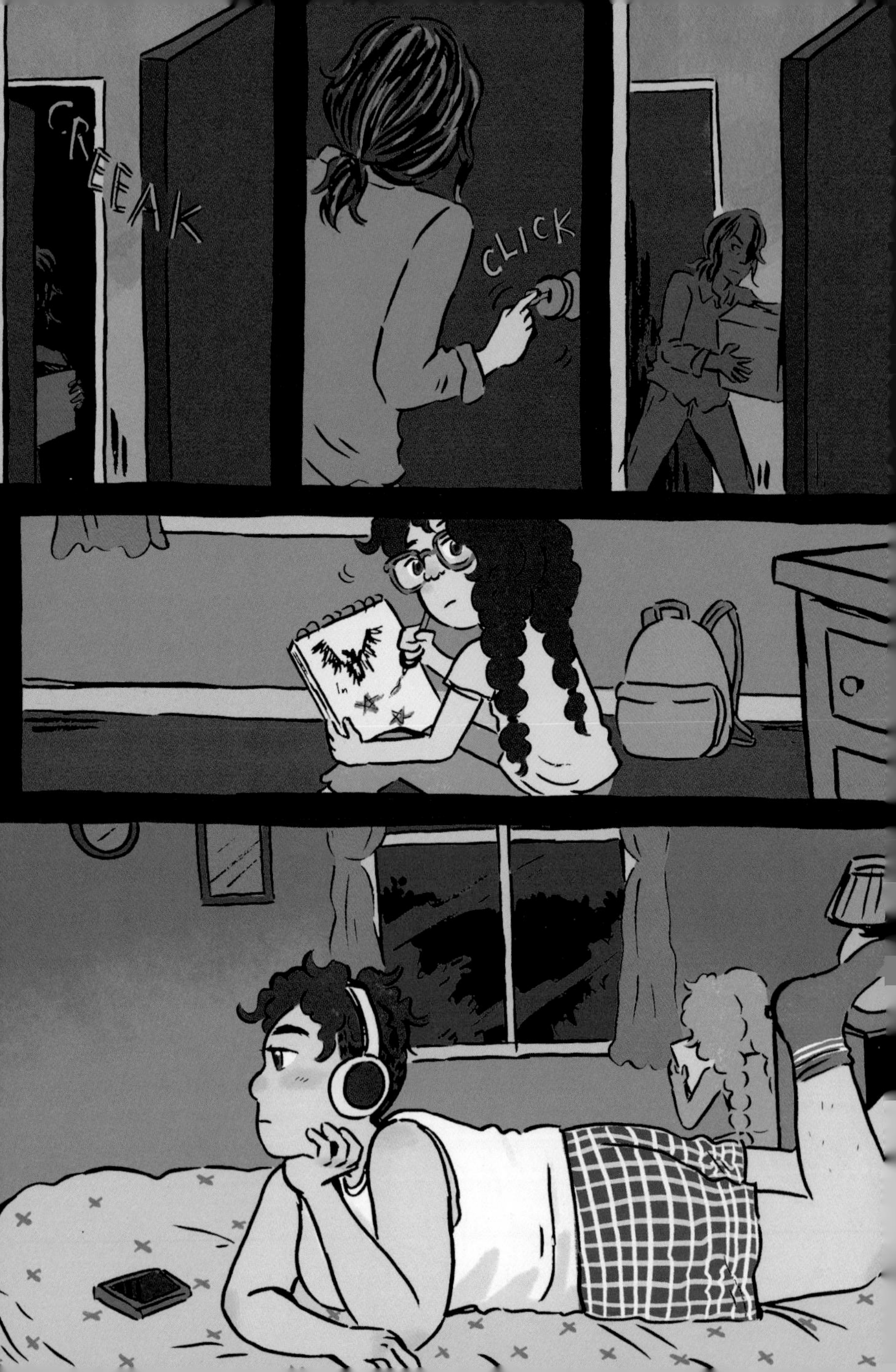
CREEAK
CLICK

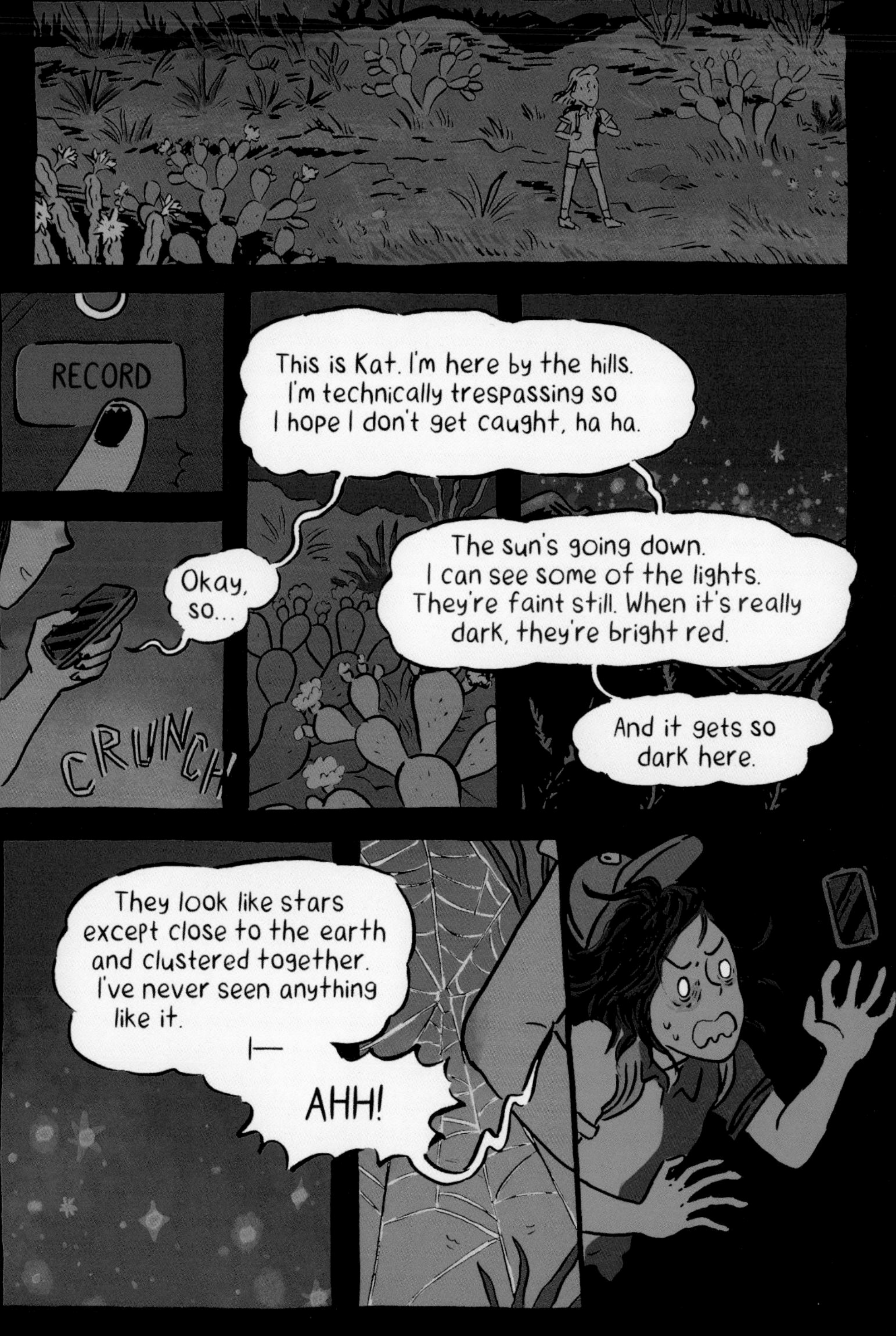
RECORD
Okay, so...
CRUNCH
This is Kat. I'm here by the hills. I'm technically trespassing so I hope I don't get caught, ha ha.
The sun's going down. I can see some of the lights. They're faint still. When it's really dark, they're bright red.
And it gets so dark here.
They look like stars except close to the earth and clustered together. I've never seen anything like it.
I—
AHH!

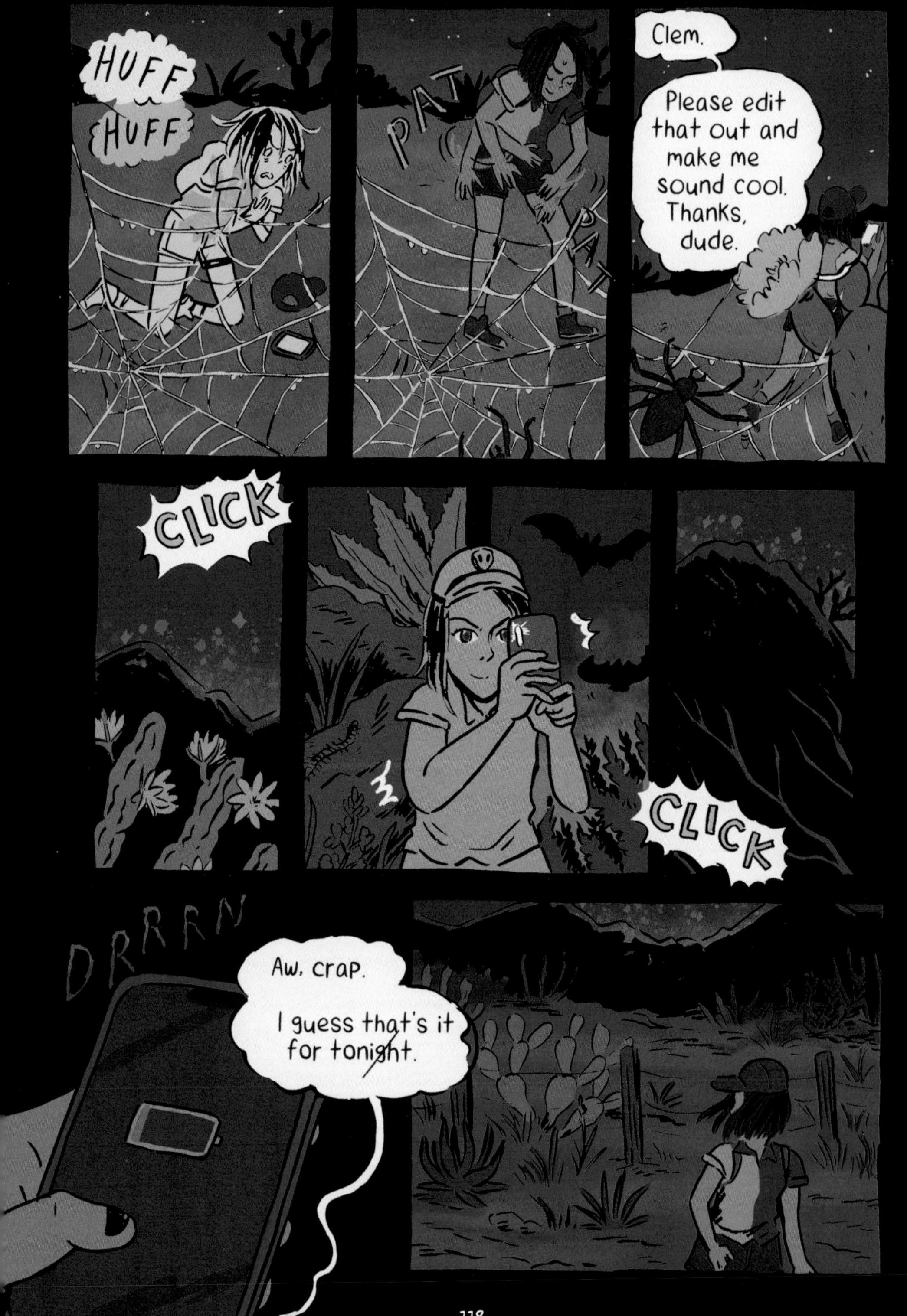
HUFF HUFF
PAT
PAT
Clem.
Please edit that out and make me sound cool. Thanks, dude.
CLICK
CLICK
DRRRN
Aw, crap.
I guess that's it for tonight.

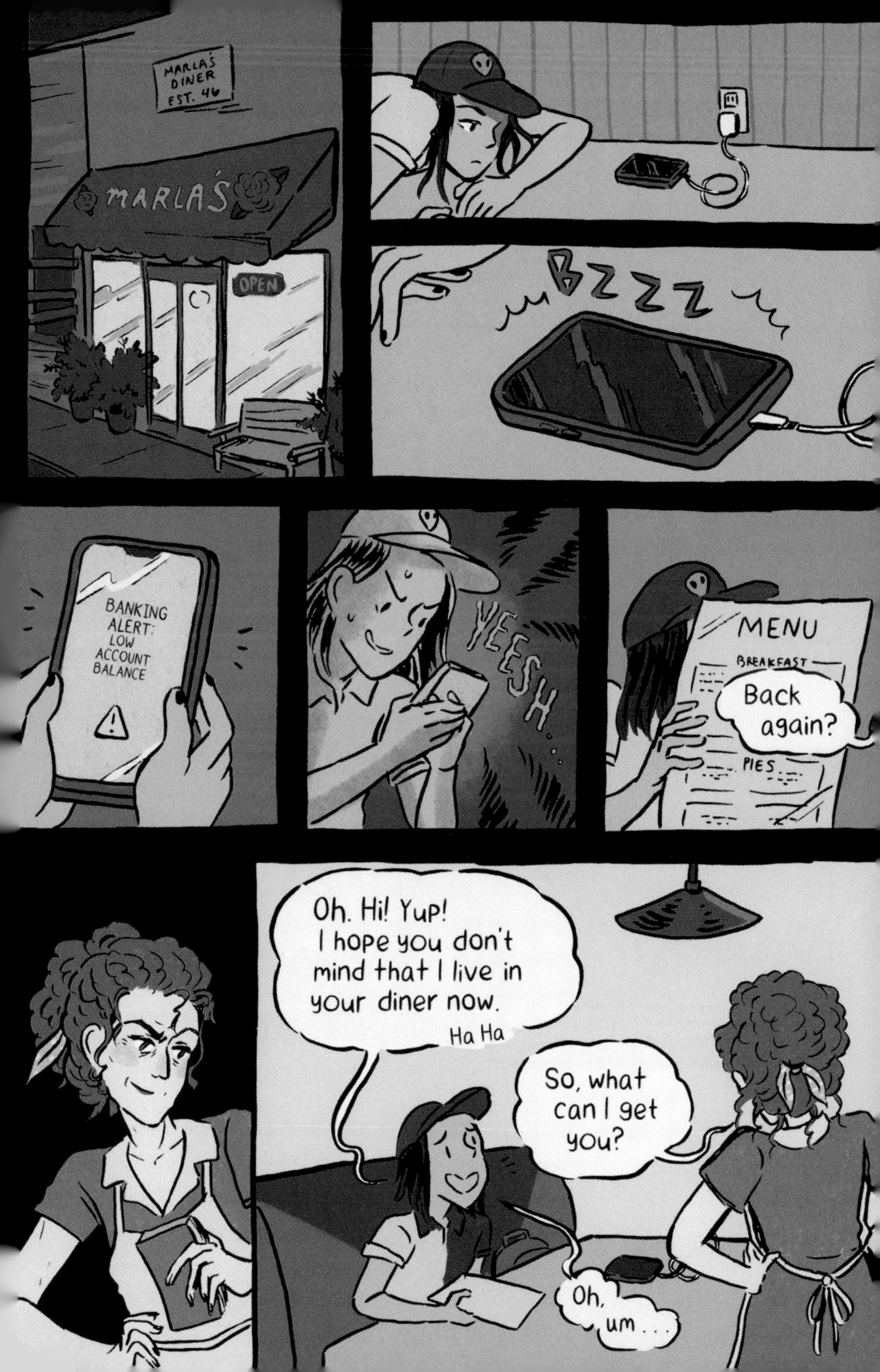
MARLA'S DINER EST. 46
MARLA'S
OPEN
BZZZZ
BANKING ALERT: LOW ACCOUNT BALANCE
YEESH...
MENU
BREAKFAST
PIES
Back again?
Oh. Hi! Yup!
I hope you don't mind that I live in your diner now.
Ha Ha
So, what can I get you?
Oh, um...

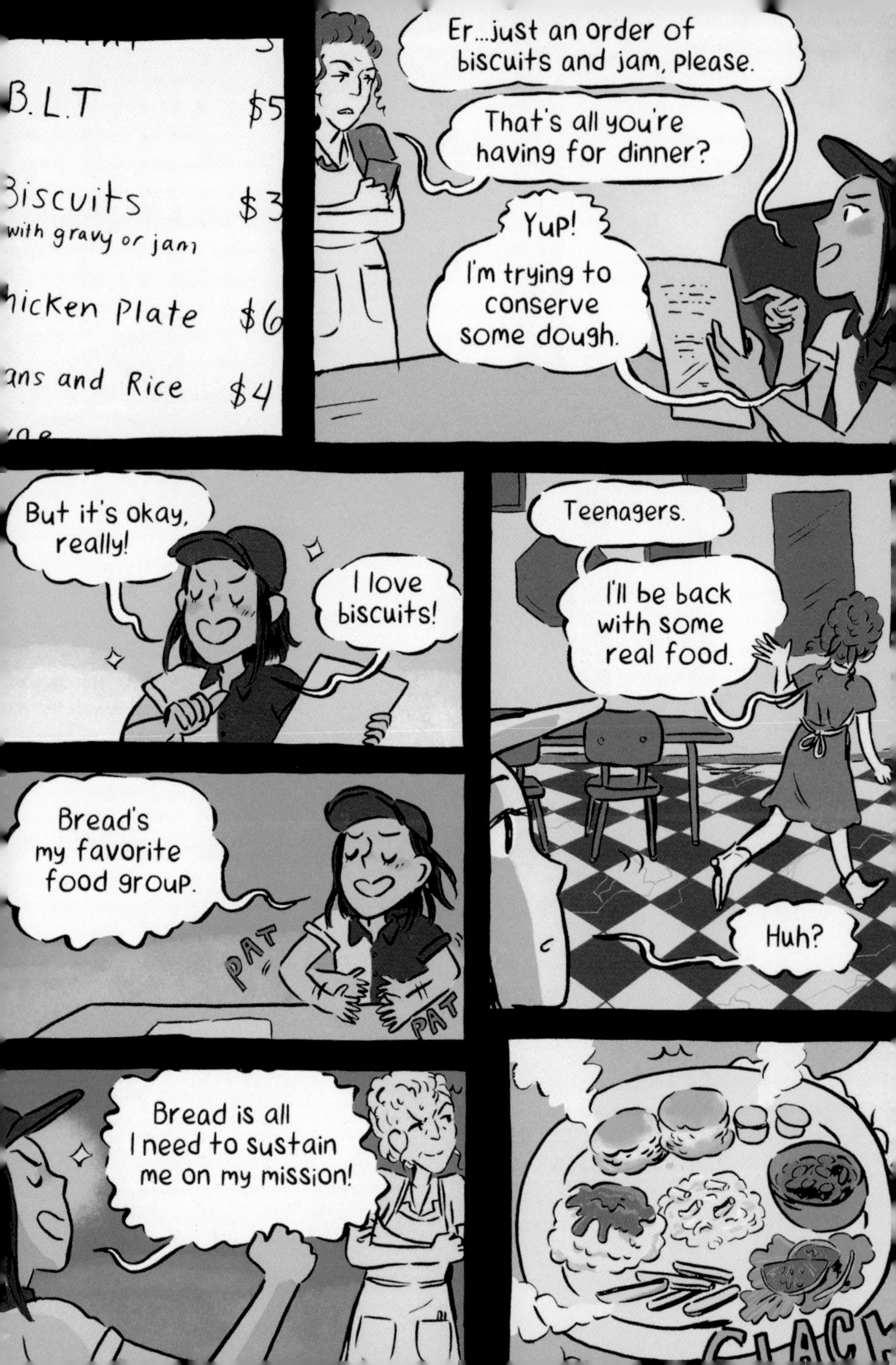
B.L.T $5
Biscuits $3
with gravy or jam
hicken Plate $6
ans and Rice $4
Er...just an order of biscuits and jam, please.
That's all you're having for dinner?
Yup!
I'm trying to conserve some dough.
But it's okay, really!
I love biscuits!
Teenagers.
I'll be back with some real food.
Huh?
Bread's my favorite food group.
PAT
PAT
Bread is all I need to sustain me on my mission!

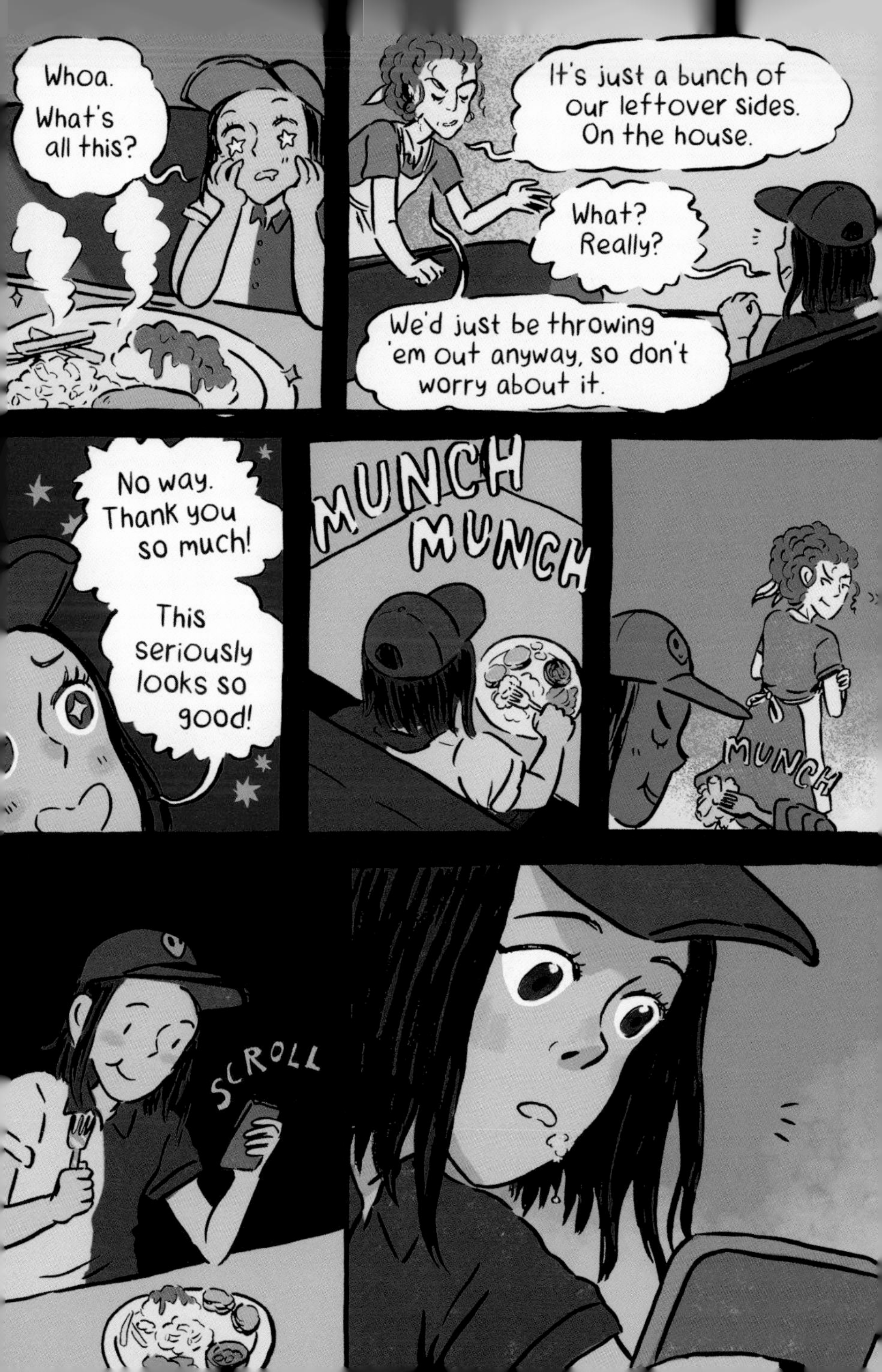
Whoa.
What's all this?
It's just a bunch of our leftover sides. On the house.
What? Really?
We'd just be throwing 'em out anyway, so don't worry about it.
No way. Thank you so much!
This seriously looks so good!
MUNCH
MUNCH
MUNCH
SCROLL

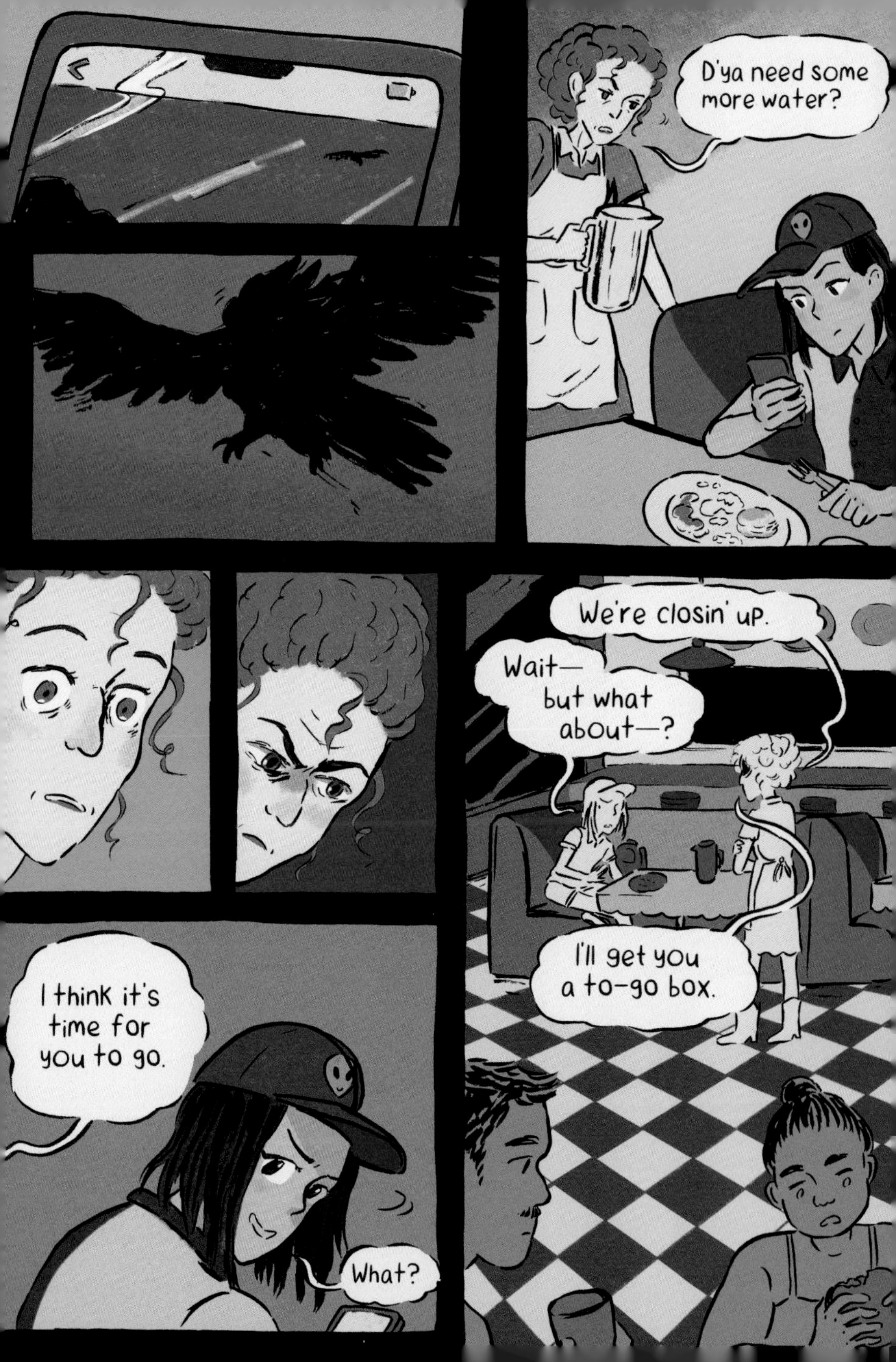
D'ya need some more water?
I think it's time for you to go.
What?
We're closin' up.
Wait— but what about—?
I'll get you a to-go box.

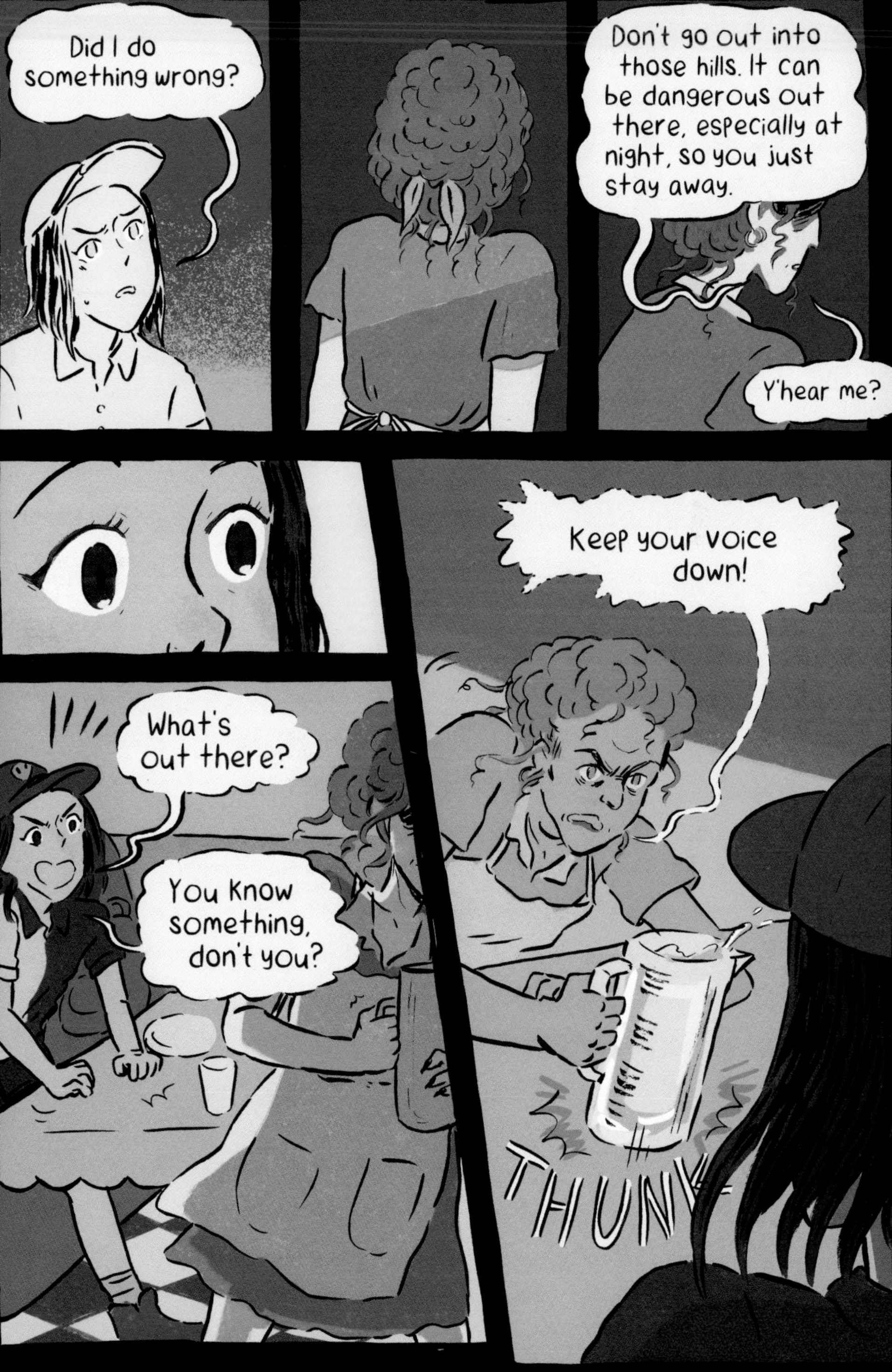
Did I do something wrong?
Don't go out into those hills. It can be dangerous out there, especially at night, so you just stay away.
Y'hear me?
What's out there?
You know something, don't you?
Keep your voice down!
THUNK

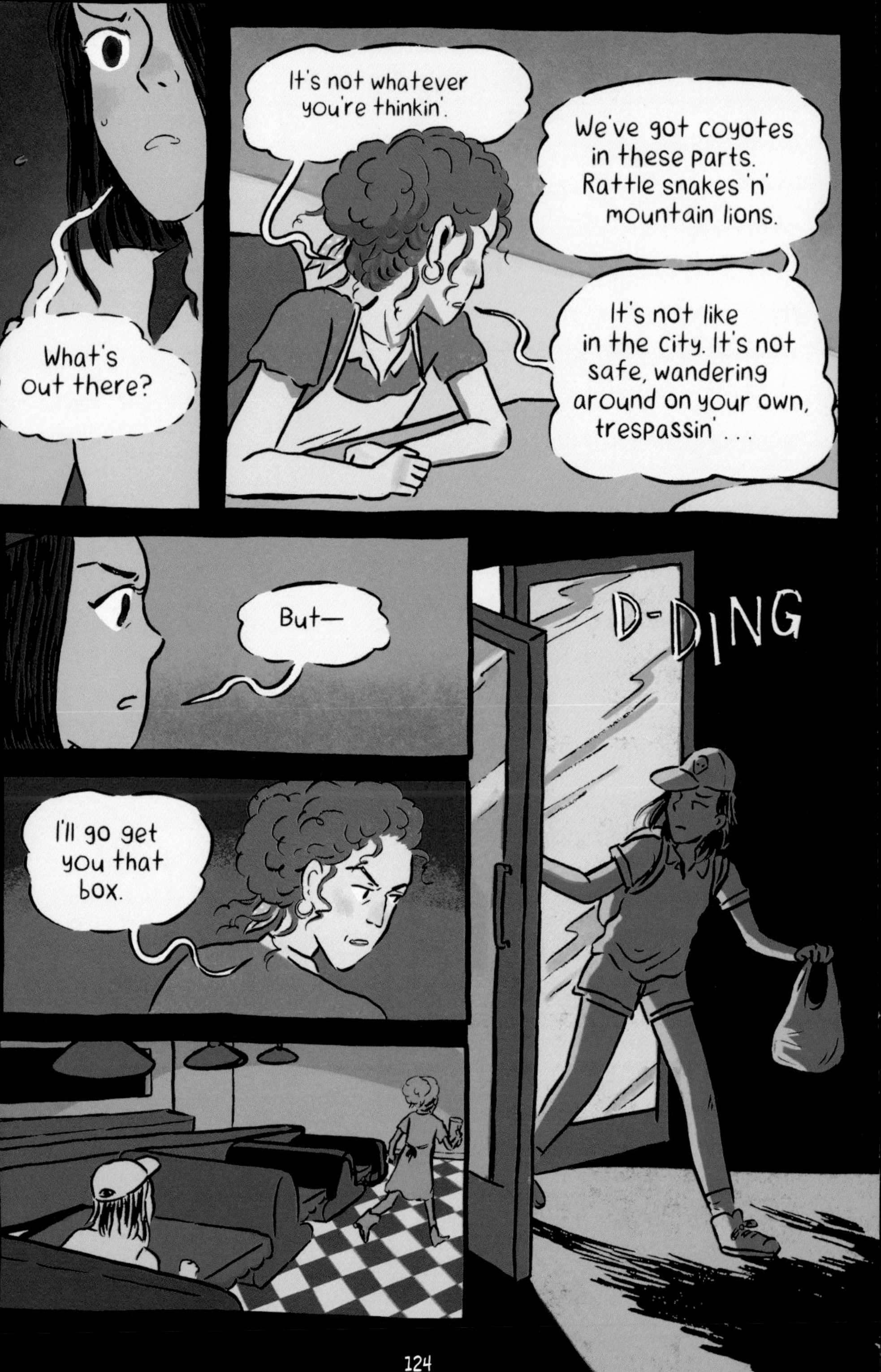
What's out there?
It's not whatever you're thinkin'.
We've got coyotes in these parts. Rattle snakes 'n' mountain lions.
It's not like in the city. It's not safe, wandering around on your own, trespassin' . . .
But—
I'll go get you that box.
D-DING

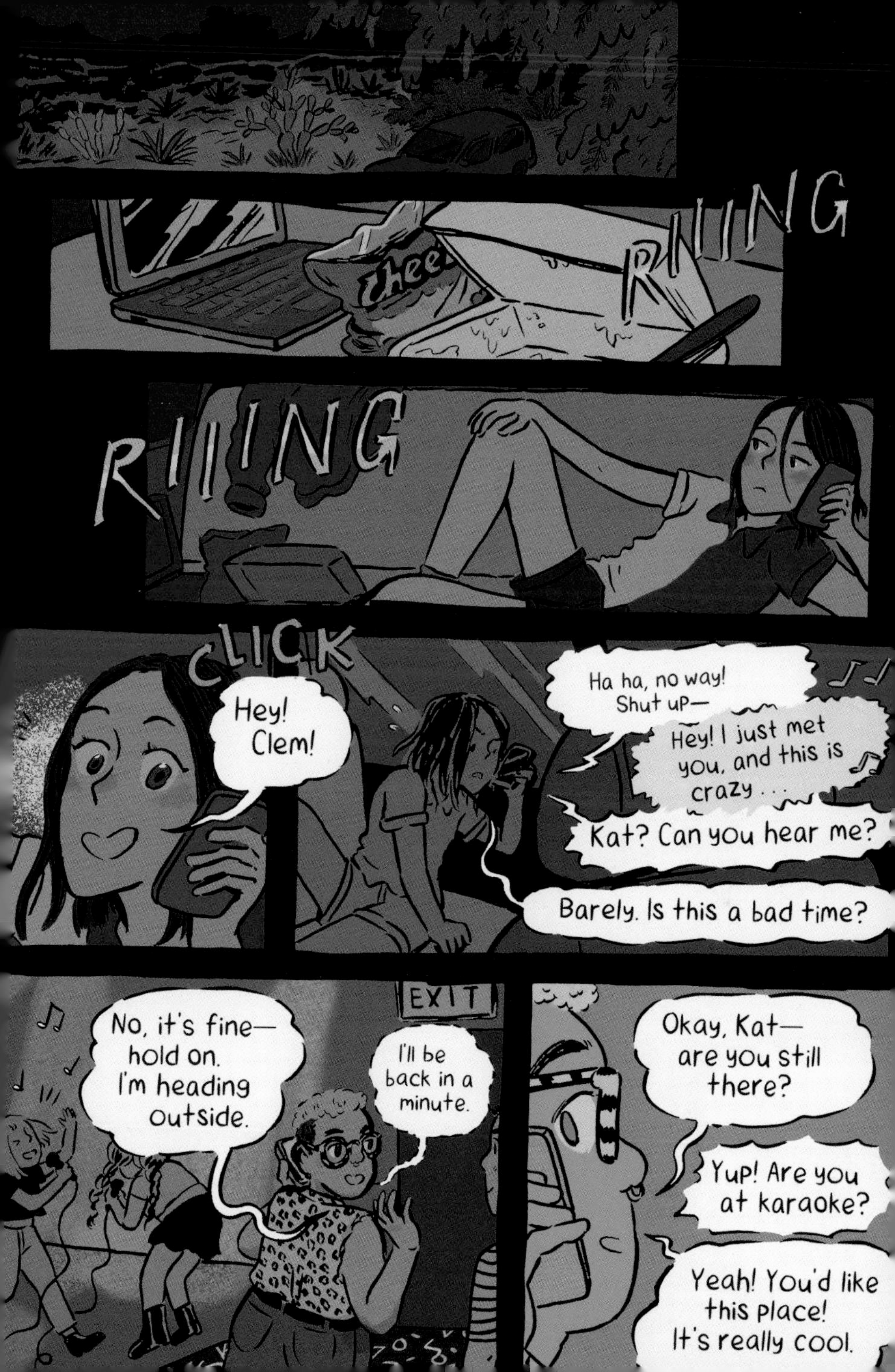
thee
RIIING
RIIING
CLICK
Hey! Clem!
Ha ha, no way! Shut up—
Hey! I just met you, and this is crazy . . .
Kat? Can you hear me?
Barely. Is this a bad time?
EXIT
No, it's fine—hold on. I'm heading outside.
I'll be back in a minute.
Okay, Kat—are you still there?
Yup! Are you at karaoke?
Yeah! You'd like this place! It's really cool.

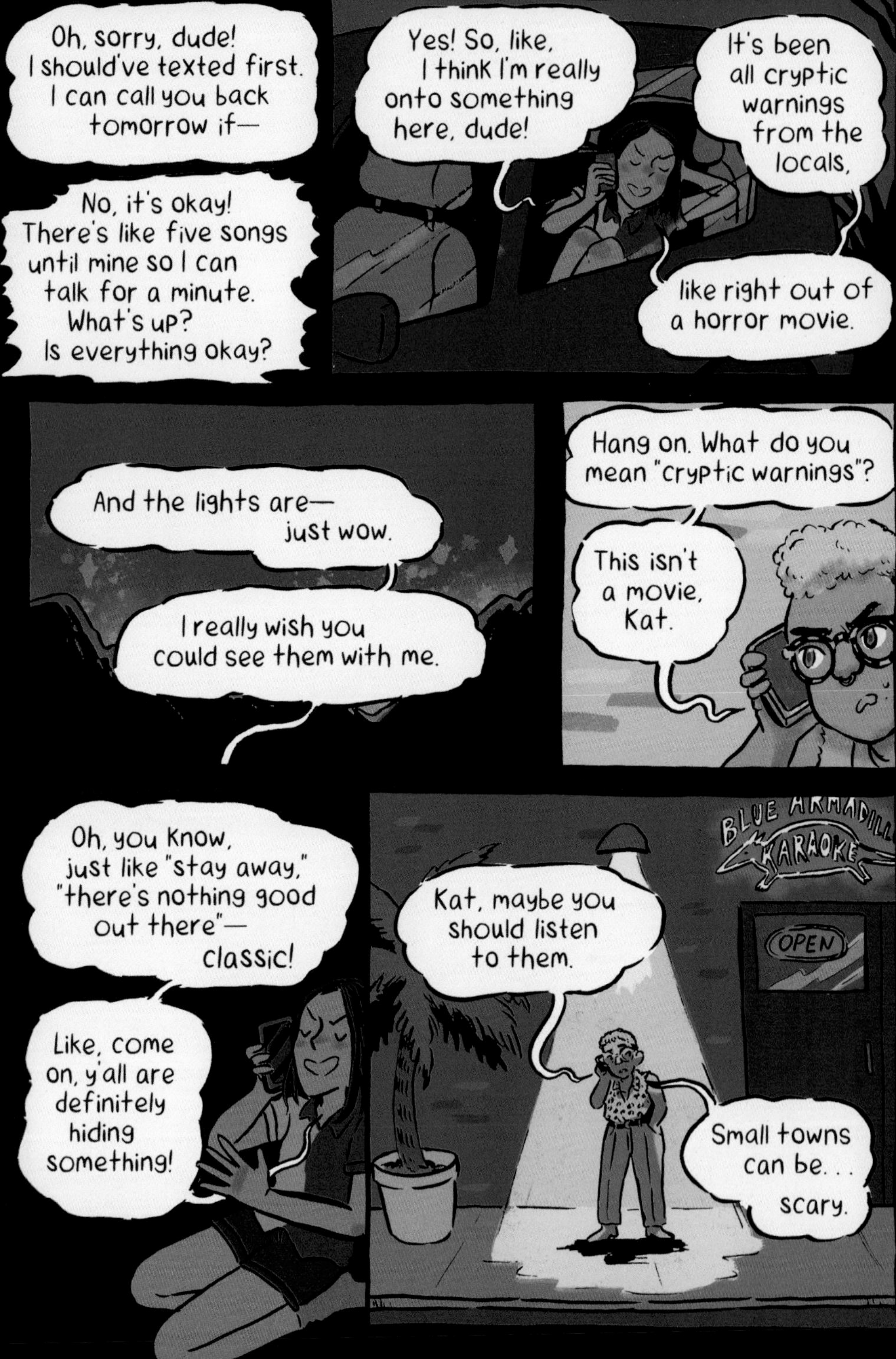
Oh, sorry, dude! I should've texted first. I can call you back tomorrow if—
No, it's okay! There's like five songs until mine so I can talk for a minute. What's up? Is everything okay?
Yes! So, like, I think I'm really onto something here, dude!
It's been all cryptic warnings from the locals,
like right out of a horror movie.
And the lights are— just wow.
I really wish you could see them with me.
Hang on. What do you mean "cryptic warnings"?
This isn't a movie, Kat.
Oh, you know, just like "stay away," "there's nothing good out there"— classic!
Like, come on, y'all are definitely hiding something!
BLUE ARMADILLO KARAOKE
OPEN
Kat, maybe you should listen to them.
Small towns can be. . . scary.

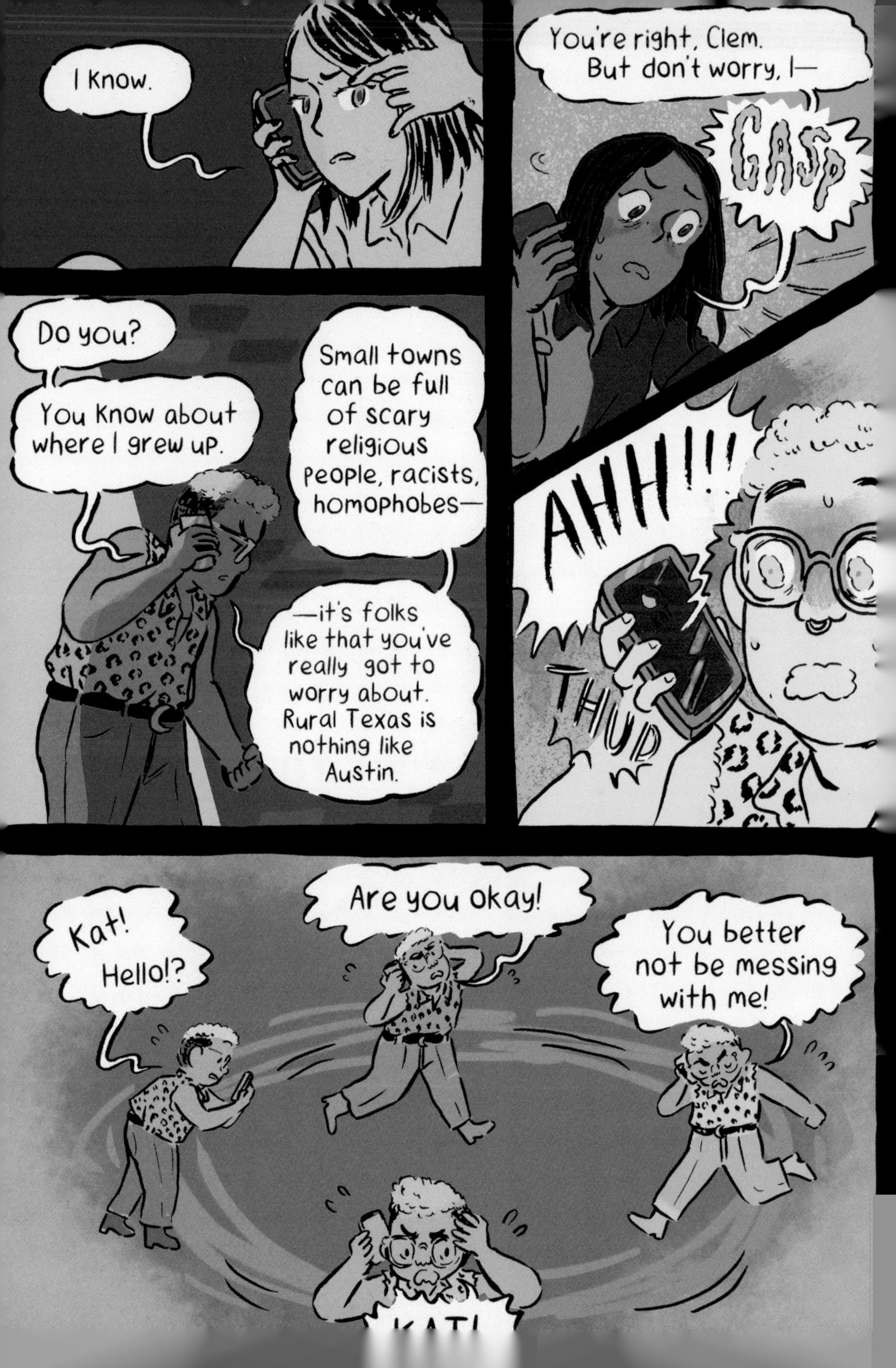
I know.
Do you?
You know about where I grew up.
Small towns can be full of scary religious people, racists, homophobes—
—it's folks like that you've really got to worry about. Rural Texas is nothing like Austin.
You're right, Clem. But don't worry, I—
GASP
AHH!!!
THUD
Kat! Hello!?
Are you okay!
You better not be messing with me!
KAT!

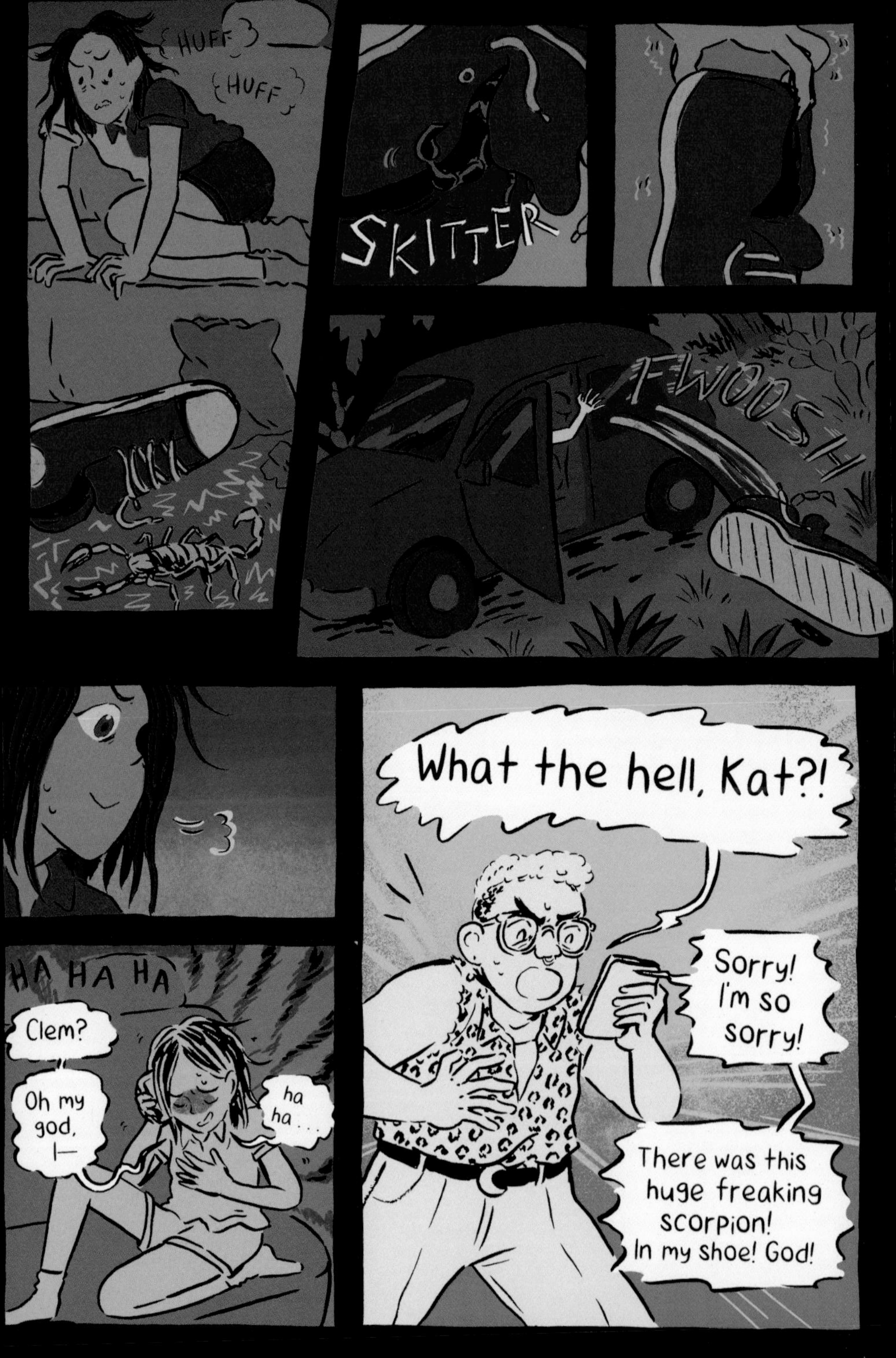
HUFF
HUFF
SKITTER
FWOOSH
What the hell, Kat?!
HA HA HA HA
Clem?
Oh my god, I—
ha ha . . .
Sorry! I'm so sorry!
There was this huge freaking scorpion! In my shoe! God!

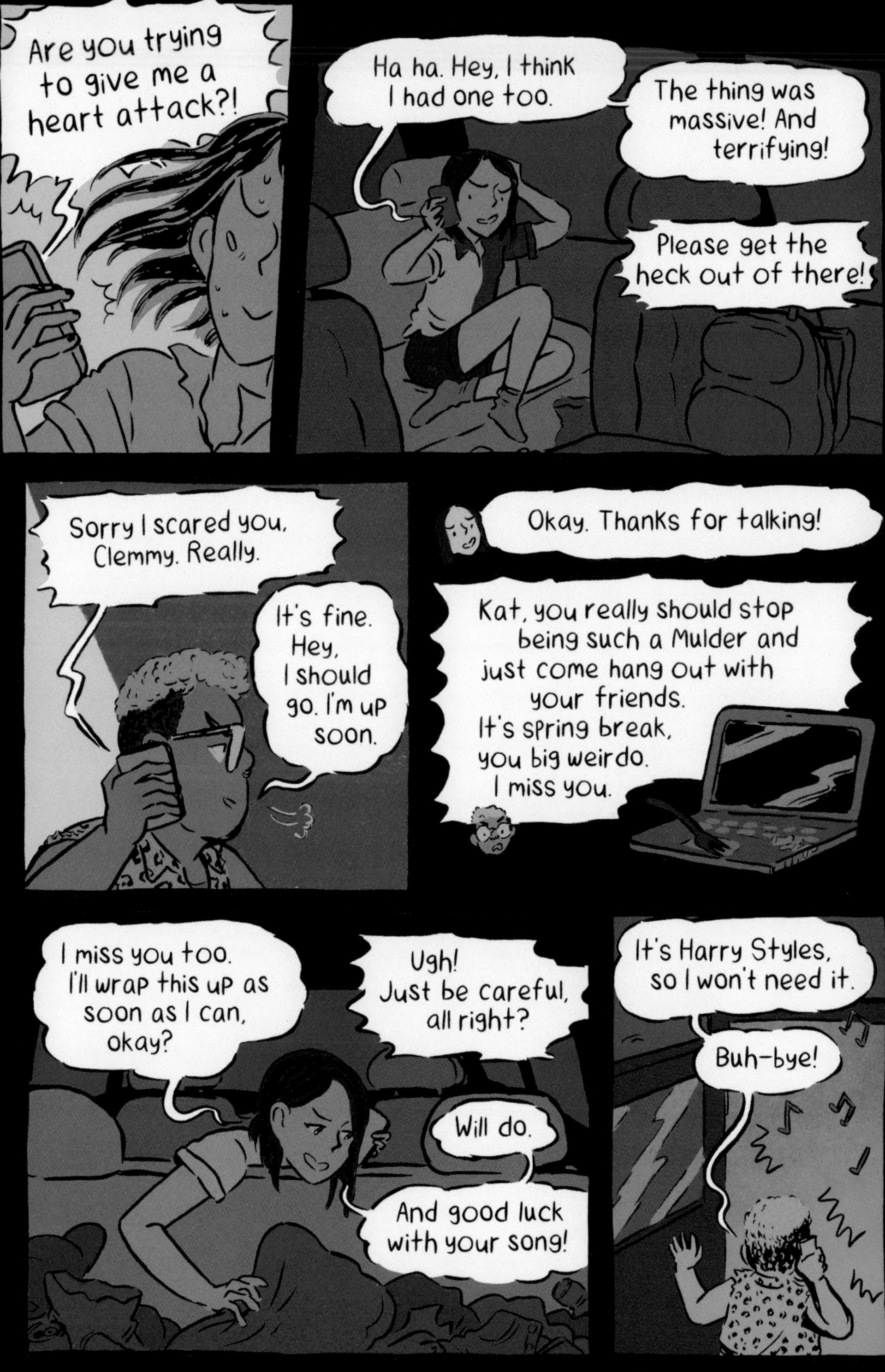
Are you trying to give me a heart attack?!
Ha ha. Hey, I think I had one too.
The thing was massive! And terrifying!
Please get the heck out of there!
Sorry I scared you, Clemmy. Really.
It's fine. Hey, I should go. I'm up soon.
Okay. Thanks for talking!
Kat, you really should stop being such a Mulder and just come hang out with your friends. It's spring break, you big weirdo. I miss you.
I miss you too. I'll wrap this up as soon as I can, okay?
Ugh! Just be careful, all right?
Will do.
And good luck with your song!
It's Harry Styles, so I won't need it.
Buh-bye!

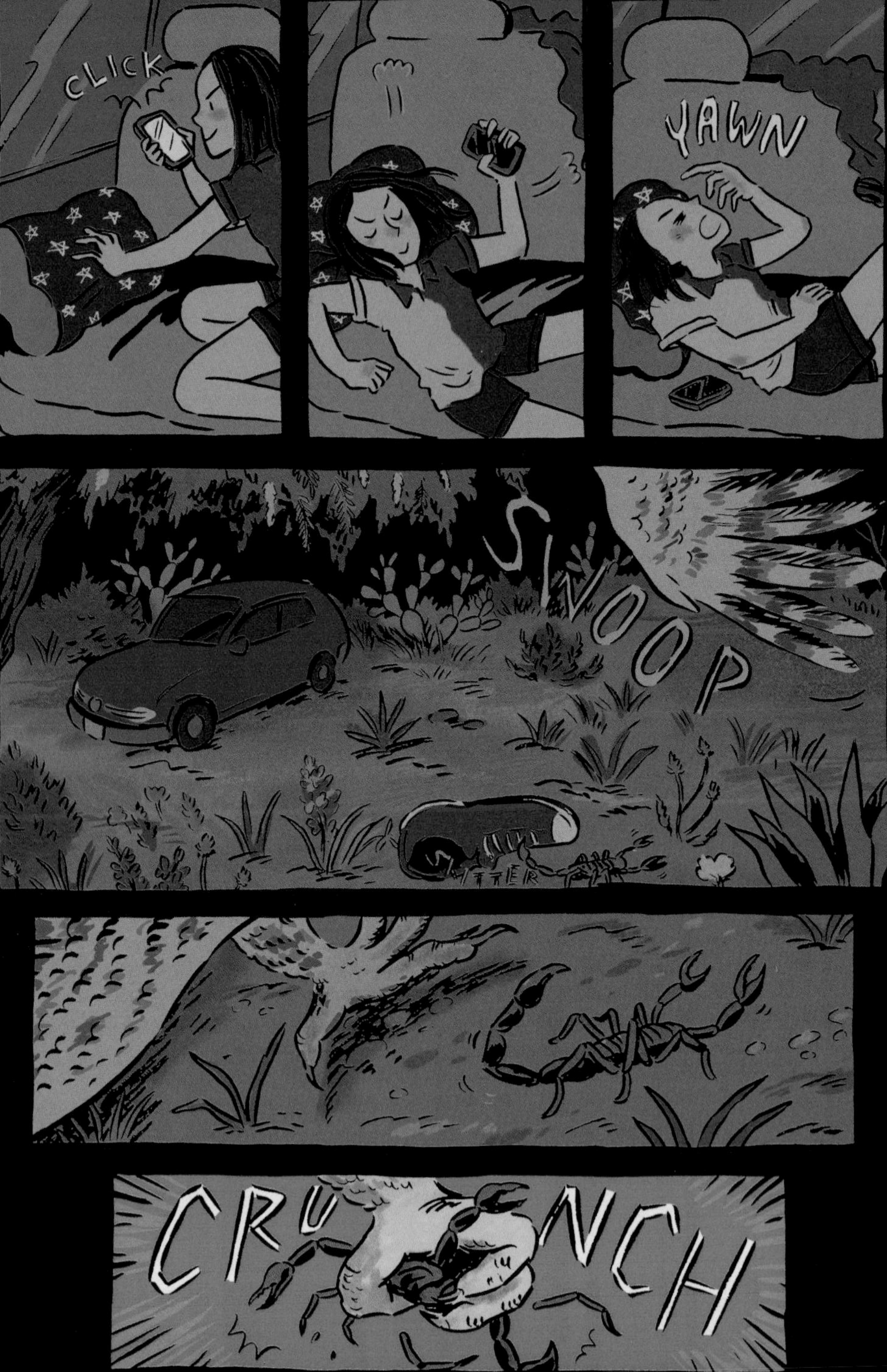
CLICK
YAWN
SWOOP
CRUNCH

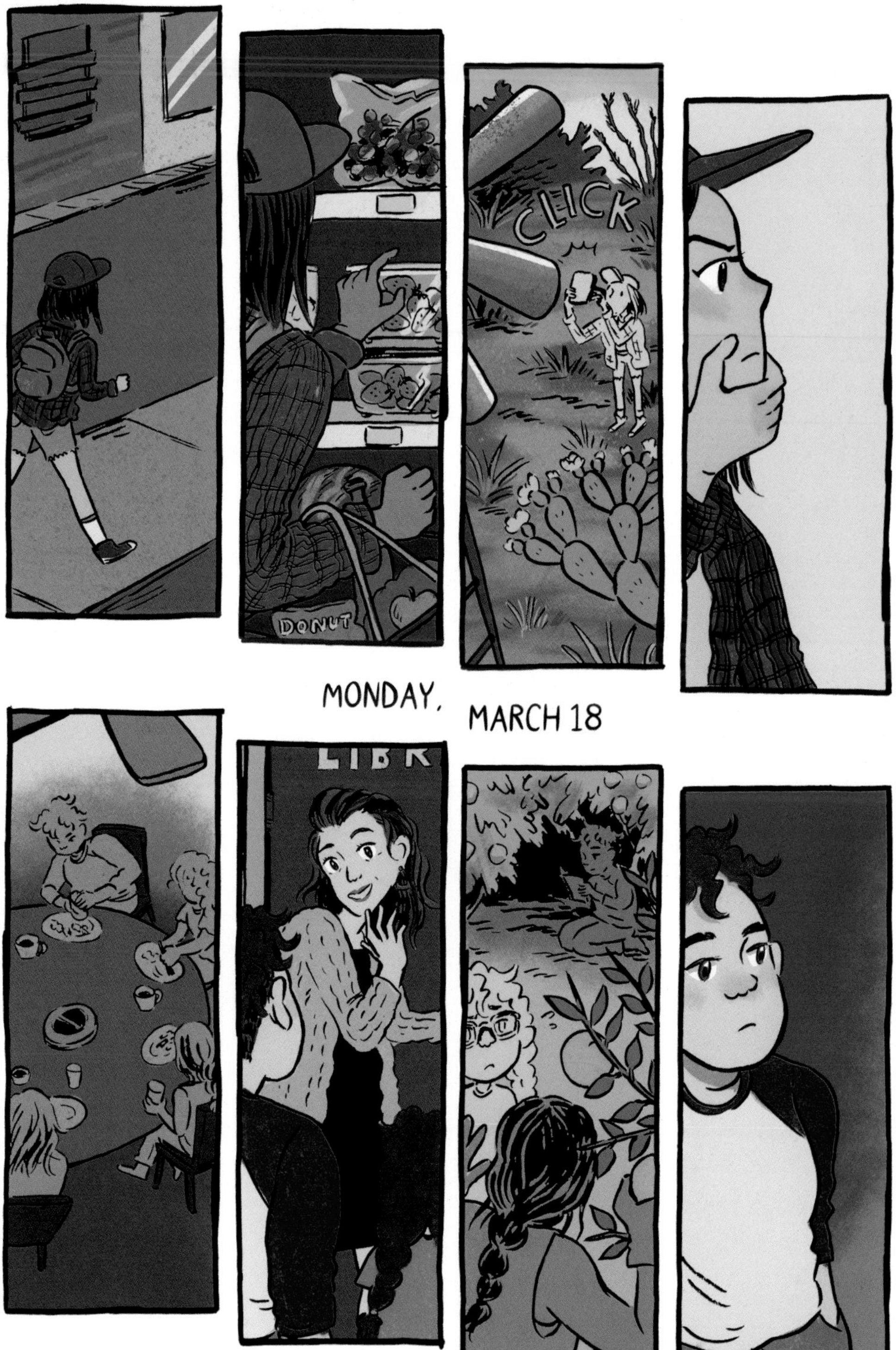
DONUT
CLICK
MONDAY, MARCH 18
LIBR

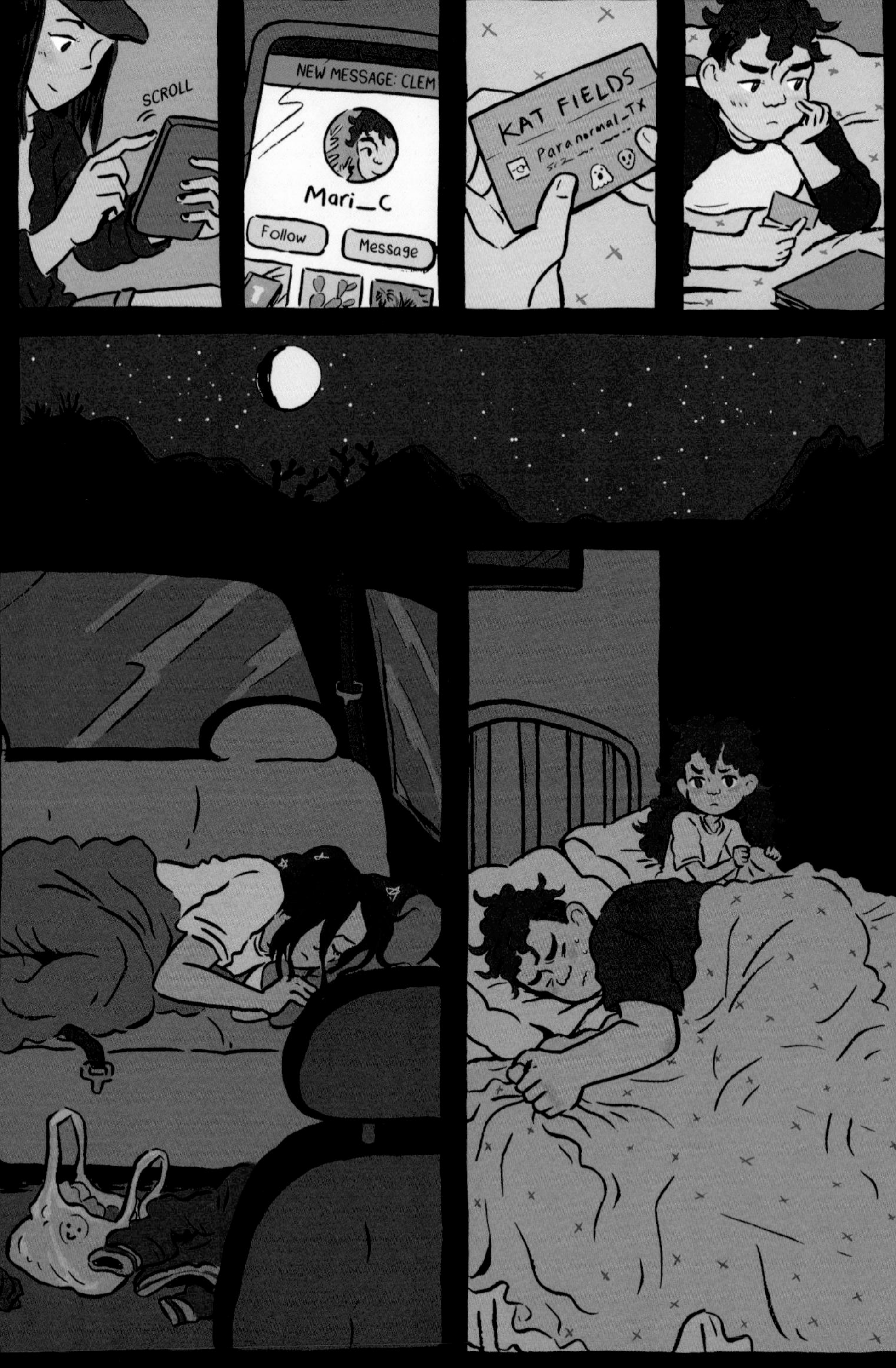
SCROLL
NEW MESSAGE: CLEM
Mari_C
Follow
Message
KAT FIELDS
Paranormal_TX

PART FOUR

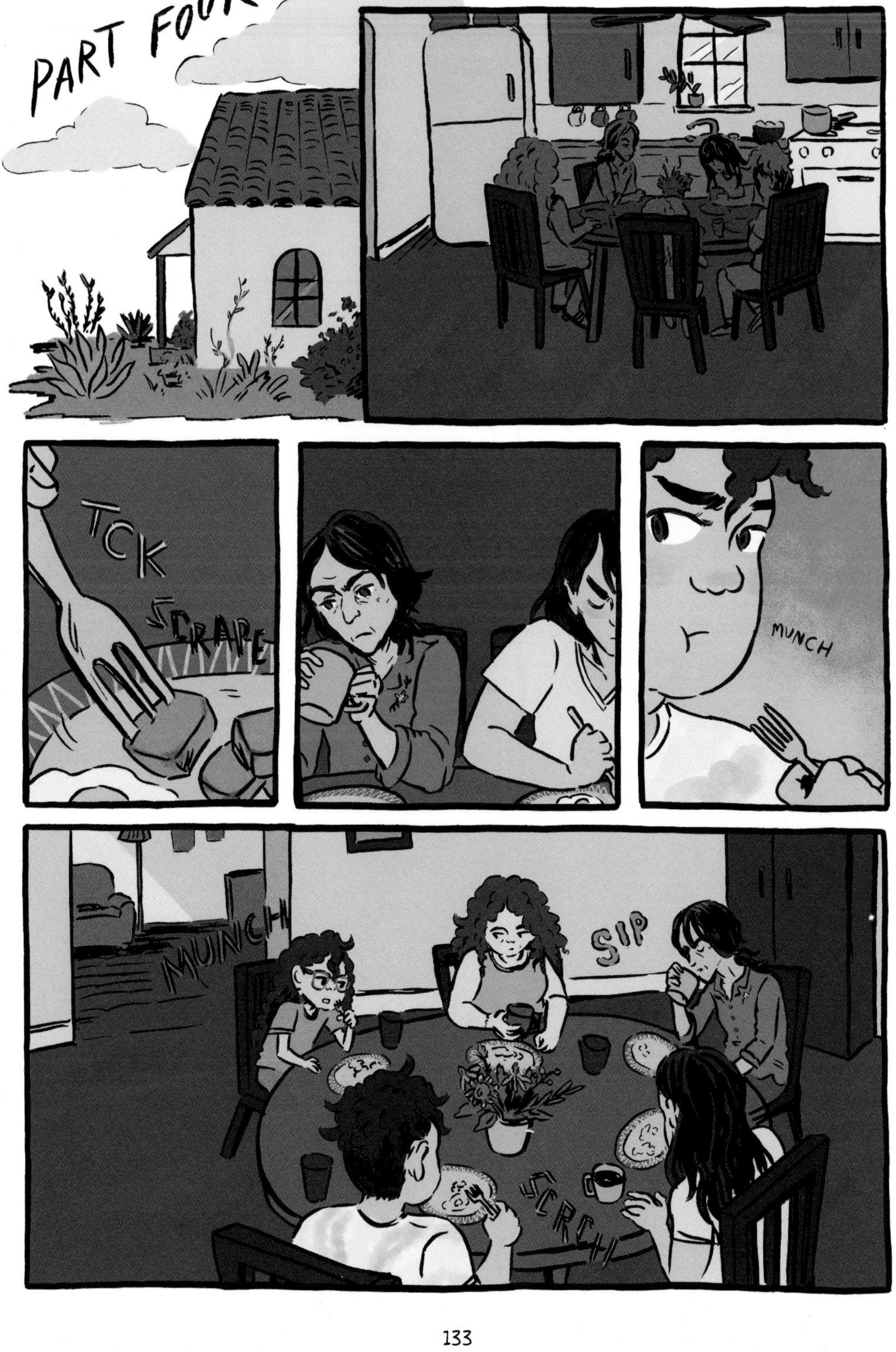
TCK
SCRAPE
MUNCH
MUNCH
SIP
SCRCH

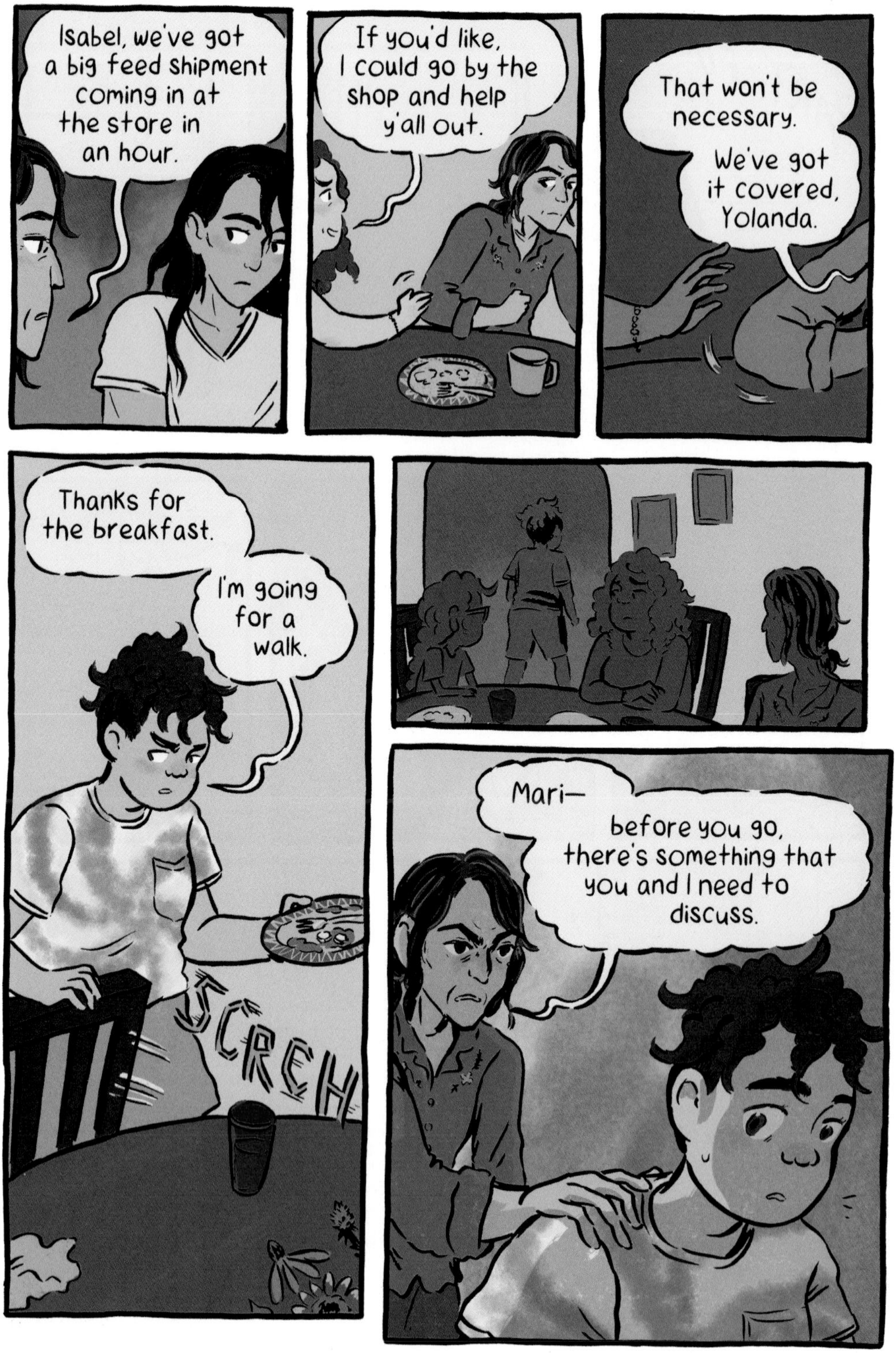

Isabel, we've got a big feed shipment coming in at the store in an hour.
If you'd like, I could go by the shop and help y'all out.
That won't be necessary.
We've got it covered, Yolanda.
Thanks for the breakfast.
I'm going for a walk.
SCRCH
Mari—
before you go, there's something that you and I need to discuss.

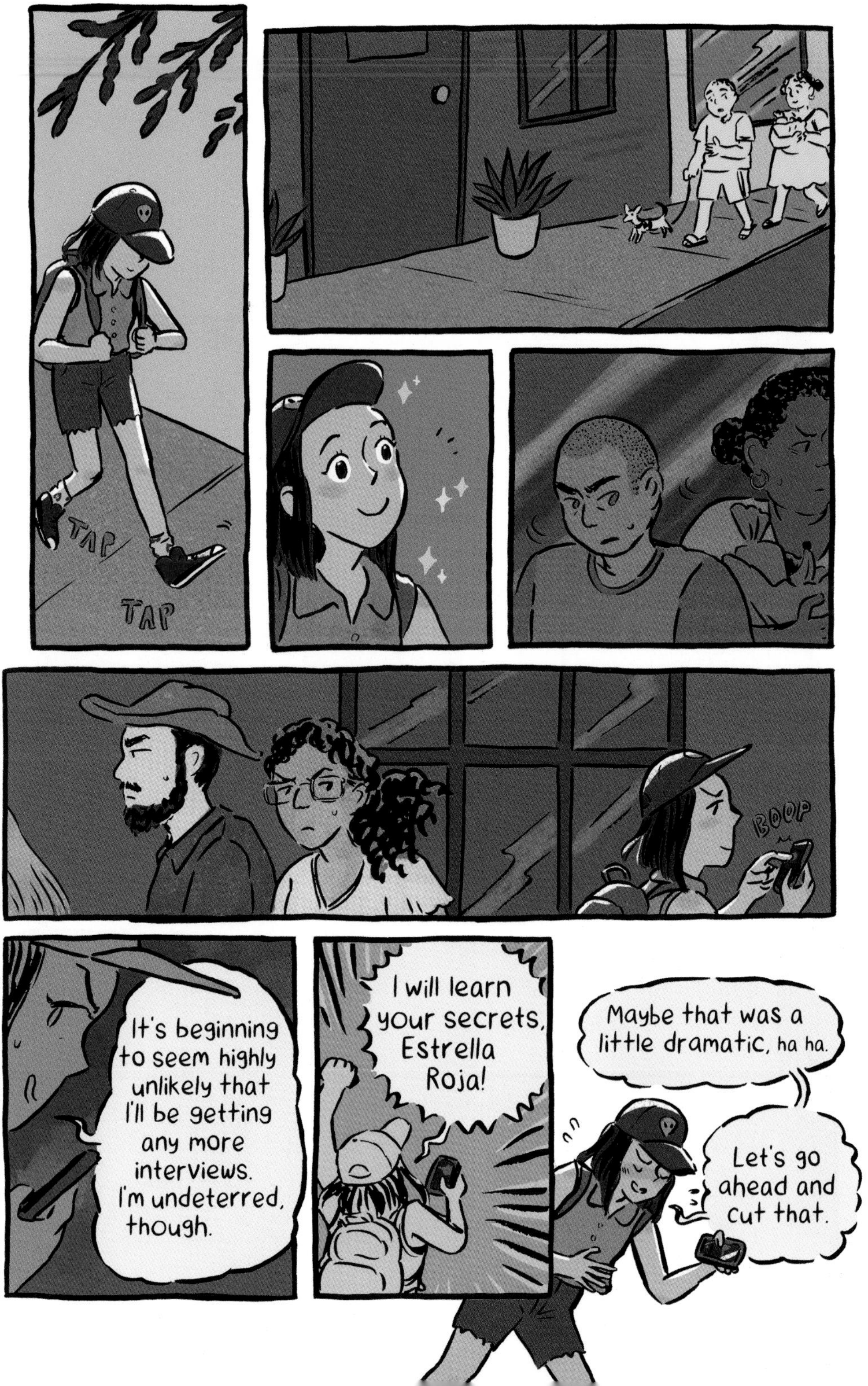
TAP
TAP
BOOP
It's beginning to seem highly unlikely that I'll be getting any more interviews. I'm undeterred, though.
I will learn your secrets, Estrella Roja!
Maybe that was a little dramatic, ha ha.
Let's go ahead and cut that.

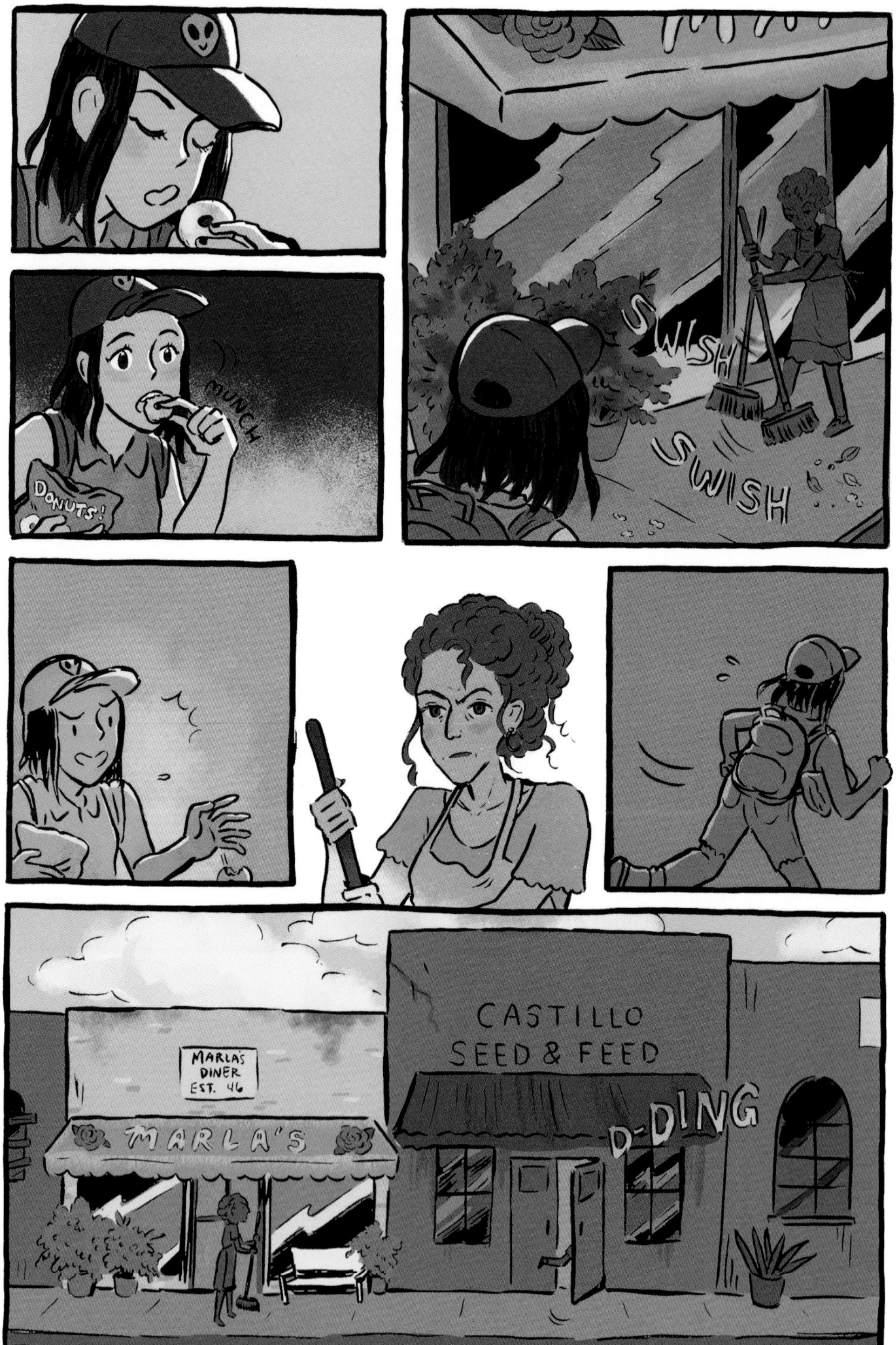
MUNCH
DONUTS!
SWISH
SWISH
CASTILLO
SEED & FEED
MARLA'S
DINER
EST. 46
MARLA'S
D-DING

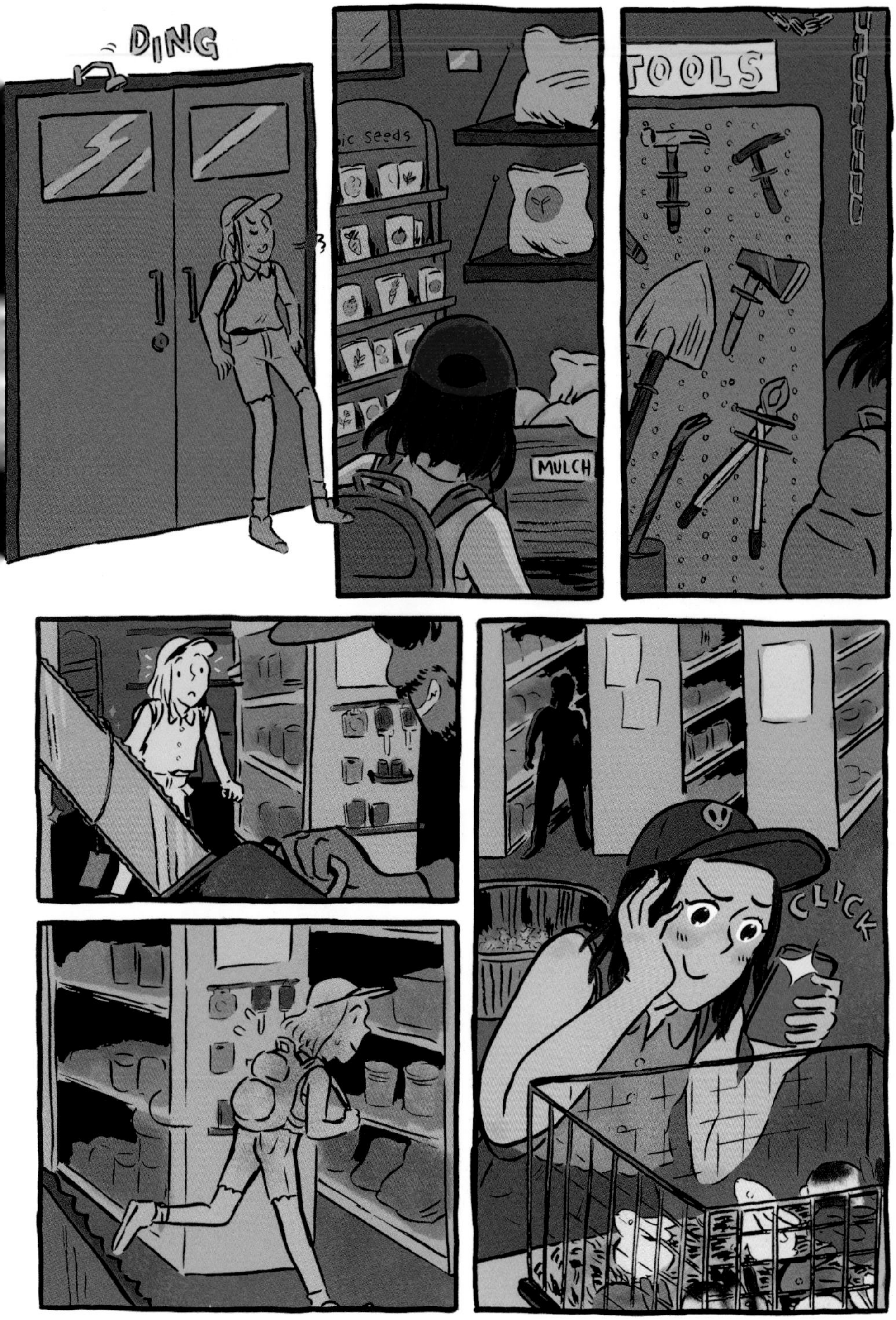
DING
ic seeds
MULCH
TOOLS
CLICK

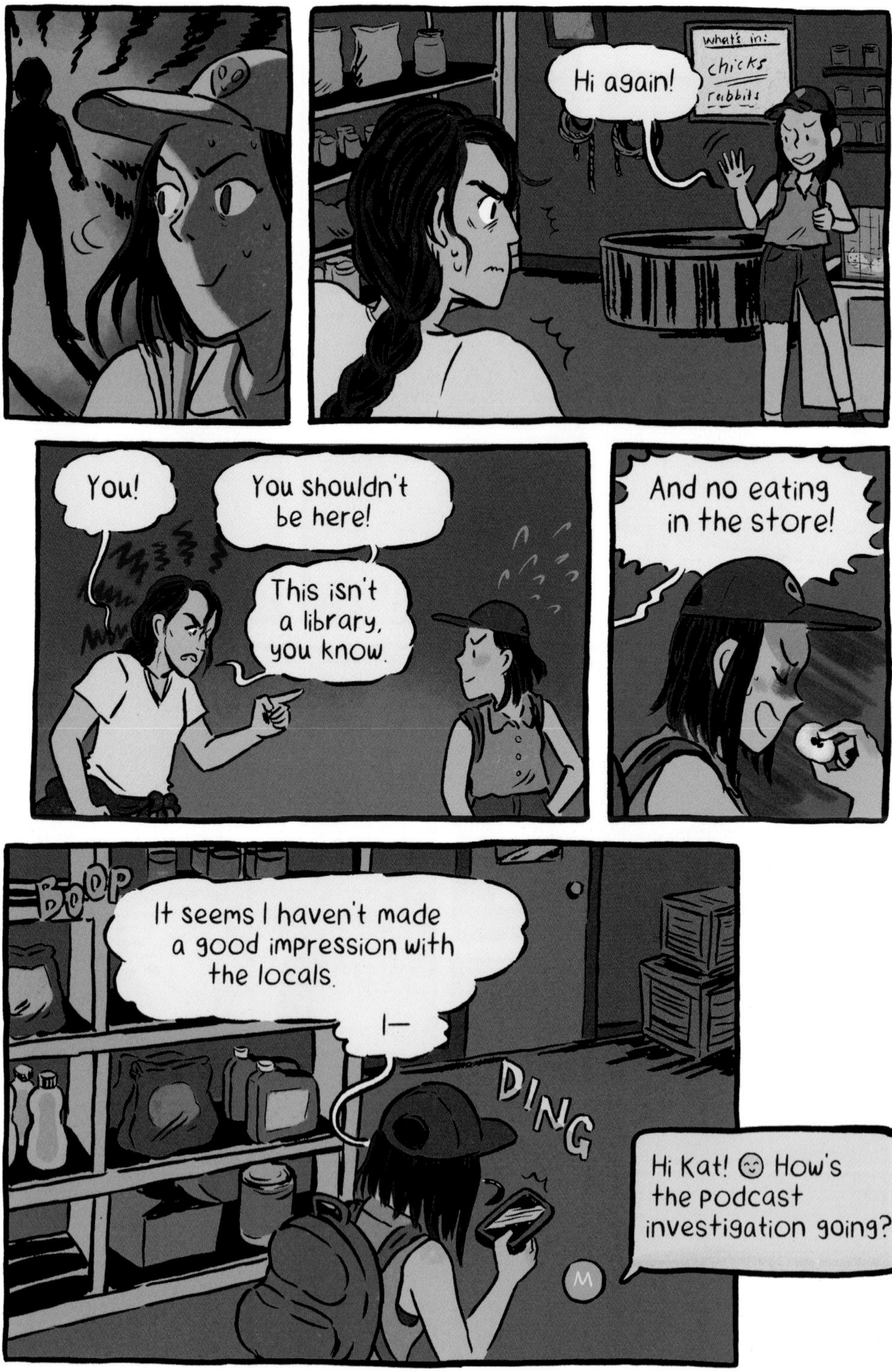
Hi again!
what's in:
chicks
rabbits
You!
You shouldn't be here!
This isn't a library, you know.
And no eating in the store!
BOOP
It seems I haven't made a good impression with the locals.
I—
DING
Hi Kat! ☺ How's the podcast investigation going?
M

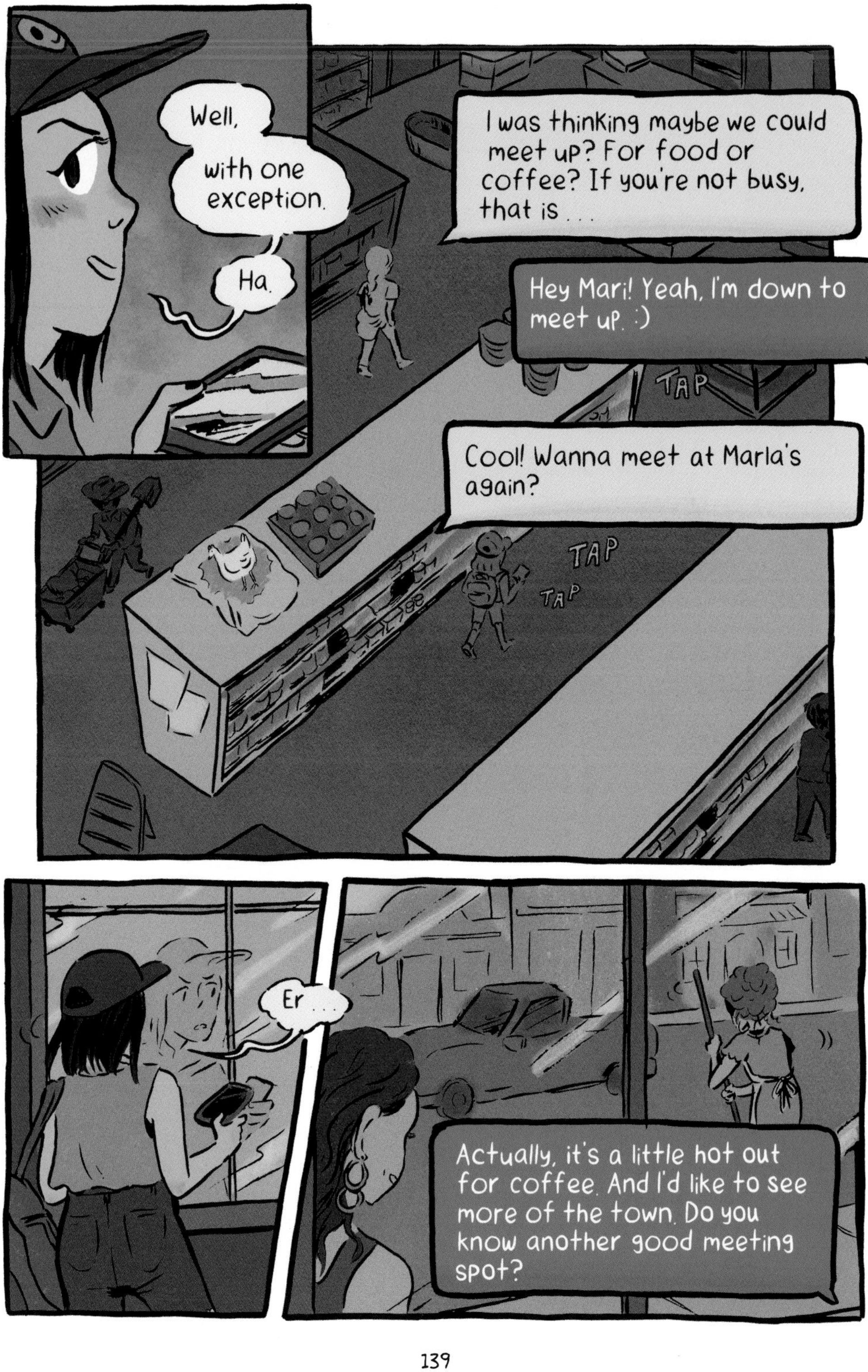
Well,
with one exception.
Ha.
I was thinking maybe we could meet up? For food or coffee? If you're not busy, that is . . .
Hey Mari! Yeah, I'm down to meet up. :)
TAP
Cool! Wanna meet at Marla's again?
TAP
TAP
Er . . .
Actually, it's a little hot out for coffee. And I'd like to see more of the town. Do you know another good meeting spot?

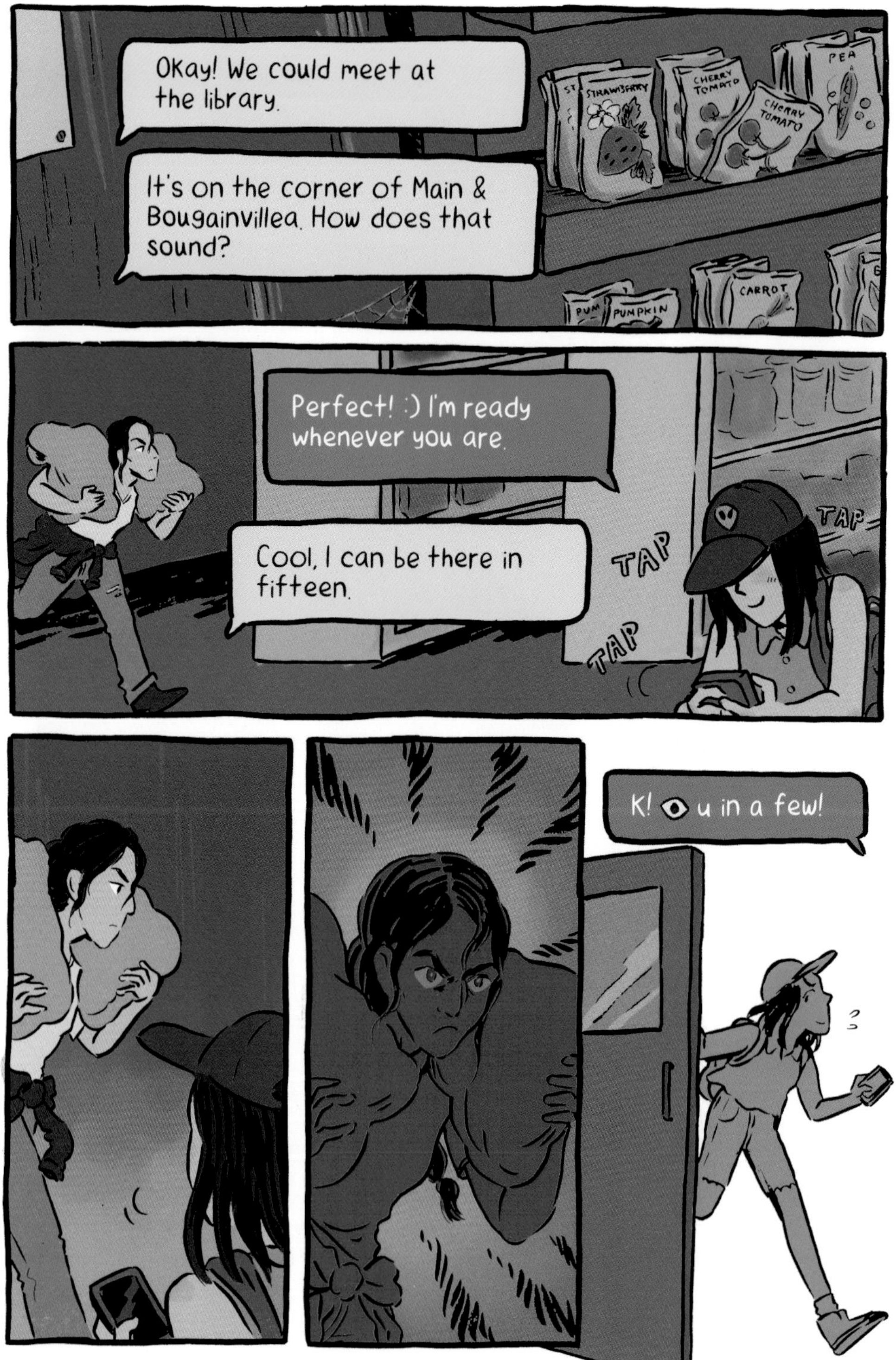
Okay! We could meet at the library.
It's on the corner of Main & Bougainvillea. How does that sound?
STRAWBERRY
CHERRY TOMATO
CHERRY TOMATO
PEA
PUMPKIN
CARROT
Perfect! :) I'm ready whenever you are.
Cool, I can be there in fifteen.
TAP
TAP
TAP
K! u in a few!

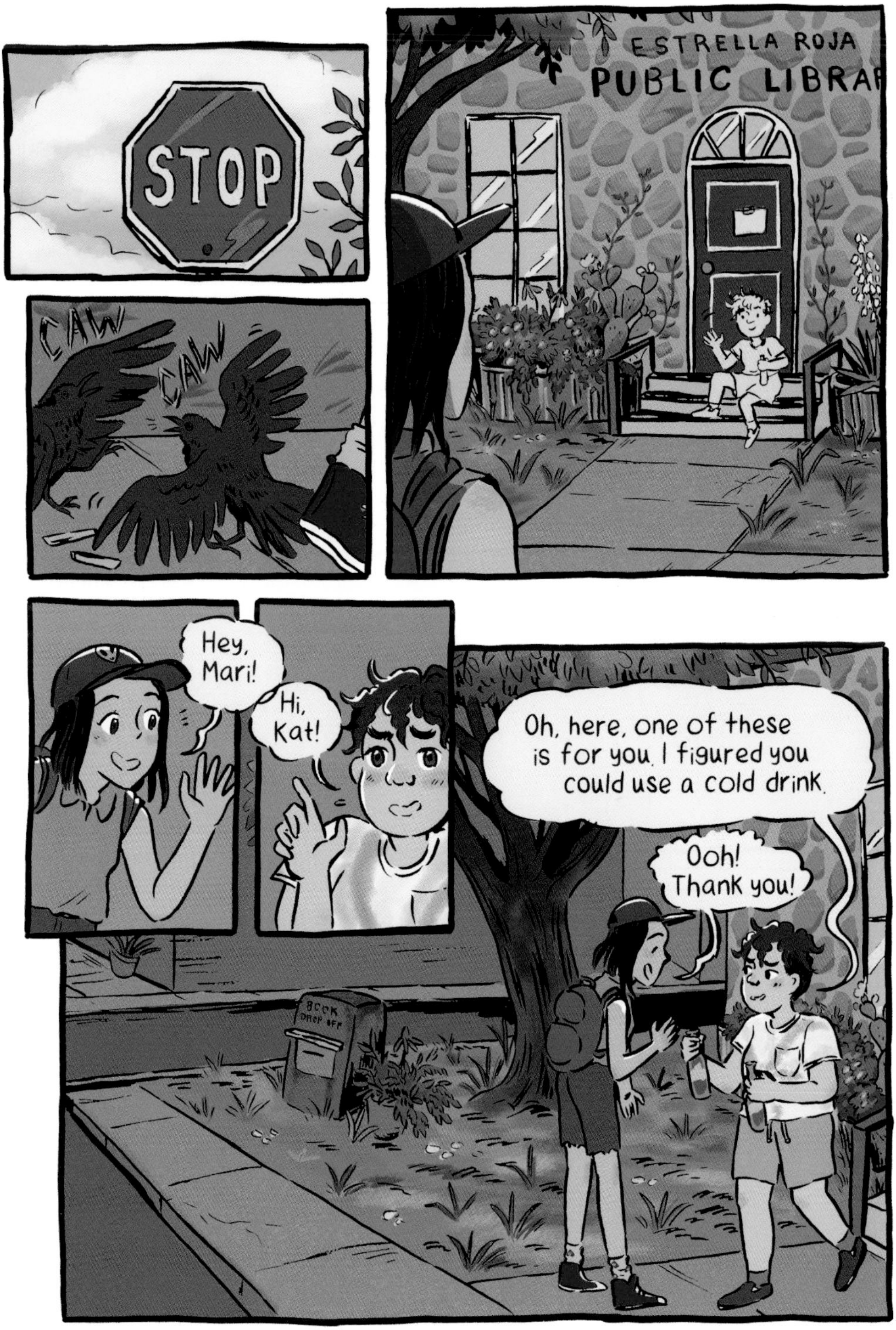
STOP
CAW
CAW
ESTRELLA ROJA
PUBLIC LIBRAR
Hey, Mari!
Hi, Kat!
Oh, here, one of these is for you. I figured you could use a cold drink.
Ooh! Thank you!
BOOK DROP OFF

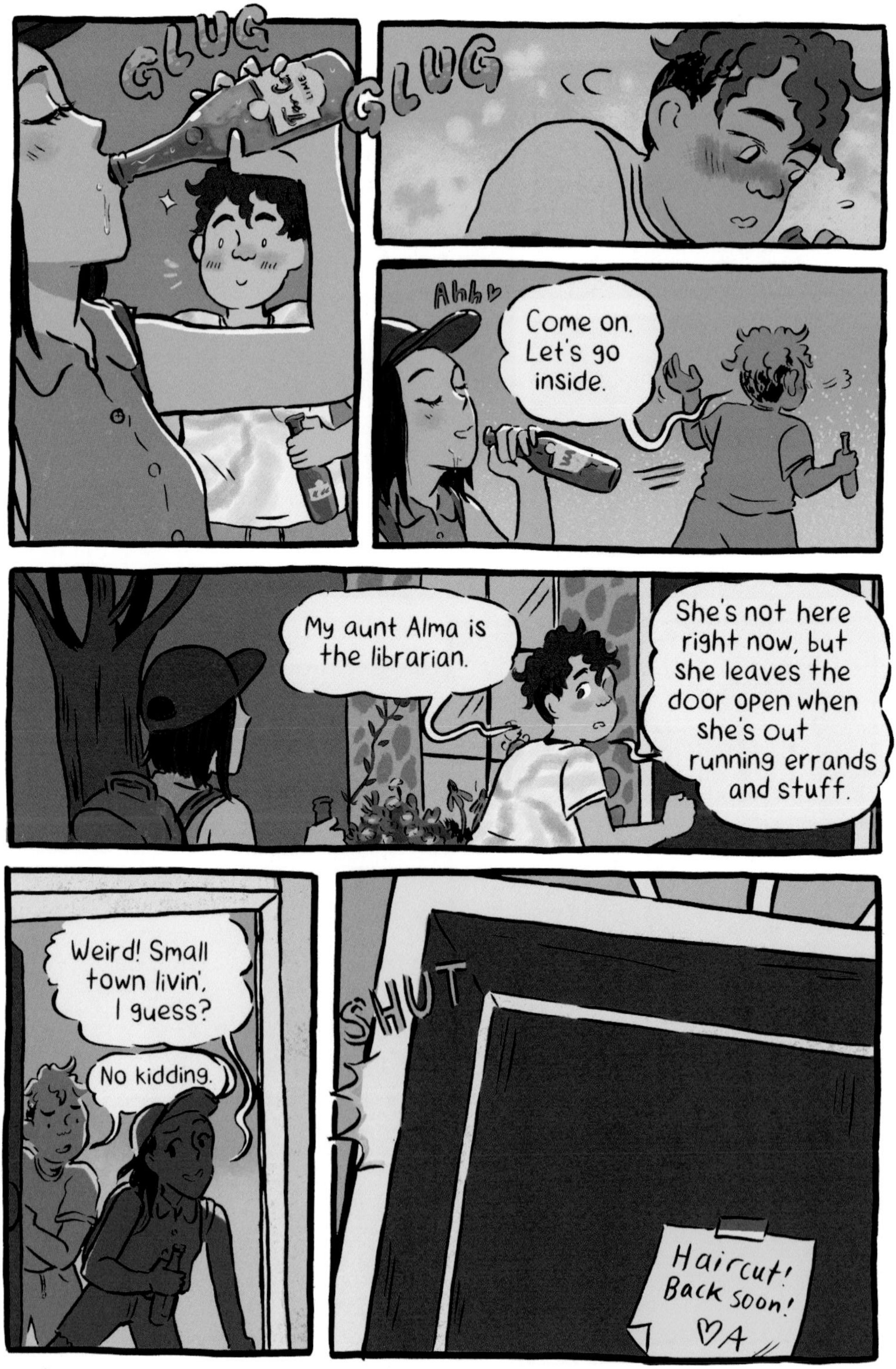
GLUG
GLUG
Ahh♥
Come on. Let's go inside.
My aunt Alma is the librarian.
She's not here right now, but she leaves the door open when she's out running errands and stuff.
Weird! Small town livin', I guess?
No kidding.
SHUT
Haircut! Back soon! ♡A

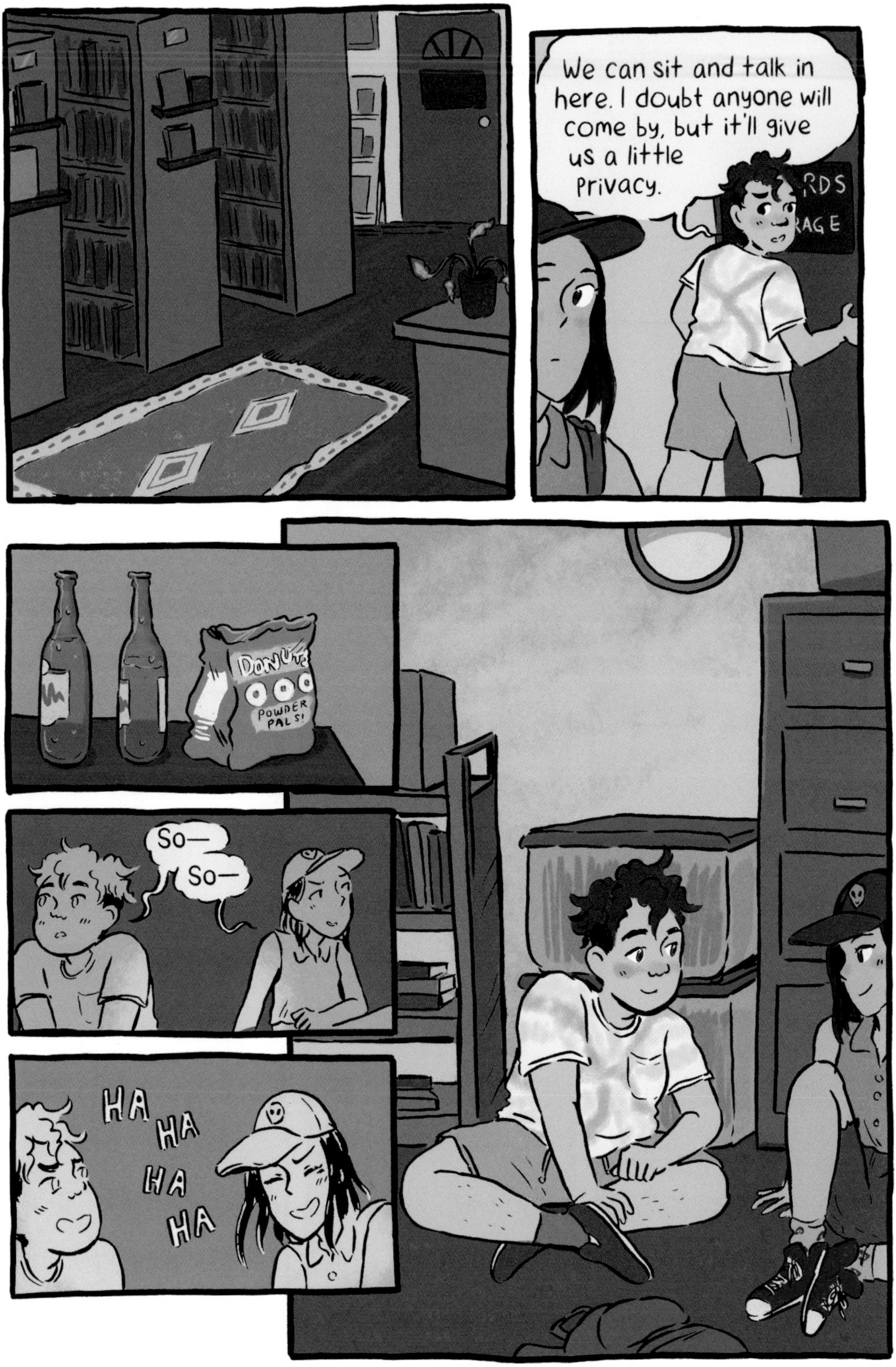
We can sit and talk in here. I doubt anyone will come by, but it'll give us a little privacy.
RDS
RAGE
DONUTS
POWDER PALS!
So—
So—
HA
HA
HA
HA

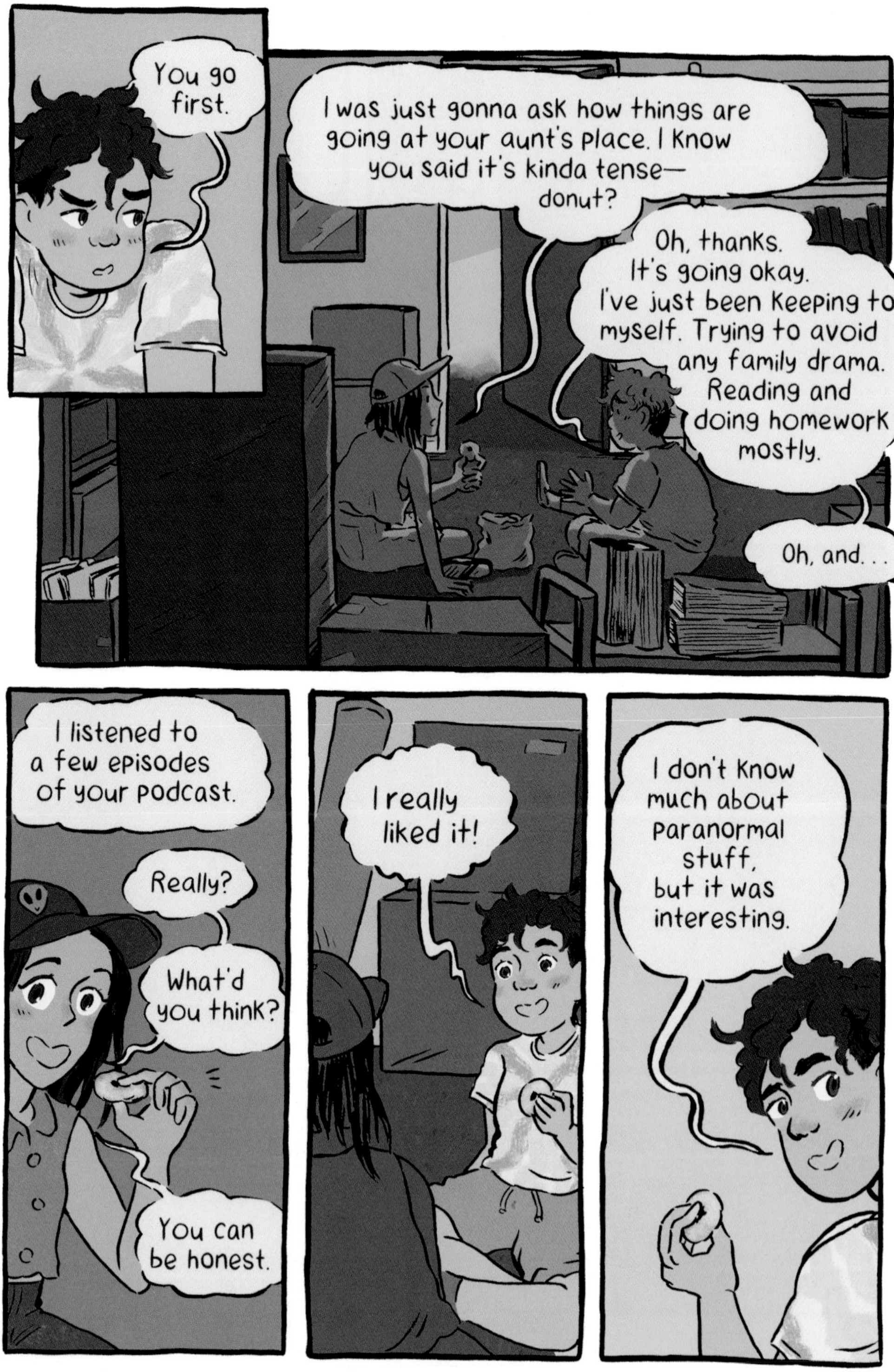
You go first.
I was just gonna ask how things are going at your aunt's place. I know you said it's kinda tense—donut?
Oh, thanks. It's going okay. I've just been keeping to myself. Trying to avoid any family drama. Reading and doing homework mostly.
Oh, and. . .
I listened to a few episodes of your podcast.
Really?
What'd you think?
You can be honest.
I really liked it!
I don't know much about paranormal stuff, but it was interesting.

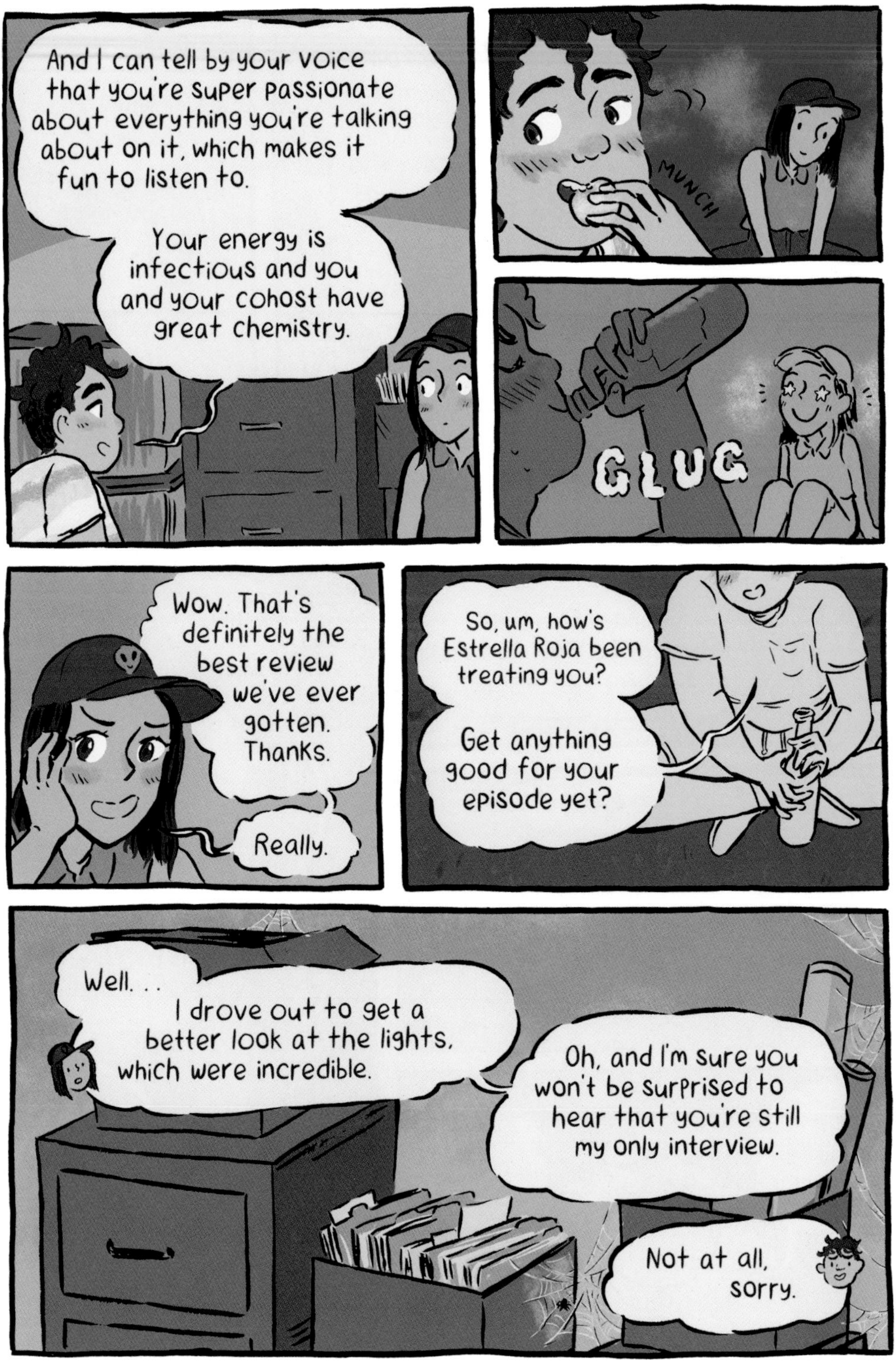
And I can tell by your voice that you're super passionate about everything you're talking about on it, which makes it fun to listen to.
Your energy is infectious and you and your cohost have great chemistry.
MUNCH
GLUG
Wow. That's definitely the best review we've ever gotten. Thanks.
Really.
So, um, how's Estrella Roja been treating you?
Get anything good for your episode yet?
Well. . .
I drove out to get a better look at the lights, which were incredible.
Oh, and I'm sure you won't be surprised to hear that you're still my only interview.
Not at all, sorry.

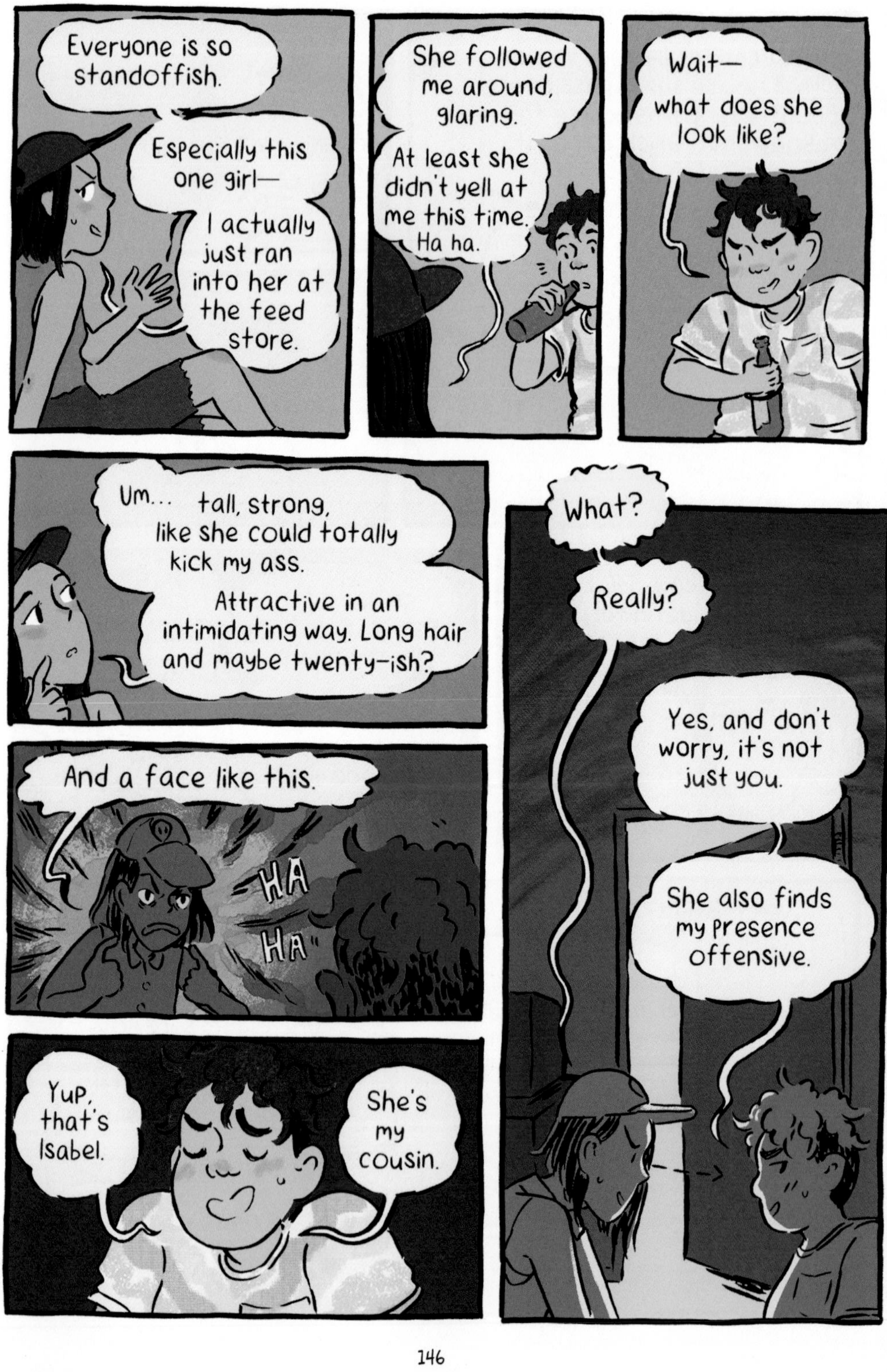
Everyone is so standoffish.
Especially this one girl—
I actually just ran into her at the feed store.
She followed me around, glaring.
At least she didn't yell at me this time. Ha ha.
Wait—
what does she look like?
Um... tall, strong, like she could totally kick my ass.
Attractive in an intimidating way. Long hair and maybe twenty-ish?
And a face like this.
HA
HA
Yup, that's Isabel.
She's my cousin.
What?
Really?
Yes, and don't worry, it's not just you.
She also finds my presence offensive.

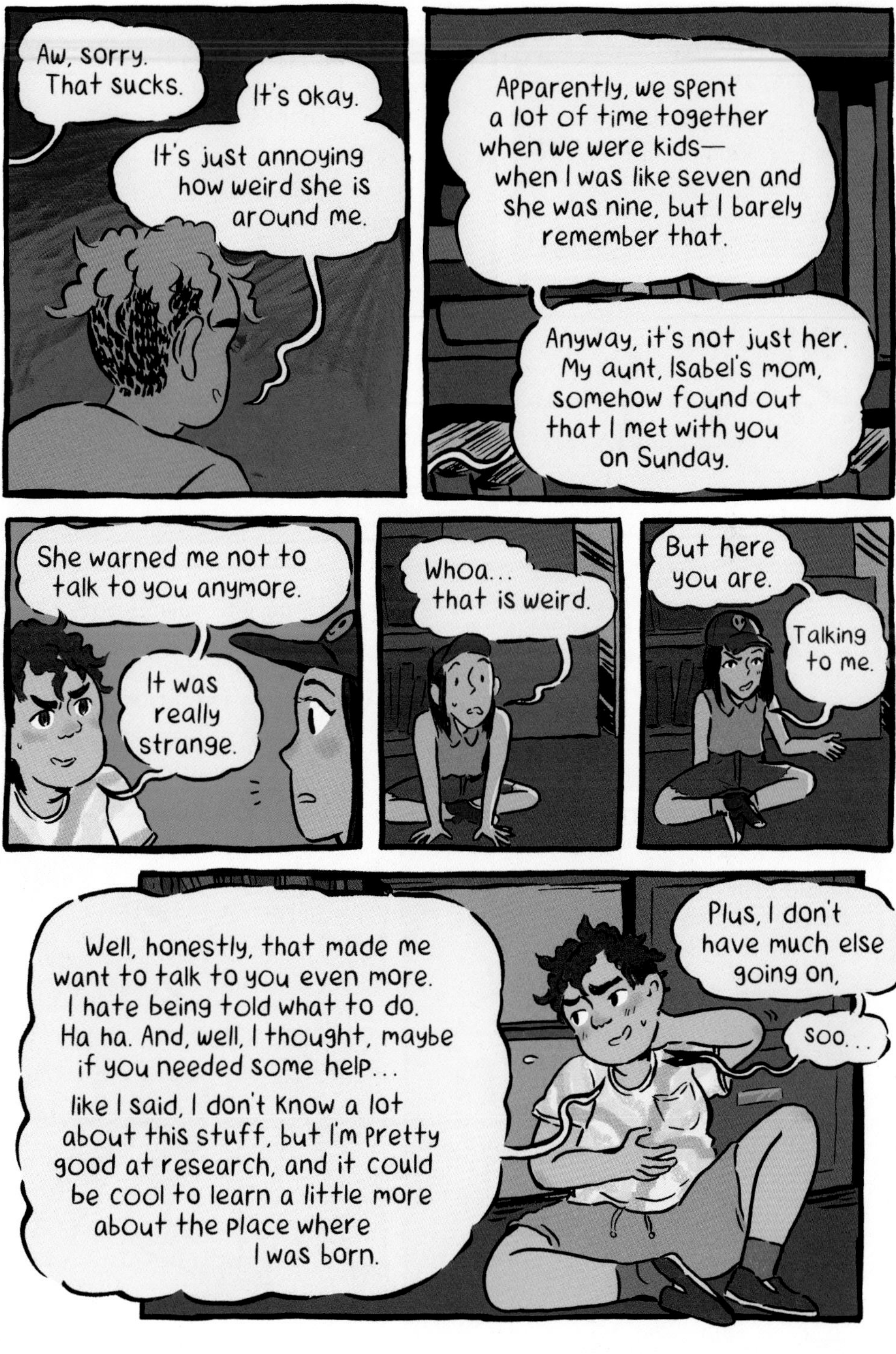
Aw, sorry. That sucks.
It's okay.
It's just annoying how weird she is around me.
Apparently, we spent a lot of time together when we were kids— when I was like seven and she was nine, but I barely remember that.
Anyway, it's not just her. My aunt, Isabel's mom, somehow found out that I met with you on Sunday.
She warned me not to talk to you anymore.
It was really strange.
Whoa... that is weird.
But here you are.
Talking to me.
Well, honestly, that made me want to talk to you even more. I hate being told what to do. Ha ha. And, well, I thought, maybe if you needed some help... like I said, I don't know a lot about this stuff, but I'm pretty good at research, and it could be cool to learn a little more about the place where I was born.
Plus, I don't have much else going on,
soo...

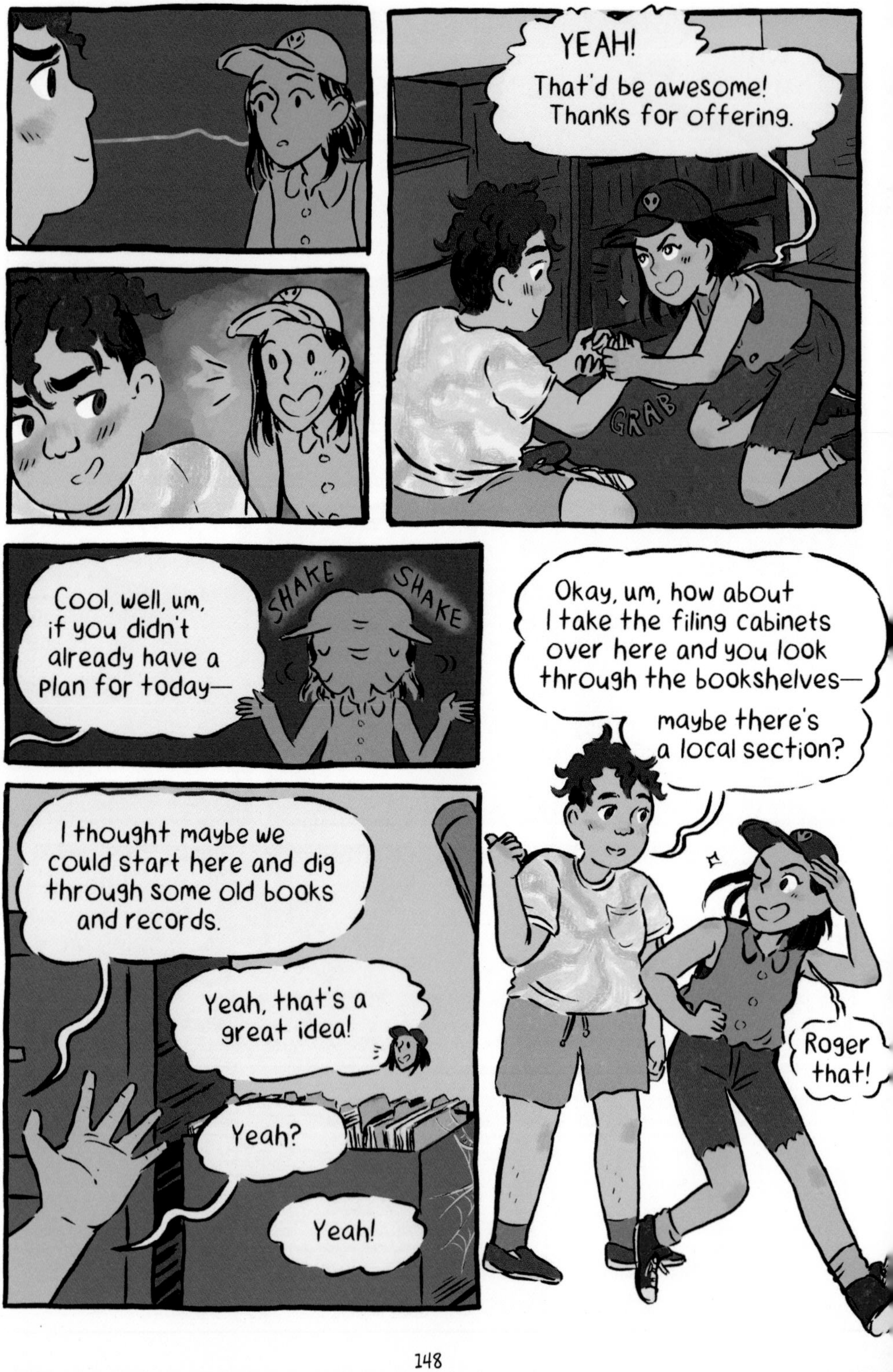
YEAH!
That'd be awesome! Thanks for offering.
GRAB
Cool, well, um, if you didn't already have a plan for today—
SHAKE SHAKE
Okay, um, how about I take the filing cabinets over here and you look through the bookshelves—
maybe there's a local section?
Roger that!
I thought maybe we could start here and dig through some old books and records.
Yeah, that's a great idea!
Yeah?
Yeah!

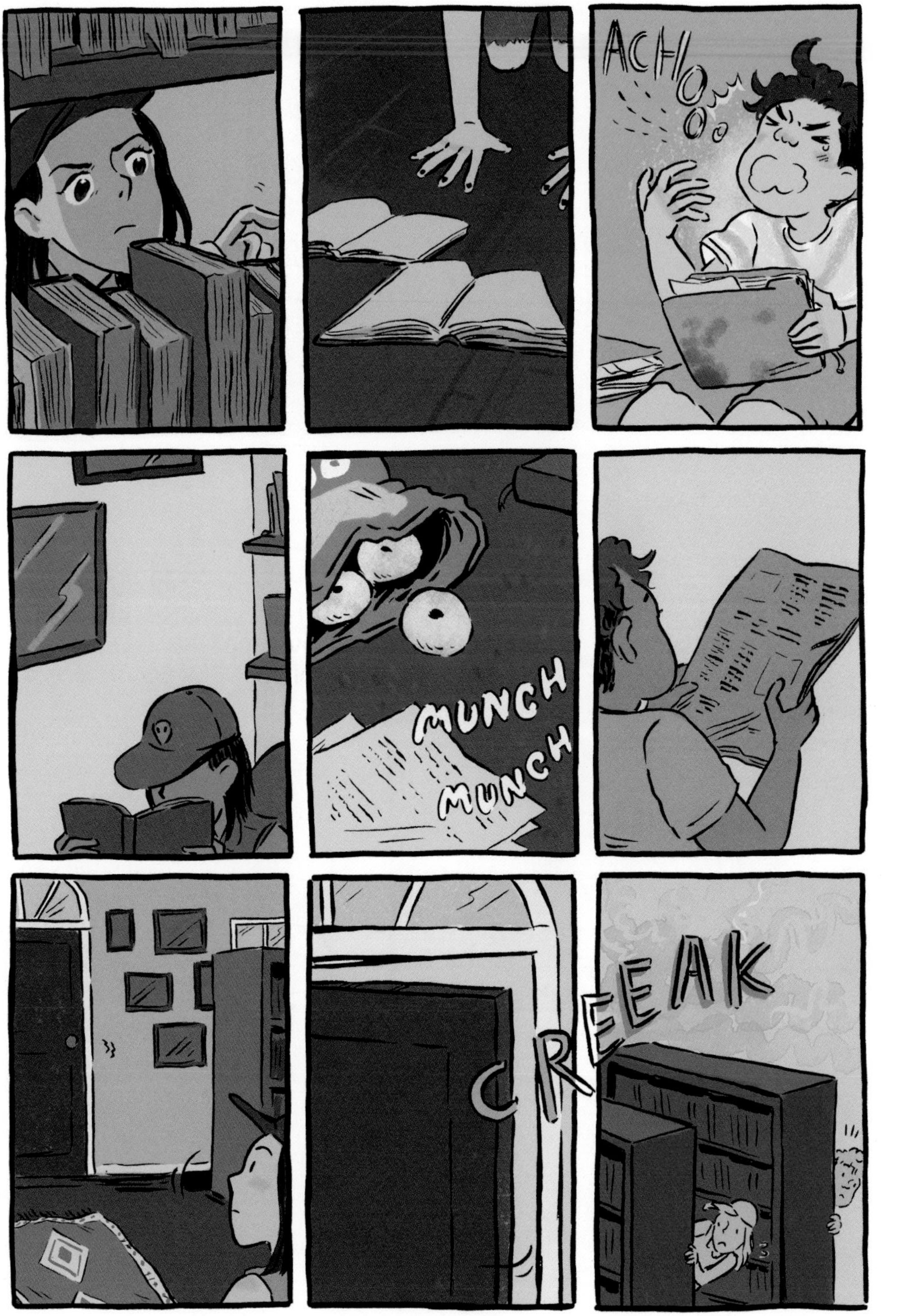
ACHOOO
MUNCH
MUNCH
CREEAK

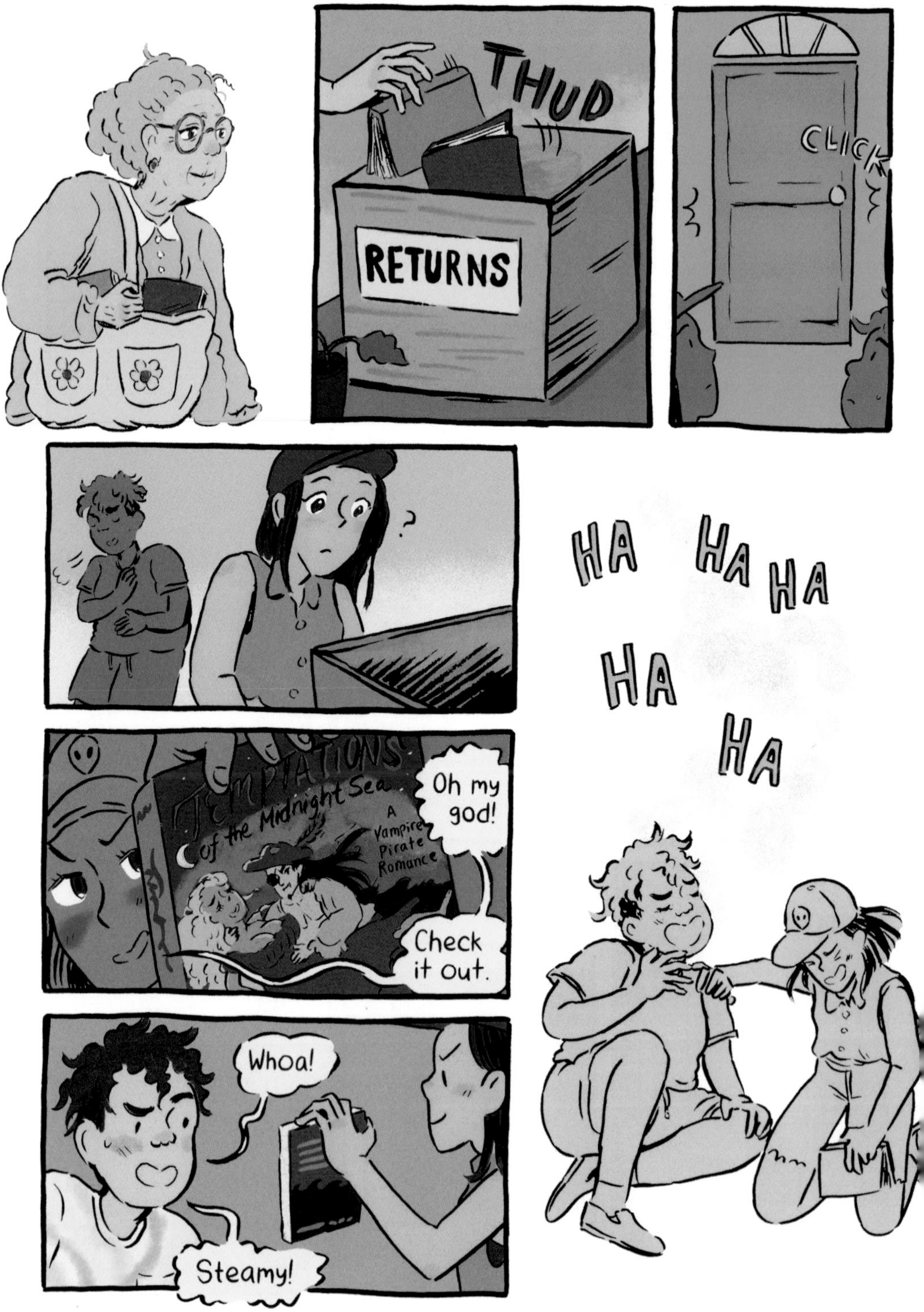
THUD
RETURNS
CLICK
?
HA HA HA HA
HA
HA
TEMPTATIONS of the Midnight Sea
A Vampire Pirate Romance
Oh my god!
Check it out.
Whoa!
Steamy!

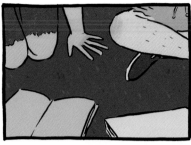

I gotta say—researching in an actual old library? Such a classic horror movie trope! I love it. All we need is some creepy microfiche to go through, ha ha. If you find any books that look like they're written in blood, please don't read them out loud.

Ha, I really wasn't planning on it.

As you can probably guess, I watch way too many horror movies.

That's not at all surprising.

So, what kind of movies are you into?

Oh, all types really. Classics, sci-fi, indie—I don't watch a lot of horror, but I do have a soft spot for a good vampire or witch movie, probably because they often read really queer?

I'm actually part of this queer movie club—

Ooh!

It's really just me and like three friends. It's low-key but really fun. Everyone brings a bunch of snacks and we meet in my friend Tala's basement. She's got a projector.

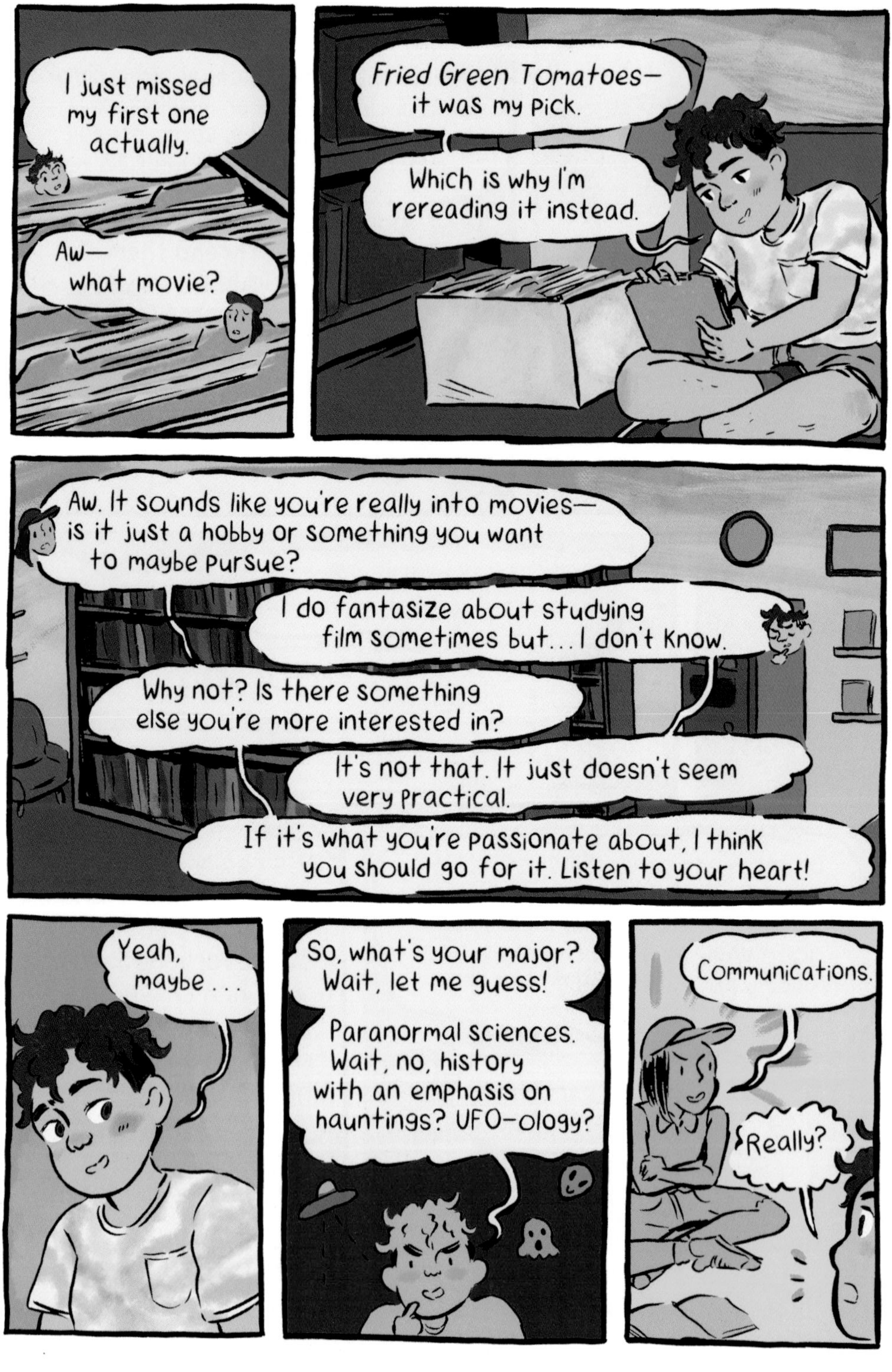
I just missed my first one actually.
Aw— what movie?
Fried Green Tomatoes— it was my pick.
Which is why I'm rereading it instead.
Aw. It sounds like you're really into movies— is it just a hobby or something you want to maybe pursue?
I do fantasize about studying film sometimes but... I don't know.
Why not? Is there something else you're more interested in?
It's not that. It just doesn't seem very practical.
If it's what you're passionate about, I think you should go for it. Listen to your heart!
Yeah, maybe...
So, what's your major? Wait, let me guess!
Paranormal sciences. Wait, no, history with an emphasis on hauntings? UFO-ology?
Communications.
Really?

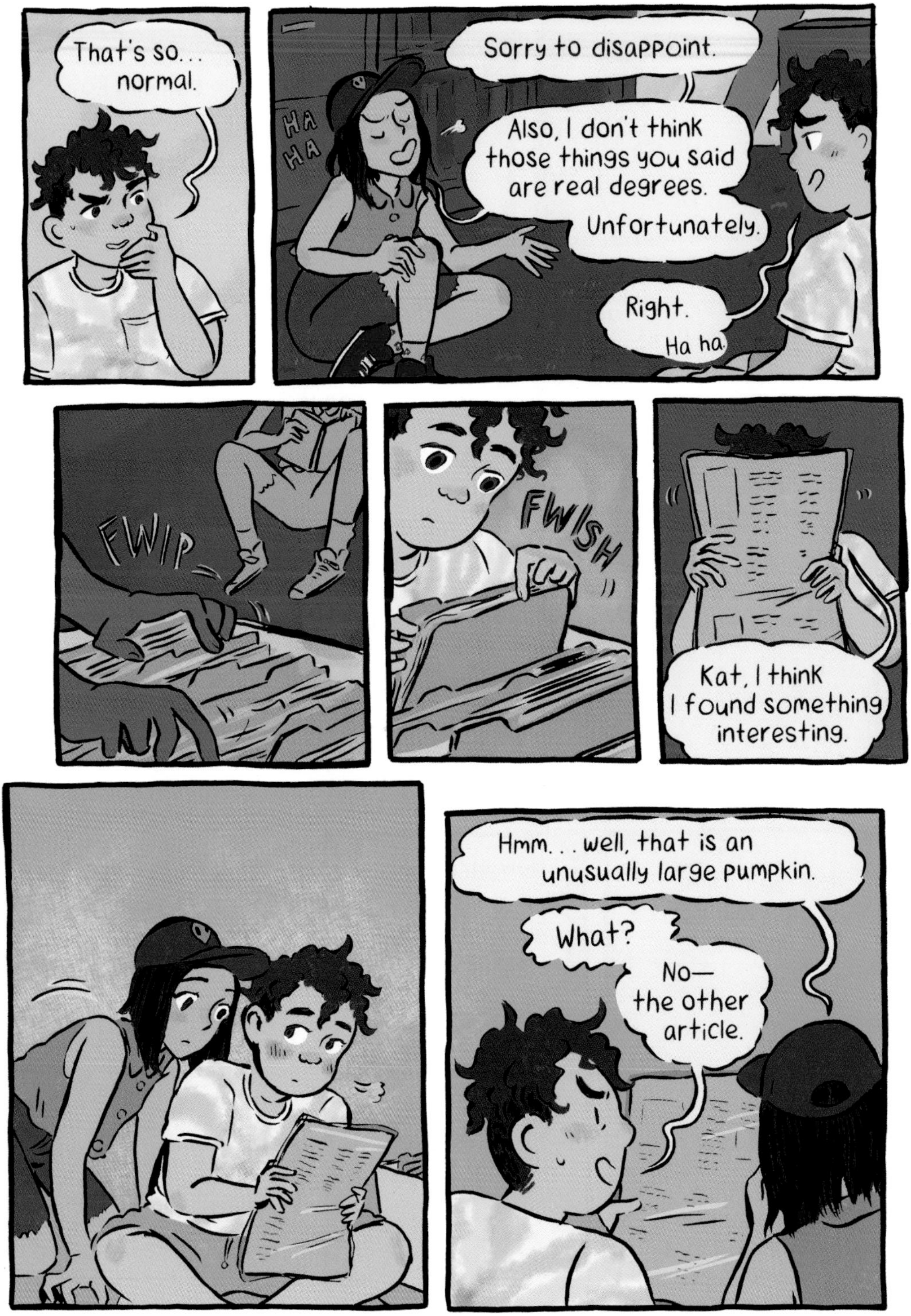
That's so... normal.
Sorry to disappoint.
HA HA
Also, I don't think those things you said are real degrees.
Unfortunately.
Right.
Ha ha.
FWIP
FWISH
Kat, I think I found something interesting.
Hmm... well, that is an unusually large pumpkin.
What?
No— the other article.

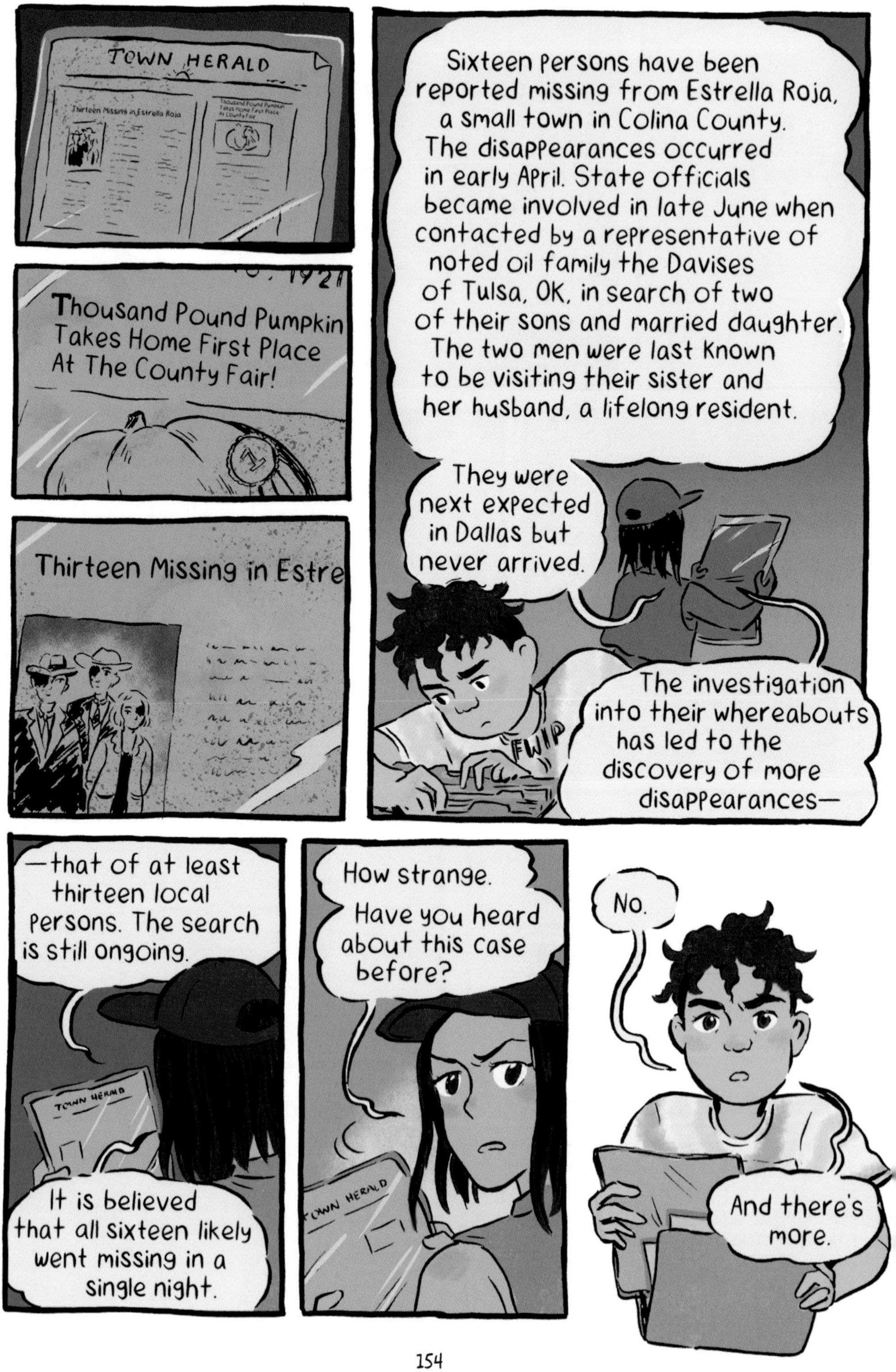
TOWN HERALD
Thirteen Missing in Estrella Roja
Thousand Pound Pumpkin Takes Home First Place At County Fair
Thousand Pound Pumpkin Takes Home First Place At The County Fair!
Thirteen Missing in Estre
Sixteen persons have been reported missing from Estrella Roja, a small town in Colina County. The disappearances occurred in early April. State officials became involved in late June when contacted by a representative of noted oil family the Davises of Tulsa, OK, in search of two of their sons and married daughter. The two men were last known to be visiting their sister and her husband, a lifelong resident.
They were next expected in Dallas but never arrived.
FWIP
The investigation into their whereabouts has led to the discovery of more disappearances—
—that of at least thirteen local persons. The search is still ongoing.
TOWN HERALD
It is believed that all sixteen likely went missing in a single night.
How strange.
Have you heard about this case before?
TOWN HERALD
No.
And there's more.

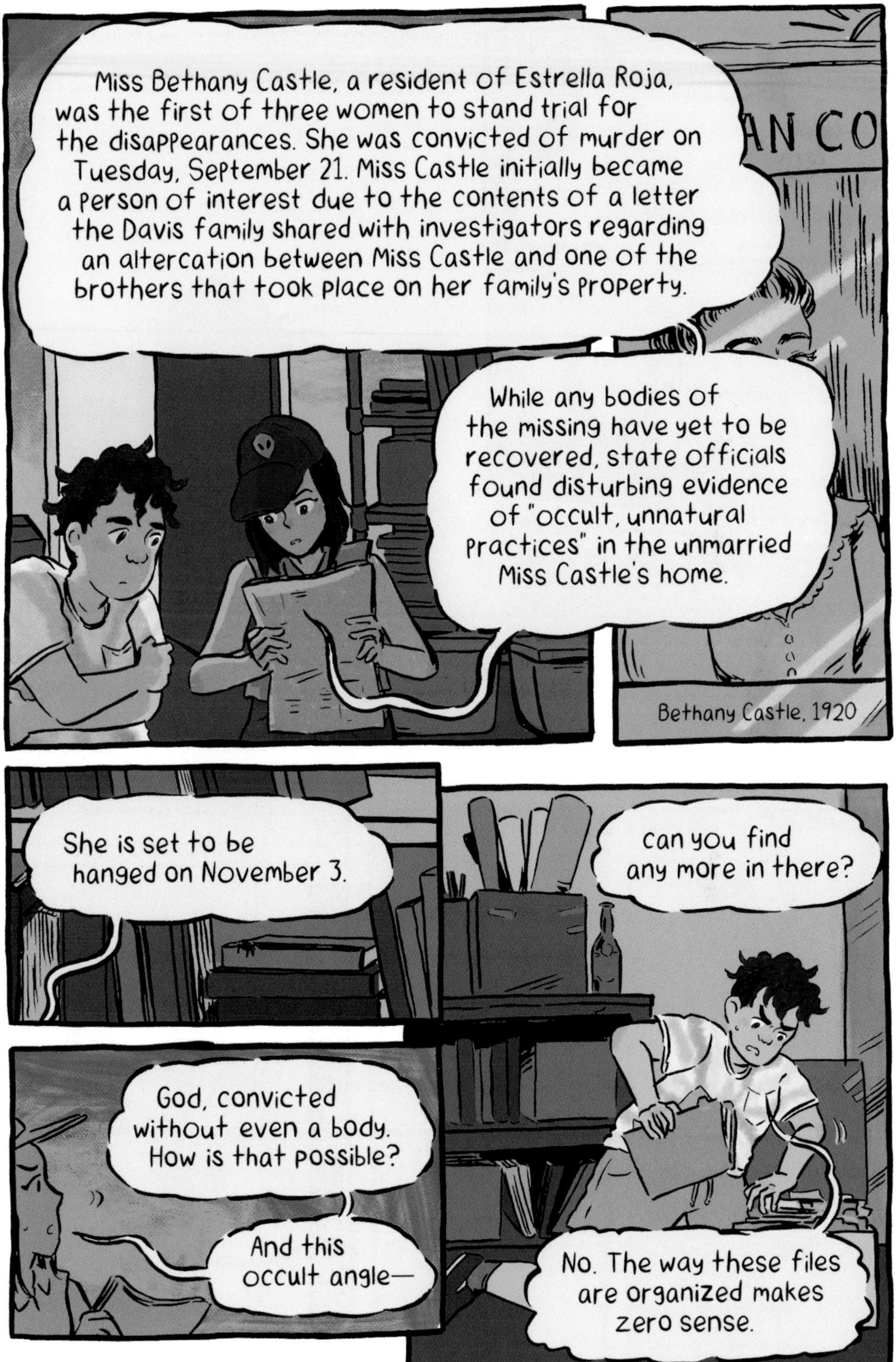
Miss Bethany Castle, a resident of Estrella Roja, was the first of three women to stand trial for the disappearances. She was convicted of murder on Tuesday, September 21. Miss Castle initially became a person of interest due to the contents of a letter the Davis family shared with investigators regarding an altercation between Miss Castle and one of the brothers that took place on her family's property.
AN CO
While any bodies of the missing have yet to be recovered, state officials found disturbing evidence of "occult, unnatural practices" in the unmarried Miss Castle's home.
Bethany Castle, 1920
She is set to be hanged on November 3.
can you find any more in there?
God, convicted without even a body. How is that possible?
And this occult angle—
No. The way these files are organized makes zero sense.

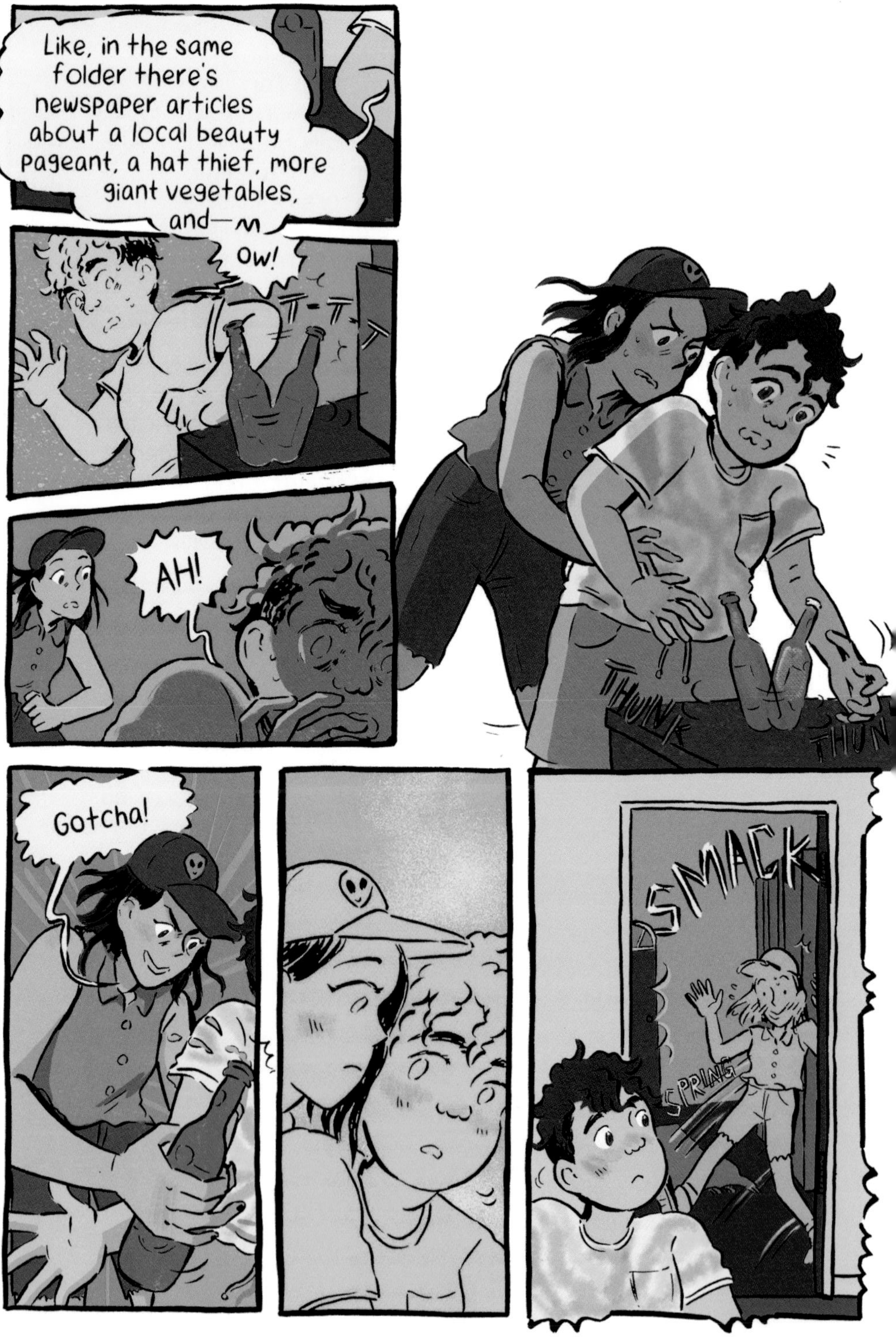
Like, in the same folder there's newspaper articles about a local beauty pageant, a hat thief, more giant vegetables, and—
OW!
AH!
THUNK
Gotcha!
SMACK
SPRING

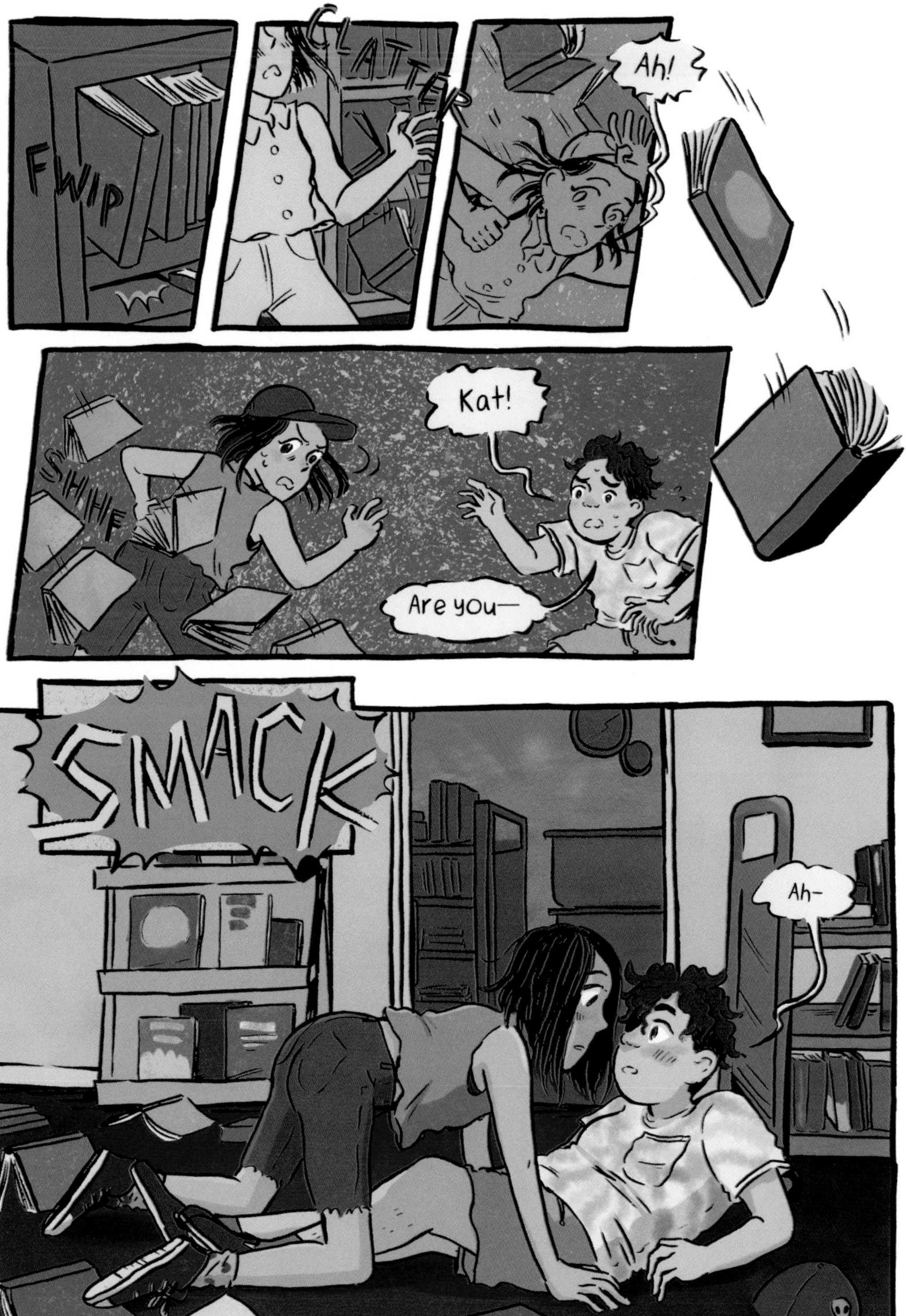
FWIP
CLATTER
Ah!
Kat!
SHHF
Are you—
SMACK
Ah-

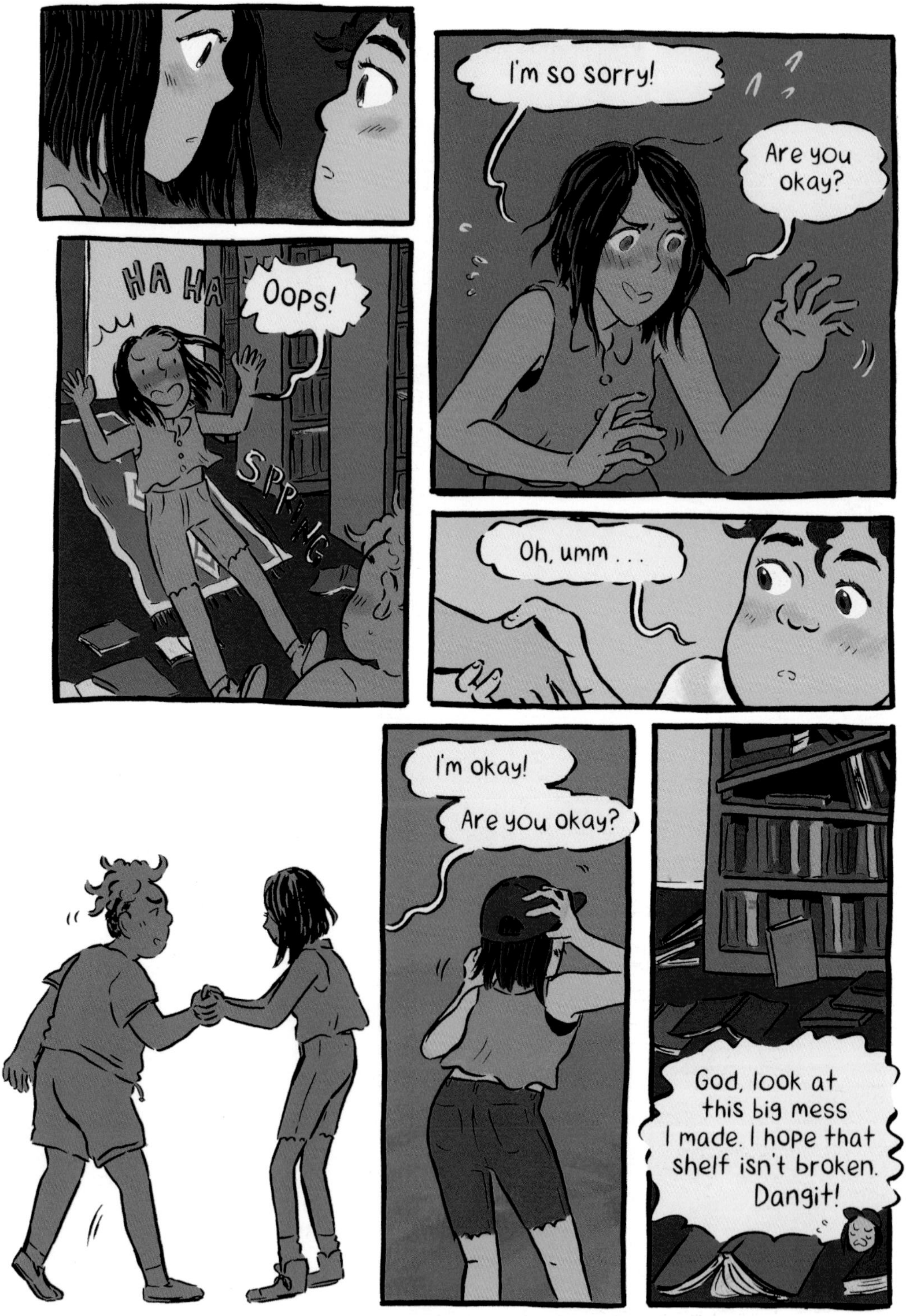
HA HA
Oops!
SPRING
I'm so sorry!
Are you okay?
Oh, umm . . .
I'm okay!
Are you okay?
God, look at this big mess I made. I hope that shelf isn't broken. Dangit!

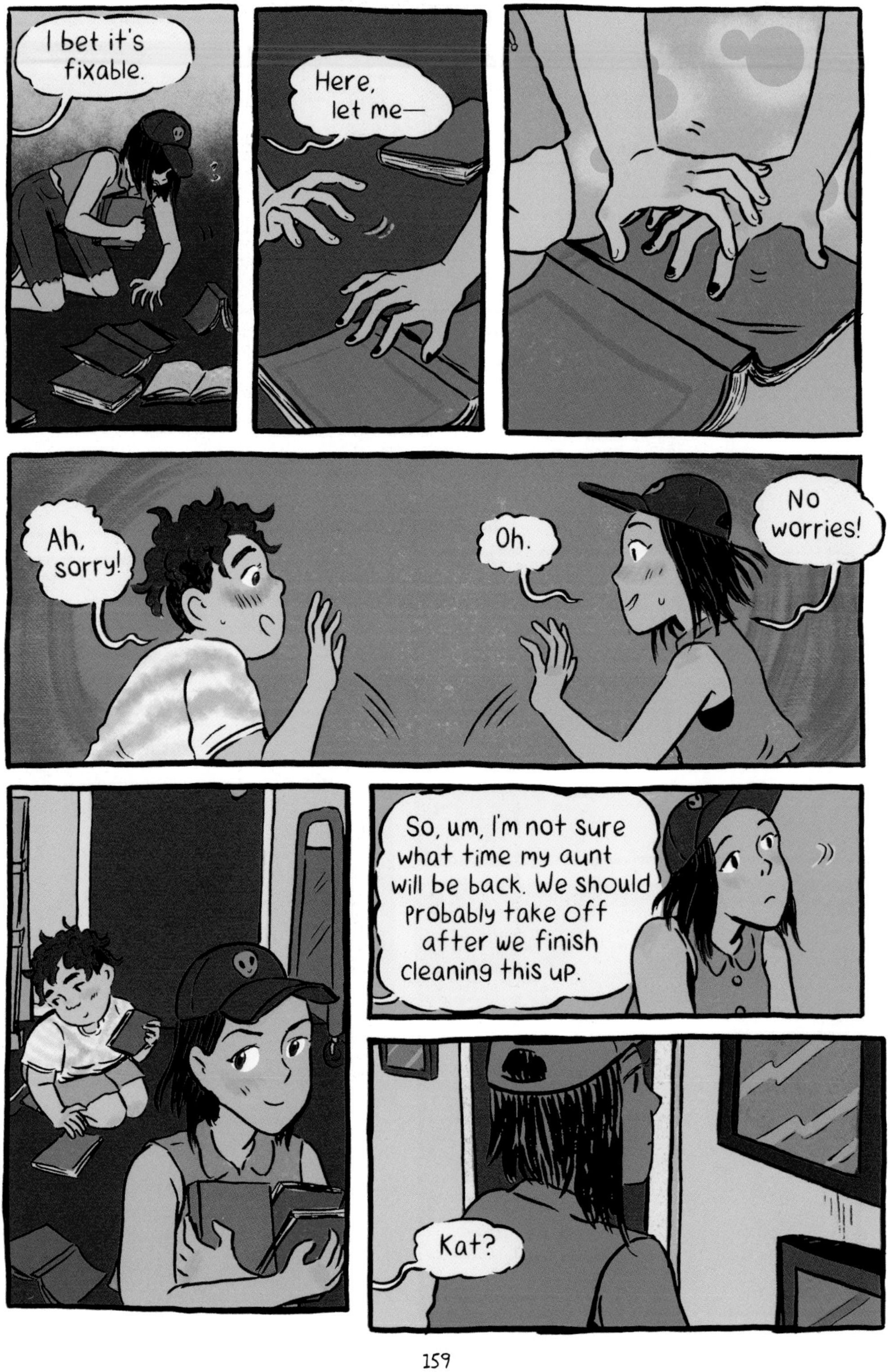
I bet it's fixable.
Here, let me—
Ah, sorry!
Oh.
No worries!
So, um, I'm not sure what time my aunt will be back. We should probably take off after we finish cleaning this up.
Kat?

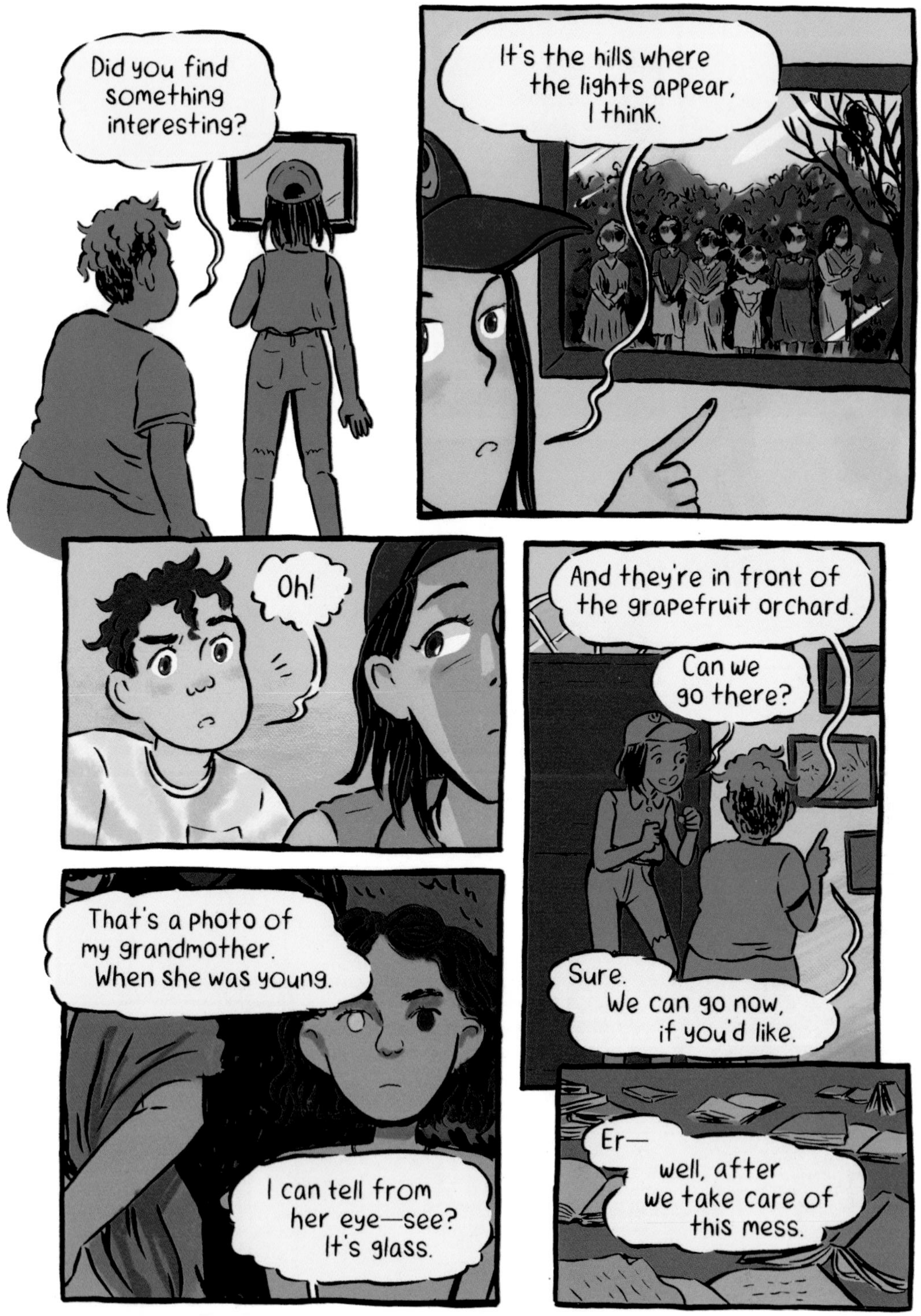
Did you find something interesting?
It's the hills where the lights appear, I think.
Oh!
And they're in front of the grapefruit orchard.
Can we go there?
Sure. We can go now, if you'd like.
That's a photo of my grandmother. When she was young.
I can tell from her eye—see? It's glass.
Er—
well, after we take care of this mess.

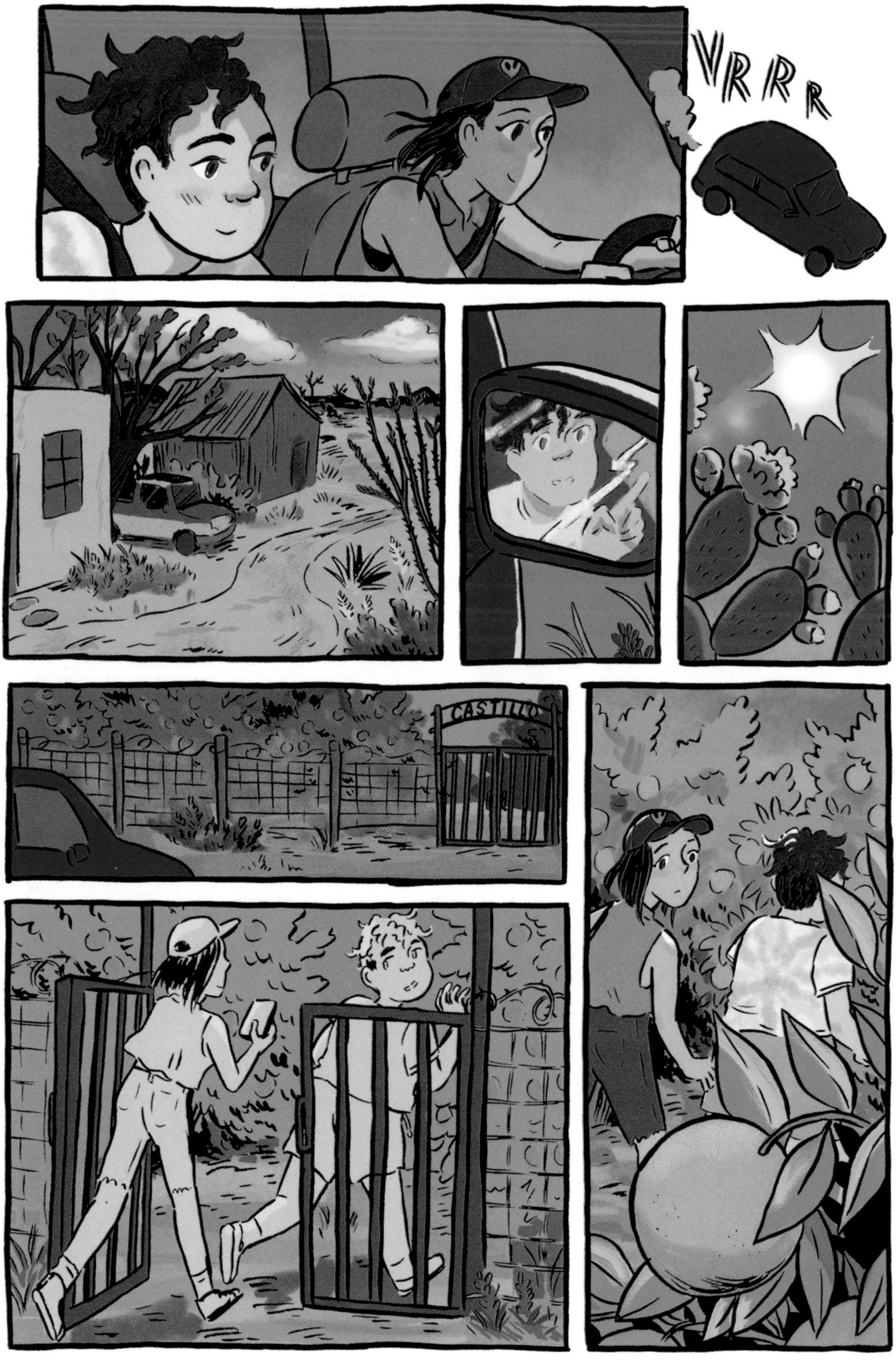
VRRR
CASTILLO

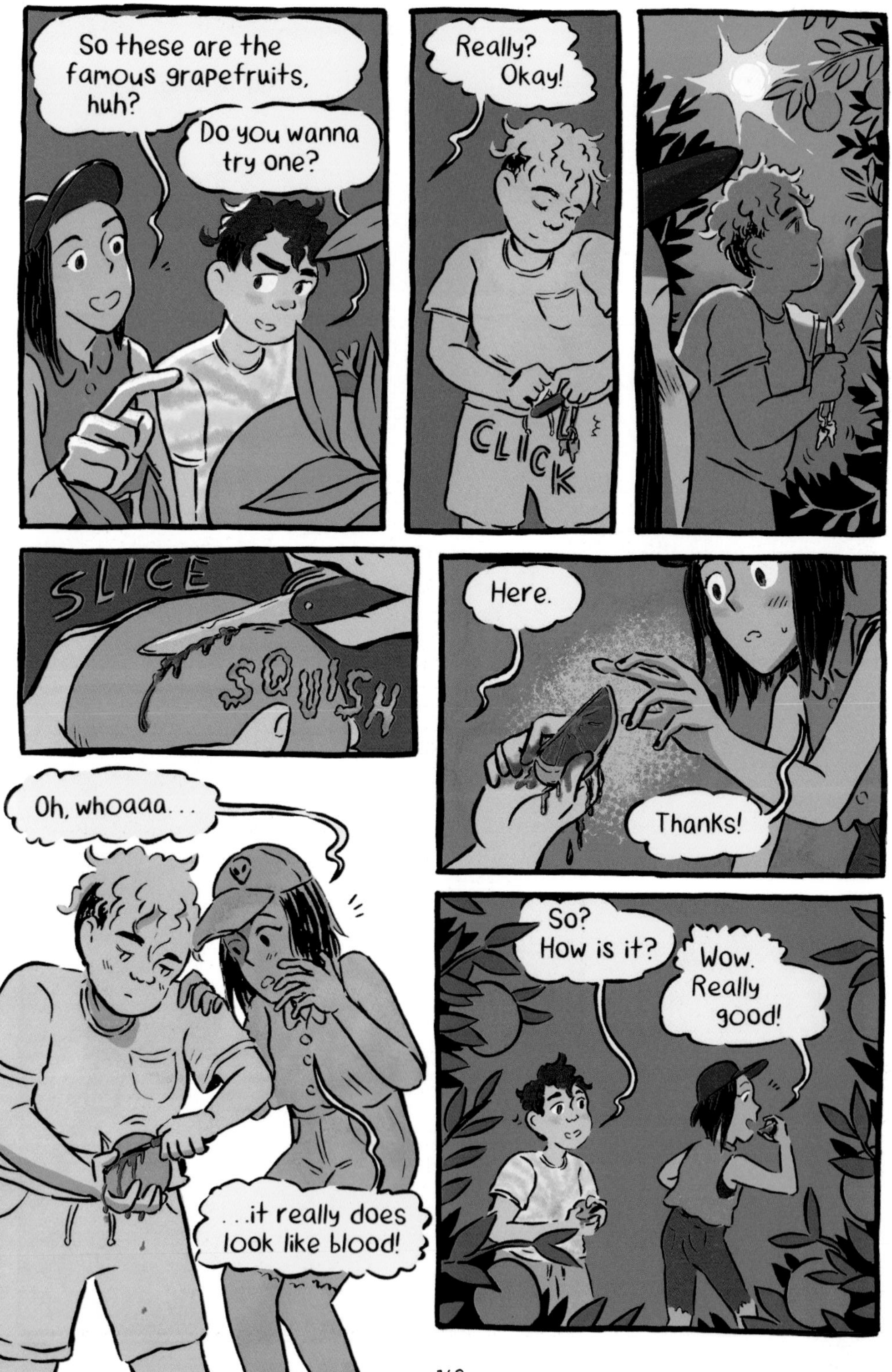

So these are the famous grapefruits, huh?
Do you wanna try one?
Really? Okay!
CLICK
SLICE
SQUISH
Here.
Thanks!
Oh, whoaaa...
...it really does look like blood!
So? How is it?
Wow. Really good!

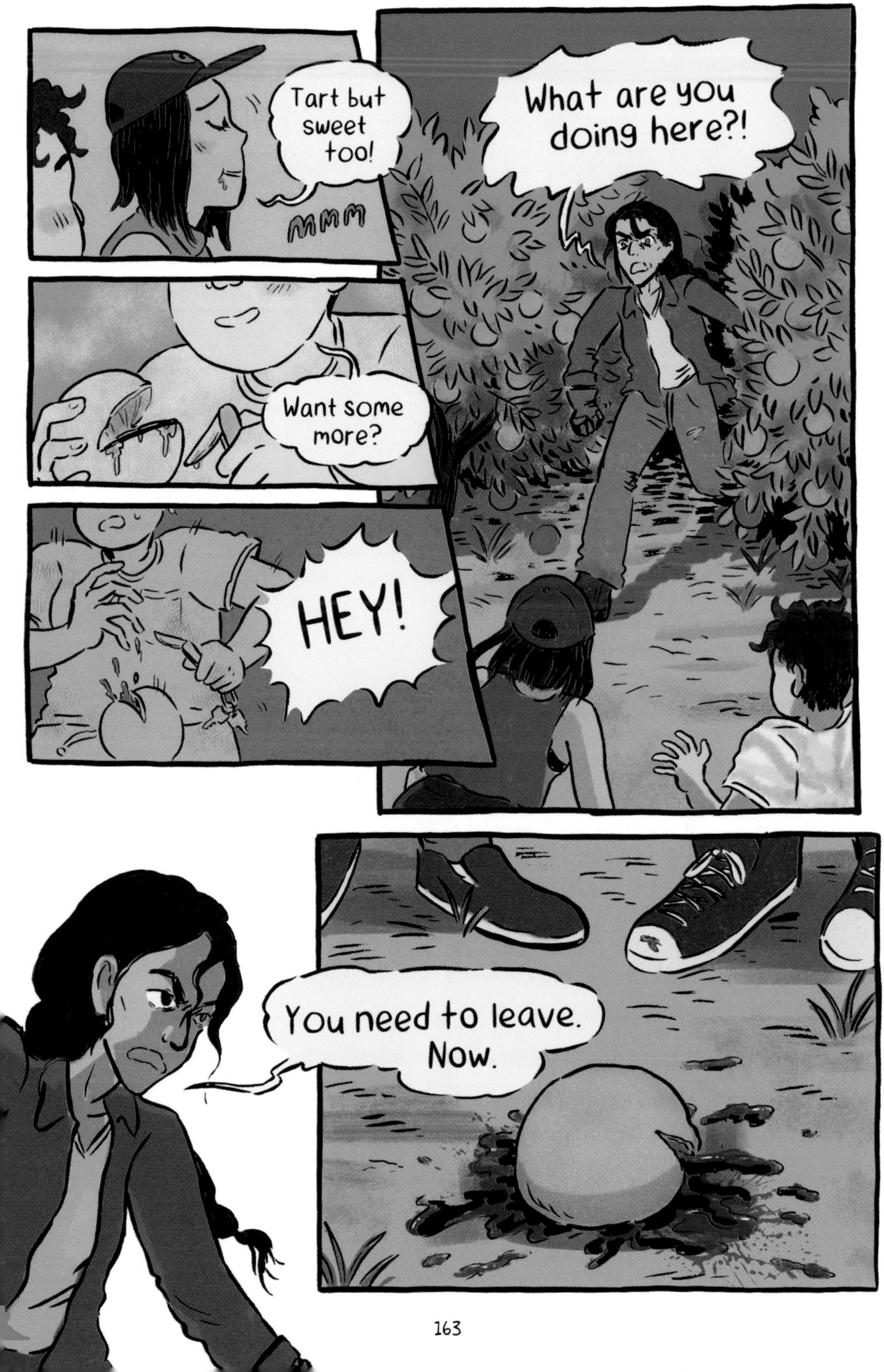
Tart but sweet too!
mmm
Want some more?
HEY!
What are you doing here?!
You need to leave. Now.

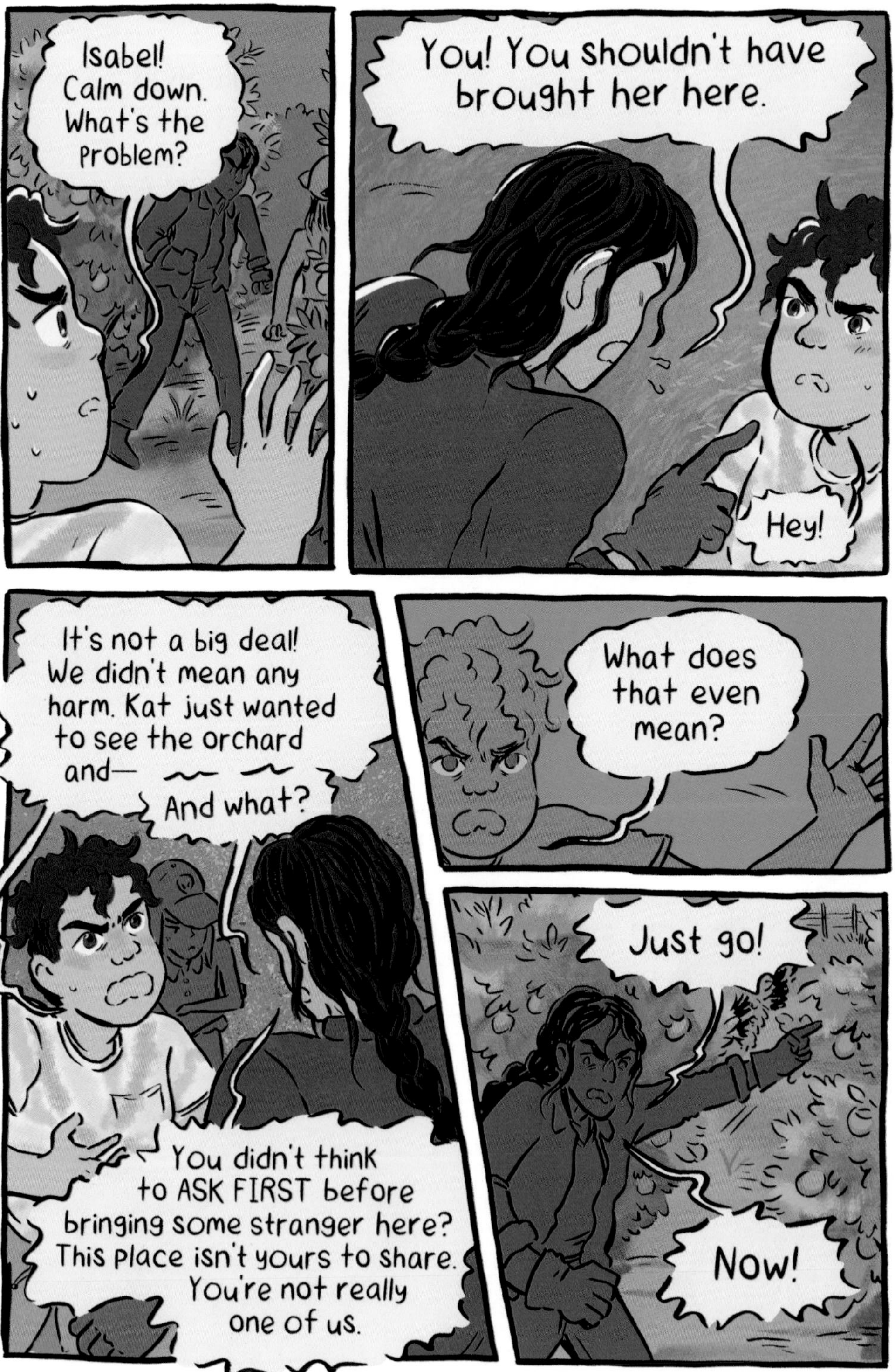
Isabel! Calm down. What's the problem?
You! You shouldn't have brought her here.
Hey!
It's not a big deal! We didn't mean any harm. Kat just wanted to see the orchard and—
And what?
You didn't think to ASK FIRST before bringing some stranger here? This place isn't yours to share. You're not really one of us.
What does that even mean?
Just go!
Now!

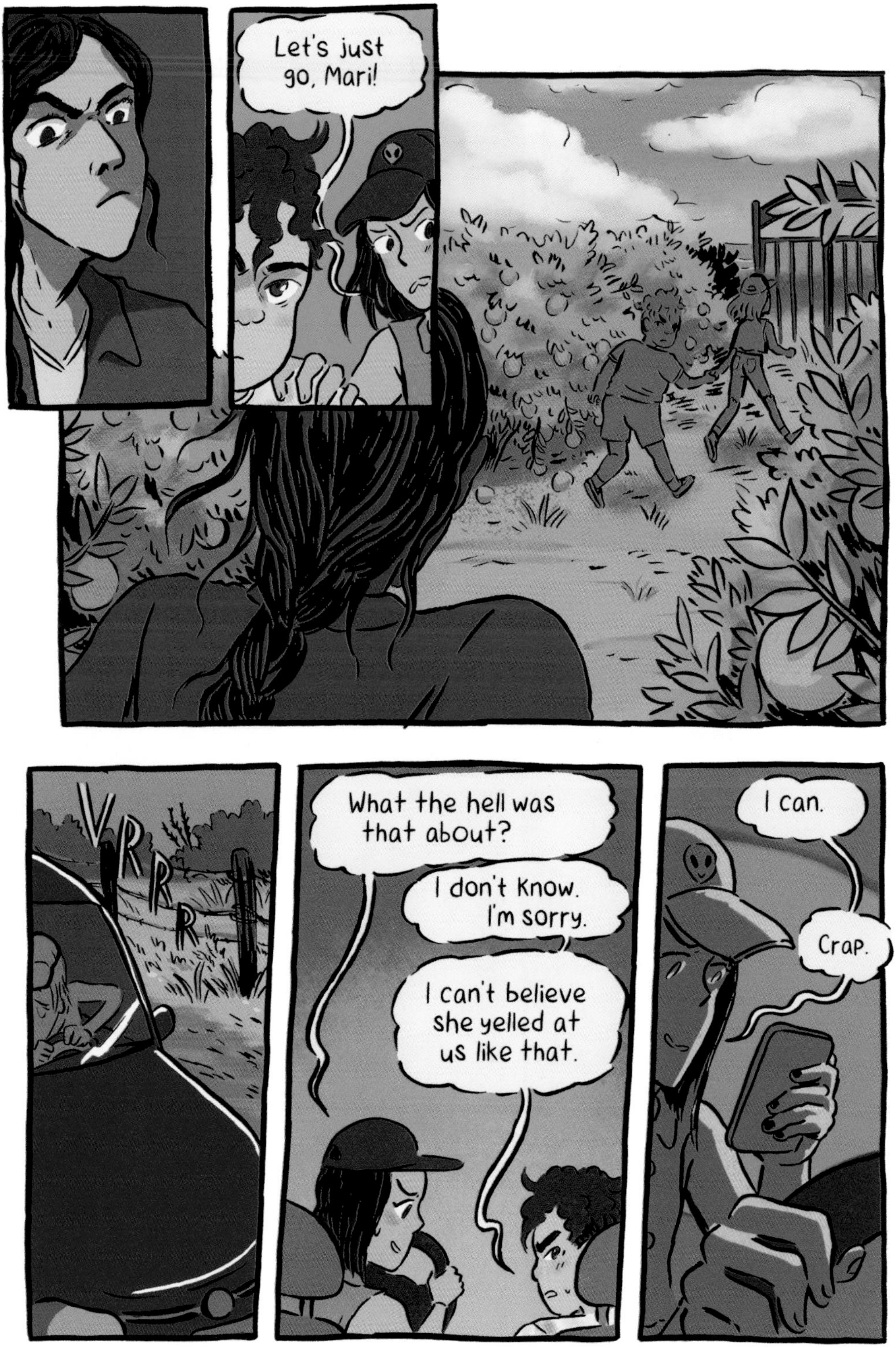
Let's just go, Mari!
VRRRR
What the hell was that about?
I don't know. I'm sorry.
I can't believe she yelled at us like that.
I can.
Crap.

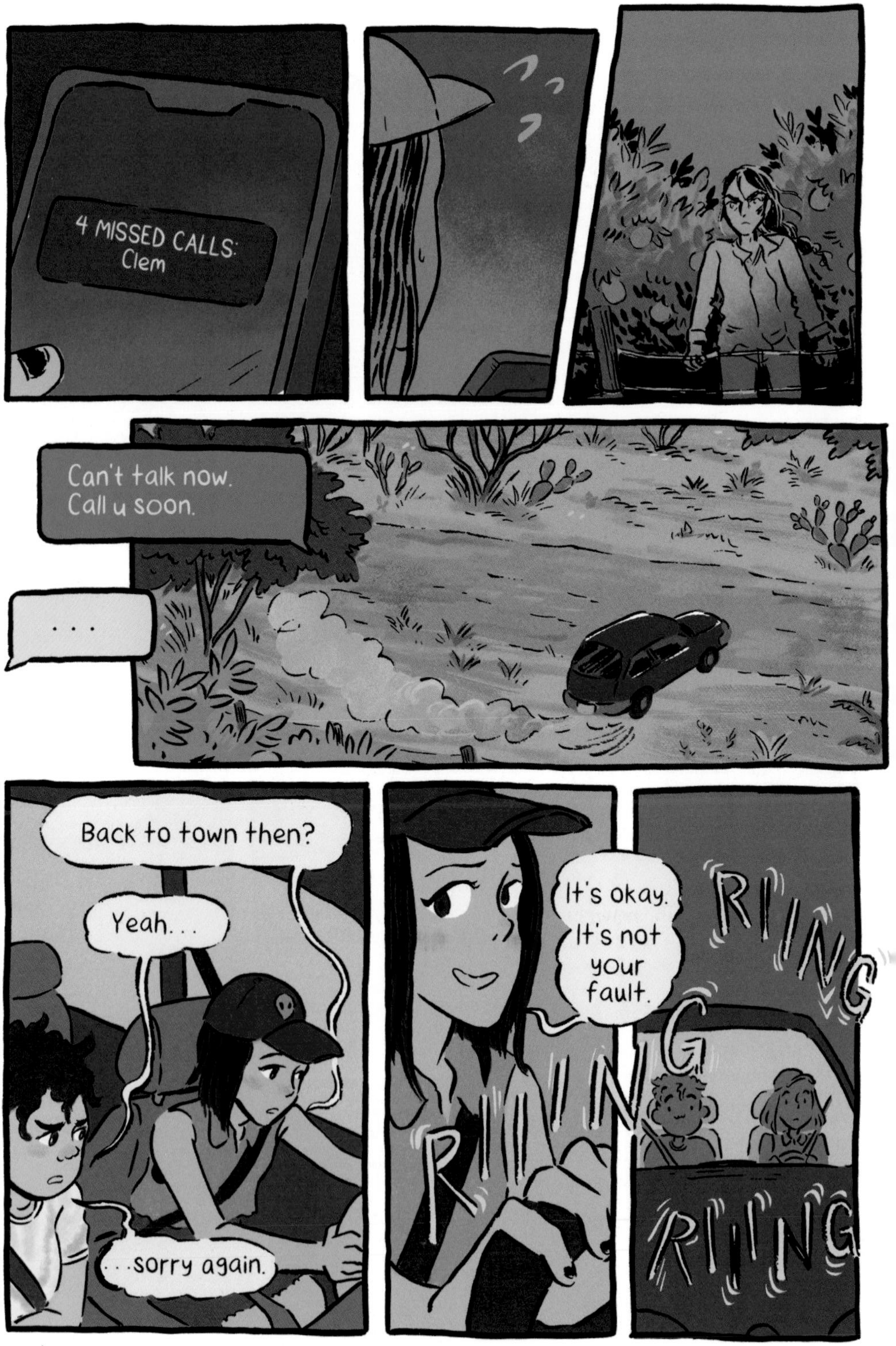
4 MISSED CALLS:
Clem
Can't talk now.
Call u soon.
. . .
Back to town then?
Yeah. . .
. . .sorry again.
It's okay.
It's not your fault.
RIING
RIIING
RIING
RIIING

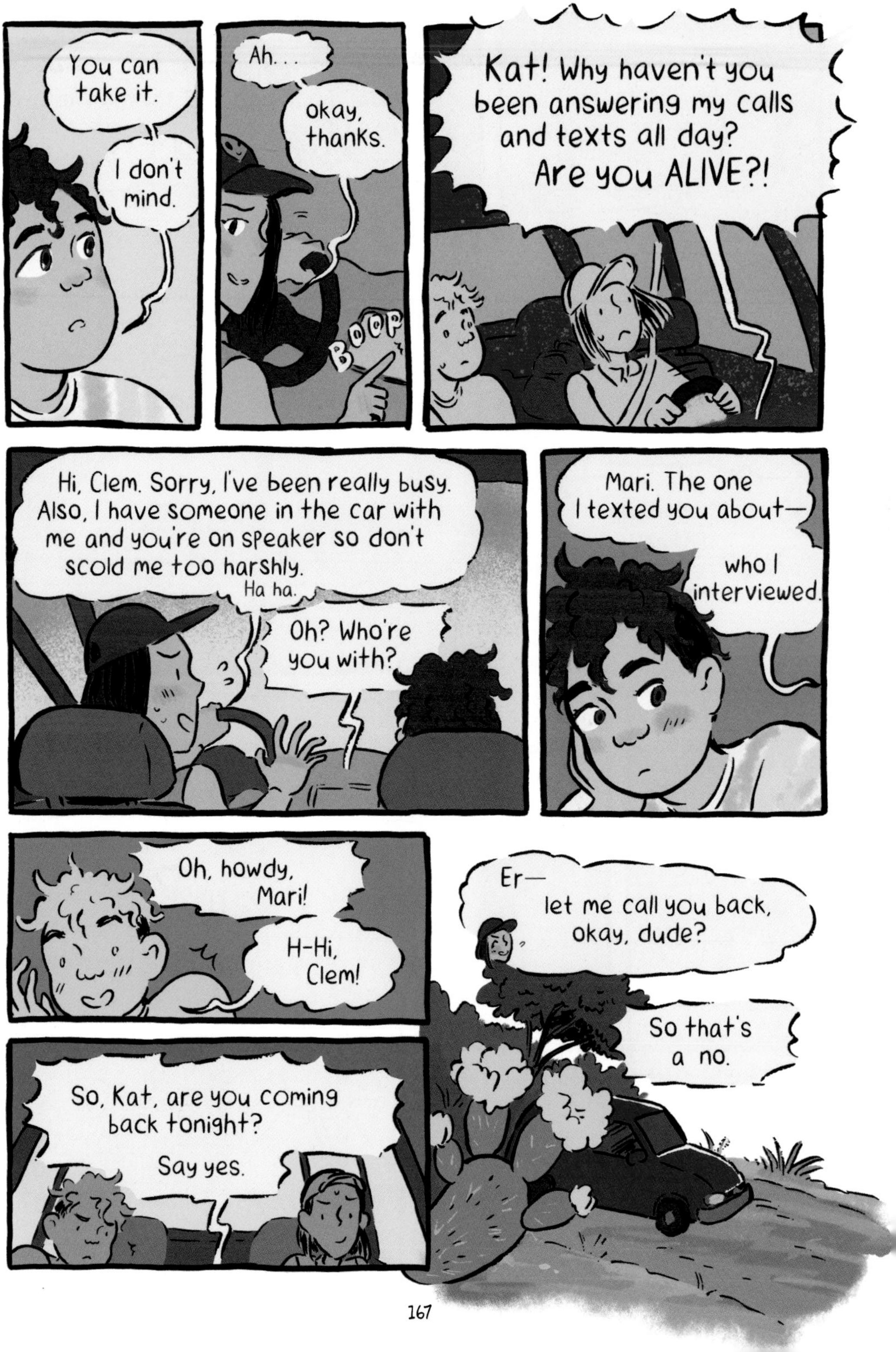
You can take it.
I don't mind.
Ah...
okay, thanks.
BOOP
Kat! Why haven't you been answering my calls and texts all day? Are you ALIVE?!
Hi, Clem. Sorry, I've been really busy. Also, I have someone in the car with me and you're on speaker so don't scold me too harshly.
Ha ha.
Oh? Who're you with?
Mari. The one I texted you about—
who I interviewed.
Oh, howdy, Mari!
H-Hi, Clem!
Er—
let me call you back, okay, dude?
So that's a no.
So, Kat, are you coming back tonight?
Say yes.

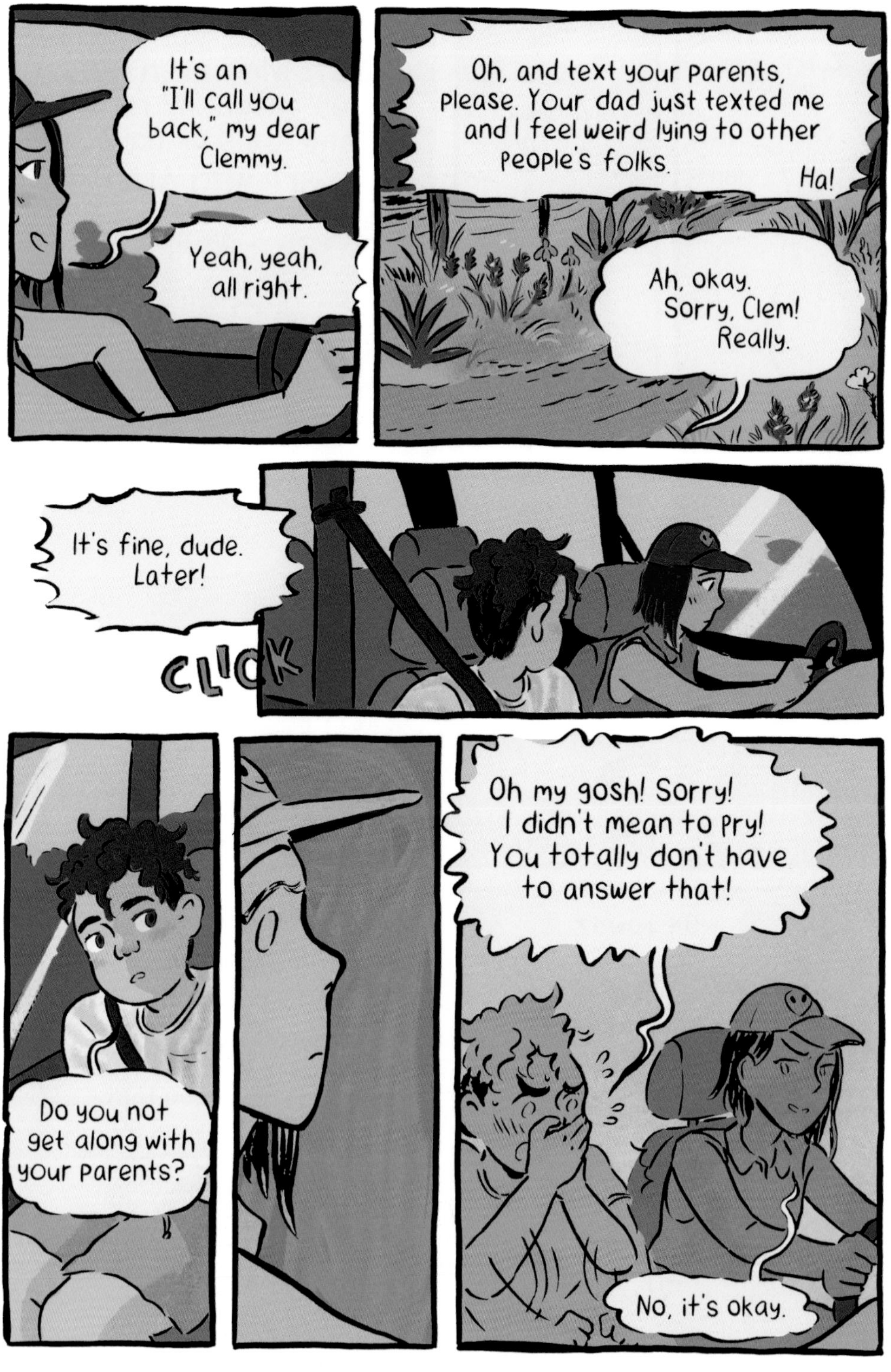
It's an "I'll call you back," my dear Clemmy.
Yeah, yeah, all right.
Oh, and text your parents, please. Your dad just texted me and I feel weird lying to other people's folks.
Ha!
Ah, okay. Sorry, Clem! Really.
It's fine, dude. Later!
CLICK
Do you not get along with your parents?
Oh my gosh! Sorry! I didn't mean to pry! You totally don't have to answer that!
No, it's okay.

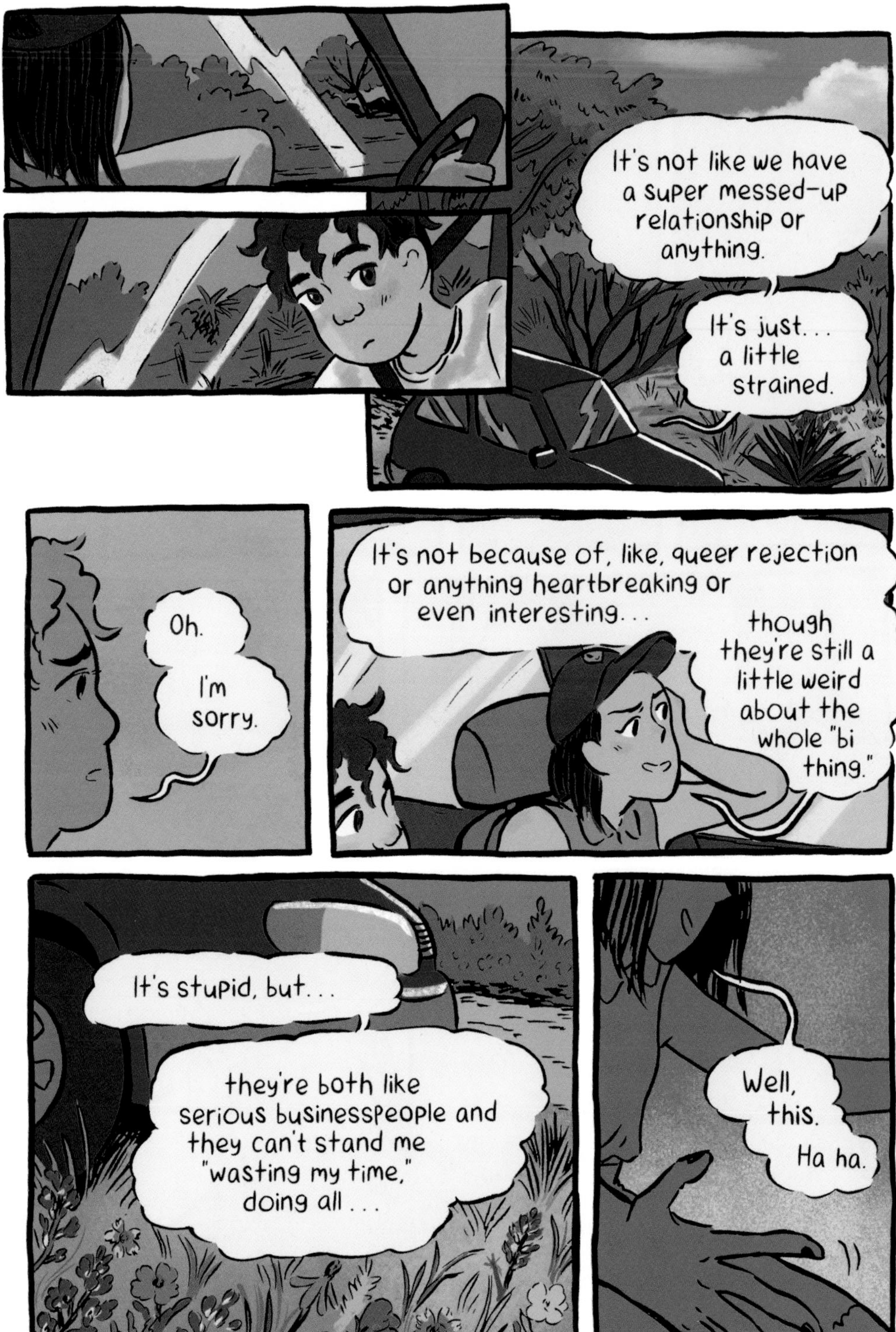
It's not like we have a super messed-up relationship or anything.
It's just... a little strained.
Oh.
I'm sorry.
It's not because of, like, queer rejection or anything heartbreaking or even interesting...
though they're still a little weird about the whole "bi thing."
It's stupid, but...
they're both like serious businesspeople and they can't stand me "wasting my time," doing all...
Well, this.
Ha ha.

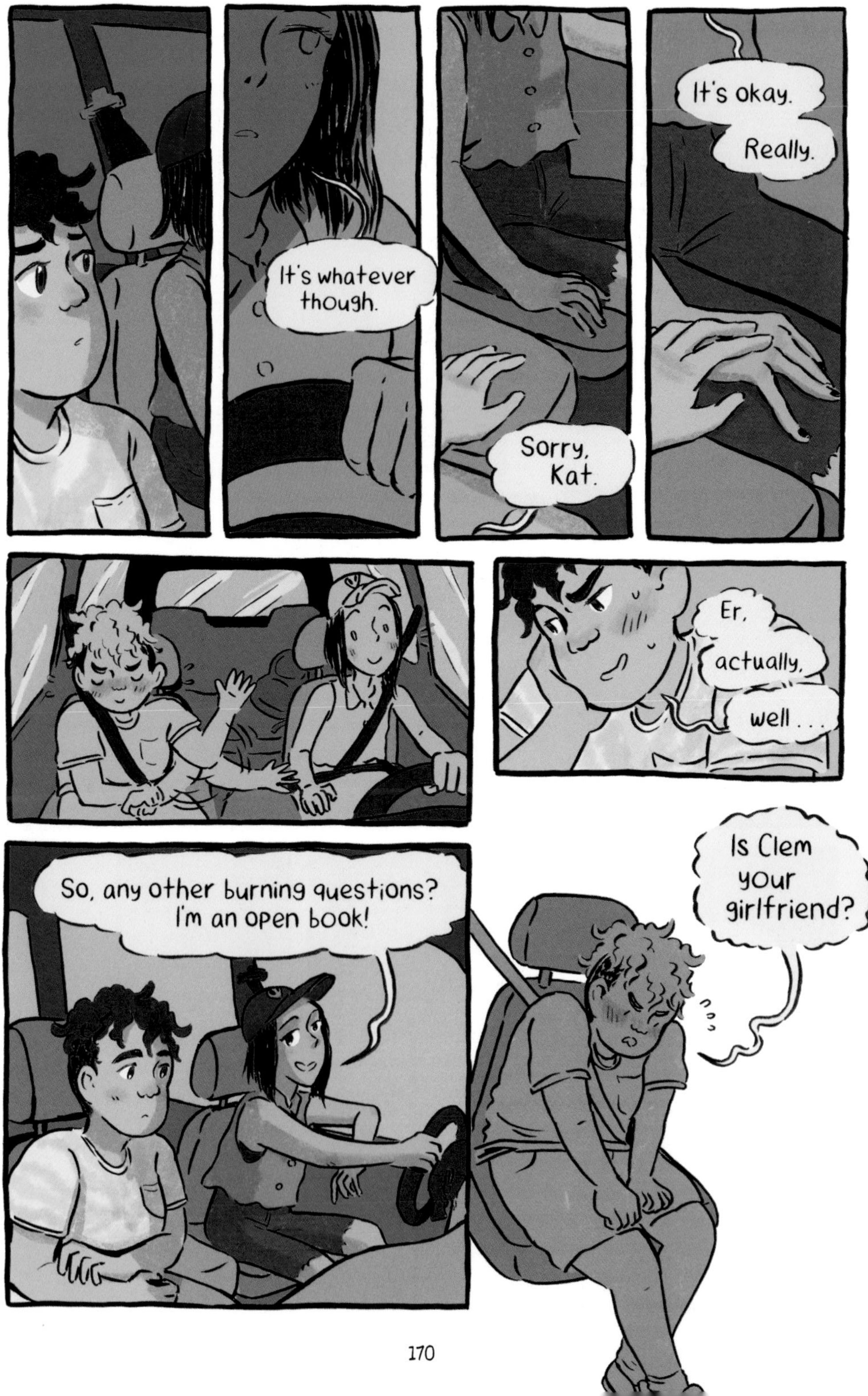
It's whatever though.
Sorry, Kat.
It's okay.
Really.
Er,
actually,
well . . .
So, any other burning questions? I'm an open book!
Is Clem your girlfriend?

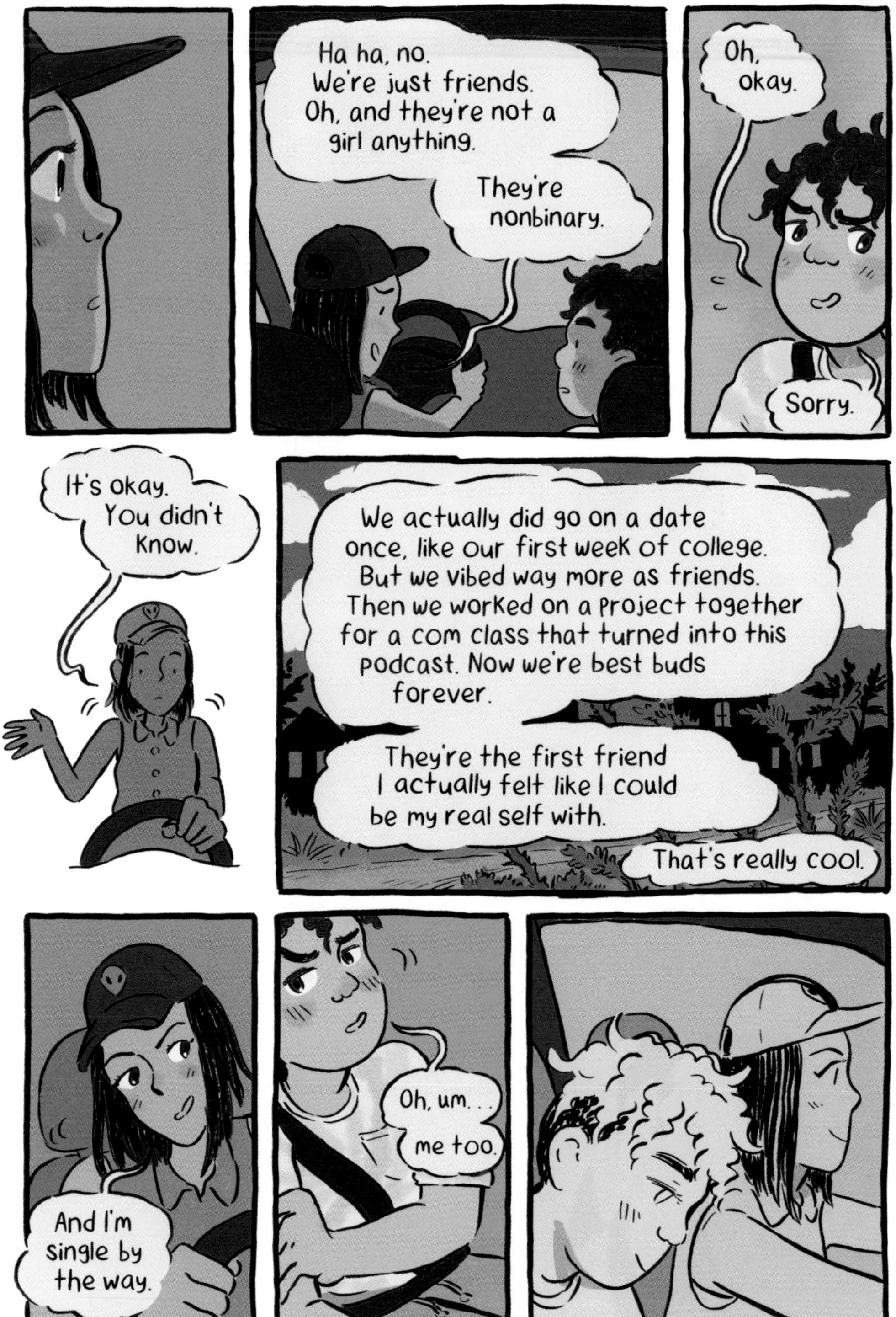
Ha ha, no. We're just friends. Oh, and they're not a girl anything.
They're nonbinary.
Oh, okay.
Sorry.
It's okay. You didn't know.
We actually did go on a date once, like our first week of college. But we vibed way more as friends. Then we worked on a project together for a com class that turned into this podcast. Now we're best buds forever.
They're the first friend I actually felt like I could be my real self with.
That's really cool.
And I'm single by the way.
Oh, um. . .
me too.

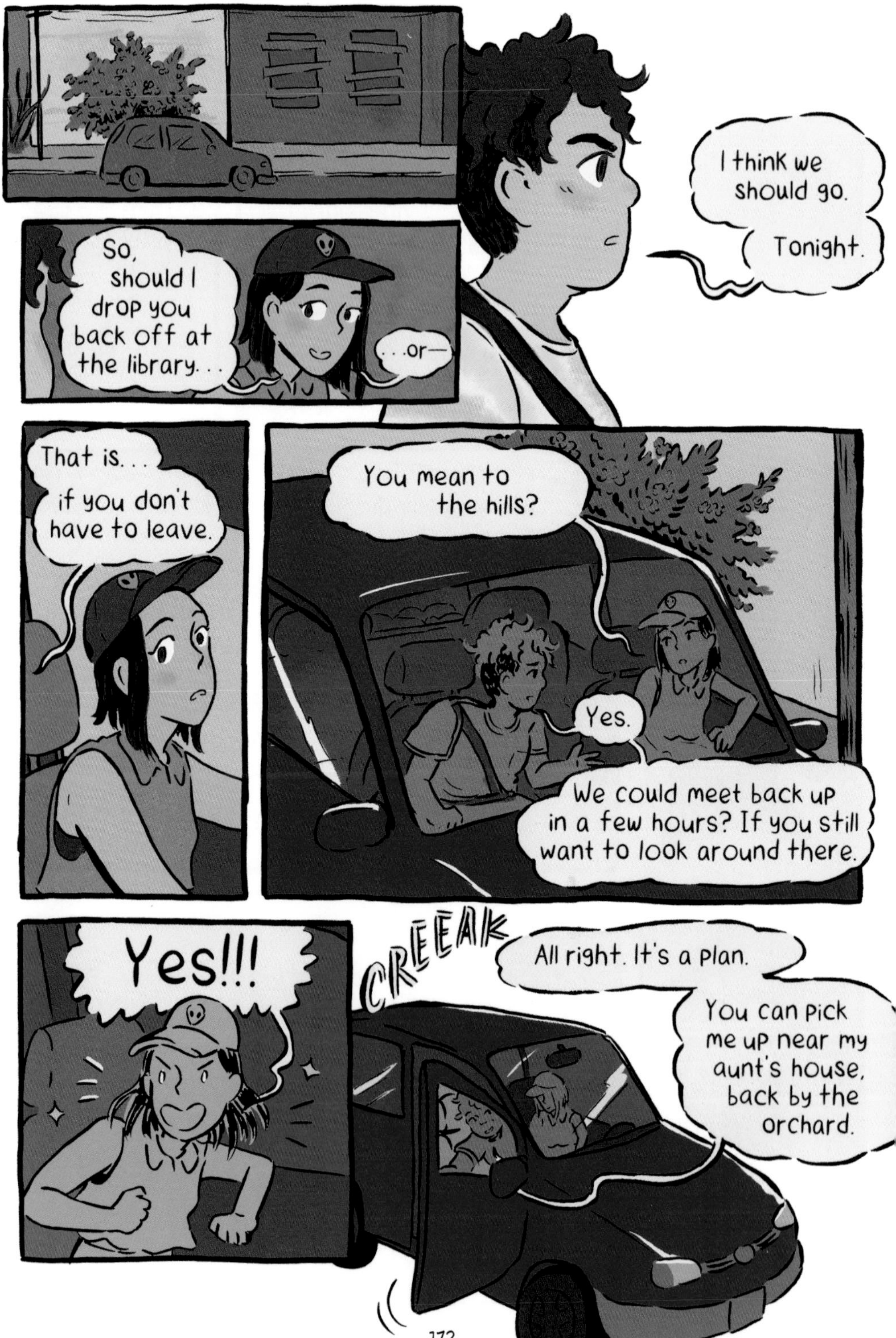
I think we should go.
Tonight.
So, should I drop you back off at the library. . .
. . .or—
That is. . .
if you don't have to leave.
You mean to the hills?
Yes.
We could meet back up in a few hours? If you still want to look around there.
Yes!!!
CREEAK
All right. It's a plan.
You can pick me up near my aunt's house, back by the orchard.

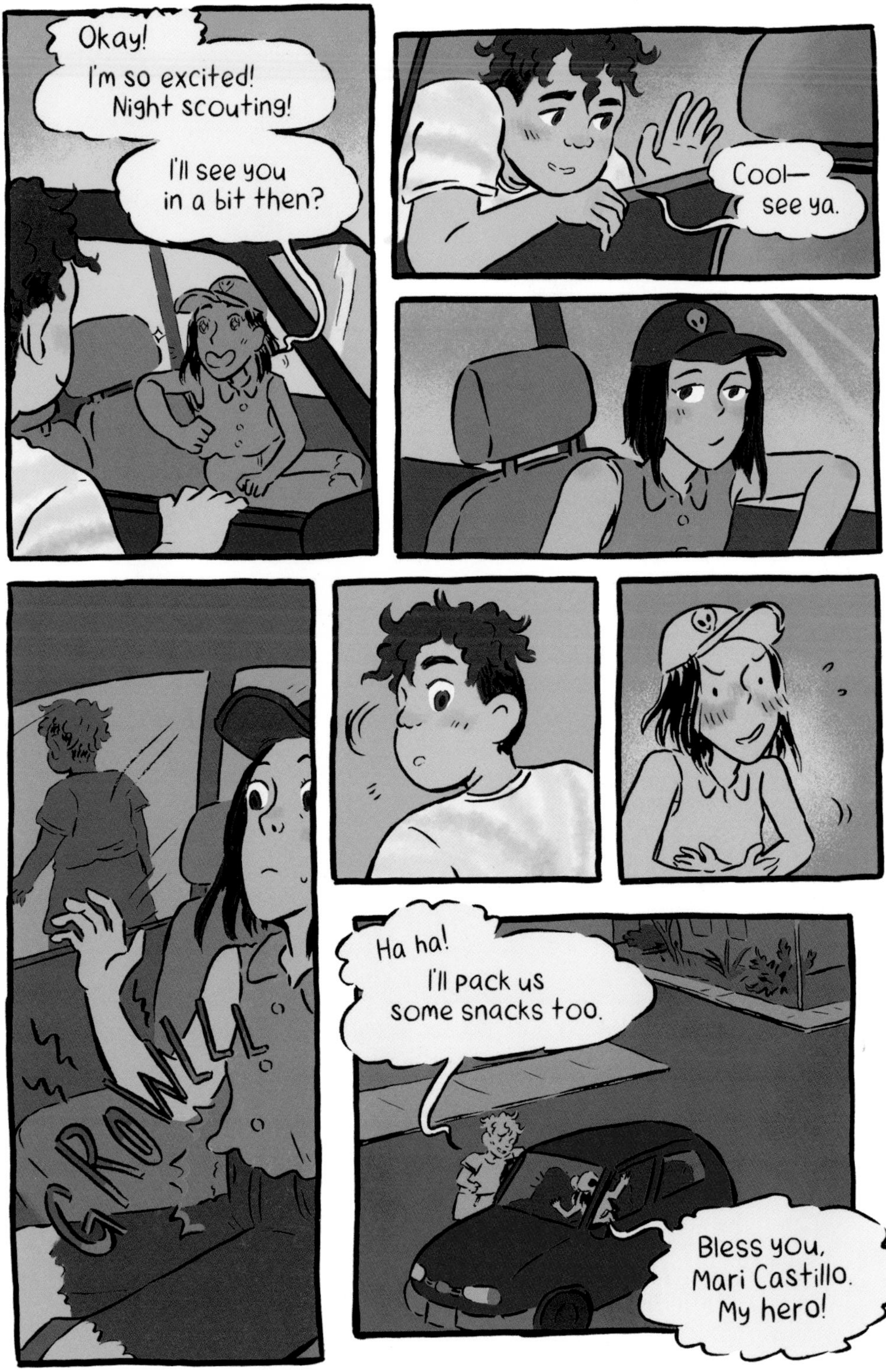
Okay!
I'm so excited! Night scouting!
I'll see you in a bit then?
Cool— see ya.
GROWLLL
Ha ha! I'll pack us some snacks too.
Bless you, Mari Castillo. My hero!

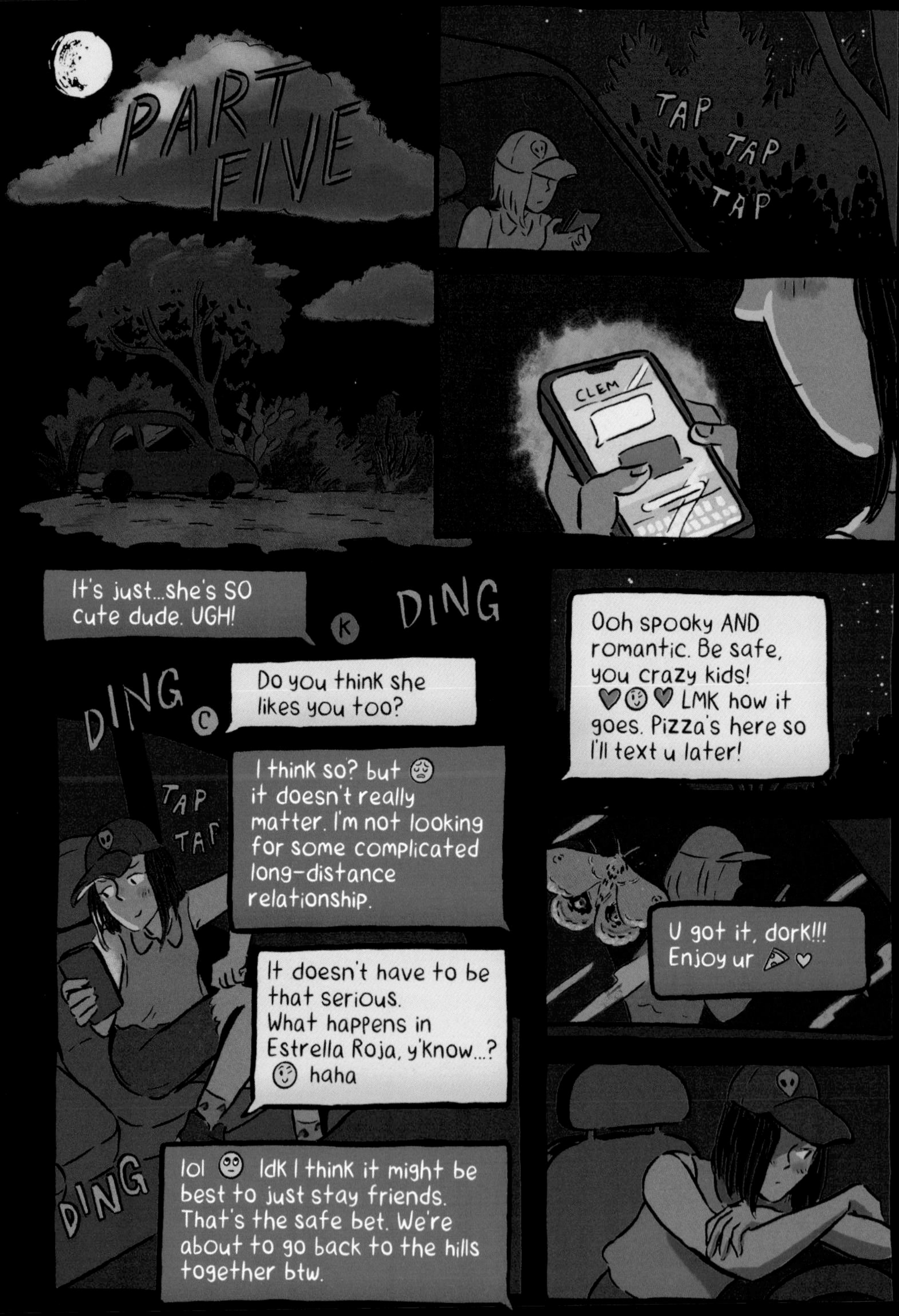
PART FIVE
TAP
TAP
TAP
CLEM
It's just...she's SO cute dude. UGH!
K
DING
DING
C
Do you think she likes you too?
TAP
TAP
I think so? but it doesn't really matter. I'm not looking for some complicated long-distance relationship.
It doesn't have to be that serious. What happens in Estrella Roja, y'know...? haha
DING
lol IdK I think it might be best to just stay friends. That's the safe bet. We're about to go back to the hills together btw.
Ooh spooky AND romantic. Be safe, you crazy kids! LMK how it goes. Pizza's here so I'll text u later!
U got it, dork!!! Enjoy ur

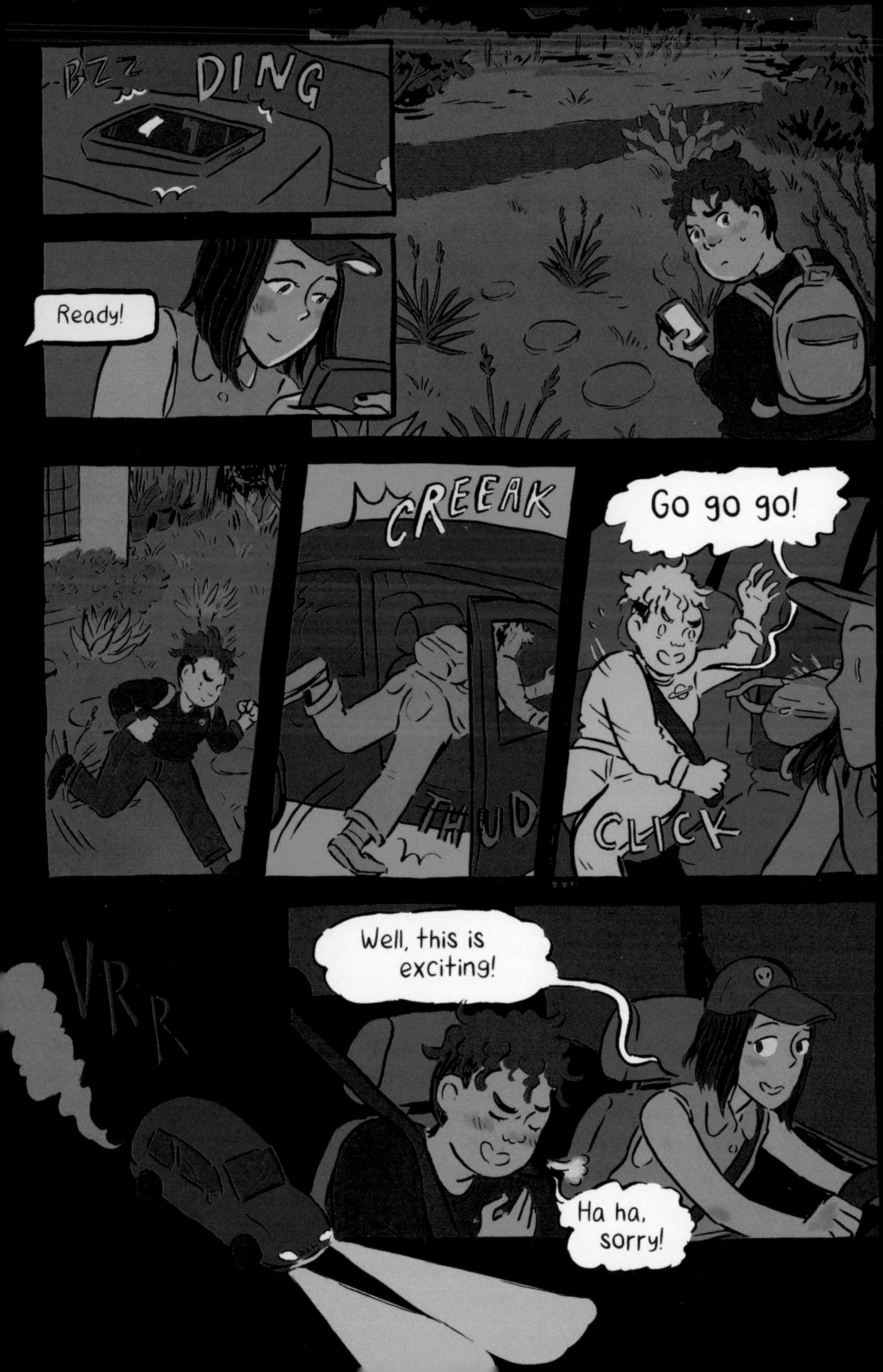
BZZ
DING
Ready!
CREEAK
THUD
Go go go!
CLICK
VRR
Well, this is exciting!
Ha ha, sorry!

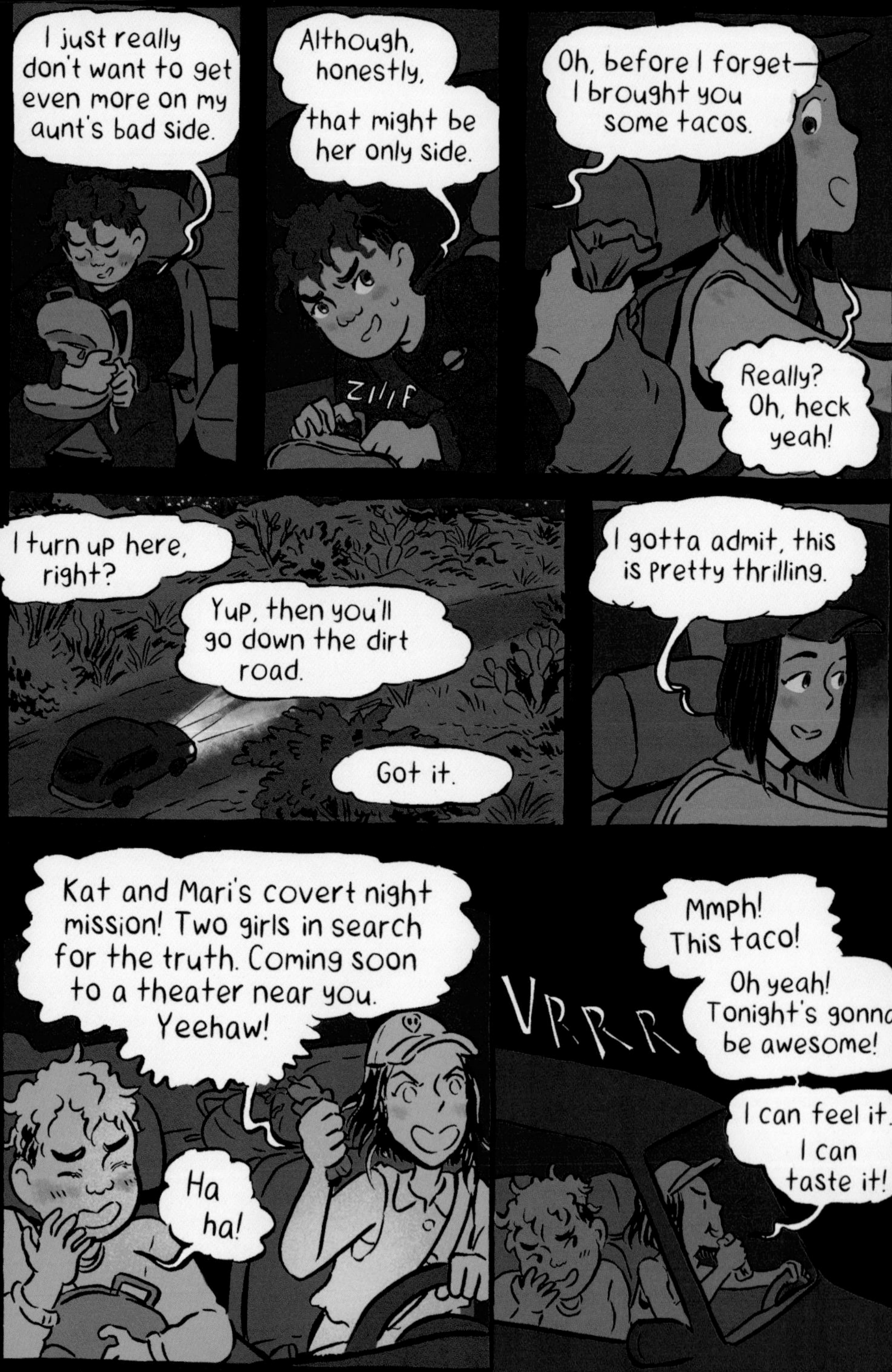

I just really don't want to get even more on my aunt's bad side.
Although, honestly,
that might be her only side.
ZIIIP
Oh, before I forget— I brought you some tacos.
Really? Oh, heck yeah!
I turn up here, right?
Yup, then you'll go down the dirt road.
Got it.
I gotta admit, this is pretty thrilling.
Kat and Mari's covert night mission! Two girls in search for the truth. Coming soon to a theater near you. Yeehaw!
Ha ha!
VRRR
Mmph! This taco!
Oh yeah! Tonight's gonna be awesome!
I can feel it. I can taste it!

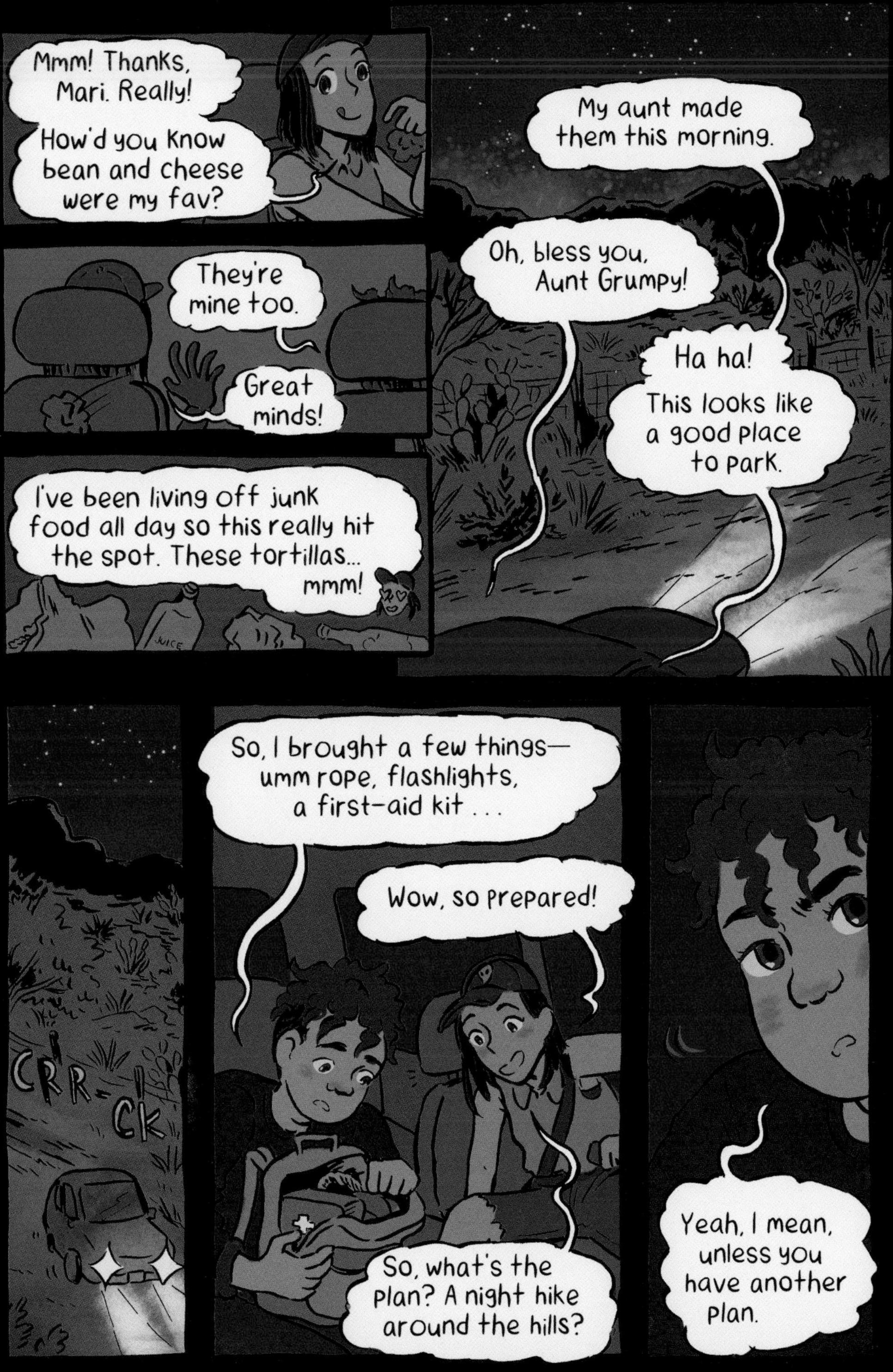
Mmm! Thanks, Mari. Really!
How'd you know bean and cheese were my fav?
They're mine too.
Great minds!
I've been living off junk food all day so this really hit the spot. These tortillas... mmm!
JUICE
My aunt made them this morning.
Oh, bless you, Aunt Grumpy!
Ha ha!
This looks like a good place to park.
CRR-CK
So, I brought a few things—umm rope, flashlights, a first-aid kit . . .
Wow, so prepared!
So, what's the plan? A night hike around the hills?
Yeah, I mean, unless you have another plan.

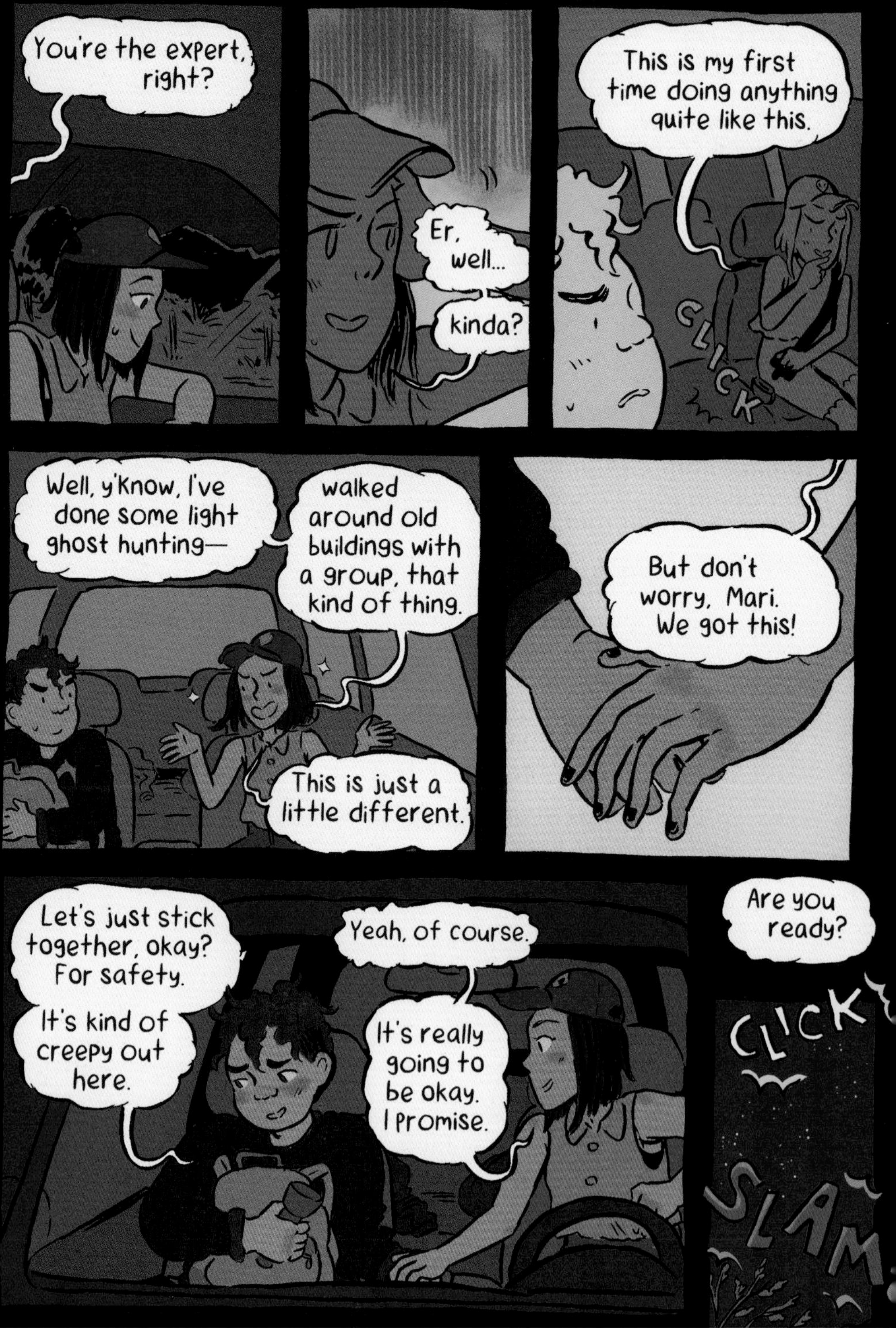
You're the expert, right?
Er, well...
kinda?
This is my first time doing anything quite like this.
CLICK
Well, y'know, I've done some light ghost hunting—
walked around old buildings with a group, that kind of thing.
This is just a little different.
But don't worry, Mari. We got this!
Let's just stick together, okay? For safety.
It's kind of creepy out here.
Yeah, of course.
It's really going to be okay. I promise.
Are you ready?
CLICK
SLAM

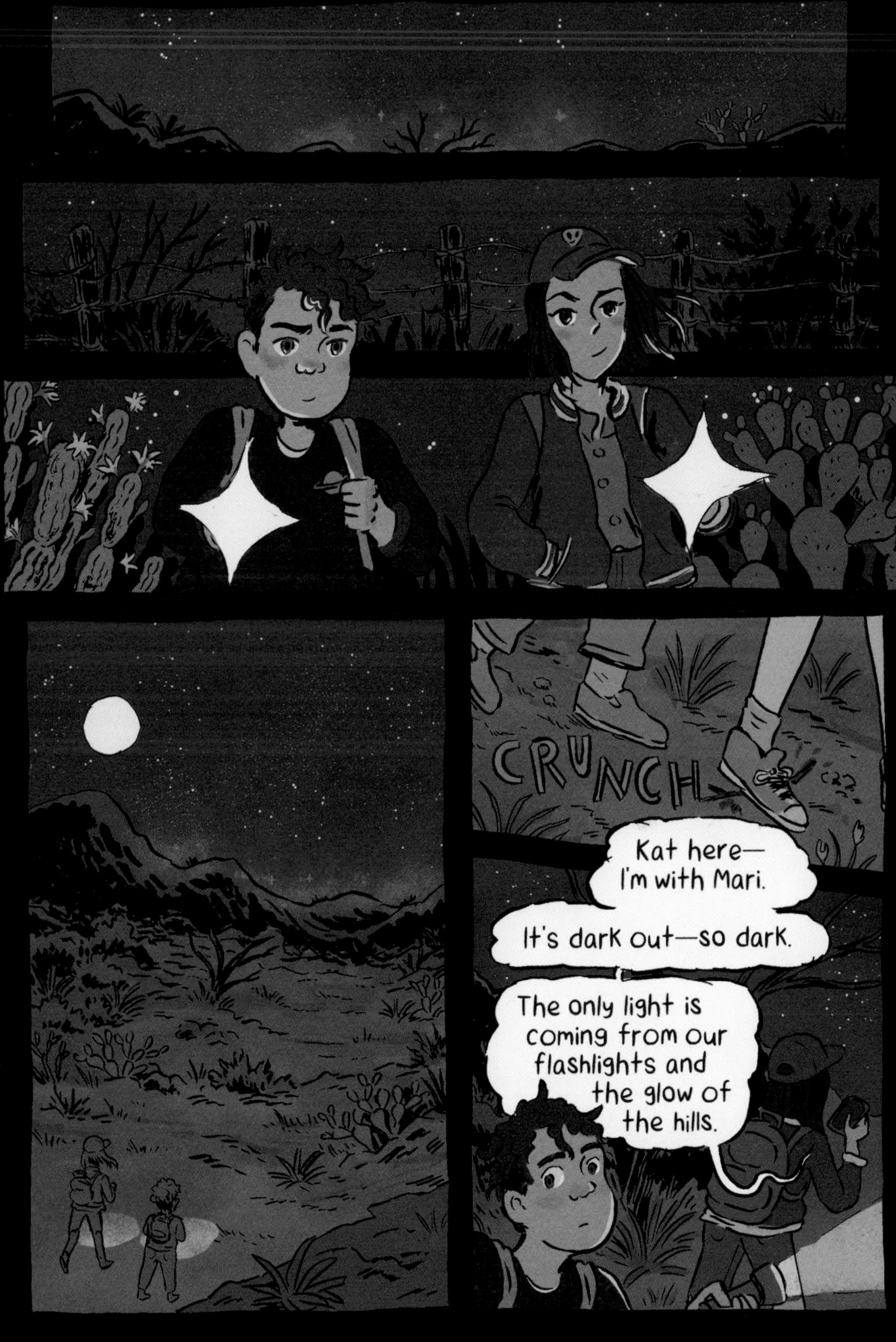
CRUNCH
Kat here— I'm with Mari.
It's dark out—so dark.
The only light is coming from our flashlights and the glow of the hills.

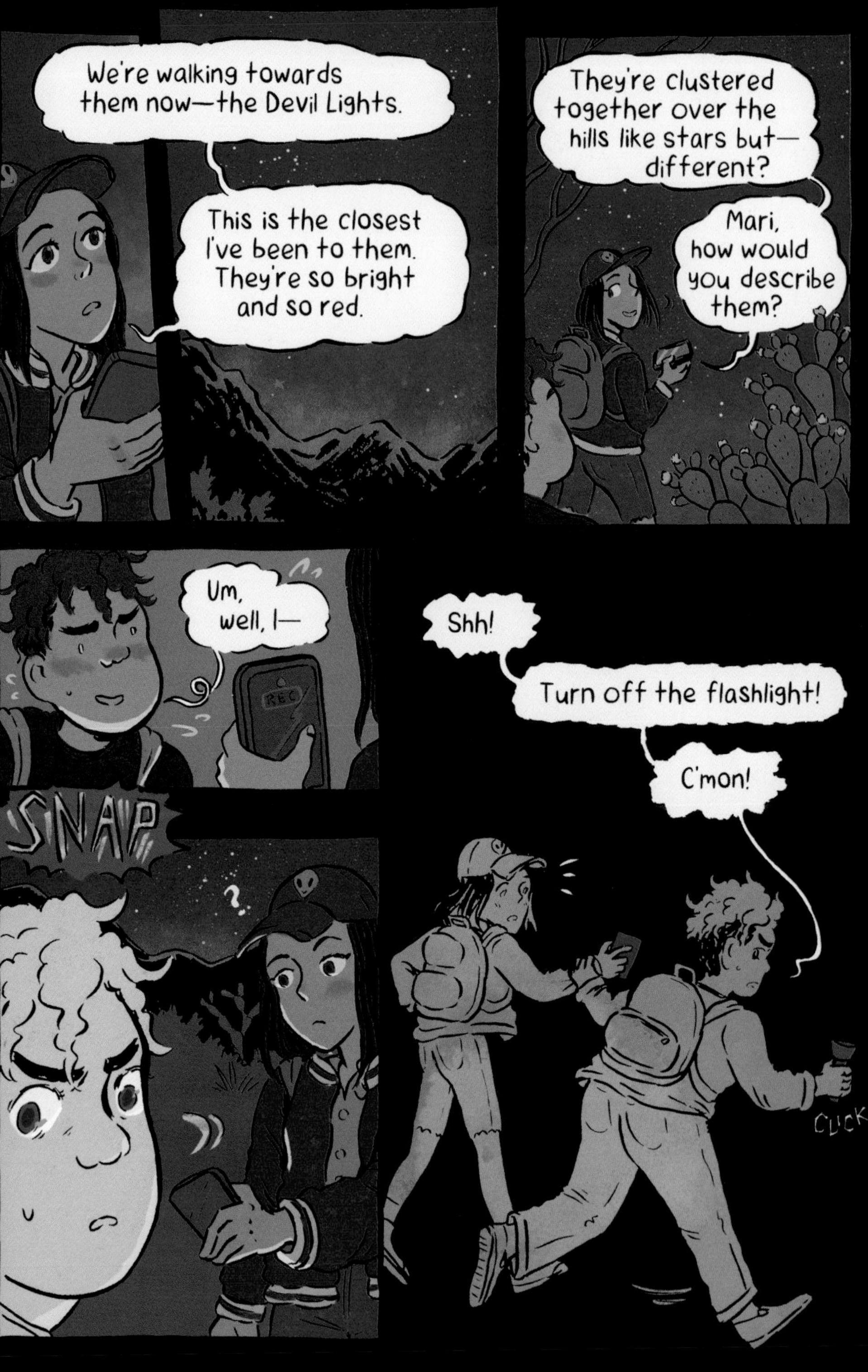

We're walking towards them now—the Devil Lights.
This is the closest I've been to them. They're so bright and so red.
They're clustered together over the hills like stars but—different?
Mari, how would you describe them?
Um, well, I—
REC
SNAP
Shh!
Turn off the flashlight!
C'mon!
CLICK

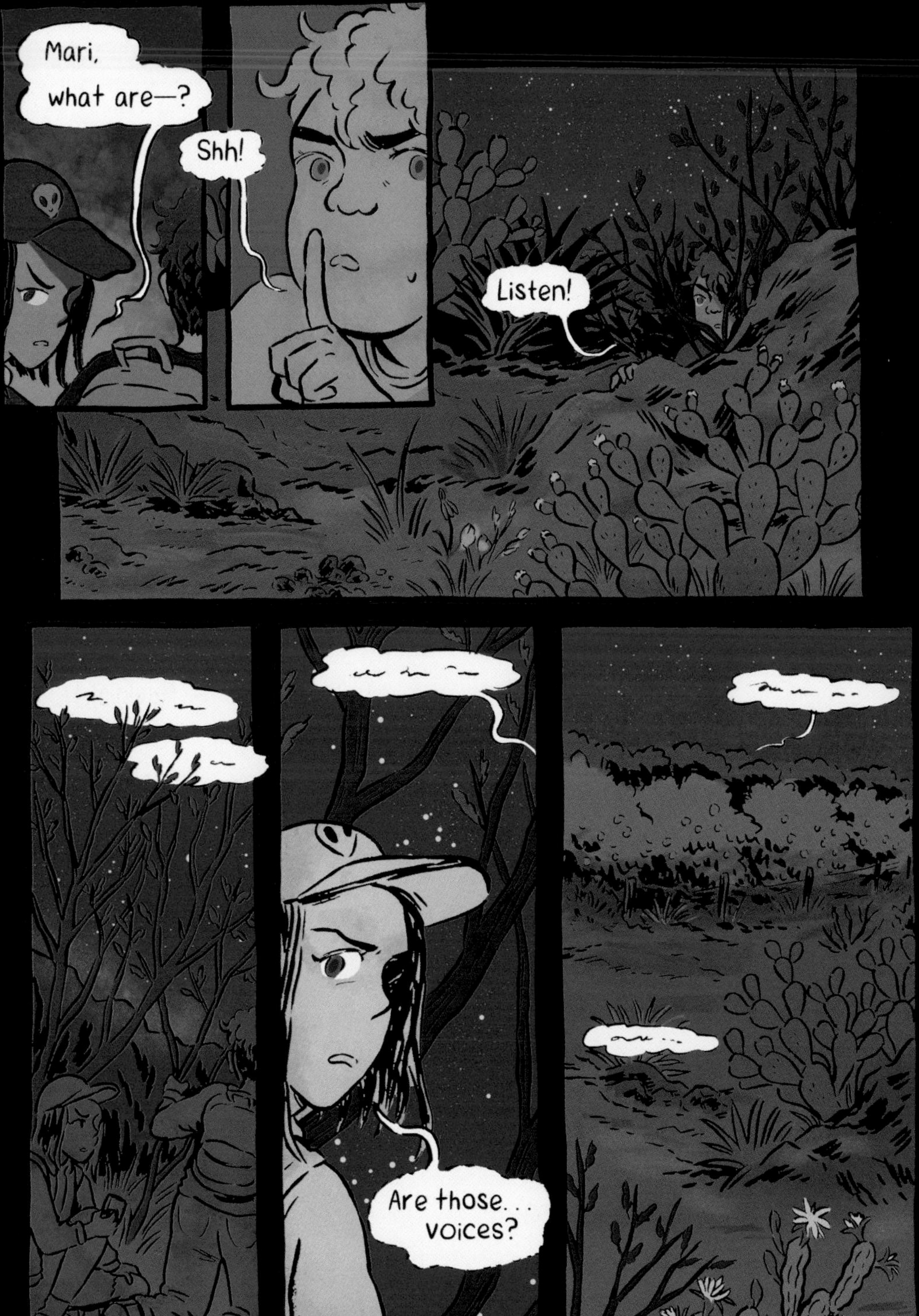
Mari, what are—?
Shh!
Listen!
Are those... voices?

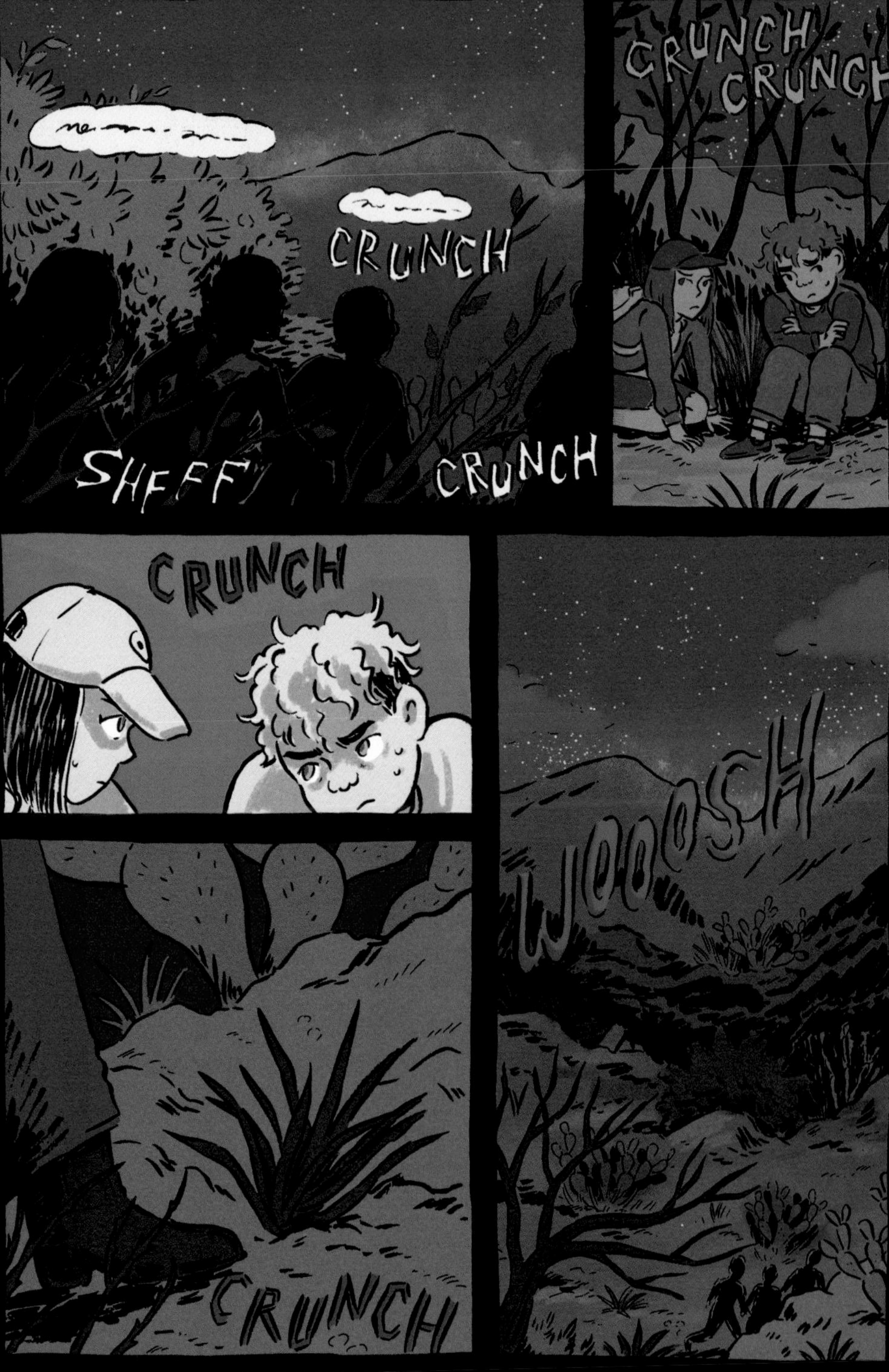
CRUNCH
SHFFF
CRUNCH
CRUNCH
CRUNCH
CRUNCH
CRUNCH
WOOOOSH

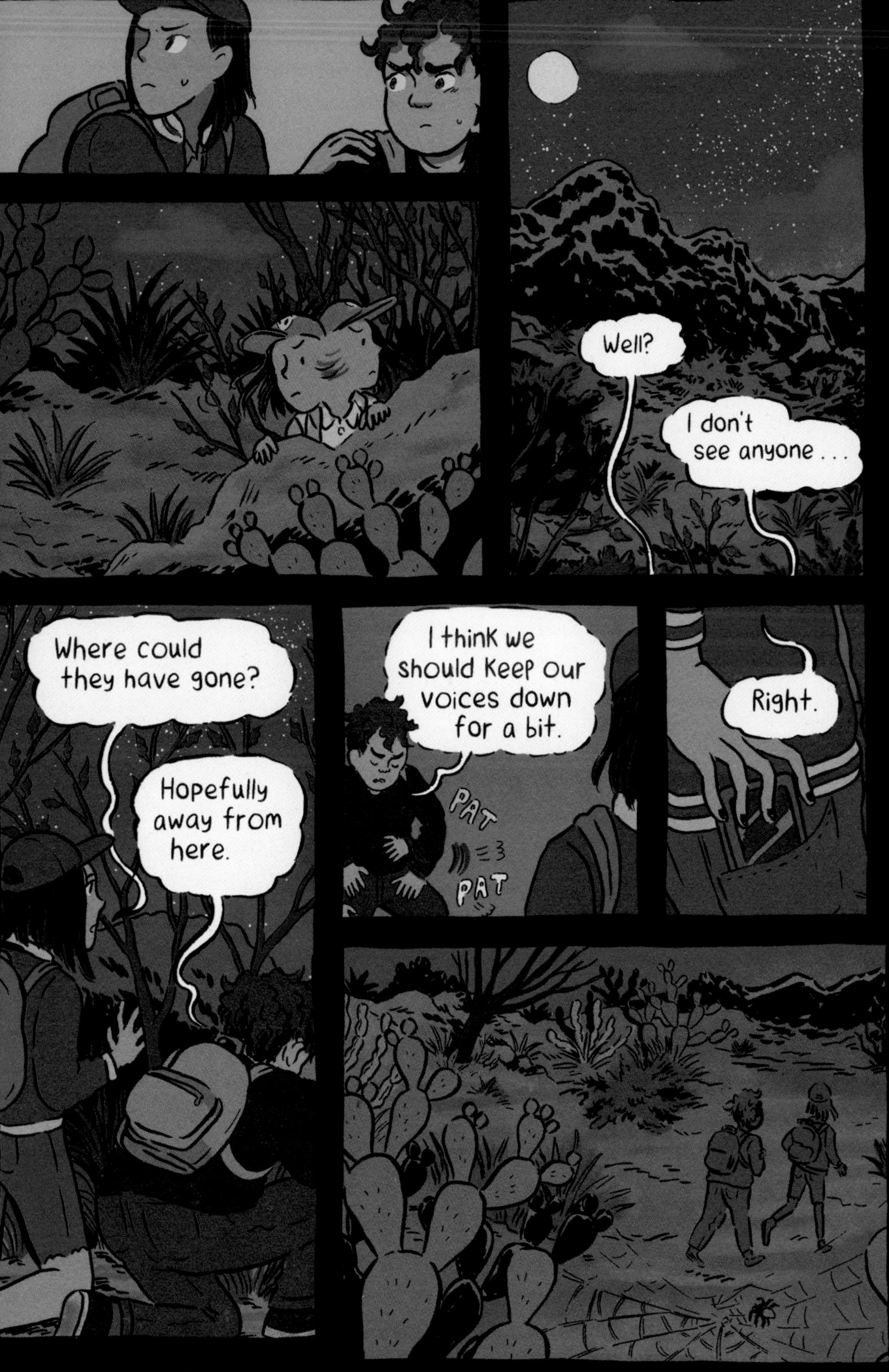
Well?
I don't see anyone . . .
Where could they have gone?
Hopefully away from here.
I think we should keep our voices down for a bit.
PAT
PAT
Right.

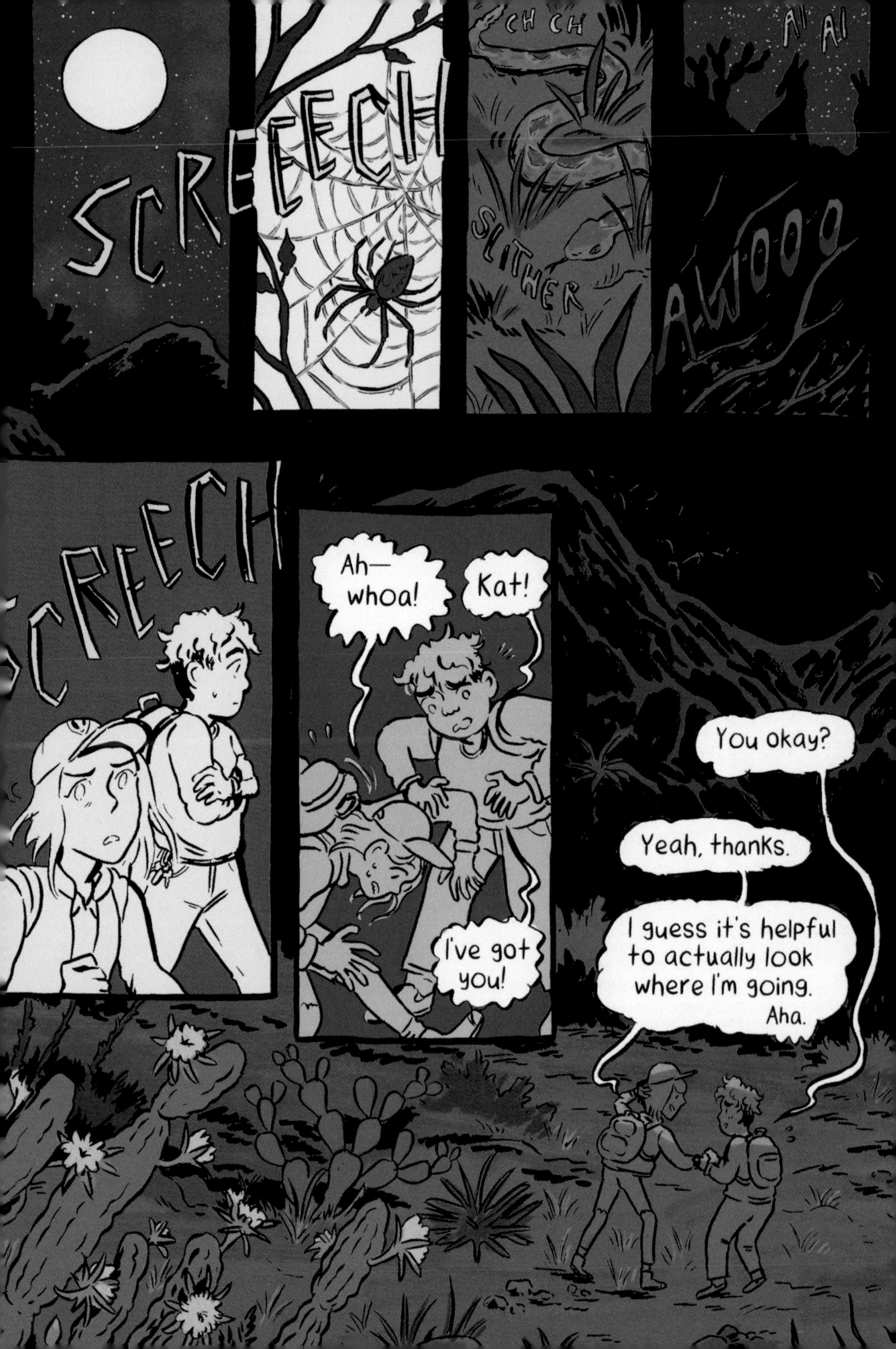
SCREEECH
CH CH
SLITHER
AI AI
AWOOOO
SCREECH
Ah—whoa!
Kat!
I've got you!
You okay?
Yeah, thanks.
I guess it's helpful to actually look where I'm going. Aha.

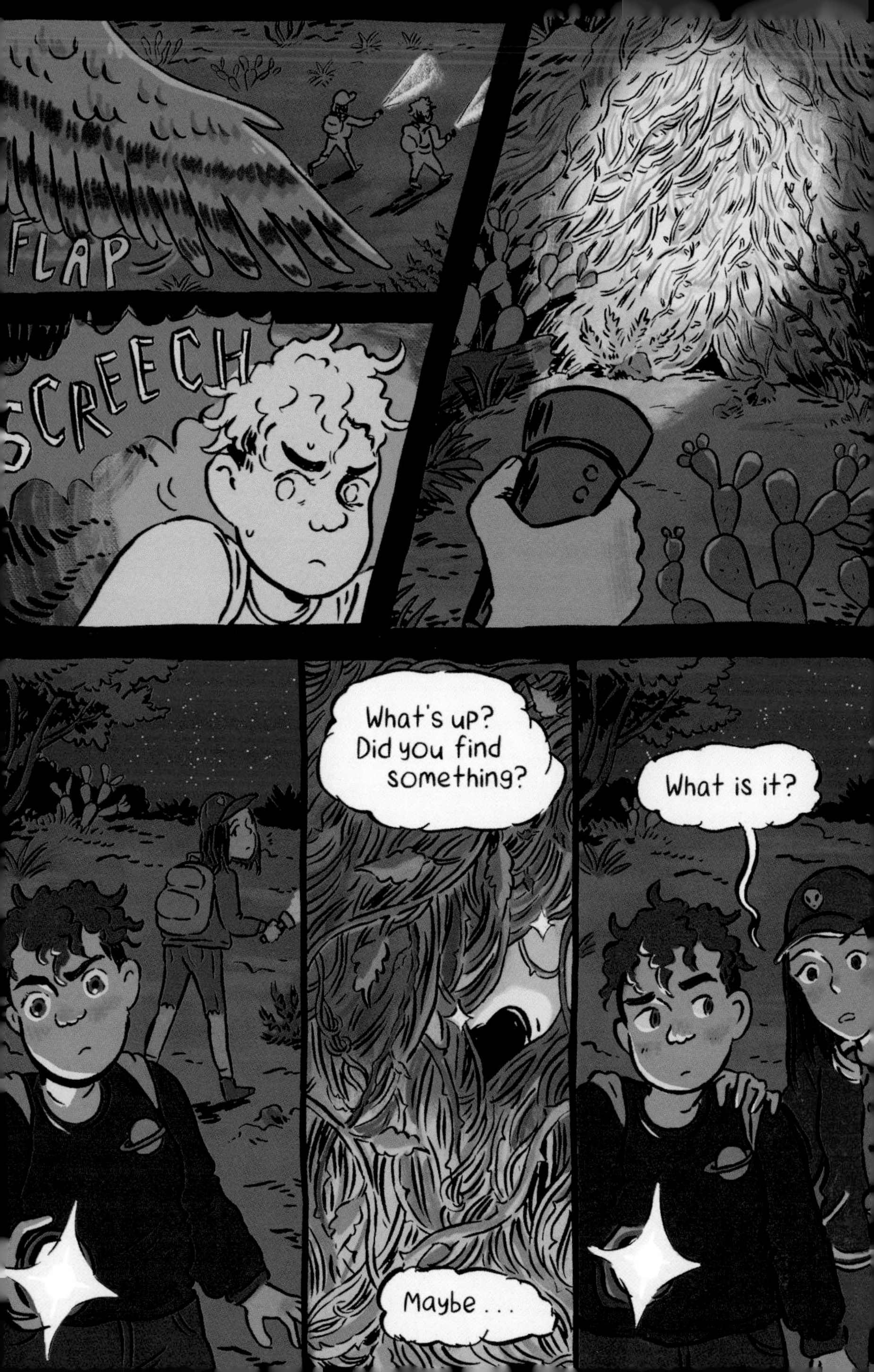
FLAP
SCREECH
What's up? Did you find something?
Maybe . . .
What is it?

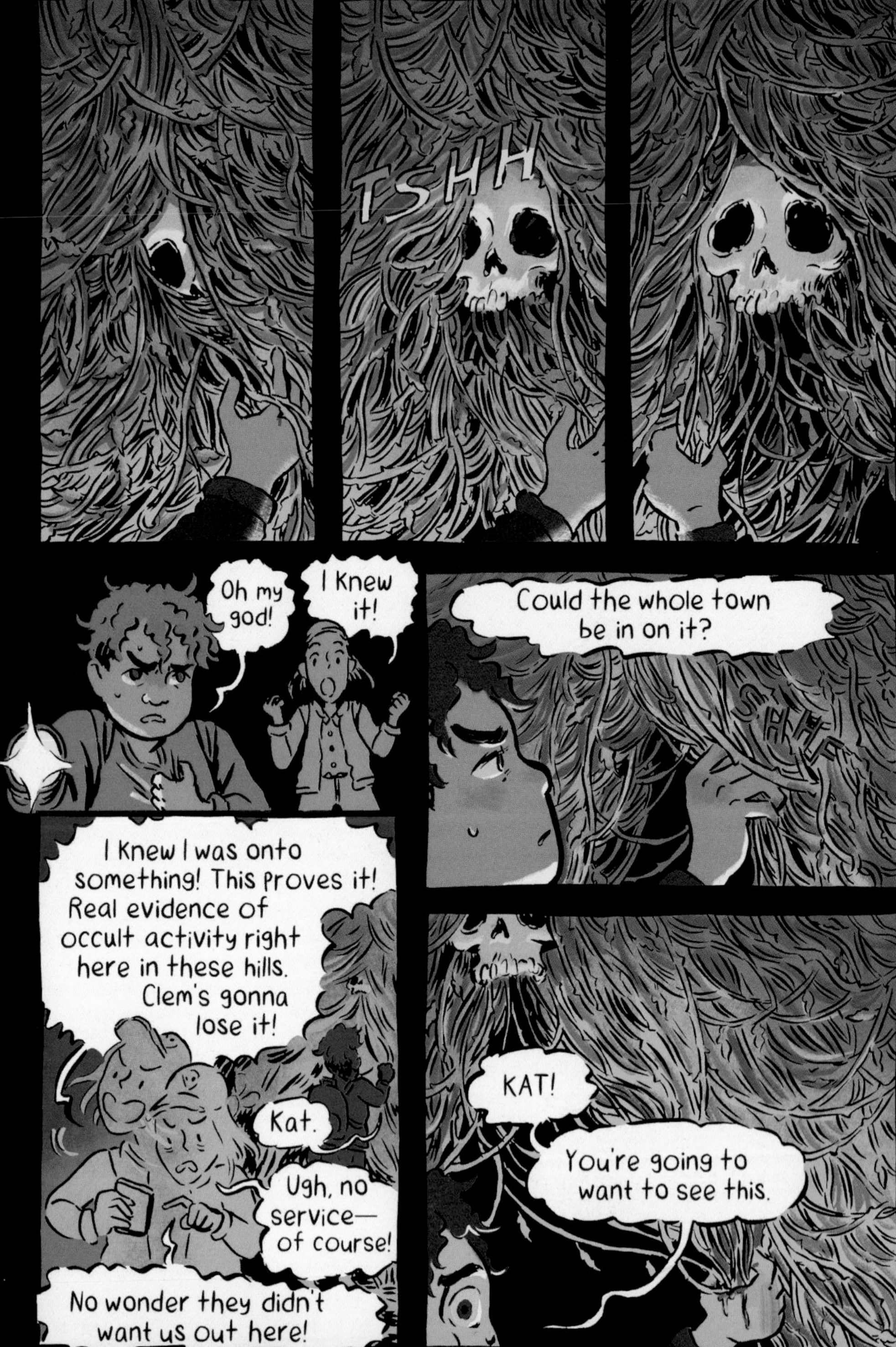
TSHH
Oh my god!
I Knew it!
Could the whole town be in on it?
SHHH
I Knew I was onto something! This proves it! Real evidence of occult activity right here in these hills. Clem's gonna lose it!
Kat.
Ugh, no service—of course!
No wonder they didn't want us out here!
KAT!
You're going to want to see this.

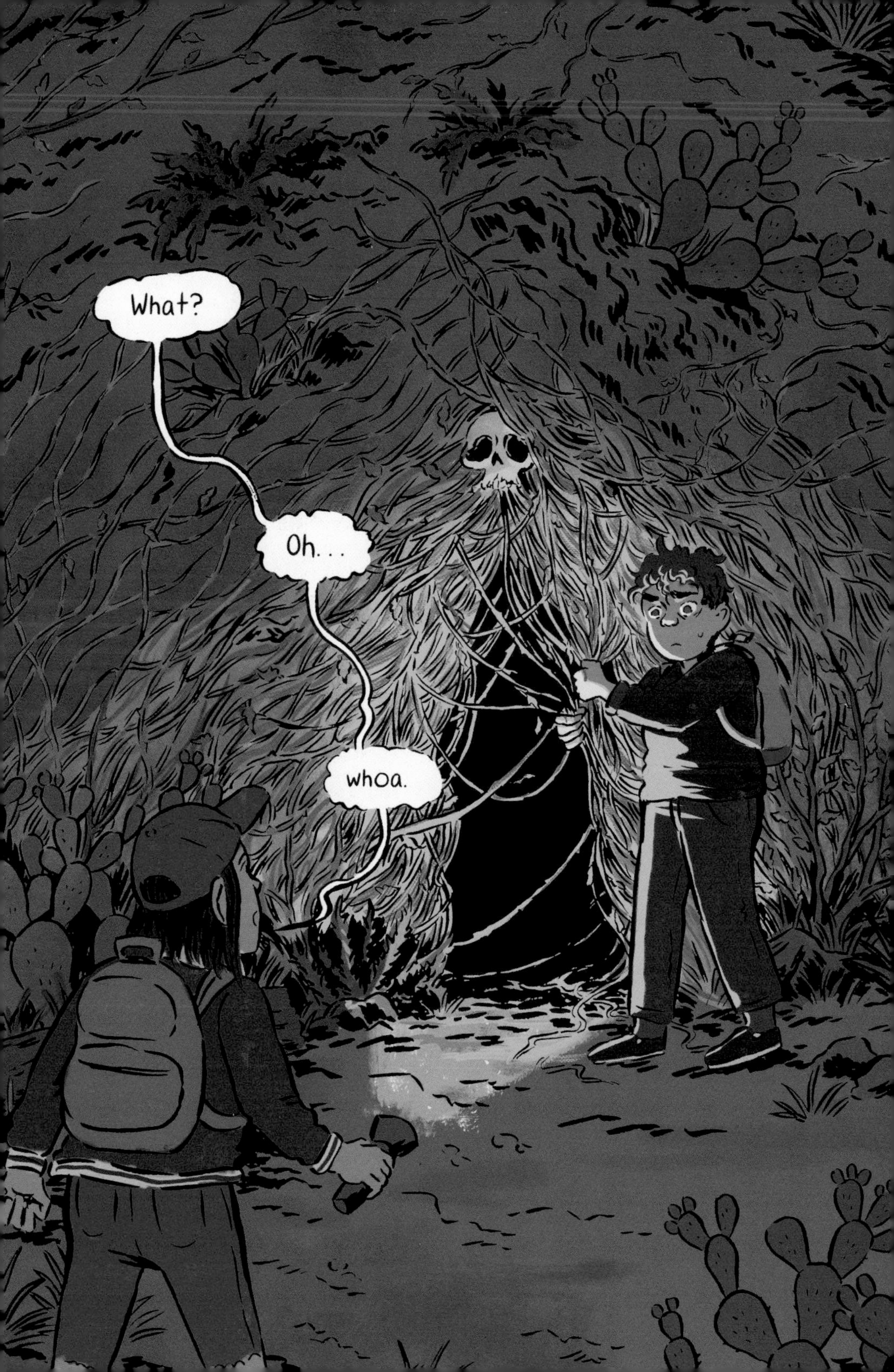
What?
Oh. . .
whoa.

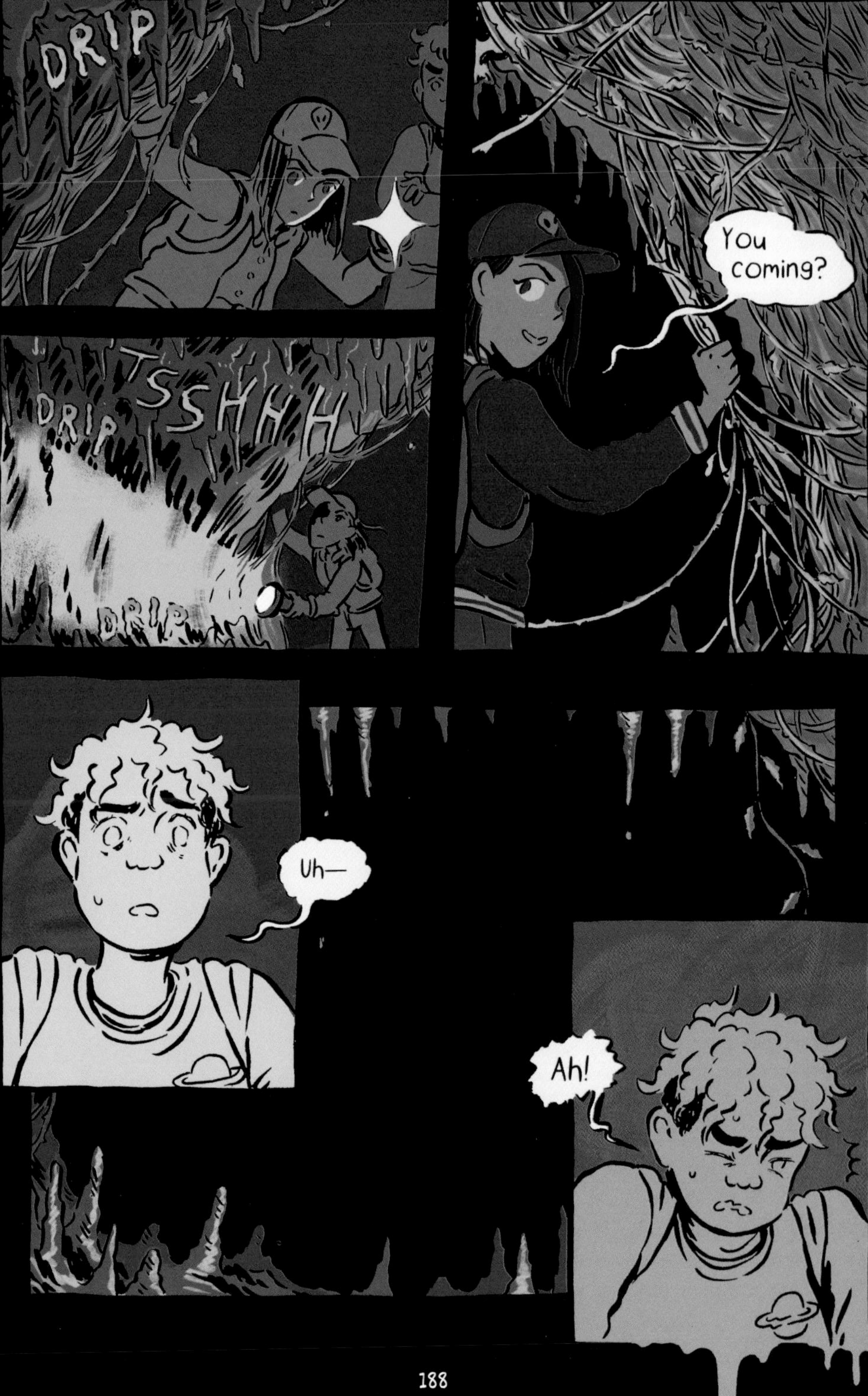
DRIP
TSSHHH
DRIP
DRIP
You coming?
Uh—
Ah!

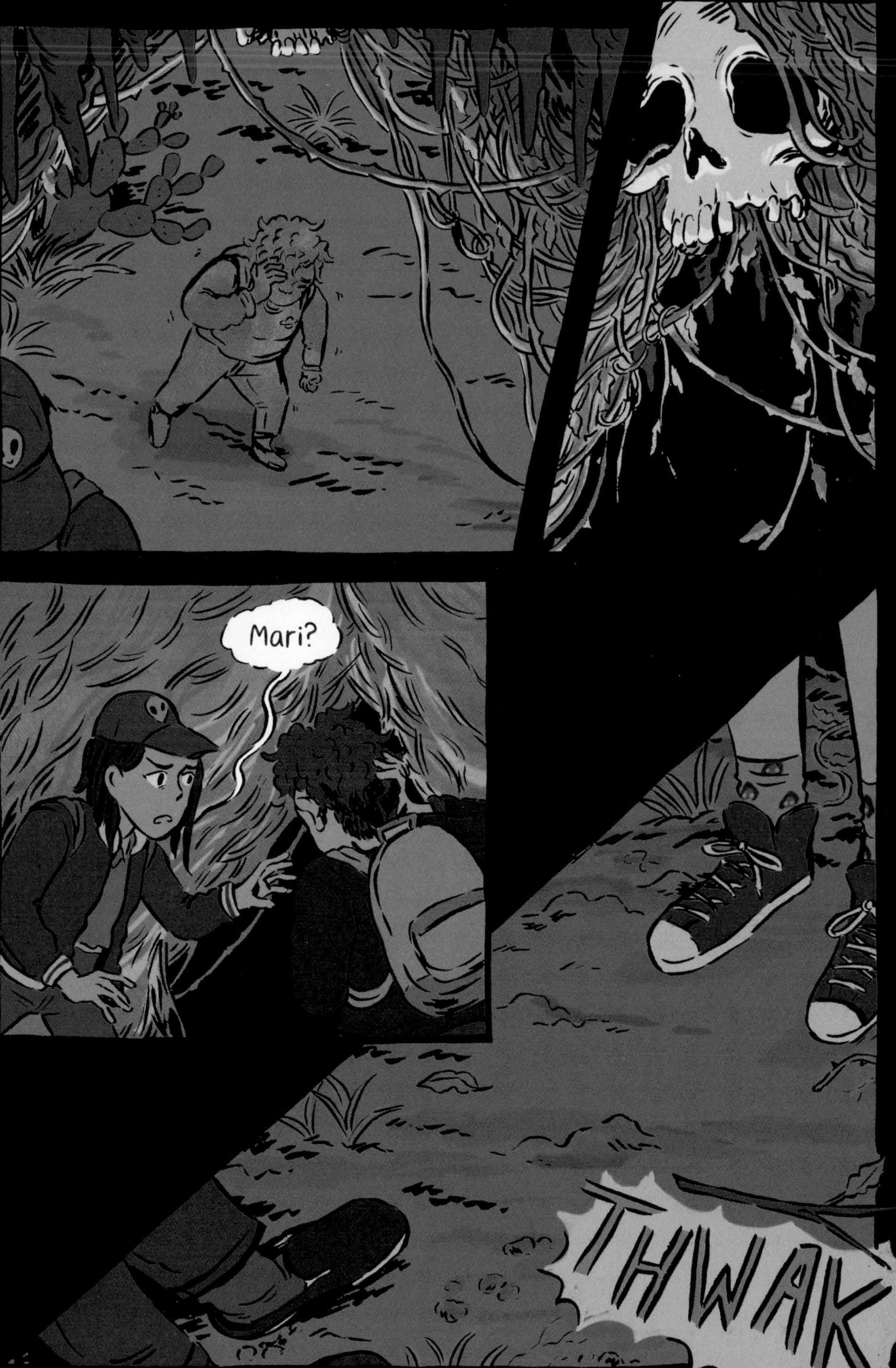
Mari?
THWAK

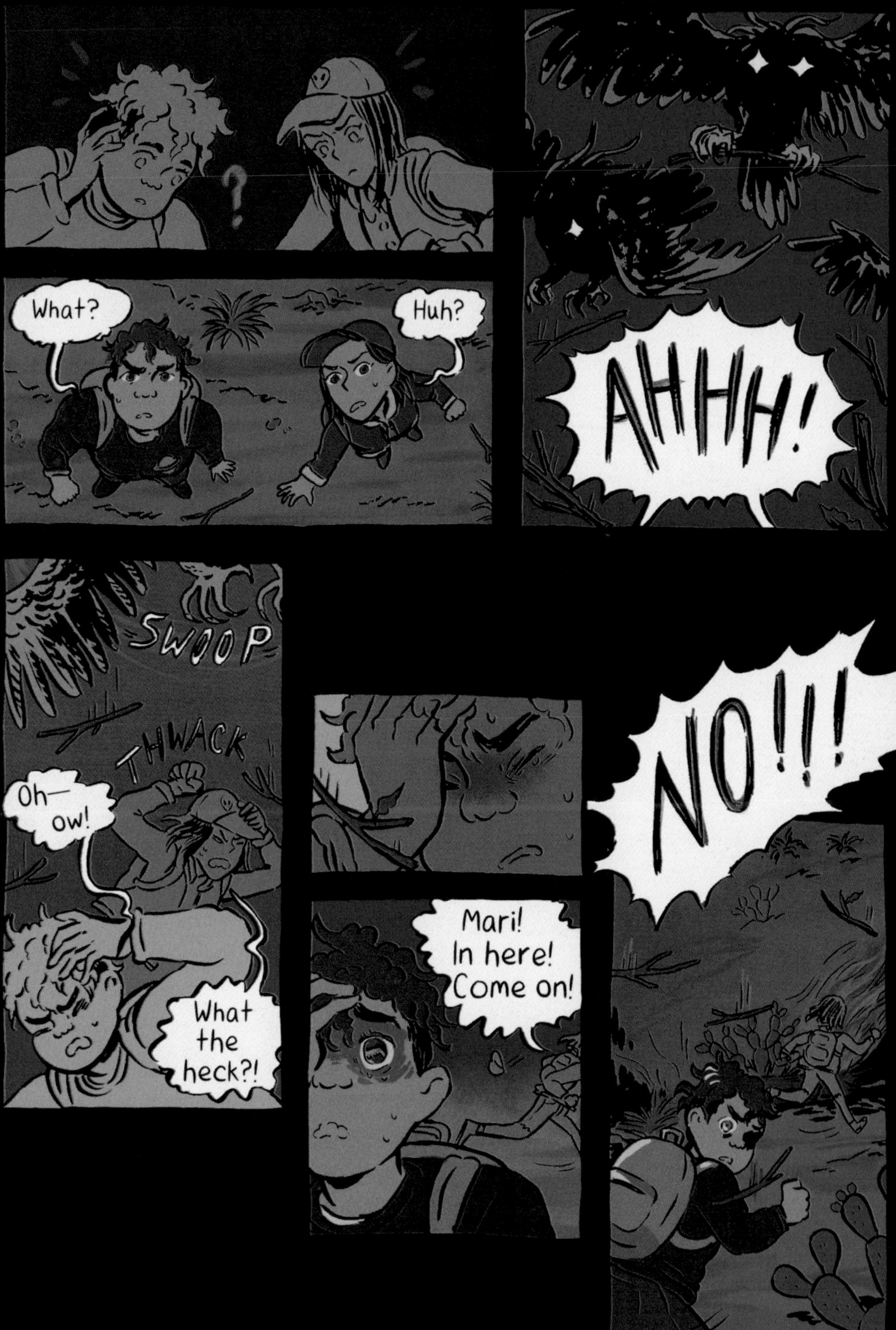
What?
Huh?
AHHH!
SWOOP
THWACK
Oh— ow!
What the heck?!
NO!!!
Mari! In here! Come on!

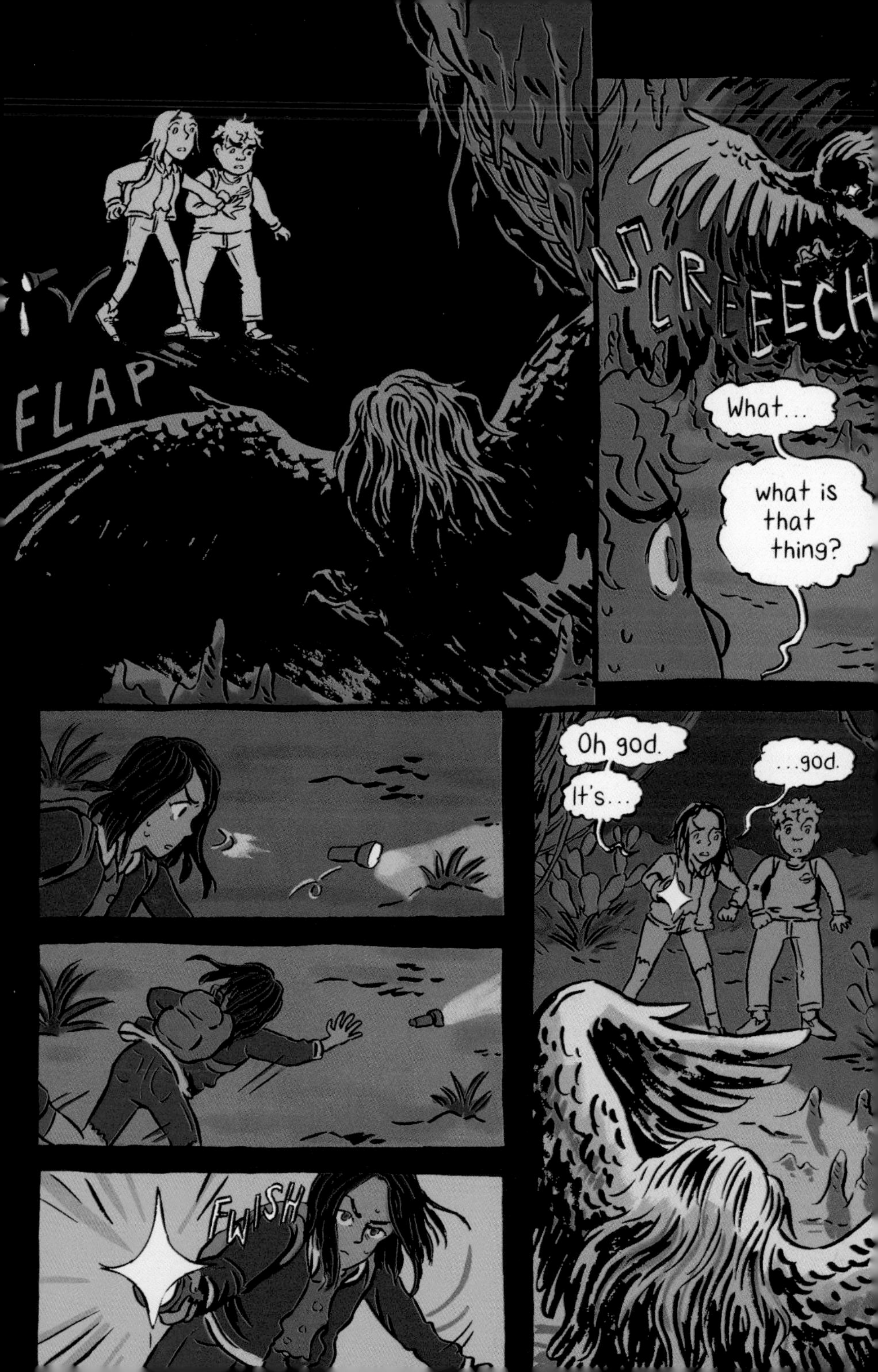
FLAP
SCREEECH
What...
what is that thing?
Oh god.
It's...
...god.
FWISH

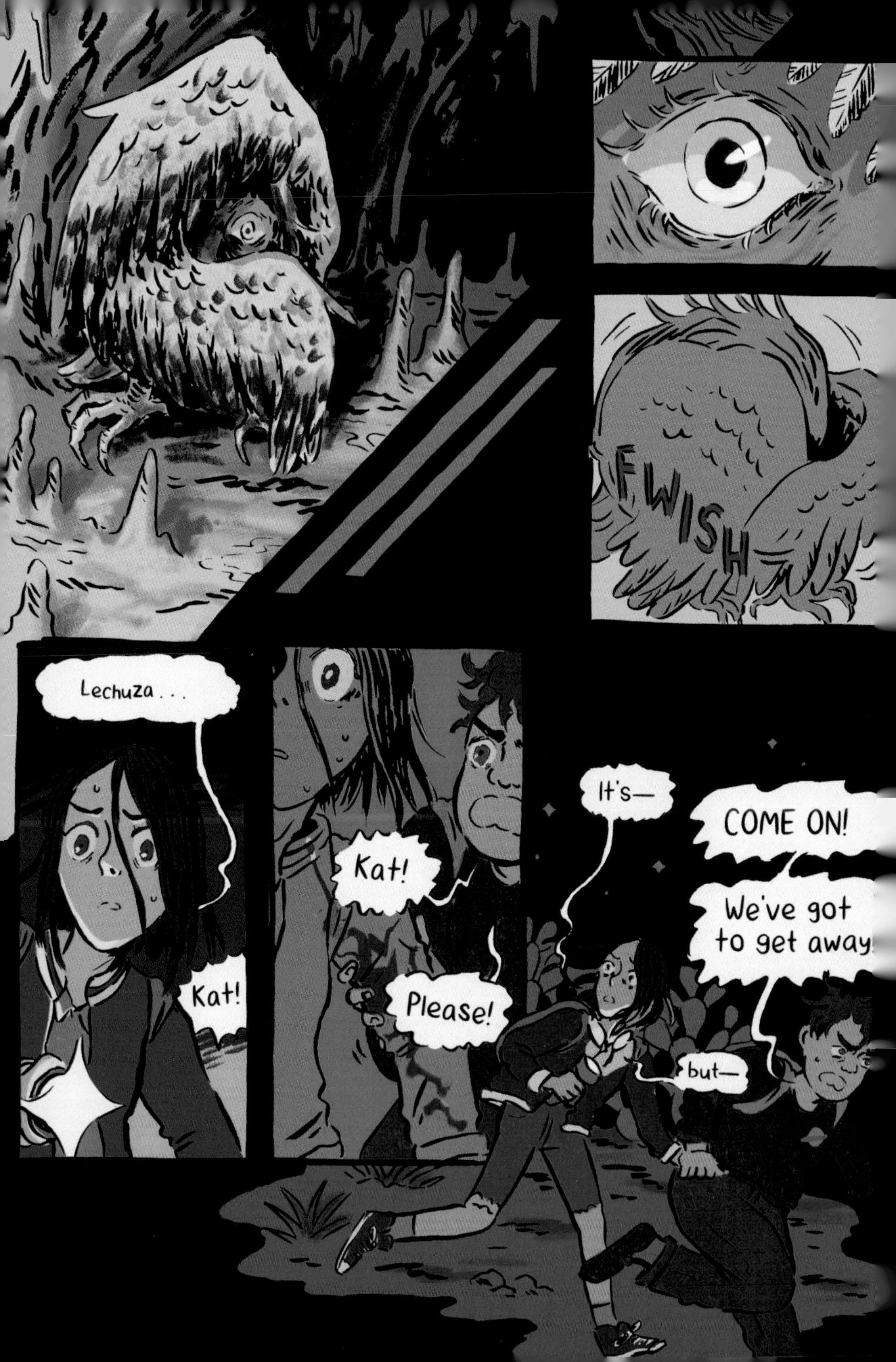
FWISH
Lechuza . . .
Kat!
Kat!
Please!
It's—
but—
COME ON!
We've got to get away!

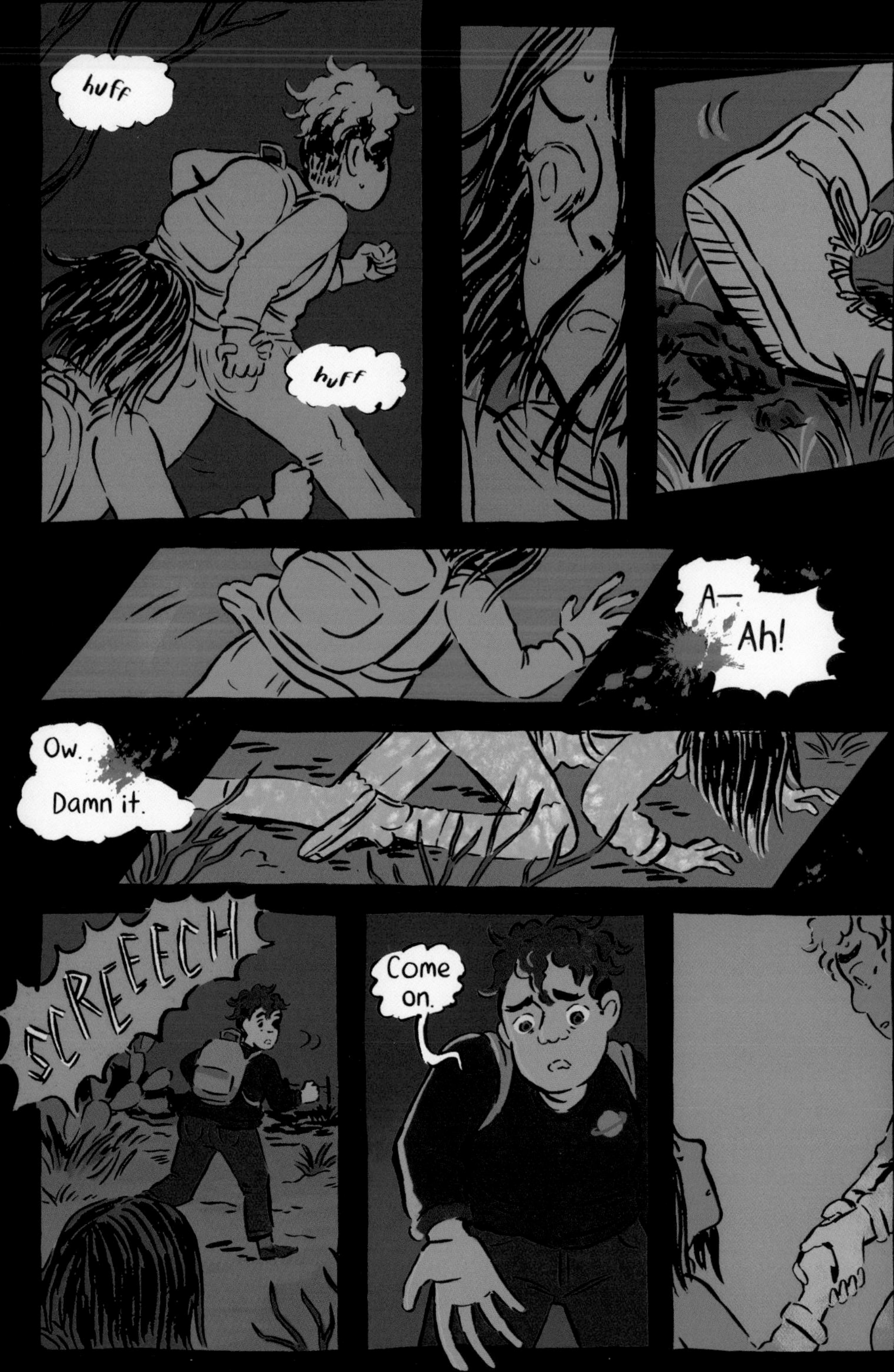
huff
huff
A—
Ah!
Ow.
Damn it.
SCREEECH
Come on.

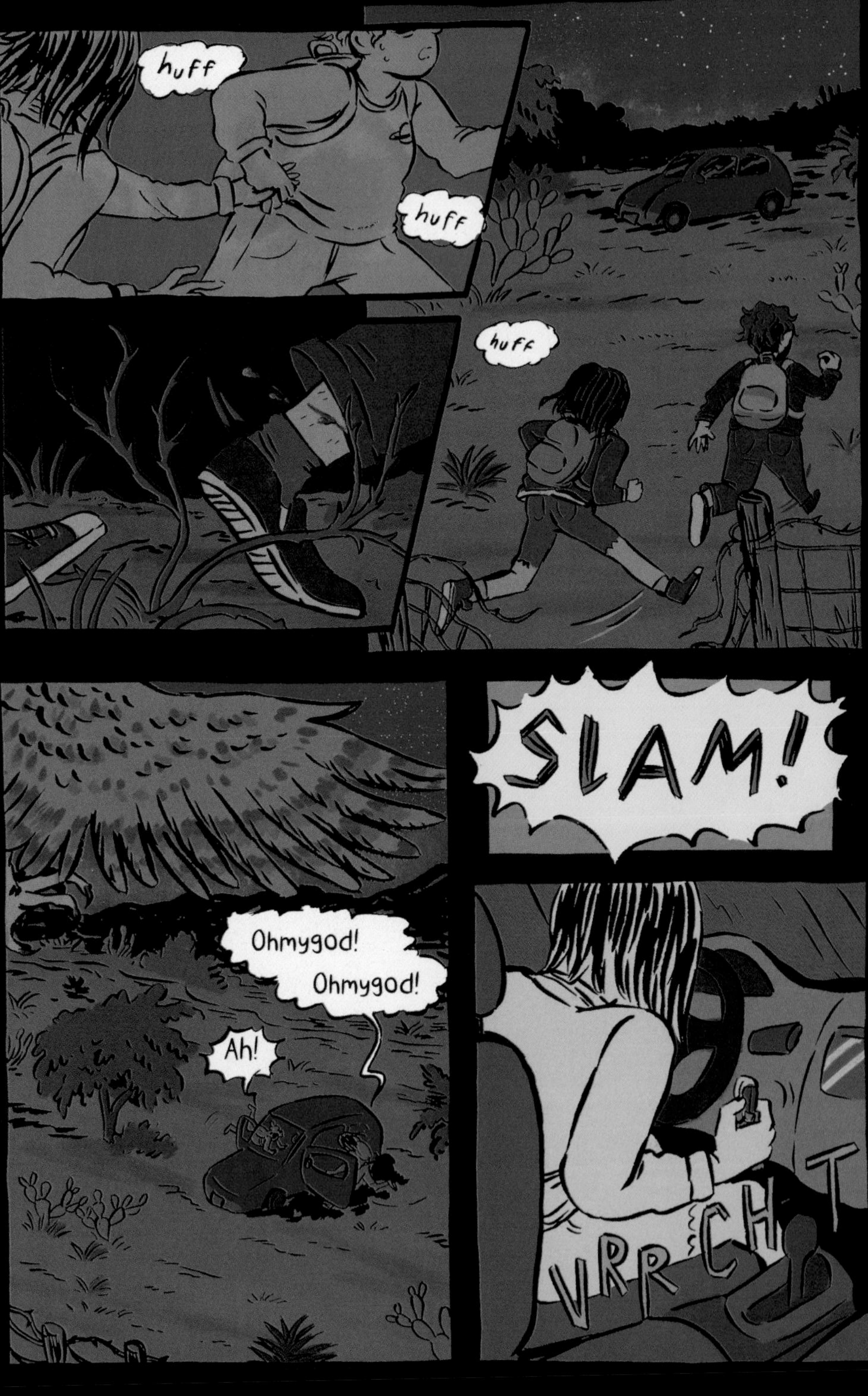
huff
huff
huff
SLAM!
Ohmygod!
Ohmygod!
Ah!
VRRCHT

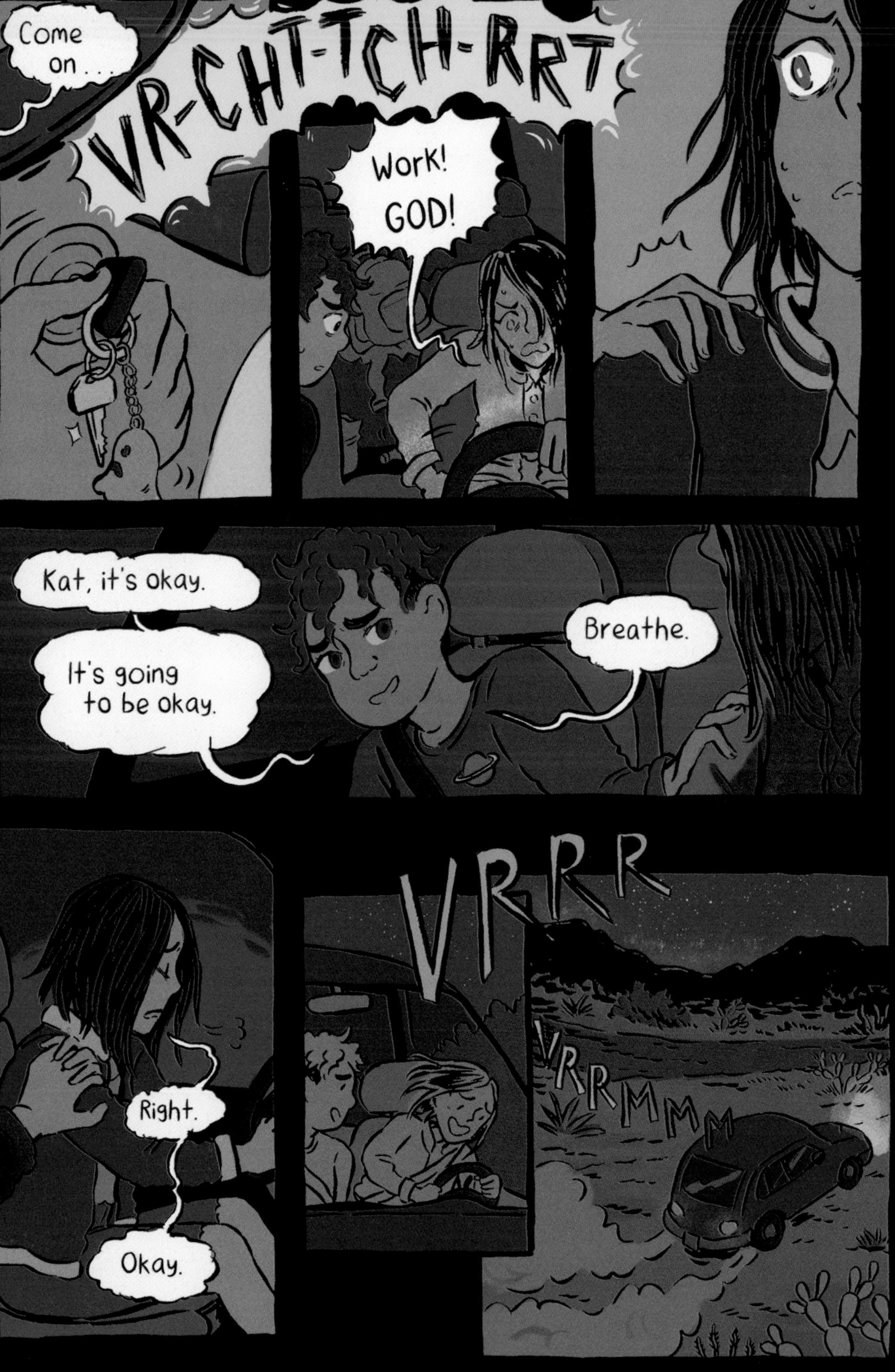
Come on . . .
VR-CHT-TCH-RRT
Work! GOD!
Kat, it's okay.
It's going to be okay.
Breathe.
Right.
Okay.
VRRR
VRRRMMM

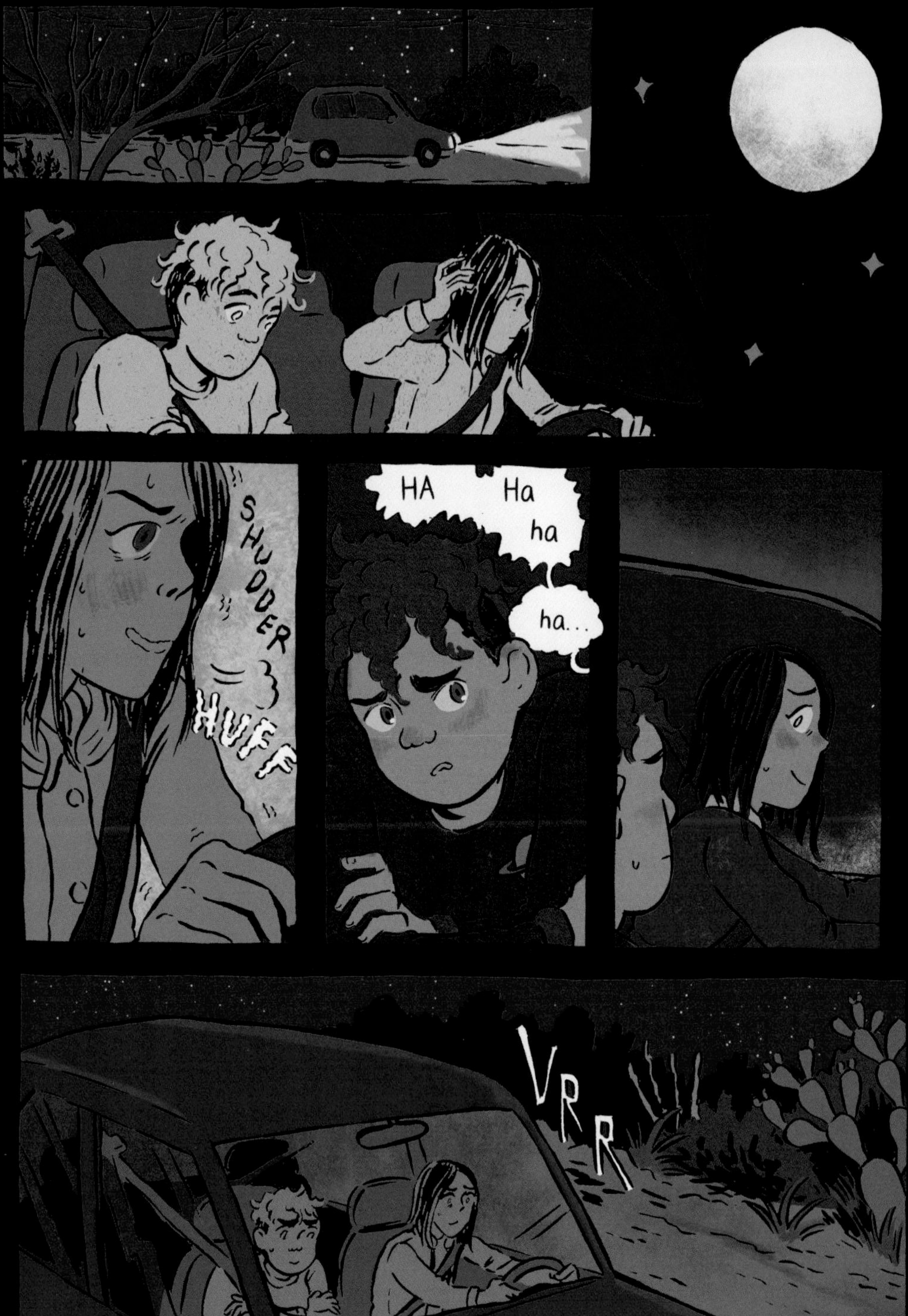
SHUDDER
HUFF
HA
Ha
ha
ha...
VRR

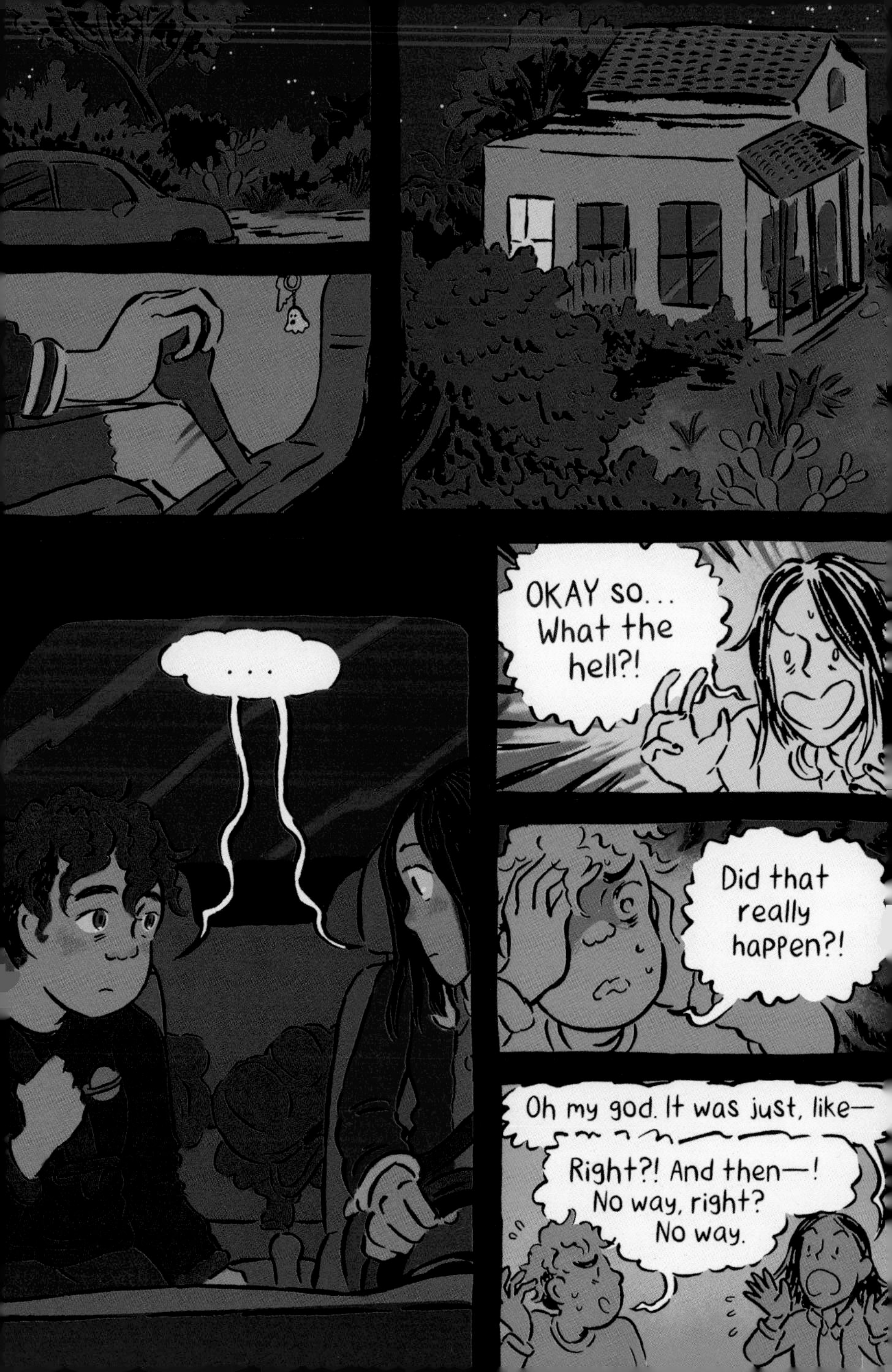
. . .
OKAY so... What the hell?!
Did that really happen?!
Oh my god. It was just, like—
Right?! And then—! No way, right? No way.

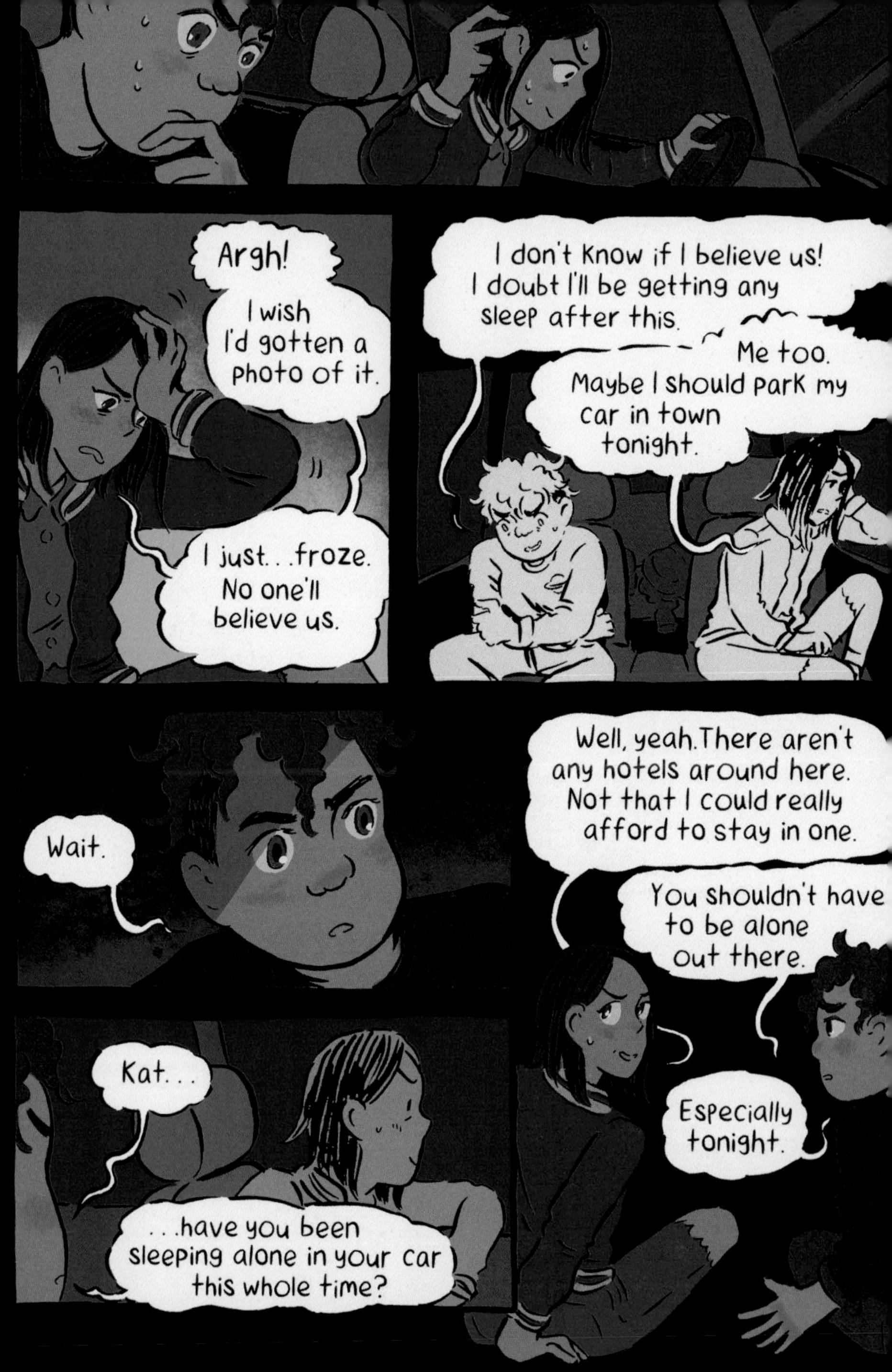
Argh!
I wish I'd gotten a photo of it.
I just. . .froze. No one'll believe us.
I don't know if I believe us! I doubt I'll be getting any sleep after this.
Me too. Maybe I should park my car in town tonight.
Wait.
Well, yeah.There aren't any hotels around here. Not that I could really afford to stay in one.
You shouldn't have to be alone out there.
Especially tonight.
Kat. . .
. . .have you been sleeping alone in your car this whole time?

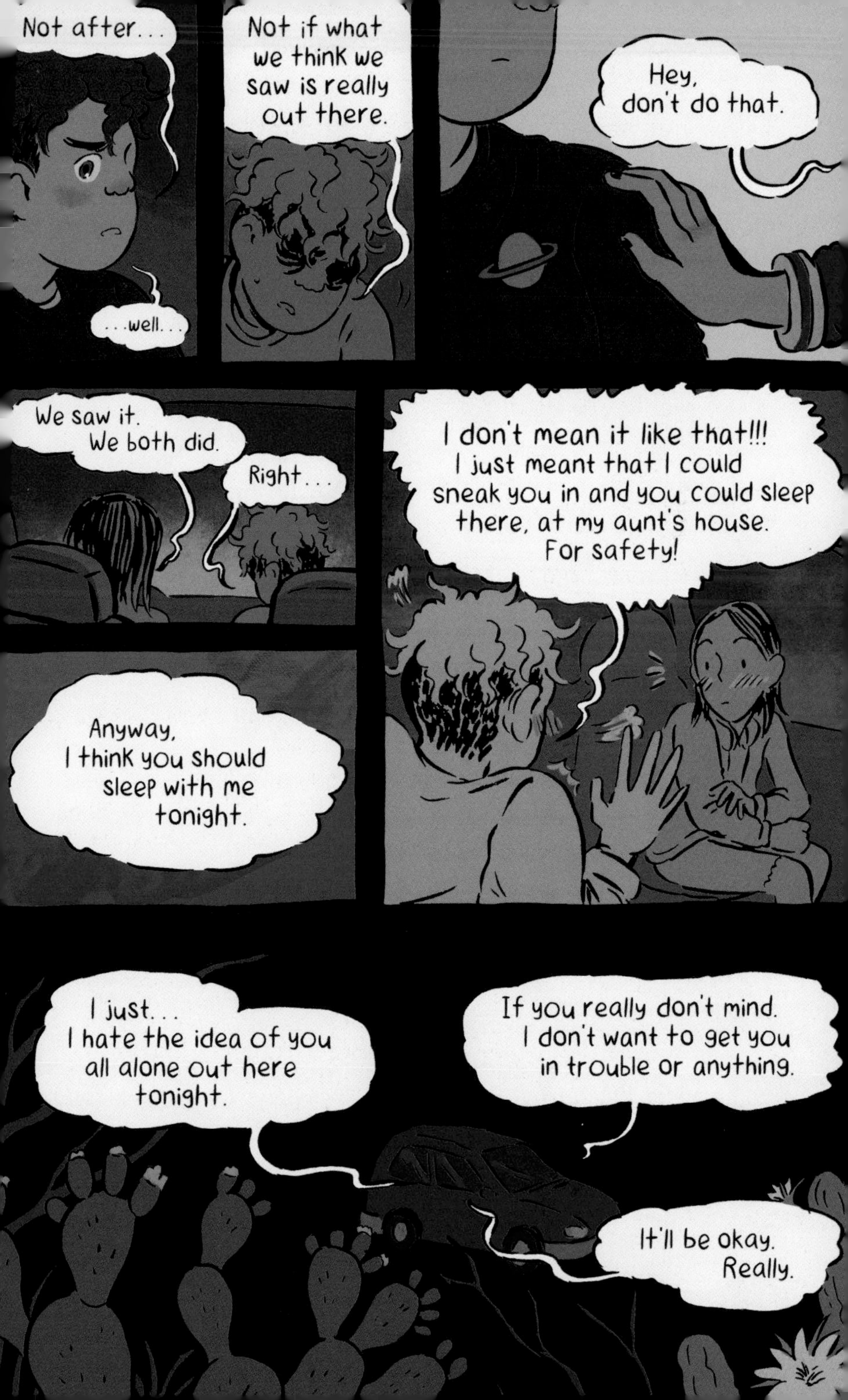
Not after...
...well...
Not if what we think we saw is really out there.
Hey, don't do that.
We saw it. We both did.
Right...
Anyway, I think you should sleep with me tonight.
I don't mean it like that!!! I just meant that I could sneak you in and you could sleep there, at my aunt's house. For safety!
I just... I hate the idea of you all alone out here tonight.
If you really don't mind. I don't want to get you in trouble or anything.
It'll be okay. Really.

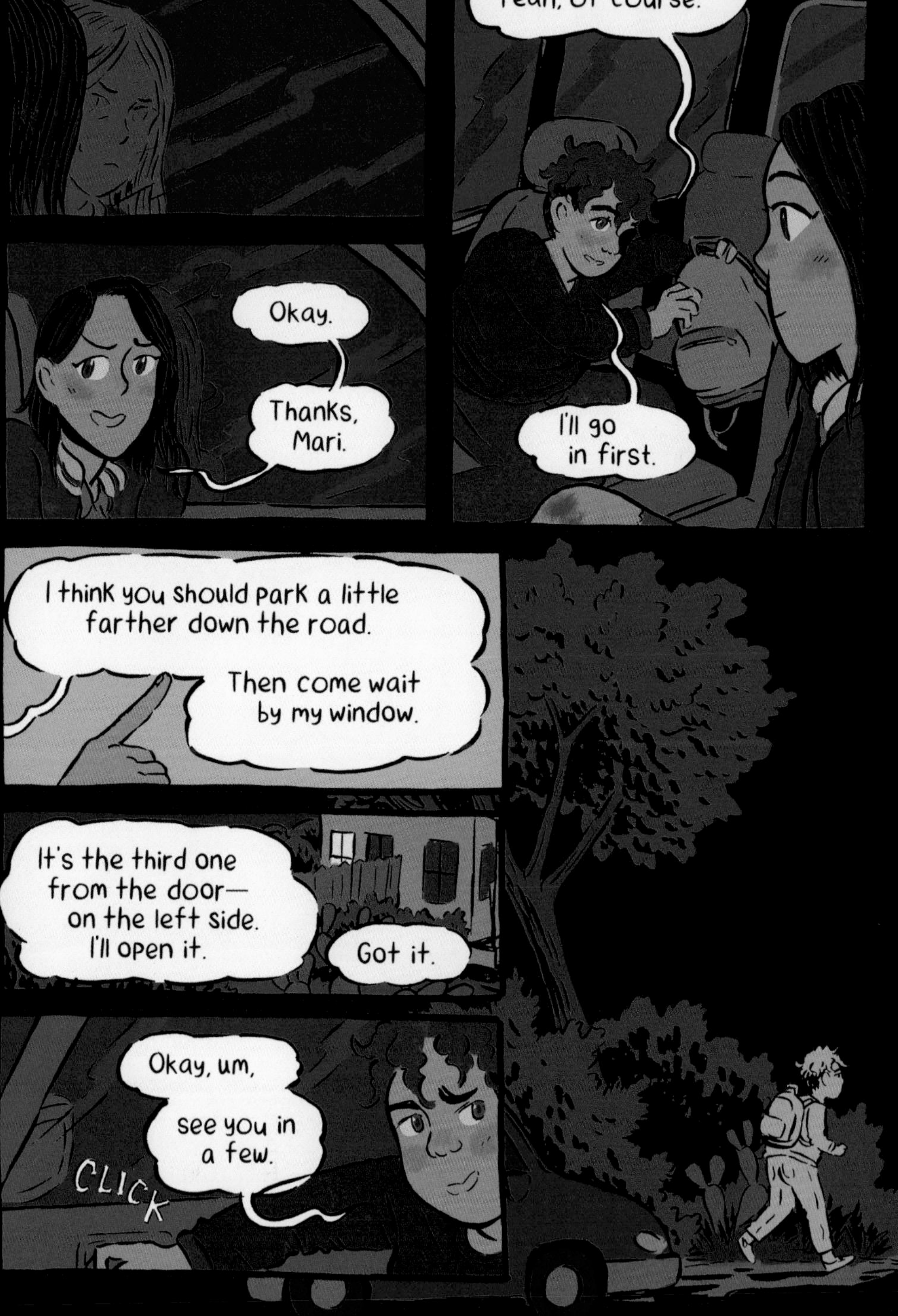
Okay.
Thanks, Mari.
I'll go in first.
I think you should park a little farther down the road.
Then come wait by my window.
It's the third one from the door— on the left side. I'll open it.
Got it.
Okay, um,
see you in a few.
CLICK

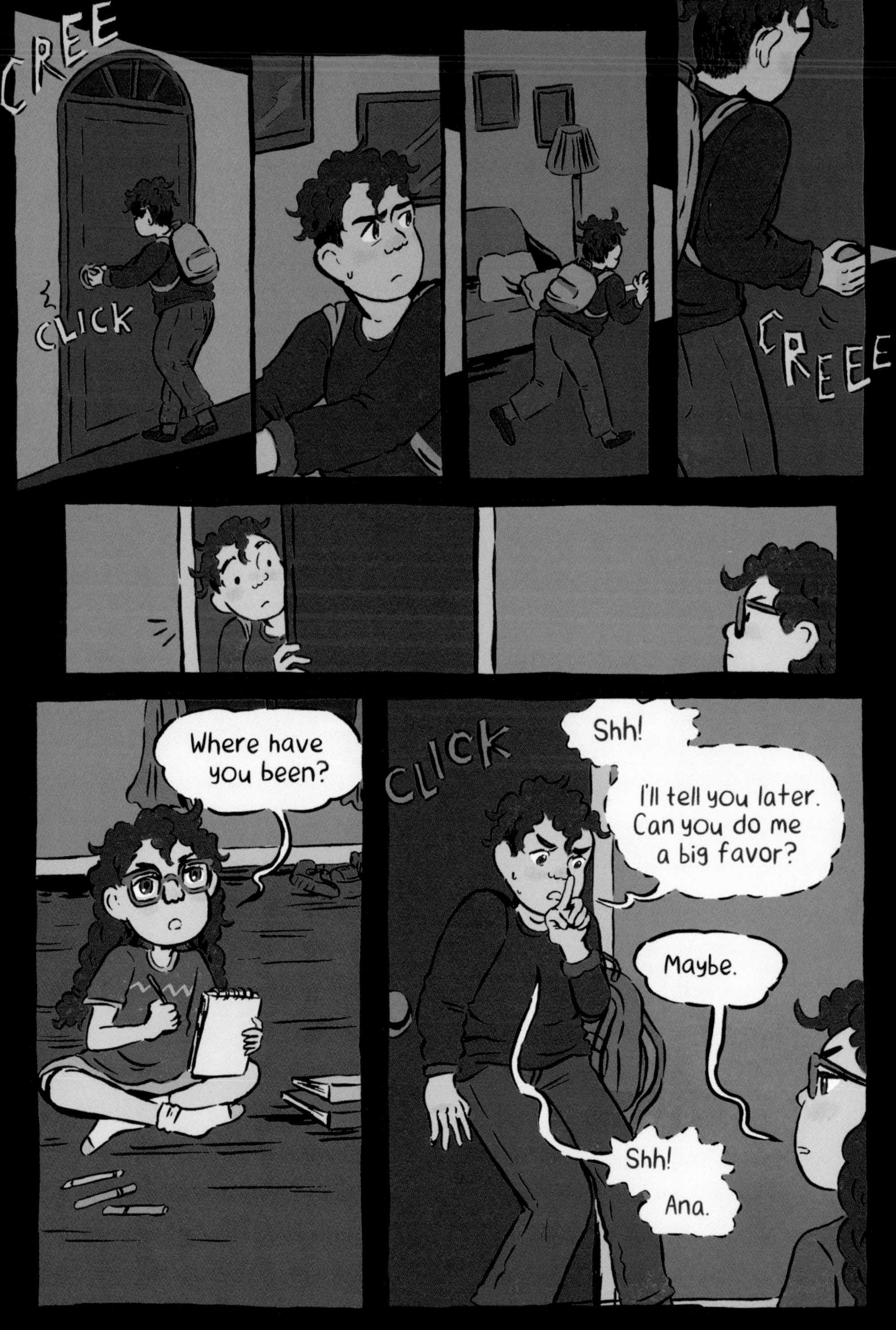
CREE
CLICK
CREEE
Where have you been?
CLICK
Shh!
I'll tell you later. Can you do me a big favor?
Maybe.
Shh!
Ana.

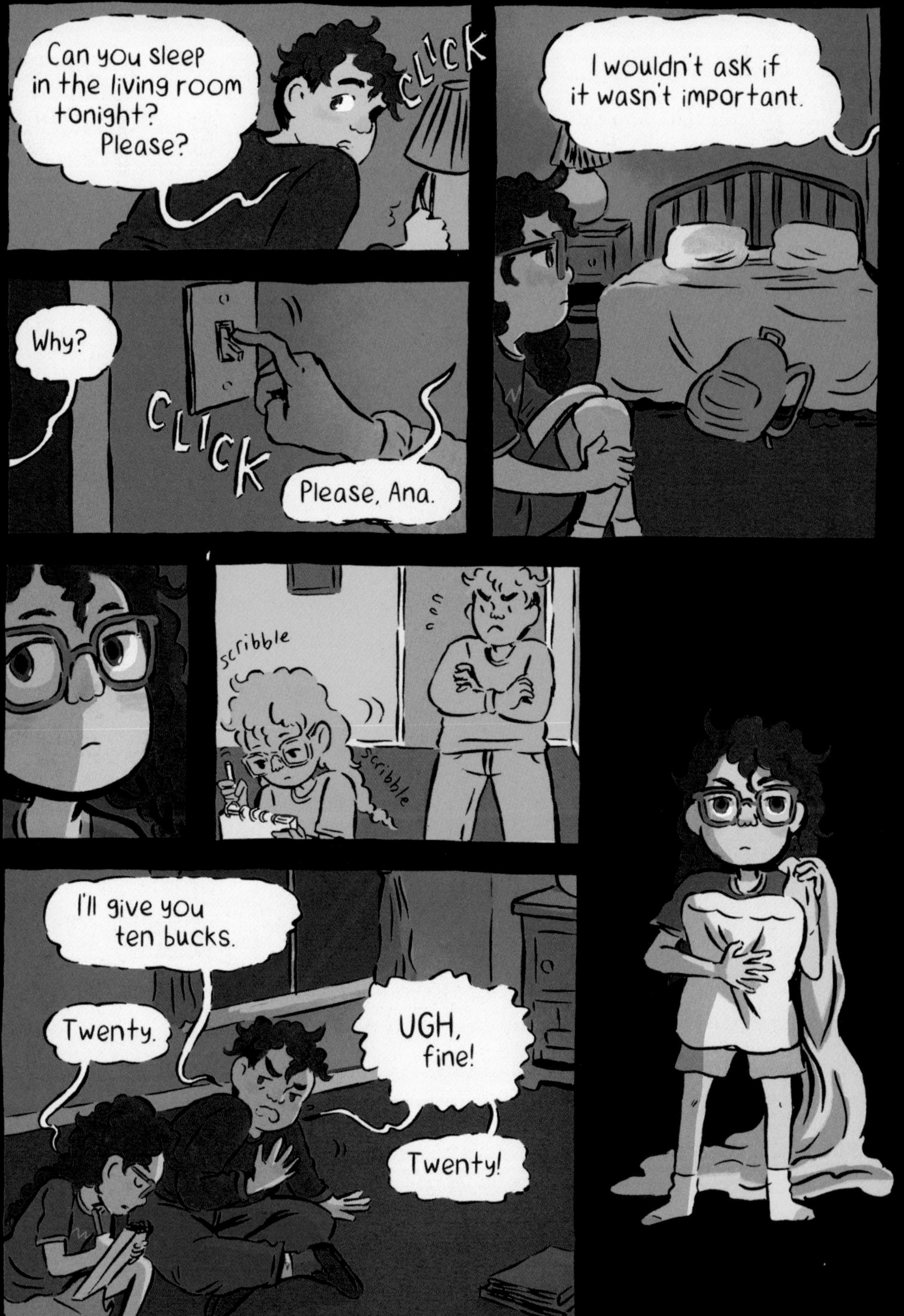
Can you sleep in the living room tonight? Please?
CLICK
I wouldn't ask if it wasn't important.
Why?
CLICK
Please, Ana.
scribble
scribble
I'll give you ten bucks.
Twenty.
UGH, fine!
Twenty!

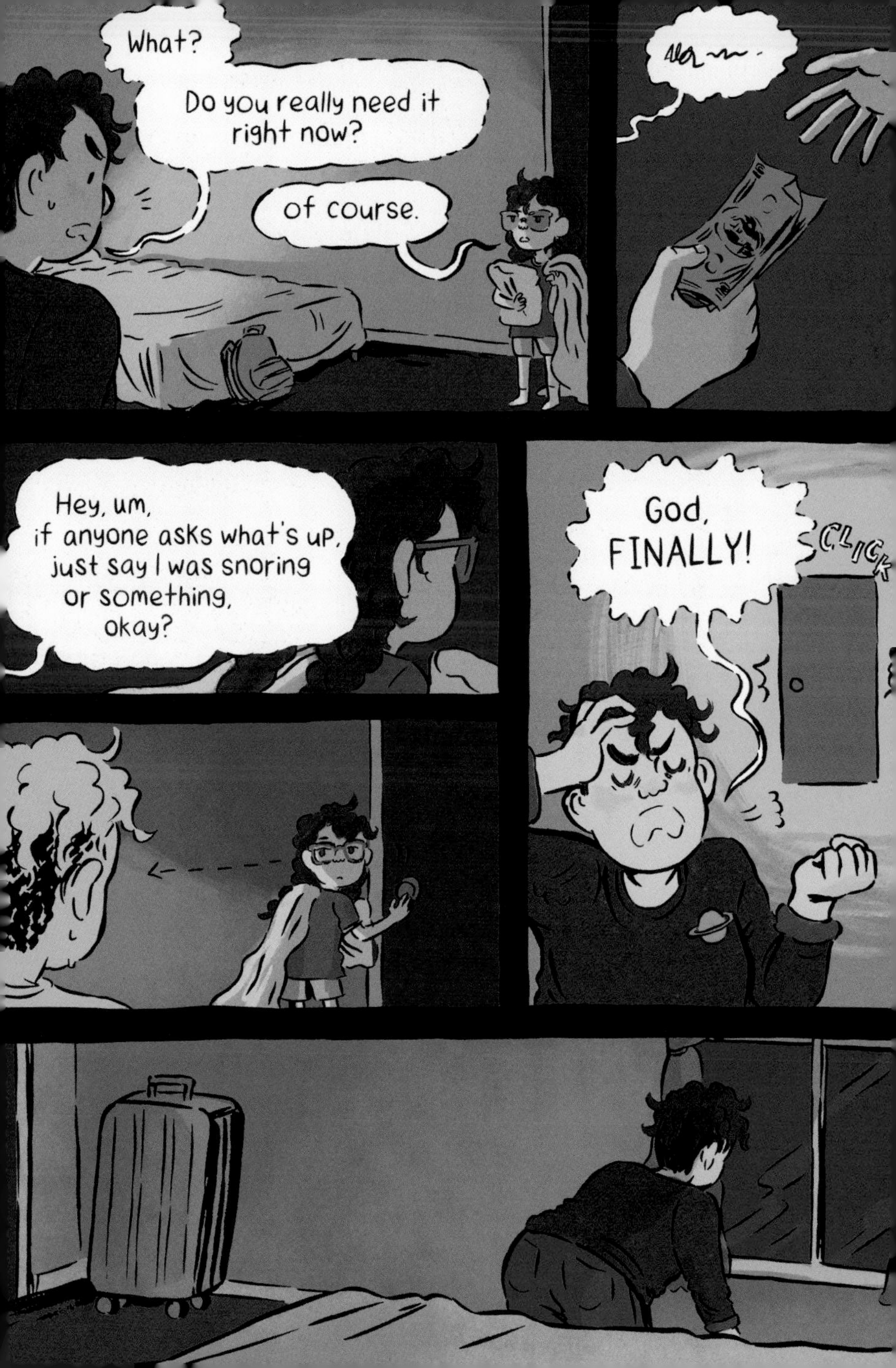

What?
Do you really need it right now?
of course.
Hey, um, if anyone asks what's up, just say I was snoring or something, okay?
God, FINALLY!
CLICK

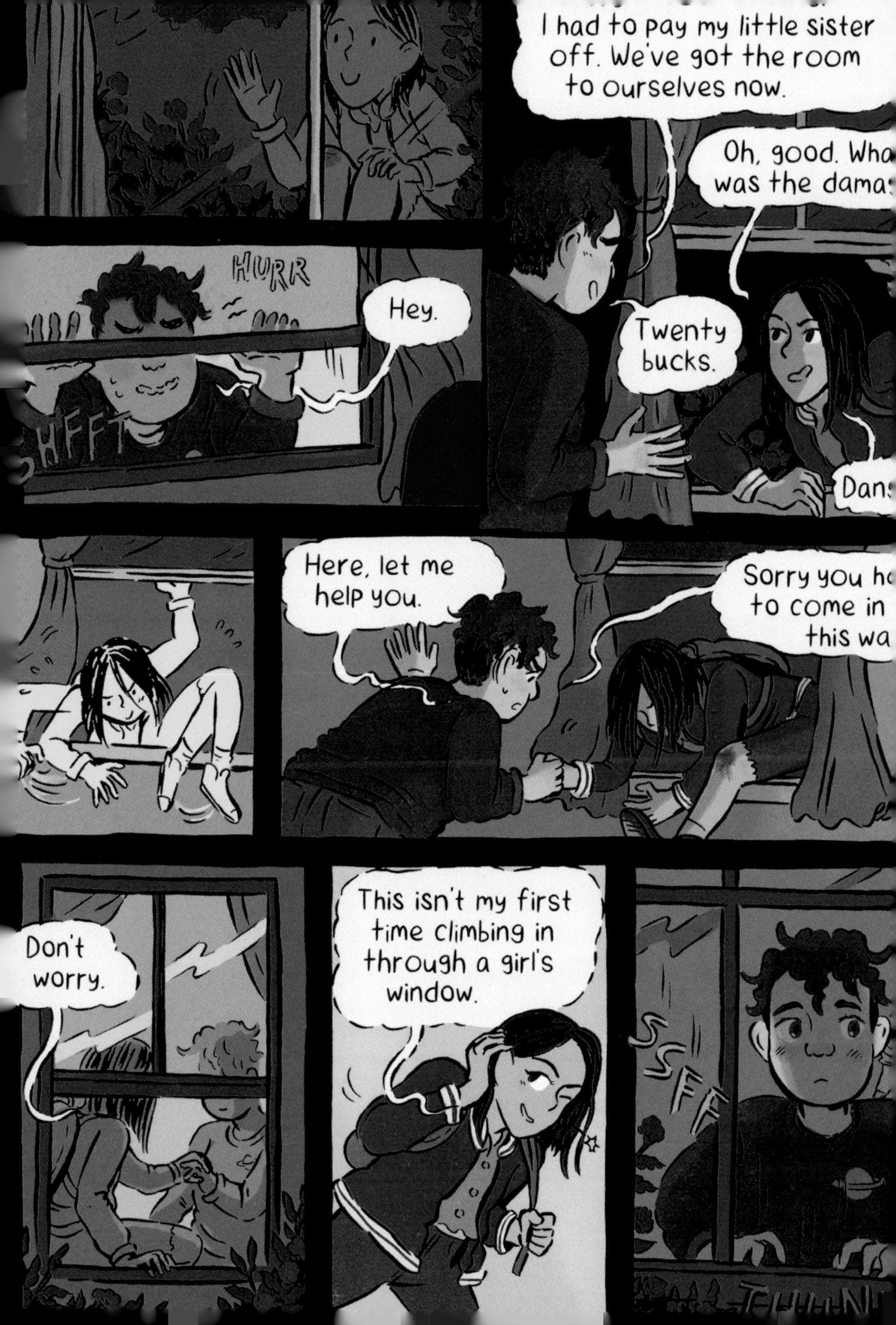
HURR
SHFFT
Hey.
I had to pay my little sister off. We've got the room to ourselves now.
Oh, good. Wha
was the dama
Twenty bucks.
Dan
Here, let me help you.
Sorry you h
to come in
this wa
Don't worry.
This isn't my first time climbing in through a girl's window.
SFF

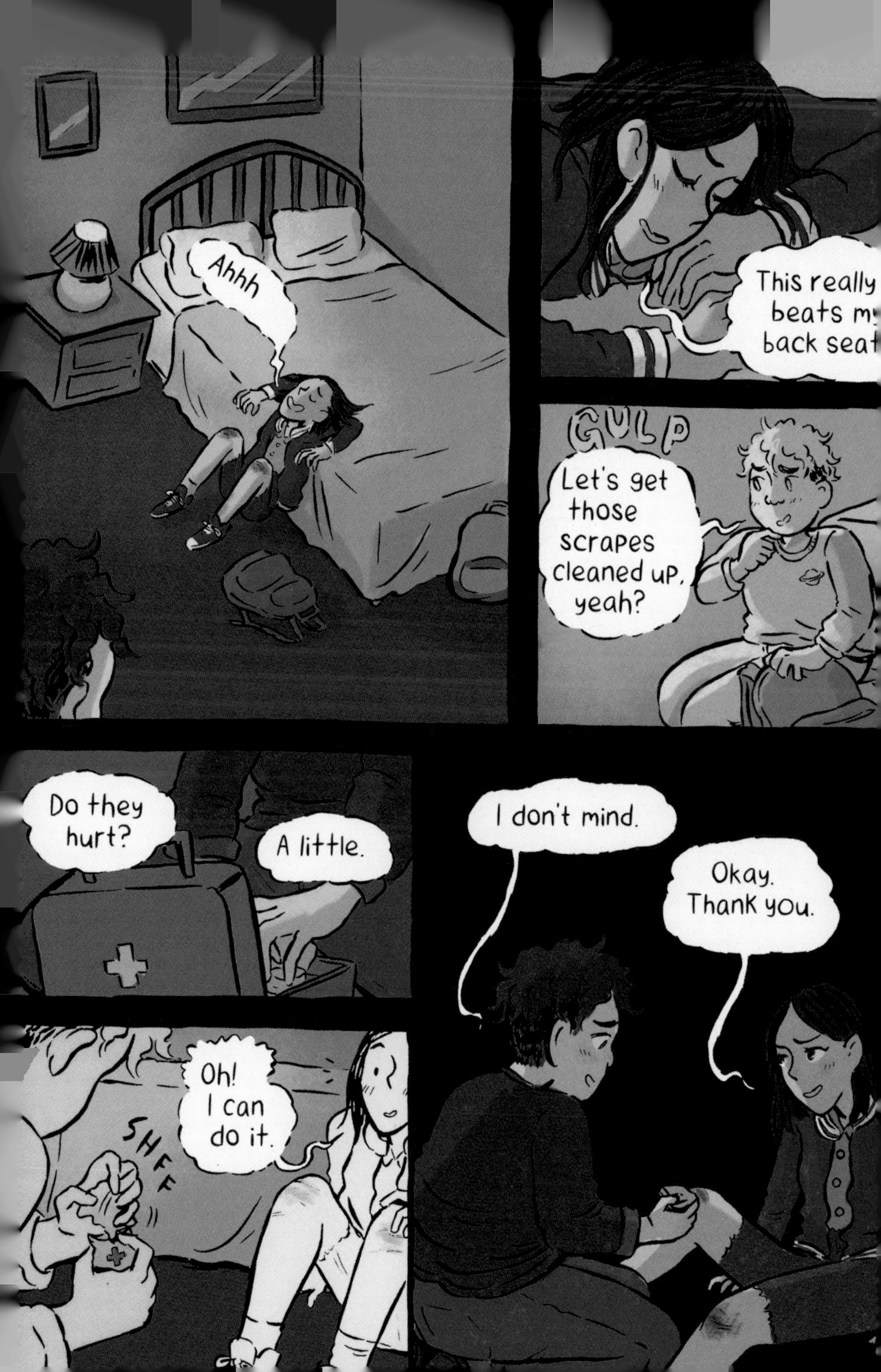
Ahhh
This really beats my back seat
GULP
Let's get those scrapes cleaned up, yeah?
Do they hurt?
A little.
Oh! I can do it.
SHFF
I don't mind.
Okay. Thank you.

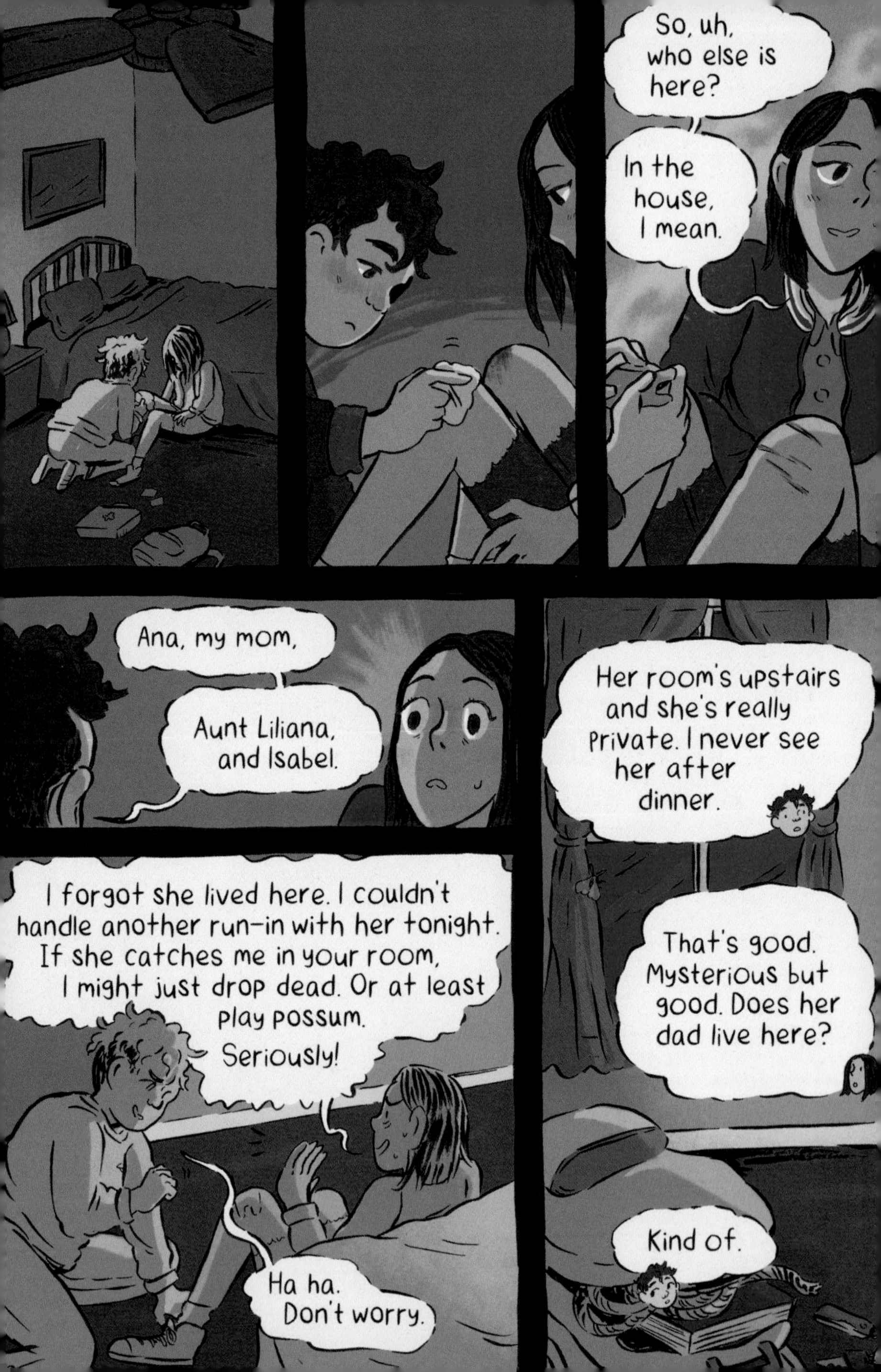
So, uh, who else is here?
In the house, I mean.
Ana, my mom,
Aunt Liliana, and Isabel.
Her room's upstairs and she's really private. I never see her after dinner.
I forgot she lived here. I couldn't handle another run-in with her tonight. If she catches me in your room, I might just drop dead. Or at least play possum.
Seriously!
Ha ha. Don't worry.
That's good. Mysterious but good. Does her dad live here?
Kind of.

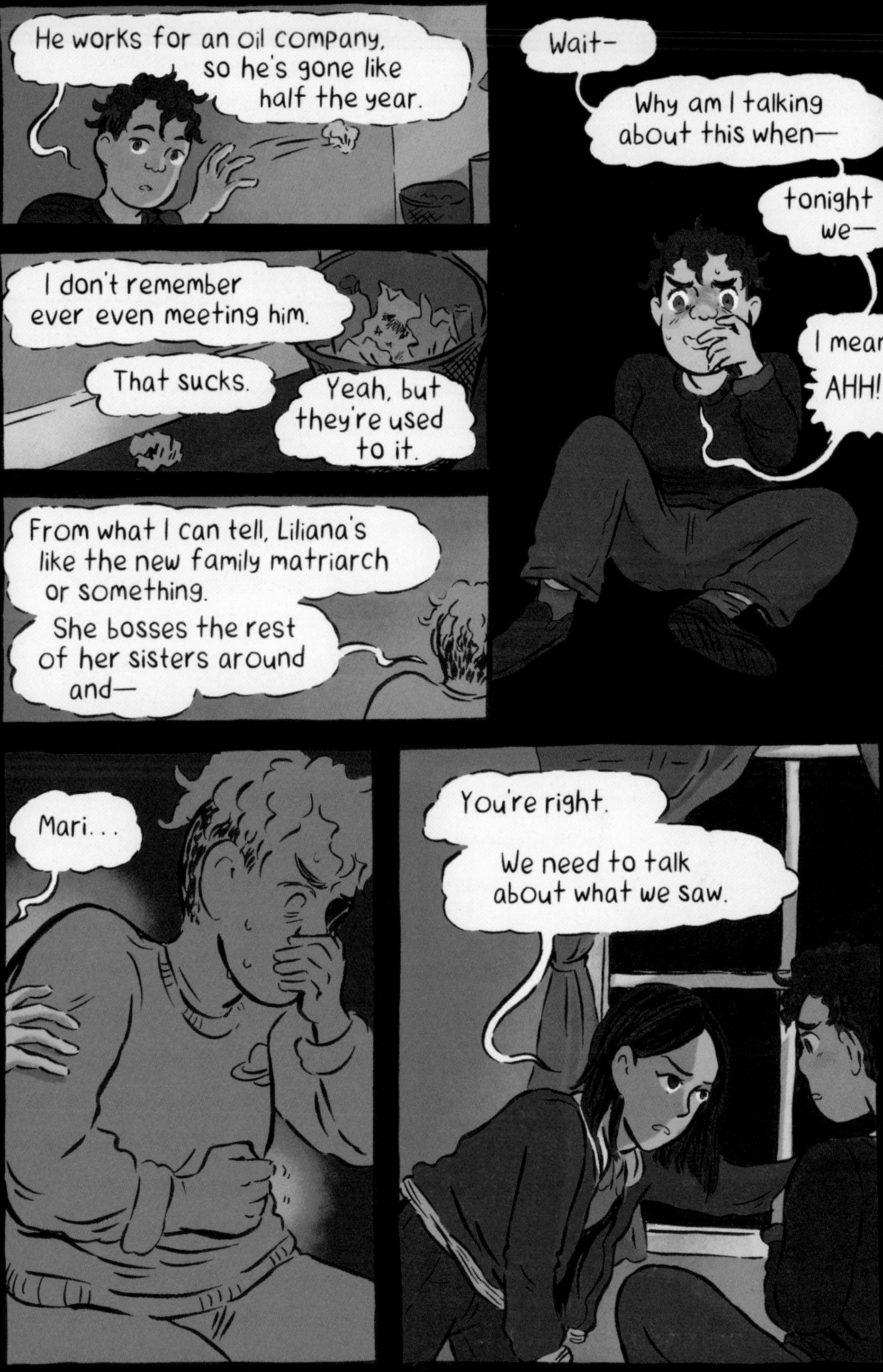
He works for an oil company, so he's gone like half the year.
I don't remember ever even meeting him.
That sucks.
Yeah, but they're used to it.
From what I can tell, Liliana's like the new family matriarch or something.
She bosses the rest of her sisters around and—
Wait-
Why am I talking about this when—
tonight we—
I mean, AHH!
Mari. . .
You're right.
We need to talk about what we saw.

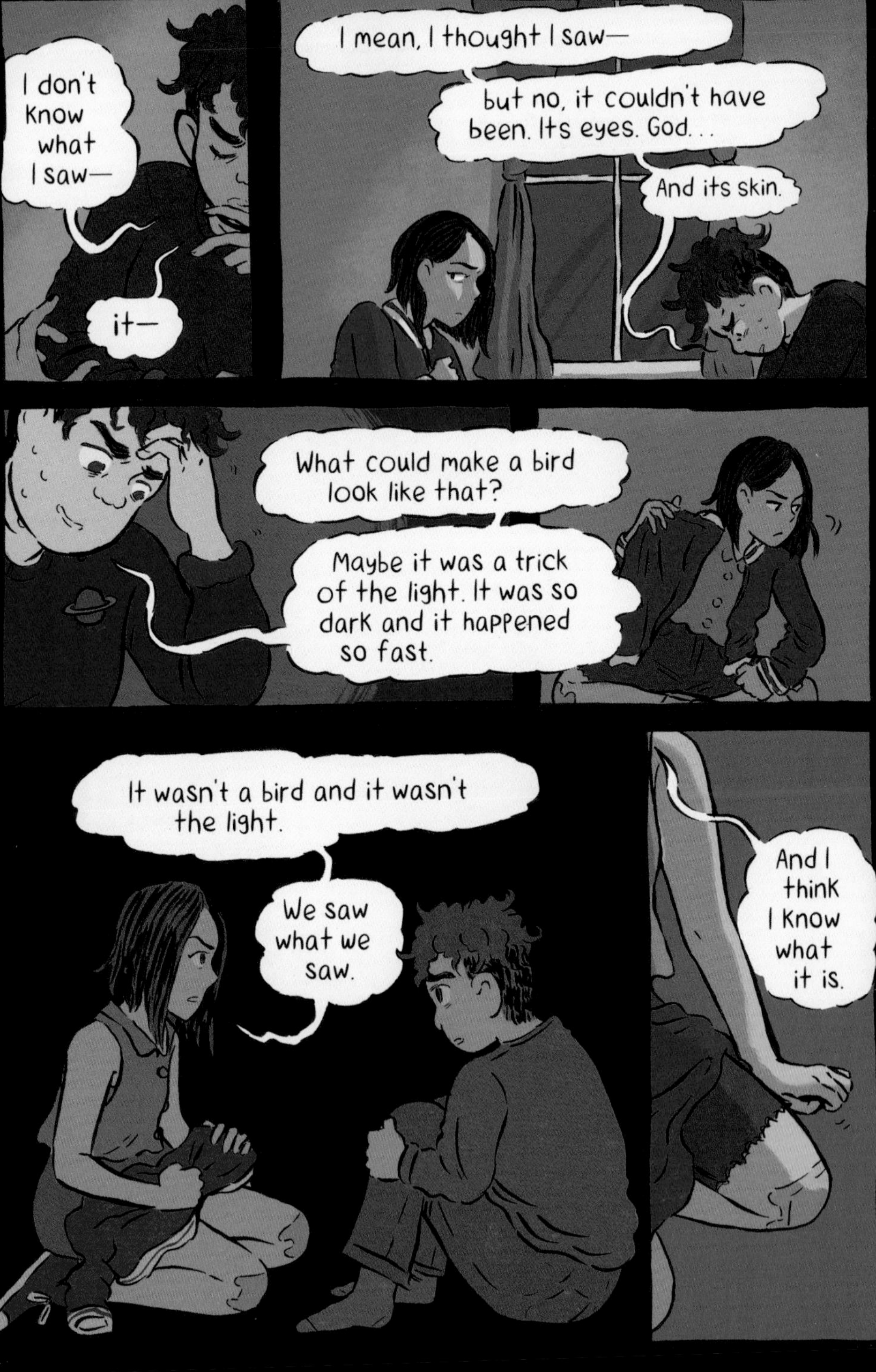
I don't know what I saw—
it—
I mean, I thought I saw—
but no, it couldn't have been. Its eyes. God. . .
And its skin.
What could make a bird look like that?
Maybe it was a trick of the light. It was so dark and it happened so fast.
It wasn't a bird and it wasn't the light.
We saw what we saw.
And I think I know what it is.

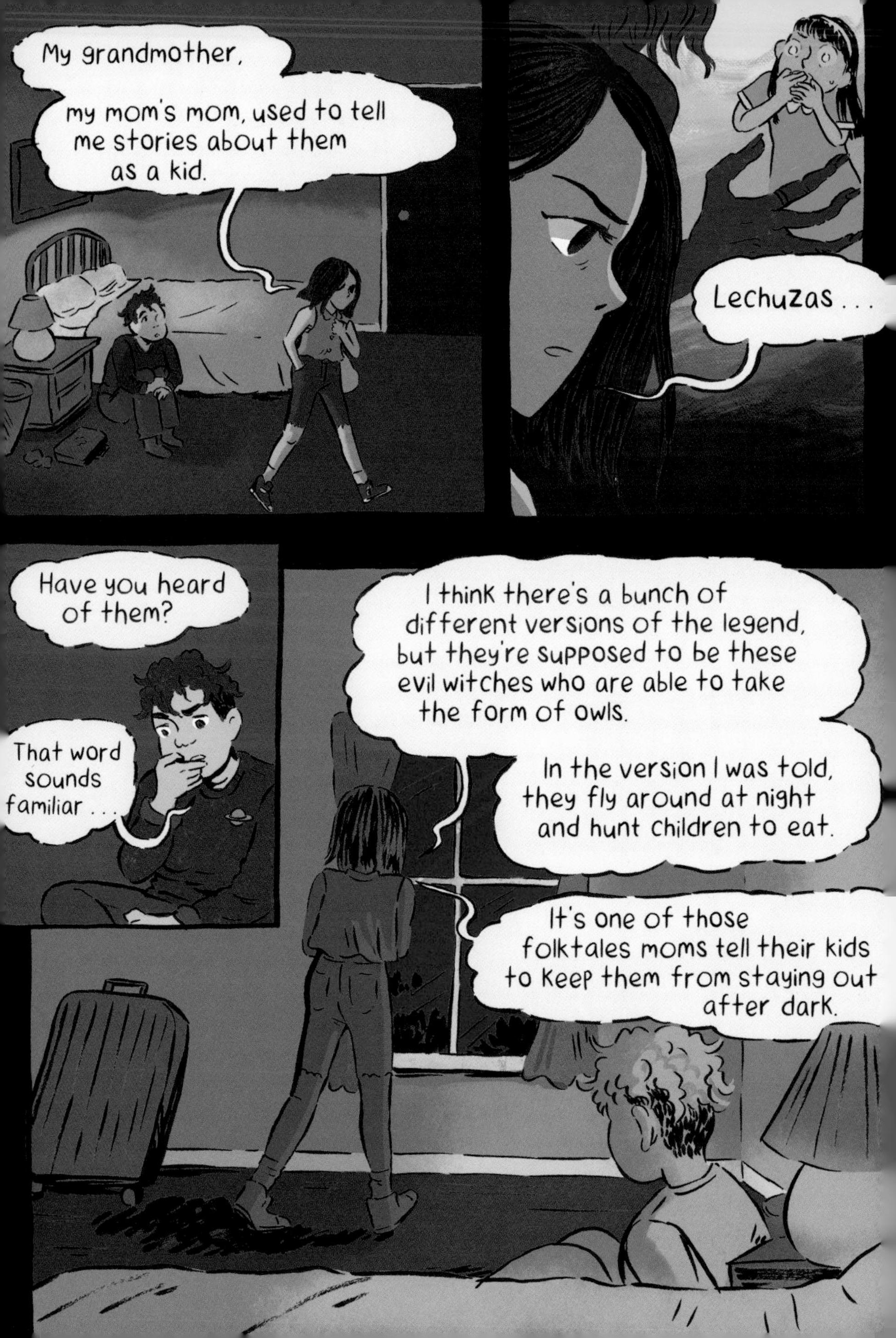
My grandmother,
my mom's mom, used to tell me stories about them as a kid.
Lechuzas . . .
Have you heard of them?
That word sounds familiar . . .
I think there's a bunch of different versions of the legend, but they're supposed to be these evil witches who are able to take the form of owls.
In the version I was told, they fly around at night and hunt children to eat.
It's one of those folktales moms tell their kids to keep them from staying out after dark.

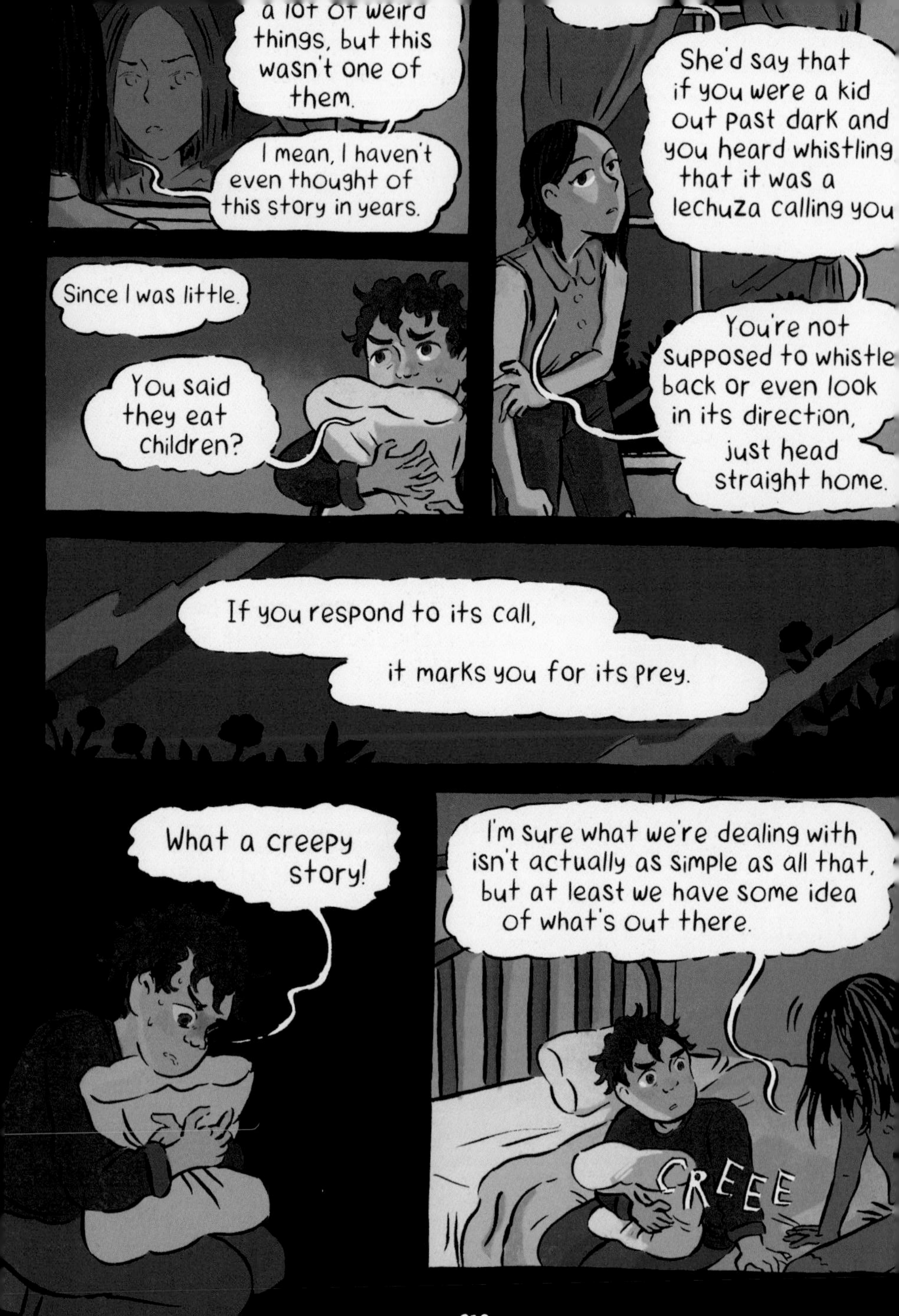
a lot of weird things, but this wasn't one of them.
I mean, I haven't even thought of this story in years.
She'd say that if you were a kid out past dark and you heard whistling that it was a lechuza calling you
Since I was little.
You said they eat children?
You're not supposed to whistle back or even look in its direction,
just head straight home.
If you respond to its call,
it marks you for its prey.
What a creepy story!
I'm sure what we're dealing with isn't actually as simple as all that, but at least we have some idea of what's out there.
CREEE

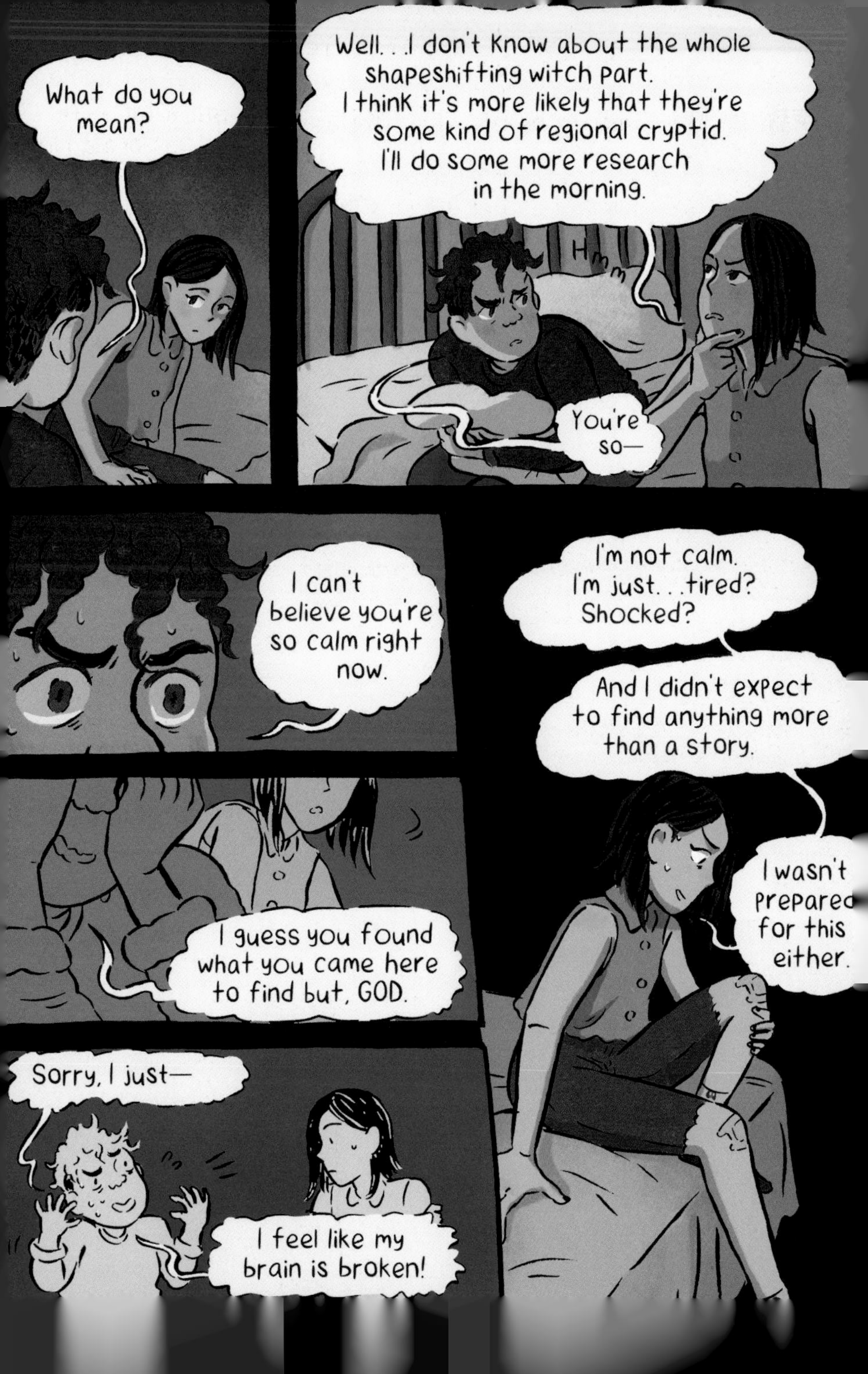
What do you mean?
Well. . .I don't know about the whole shapeshifting witch part. I think it's more likely that they're some kind of regional cryptid. I'll do some more research in the morning.
Hmm
You're so—
I can't believe you're so calm right now.
I'm not calm. I'm just. . .tired? Shocked?
And I didn't expect to find anything more than a story.
I guess you found what you came here to find but, GOD.
Sorry, I just—
I feel like my brain is broken!
I wasn't prepared for this either.

I think we should try and get some sleep. I'm setting my alarm really early, so we can sneek you out of here before everyone gets up.

Sorry.

That's okay. I'm really just glad to get a break from my car.

So, you can take the bed. I don't mind sleeping on the floor.

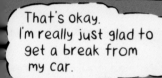

What? No way!

I'm not kicking you out of your bed.

Anyway, it's pretty big— there's enough room for both of us.

Oh.

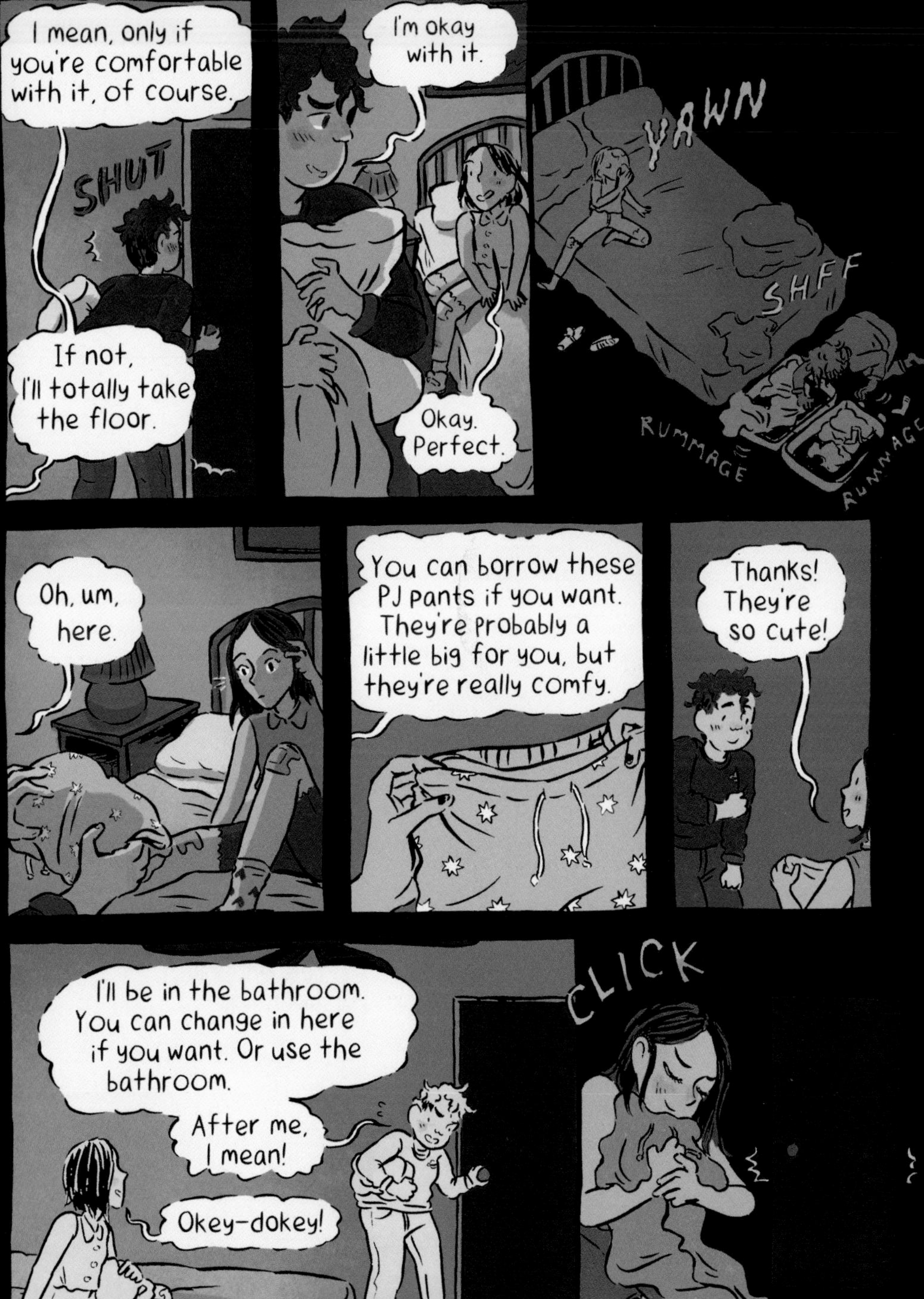
I mean, only if you're comfortable with it, of course.
SHUT
If not, I'll totally take the floor.
I'm okay with it.
Okay. Perfect.
YAWN
SHFF
RUMMAGE
RUMMAGE
Oh, um, here.
You can borrow these PJ pants if you want. They're probably a little big for you, but they're really comfy.
Thanks! They're so cute!
I'll be in the bathroom. You can change in here if you want. Or use the bathroom.
After me, I mean!
Okey-dokey!
CLICK

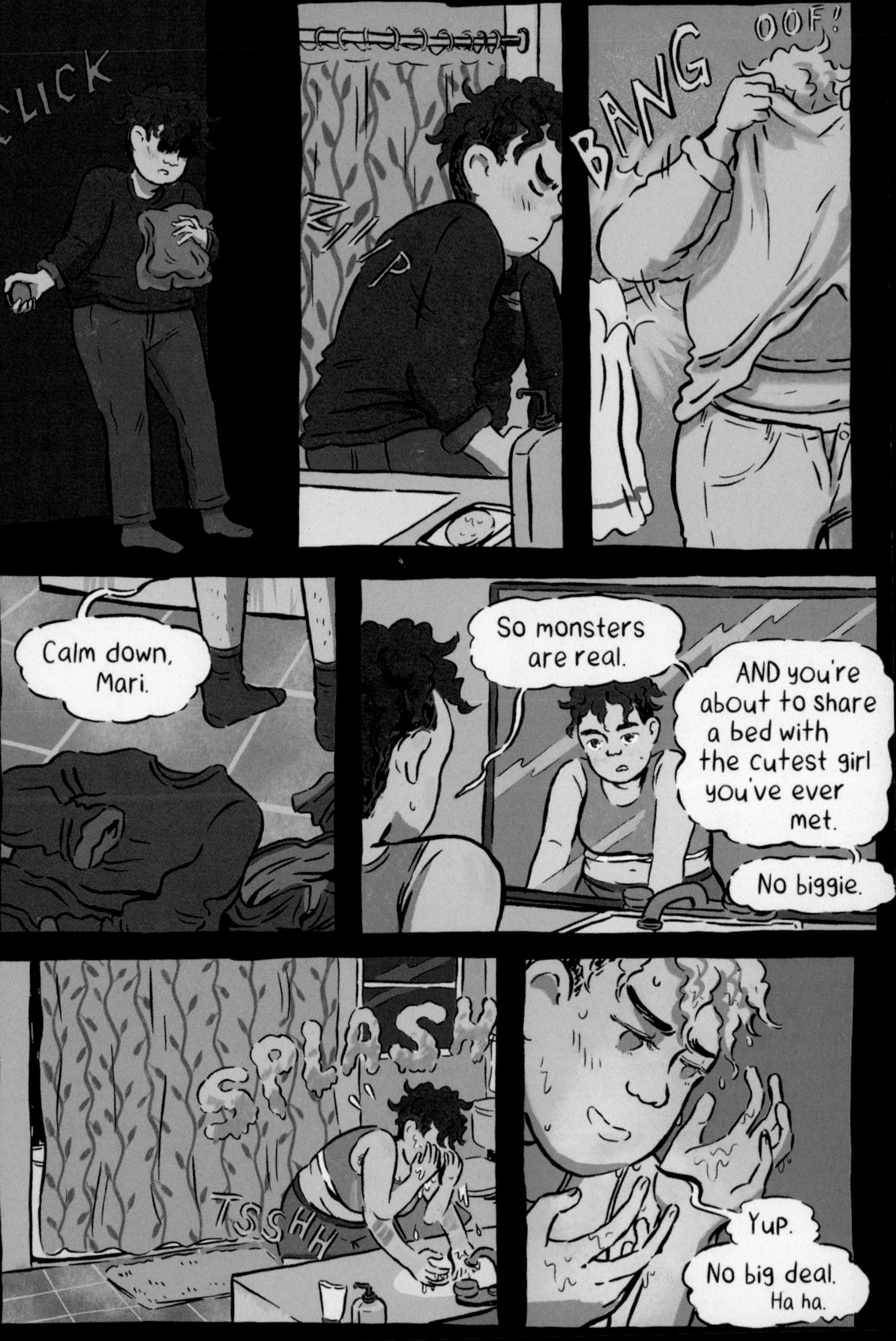
CLICK
ZIP
BANG
OOF!
Calm down, Mari.
So monsters are real.
AND you're about to share a bed with the cutest girl you've ever met.
No biggie.
SPLASH
TSSHH
Yup.
No big deal. Ha ha.

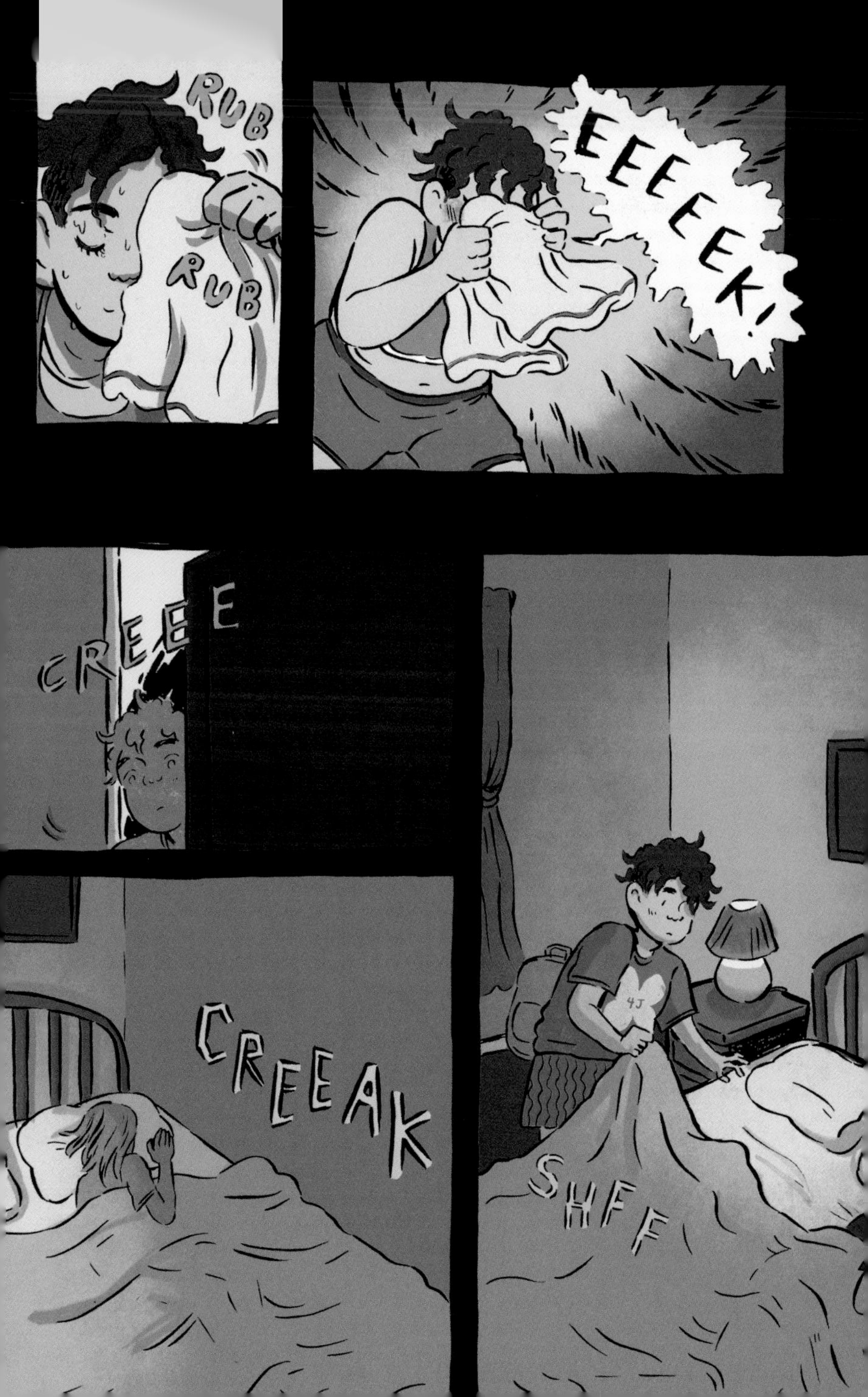
RUB
RUB
EEEEEK!
CREEE
CREEAK
4J
SHFF

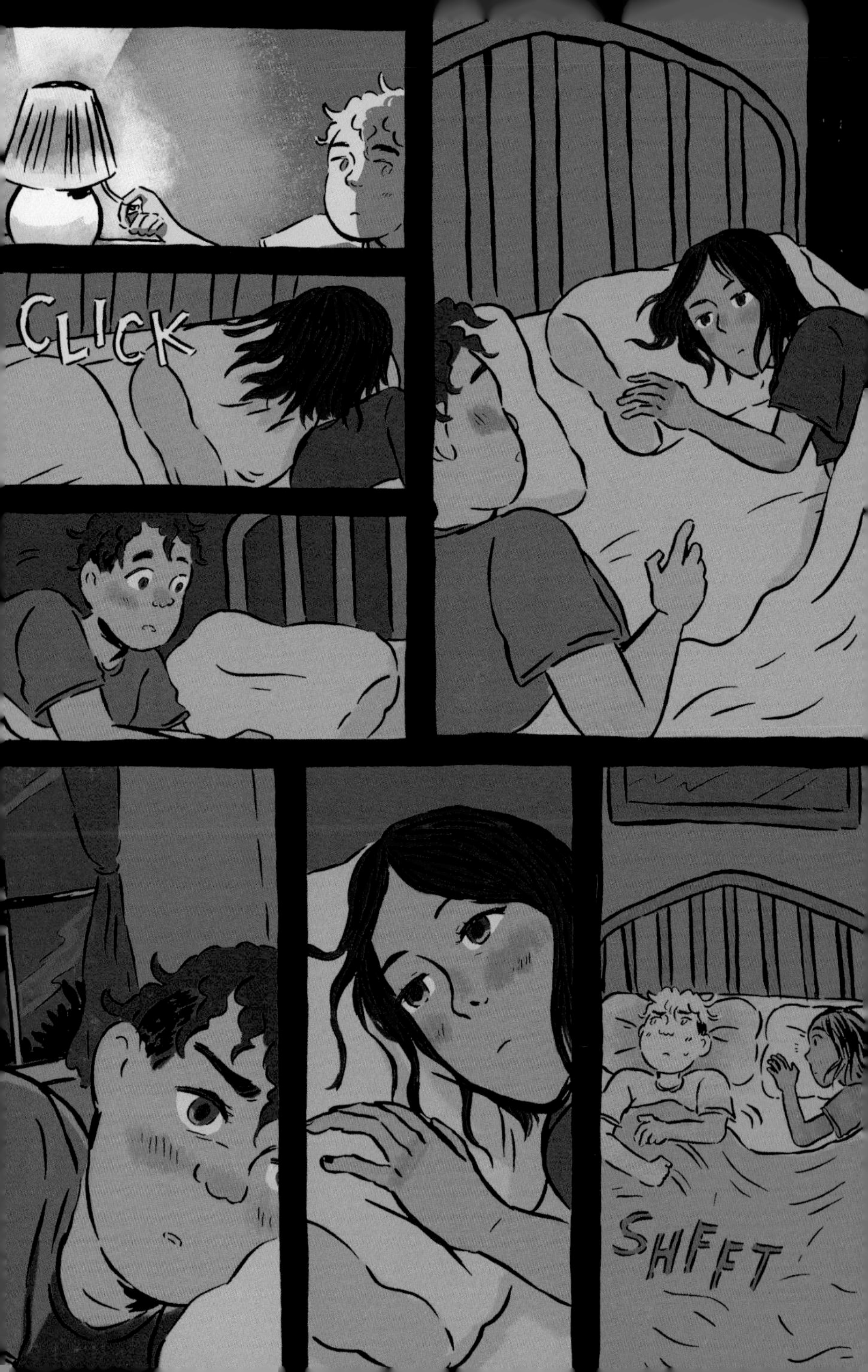
CLICK
SHFFT

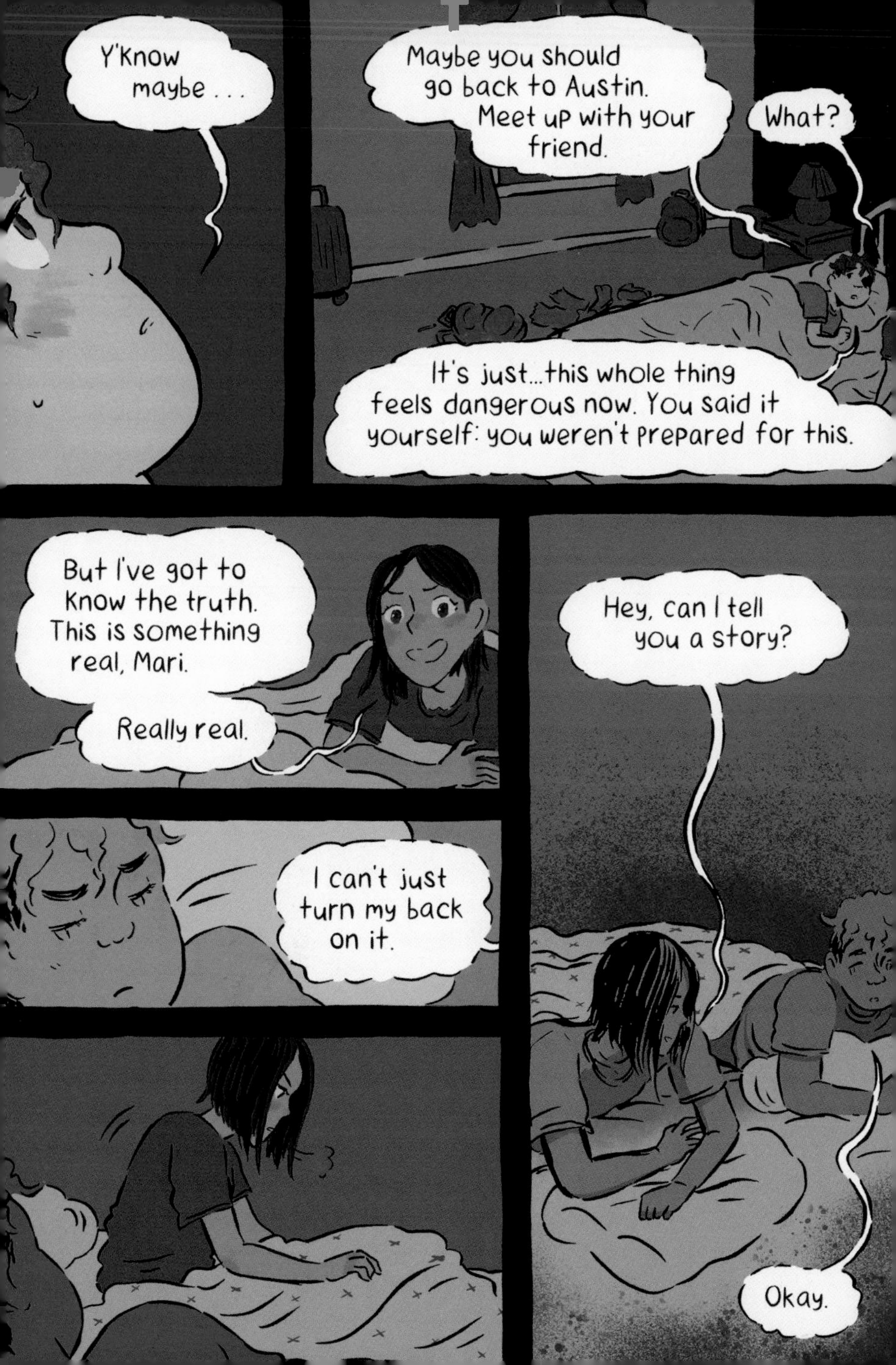
Y'know maybe . . .
Maybe you should go back to Austin. Meet up with your friend.
What?
It's just...this whole thing feels dangerous now. You said it yourself: you weren't prepared for this.
But I've got to know the truth. This is something real, Mari.
Really real.
I can't just turn my back on it.
Hey, can I tell you a story?
Okay.

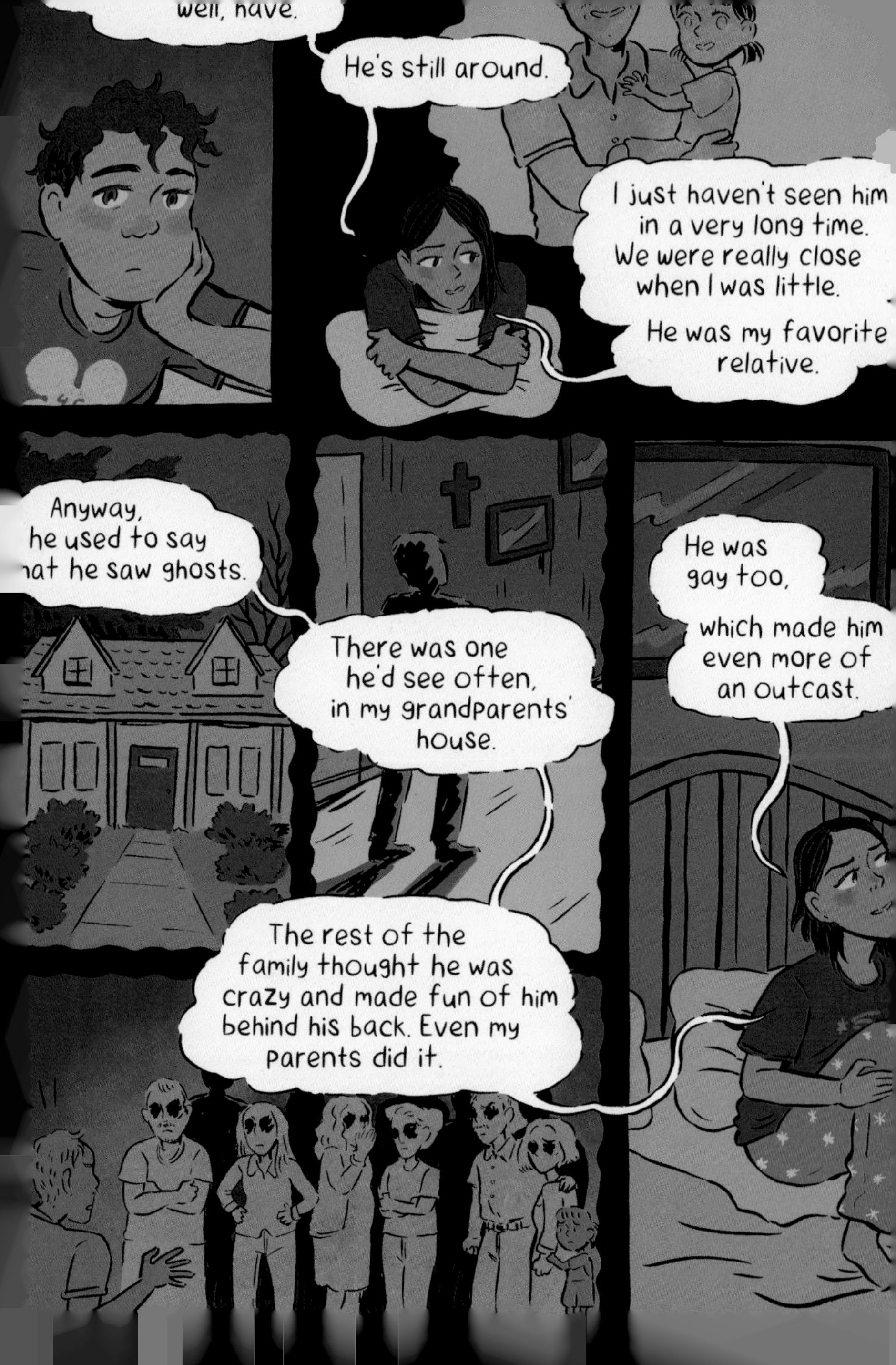

well, have.
He's still around.
I just haven't seen him in a very long time. We were really close when I was little.
He was my favorite relative.
Anyway, he used to say hat he saw ghosts.
There was one he'd see often, in my grandparents' house.
He was gay too,
which made him even more of an outcast.
The rest of the family thought he was crazy and made fun of him behind his back. Even my parents did it.

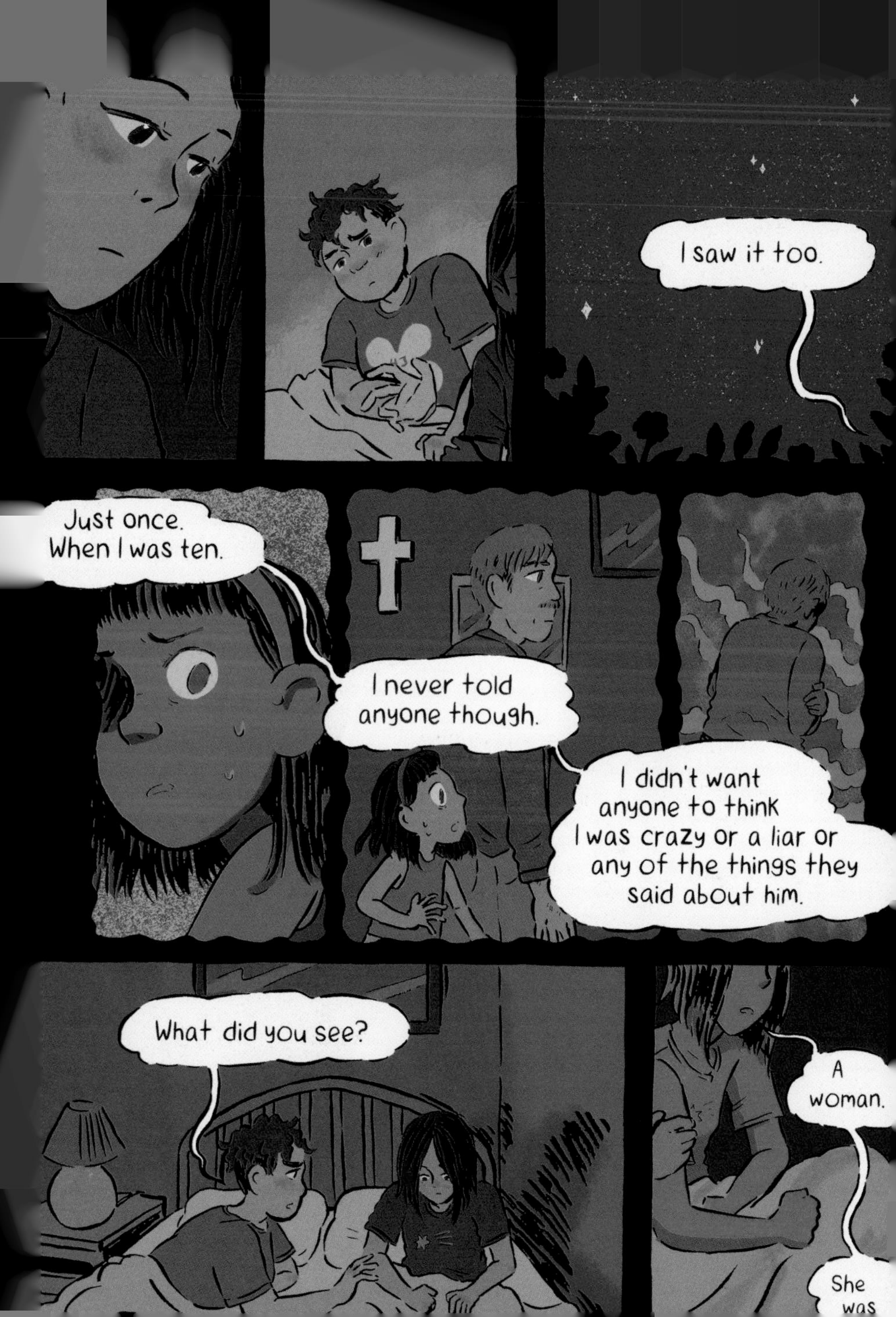
I saw it too.
Just once. When I was ten.
I never told anyone though.
I didn't want anyone to think I was crazy or a liar or any of the things they said about him.
What did you see?
A woman.
She was

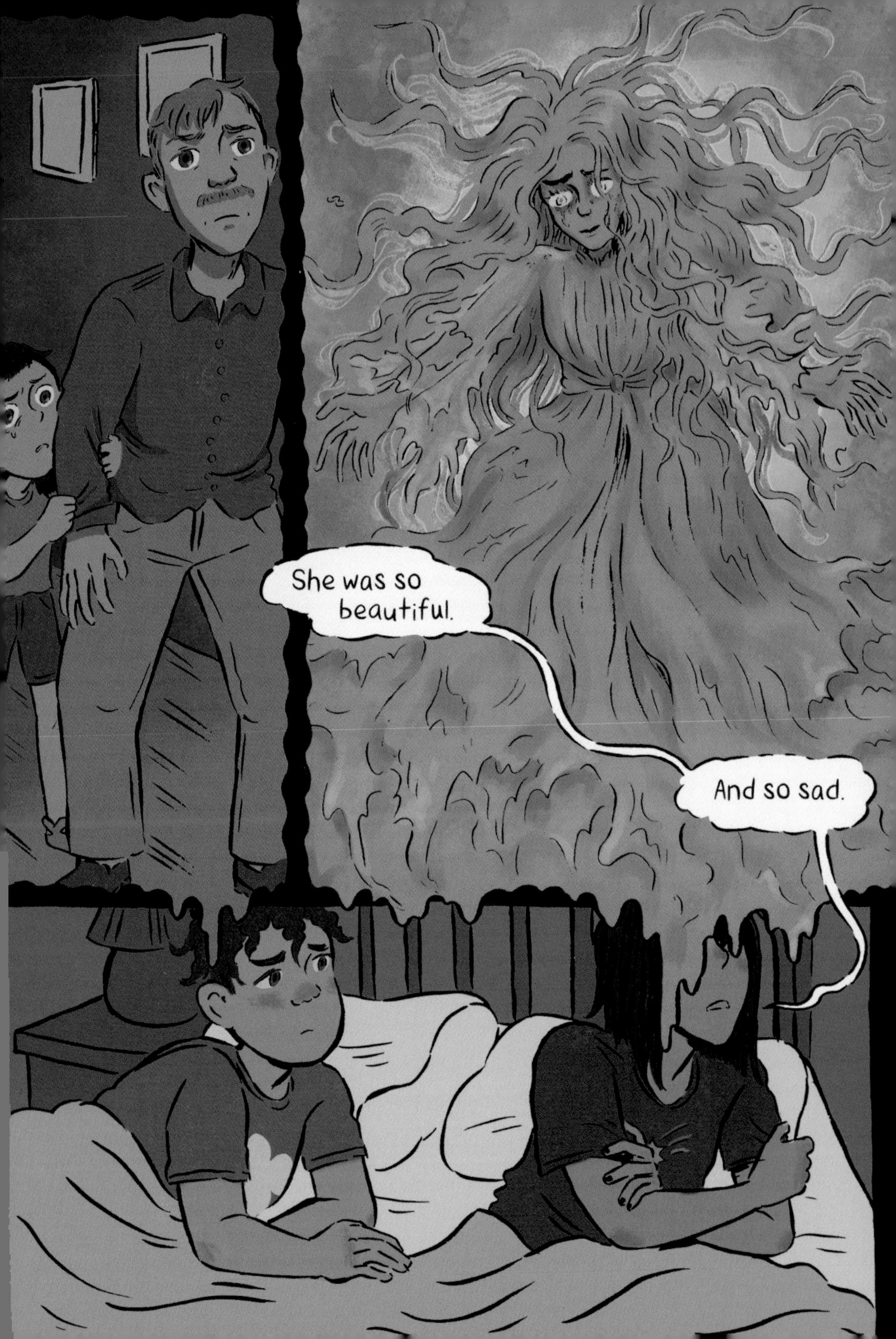
She was so beautiful.
And so sad.

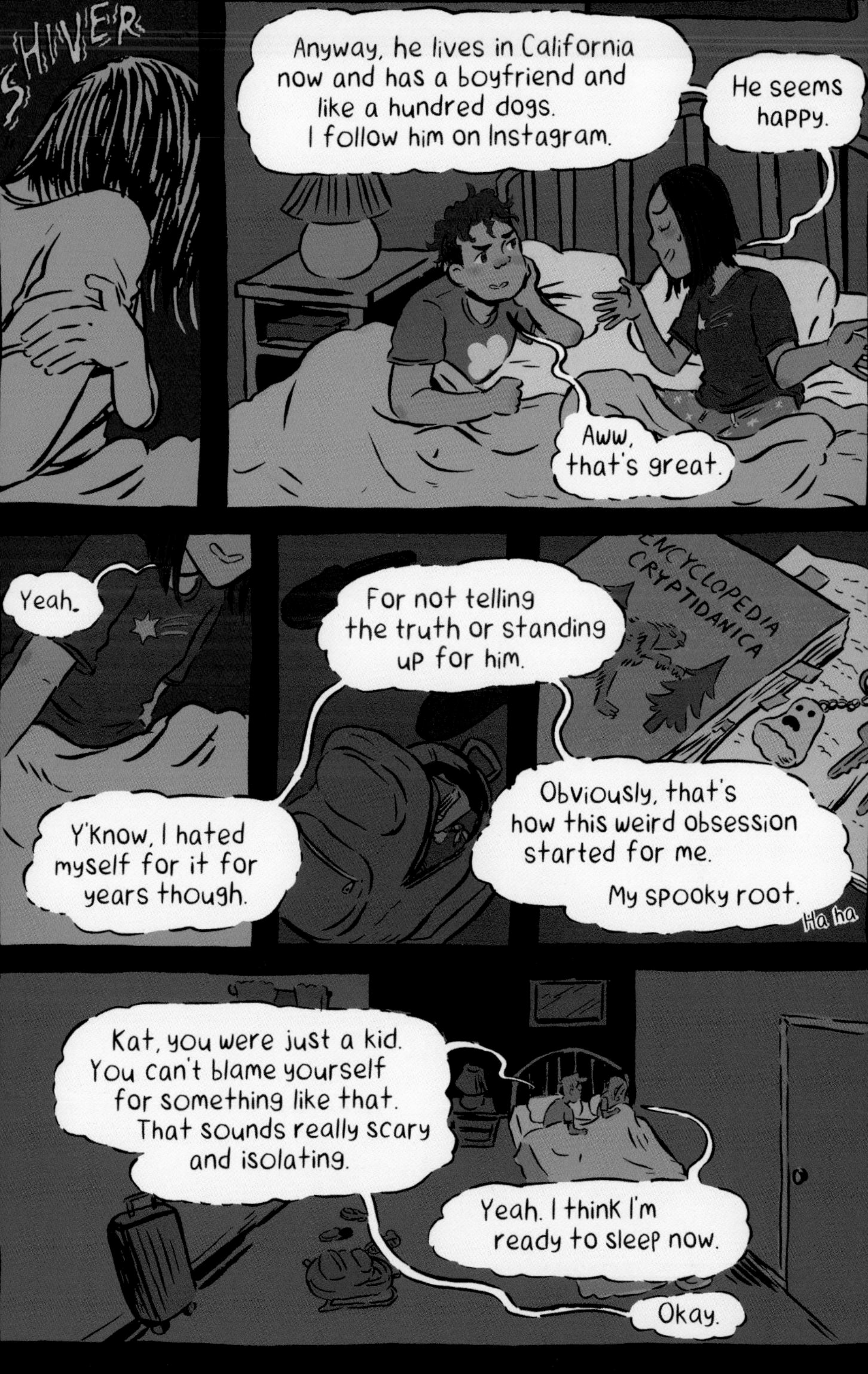
SHIVER
Anyway, he lives in California now and has a boyfriend and like a hundred dogs. I follow him on Instagram.
He seems happy.
Aww, that's great.
Yeah.
For not telling the truth or standing up for him.
ENCYCLOPEDIA CRYPTIDANICA
Y'Know, I hated myself for it for years though.
Obviously, that's how this weird obsession started for me.
My spooky root.
Ha ha
Kat, you were just a kid. You can't blame yourself for something like that. That sounds really scary and isolating.
Yeah. I think I'm ready to sleep now.
Okay.

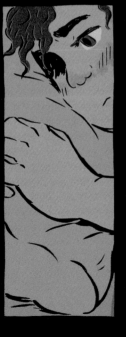

Hey,
Mari...

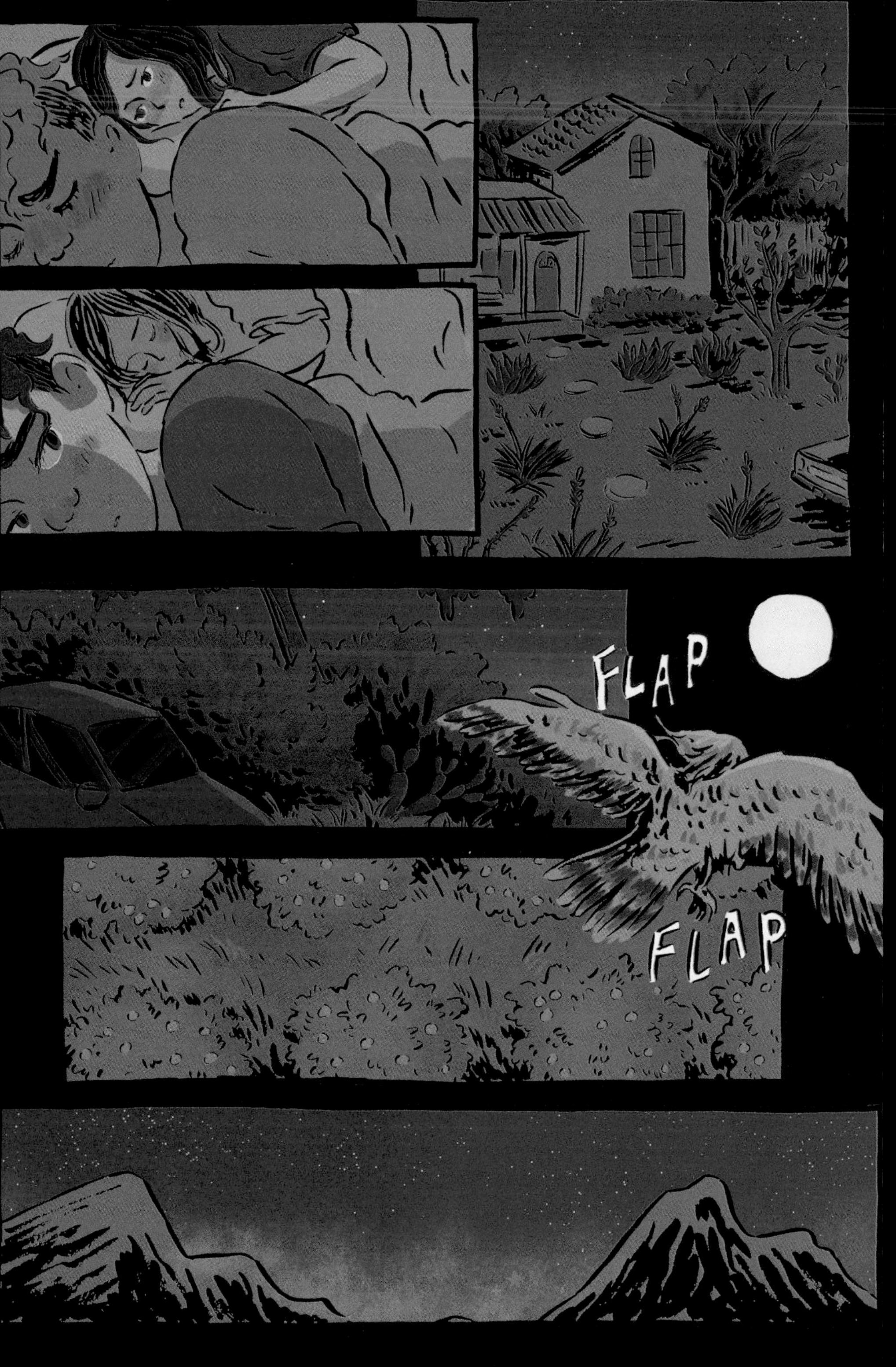
FLAP
FLAP

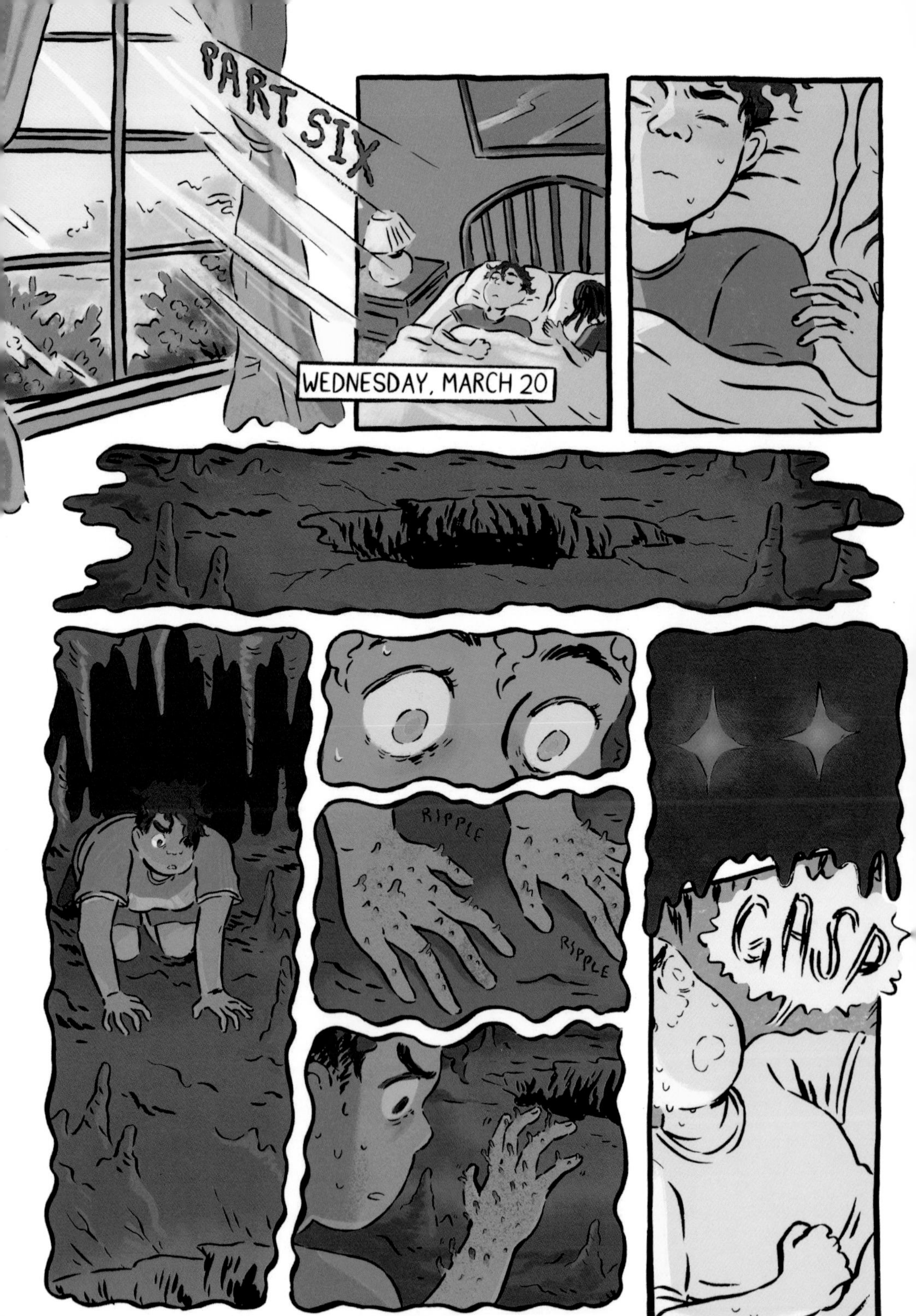
PART SIX
WEDNESDAY, MARCH 20
RIPPLE
RIPPLE
GASP

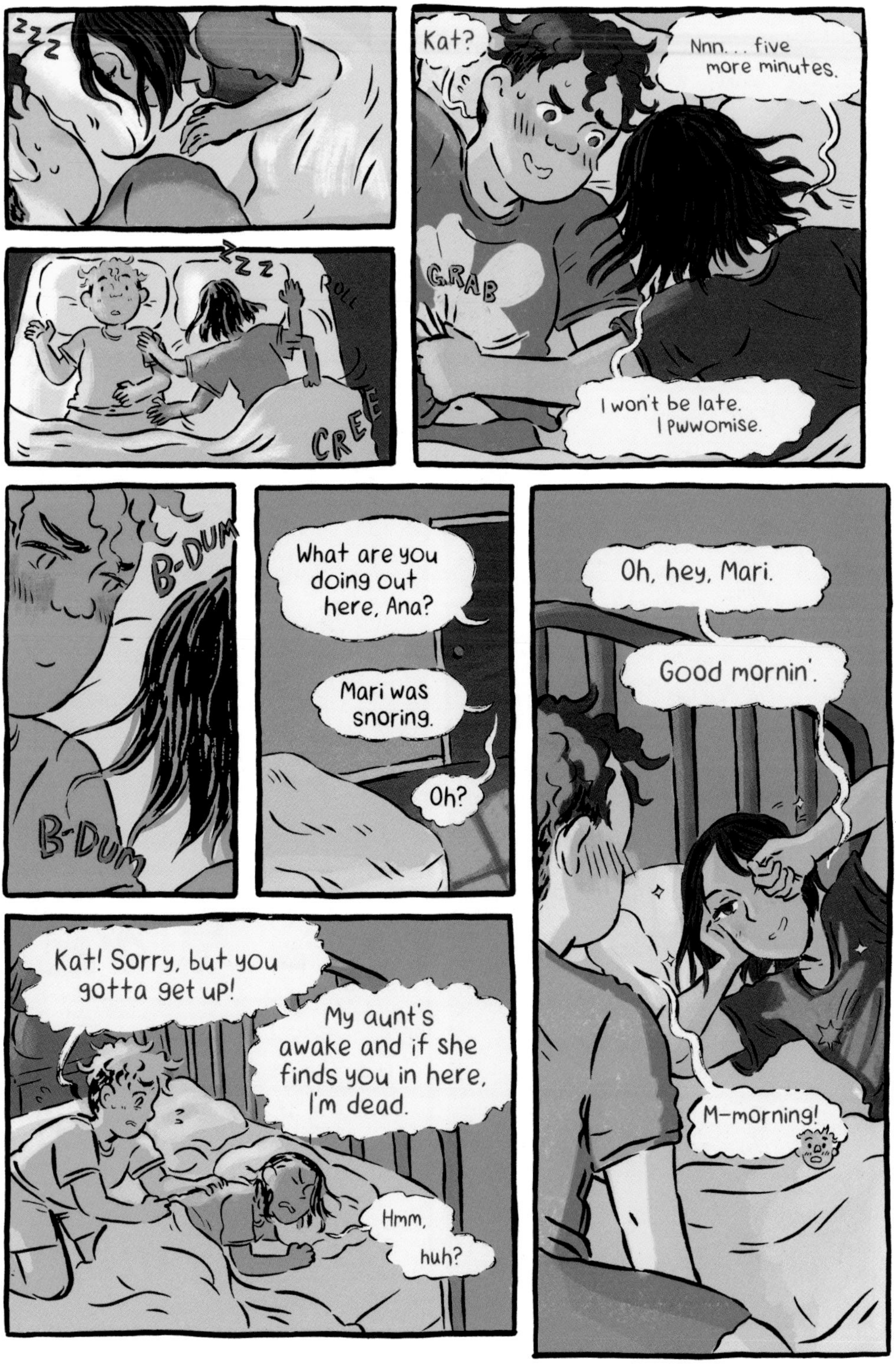
ZZZ
ZZZ
ROLL
CREEE
Kat?
Nnn. . . five more minutes.
GRAB
I won't be late. I pwwomise.
B-DUM
B-DUM
What are you doing out here, Ana?
Mari was snoring.
Oh?
Oh, hey, Mari.
Good mornin'.
M-morning!
Kat! Sorry, but you gotta get up!
My aunt's awake and if she finds you in here, I'm dead.
Hmm,
huh?

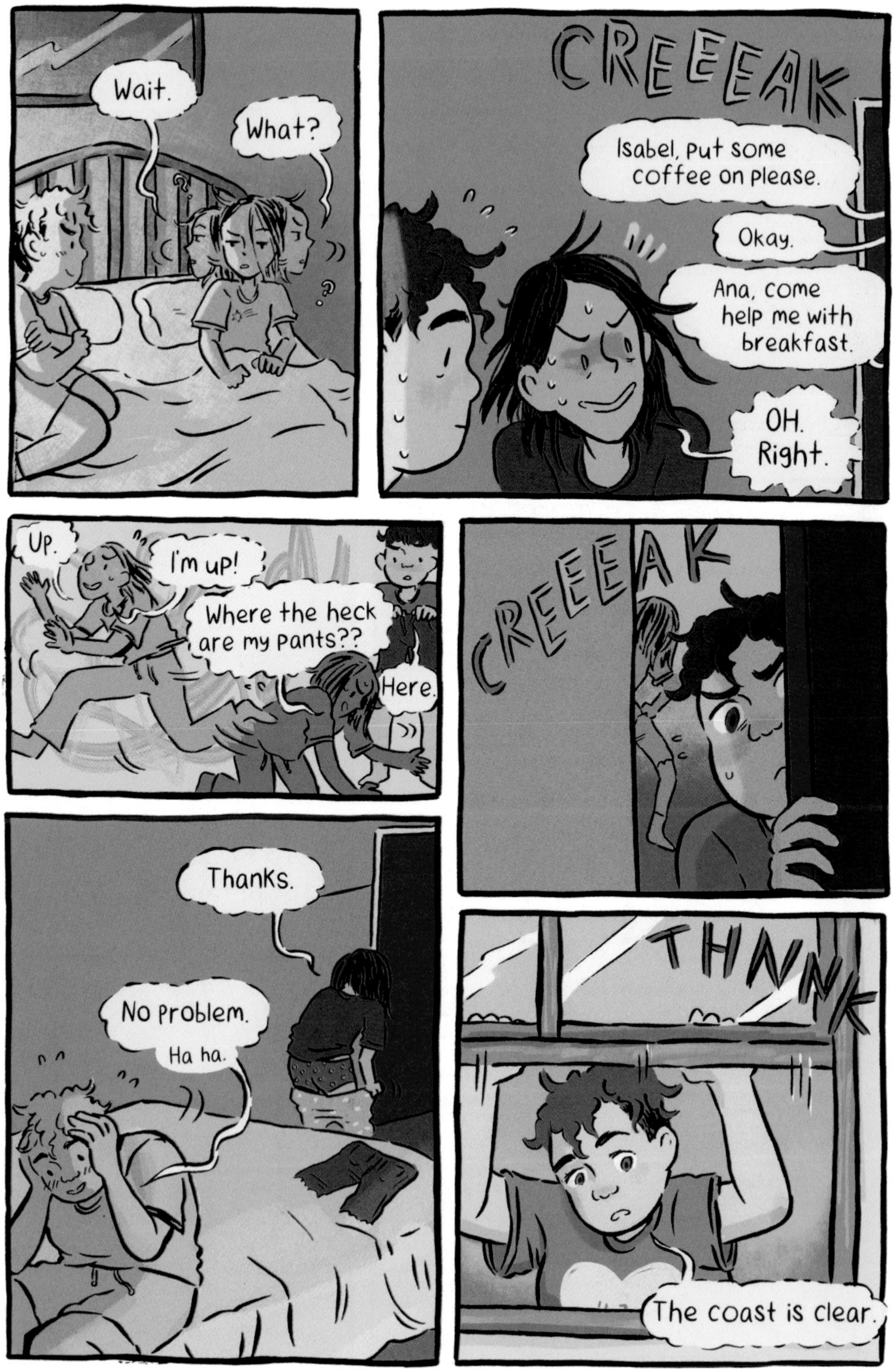
Wait.
What?
CREEEAK
Isabel, put some coffee on please.
Okay.
Ana, come help me with breakfast.
OH. Right.
Up.
I'm up!
Where the heck are my pants??
Here.
CREEEAK
Thanks.
No problem.
Ha ha.
THNNK
The coast is clear.

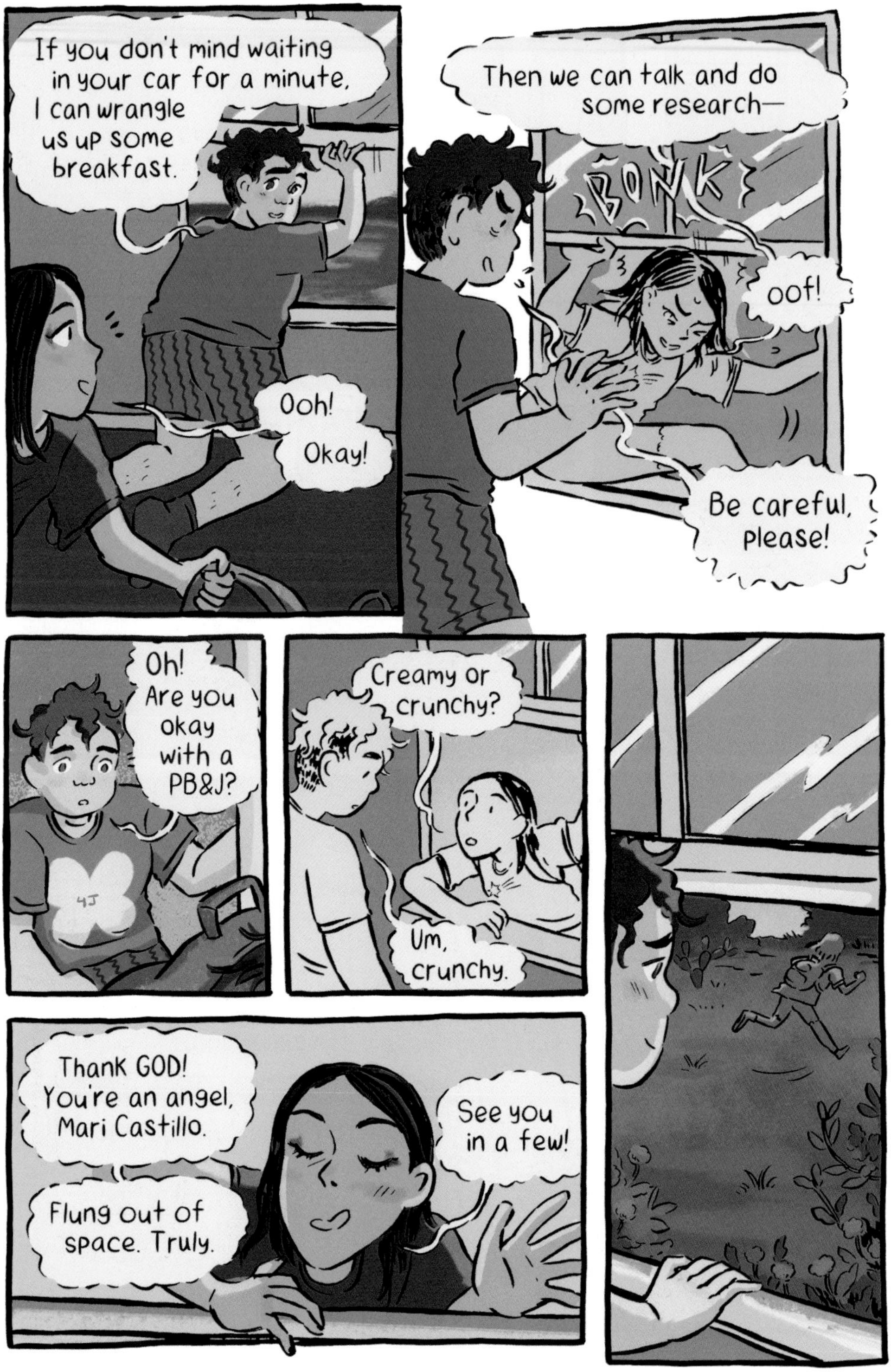
If you don't mind waiting in your car for a minute, I can wrangle us up some breakfast.
Ooh!
Okay!
Then we can talk and do some research—
BONK
oof!
Be careful, please!
Oh! Are you okay with a PB&J?
4J
Creamy or crunchy?
Um, crunchy.
Thank GOD! You're an angel, Mari Castillo.
Flung out of space. Truly.
See you in a few!

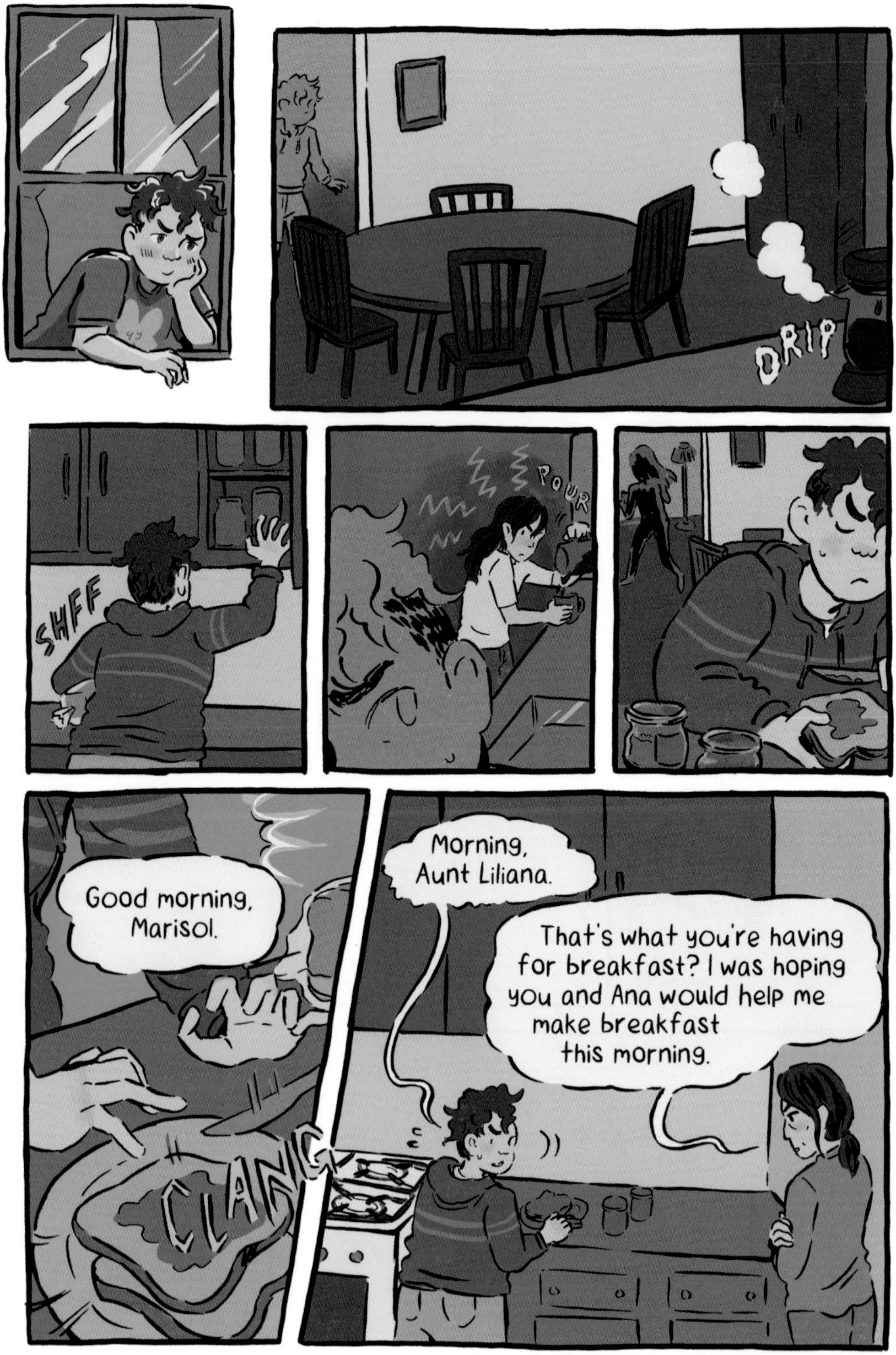
DRIP
SHFF
POUR
Good morning, Marisol.
Morning, Aunt Liliana.
That's what you're having for breakfast? I was hoping you and Ana would help me make breakfast this morning.
CLANG

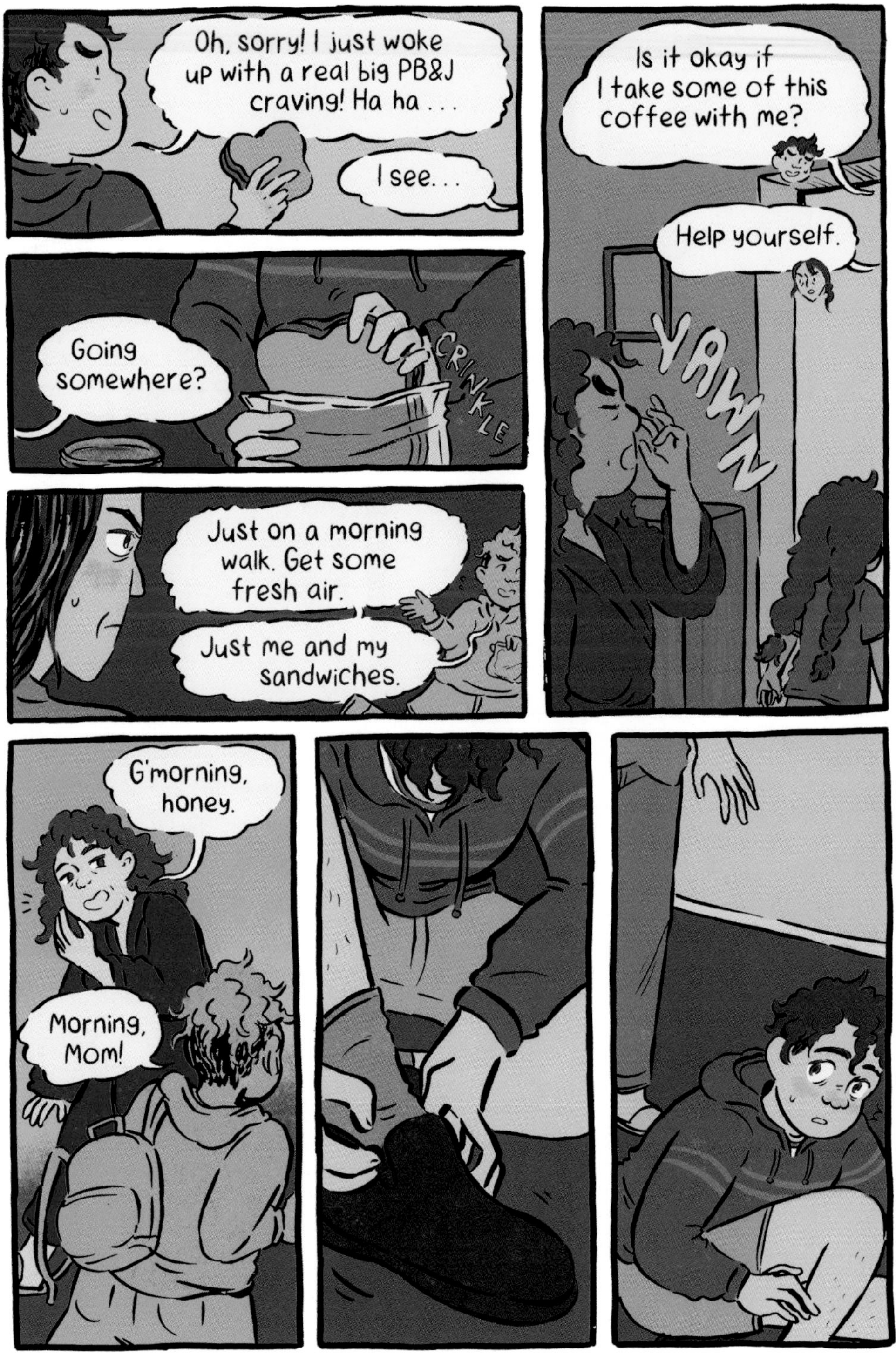
Oh, sorry! I just woke up with a real big PB&J craving! Ha ha . . .
I see. . .
Is it okay if I take some of this coffee with me?
Help yourself.
YAWN
Going somewhere?
CRINKLE
Just on a morning walk. Get some fresh air.
Just me and my sandwiches.
G'morning, honey.
Morning, Mom!

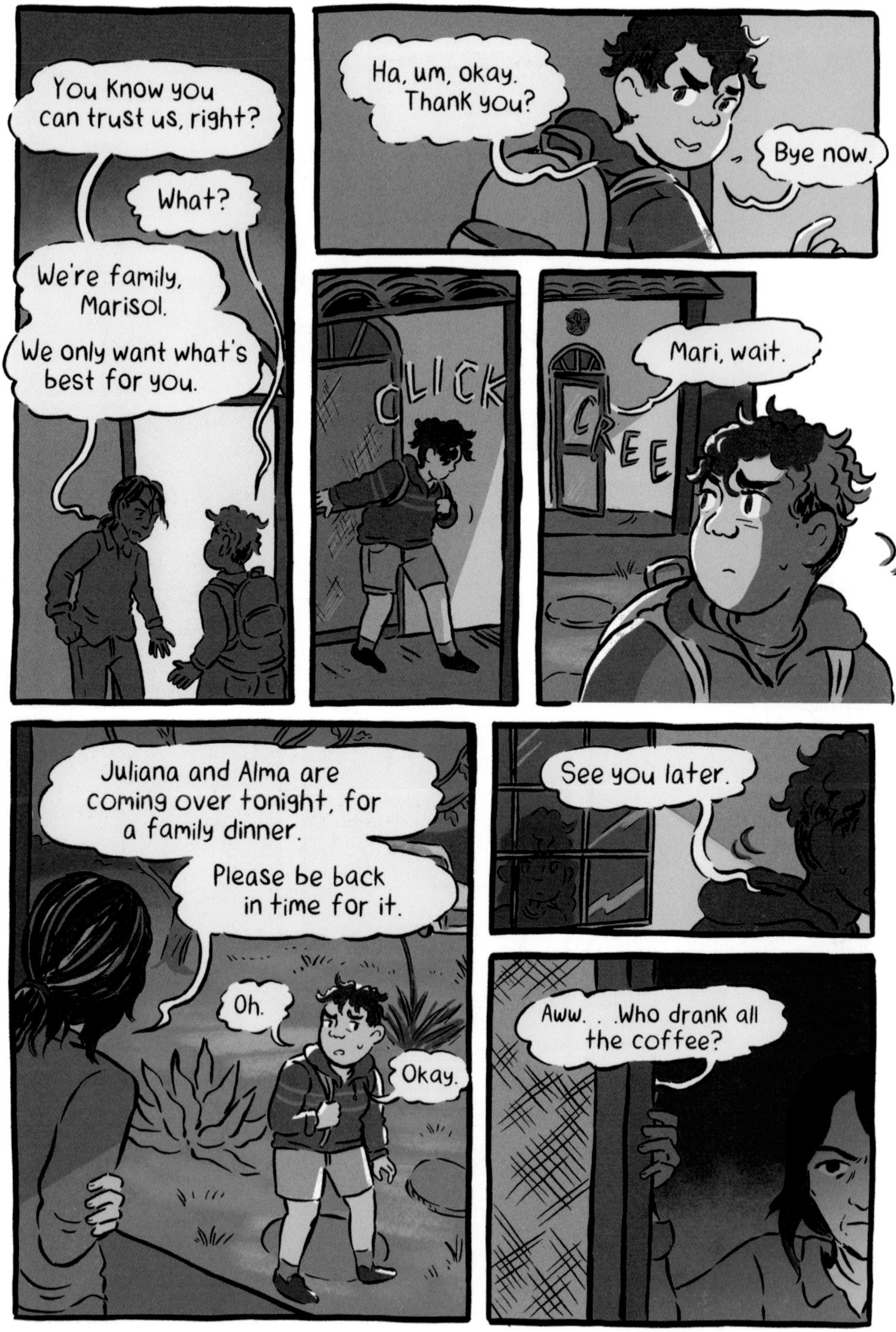

You know you can trust us, right?
What?
We're family, Marisol.
We only want what's best for you.
Ha, um, okay. Thank you?
Bye now.
CLICK
Mari, wait.
CREEE
Juliana and Alma are coming over tonight, for a family dinner.
Please be back in time for it.
Oh.
Okay.
See you later.
Aww. . .Who drank all the coffee?

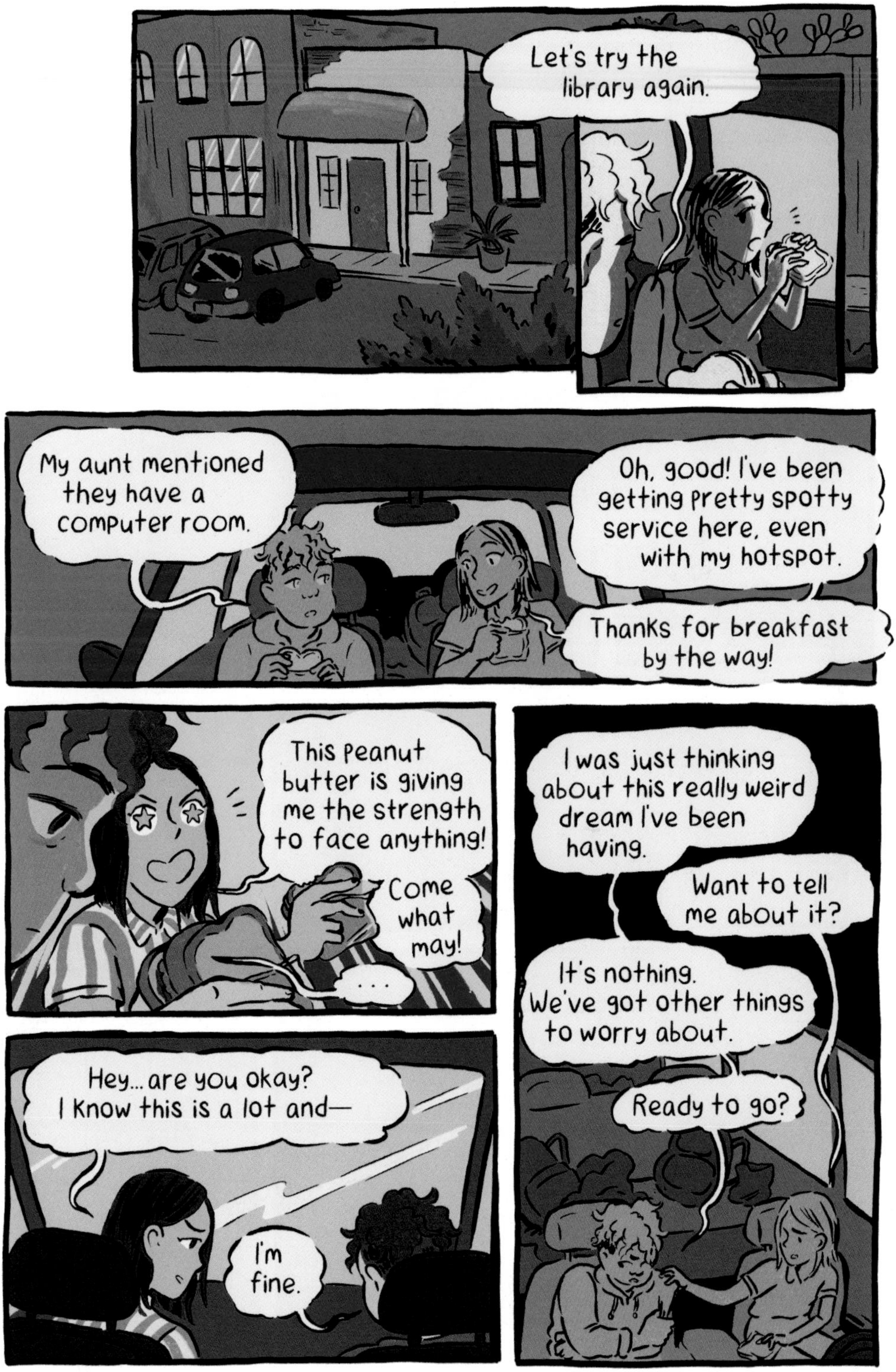

Let's try the library again.
My aunt mentioned they have a computer room.
Oh, good! I've been getting pretty spotty service here, even with my hotspot.
Thanks for breakfast by the way!
This peanut butter is giving me the strength to face anything!
Come what may!
...
Hey... are you okay? I know this is a lot and—
I'm fine.
I was just thinking about this really weird dream I've been having.
Want to tell me about it?
It's nothing. We've got other things to worry about.
Ready to go?

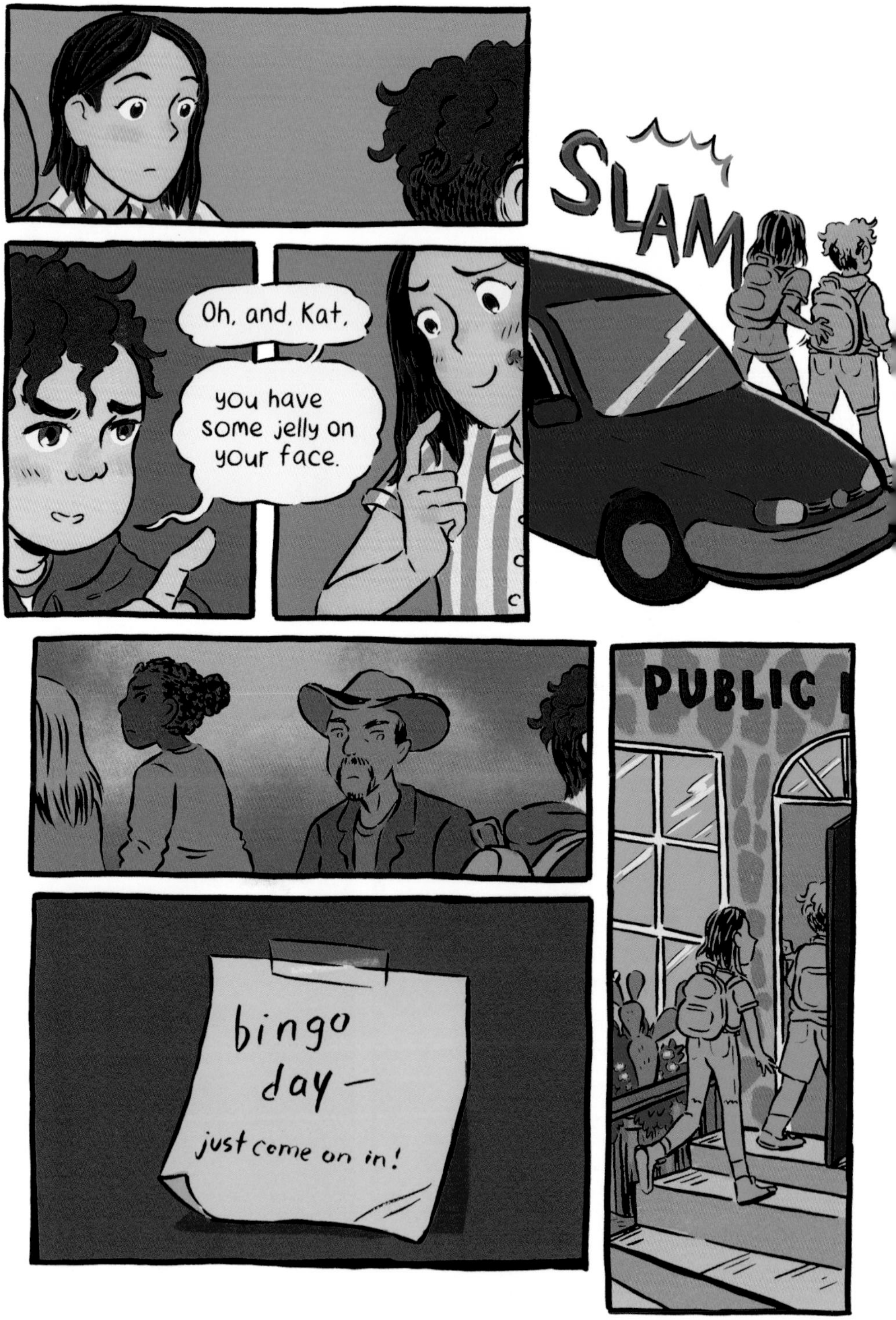
SLAM
Oh, and, Kat,
you have some jelly on your face.
PUBLIC
bingo day —
just come on in!

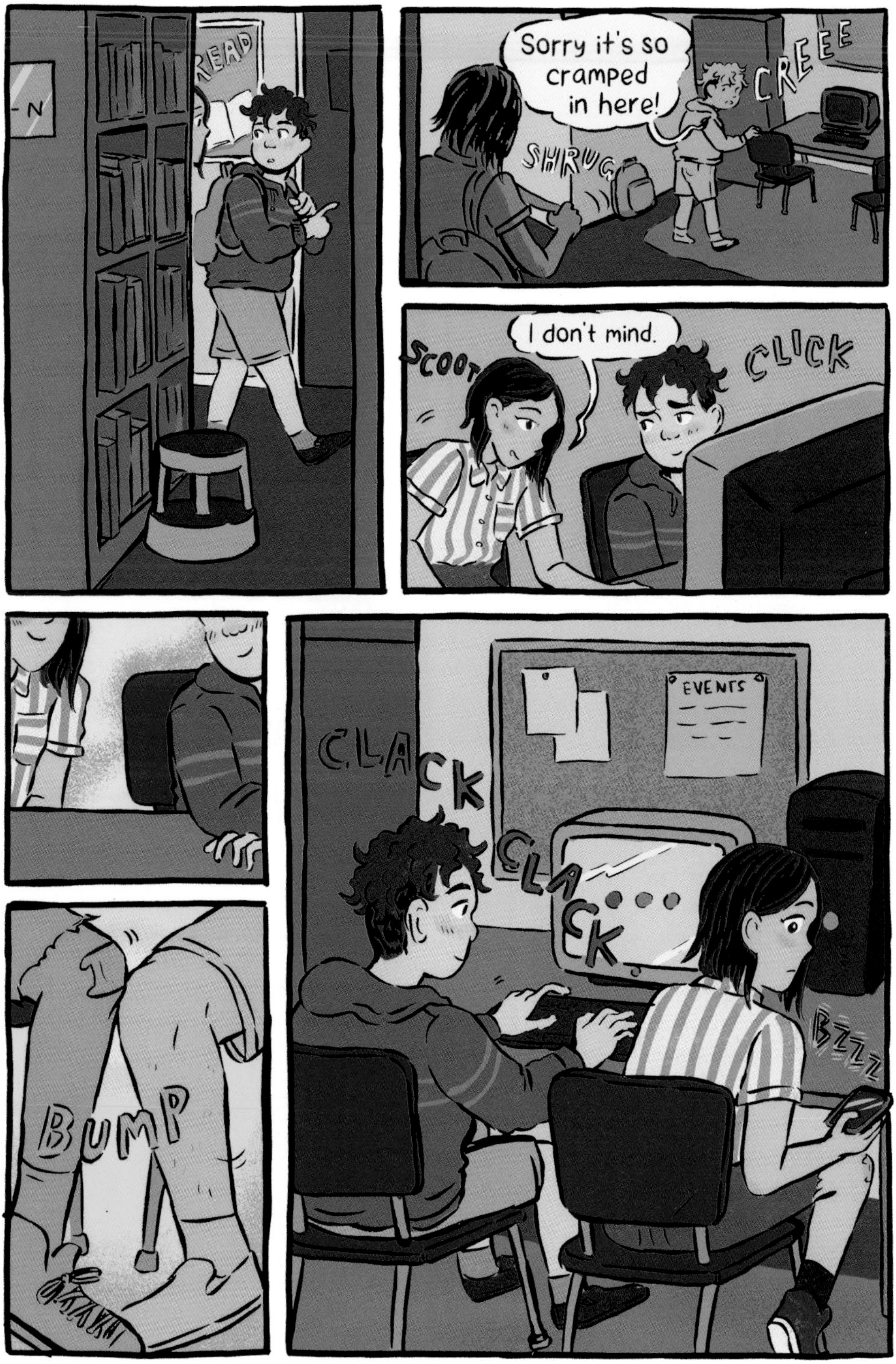
READ
Sorry it's so cramped in here!
SHRUG
CREEE
I don't mind.
SCOOT
CLICK
EVENTS
CLACK
CLACK
BZZZ
BUMP

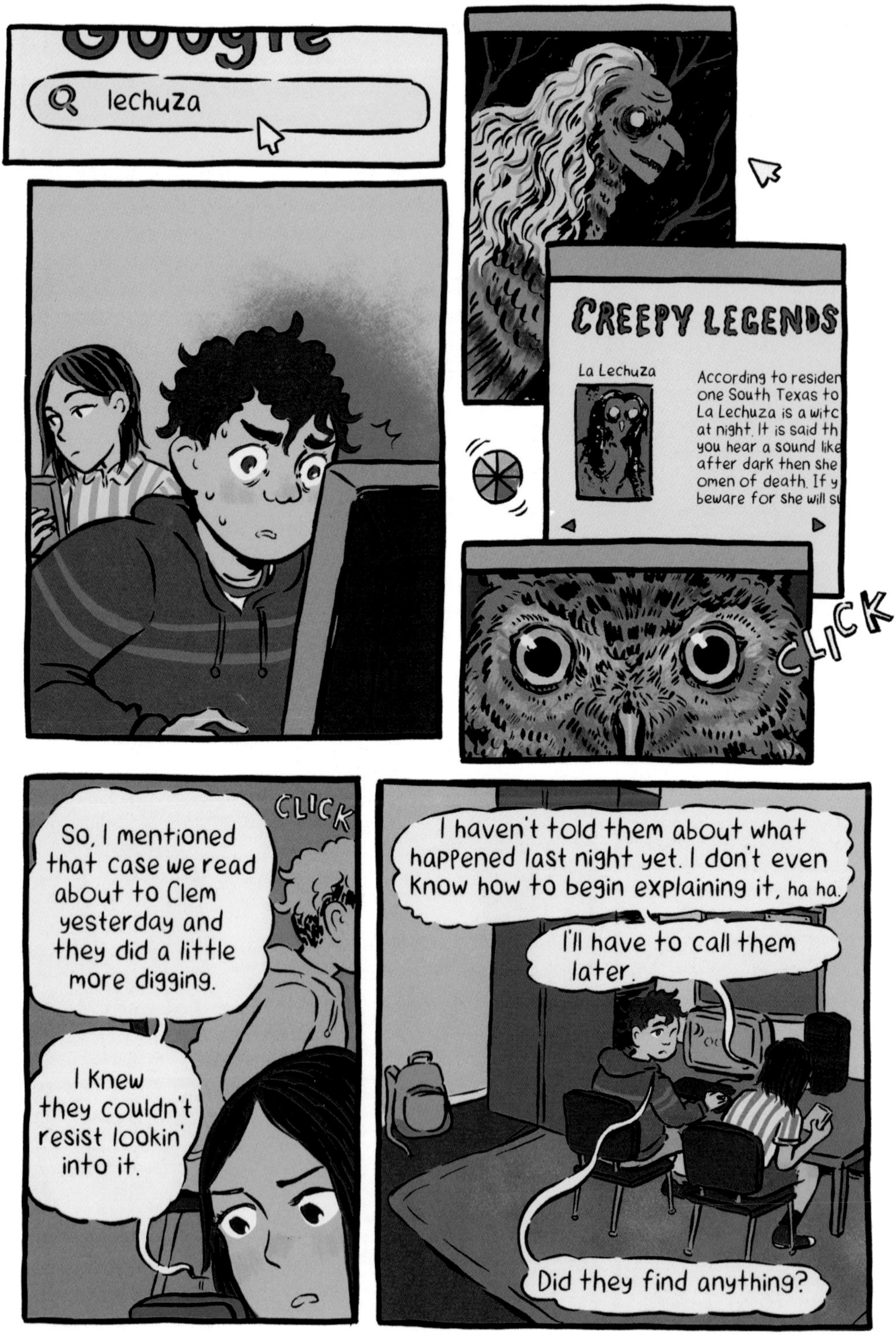

Google
lechuza
CREEPY LEGENDS
La Lechuza
According to residen
one South Texas to
La Lechuza is a witc
at night. It is said th
you hear a sound like
after dark then she
omen of death. If y
beware for she will s
CLICK
CLICK
So, I mentioned that case we read about to Clem yesterday and they did a little more digging.
I knew they couldn't resist lookin' into it.
I haven't told them about what happened last night yet. I don't even know how to begin explaining it, ha ha.
I'll have to call them later.
Did they find anything?

They couldn't find much— a few more old articles about the disappearances.

And. . .

Hmm...

And?

Oh!

Sorry!

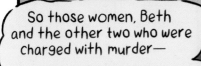

So those women, Beth and the other two who were charged with murder—

they all went missing right before they were supposed to be executed and were never heard from again.

None of the bodies ever turned up either.

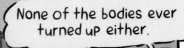

Clem couldn't find much else.

They're a little preoccupied with youthful fun though. Whatever that is, ha ha.

Do you think they could have been. . . lechuzas?

I don't know. Maybe.

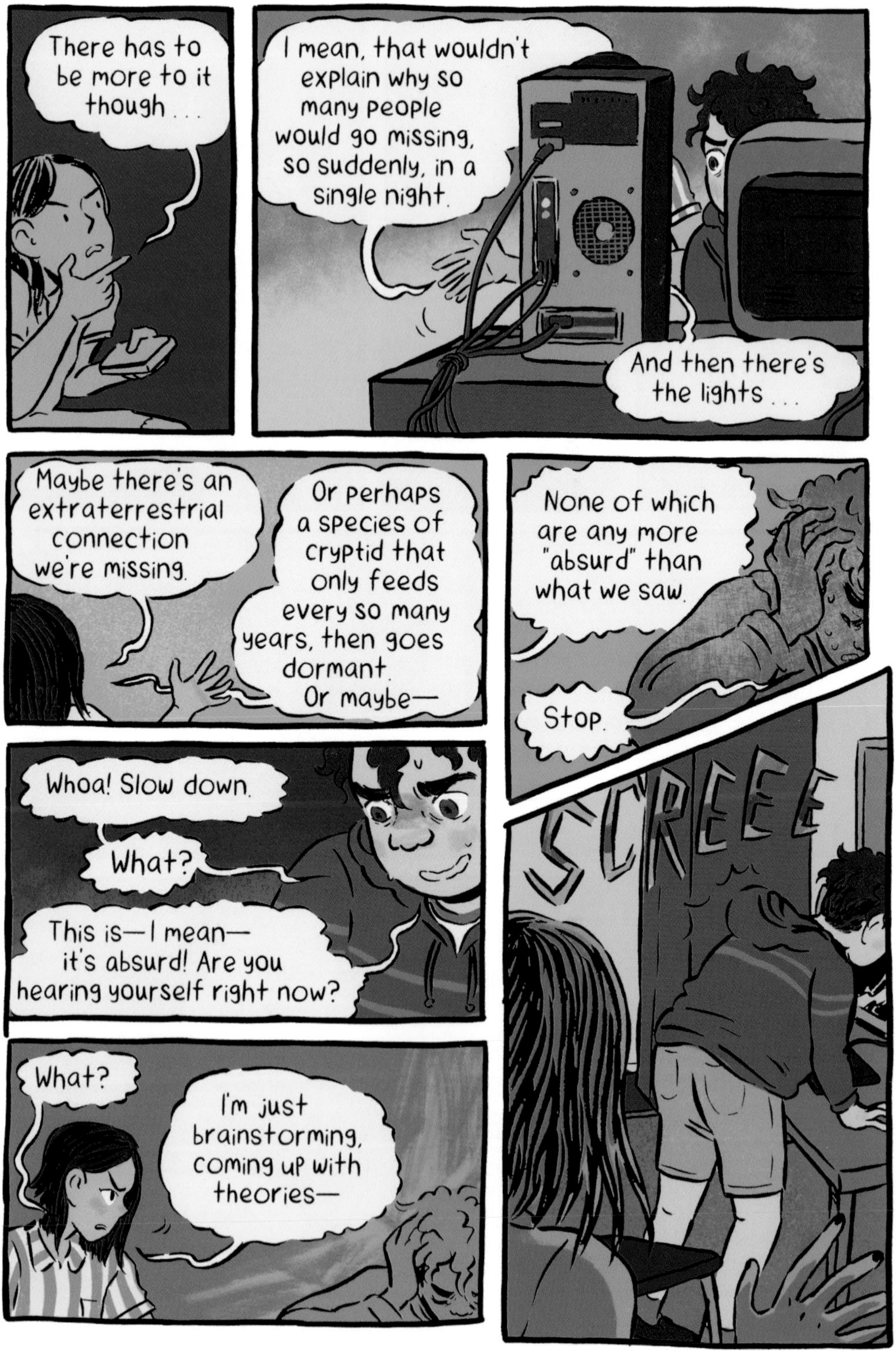
There has to be more to it though . . .
I mean, that wouldn't explain why so many people would go missing, so suddenly, in a single night.
And then there's the lights . . .
Maybe there's an extraterrestrial connection we're missing.
Or perhaps a species of cryptid that only feeds every so many years, then goes dormant.
Or maybe—
Whoa! Slow down.
What?
This is—I mean— it's absurd! Are you hearing yourself right now?
What?
I'm just brainstorming, coming up with theories—
None of which are any more "absurd" than what we saw.
Stop.
SCREEE

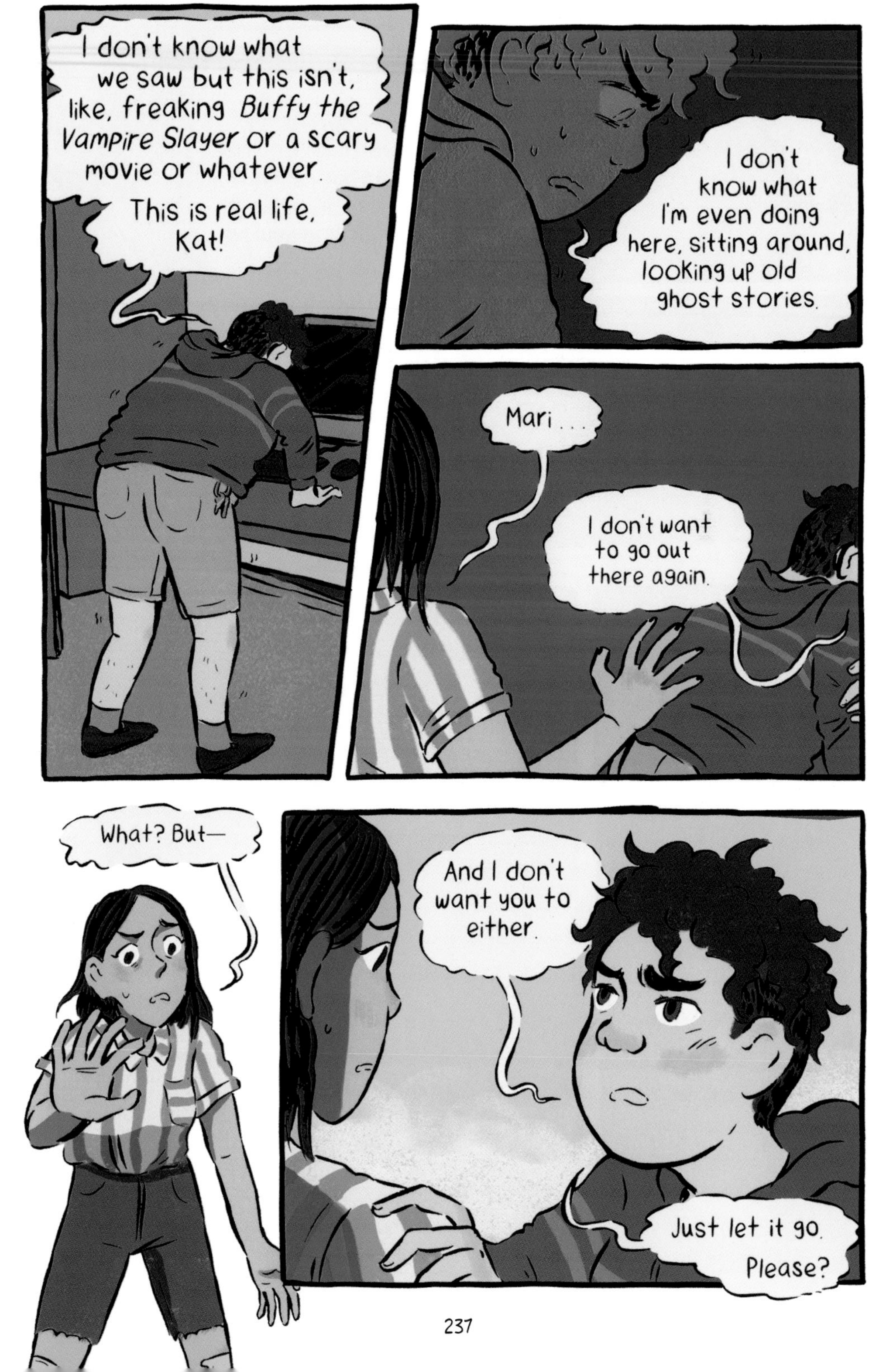
I don't know what we saw but this isn't, like, freaking *Buffy the Vampire Slayer* or a scary movie or whatever.
This is real life, Kat!
I don't know what I'm even doing here, sitting around, looking up old ghost stories.
Mari . . .
I don't want to go out there again.
What? But—
And I don't want you to either.
Just let it go.
Please?

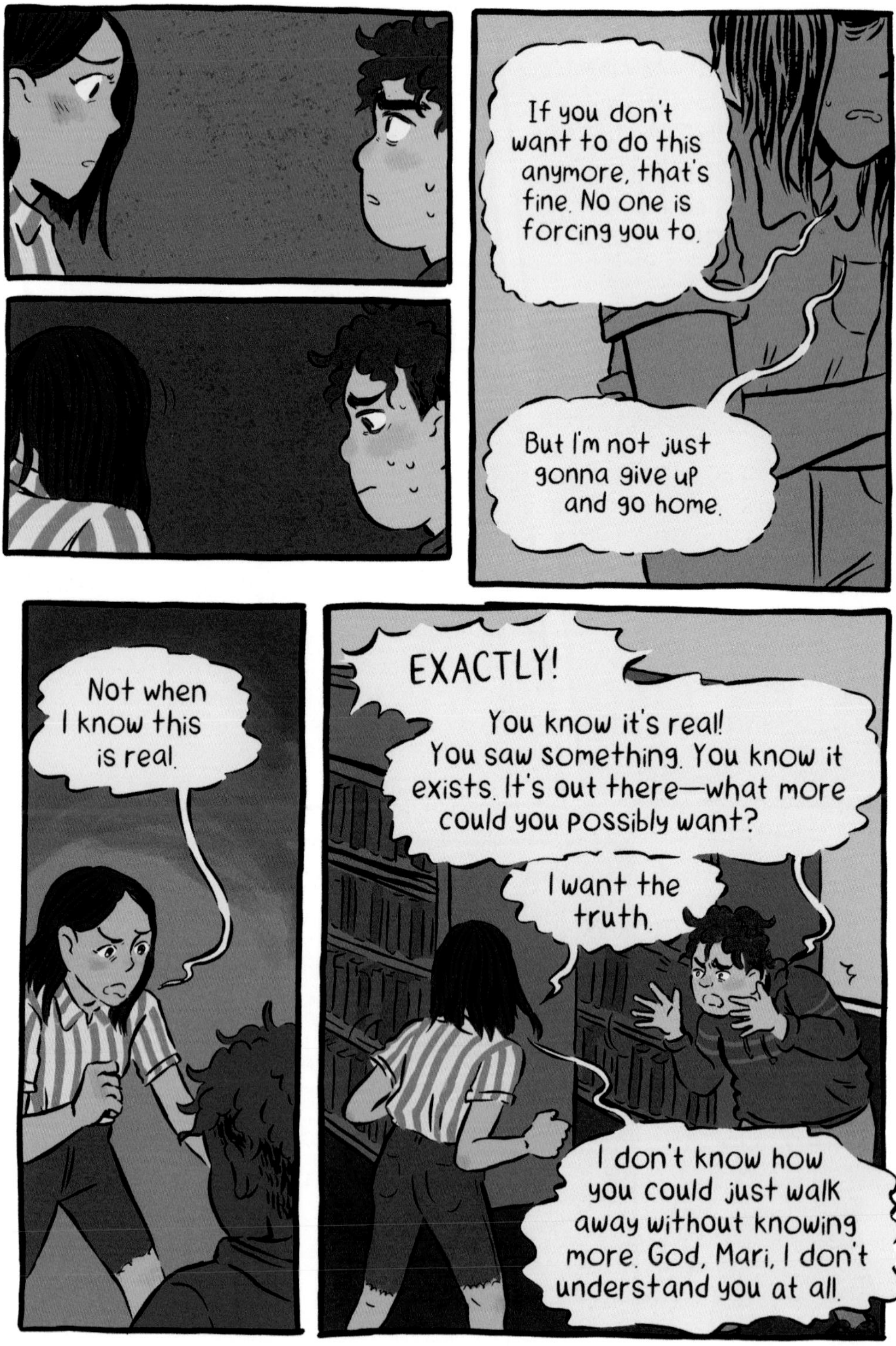
If you don't want to do this anymore, that's fine. No one is forcing you to.
But I'm not just gonna give up and go home.
Not when I know this is real.
EXACTLY!
You know it's real! You saw something. You know it exists. It's out there—what more could you possibly want?
I want the truth.
I don't know how you could just walk away without knowing more. God, Mari, I don't understand you at all.

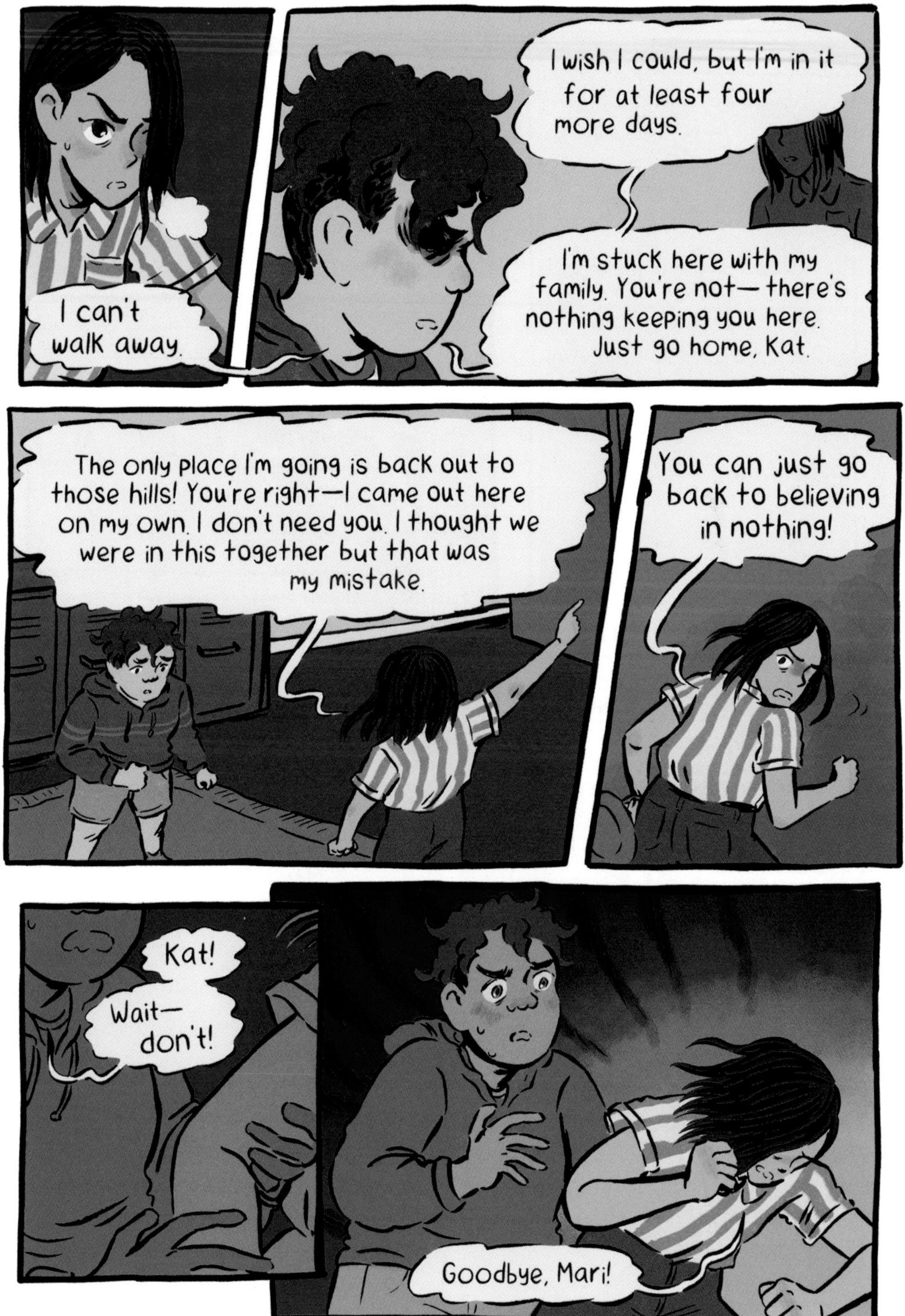
I can't walk away.
I wish I could, but I'm in it for at least four more days.
I'm stuck here with my family. You're not— there's nothing keeping you here. Just go home, Kat.
The only place I'm going is back out to those hills! You're right—I came out here on my own. I don't need you. I thought we were in this together but that was my mistake.
You can just go back to believing in nothing!
Kat!
Wait— don't!
Goodbye, Mari!

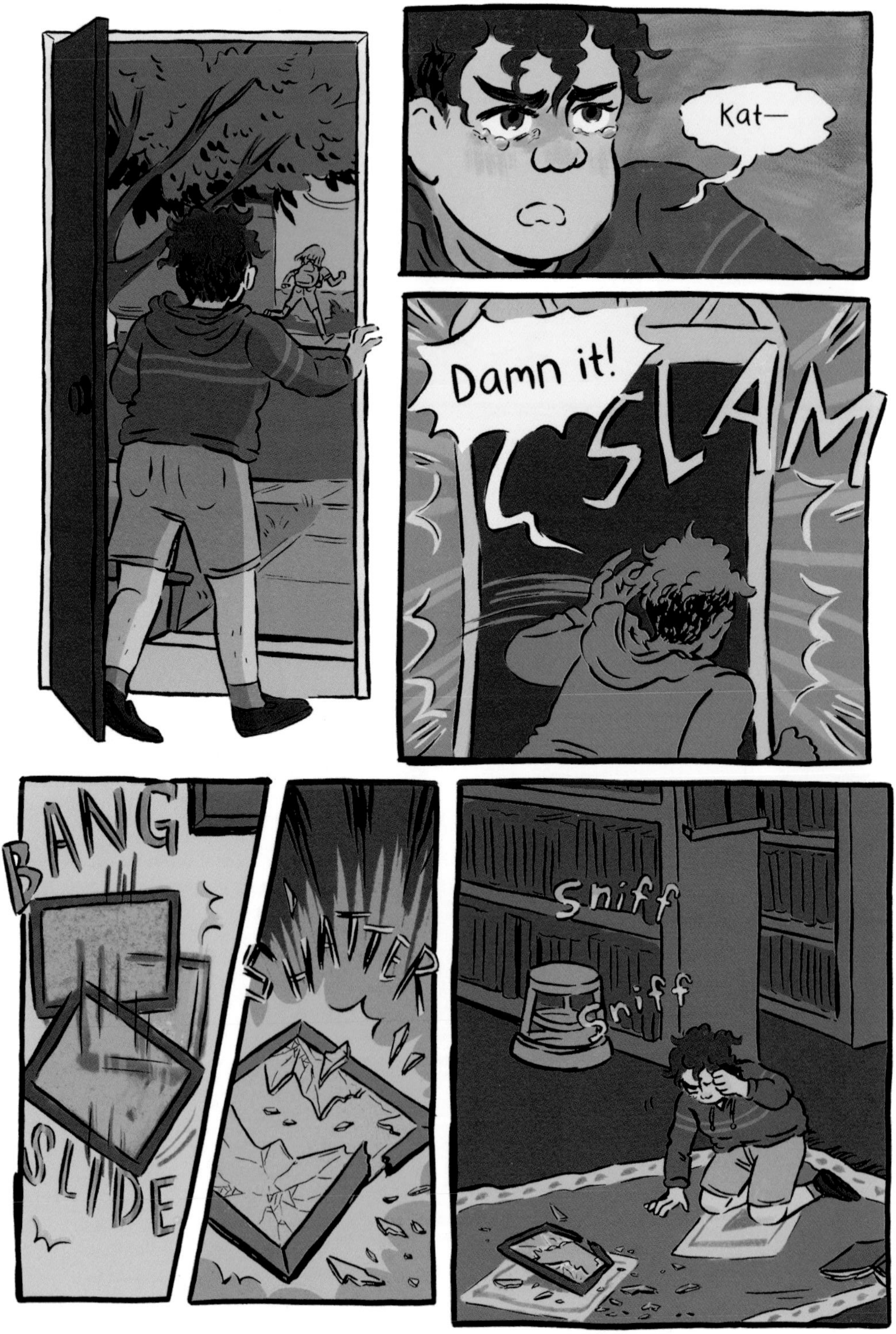
Kat—
Damn it!
SLAM
BANG
SLIDE
SHATTER
Sniff
Sniff

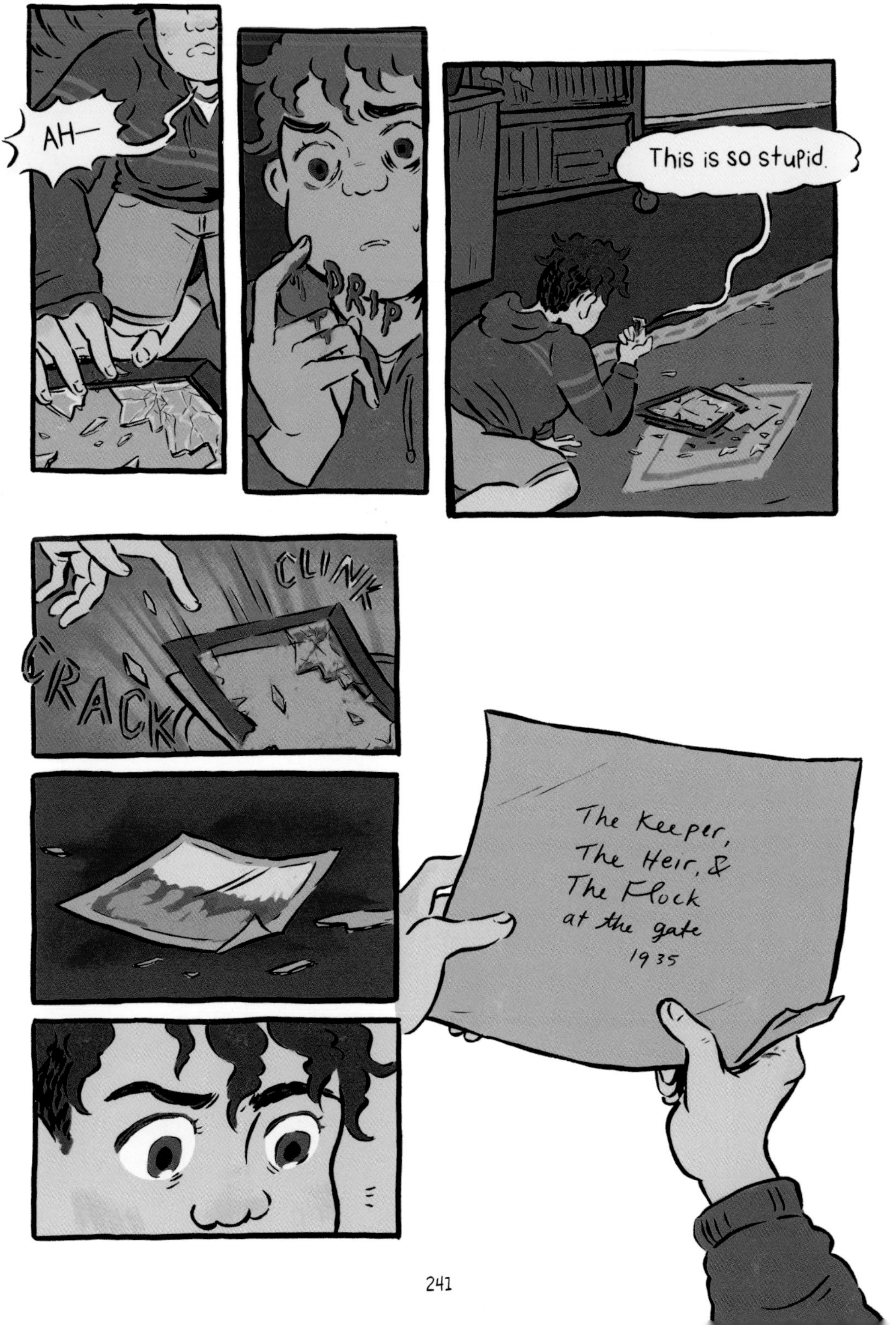

AH—
DRIP
This is so stupid.
CLINK
CRACK
The Keeper,
The Heir, &
The Flock
at the gate
1935

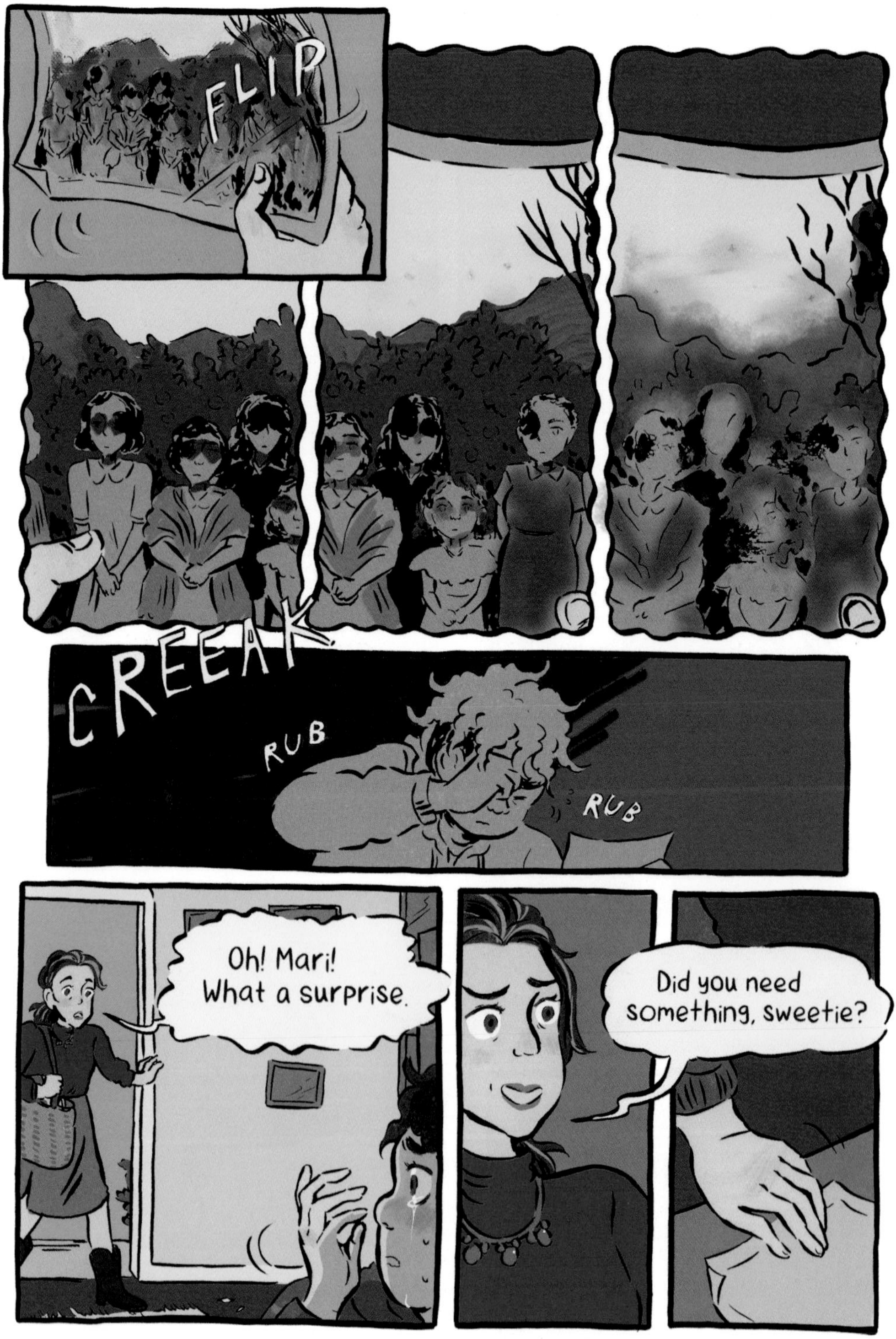
FLIP
CREEAK
RUB
RUB
Oh! Mari! What a surprise.
Did you need something, sweetie?

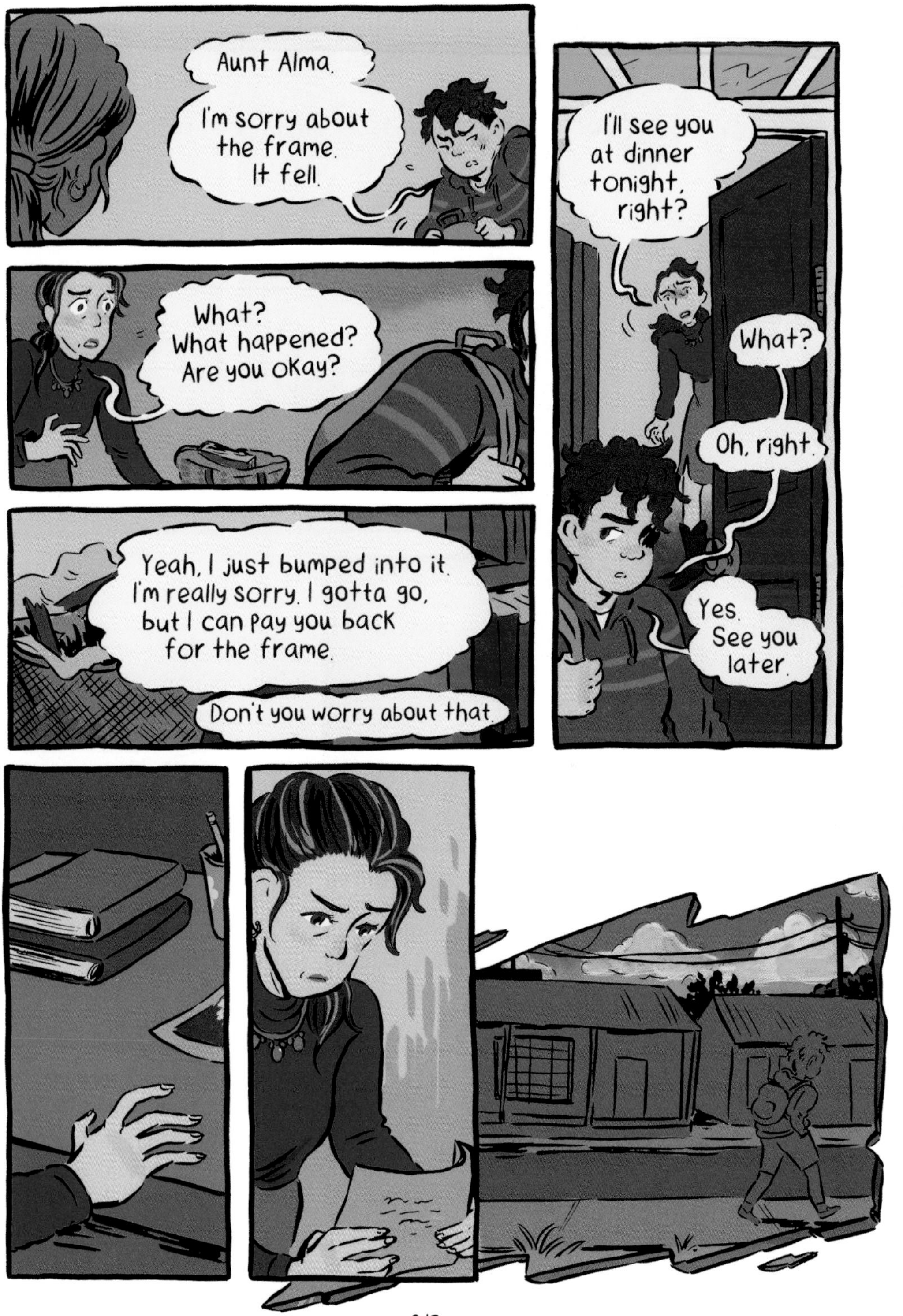
Aunt Alma.
I'm sorry about the frame. It fell.
What? What happened? Are you okay?
Yeah, I just bumped into it. I'm really sorry. I gotta go, but I can pay you back for the frame.
Don't you worry about that.
I'll see you at dinner tonight, right?
What?
Oh, right.
Yes. See you later.

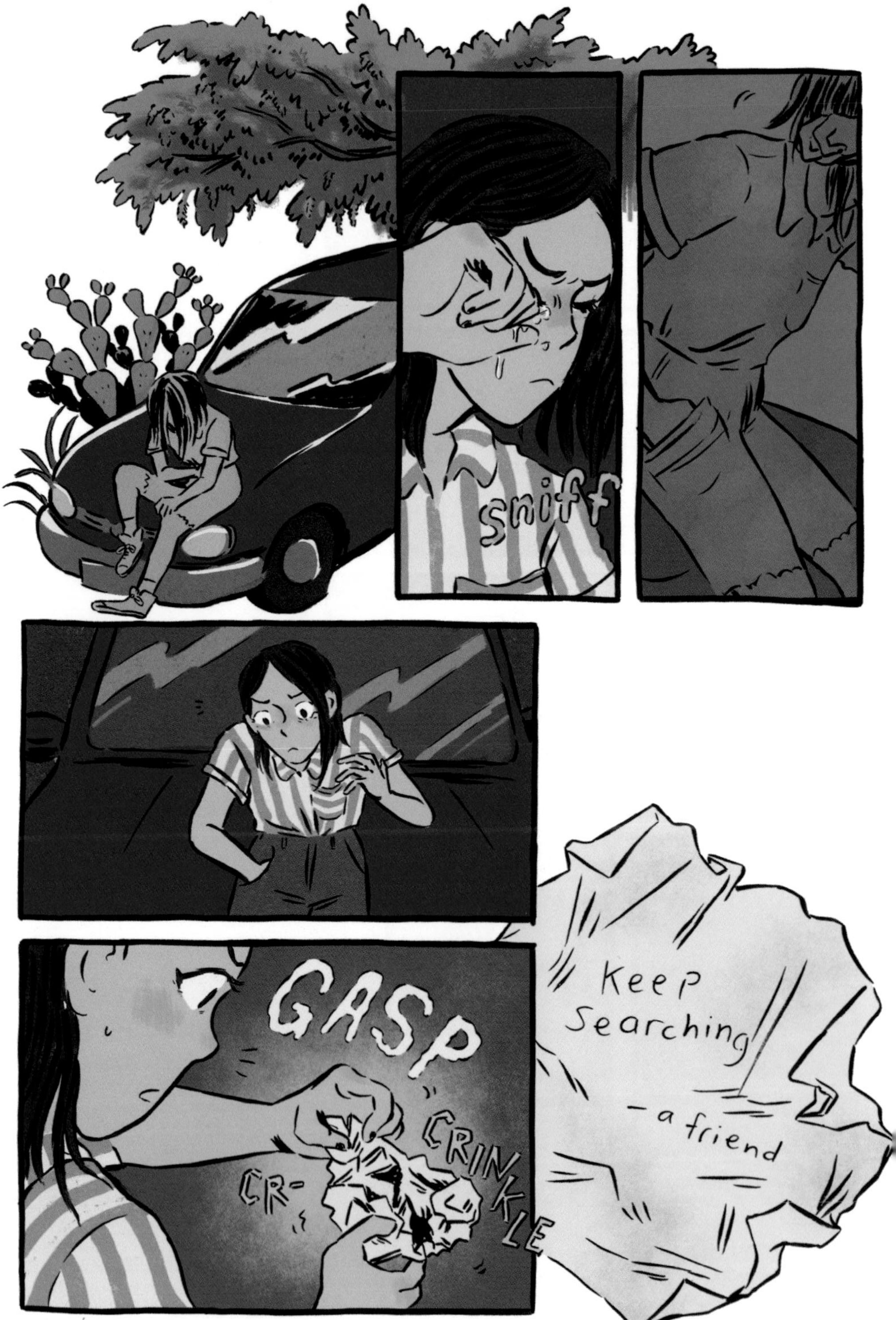
sniff
GASP
CR-
CRINKLE
Keep Searching
-a friend

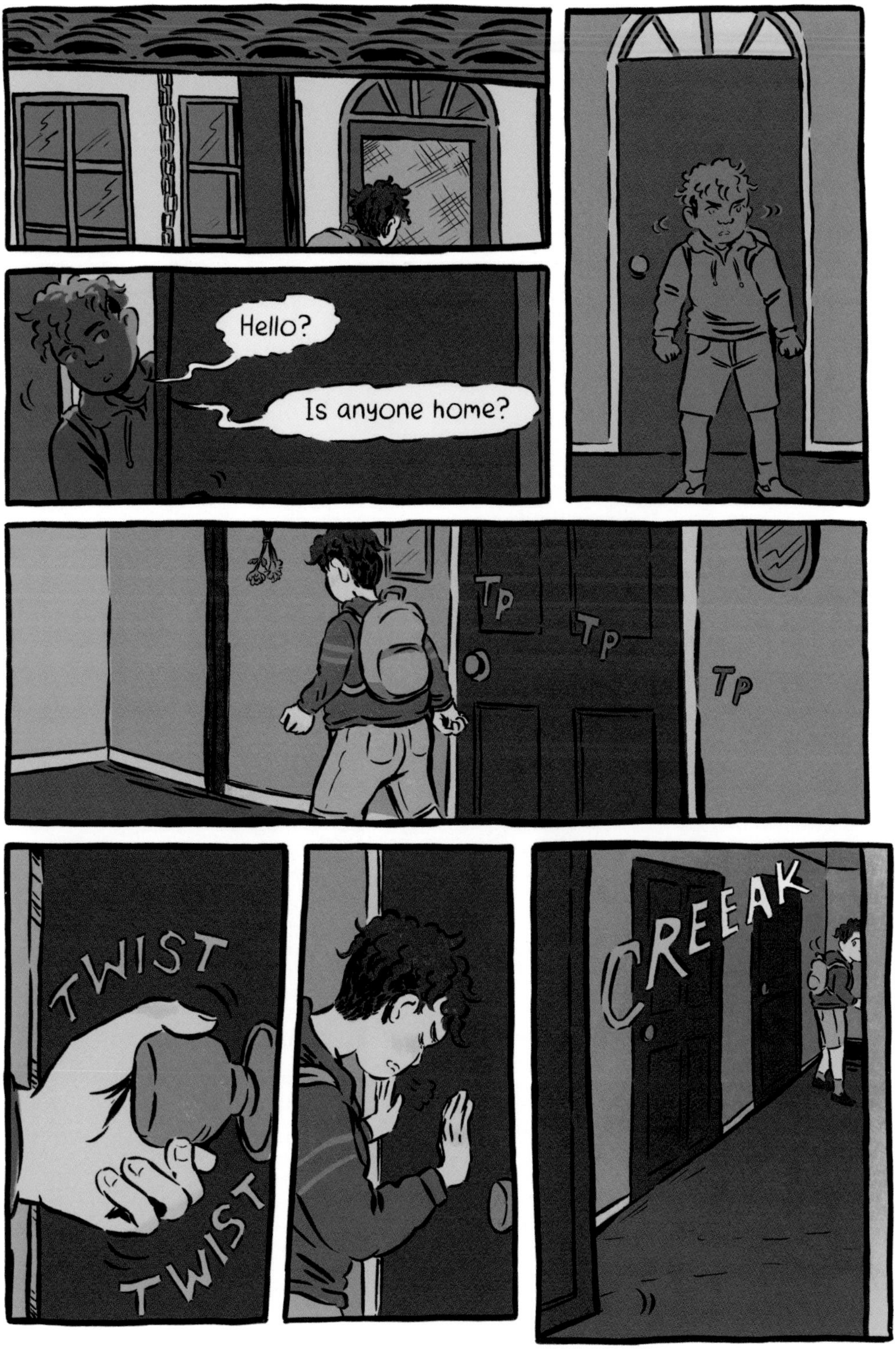
Hello?
Is anyone home?
Tp
Tp
Tp
TWIST
TWIST
CREEAK

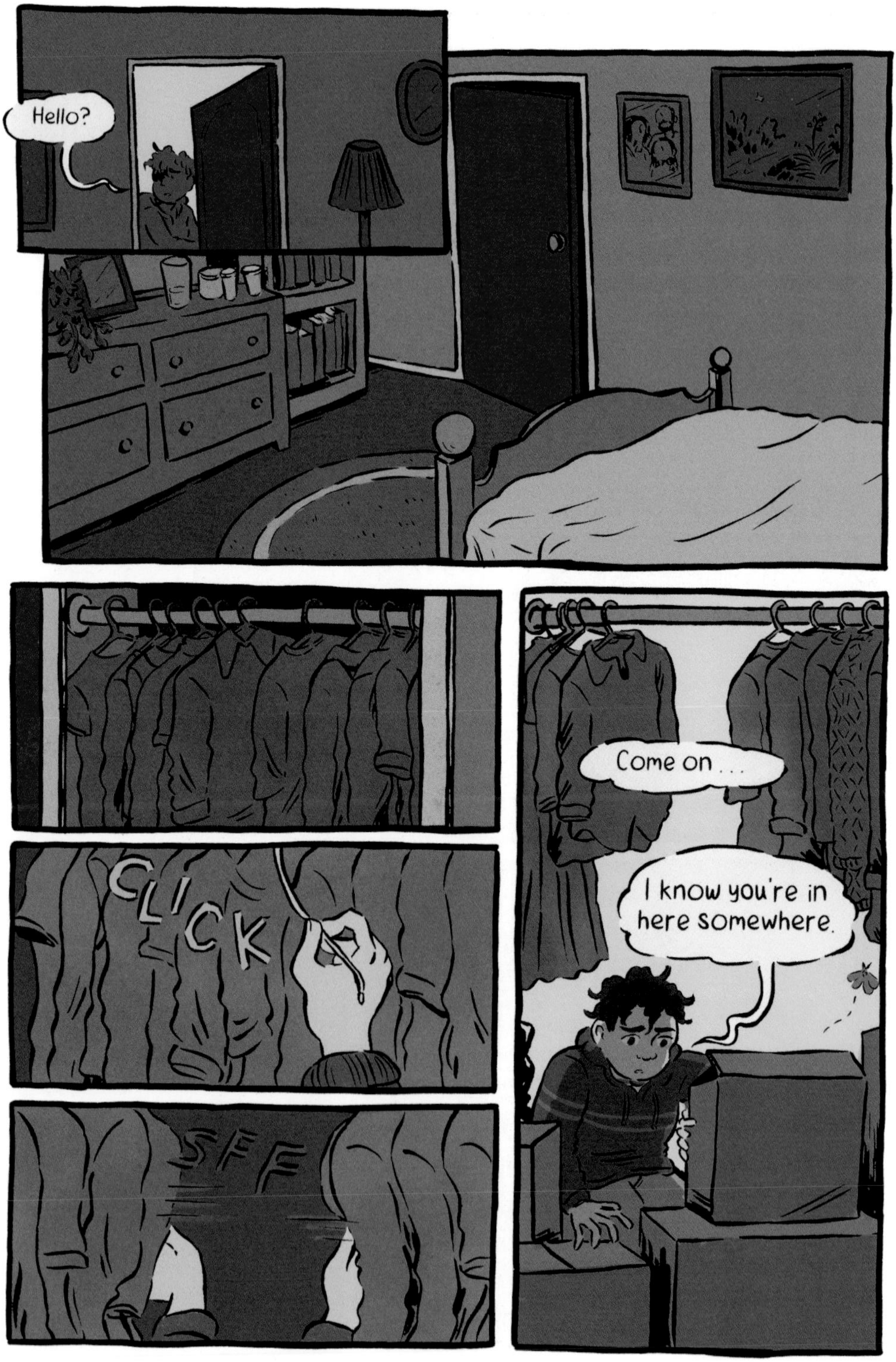
Hello?
CLICK
SFF
Come on . . .
I know you're in here somewhere.

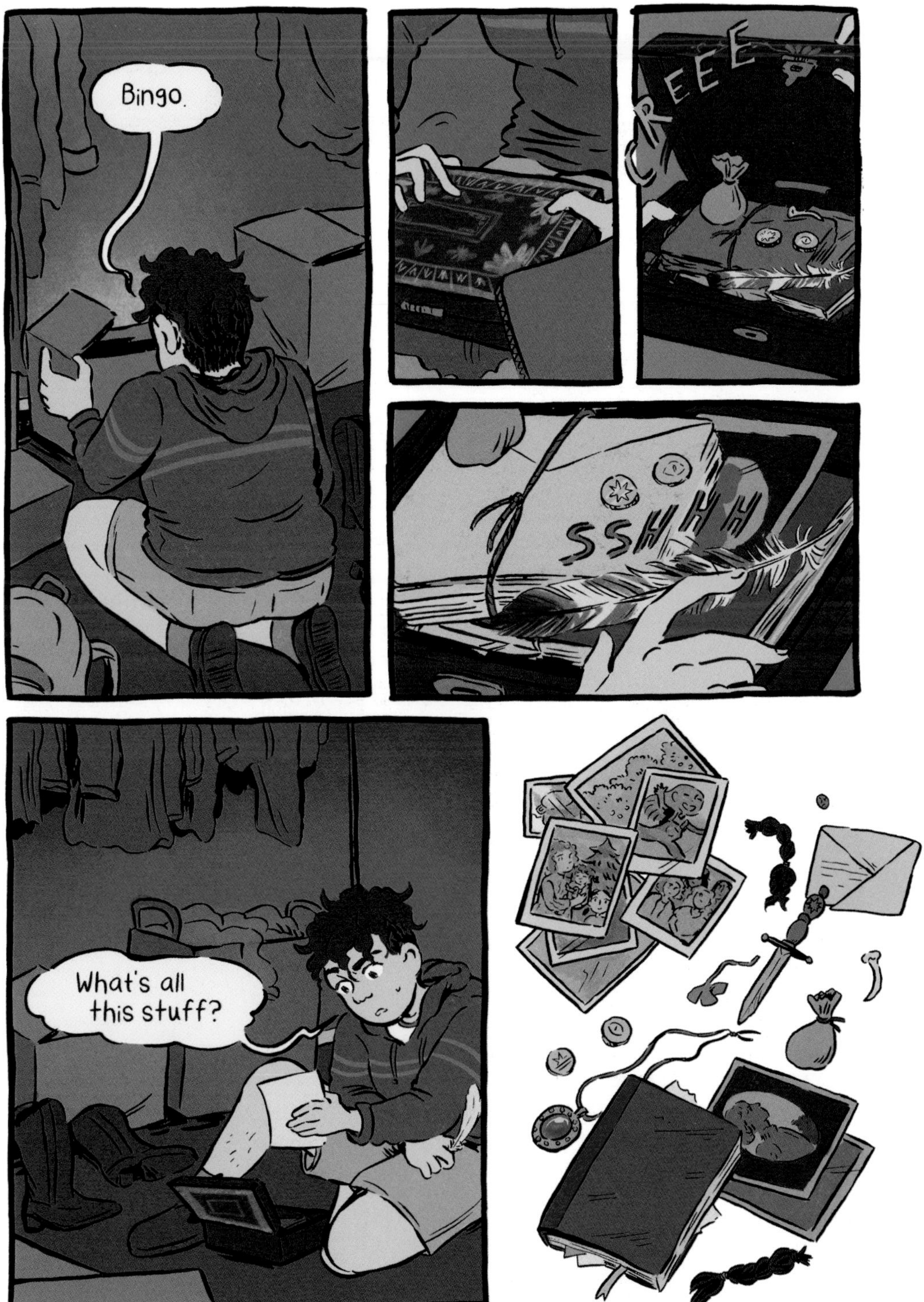
Bingo.
REEE
SSHHH
What's all this stuff?

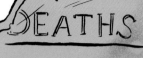

DEATHS

Elizabeth Castillo is still missing and is, at this time, presumed dead. She leaves behind a three-year-old daughter, now in the care of relatives in Estrella Roja. Any information regarding her whereabouts should be sent to

FLIP

FLUTTER

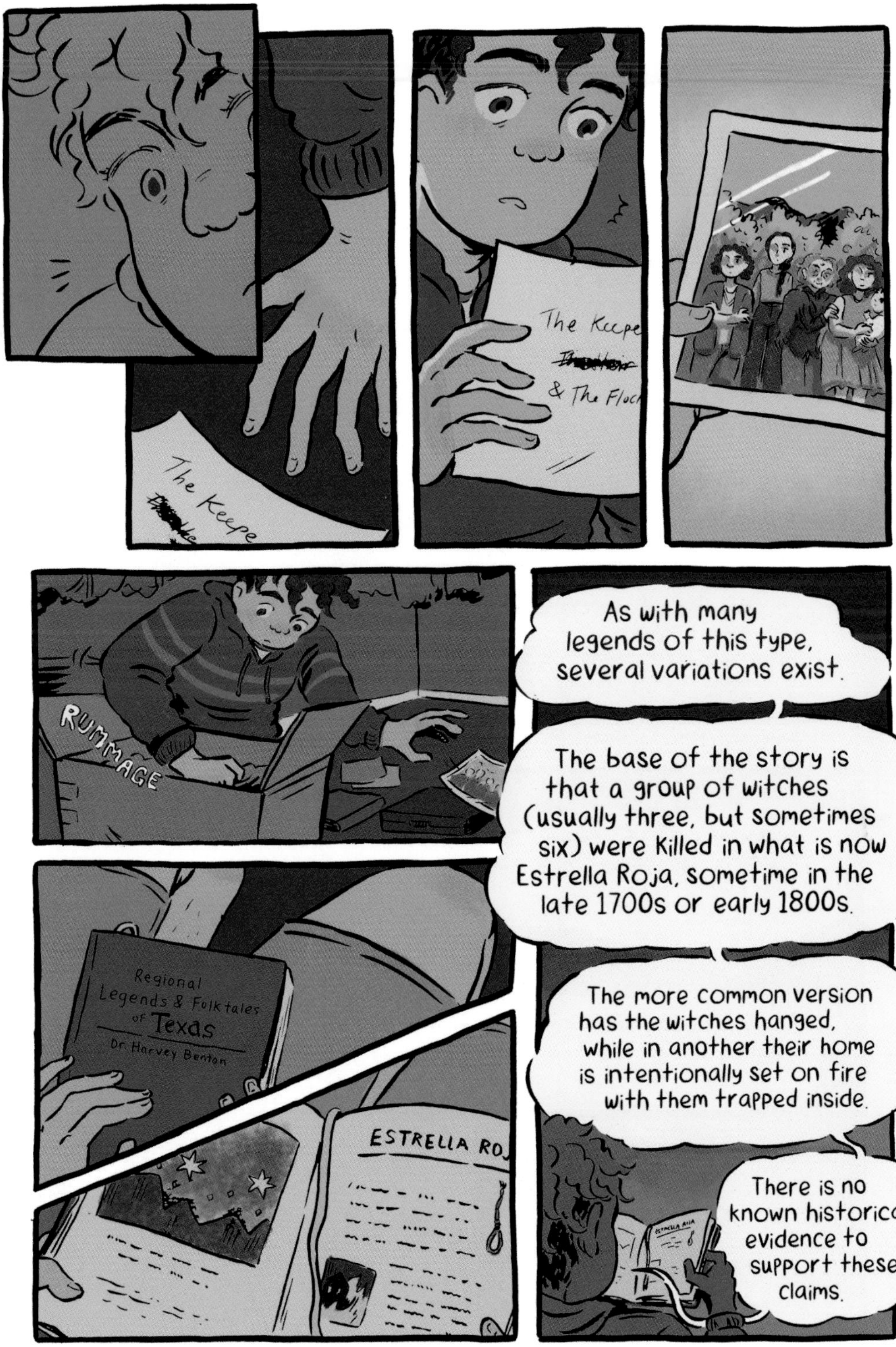
The Keepe
The Keepe
& The Floc
RUMMAGE
As with many legends of this type, several variations exist.
The base of the story is that a group of witches (usually three, but sometimes six) were killed in what is now Estrella Roja, sometime in the late 1700s or early 1800s.
Regional Legends & Folktales of Texas
Dr Harvey Benton
ESTRELLA ROJ
The more common version has the witches hanged, while in another their home is intentionally set on fire with them trapped inside.
There is no known historical evidence to support these claims.

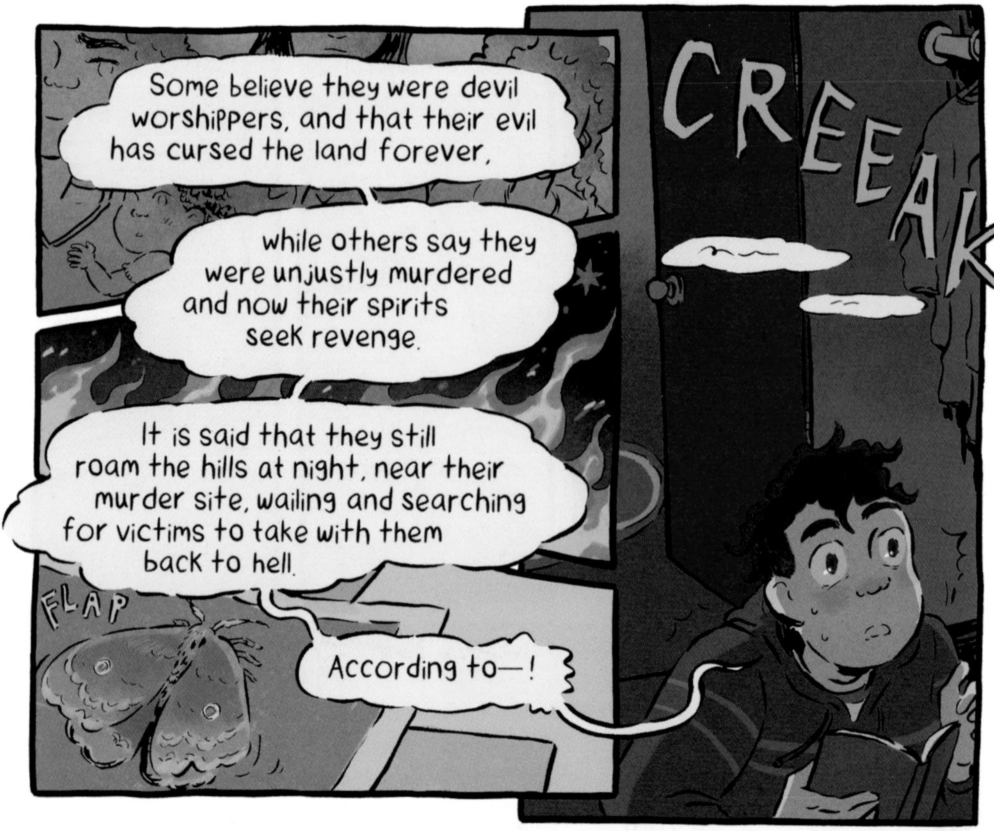
Some believe they were devil worshippers, and that their evil has cursed the land forever,
while others say they were unjustly murdered and now their spirits seek revenge.
It is said that they still roam the hills at night, near their murder site, wailing and searching for victims to take with them back to hell.
FLAP
According to—!
CREEAK

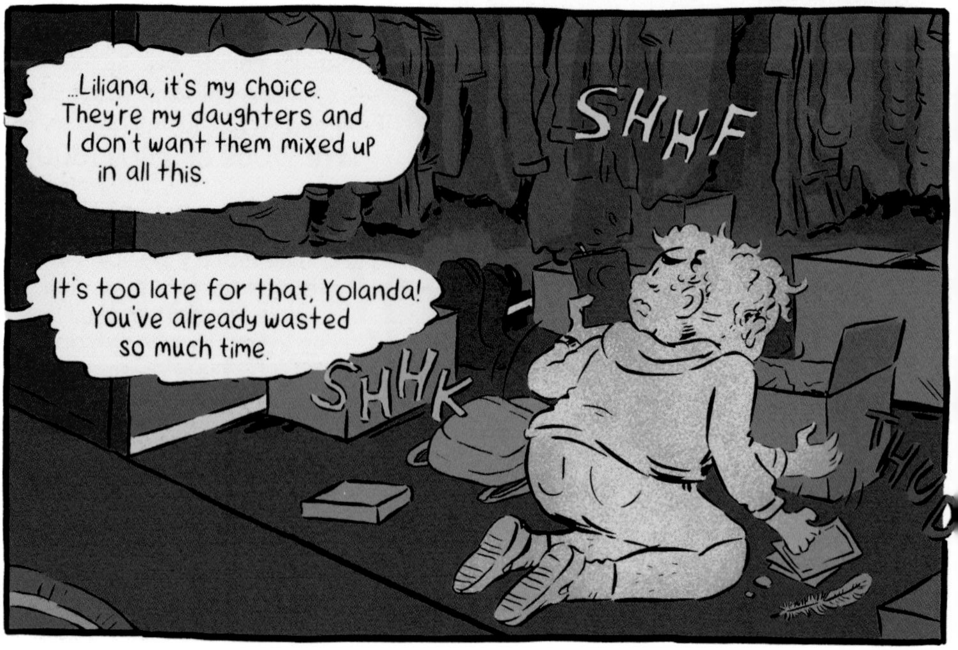
...Liliana, it's my choice. They're my daughters and I don't want them mixed up in all this.
SHHF
It's too late for that, Yolanda! You've already wasted so much time.
SHHK

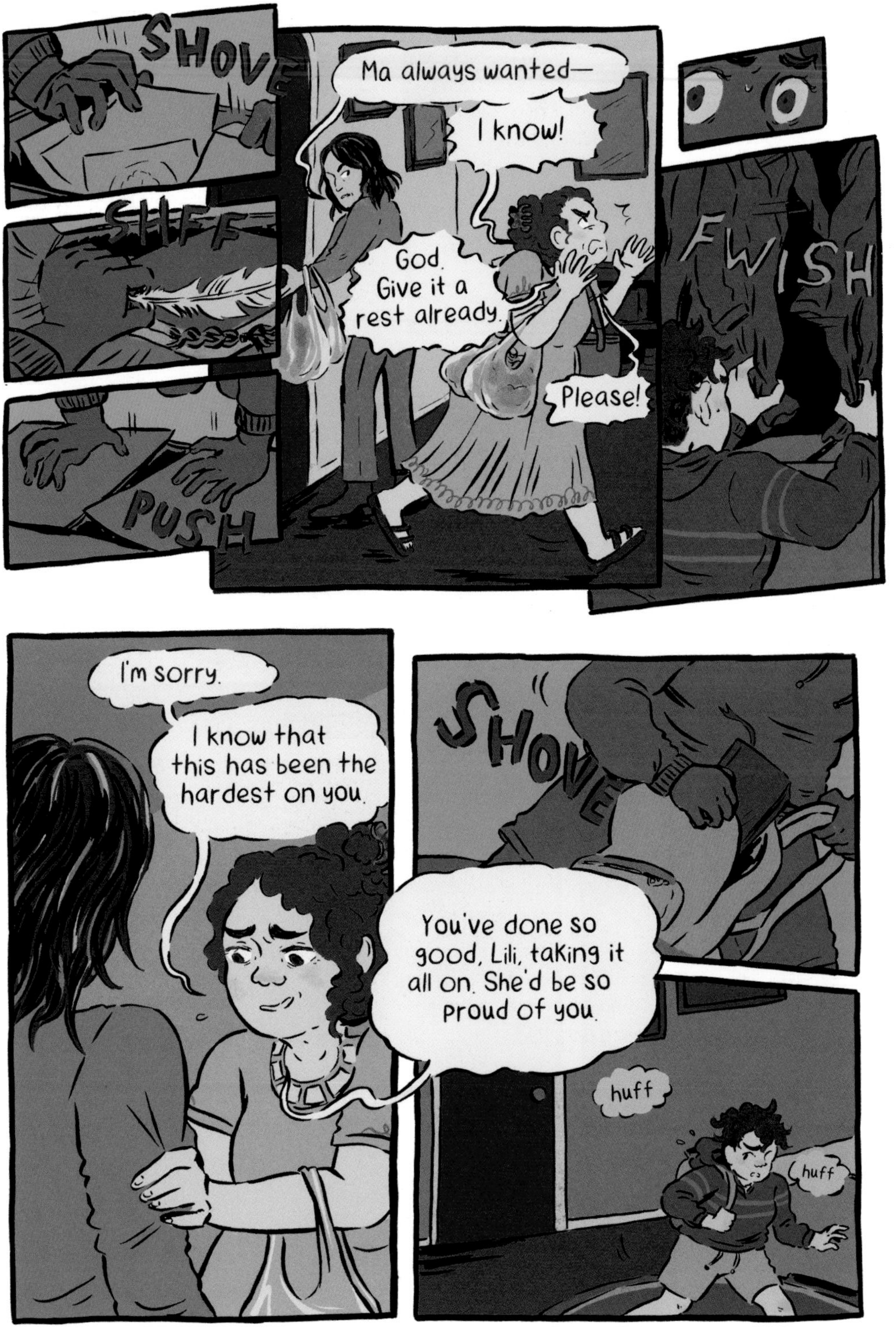
SHOVE
SHFF
PUSH
Ma always wanted—
I know!
God. Give it a rest already.
Please!
FWISH
I'm sorry.
I know that this has been the hardest on you.
You've done so good, Lili, taking it all on. She'd be so proud of you.
SHOVE
huff
huff

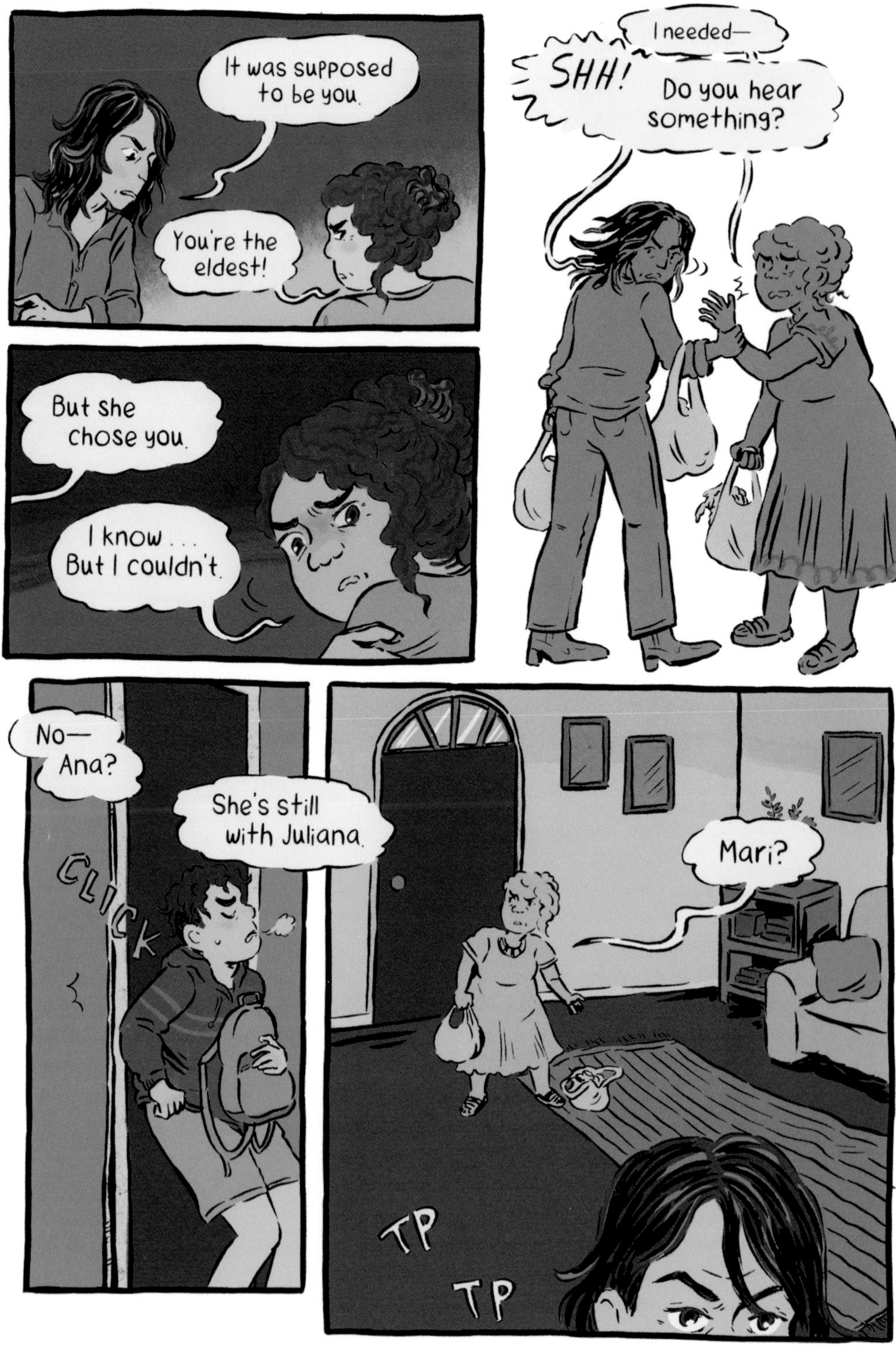
It was supposed to be you.
You're the eldest!
But she chose you.
I know . . . But I couldn't.
I needed—
SHH! Do you hear something?
No— Ana?
She's still with Juliana.
CLICK
Mari?
TP
TP

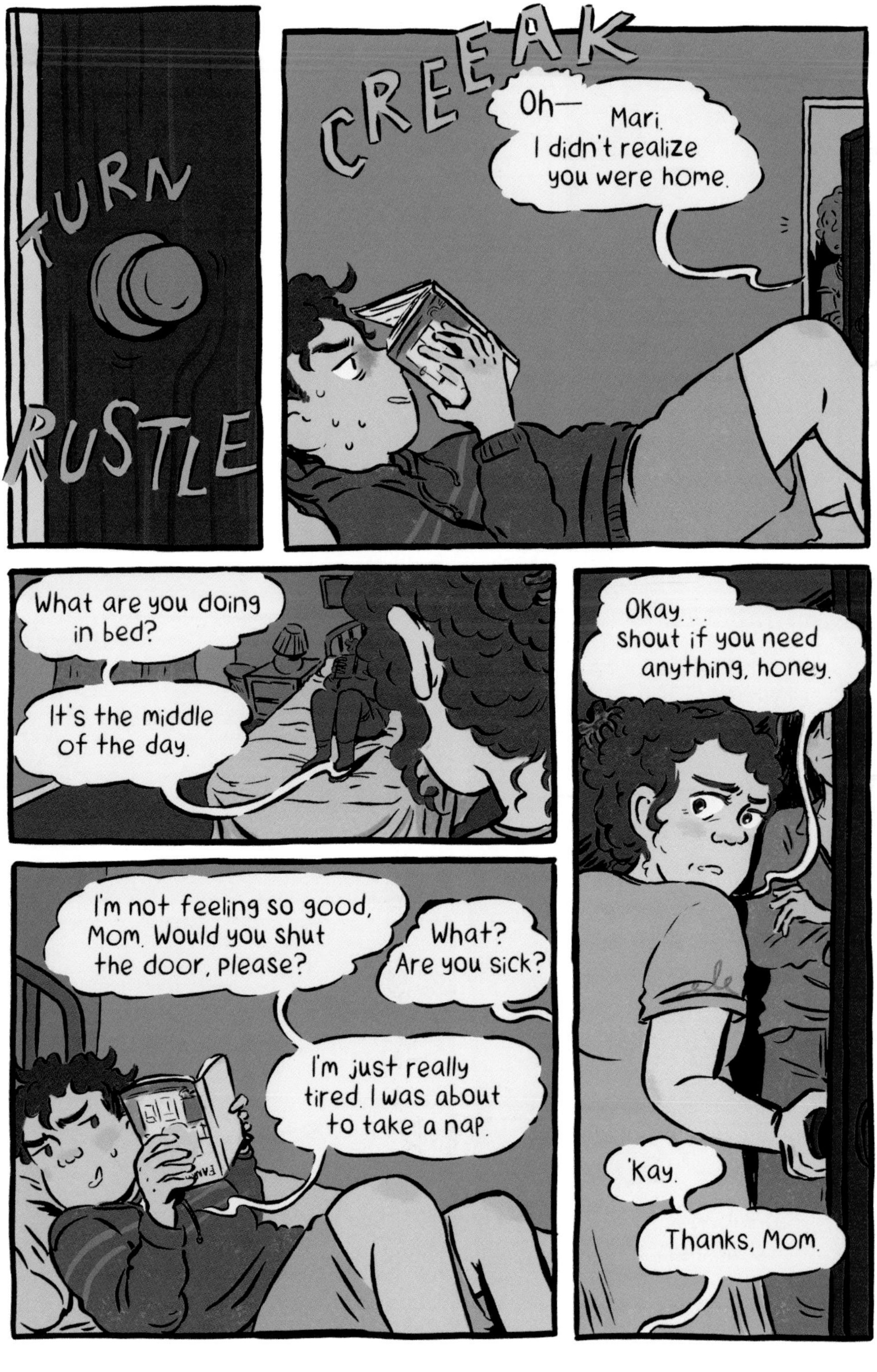
TURN
RUSTLE
CREEAK
Oh— Mari. I didn't realize you were home.
What are you doing in bed?
It's the middle of the day.
I'm not feeling so good, Mom. Would you shut the door, please?
What? Are you sick?
I'm just really tired. I was about to take a nap.
Okay. . . shout if you need anything, honey.
'Kay.
Thanks, Mom.

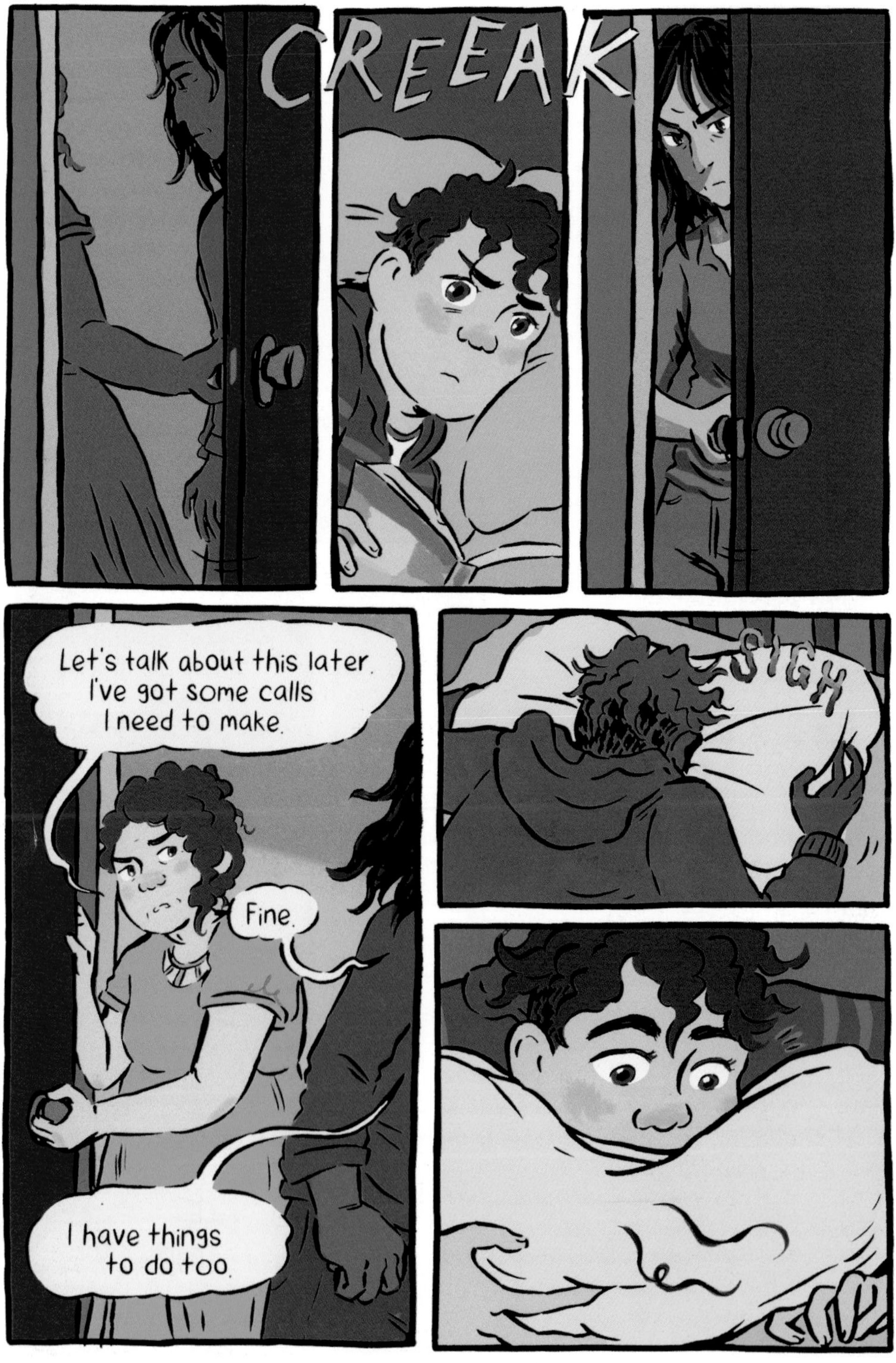
CREEAK
Let's talk about this later. I've got some calls I need to make.
Fine.
I have things to do too.
SIGH

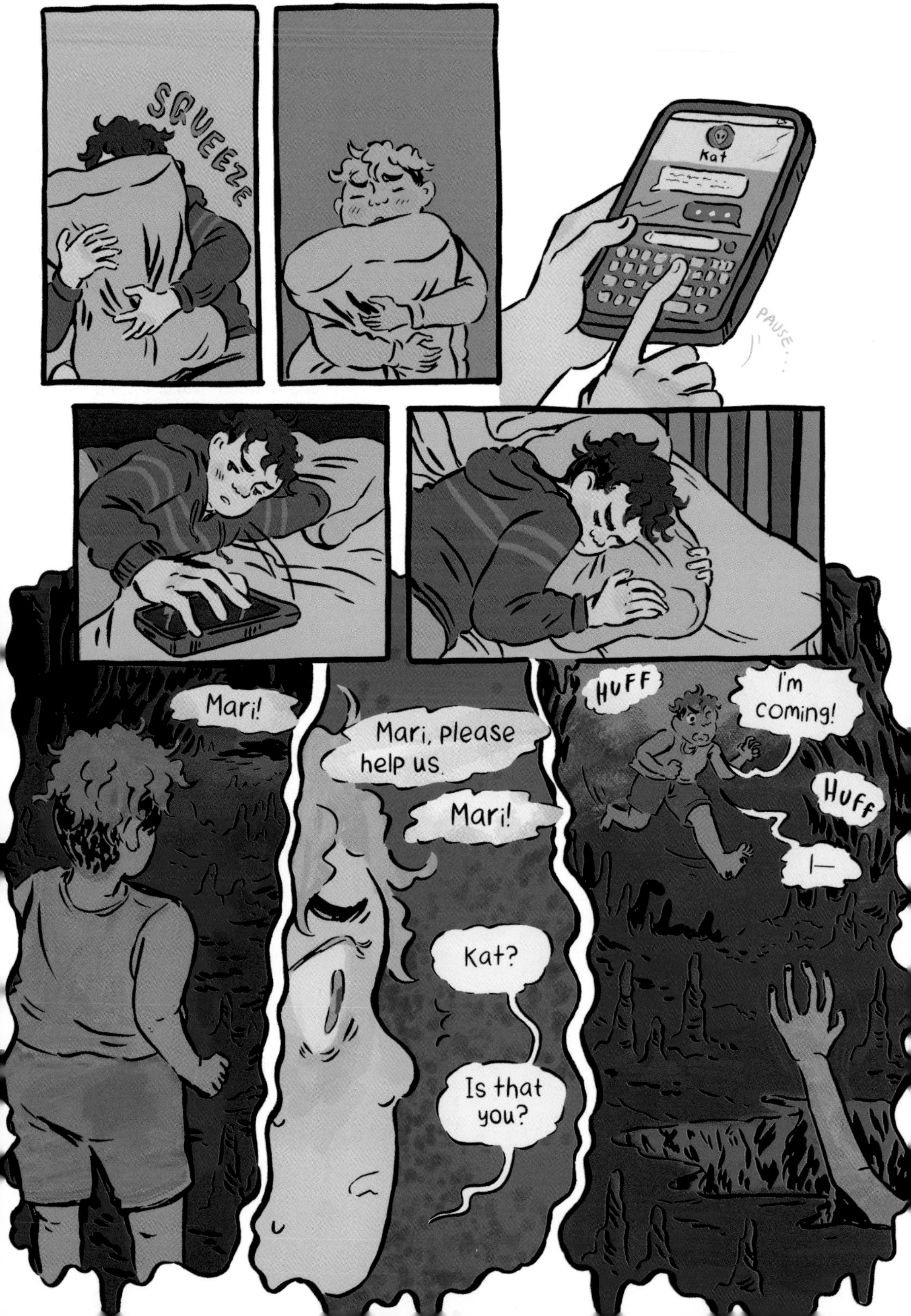
SQUEEZE
Kat
PAUSE...
Mari!
Mari, please help us.
Mari!
Kat?
Is that you?
HUFF
I'm coming!
HUFF
I—

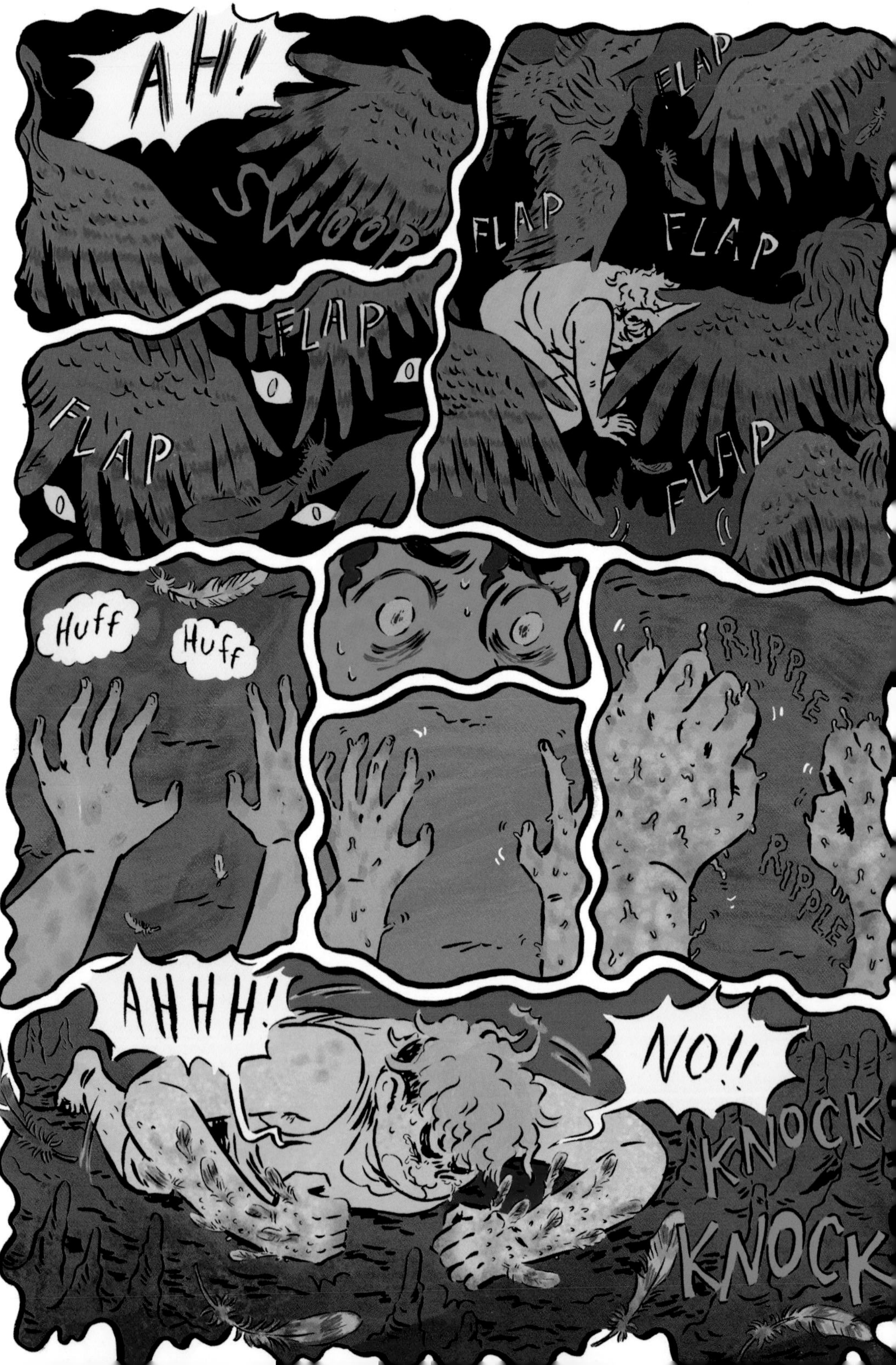
AH!
SWOOP
FLAP
FLAP
FLAP
FLAP
FLAP
FLAP
Huff
Huff
RIPPLE
RIPPLE
AHHH!
NO!!
KNOCK
KNOCK

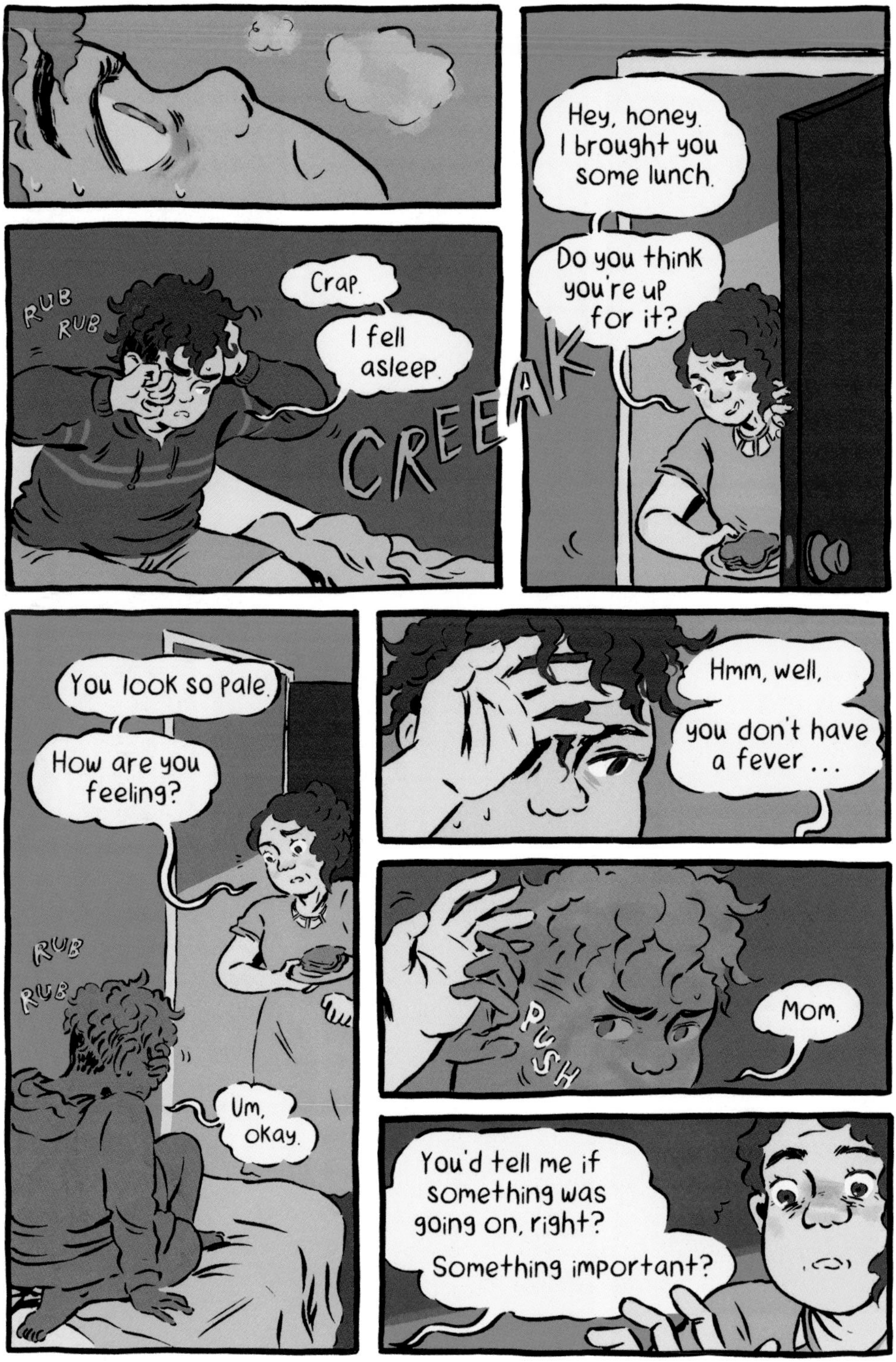
RUB RUB
Crap.
I fell asleep.
CREEAK
Hey, honey. I brought you some lunch.
Do you think you're up for it?
You look so pale.
How are you feeling?
RUB RUB
Um, okay.
Hmm, well,
you don't have a fever ...
PUSH
Mom.
You'd tell me if something was going on, right?
Something important?

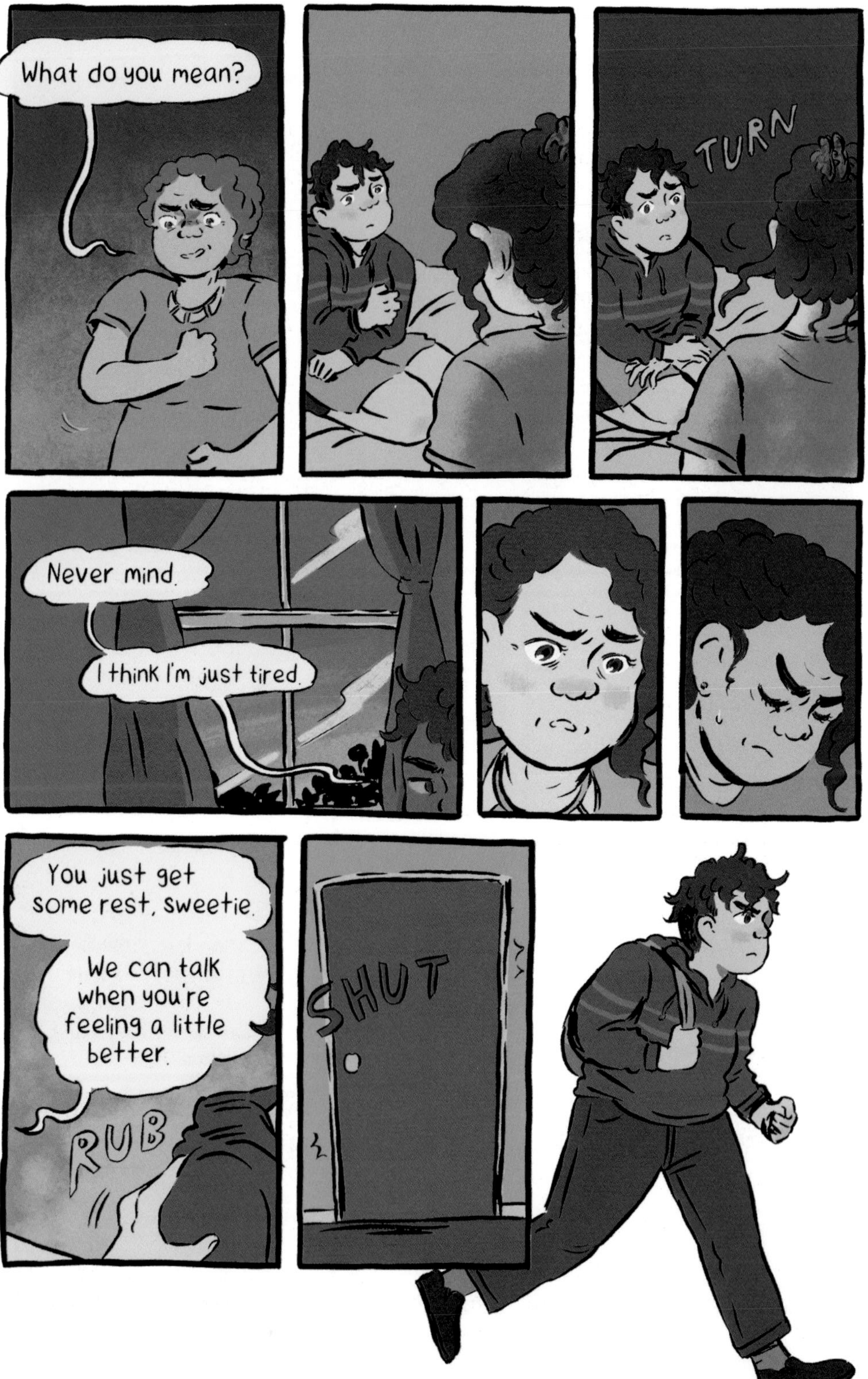
What do you mean?
TURN
Never mind.
I think I'm just tired.
You just get some rest, sweetie.
We can talk when you're feeling a little better.
RUB
SHUT

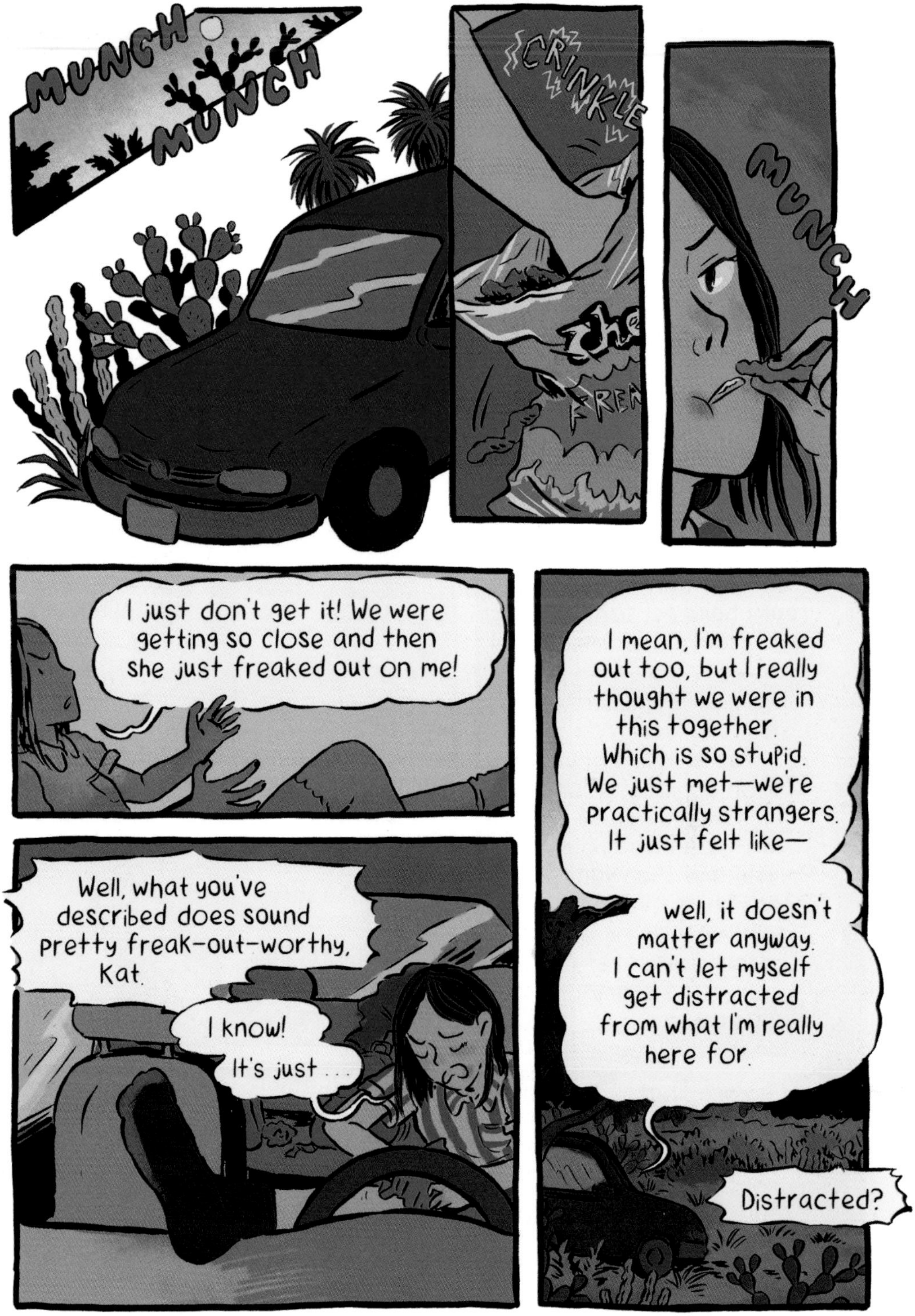
MUNCH MUNCH
CRINKLE
MUNCH
I just don't get it! We were getting so close and then she just freaked out on me!
I mean, I'm freaked out too, but I really thought we were in this together. Which is so stupid. We just met—we're practically strangers. It just felt like—
Well, what you've described does sound pretty freak-out-worthy, Kat.
I know!
It's just . . .
well, it doesn't matter anyway. I can't let myself get distracted from what I'm really here for.
Distracted?

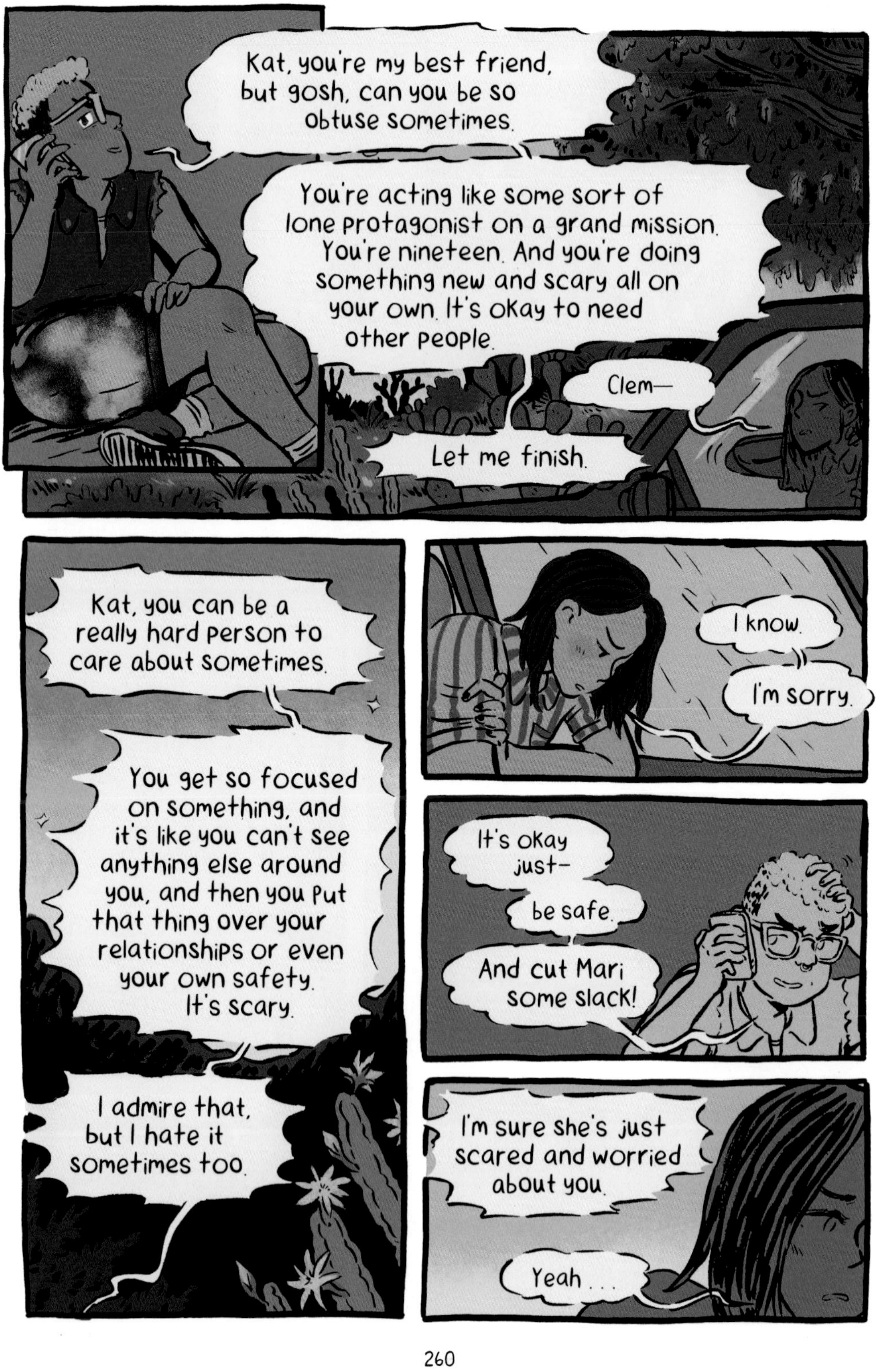
Kat, you're my best friend, but gosh, can you be so obtuse sometimes.
You're acting like some sort of lone protagonist on a grand mission. You're nineteen. And you're doing something new and scary all on your own. It's okay to need other people.
Clem—
Let me finish.
Kat, you can be a really hard person to care about sometimes.
You get so focused on something, and it's like you can't see anything else around you, and then you put that thing over your relationships or even your own safety. It's scary.
I admire that, but I hate it sometimes too.
I know.
I'm sorry.
It's okay just—
be safe.
And cut Mari some slack!
I'm sure she's just scared and worried about you.
Yeah . . .

I shouldn't have yelled at her. God, I'm such a fool!

UGH.

Well, yeah.

But you're my favorite fool. ♡

HEY!

HA HA

Okay, bud, I've got to go. I'm supposed to be helping Cam with the grill, and I think I smell the first batch of veggie dogs burning. There may or may not be a small fire. Look, don't go back to that cave solo, okay? Promise me that.

Clemy . . .

I'm serious. If you get eaten or sacrificed or possessed or whatever, I'll never forgive you! If Mari's not in, then wait. We can return together. I mean it.

Fine, okay.

Good! Now go apologize to her already.

Got it.

Go save your dogs already.

And hey...

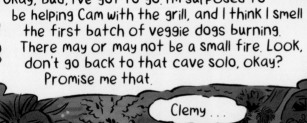

Yeah?

Thanks. You know you're the best, right? I don't know what I'd do without you.

Yeah, yeah.

Love you too, dork.

CLICK

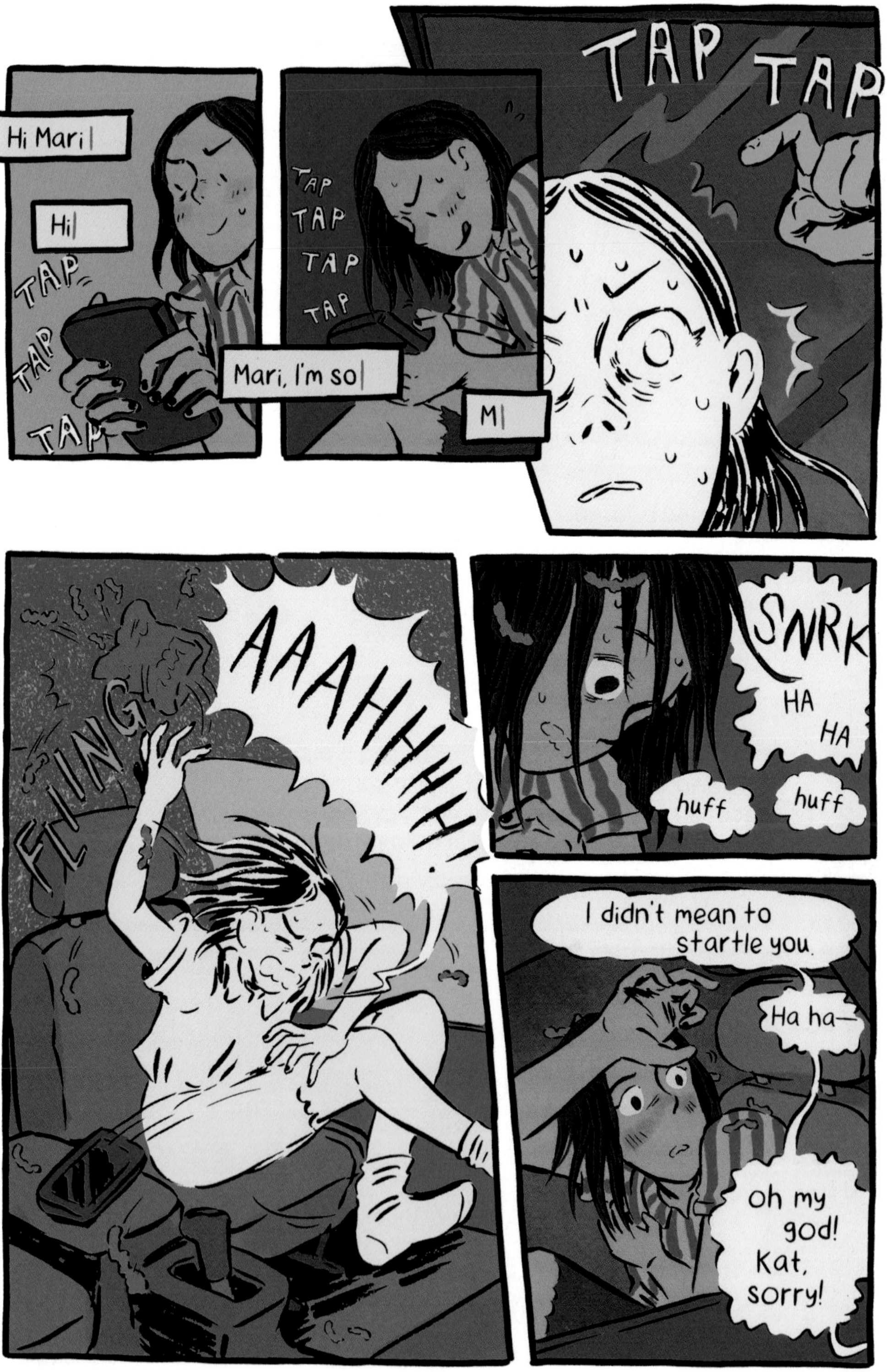
Hi Mari
Hi
TAP
TAP
TAP
TAP
TAP
TAP
TAP
Mari, I'm so
M
TAP TAP
FLING
AAAHHHH!!
SNRK
HA
HA
huff
huff
I didn't mean to startle you.
Ha ha—
Oh my god! Kat, sorry!

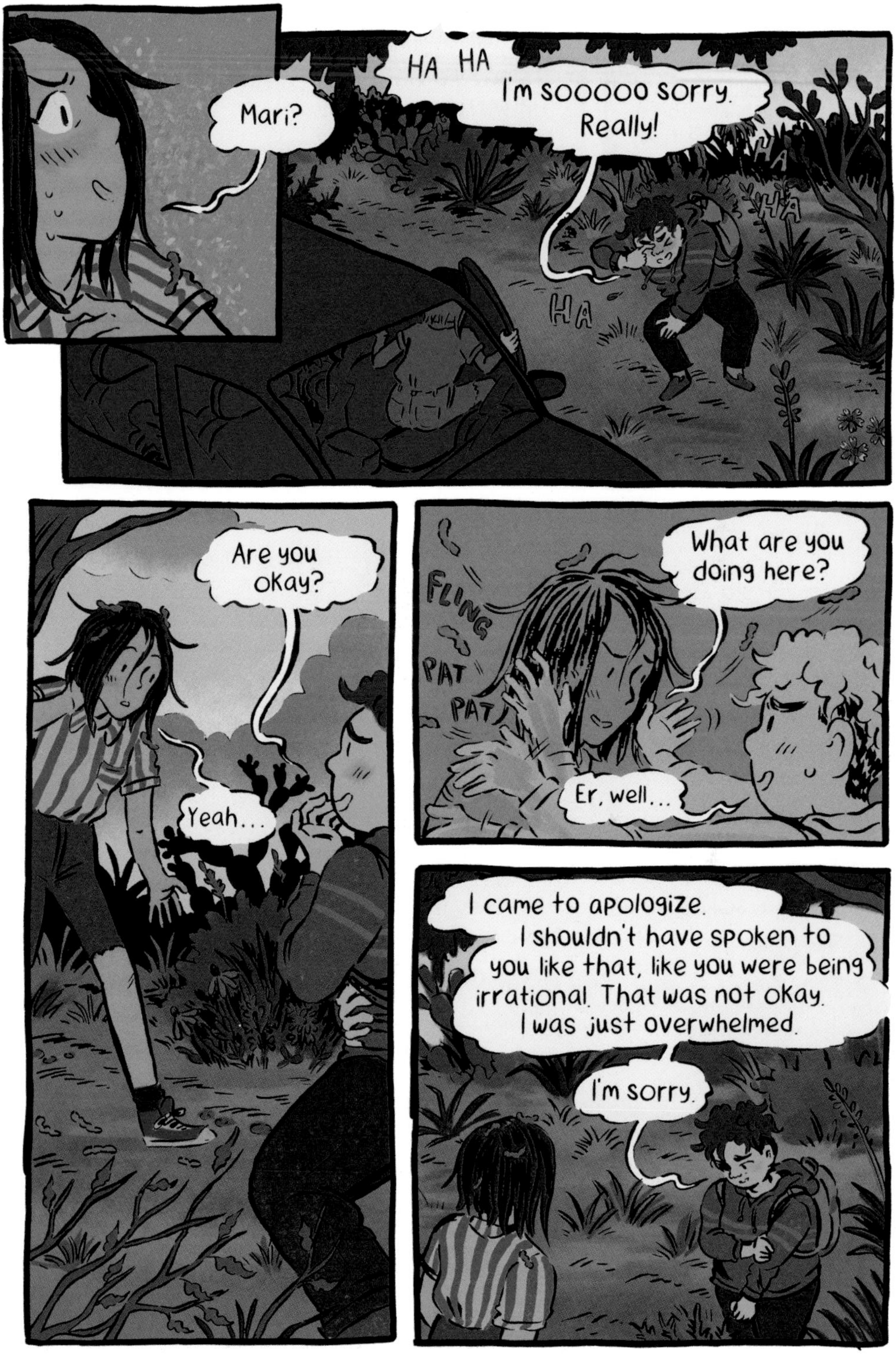
Mari?
HA HA
I'm sooooo sorry. Really!
HA
HA
HA
Are you okay?
Yeah...
FLING
PAT
PAT
What are you doing here?
Er, well...
I came to apologize. I shouldn't have spoken to you like that, like you were being irrational. That was not okay. I was just overwhelmed.
I'm sorry.

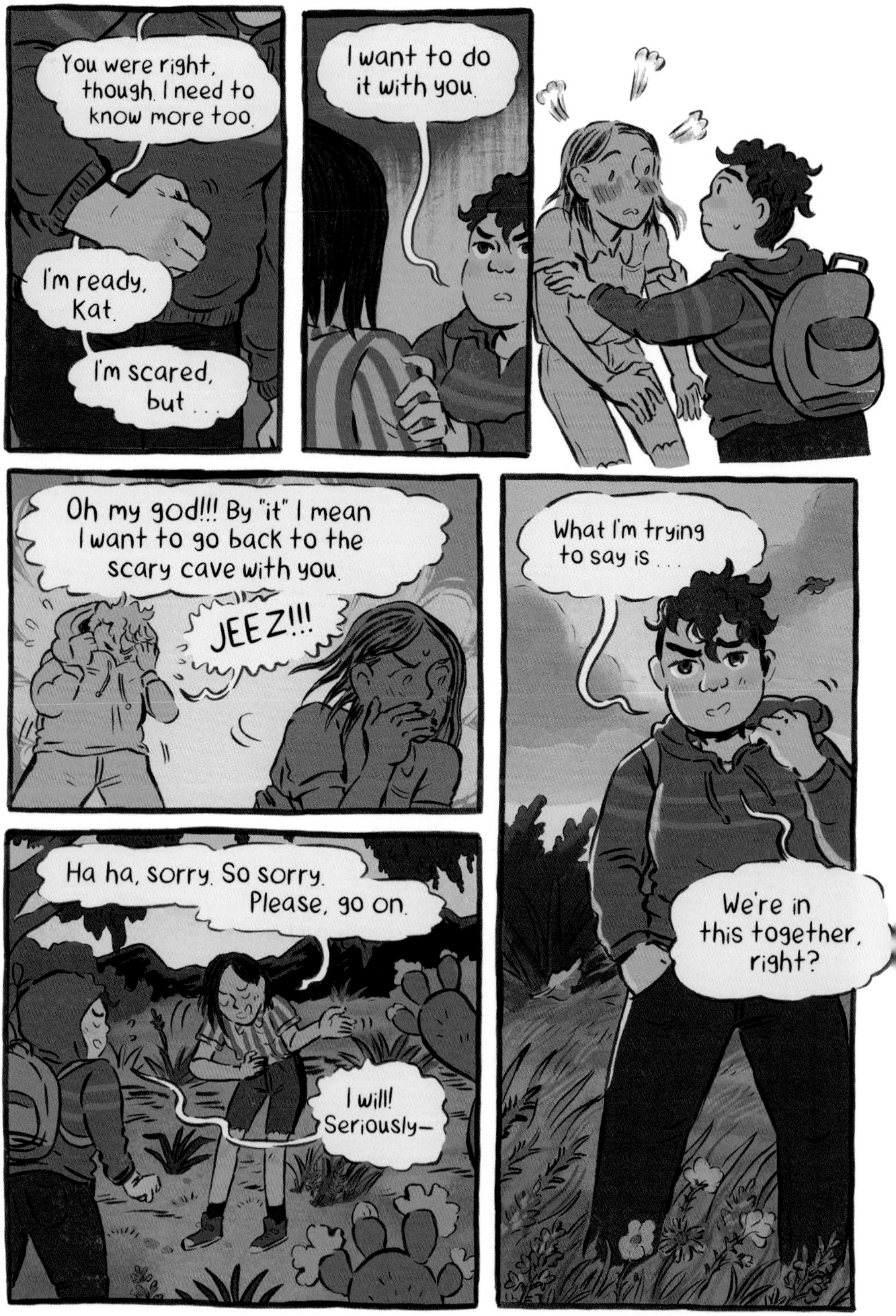
You were right, though. I need to know more too.
I'm ready, Kat.
I'm scared, but . . .
I want to do it with you.
Oh my god!!! By "it" I mean I want to go back to the scary cave with you.
JEEZ!!!
Ha ha, sorry. So sorry. Please, go on.
I will! Seriously—
What I'm trying to say is . . .
We're in this together, right?

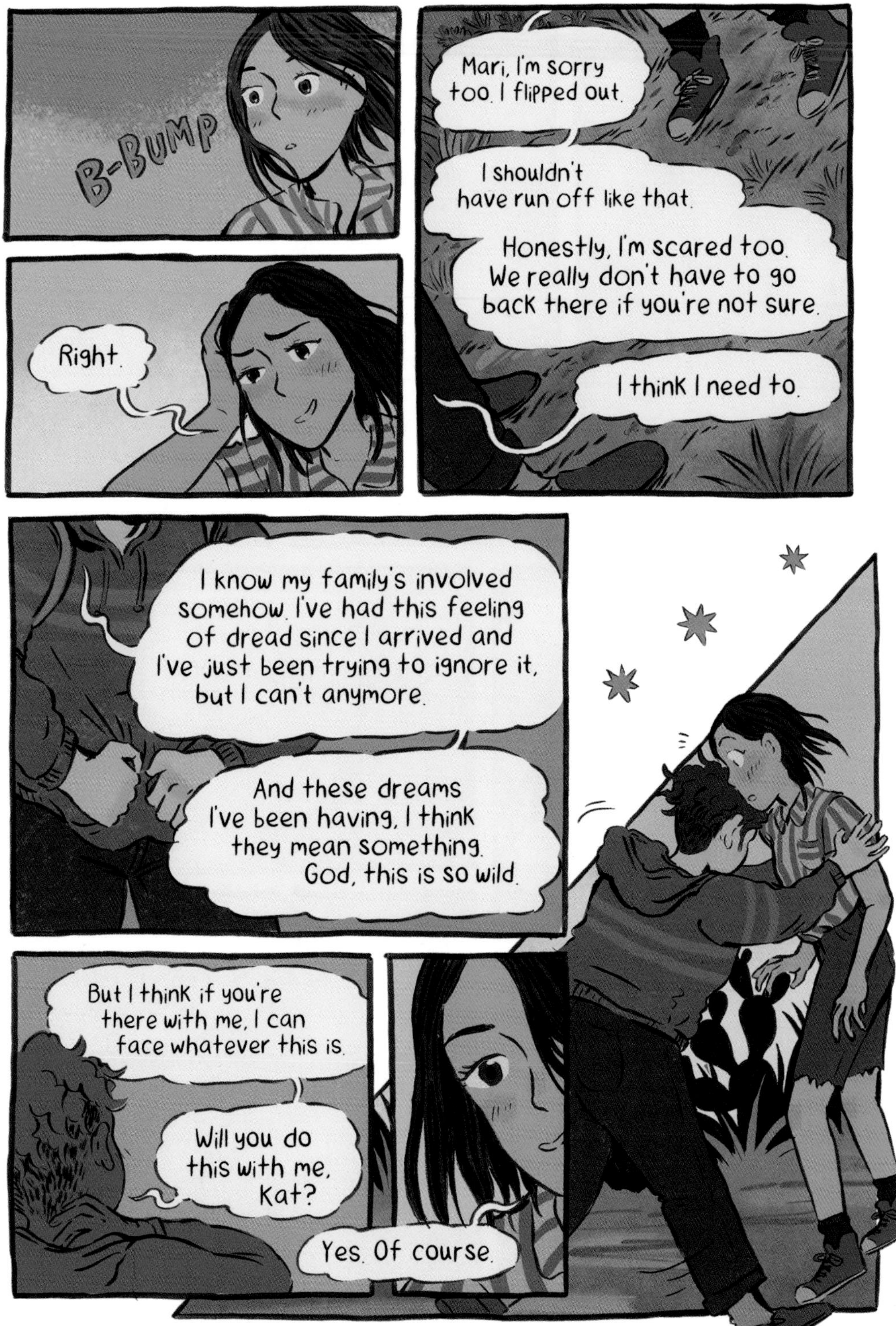
B-BUMP
Right.
Mari, I'm sorry too. I flipped out.
I shouldn't have run off like that.
Honestly, I'm scared too. We really don't have to go back there if you're not sure.
I think I need to.
I know my family's involved somehow. I've had this feeling of dread since I arrived and I've just been trying to ignore it, but I can't anymore.
And these dreams I've been having, I think they mean something. God, this is so wild.
But I think if you're there with me, I can face whatever this is.
Will you do this with me, Kat?
Yes. Of course.

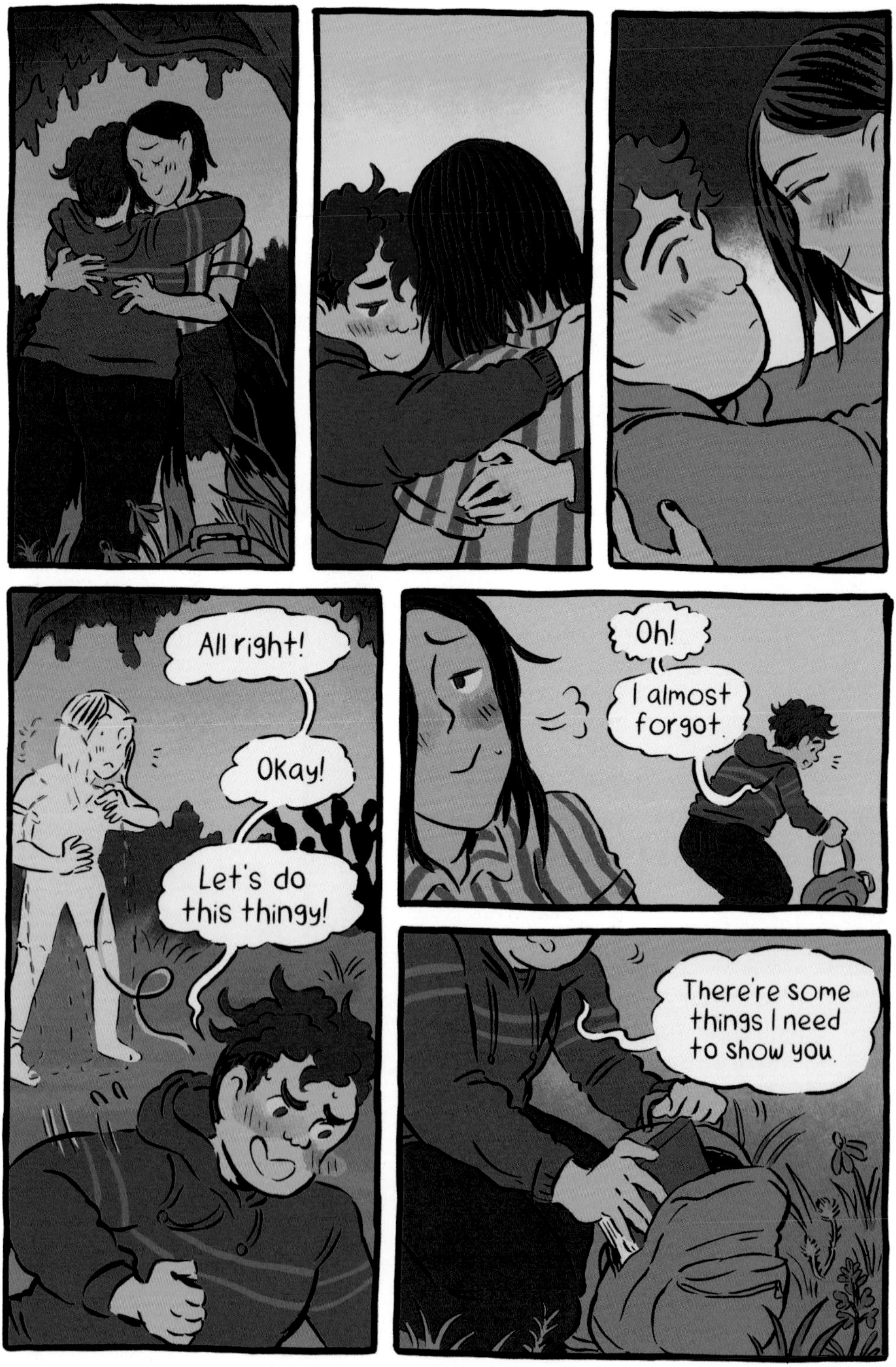
All right!
Okay!
Let's do this thingy!
Oh!
I almost forgot.
There're some things I need to show you.

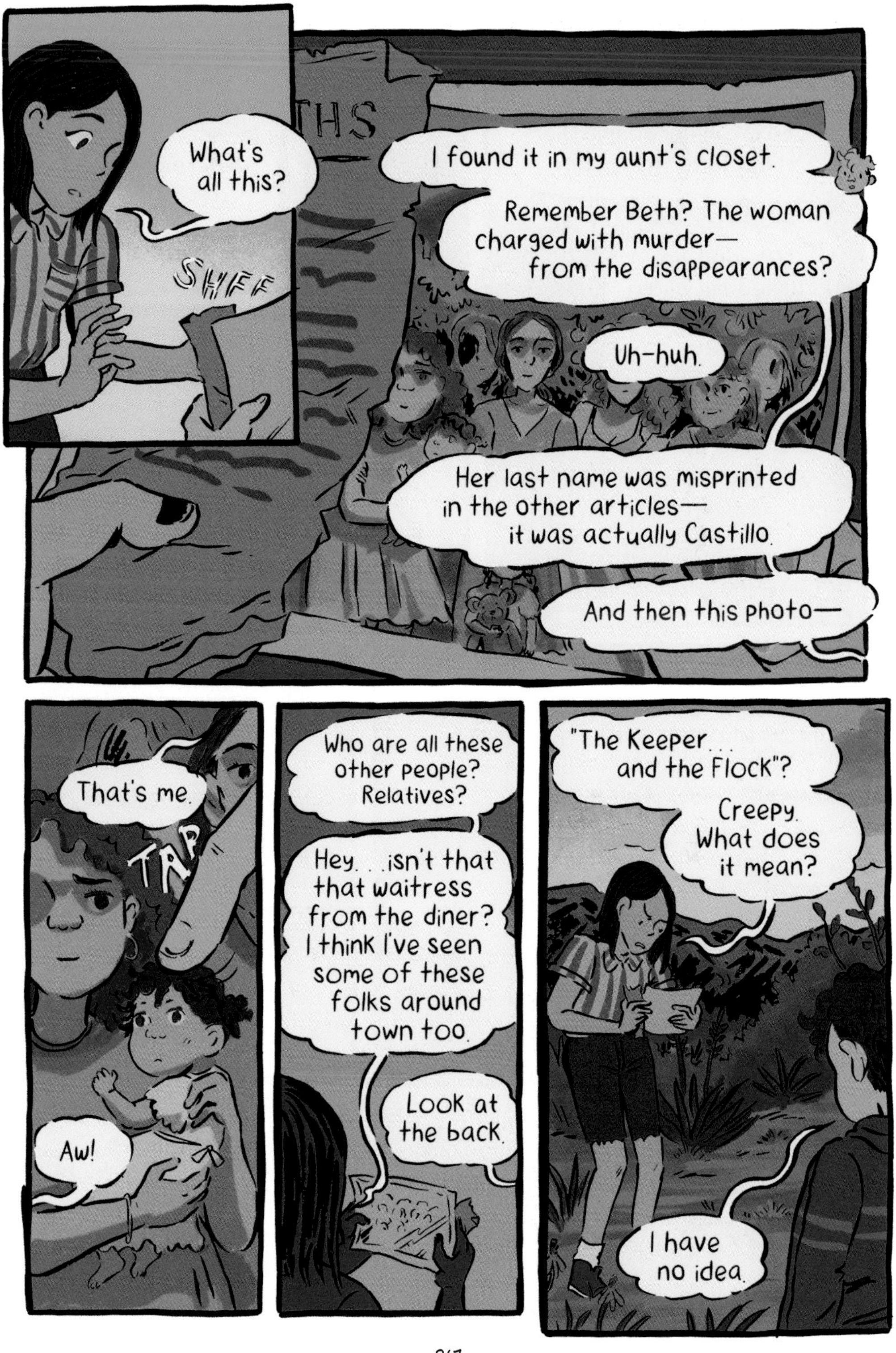
What's all this?
SHFF
THS
I found it in my aunt's closet.
Remember Beth? The woman charged with murder— from the disappearances?
Uh-huh.
Her last name was misprinted in the other articles— it was actually Castillo.
And then this photo—
That's me.
TAP
Aw!
Who are all these other people? Relatives?
Hey. . .isn't that that waitress from the diner? I think I've seen some of these folks around town too.
Look at the back.
"The Keeper. . . and the Flock"?
Creepy. What does it mean?
I have no idea.

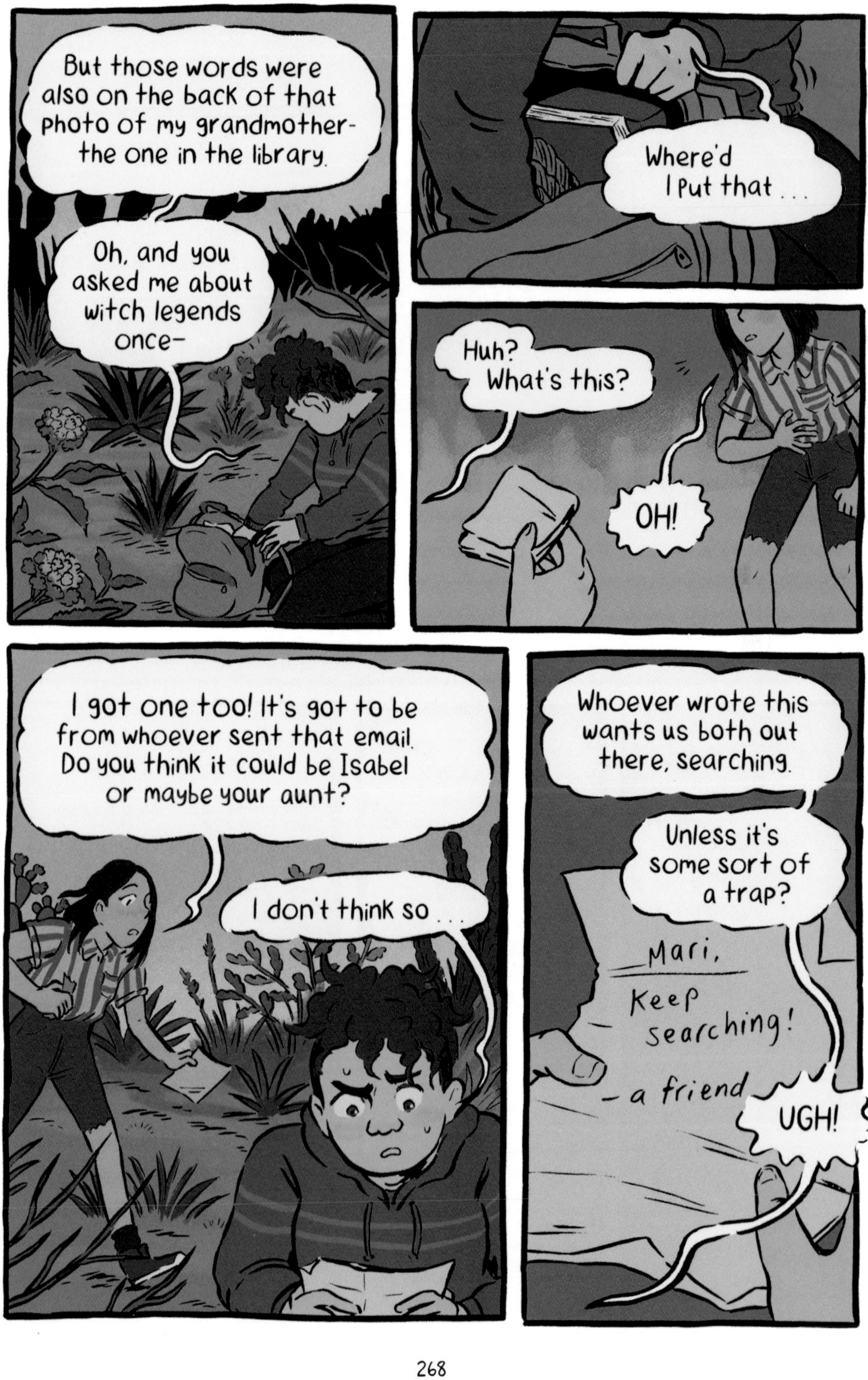
But those words were also on the back of that photo of my grandmother- the one in the library.
Oh, and you asked me about witch legends once-
Where'd I put that . . .
Huh? What's this?
OH!
I got one too! It's got to be from whoever sent that email. Do you think it could be Isabel or maybe your aunt?
I don't think so . . .
Whoever wrote this wants us both out there, searching.
Unless it's some sort of a trap?
Mari,
Keep searching!
- a friend
UGH!

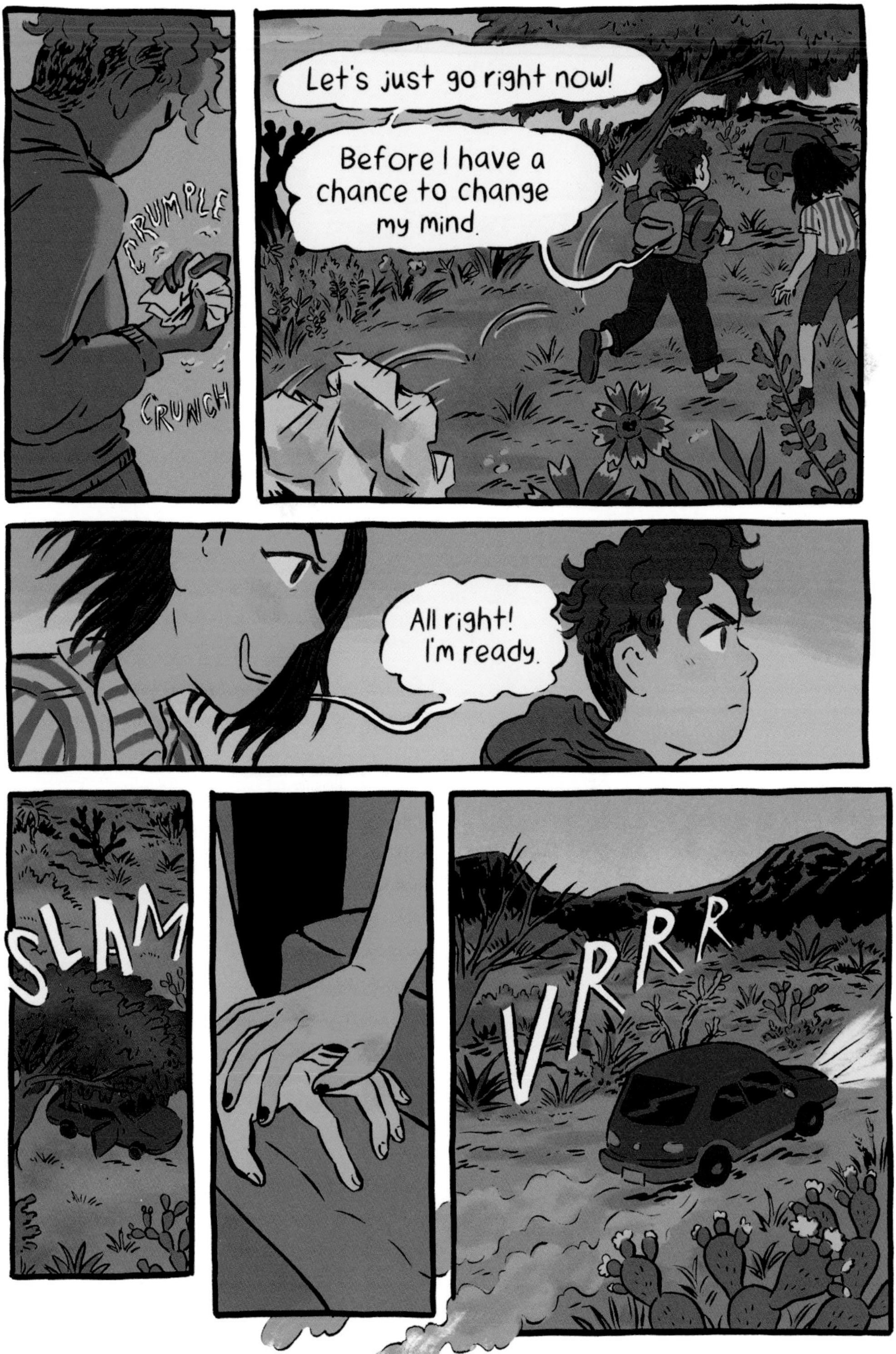
CRUMPLE
CRUNCH
Let's just go right now!
Before I have a chance to change my mind.
All right! I'm ready.
SLAM
VRRRR

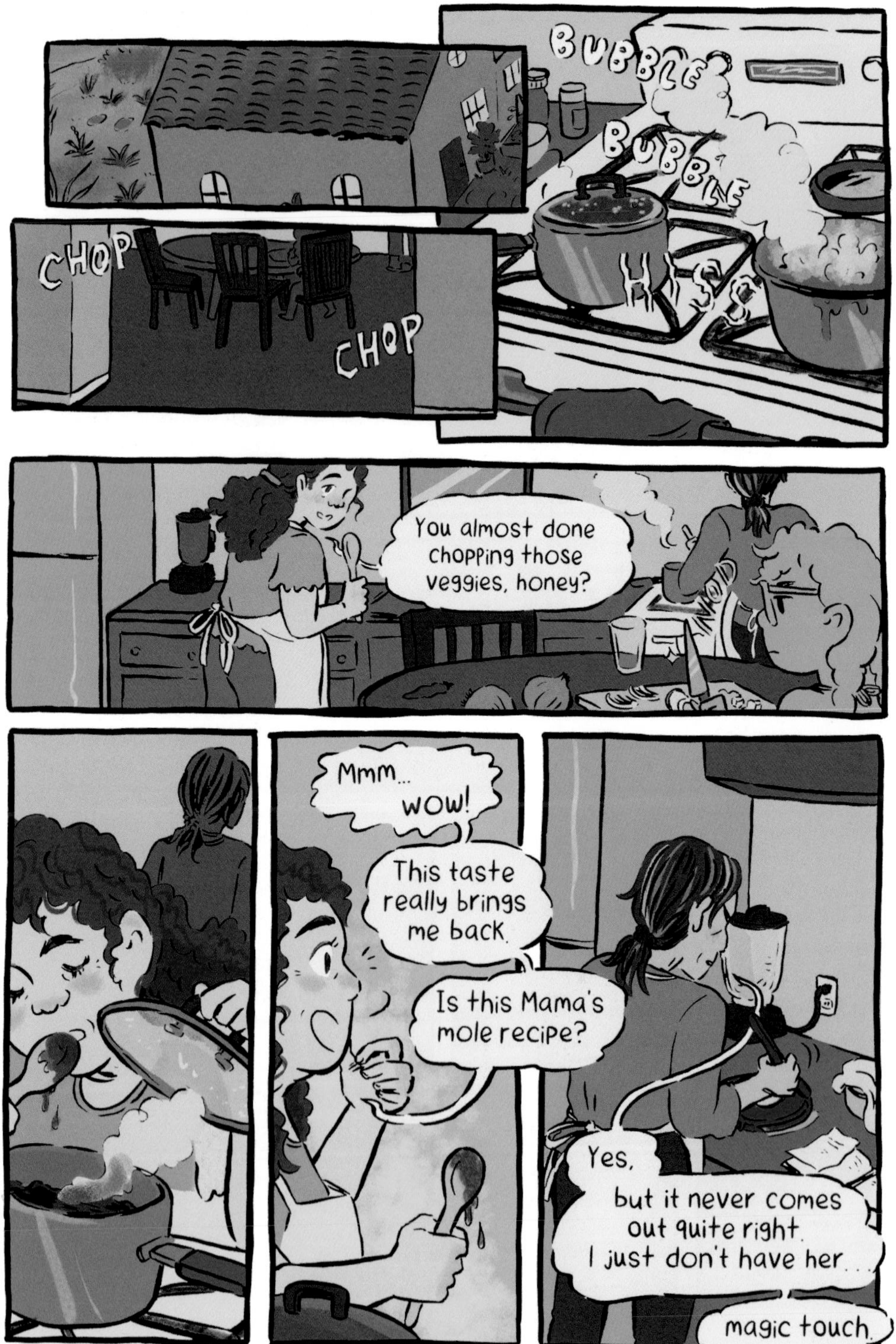
BUBBLE
BUBBLE
HISS
CHOP
CHOP
You almost done chopping those veggies, honey?
Mmm... WOW!
This taste really brings me back.
Is this Mama's mole recipe?
Yes,
but it never comes out quite right. I just don't have her...
magic touch.

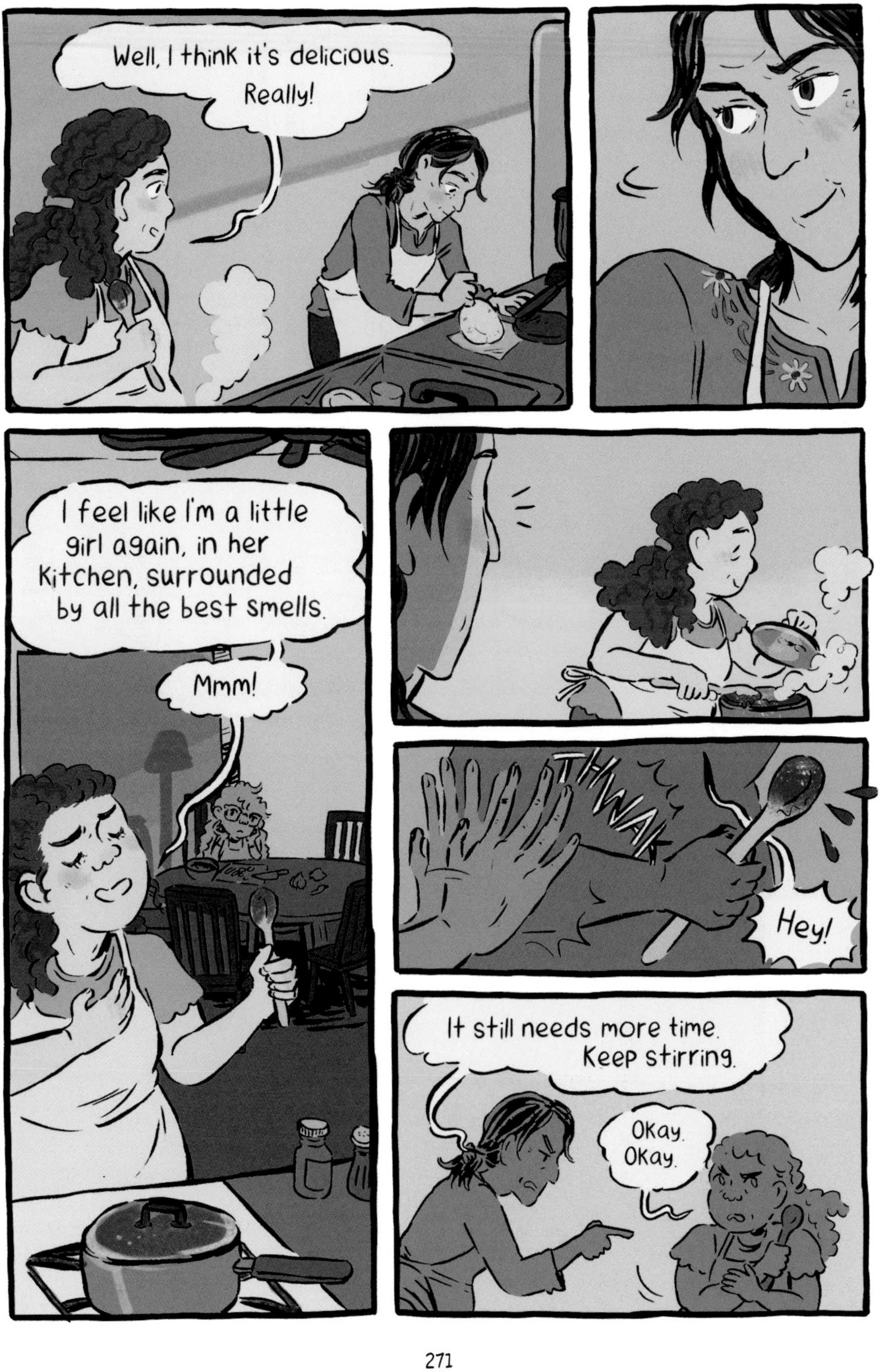

Well, I think it's delicious.
Really!
I feel like I'm a little girl again, in her kitchen, surrounded by all the best smells.
Mmm!
THWAK
Hey!
It still needs more time. Keep stirring.
Okay. Okay.

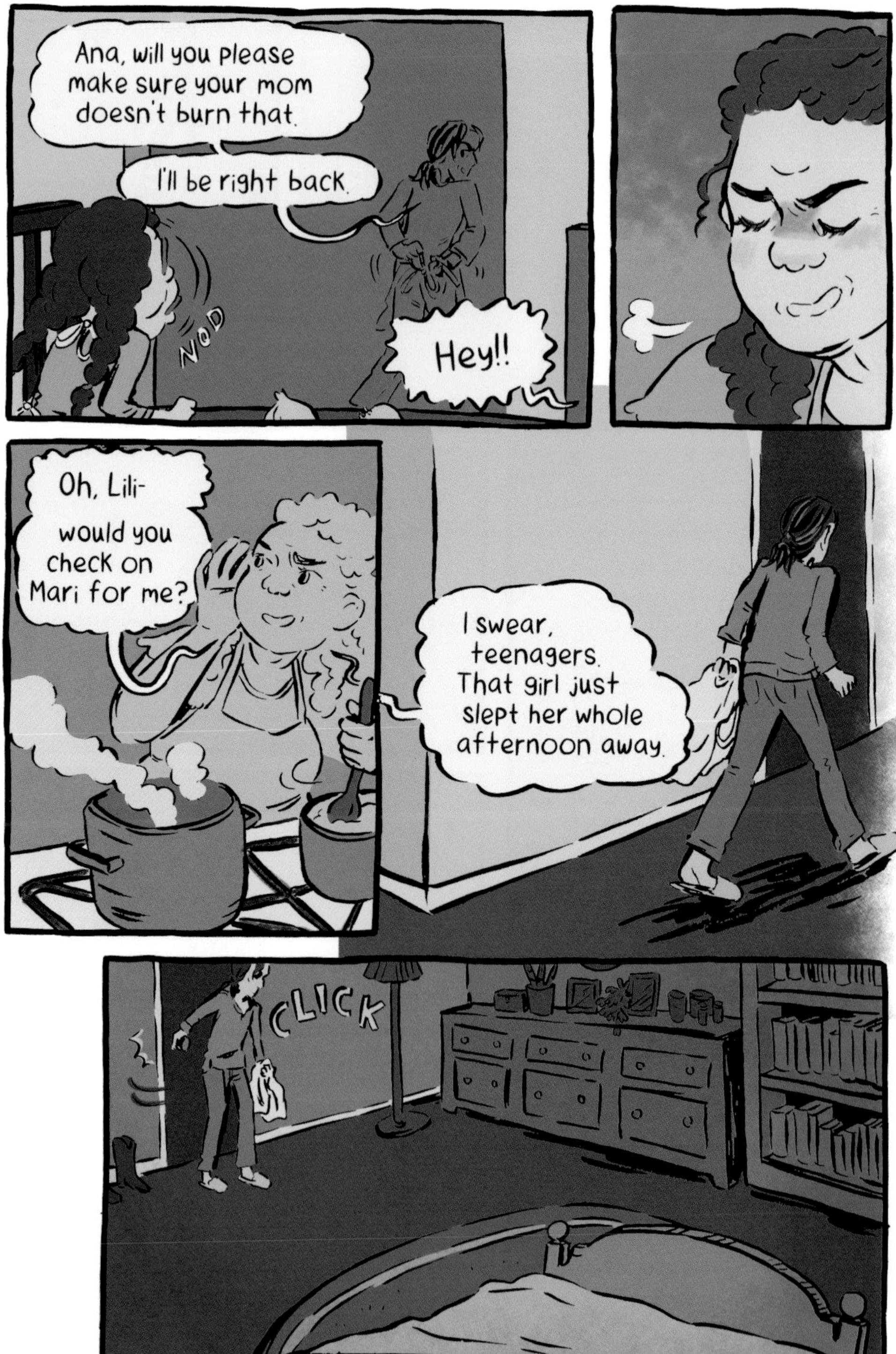
Ana, will you please make sure your mom doesn't burn that.
I'll be right back.
NOD
Hey!!
Oh, Lili-
would you check on Mari for me?
I swear, teenagers. That girl just slept her whole afternoon away.
CLICK

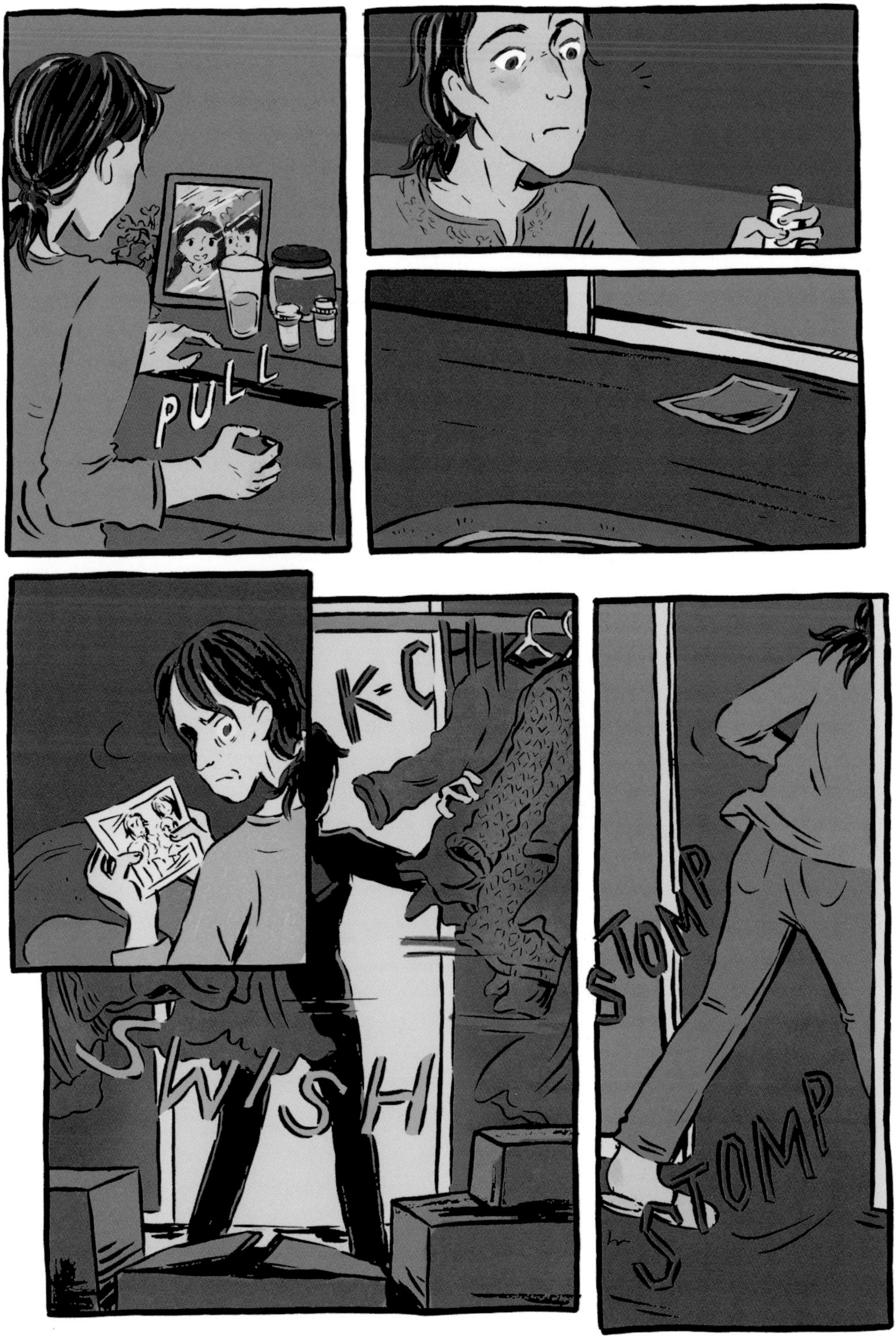
PULL
K-CHK
SWISH
STOMP
STOMP

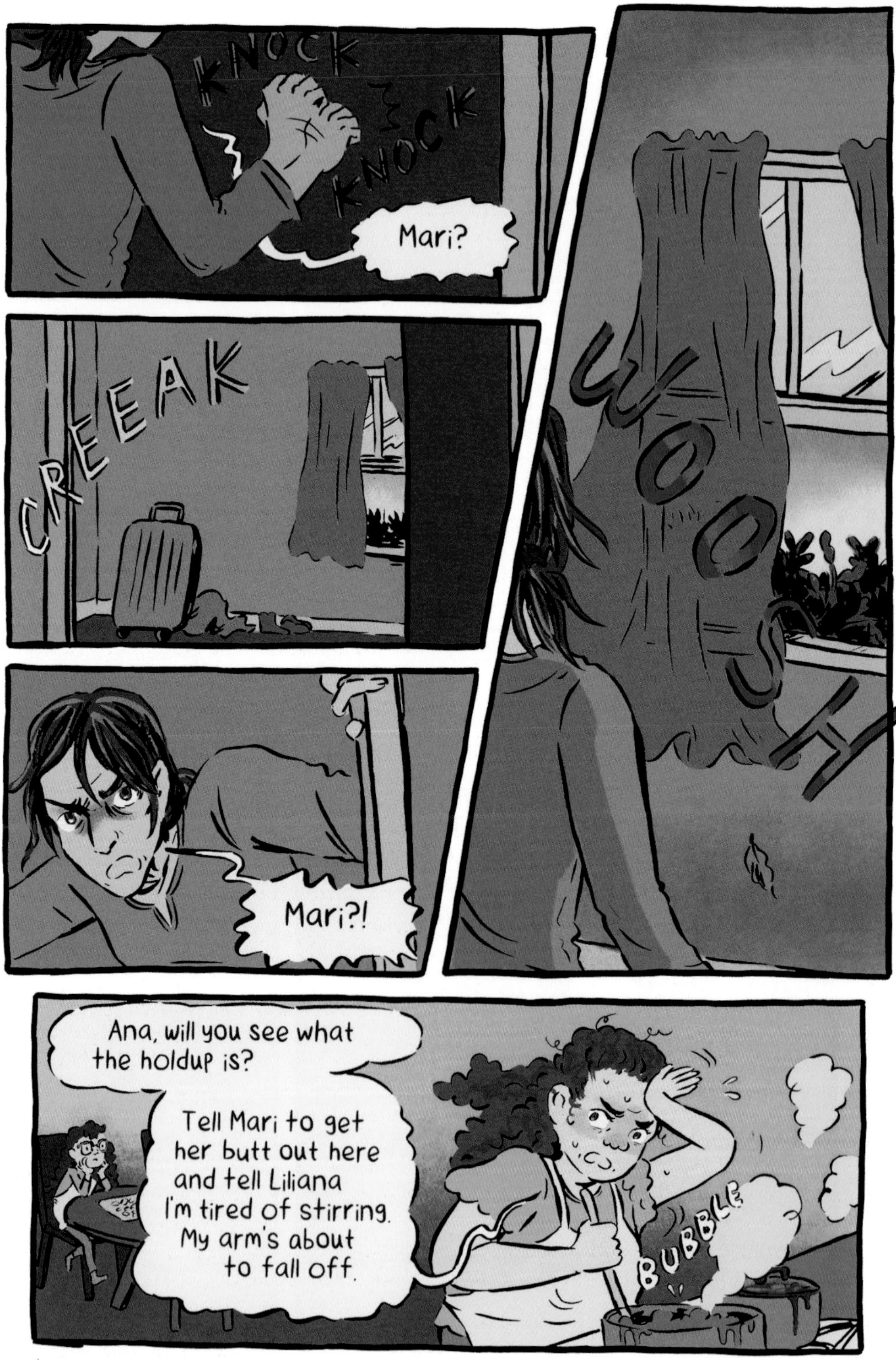
KNOCK
KNOCK
KNOCK
Mari?
CREEAK
WOOOOSH
Mari?!
Ana, will you see what the holdup is?
Tell Mari to get her butt out here and tell Liliana I'm tired of stirring. My arm's about to fall off.
BUBBLE

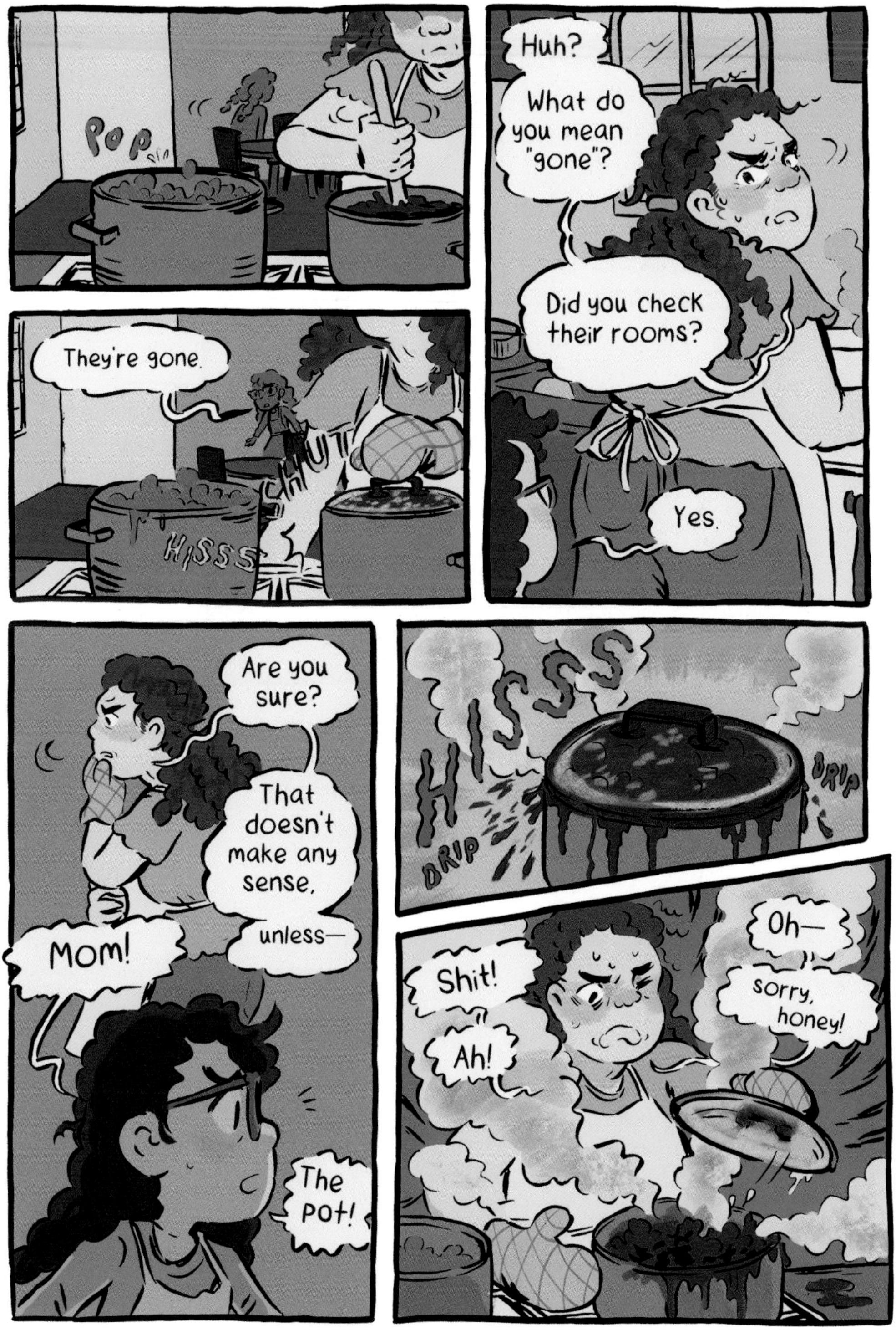
POP
They're gone.
CHUNK
HISSS
Huh?
What do you mean "gone"?
Did you check their rooms?
Yes.
Are you sure?
That doesn't make any sense,
unless—
MOM!
The pot!
HISSS
DRIP
DRIP
Oh—
Shit!
sorry, honey!
Ah!

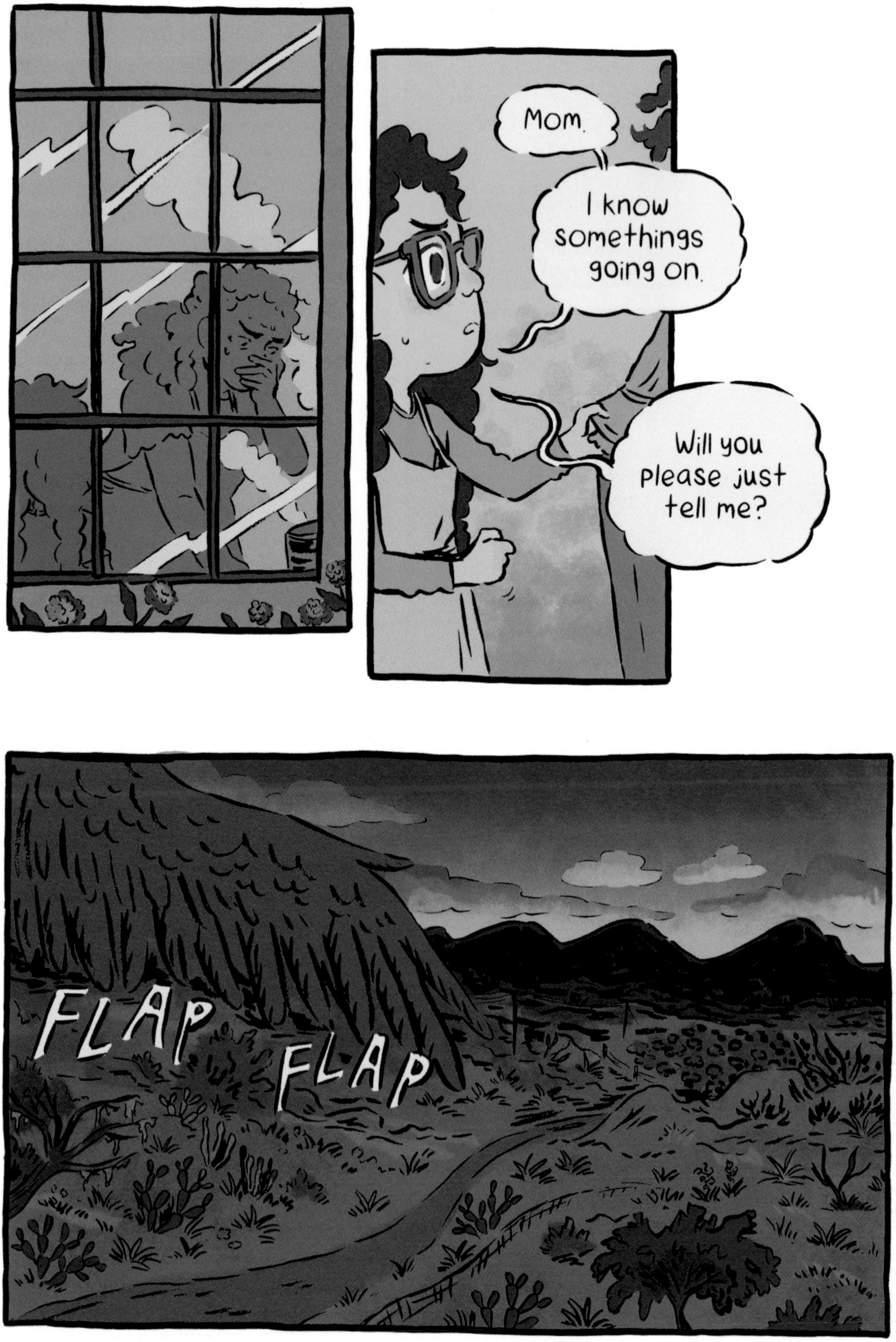
Mom.
I know somethings going on.
Will you please just tell me?
FLAP
FLAP

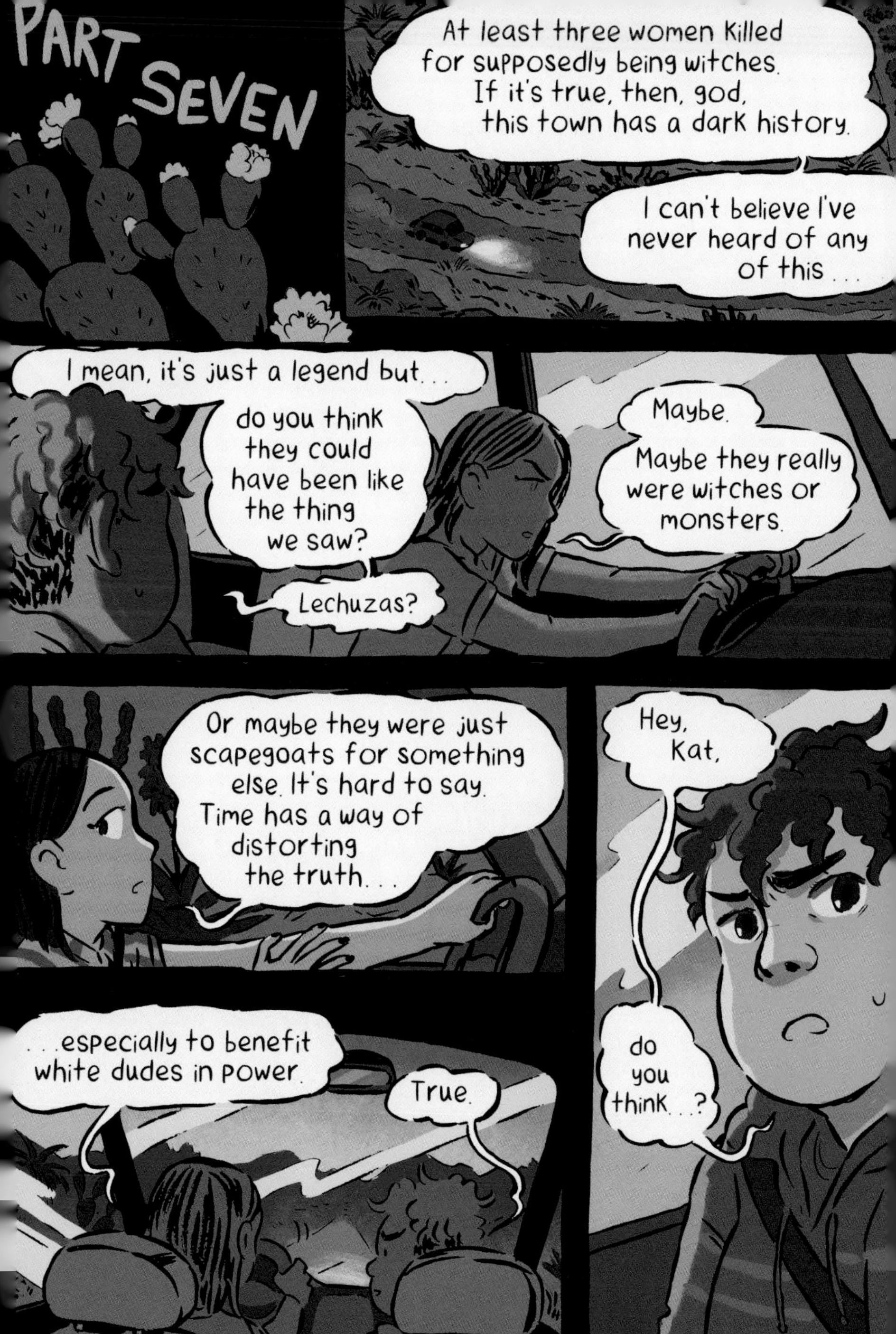
PART SEVEN
At least three women killed for supposedly being witches. If it's true, then, god, this town has a dark history.
I can't believe I've never heard of any of this . . .
I mean, it's just a legend but . . .
do you think they could have been like the thing we saw?
Lechuzas?
Maybe.
Maybe they really were witches or monsters.
Or maybe they were just scapegoats for something else. It's hard to say. Time has a way of distorting the truth . . .
. . . especially to benefit white dudes in power.
True.
Hey, Kat,
do you think . . . ?

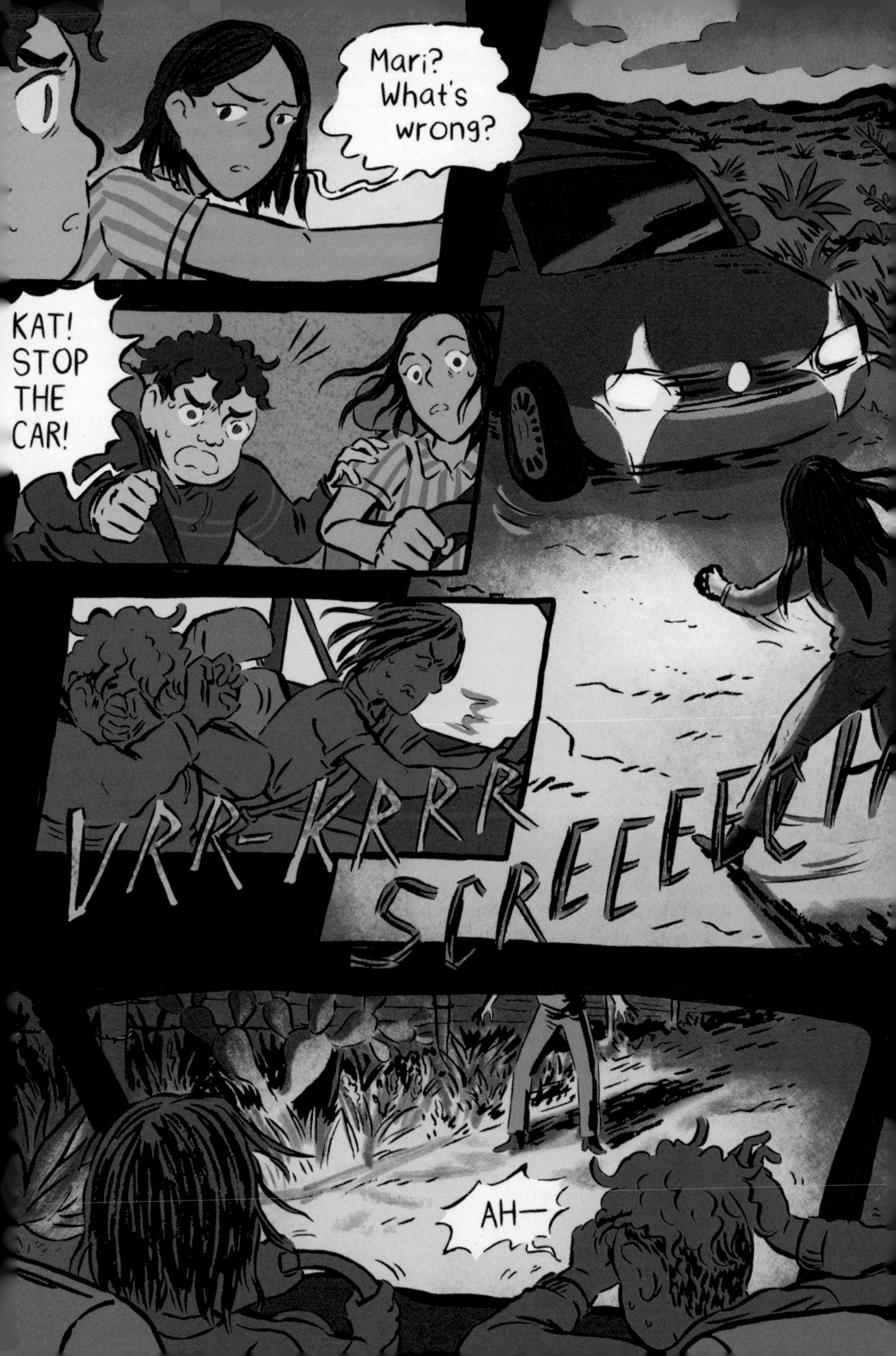
Mari? What's wrong?
KAT! STOP THE CAR!
VRR-KRRR
SCREEEECH
AH—

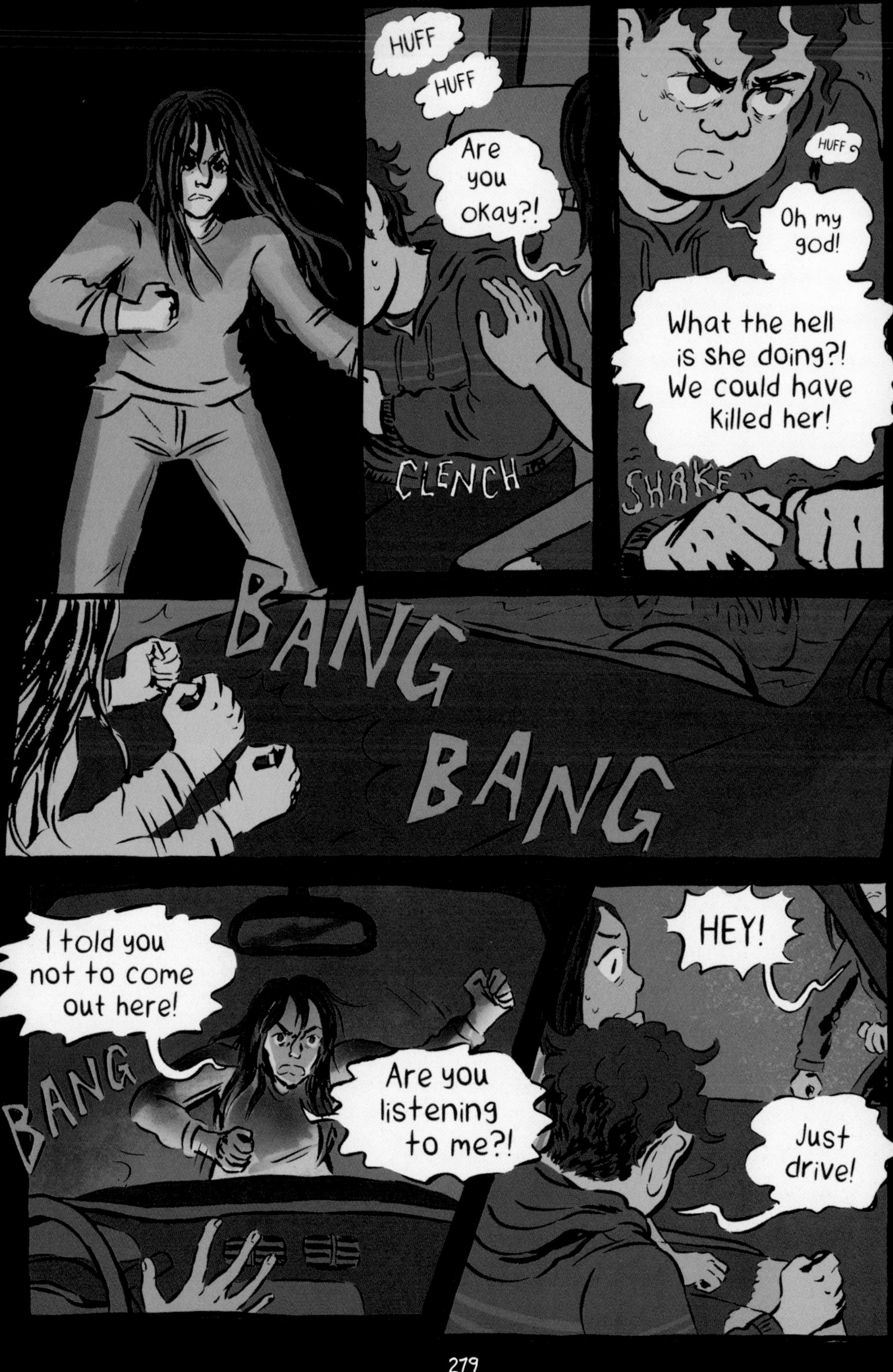
HUFF
HUFF
Are you okay?!
CLENCH
HUFF
Oh my god!
What the hell is she doing?! We could have killed her!
SHAKE
BANG
BANG
I told you not to come out here!
BANG
Are you listening to me?!
HEY!
Just drive!

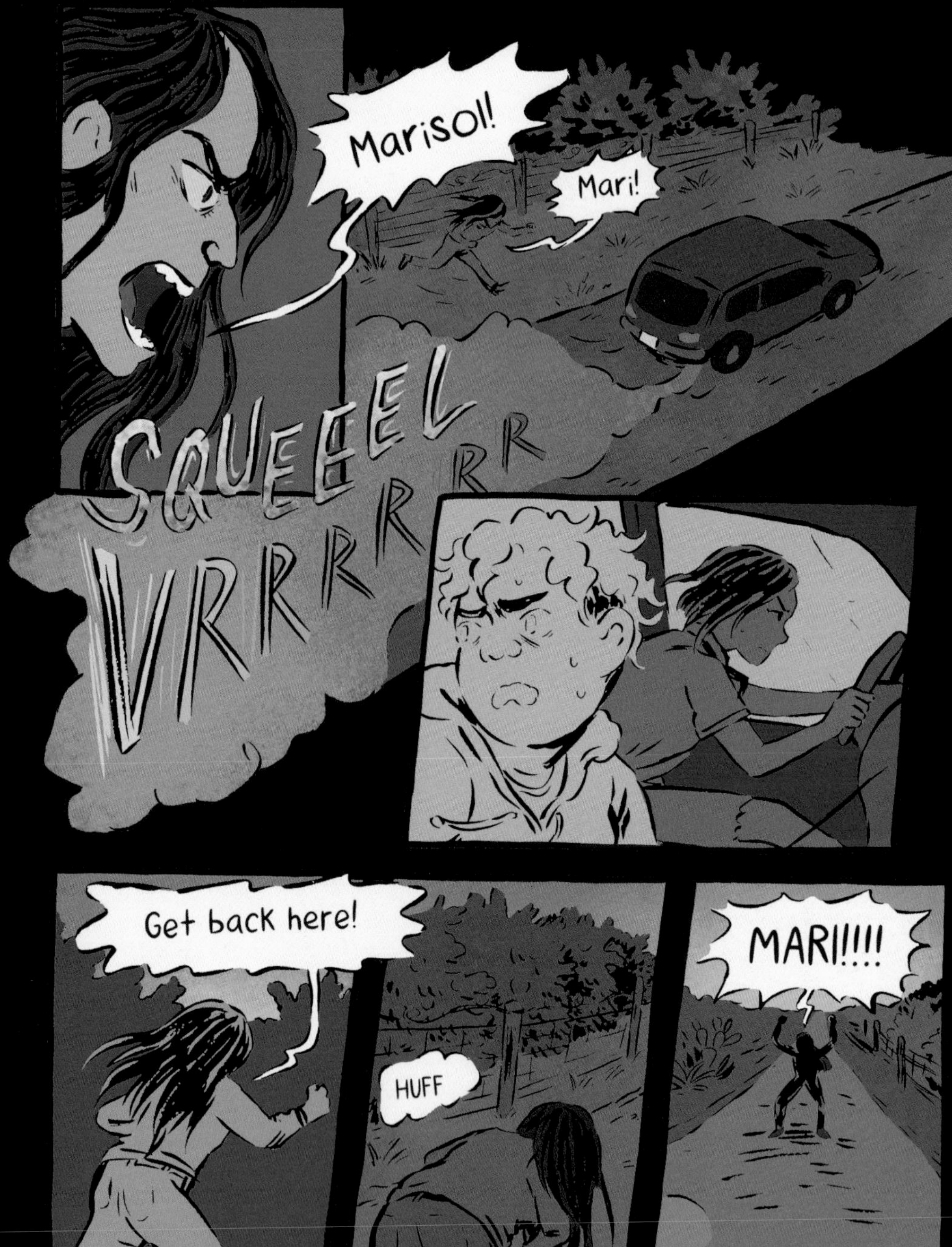

Marisol!
Mari!
SQUEEEL
VRRRRRRR
Get back here!
HUFF
HUFF
MARI!!!!

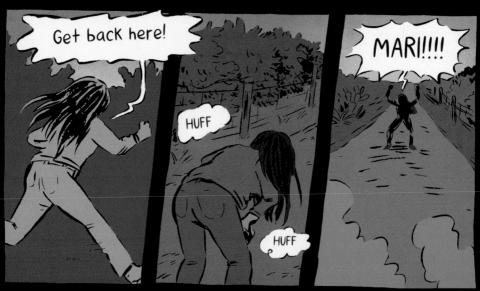

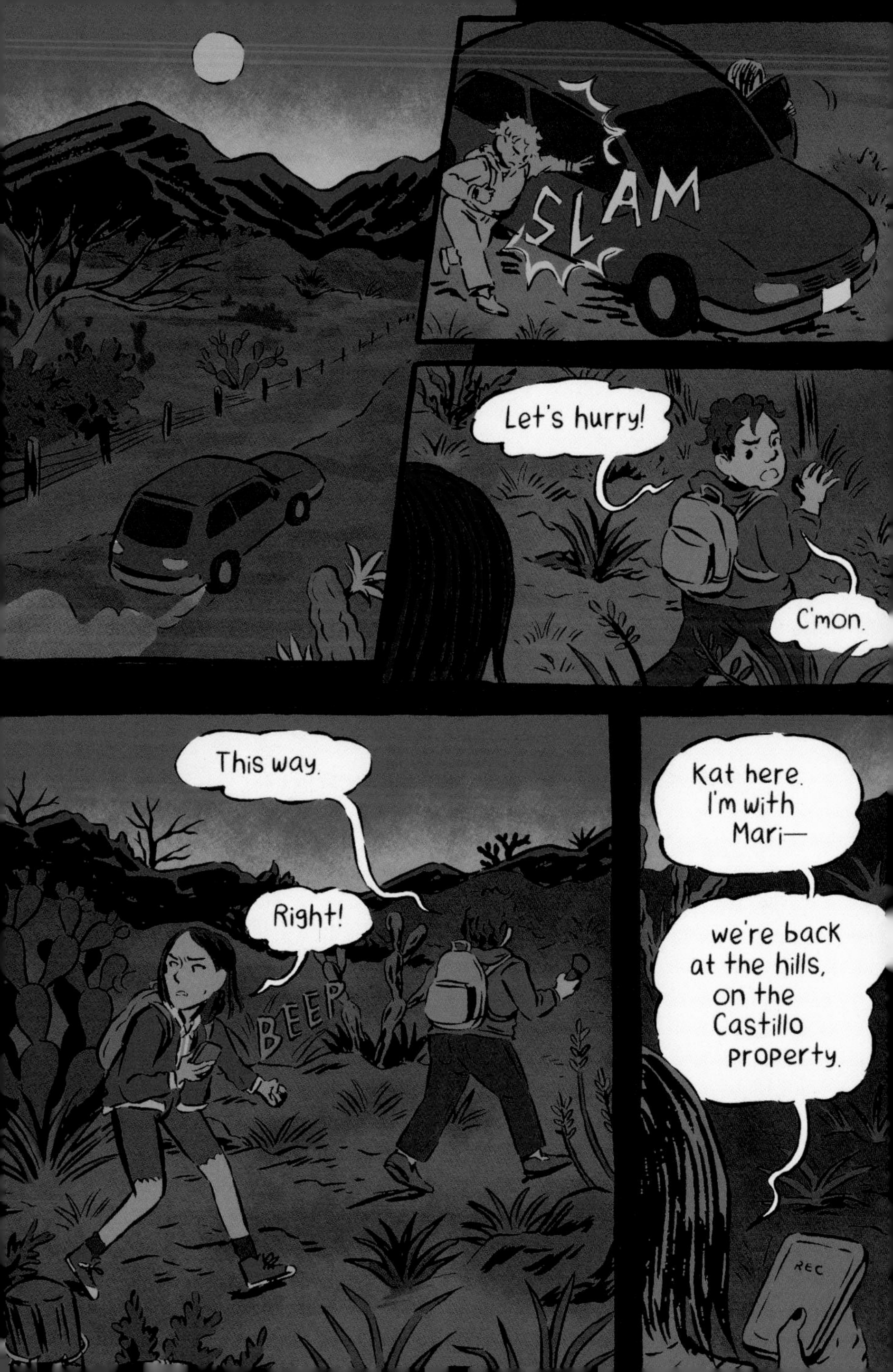
SLAM
Let's hurry!
C'mon.
This way.
Right!
BEEP
Kat here. I'm with Mari—
we're back at the hills, on the Castillo property.
REC

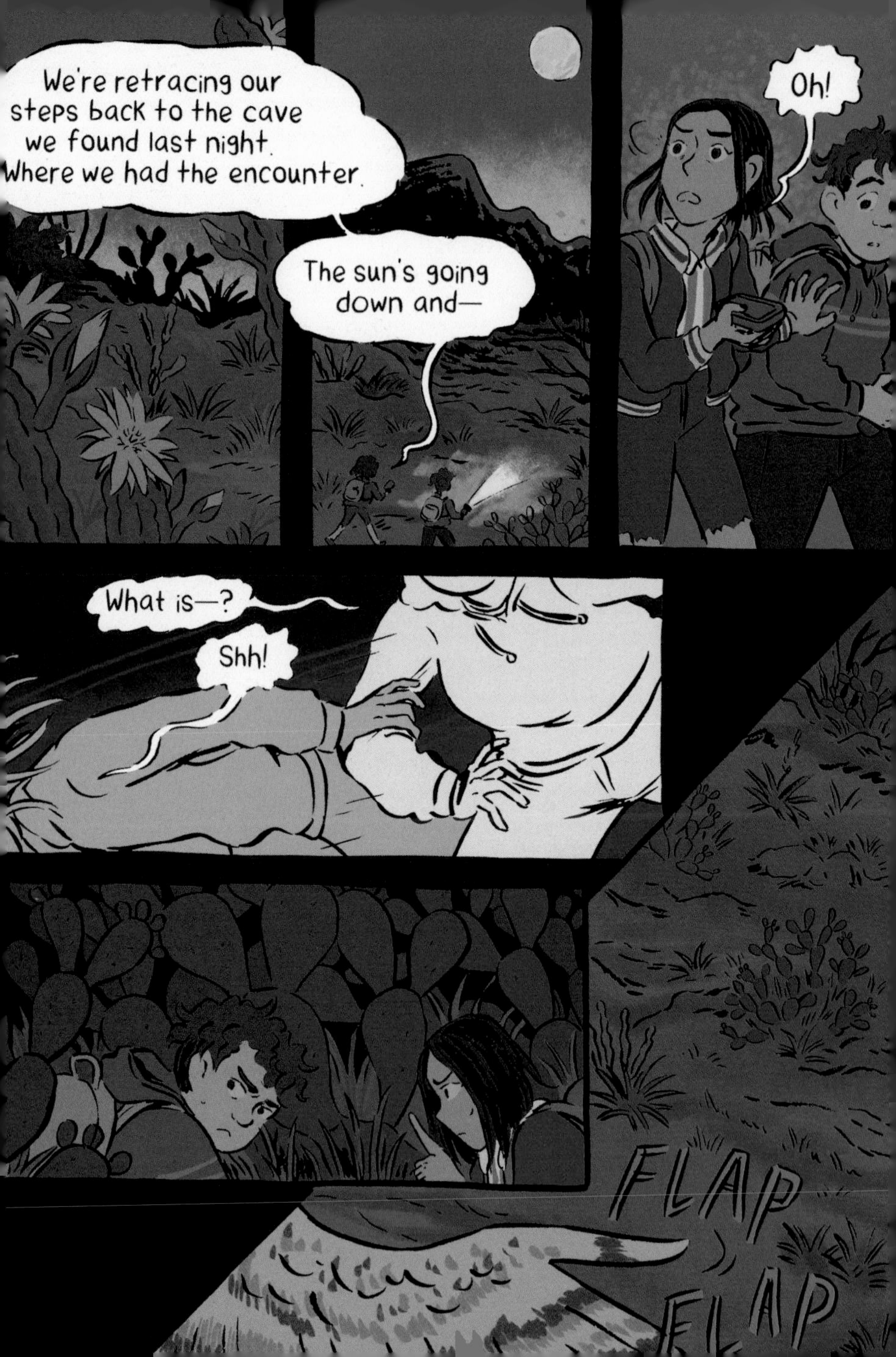
We're retracing our steps back to the cave we found last night. Where we had the encounter.
The sun's going down and—
Oh!
What is—?
Shh!
FLAP
FLAP

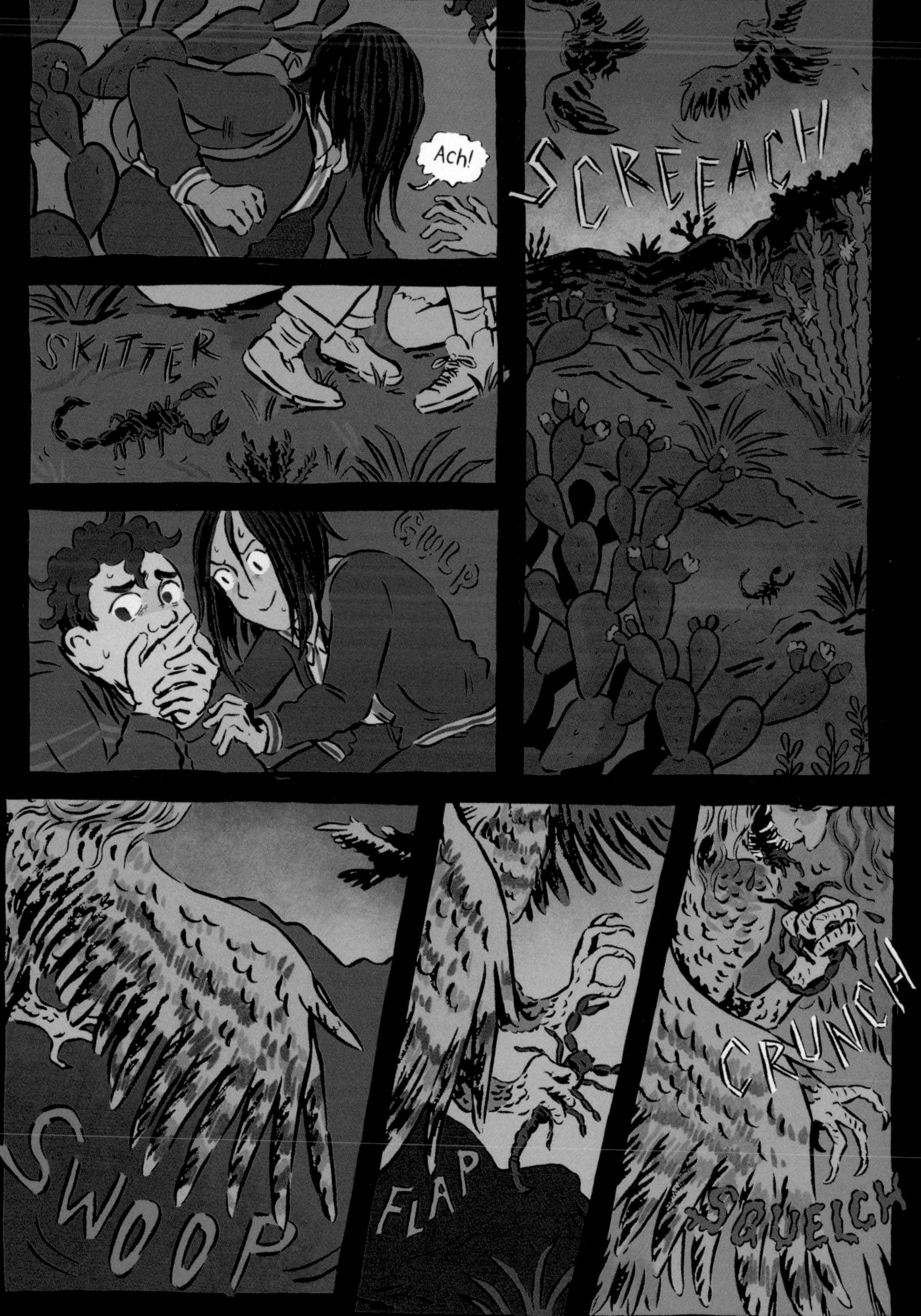
Ach!
SCREEACH
SKITTER
GULP
SWOOP
FLAP
CRUNCH
SQUELCH

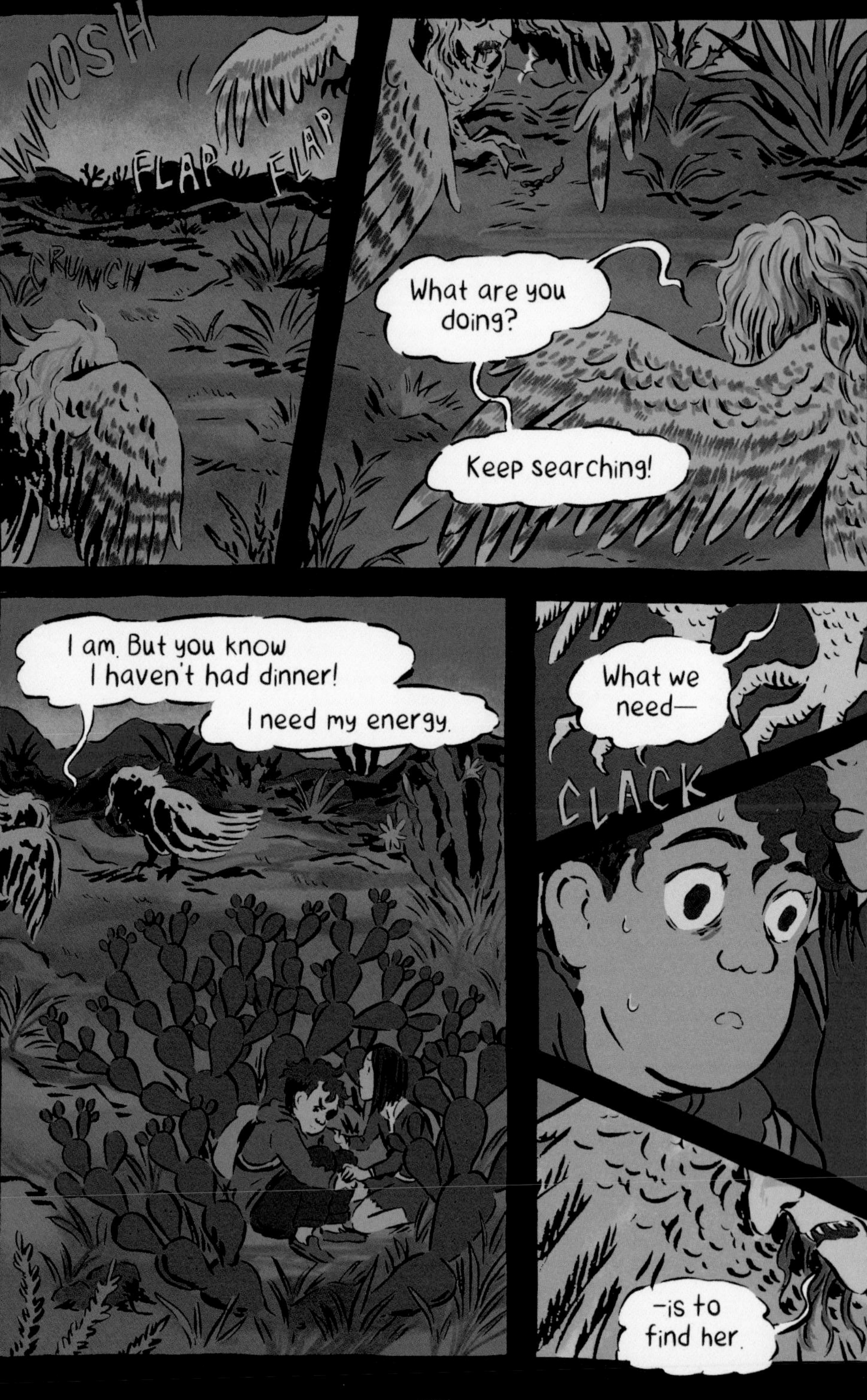
WOOSH
FLAP
FLAP
CRUNCH
What are you doing?
Keep searching!
I am. But you know I haven't had dinner!
I need my energy.
What we need—
CLACK
–is to find her.

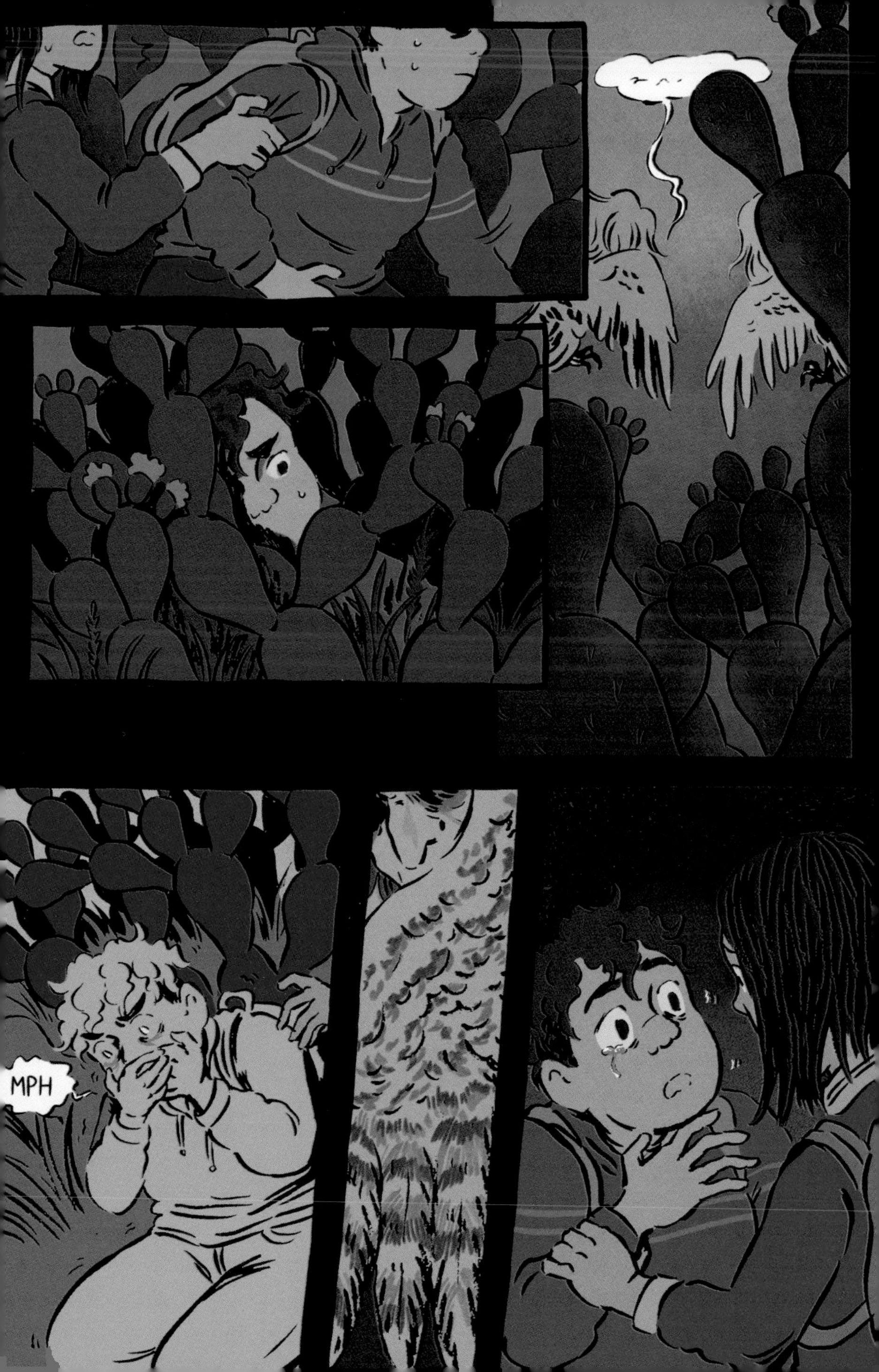
MPH

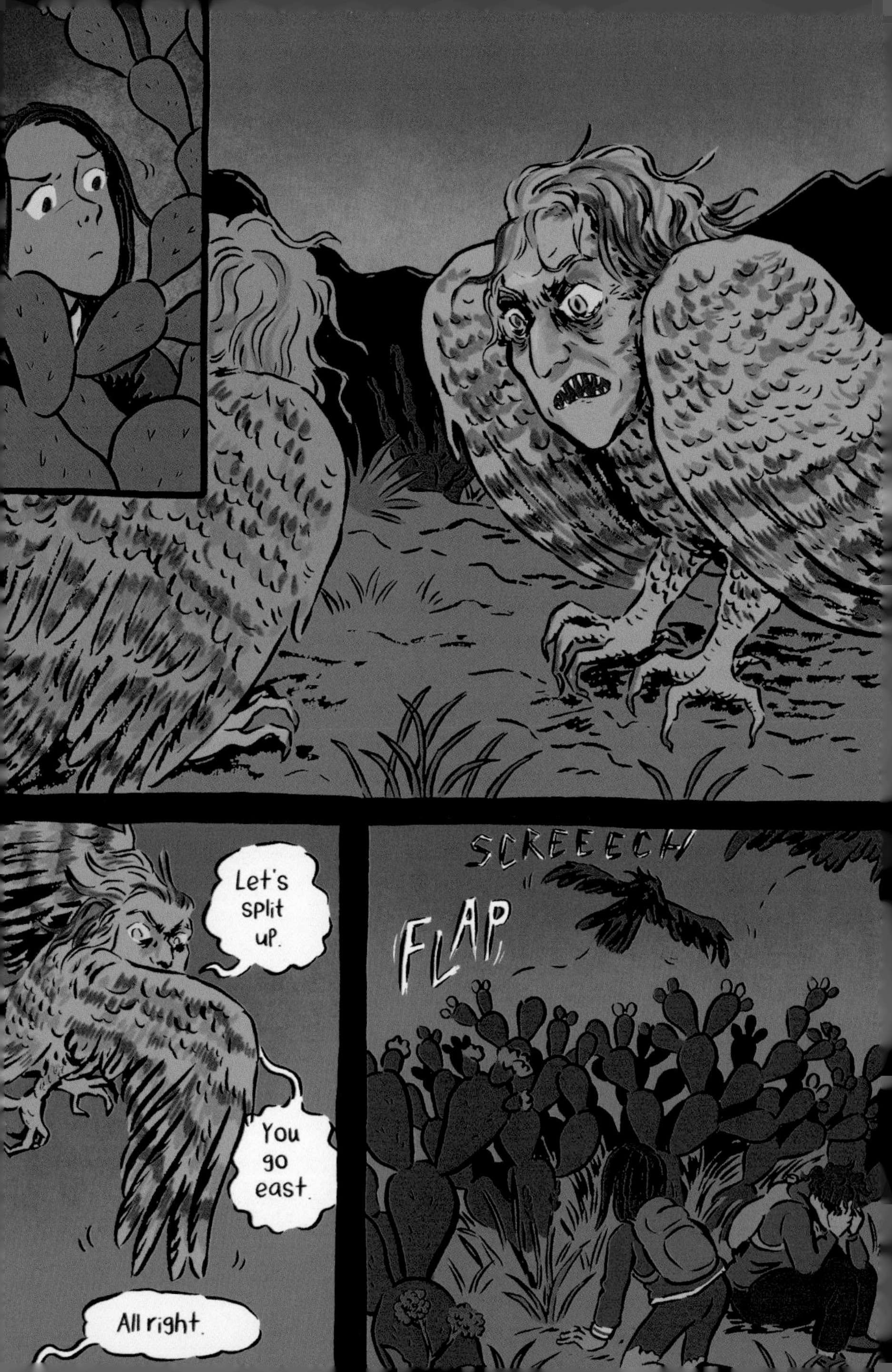
Let's split up.
You go east.
All right.
SCREEECH
FLAP

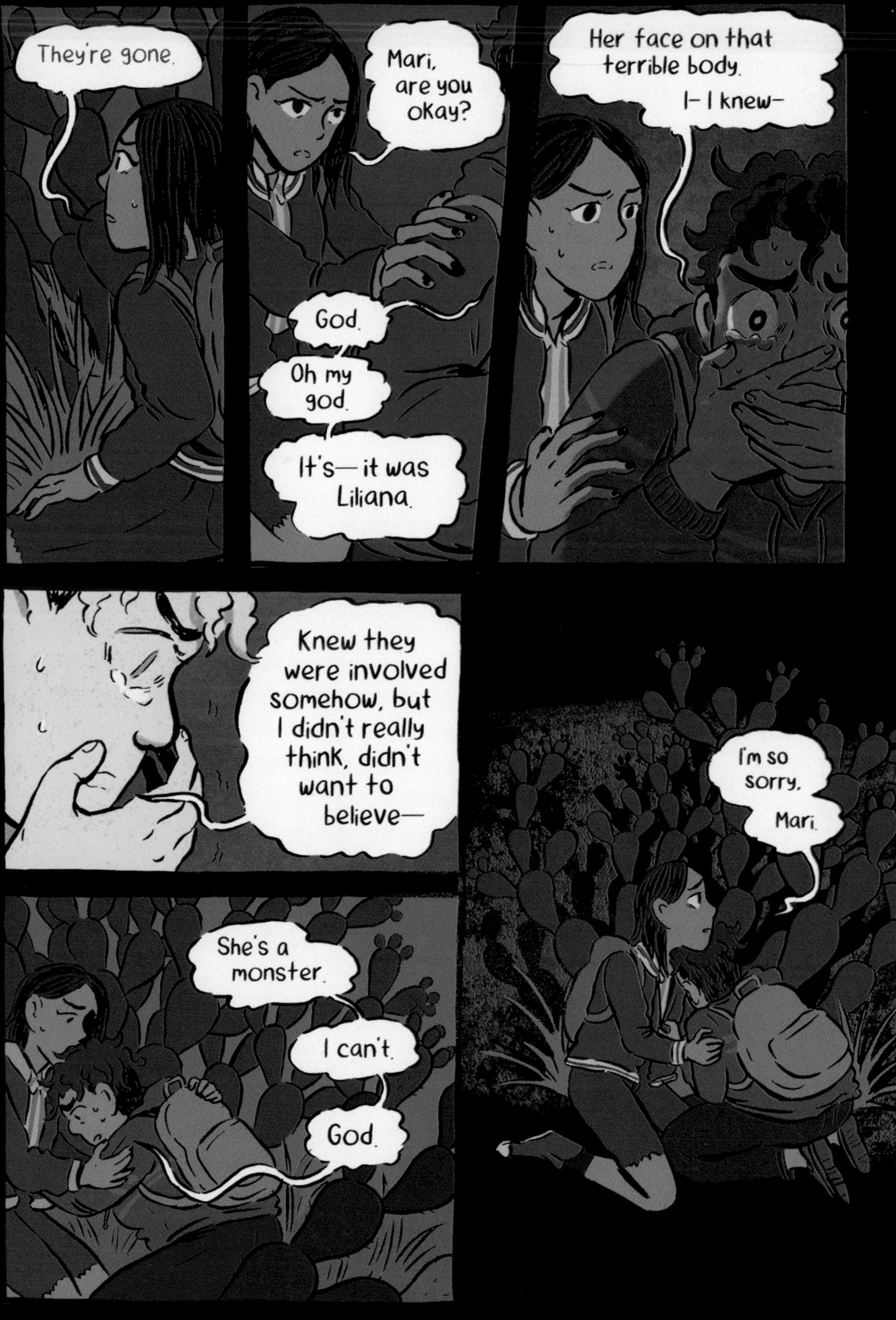
They're gone.
Mari, are you okay?
God.
Oh my god.
It's— it was Liliana.
Her face on that terrible body.
I- I knew-
Knew they were involved somehow, but I didn't really think, didn't want to believe—
She's a monster.
I can't.
God.
I'm so sorry, Mari.

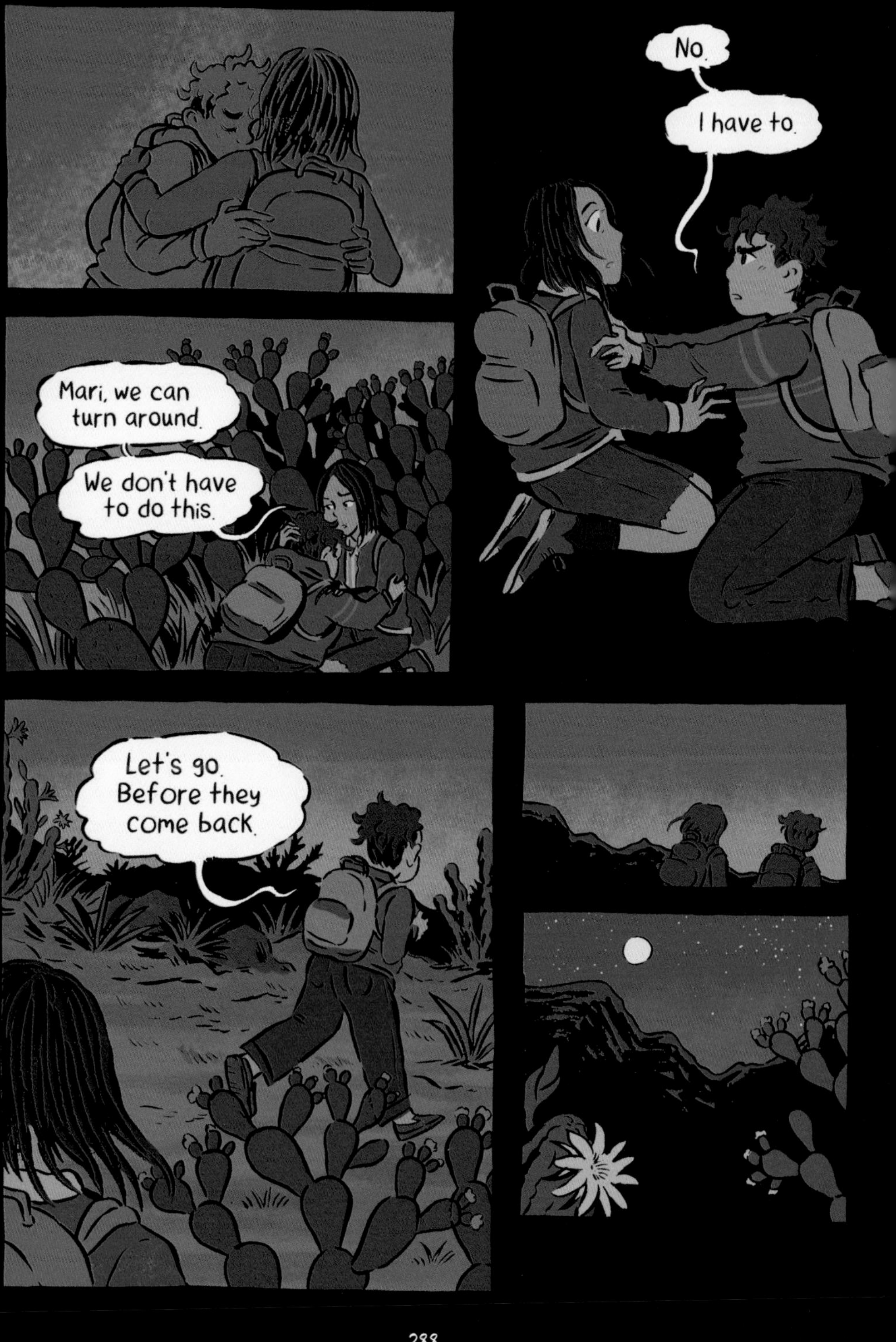
No.
I have to.
Mari, we can turn around.
We don't have to do this.
Let's go. Before they come back.

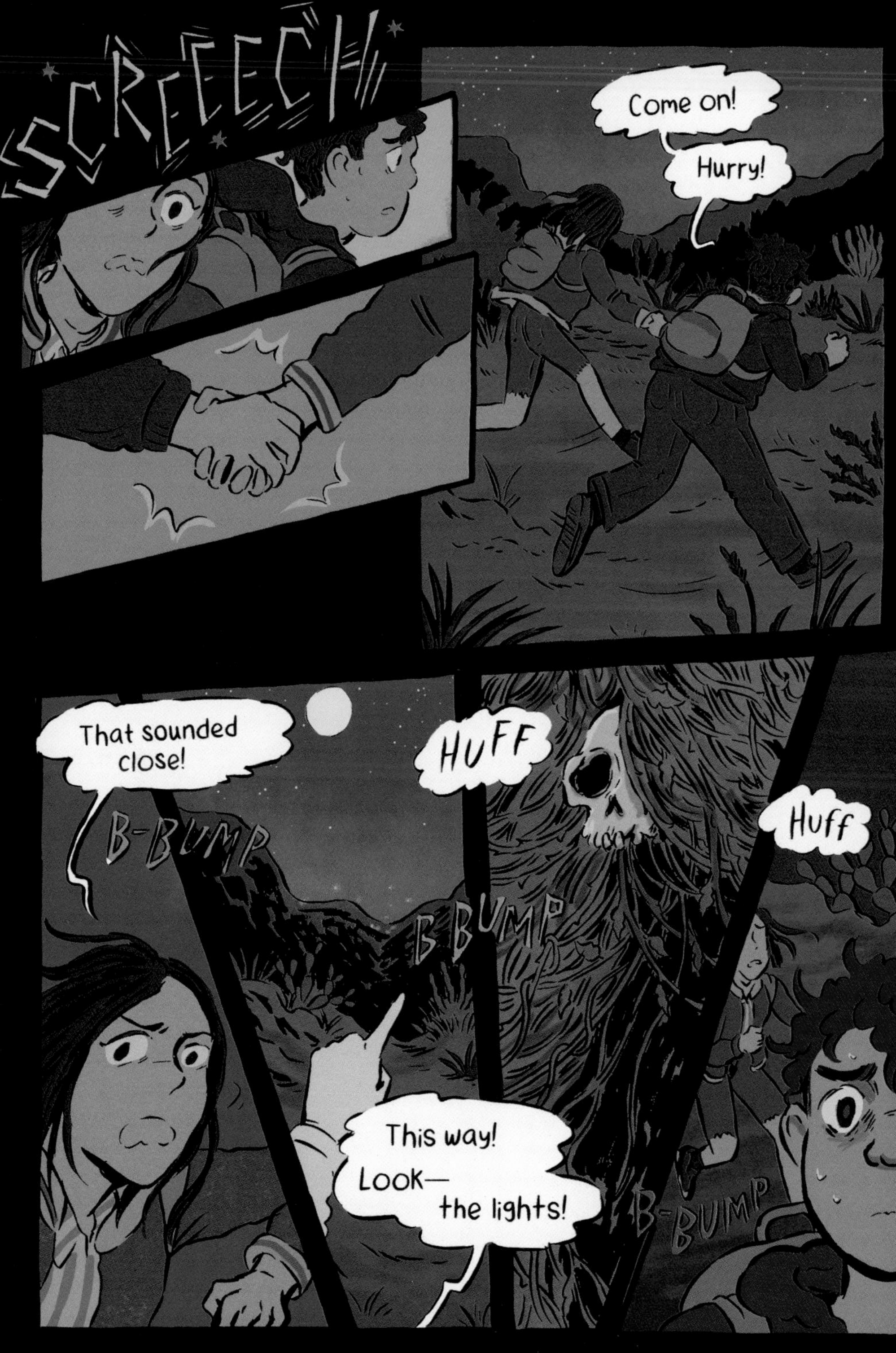
SCREEECH
Come on!
Hurry!
That sounded close!
B-BUMP
HUFF
Huff
B-BUMP
This way!
Look—
the lights!
B-BUMP

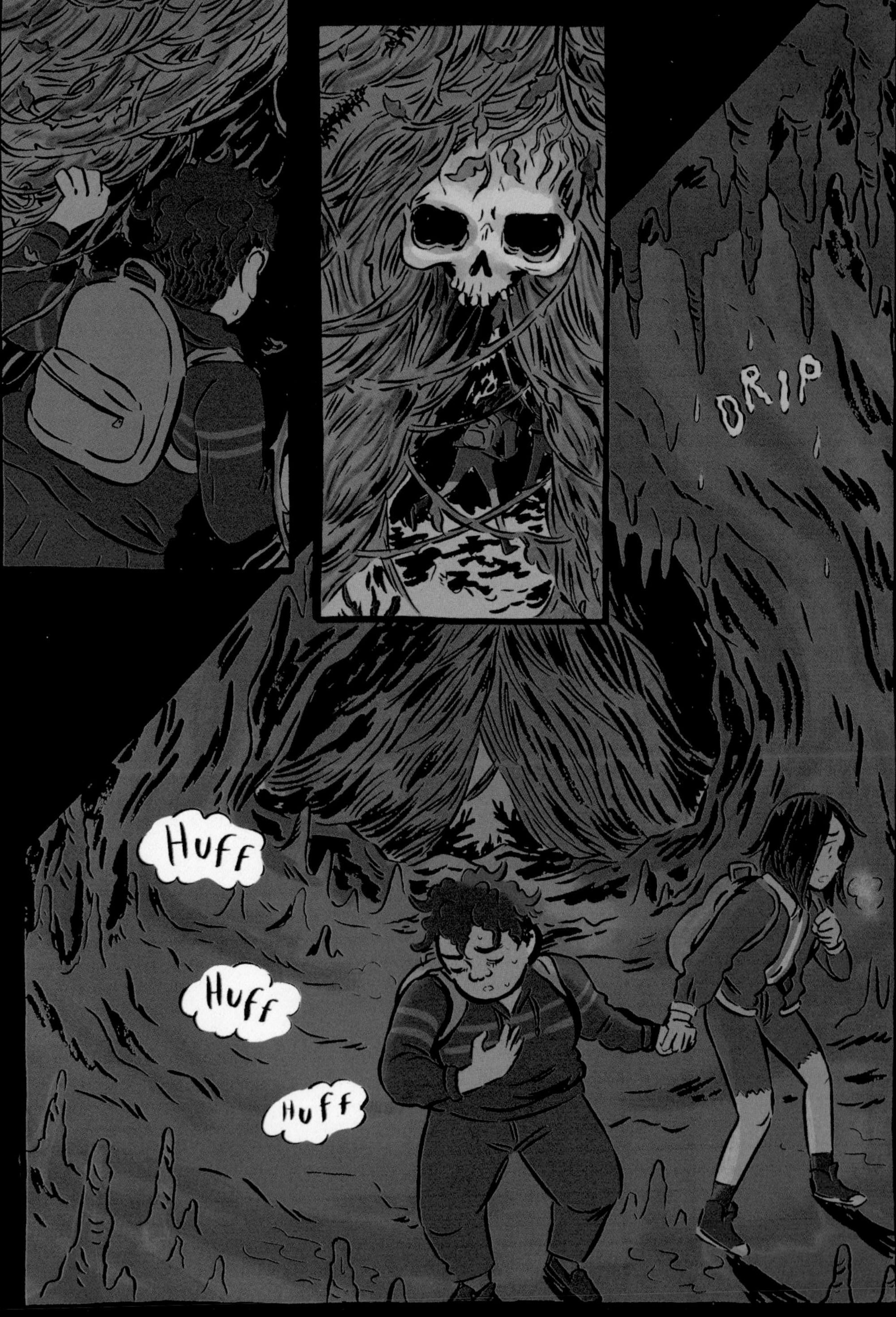
DRIP
HUFF
HUFF
HUFF

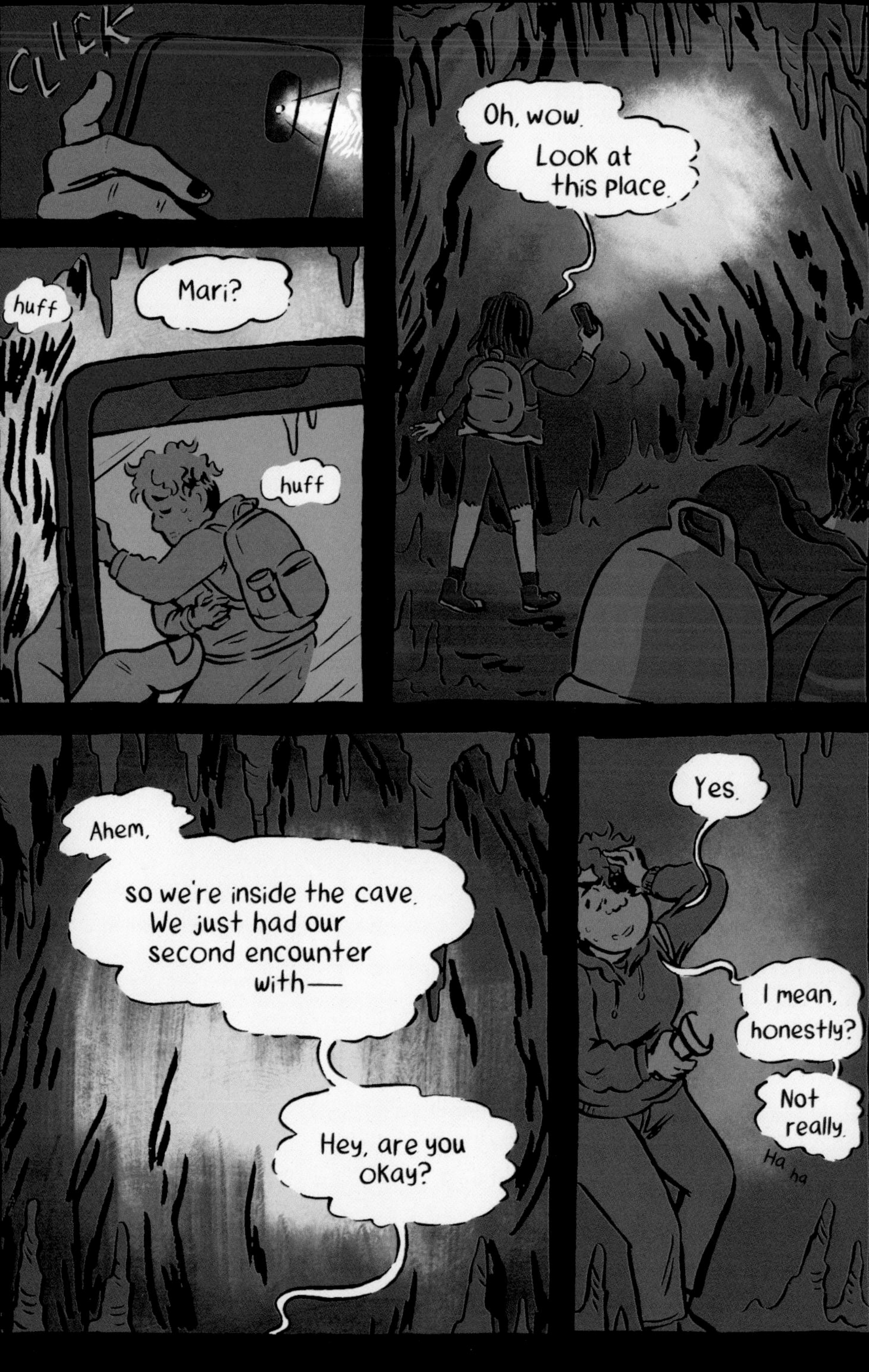
CLICK
huff
Mari?
huff
Oh, wow.
Look at this place.
Ahem,
so we're inside the cave. We just had our second encounter with—
Hey, are you okay?
Yes.
I mean, honestly?
Not really.
Ha ha

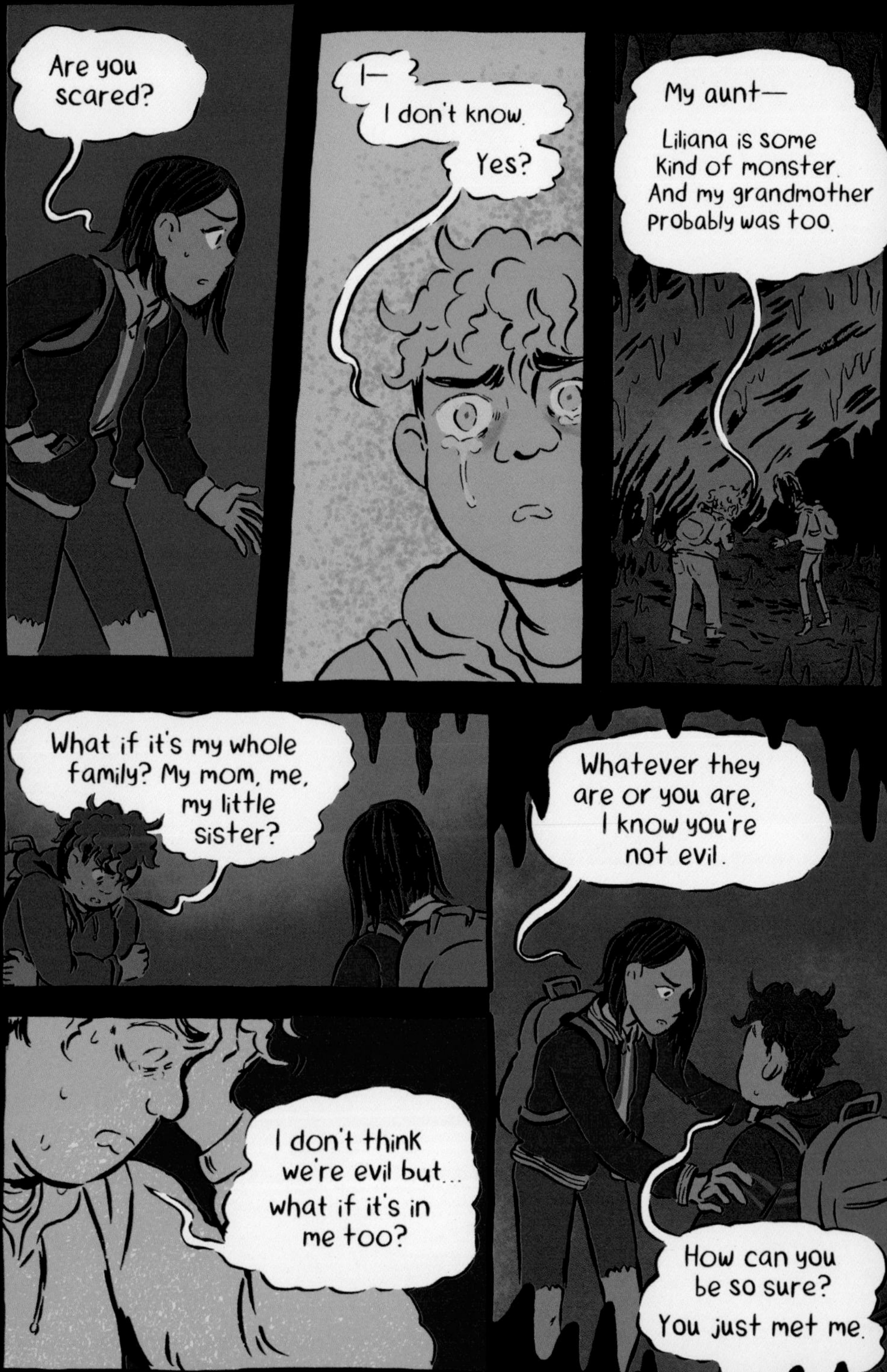
Are you scared?
I—
I don't know.
Yes?
My aunt—
Liliana is some kind of monster. And my grandmother probably was too.
What if it's my whole family? My mom, me, my little sister?
Whatever they are or you are, I know you're not evil.
I don't think we're evil but... what if it's in me too?
How can you be so sure?
You just met me.

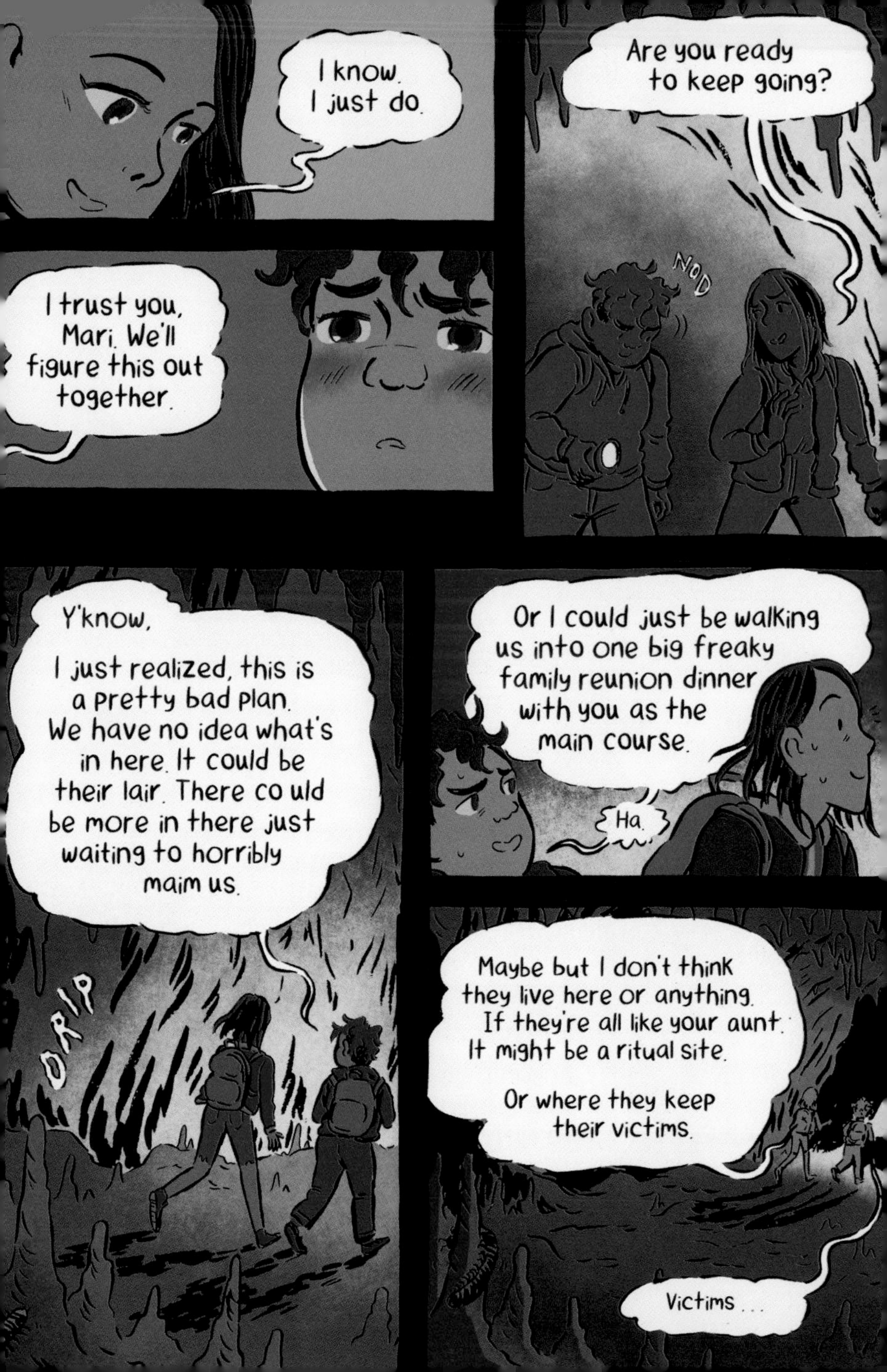
I know. I just do.
Are you ready to keep going?
I trust you, Mari. We'll figure this out together.
NOD
Y'know,
I just realized, this is a pretty bad plan. We have no idea what's in here. It could be their lair. There co uld be more in there just waiting to horribly maim us.
DRIP
Or I could just be walking us into one big freaky family reunion dinner with you as the main course.
Ha.
Maybe but I don't think they live here or anything. If they're all like your aunt. It might be a ritual site.
Or where they keep their victims.
Victims . . .

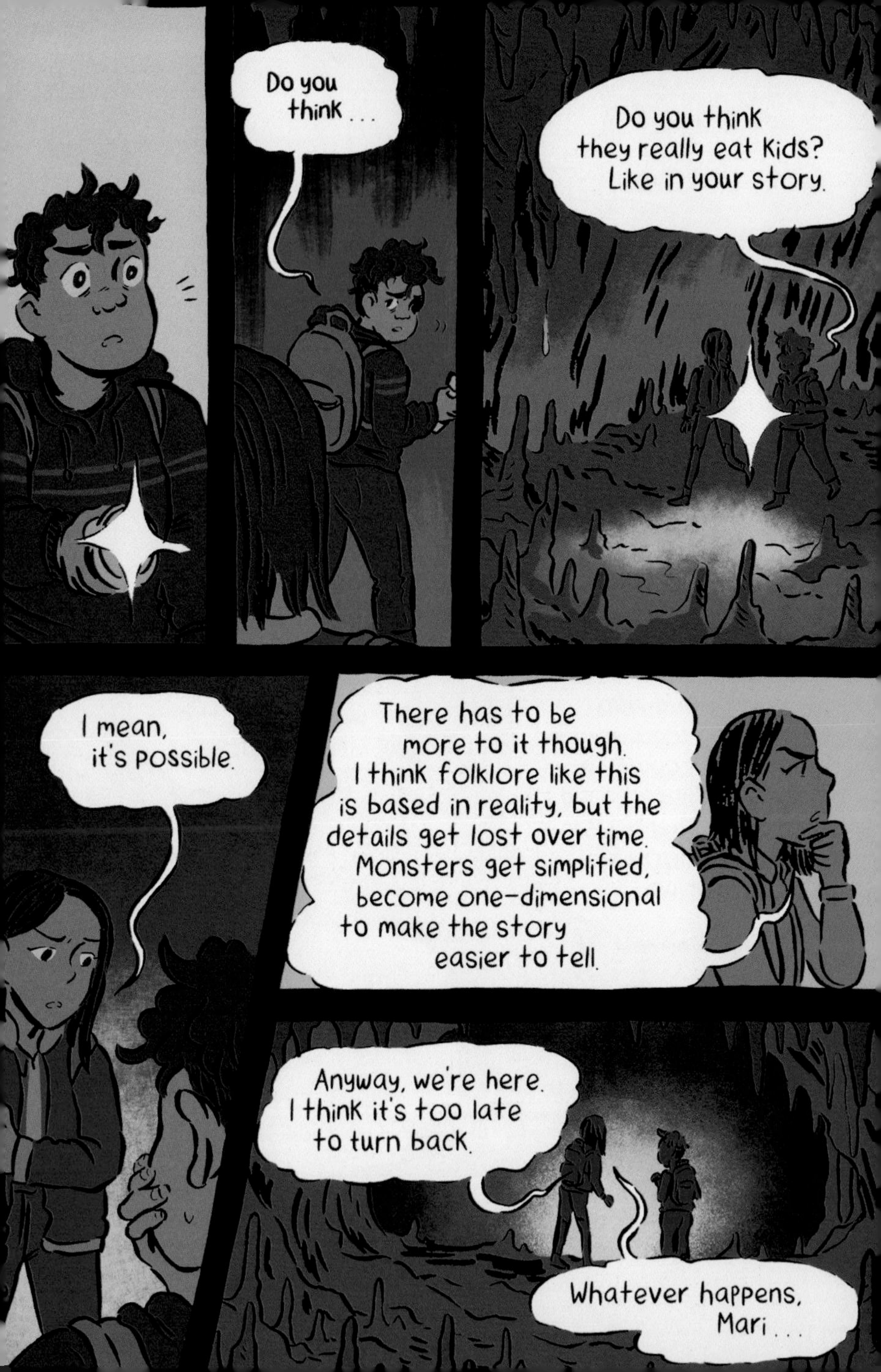
Do you think . . .
Do you think they really eat kids? Like in your story.
I mean, it's possible.
There has to be more to it though. I think folklore like this is based in reality, but the details get lost over time. Monsters get simplified, become one-dimensional to make the story easier to tell.
Anyway, we're here. I think it's too late to turn back.
Whatever happens, Mari . . .

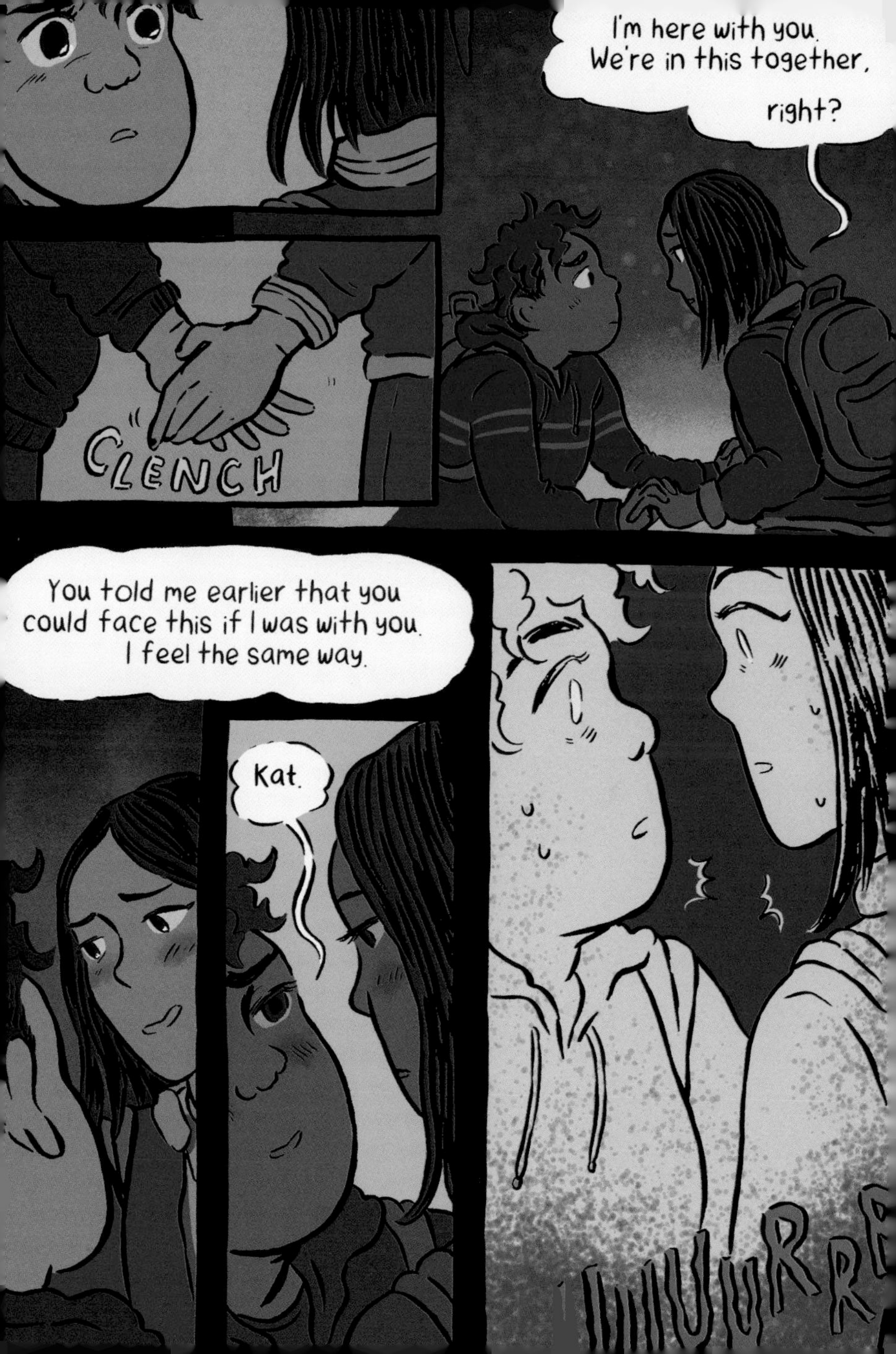

CLENCH
I'm here with you. We're in this together, right?
You told me earlier that you could face this if I was with you. I feel the same way.
Kat.
IIIIIUURRE

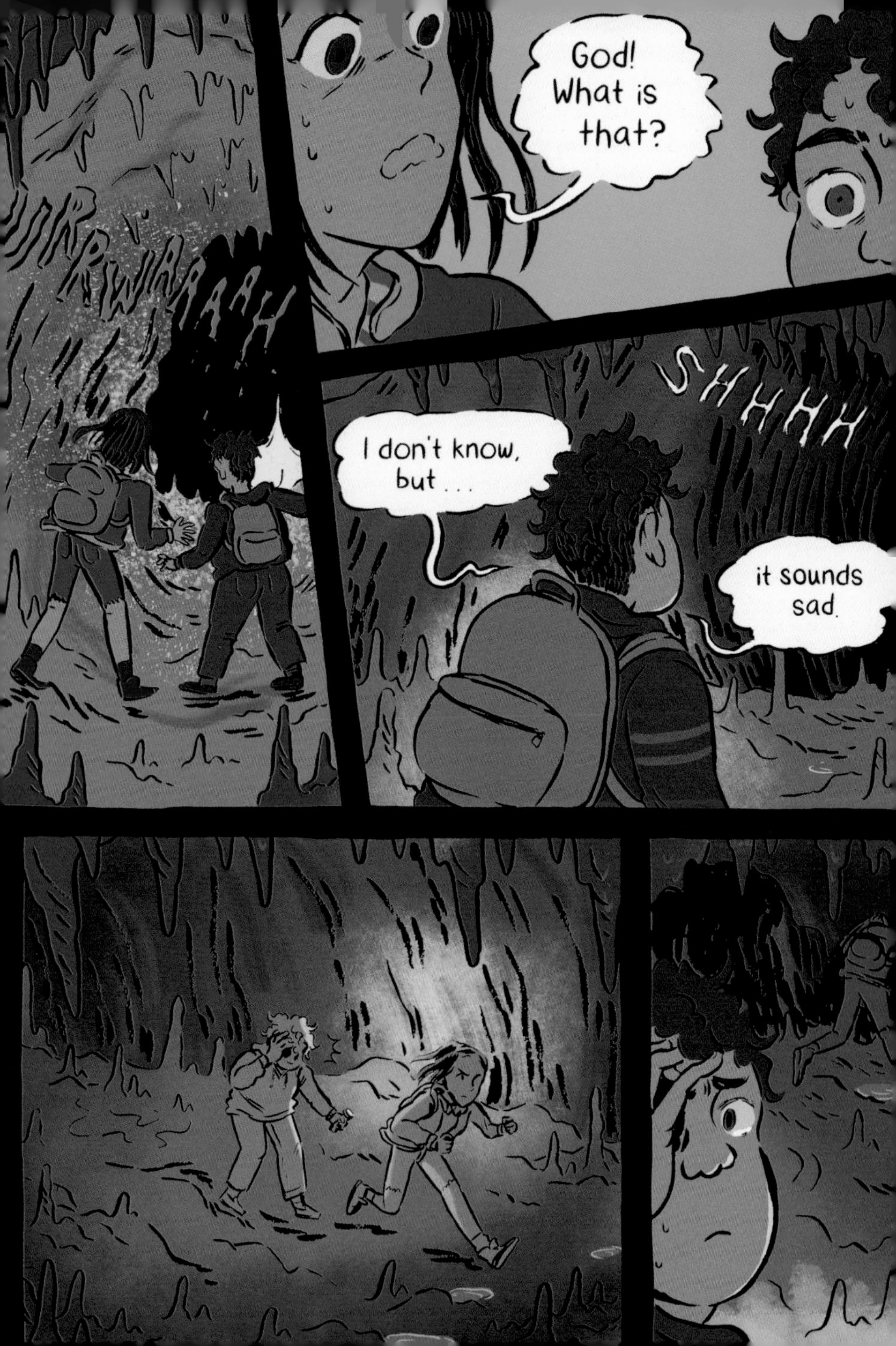
RRRWAAAAH
God! What is that?
SHHHH
I don't know, but . . .
it sounds sad.

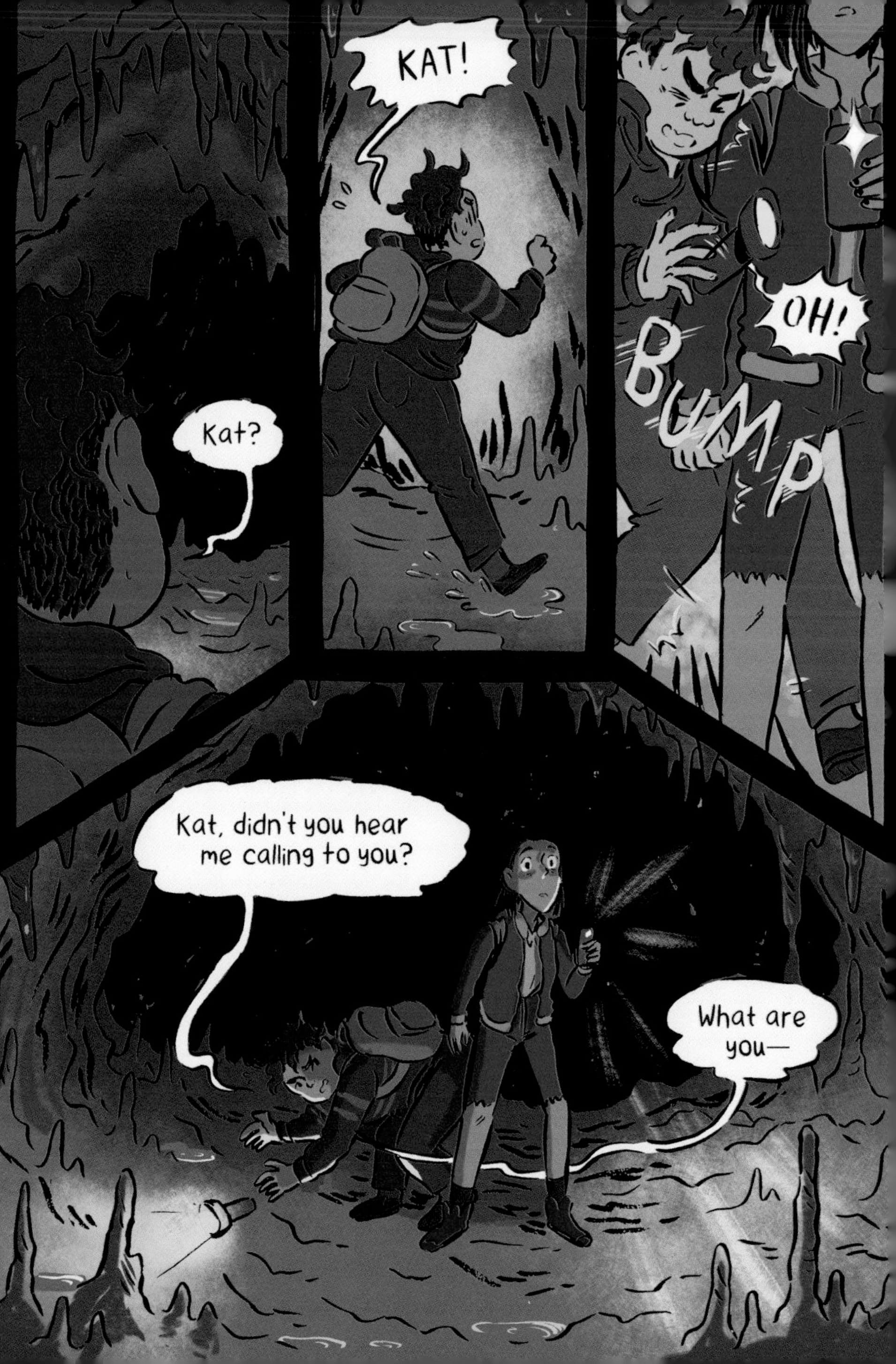
Kat?
KAT!
OH!
BUMP
Kat, didn't you hear me calling to you?
What are you—

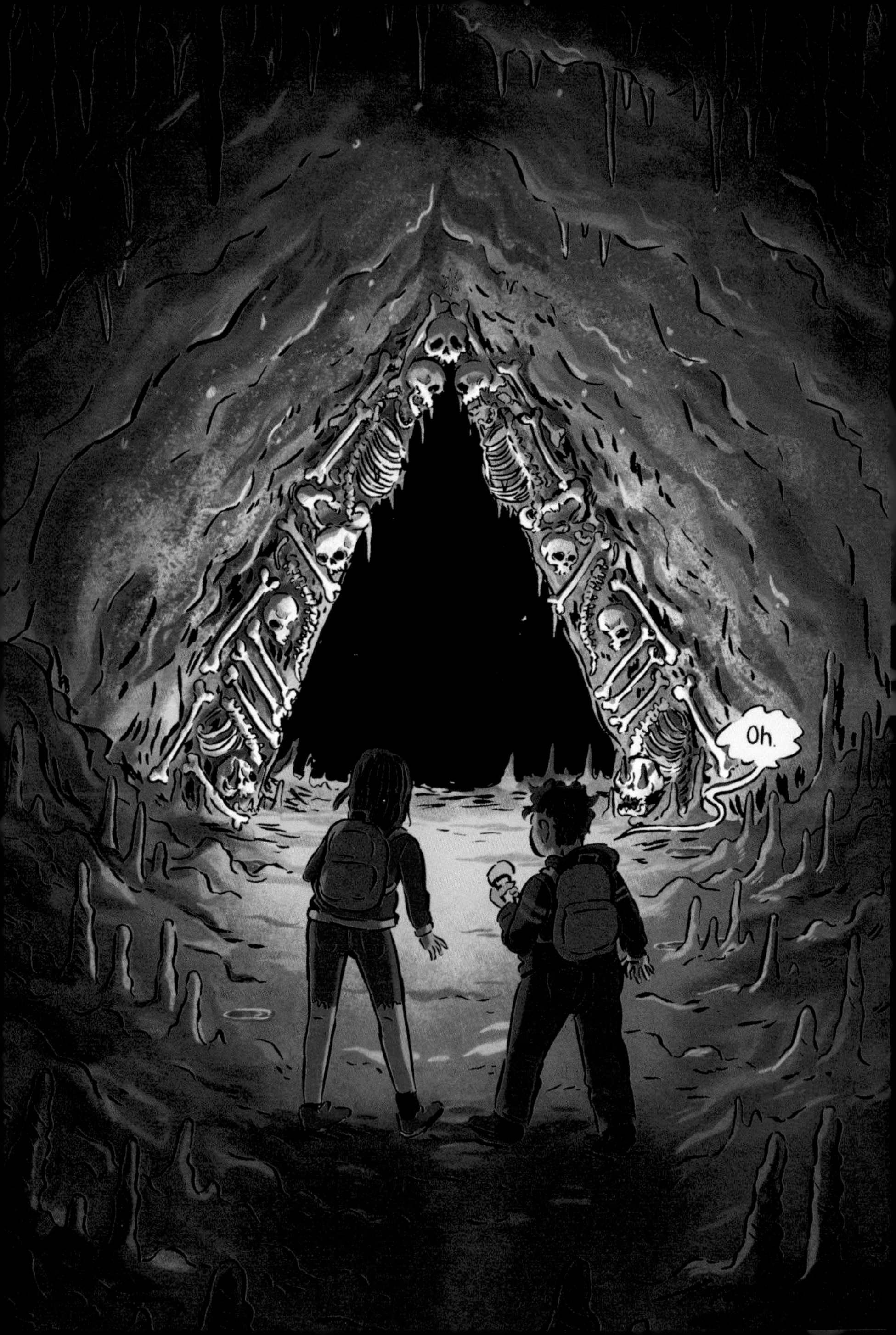
Oh.

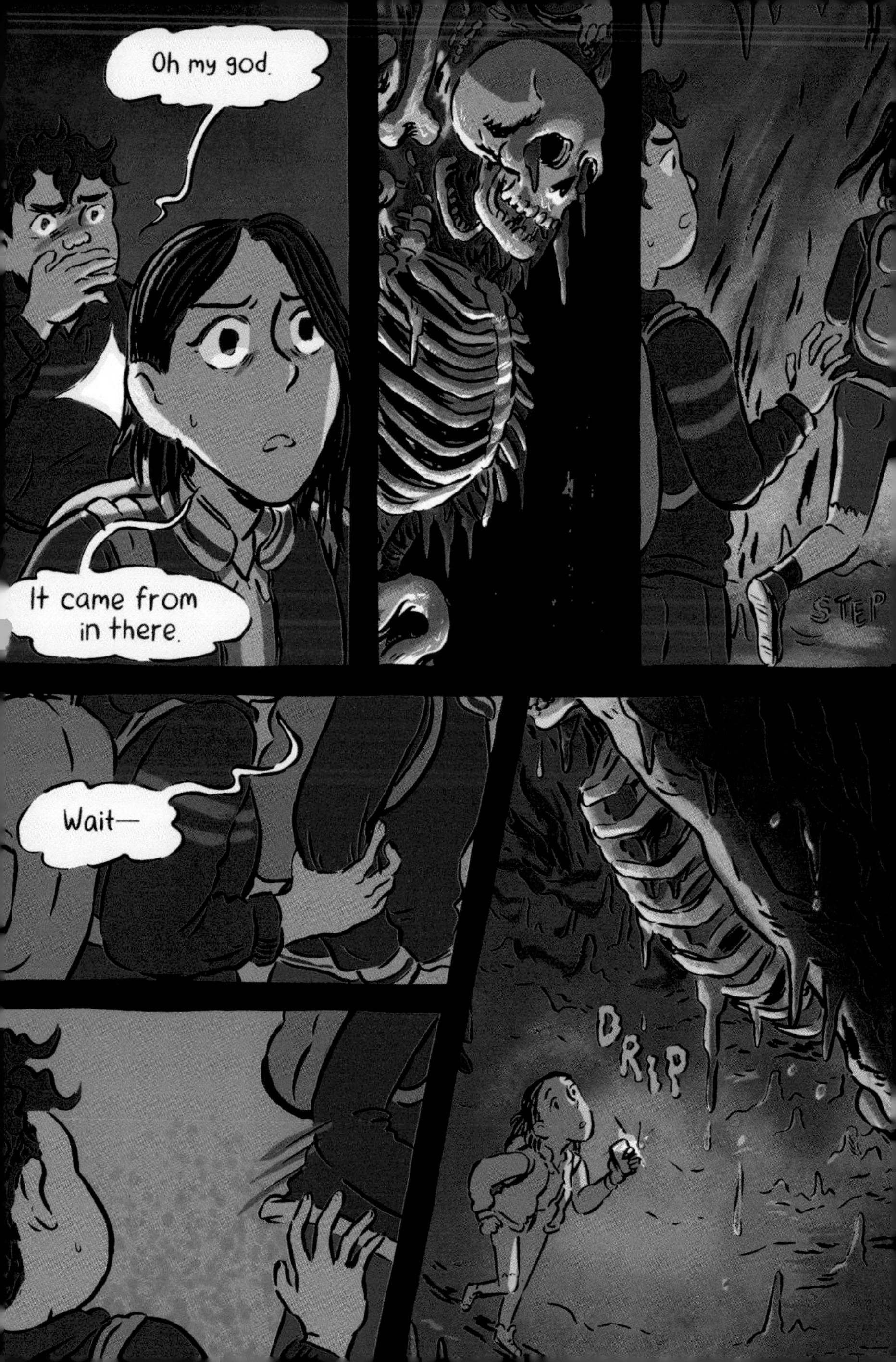
Oh my god.
It came from in there.
STEP
Wait—
DRIP

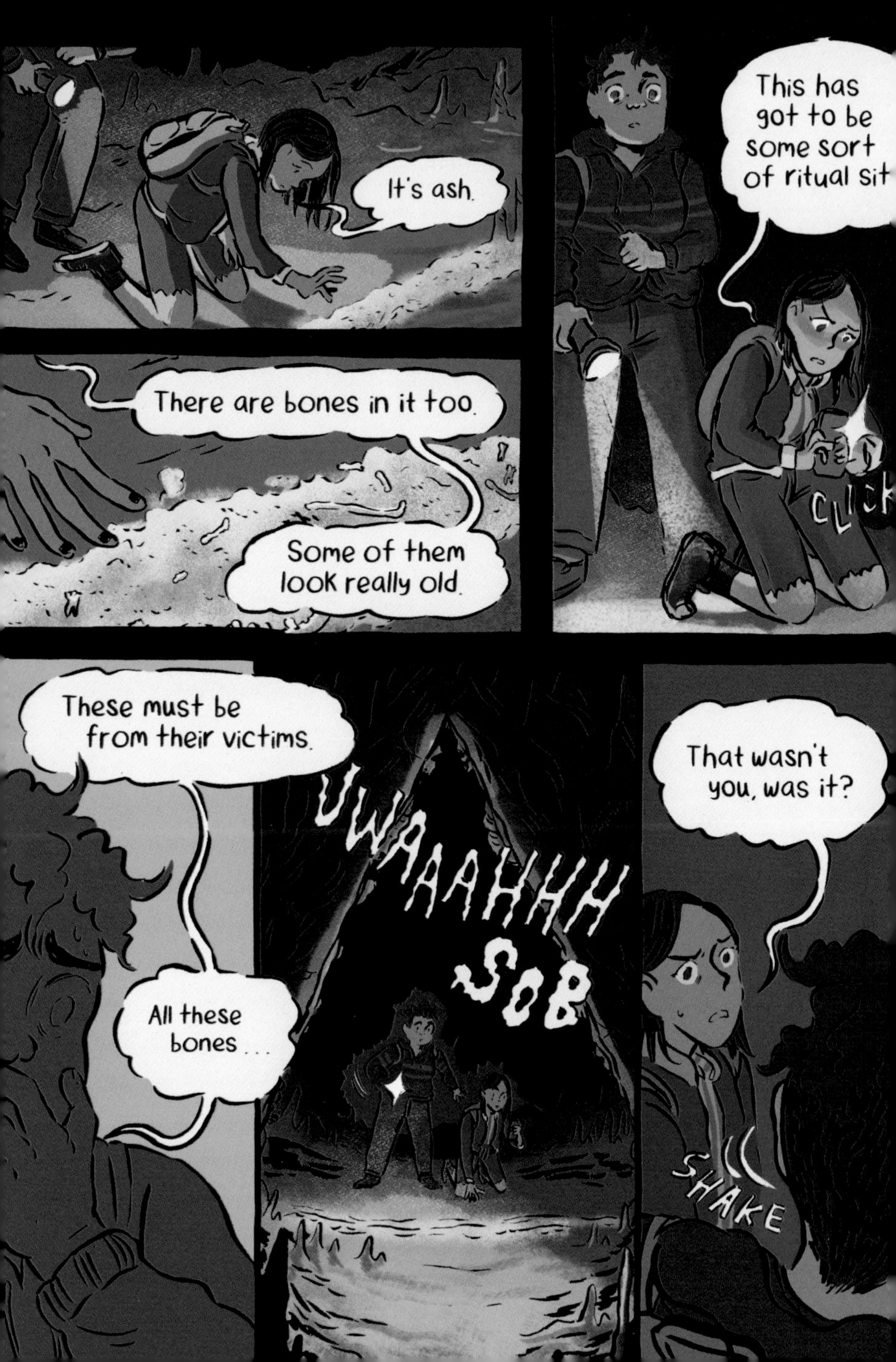
It's ash.
This has got to be some sort of ritual sit
There are bones in it too.
Some of them look really old.
CLICK
These must be from their victims.
All these bones . . .
UWAAAHHH
SOB
That wasn't you, was it?
SHAKE

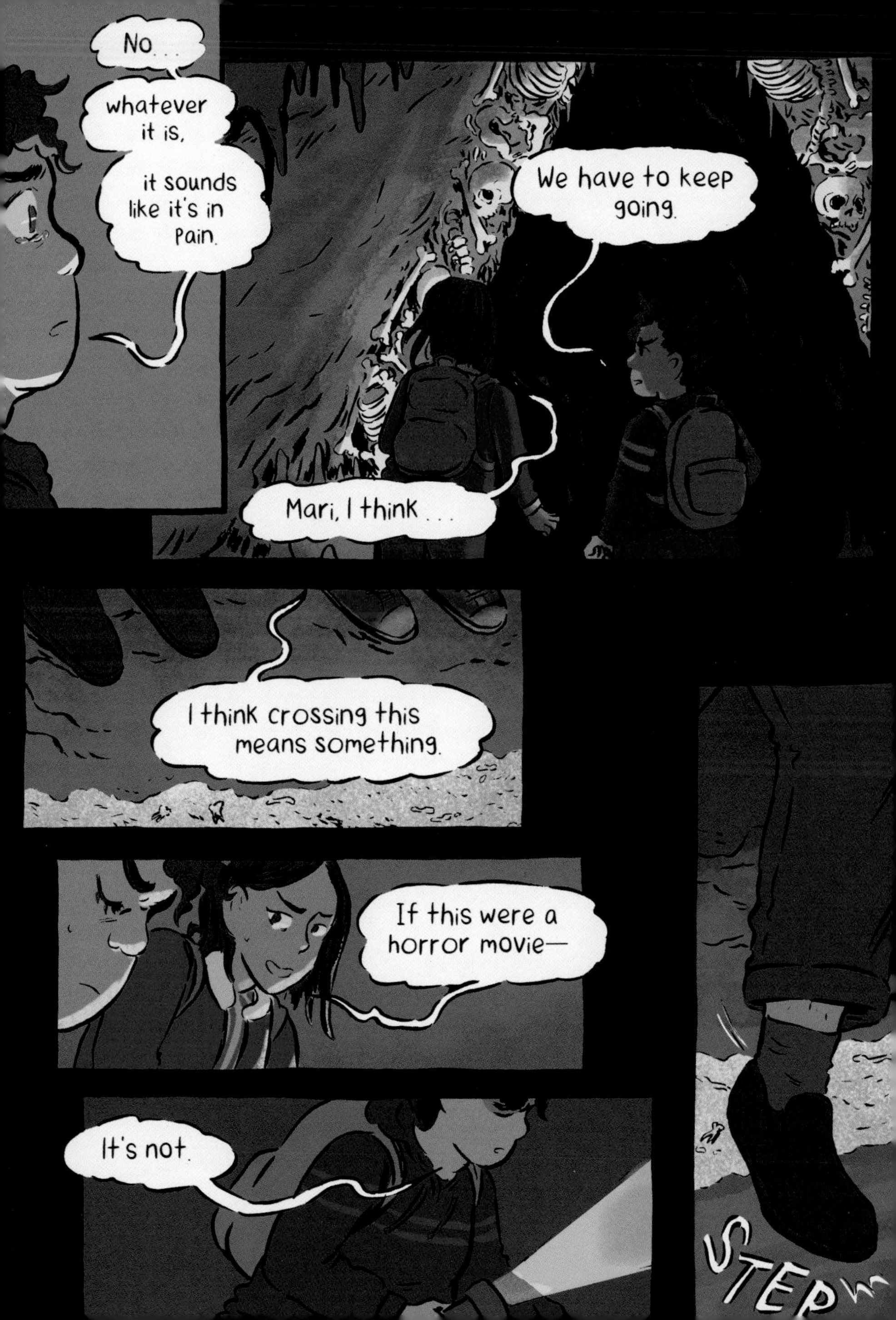
No . . .
whatever it is,
it sounds like it's in pain.
We have to keep going.
Mari, I think . . .
I think crossing this means something.
If this were a horror movie—
It's not.
STEP

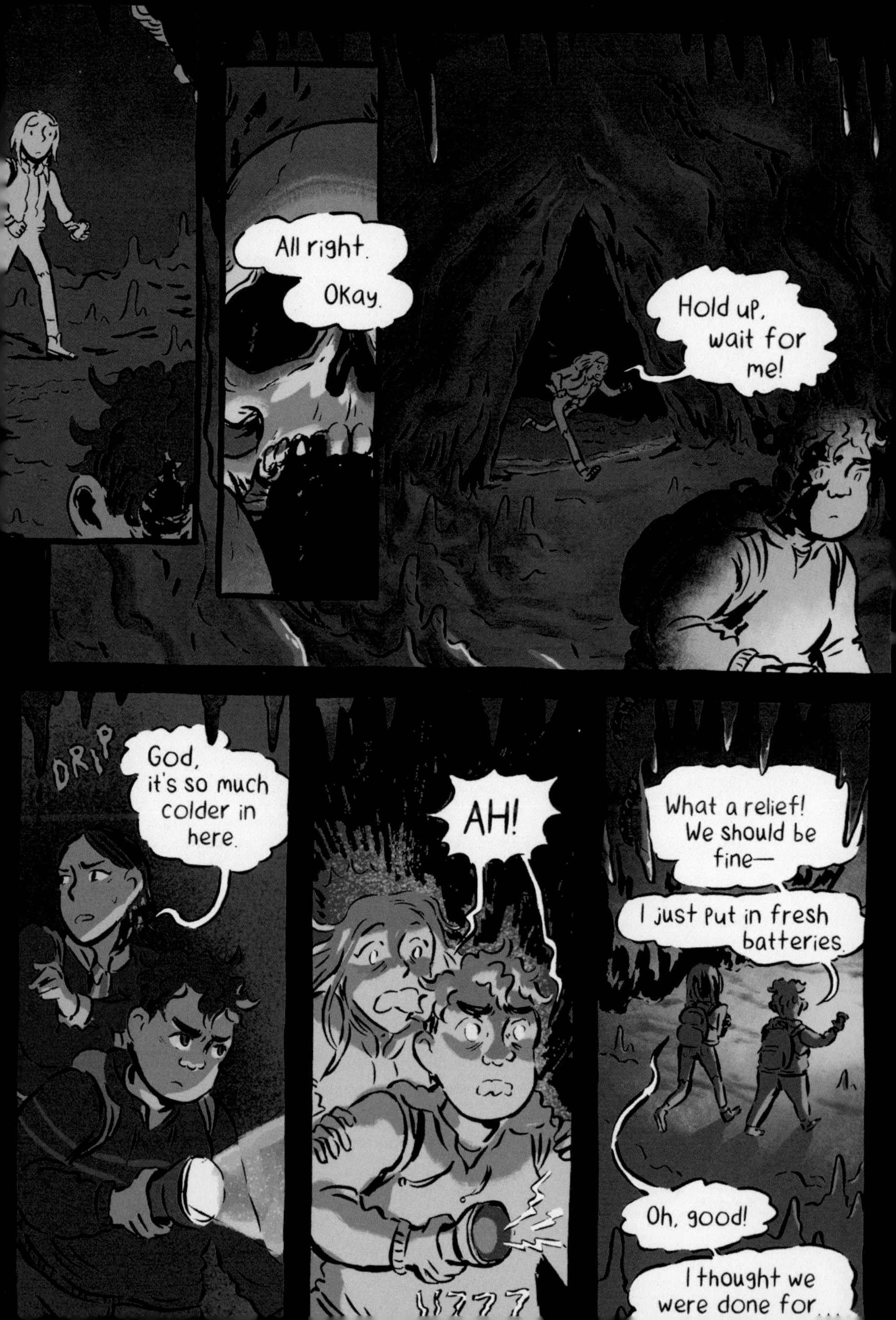
All right.
Okay.
Hold up, wait for me!
DRIP
God, it's so much colder in here.
AH!
BZZZ
What a relief! We should be fine—
I just put in fresh batteries.
Oh, good!
I thought we were done for...

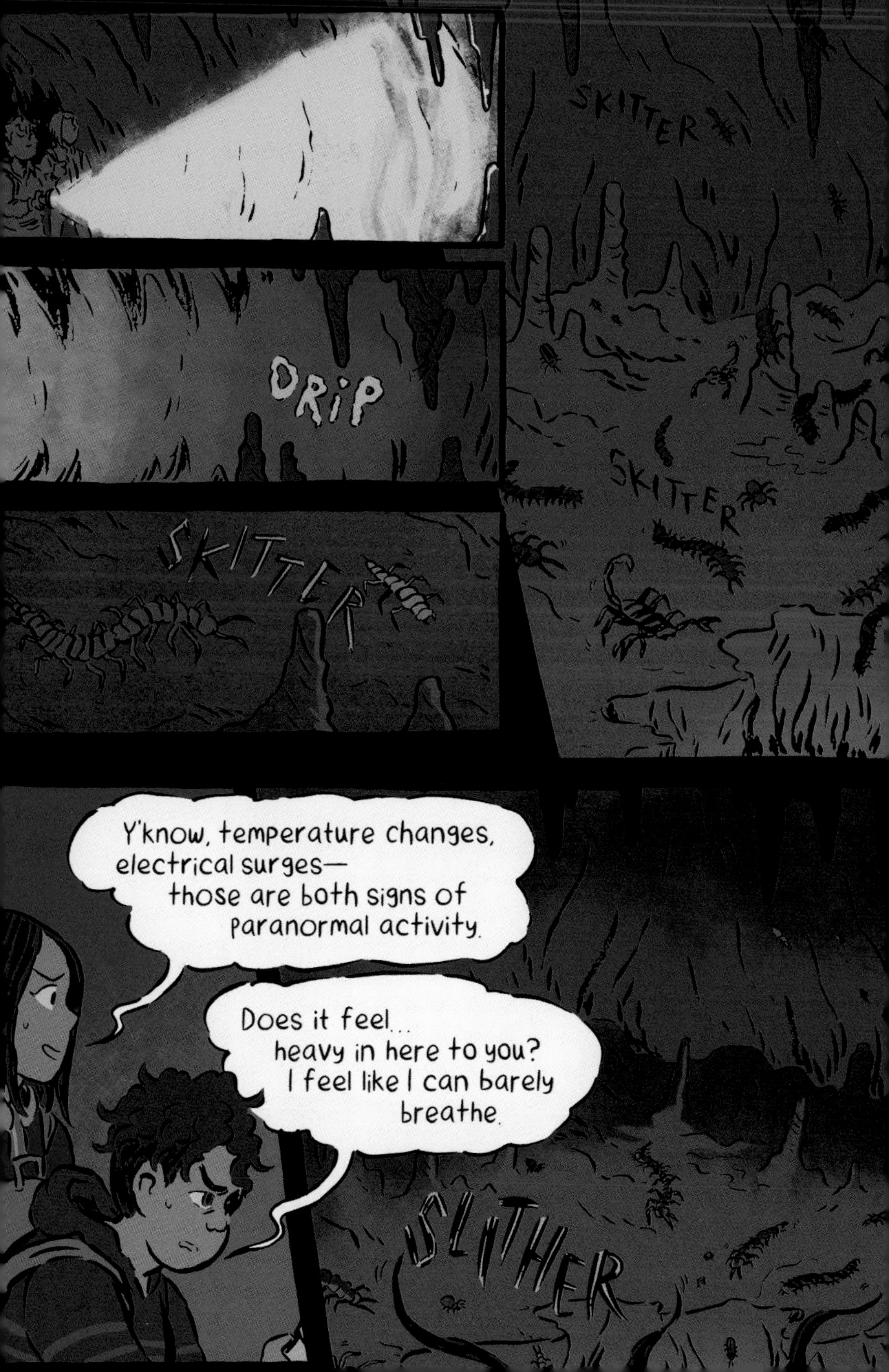

SKITTER
DRIP
SKITTER
SKITTER
Y'know, temperature changes, electrical surges— those are both signs of paranormal activity.
Does it feel... heavy in here to you? I feel like I can barely breathe.
SLITHER

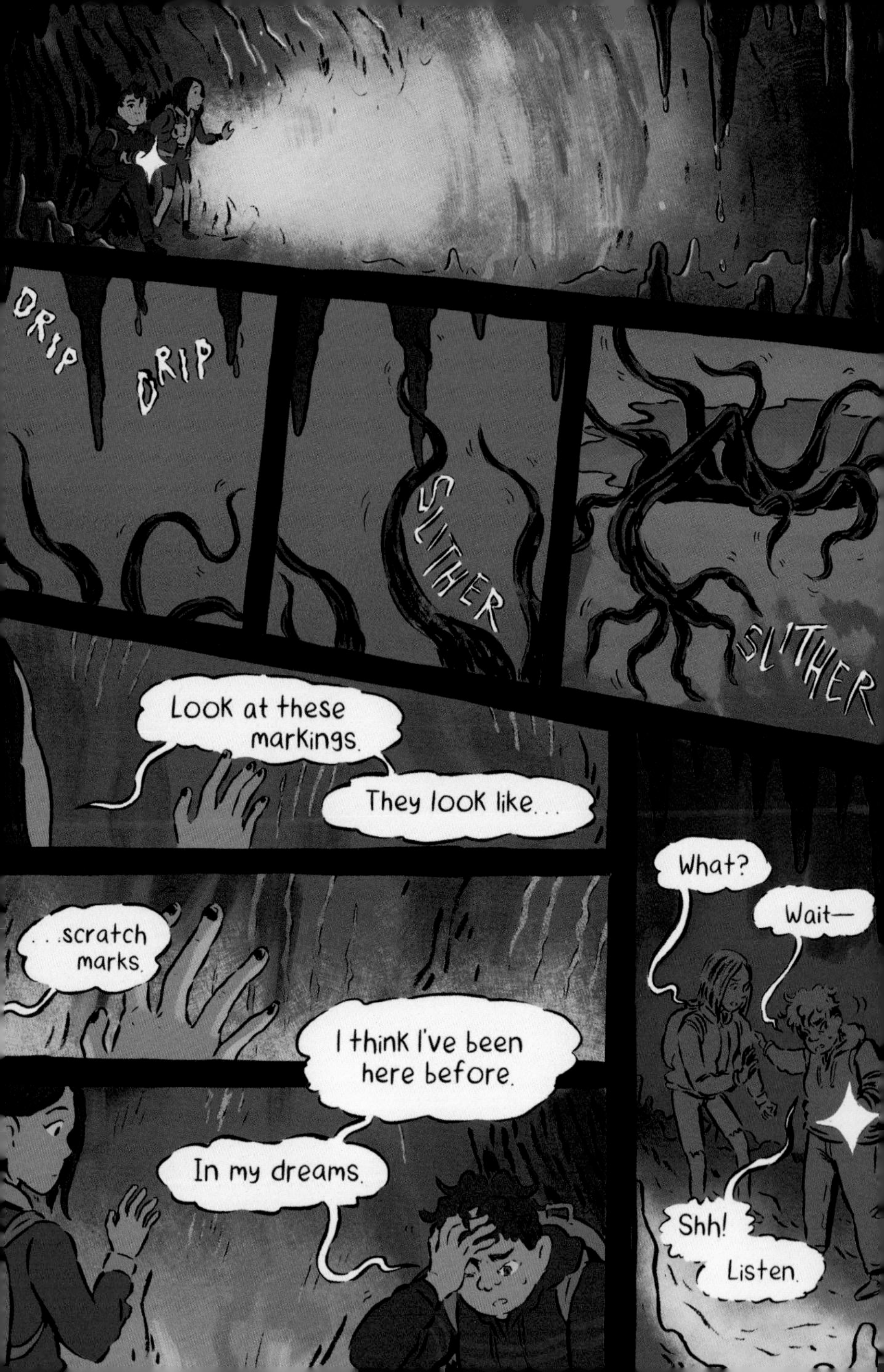
DRIP
DRIP
SLITHER
SLITHER
Look at these markings.
They look like...
...scratch marks.
I think I've been here before.
In my dreams.
What?
Wait—
Shh!
Listen.

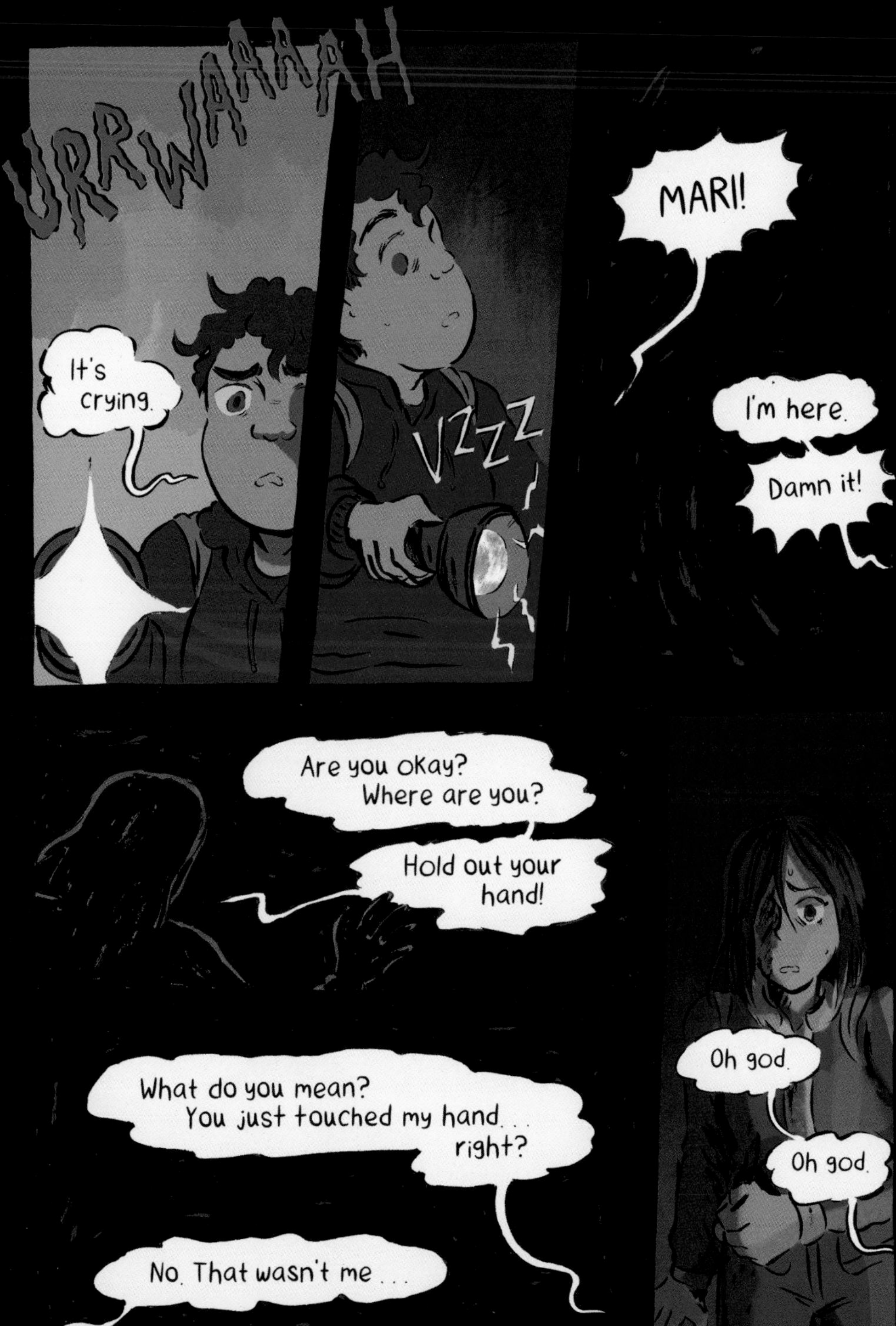
URRWAAAAAH
It's crying.
VZZZ
MARI!
I'm here.
Damn it!
Are you okay? Where are you?
Hold out your hand!
What do you mean? You just touched my hand . . . right?
No. That wasn't me . . .
Oh god.
Oh god.

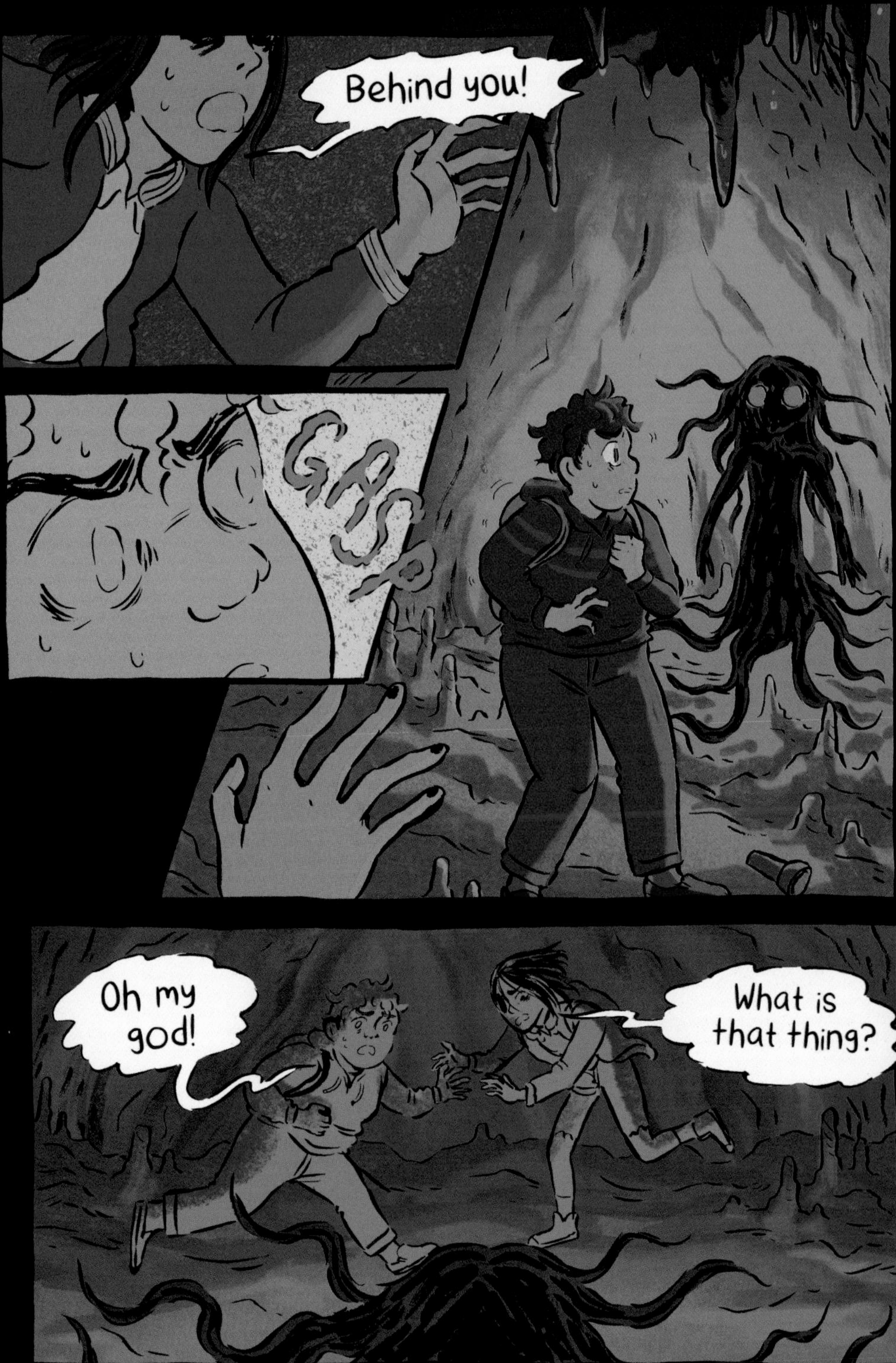
Behind you!
GASP
Oh my god!
What is that thing?

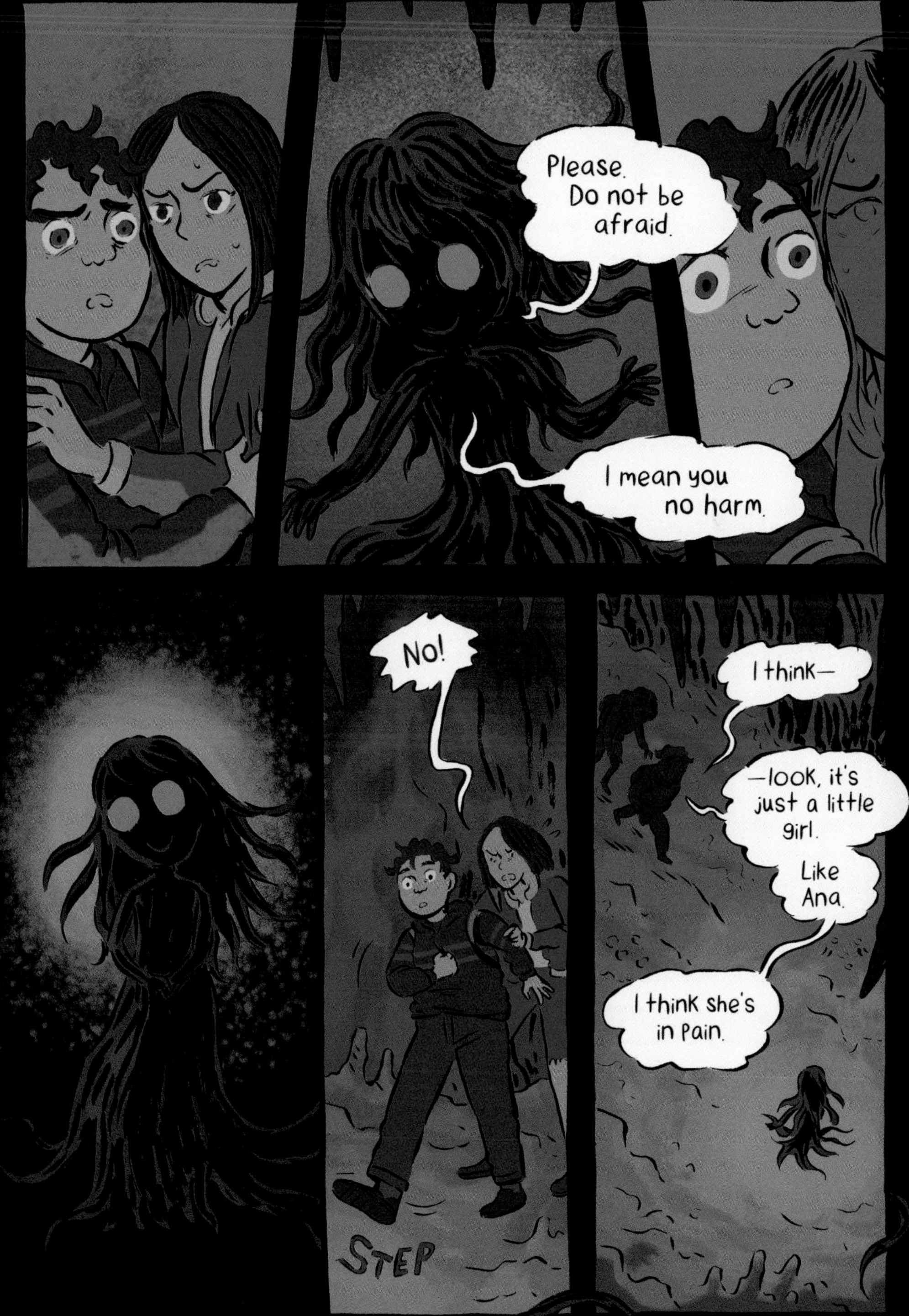
Please. Do not be afraid.
I mean you no harm.
No!
STEP
I think—
—look, it's just a little girl.
Like Ana.
I think she's in pain.

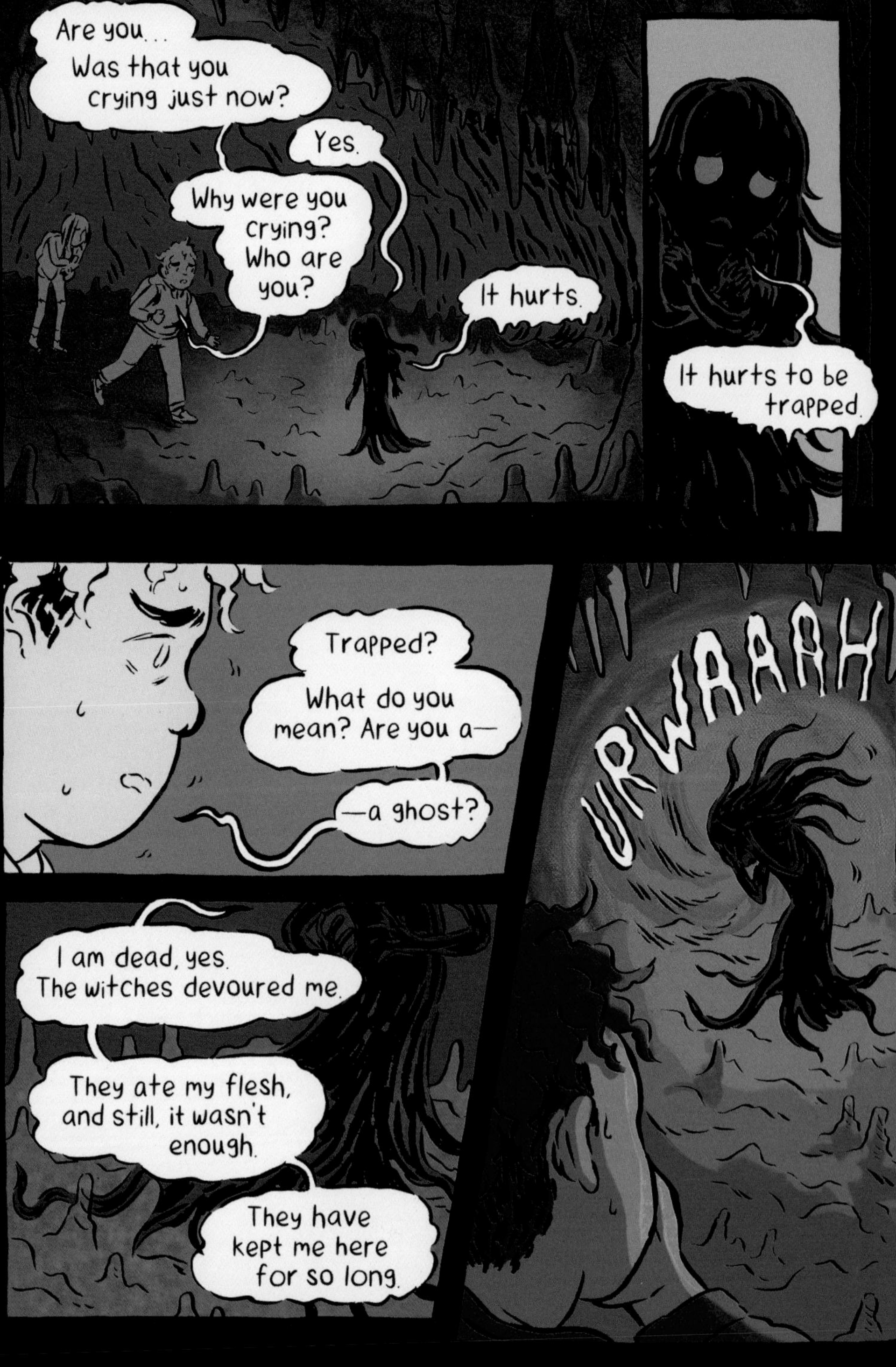
Are you...
Was that you crying just now?
Yes.
Why were you crying? Who are you?
It hurts.
It hurts to be trapped.
Trapped?
What do you mean? Are you a—
—a ghost?
URWAAAH
I am dead, yes. The witches devoured me.
They ate my flesh, and still, it wasn't enough.
They have kept me here for so long.

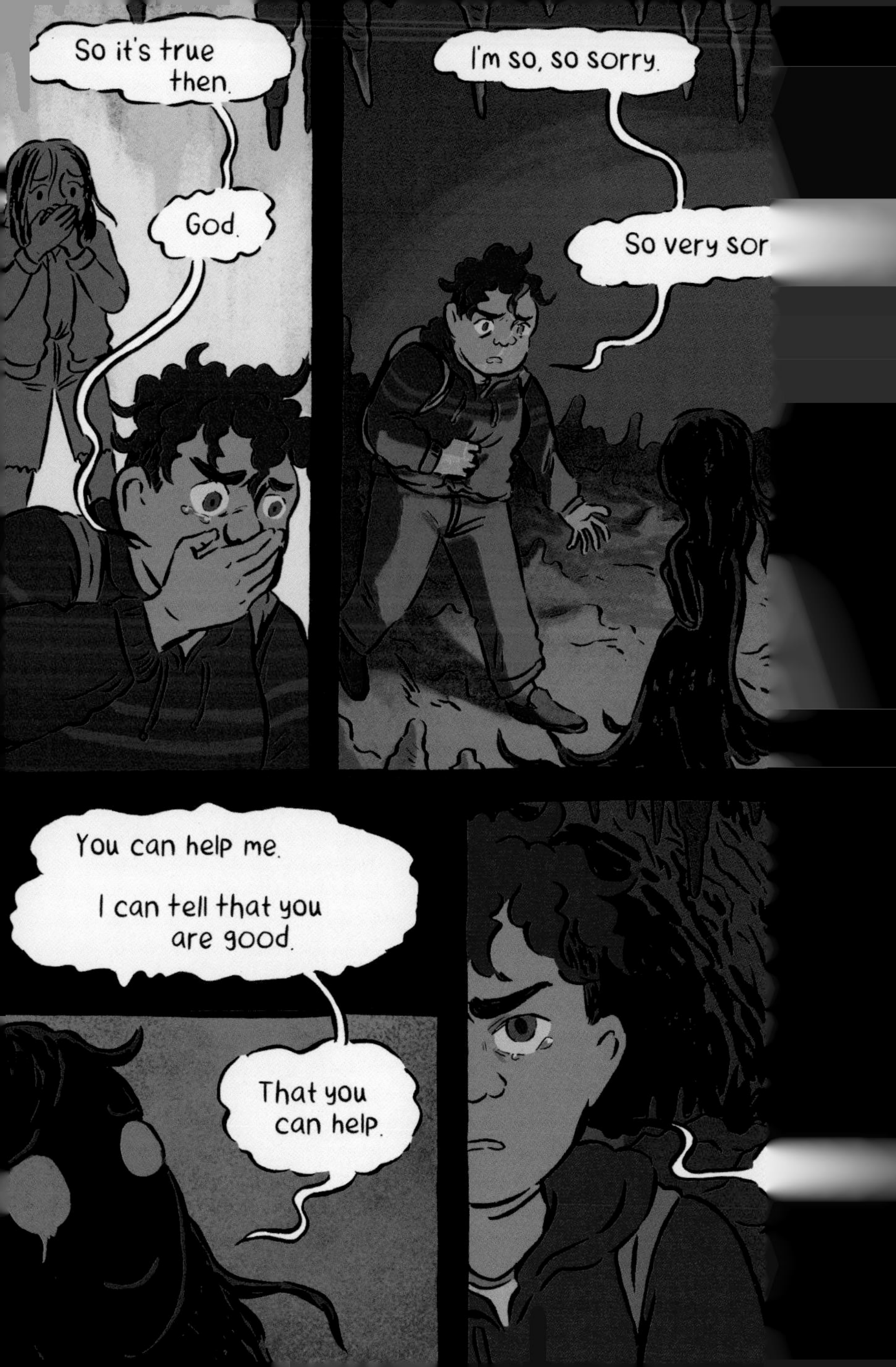
So it's true then.
God.
I'm so, so sorry.
So very sor
You can help me.
I can tell that you are good.
That you can help.

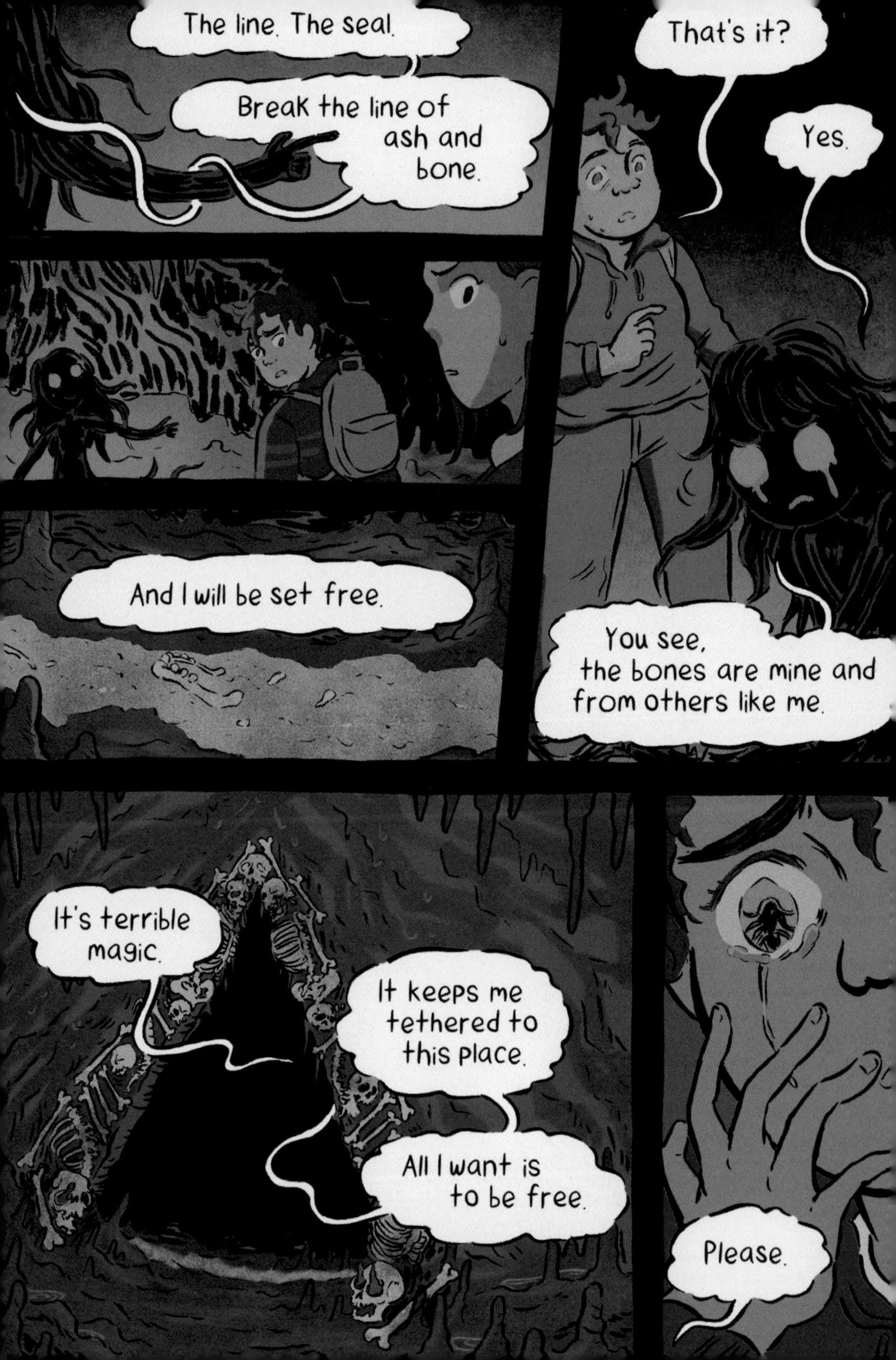
The line. The seal.
Break the line of ash and bone.
That's it?
Yes.
And I will be set free.
You see, the bones are mine and from others like me.
It's terrible magic.
It keeps me tethered to this place.
All I want is to be free.
Please.

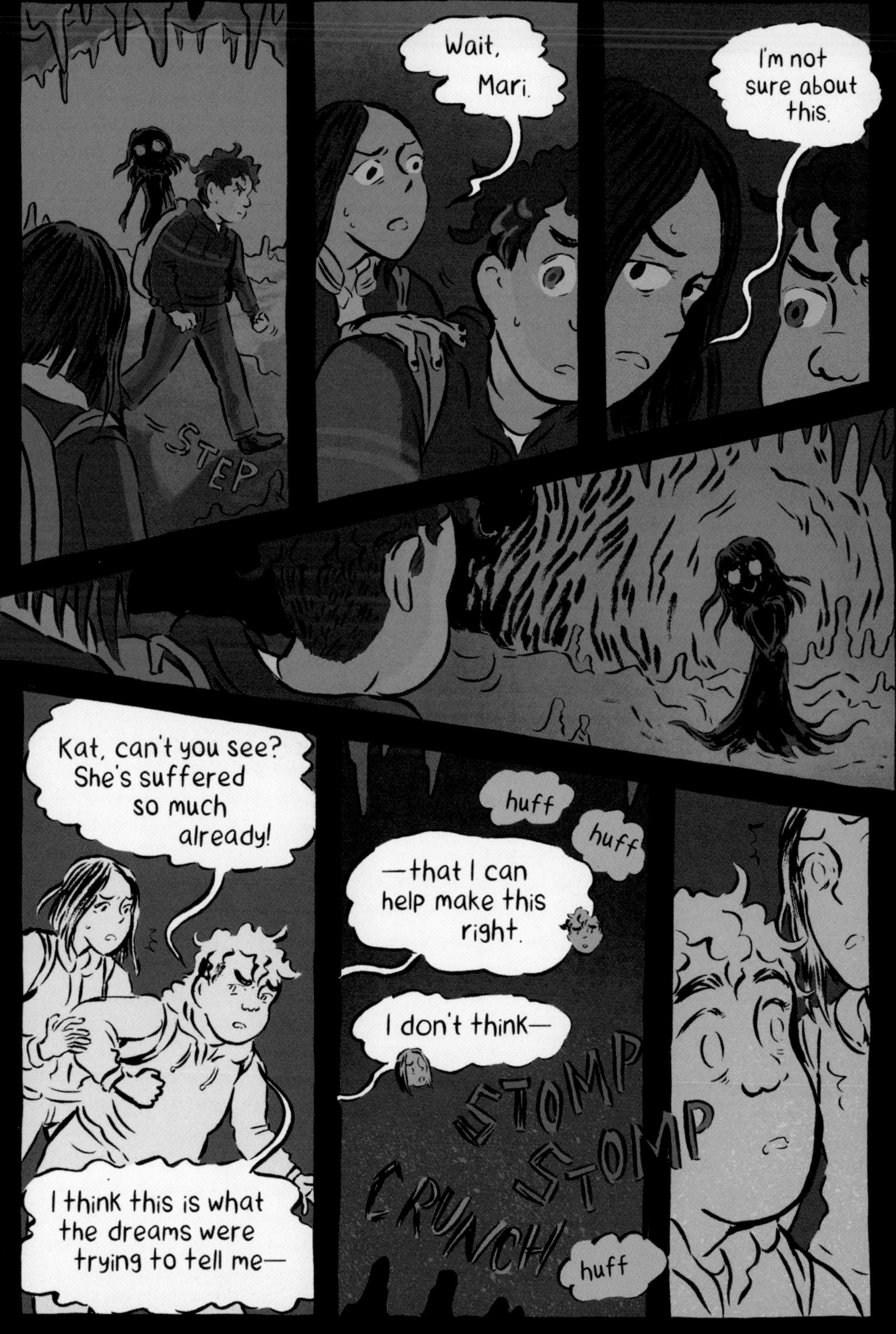

STEP
Wait, Mari.
I'm not sure about this.
Kat, can't you see? She's suffered so much already!
I think this is what the dreams were trying to tell me—
huff
huff
—that I can help make this right.
I don't think—
STOMP
STOMP
CRUNCH
huff

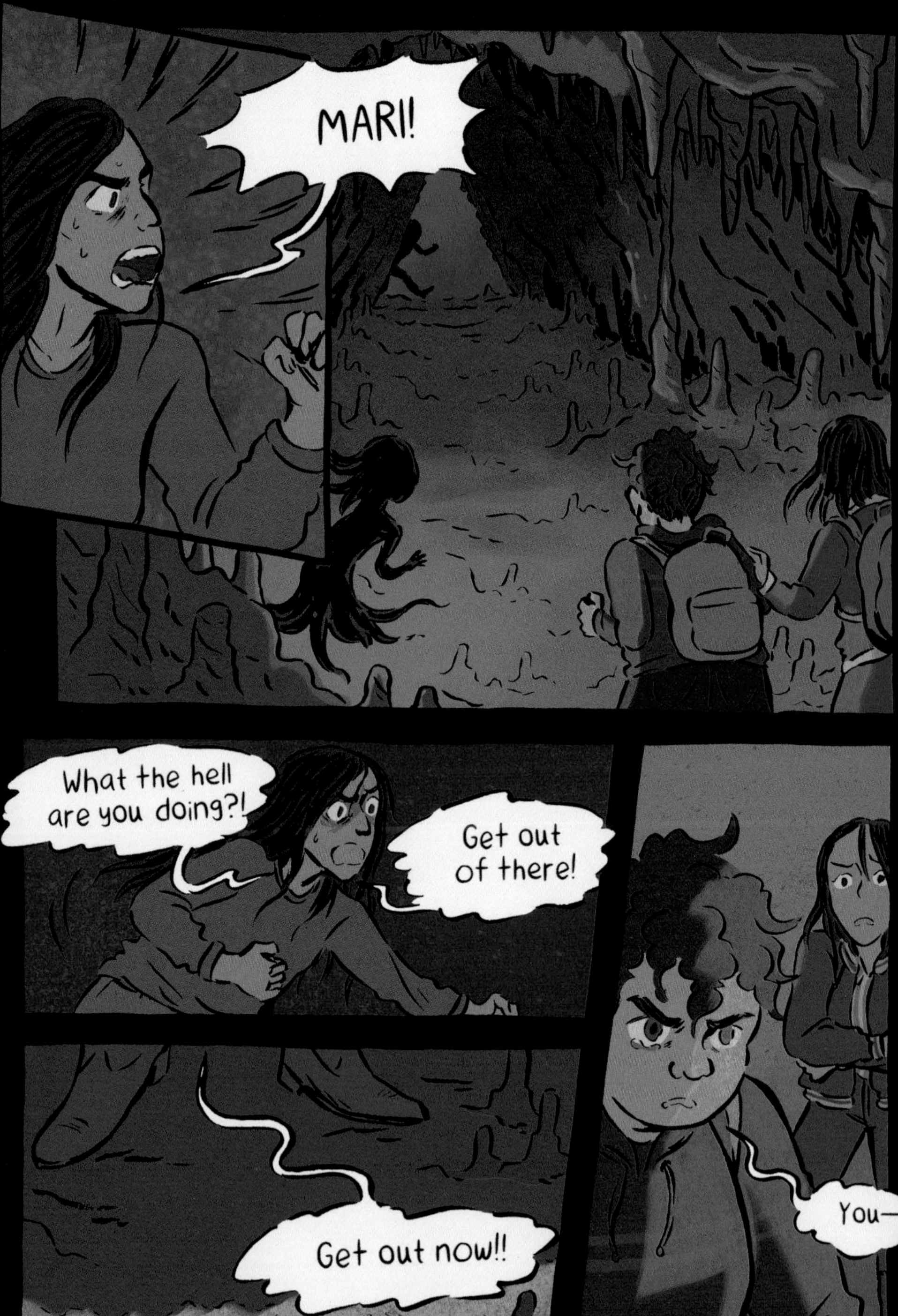

MARI!
What the hell are you doing?!
Get out of there!
Get out now!!
You—

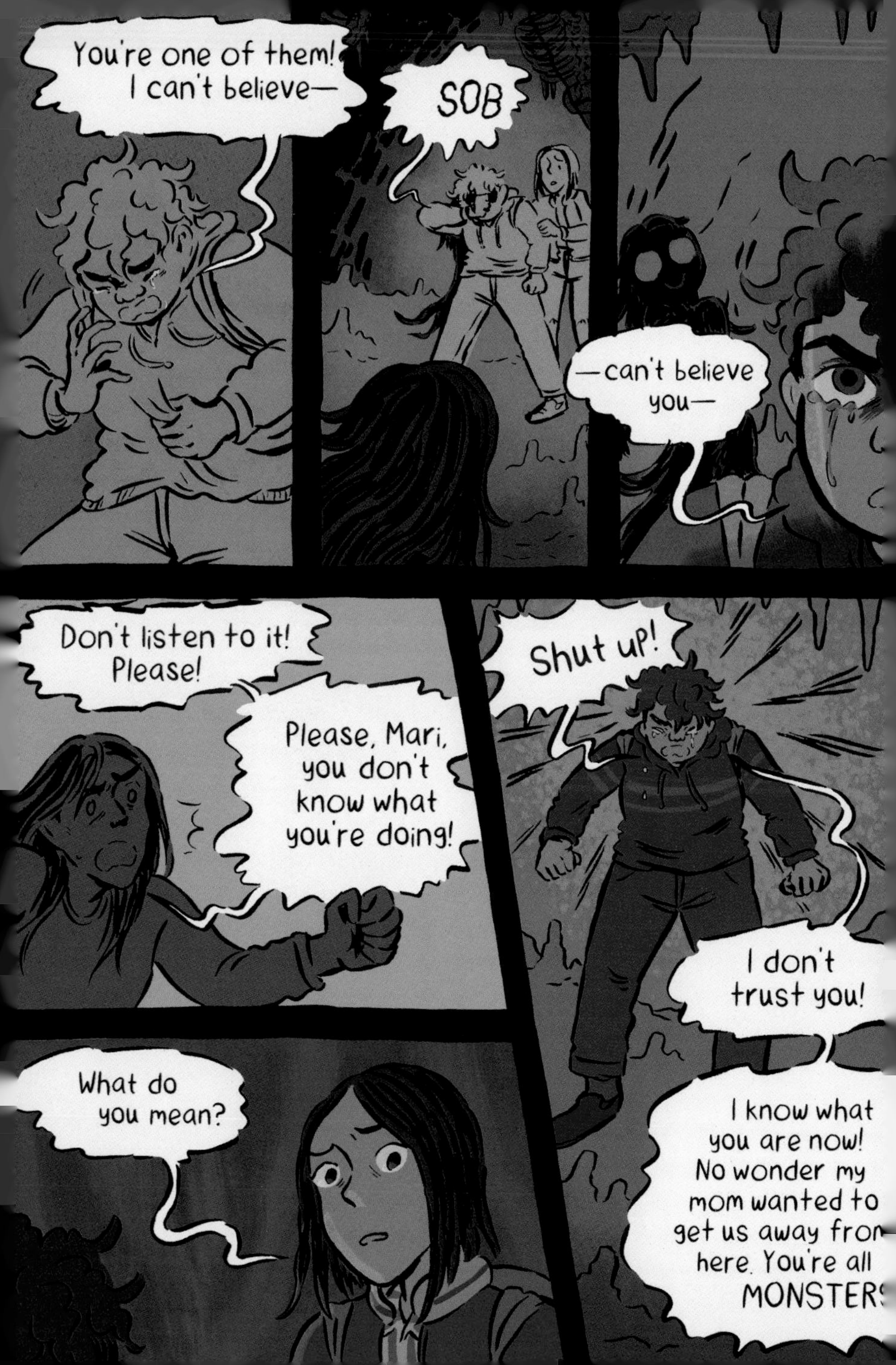
You're one of them! I can't believe—
SOB
—can't believe you—
Don't listen to it! Please!
Please, Mari, you don't know what you're doing!
Shut up!
I don't trust you!
What do you mean?
I know what you are now! No wonder my mom wanted to get us away from here. You're all MONSTERS

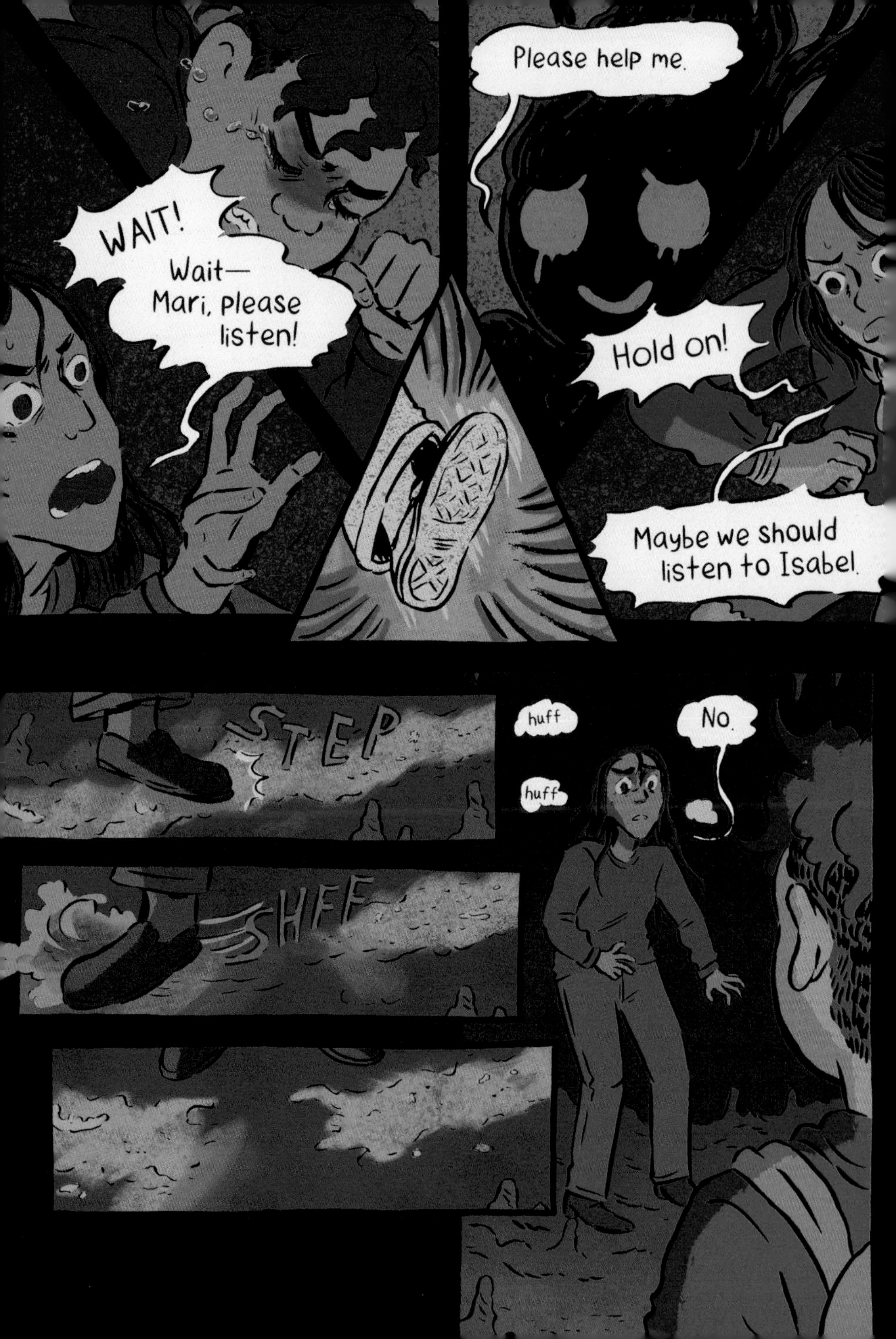
WAIT!
Wait— Mari, please listen!
Please help me.
Hold on!
Maybe we should listen to Isabel.
STEP
SHFF
huff
huff
No.

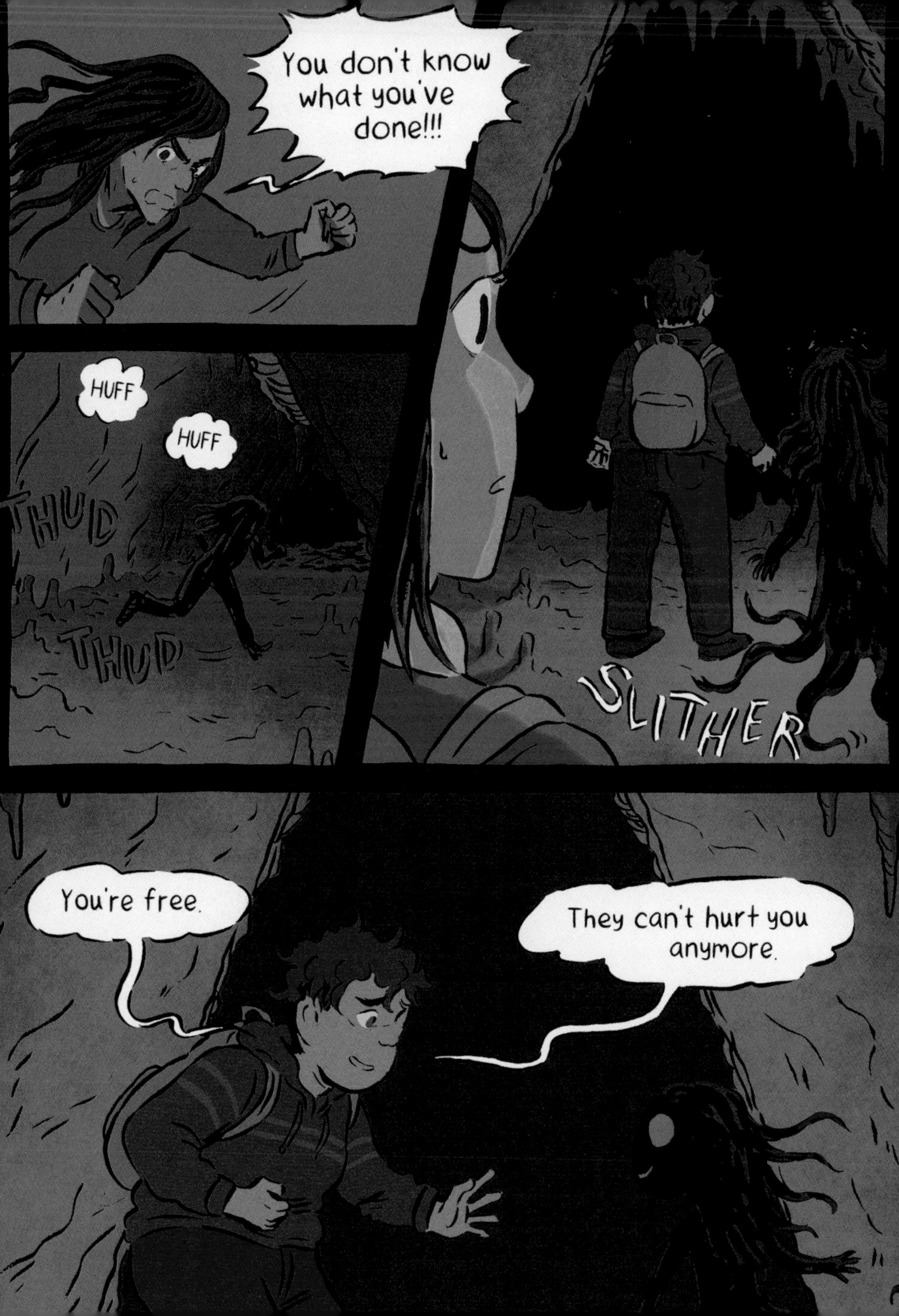
You don't know what you've done!!!
HUFF
HUFF
THUD
THUD
SLITHER
You're free.
They can't hurt you anymore.

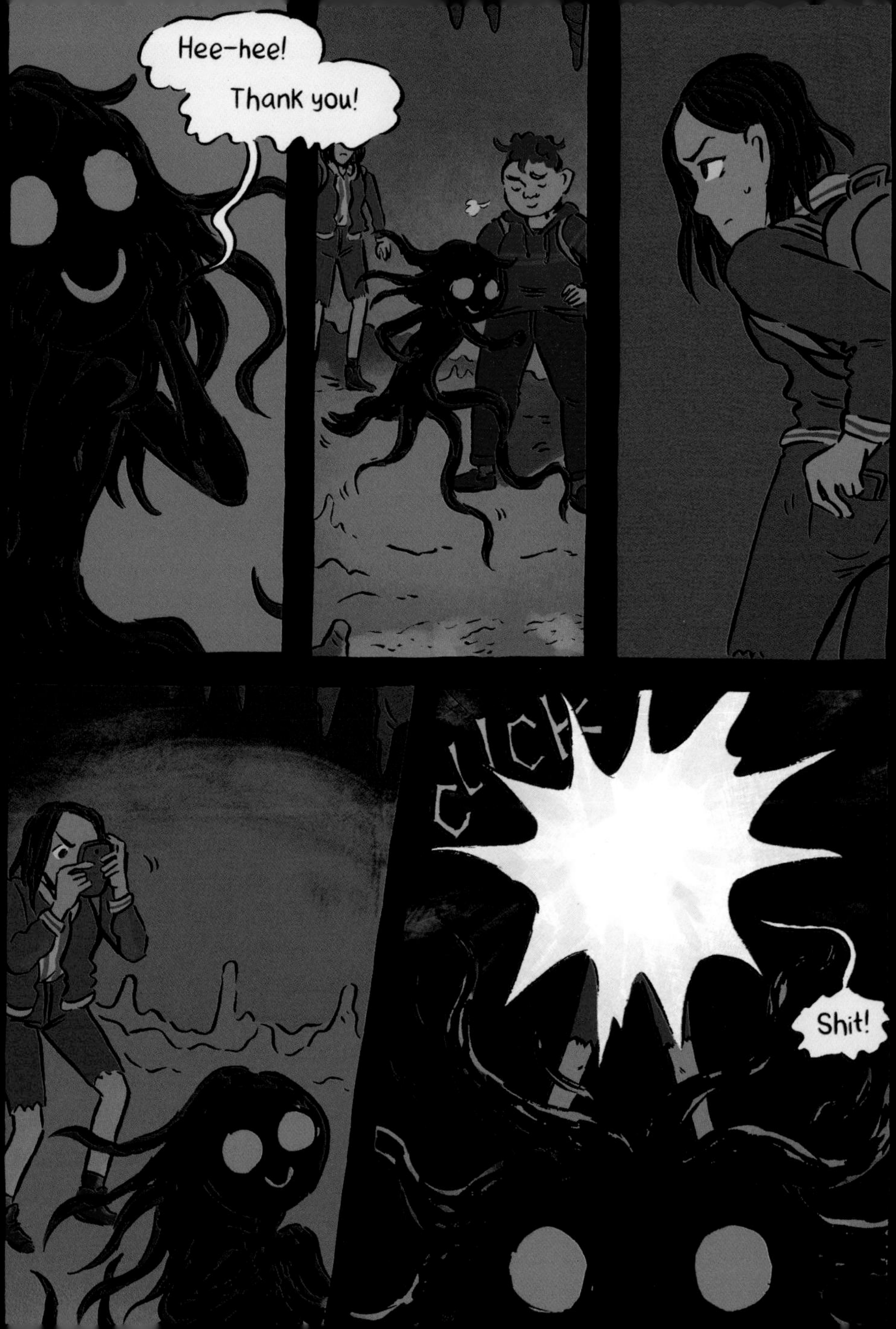
Hee-hee!
Thank you!
CLICK
Shit!

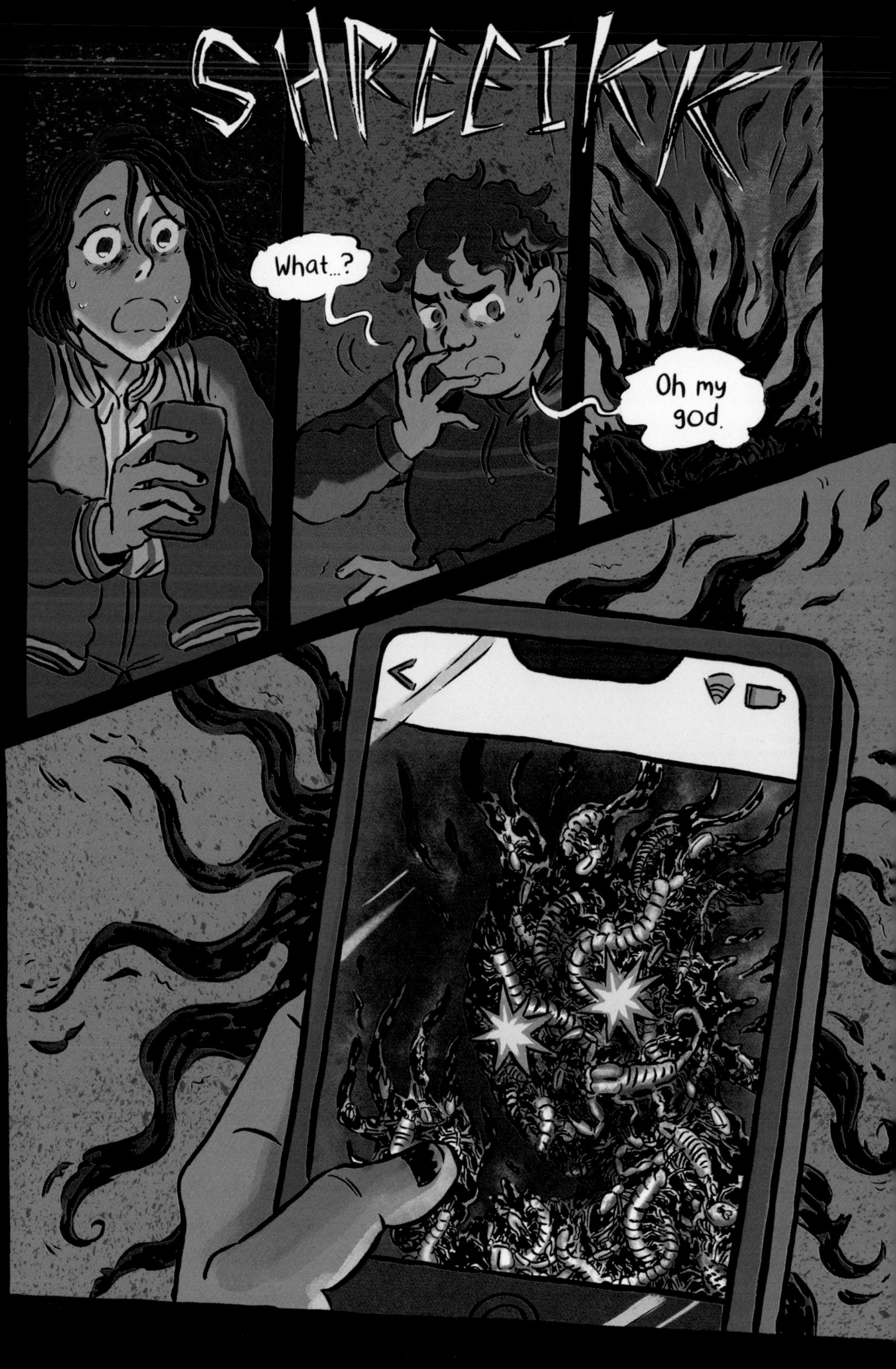
SHREEIKK
What...?
Oh my god.

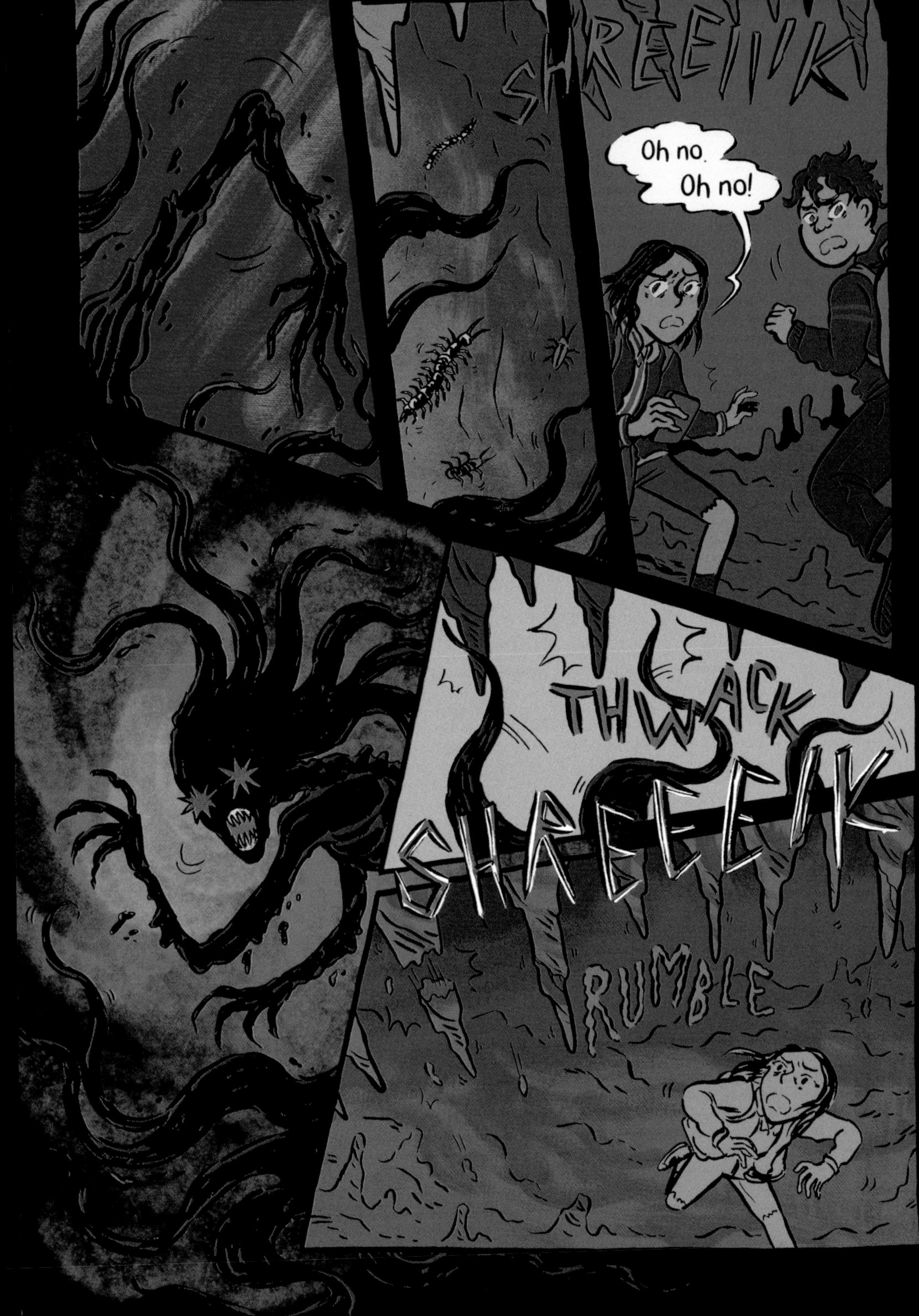
SHREEEIIIK
Oh no.
Oh no!
THWACK
SHREEEIIK
RUMBLE

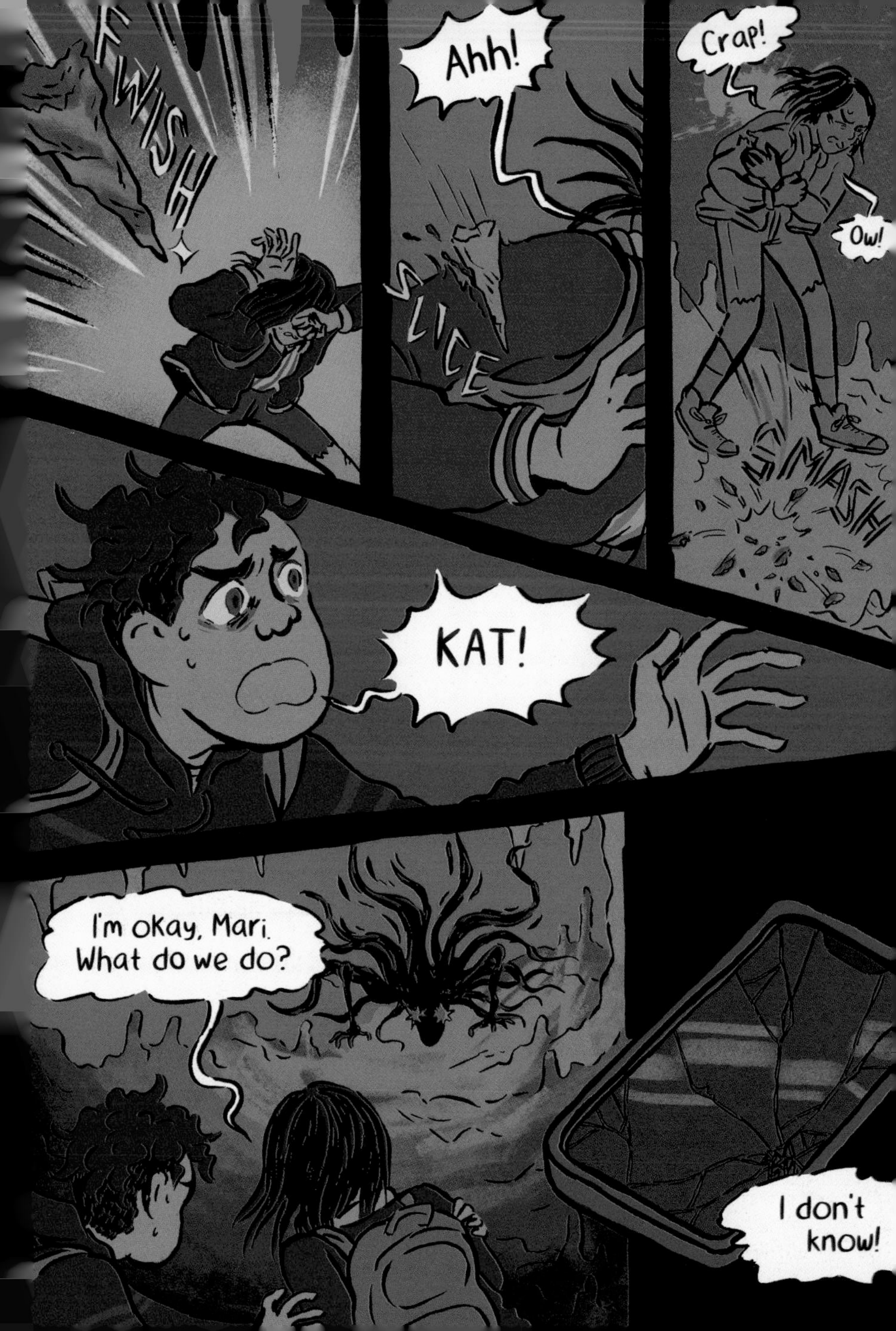
FWISH
Ahh!
SLICE
Crap!
Ow!
SMASH
KAT!
I'm okay, Mari.
What do we do?
I don't
know!

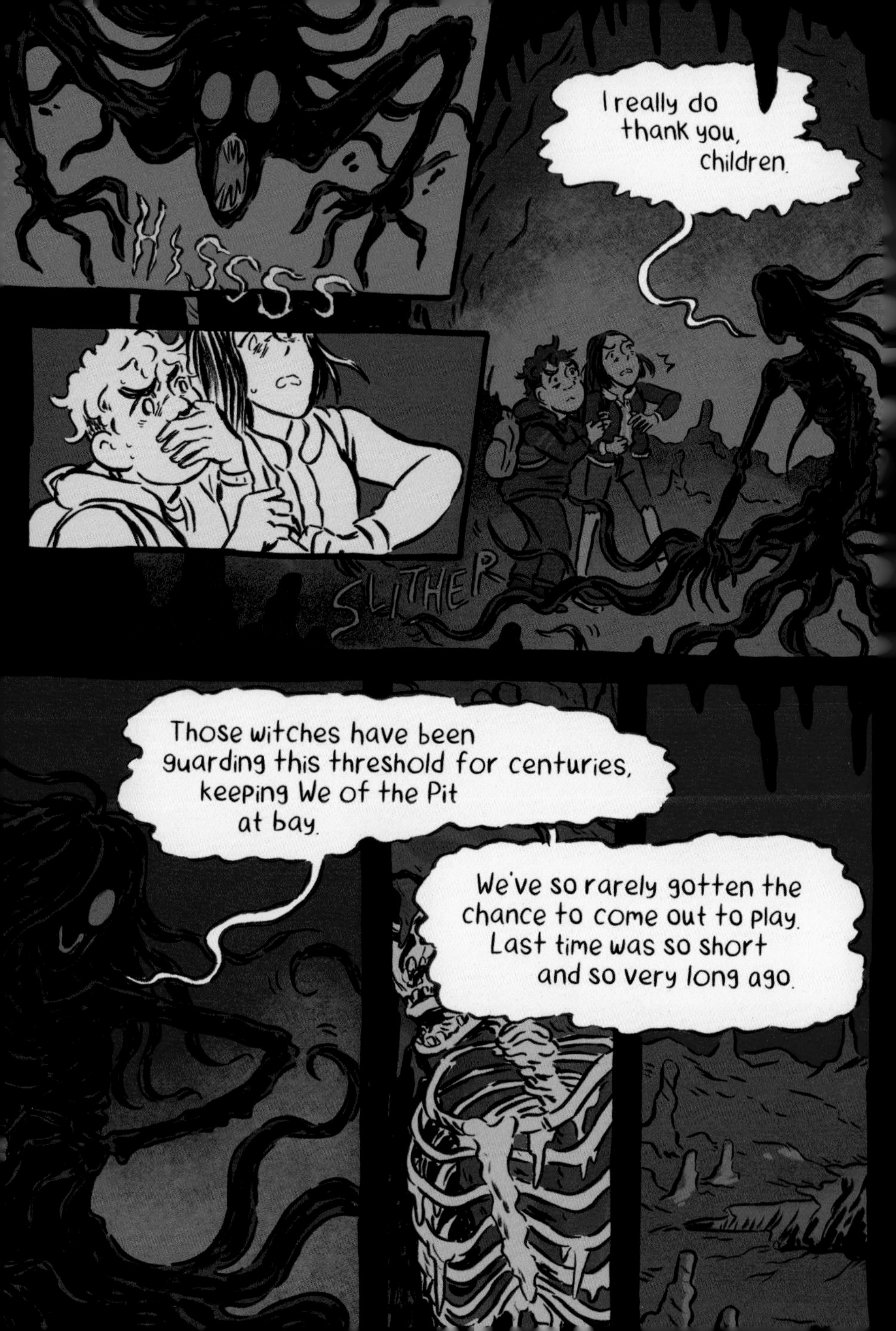
HISSSSS
I really do thank you, children.
SLITHER
Those witches have been guarding this threshold for centuries, keeping We of the Pit at bay.
We've so rarely gotten the chance to come out to play. Last time was so short and so very long ago.

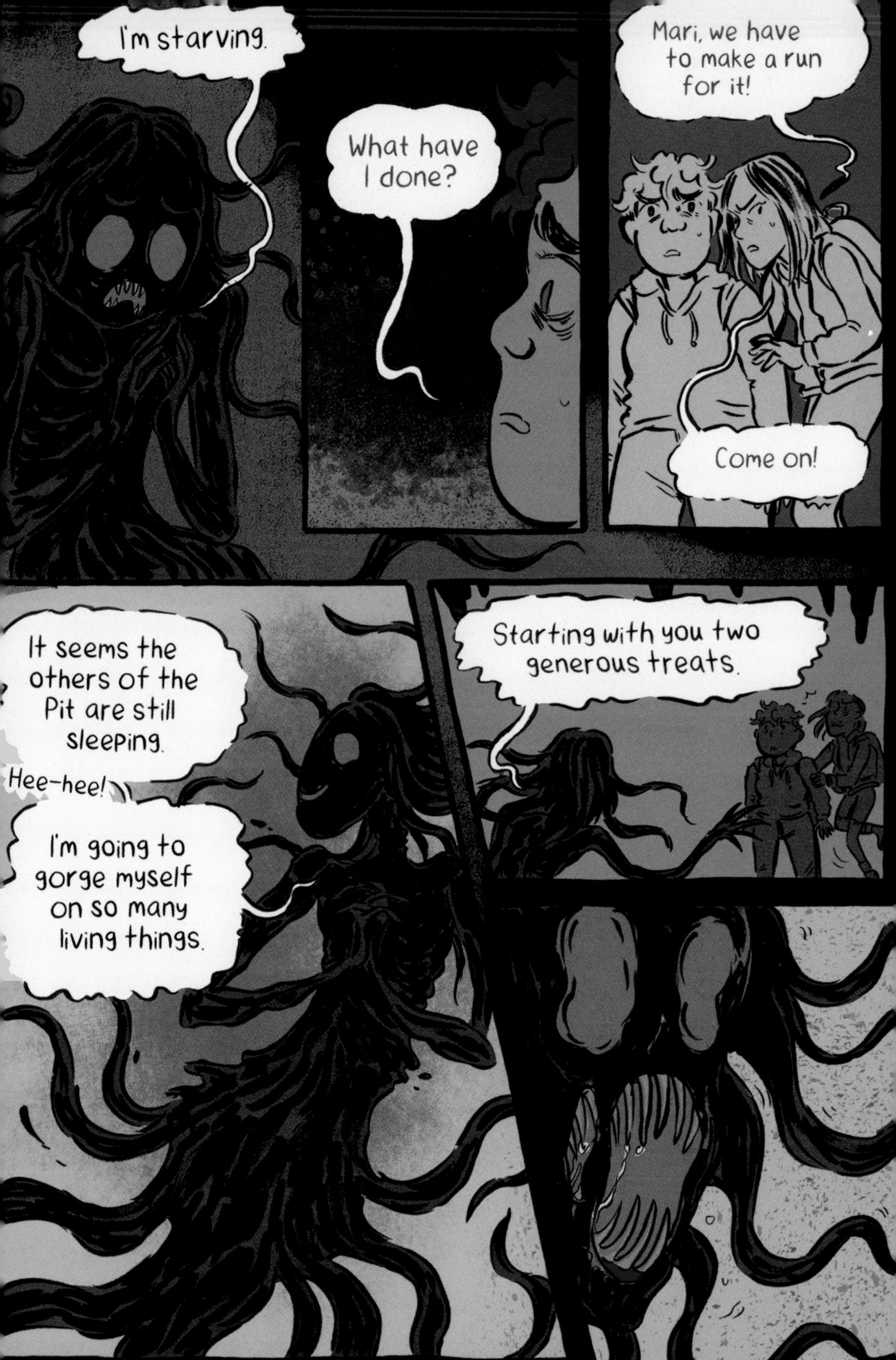
I'm starving.
What have I done?
Mari, we have to make a run for it!
Come on!
It seems the others of the Pit are still sleeping.
Hee-hee!
I'm going to gorge myself on so many living things.
Starting with you two generous treats.

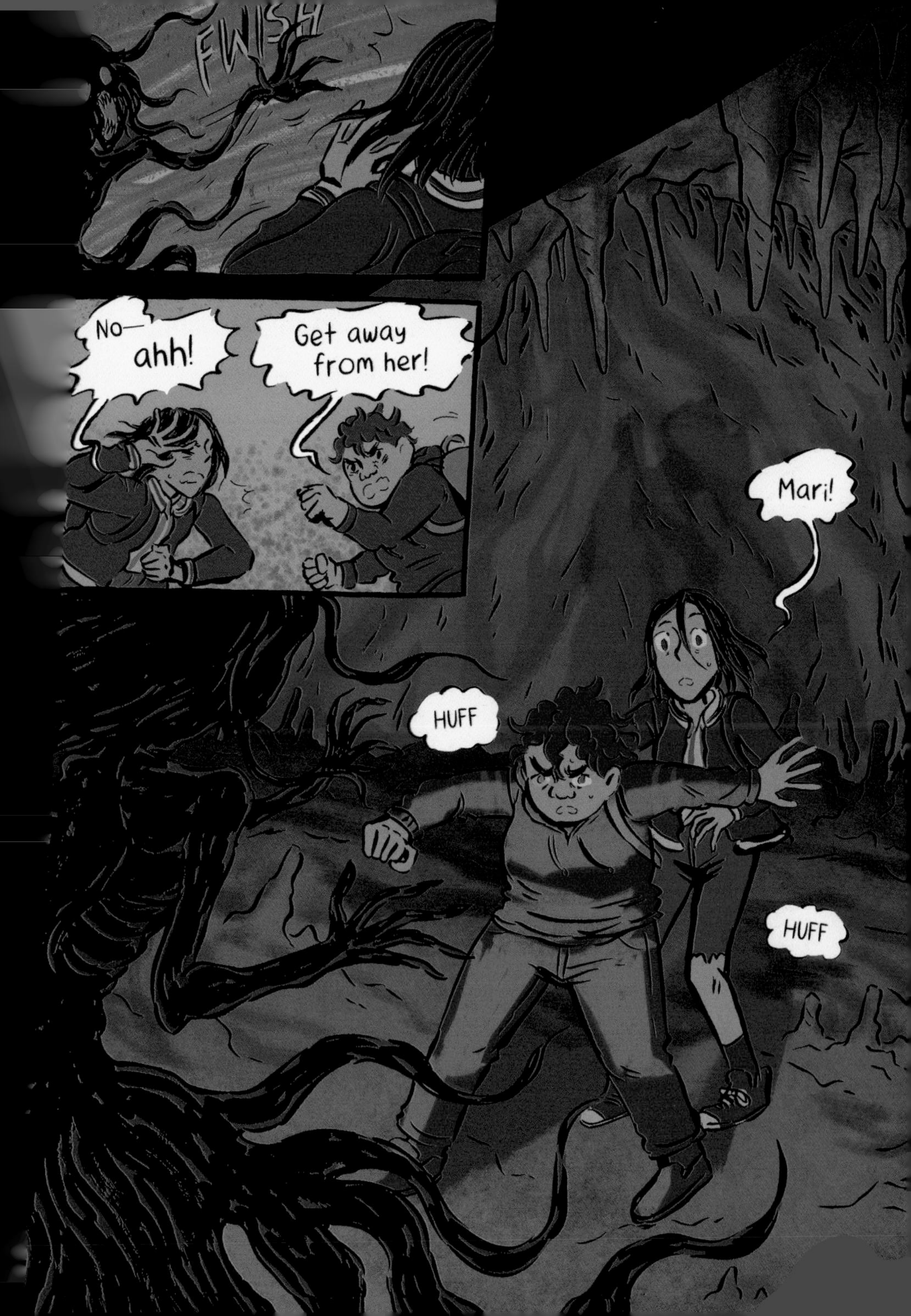
FWISH
No— ahh!
Get away from her!
Mari!
HUFF
HUFF

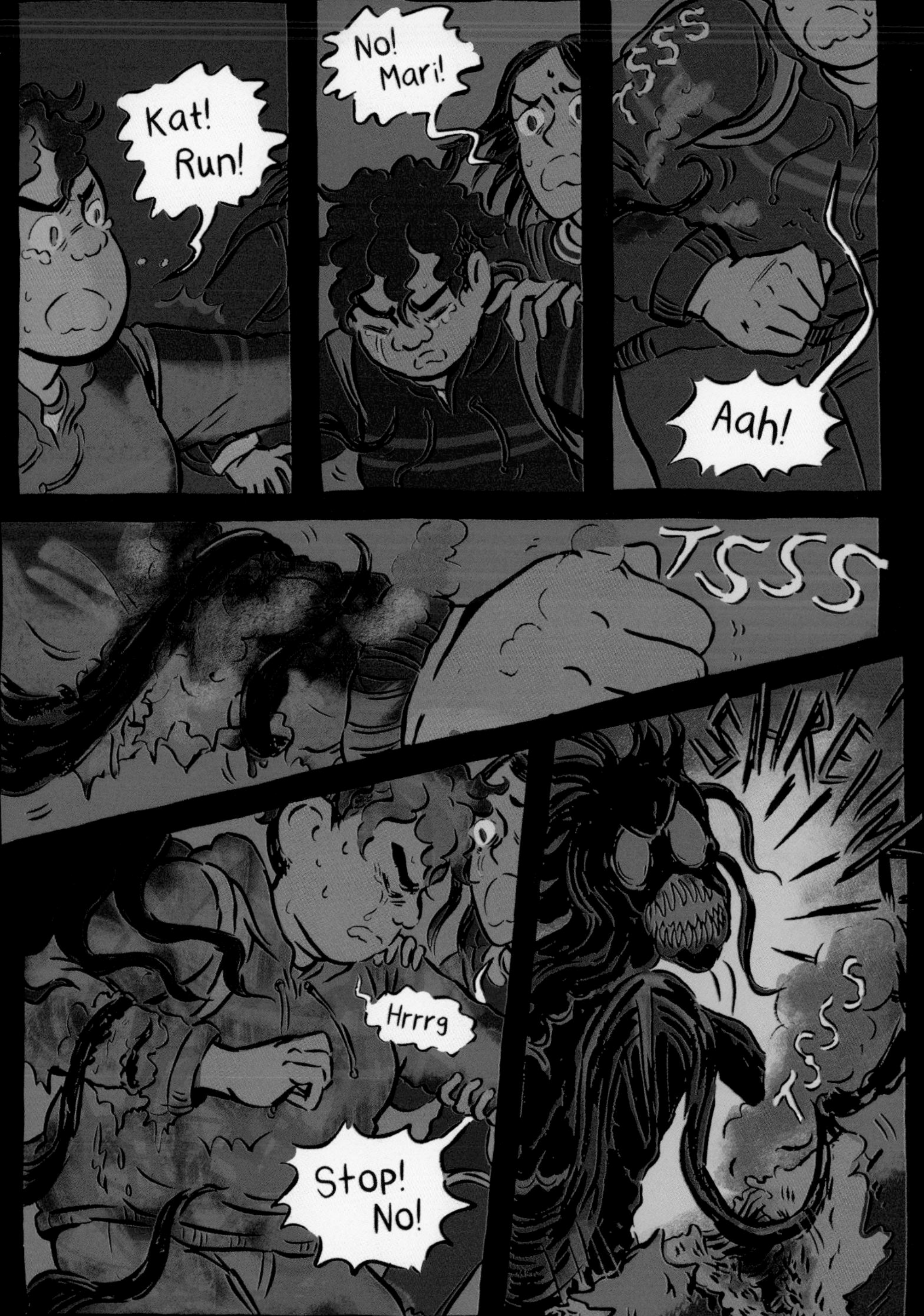
Kat!
Run!
No!
Mari!
TSSS
Aah!
TSSS
SHREE
Hrrrg
Stop!
No!
TSSS

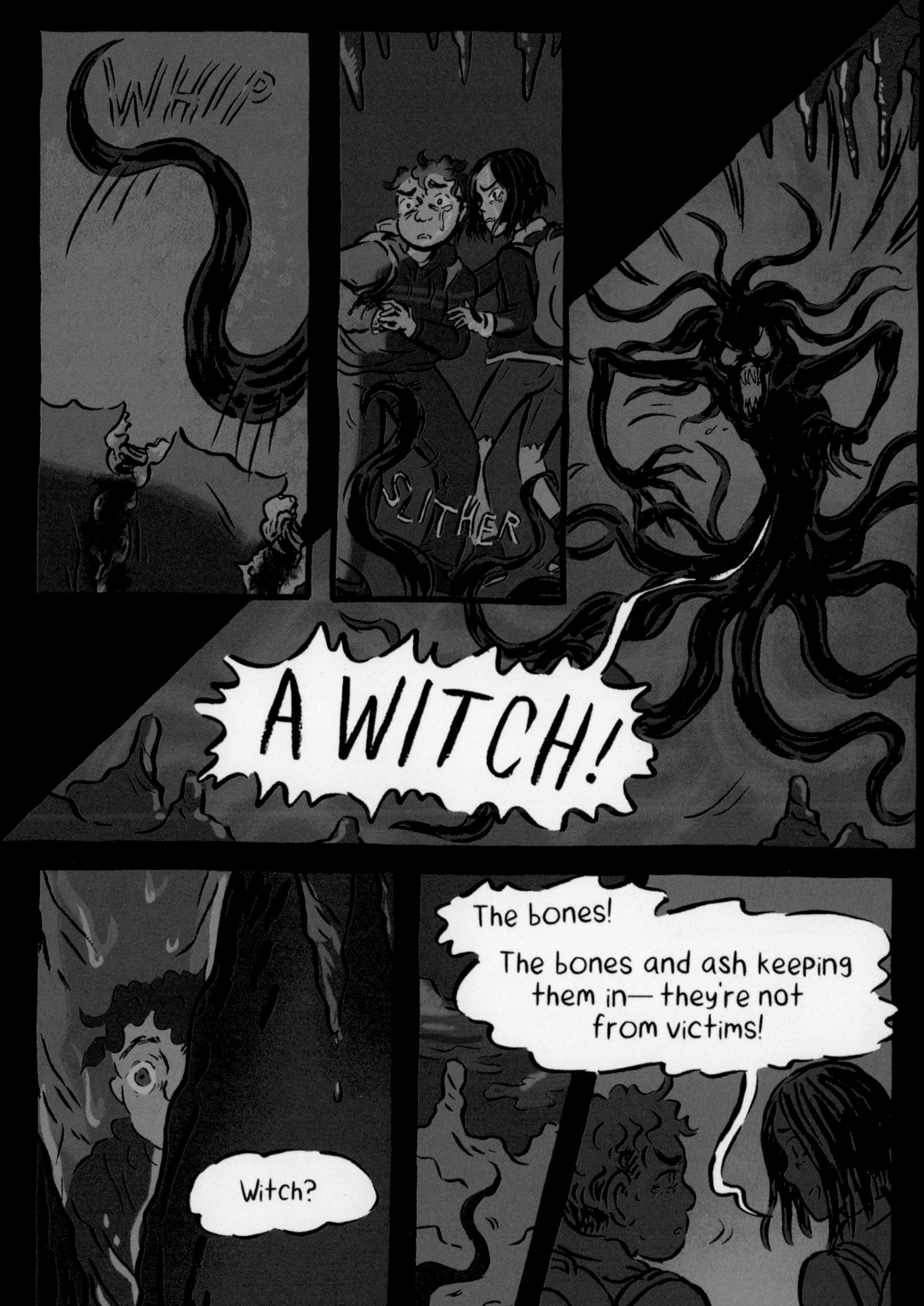
WHIP
SLITHER
A WITCH!
Witch?
The bones!
The bones and ash keeping them in— they're not from victims!

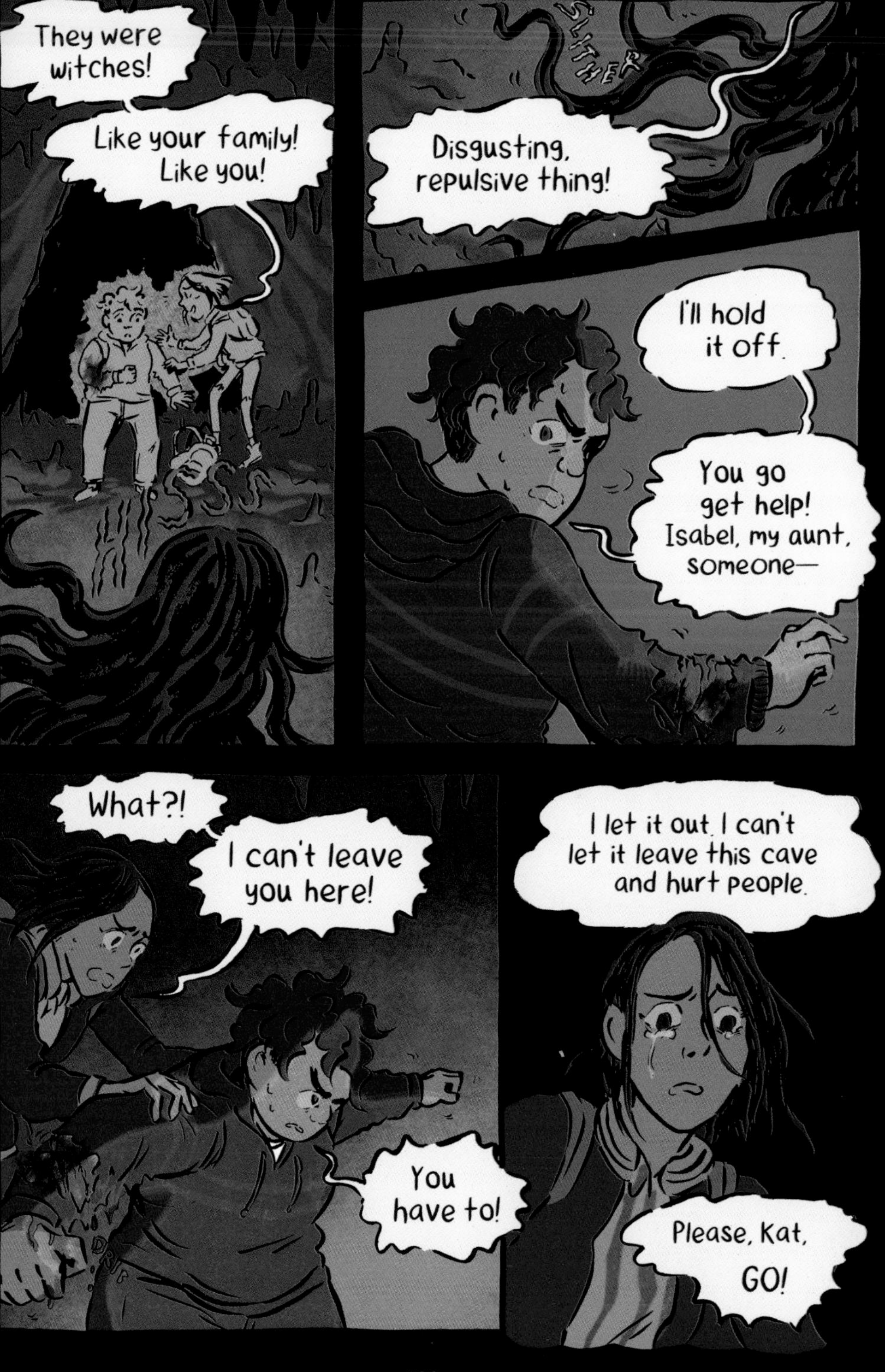

They were witches!
Like your family! Like you!
SLITHER
Disgusting, repulsive thing!
I'll hold it off.
You go get help! Isabel, my aunt, someone—
What?!
I can't leave you here!
You have to!
I let it out. I can't let it leave this cave and hurt people.
Please, Kat, GO!

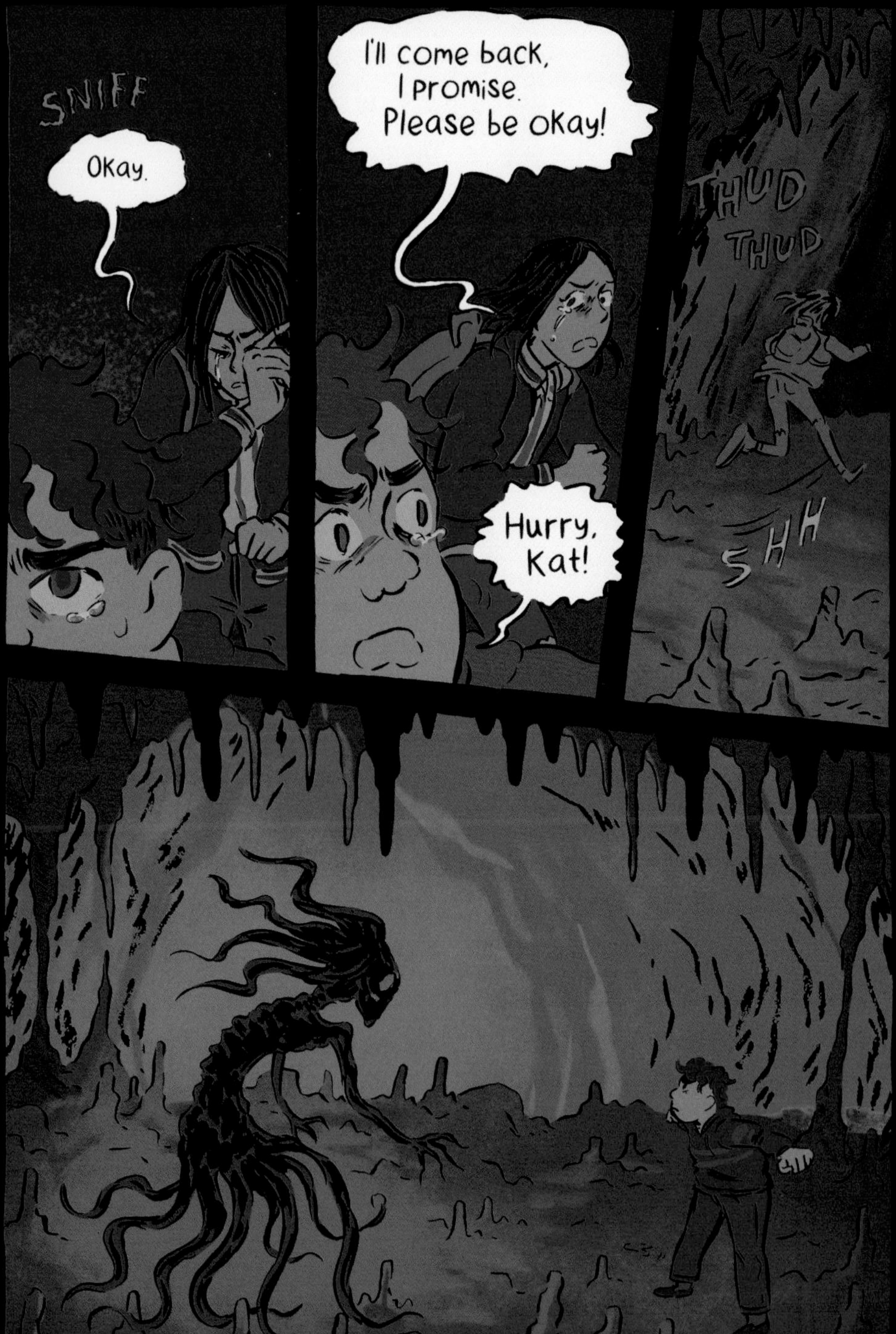
SNIFF
Okay.
I'll come back, I promise. Please be okay!
Hurry, Kat!
THUD THUD
SHH

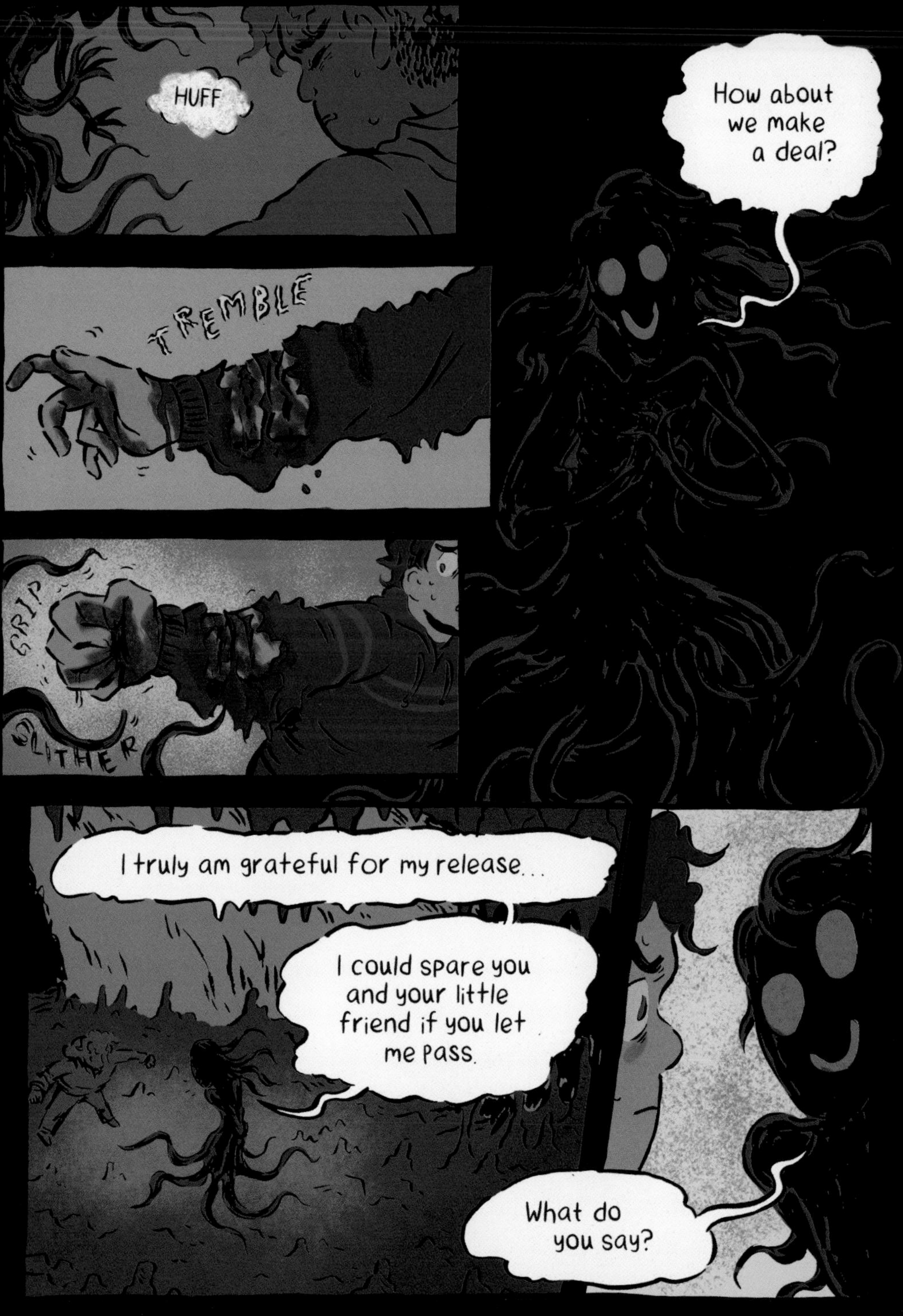
HUFF
How about we make a deal?
TREMBLE
GRIP
SLITHER
I truly am grateful for my release...
I could spare you and your little friend if you let me pass.
What do you say?

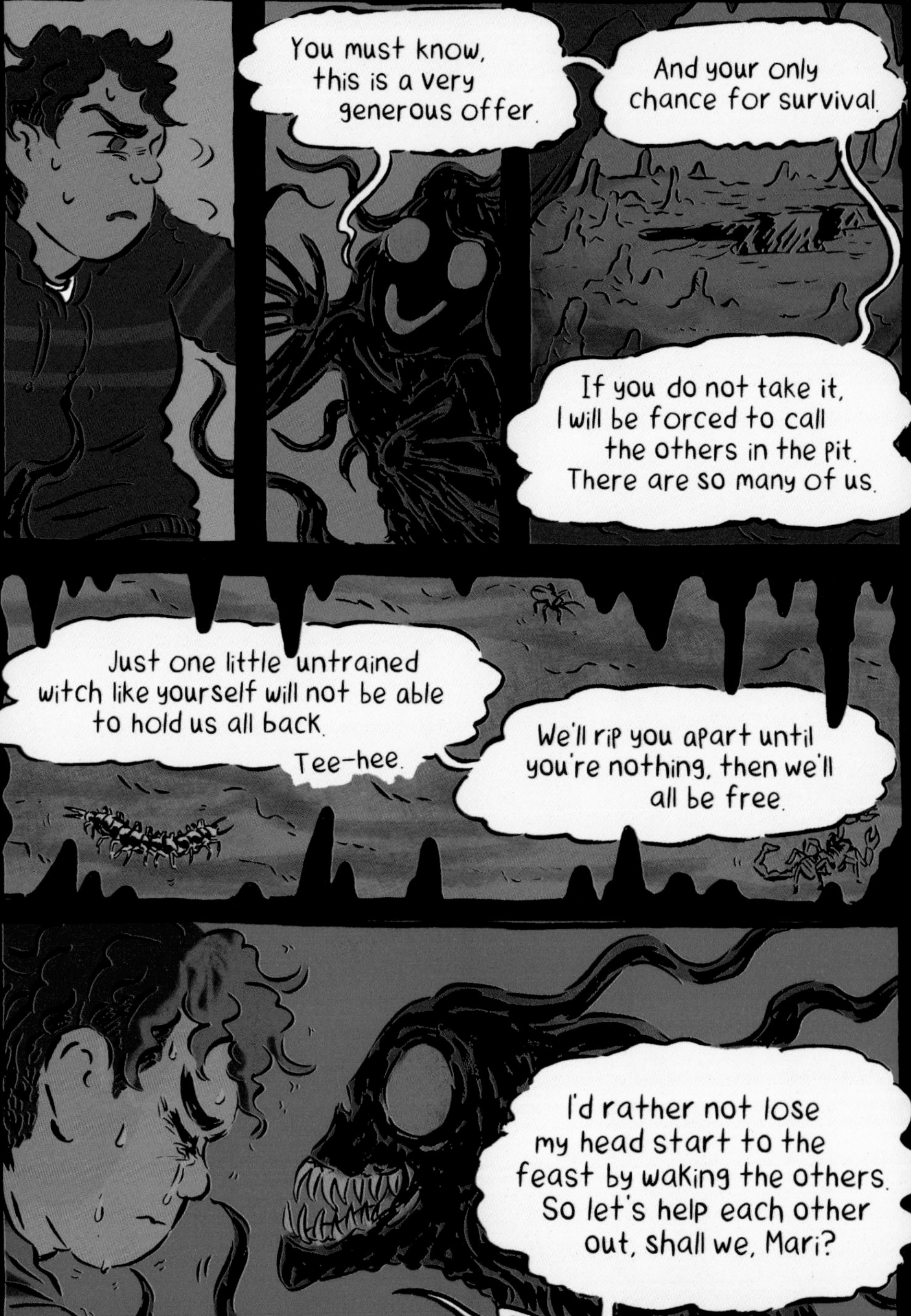
You must know, this is a very generous offer.
And your only chance for survival.
If you do not take it, I will be forced to call the others in the pit. There are so many of us.
Just one little untrained witch like yourself will not be able to hold us all back.
Tee-hee.
We'll rip you apart until you're nothing, then we'll all be free.
I'd rather not lose my head start to the feast by waking the others. So let's help each other out, shall we, Mari?

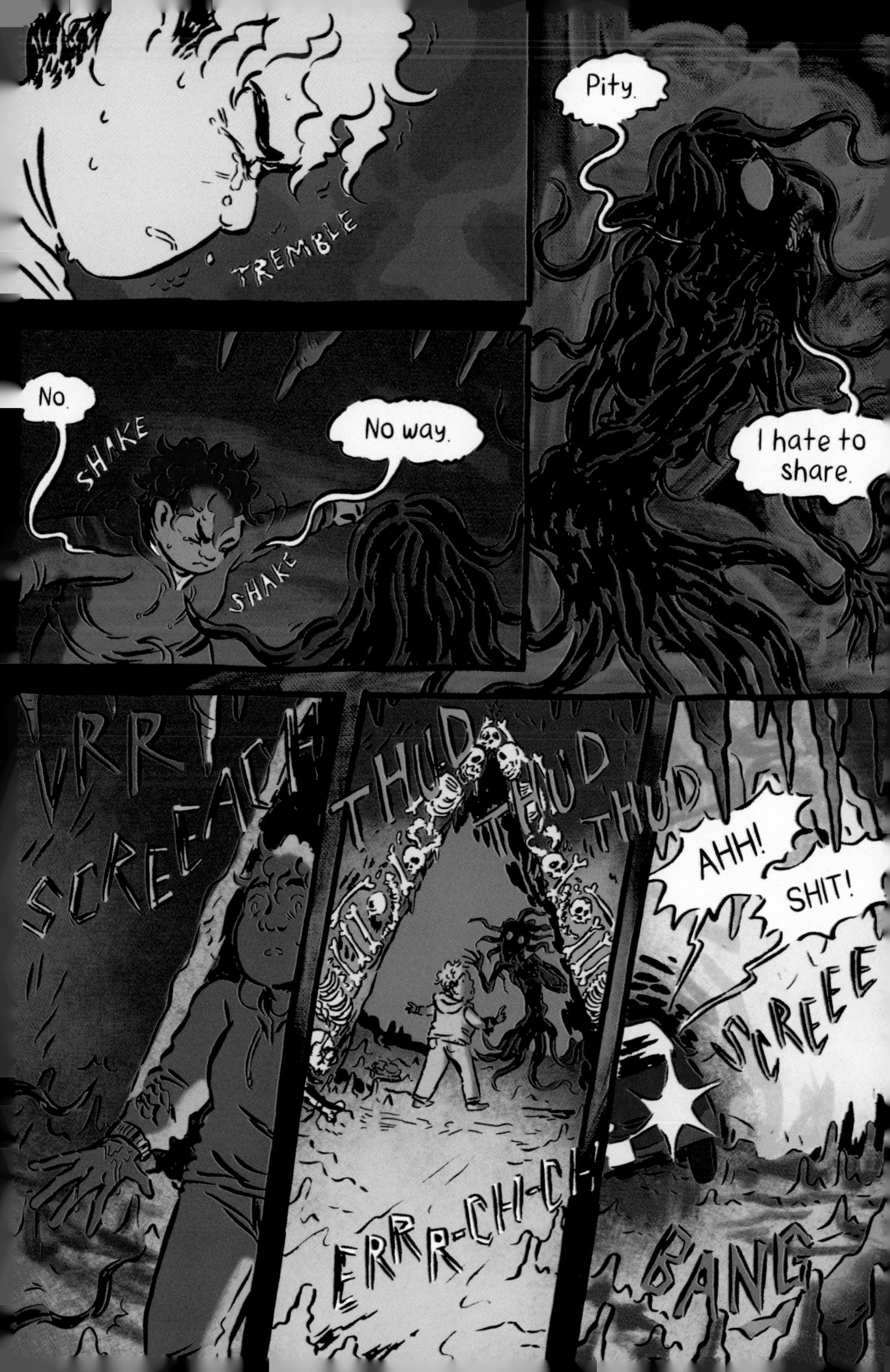
TREMBLE
Pity.
No.
SHAKE
No way.
SHAKE
I hate to share.
VRR
SCREEACH
THUD
THUD
THUD
ERRR-CH-CH
AHH!
SHIT!
SCREEE
BANG

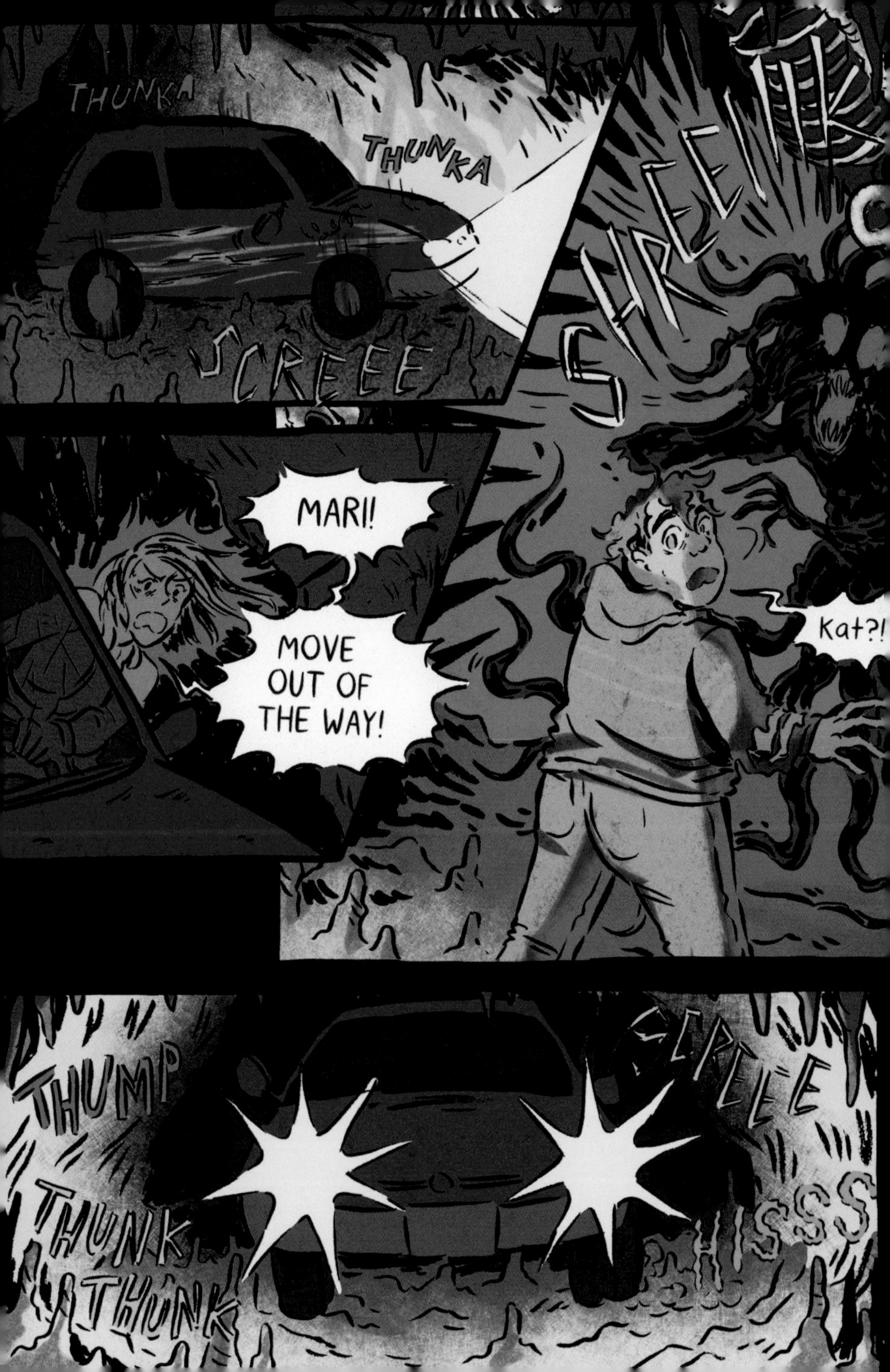
THUNKA
THUNKA
SCREEE
SCREEEK
MARI!
MOVE OUT OF THE WAY!
Kat?!
THUMP
THUNK
THUNK
SCREEE
HISSS

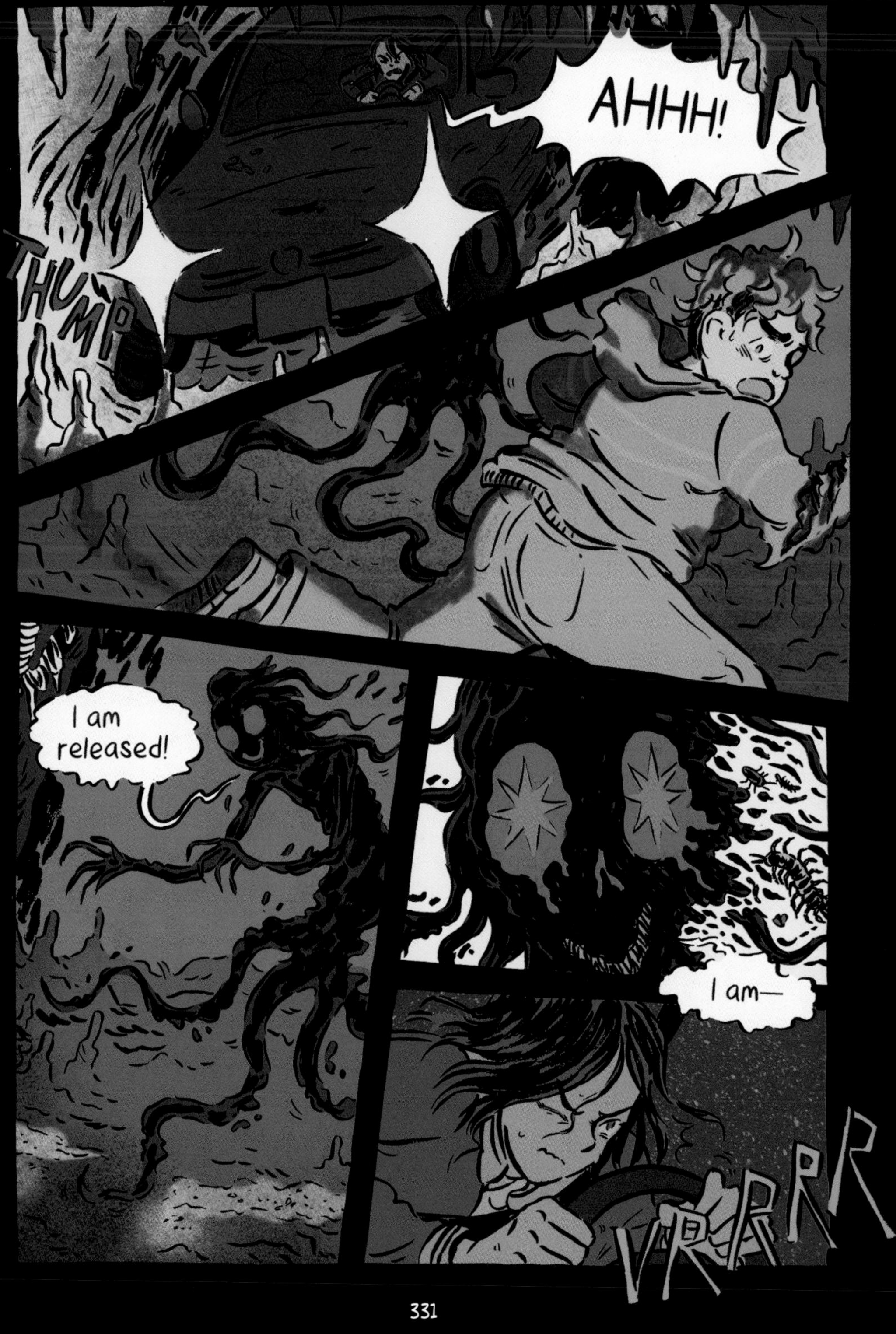
AHHH!
THUMP
I am released!
I am—
VRRRRR

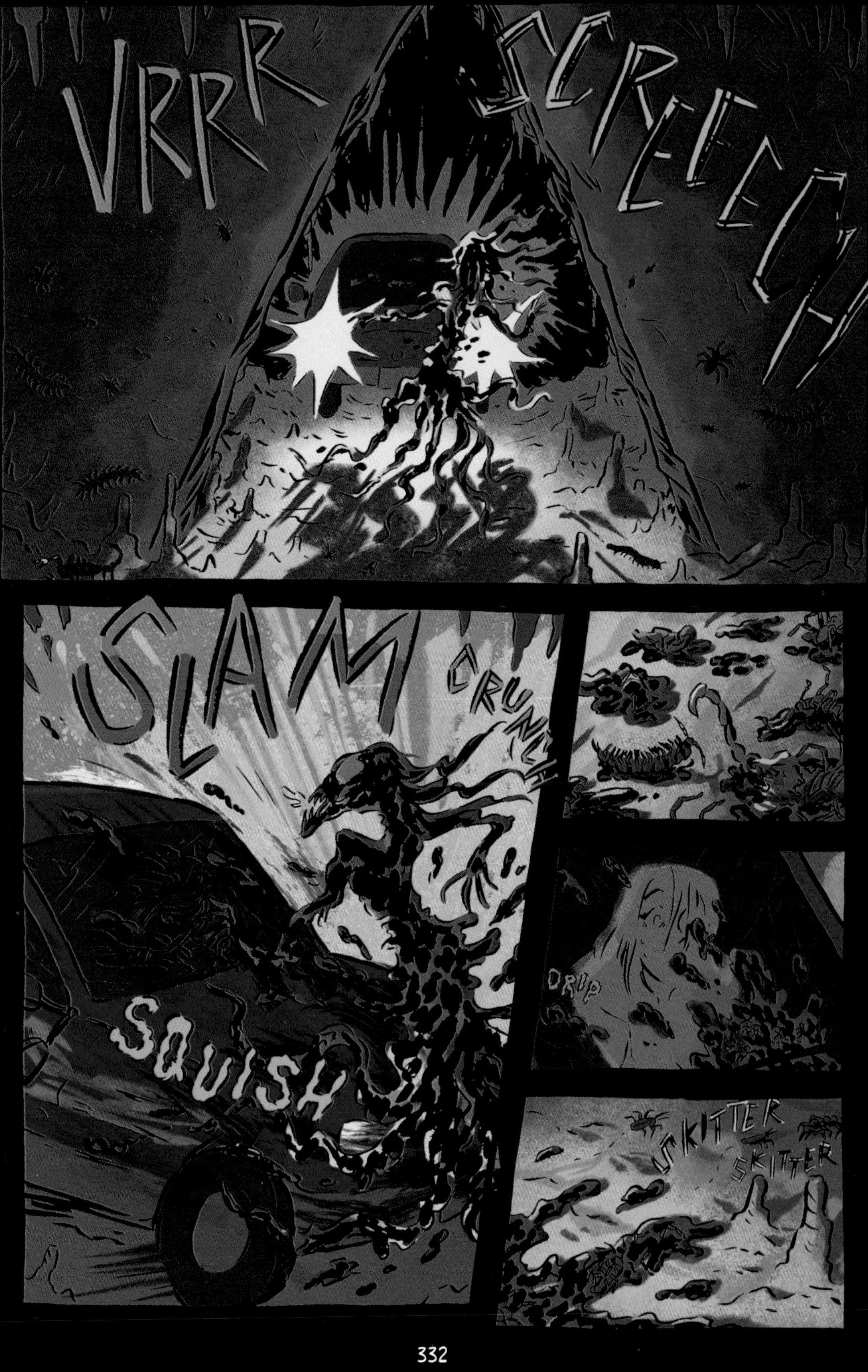
VRRR
SCREEECH
SLAM
CRUNCH
SQUISH
DRIP
SKITTER
SKITTER

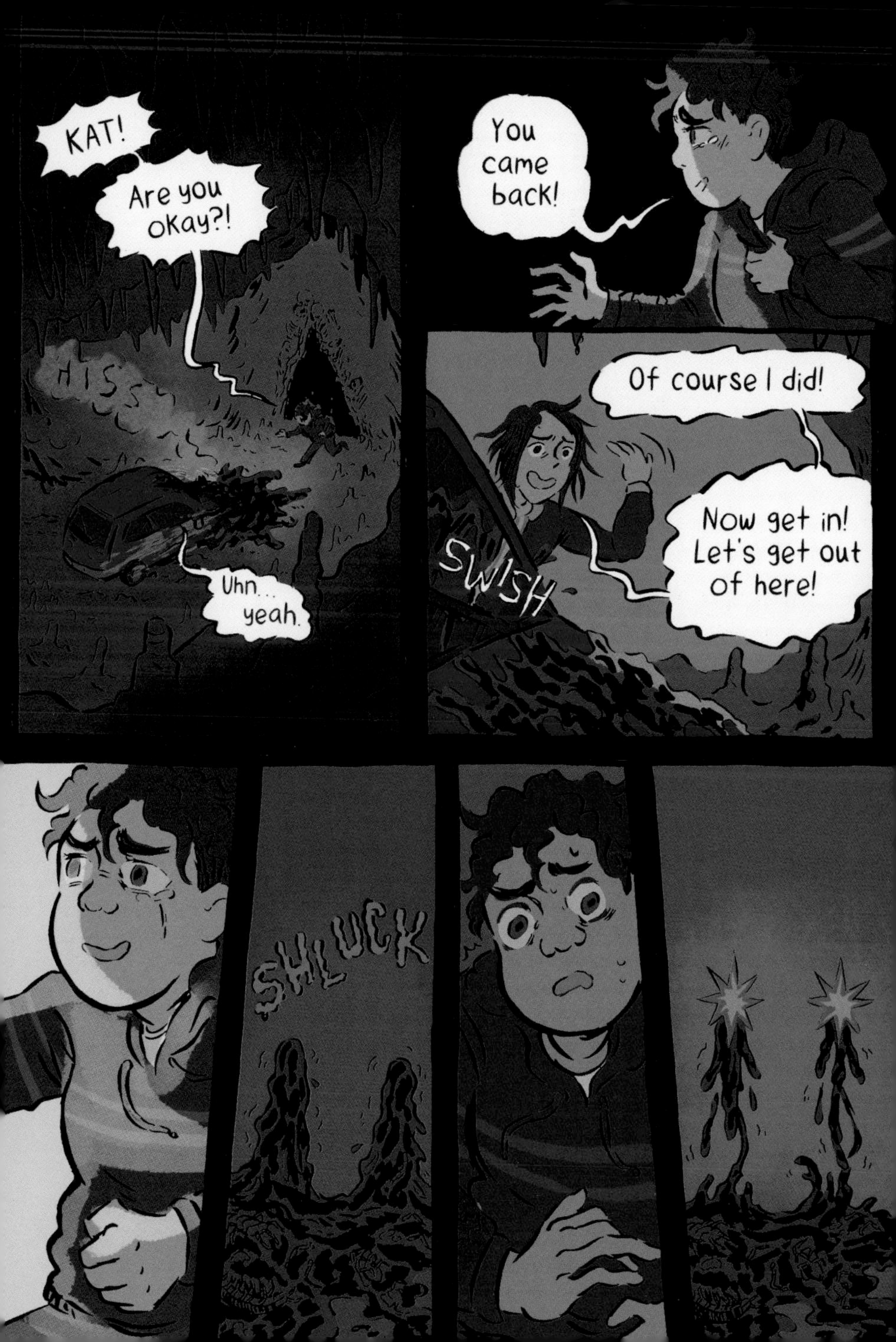
KAT!
Are you okay?!
HISS
Uhn... yeah.
You came back!
Of course I did!
Now get in! Let's get out of here!
SWISH
SHLUCK

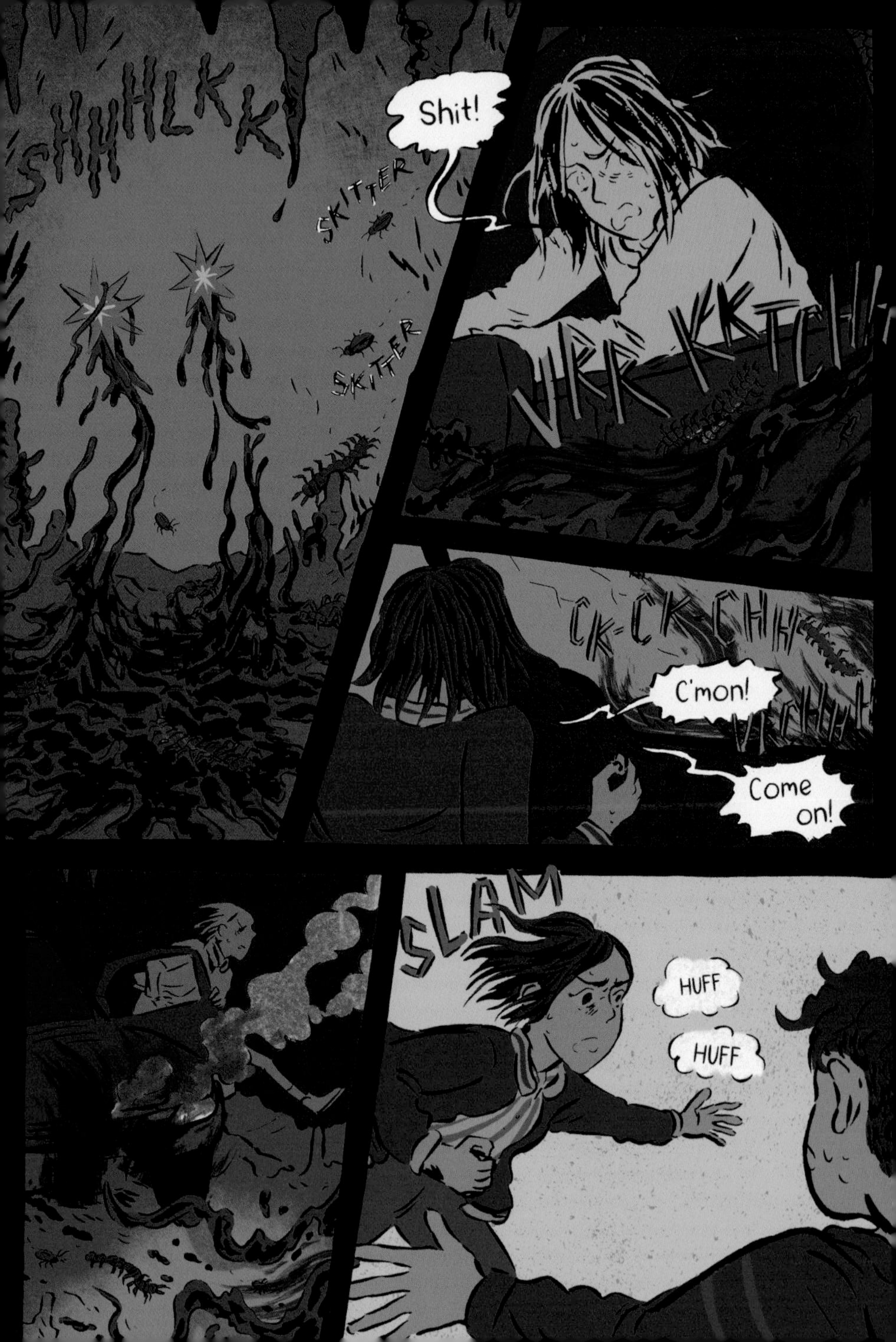
SHHHLKKK
SKITTER
SKITTER
Shit!
NRRR KRTCHH
CK-CK CHHH
C'mon!
Come on!
SLAM
HUFF
HUFF

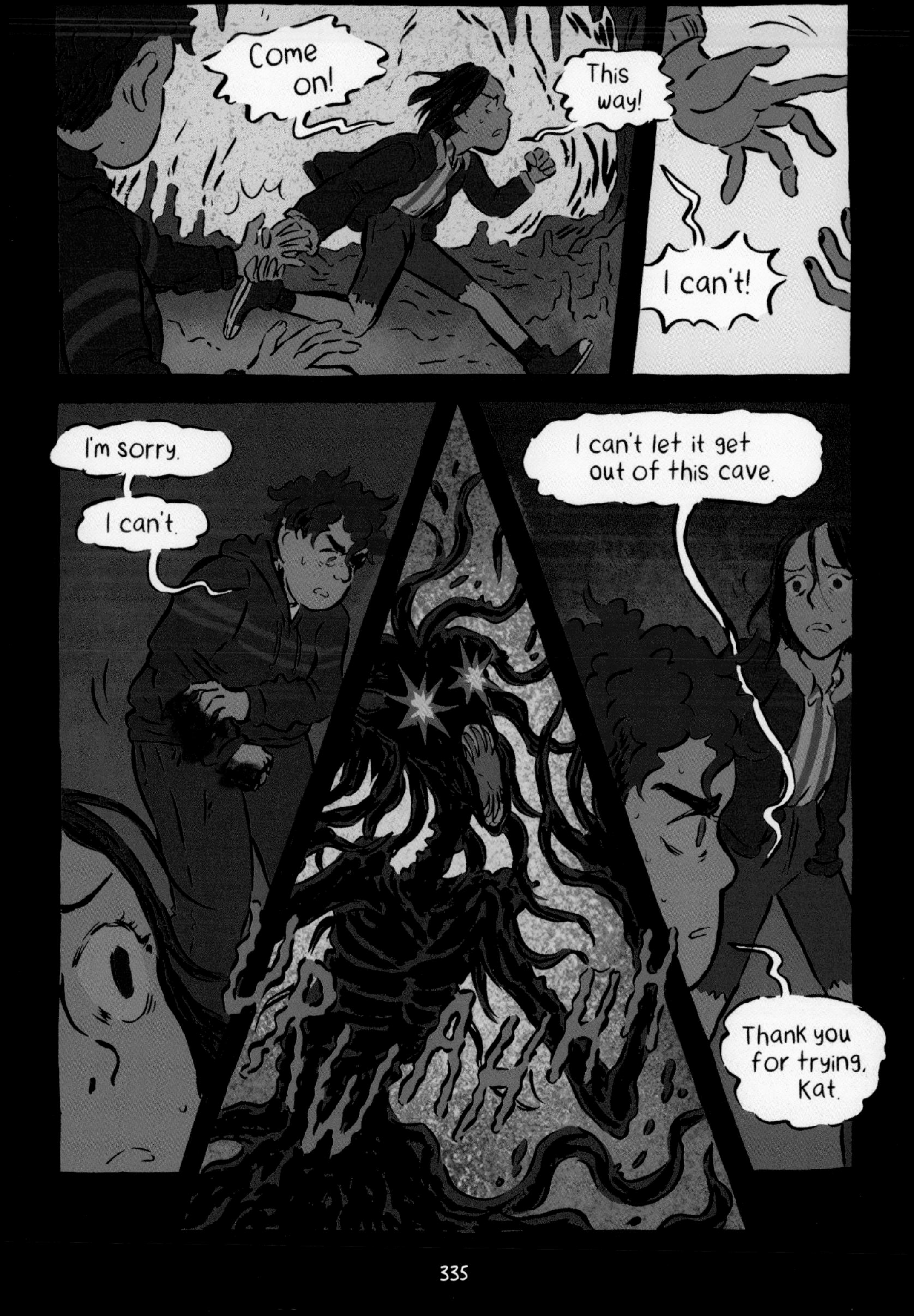
Come on!
This way!
I can't!
I'm sorry.
I can't.
I can't let it get out of this cave.
Thank you for trying, Kat.

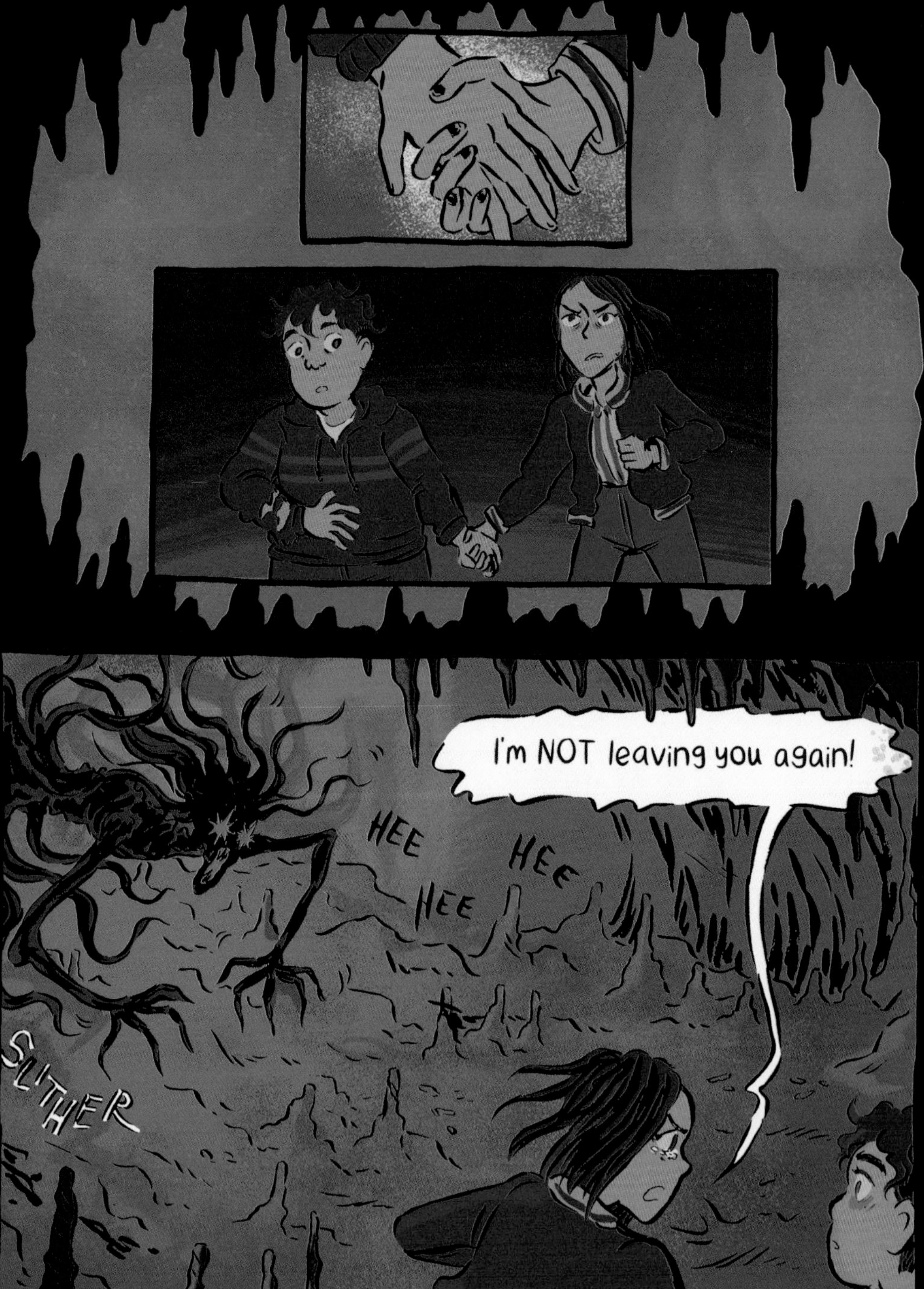
I'm NOT leaving you again!
HEE
HEE
HEE
SLITHER

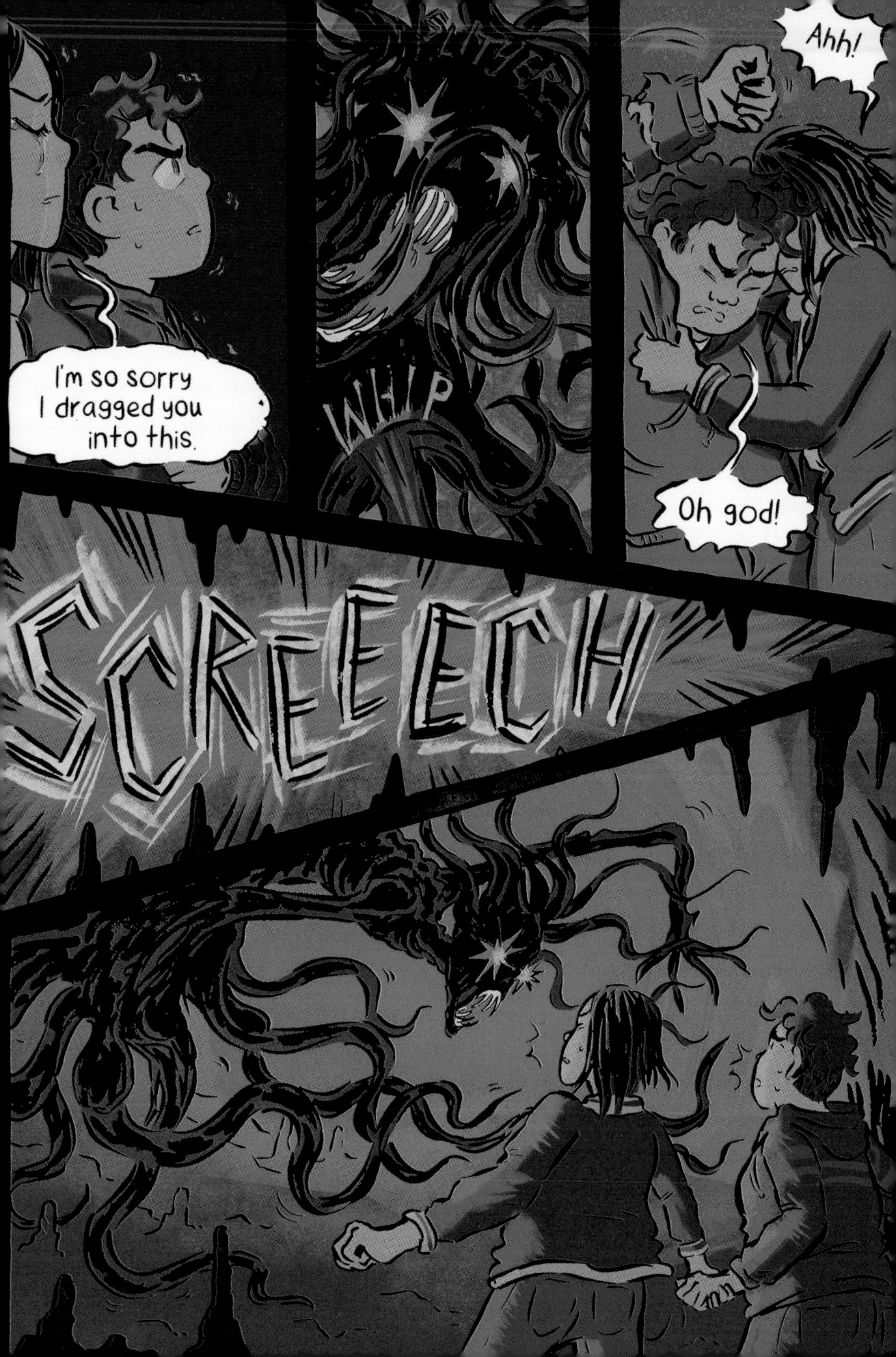
I'm so sorry I dragged you into this.
WHIP
Ahh!
Oh god!
SCREEECH

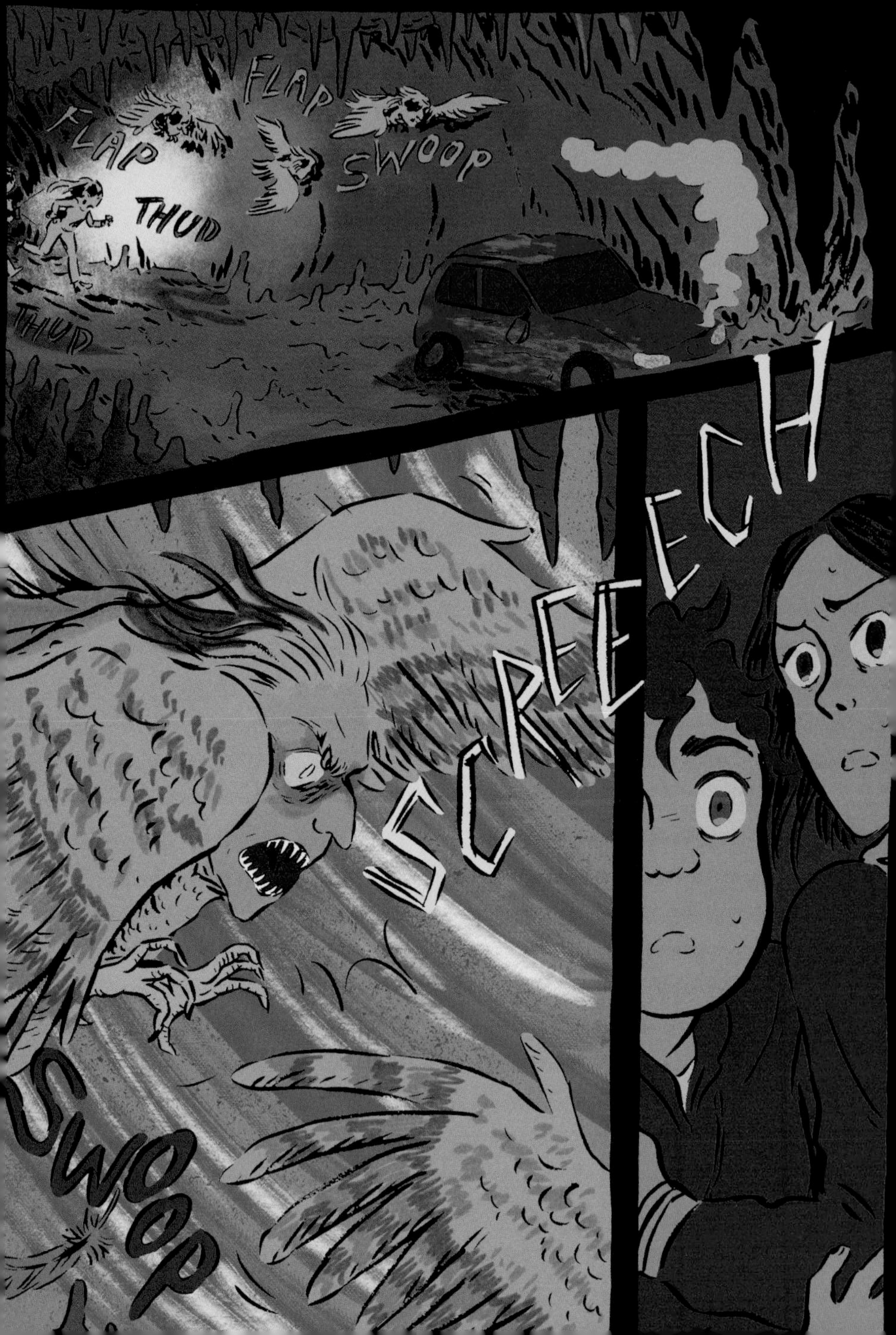
FLAP
FLAP
SWOOP
THUD
THUD
SCREEECH
SWOOP

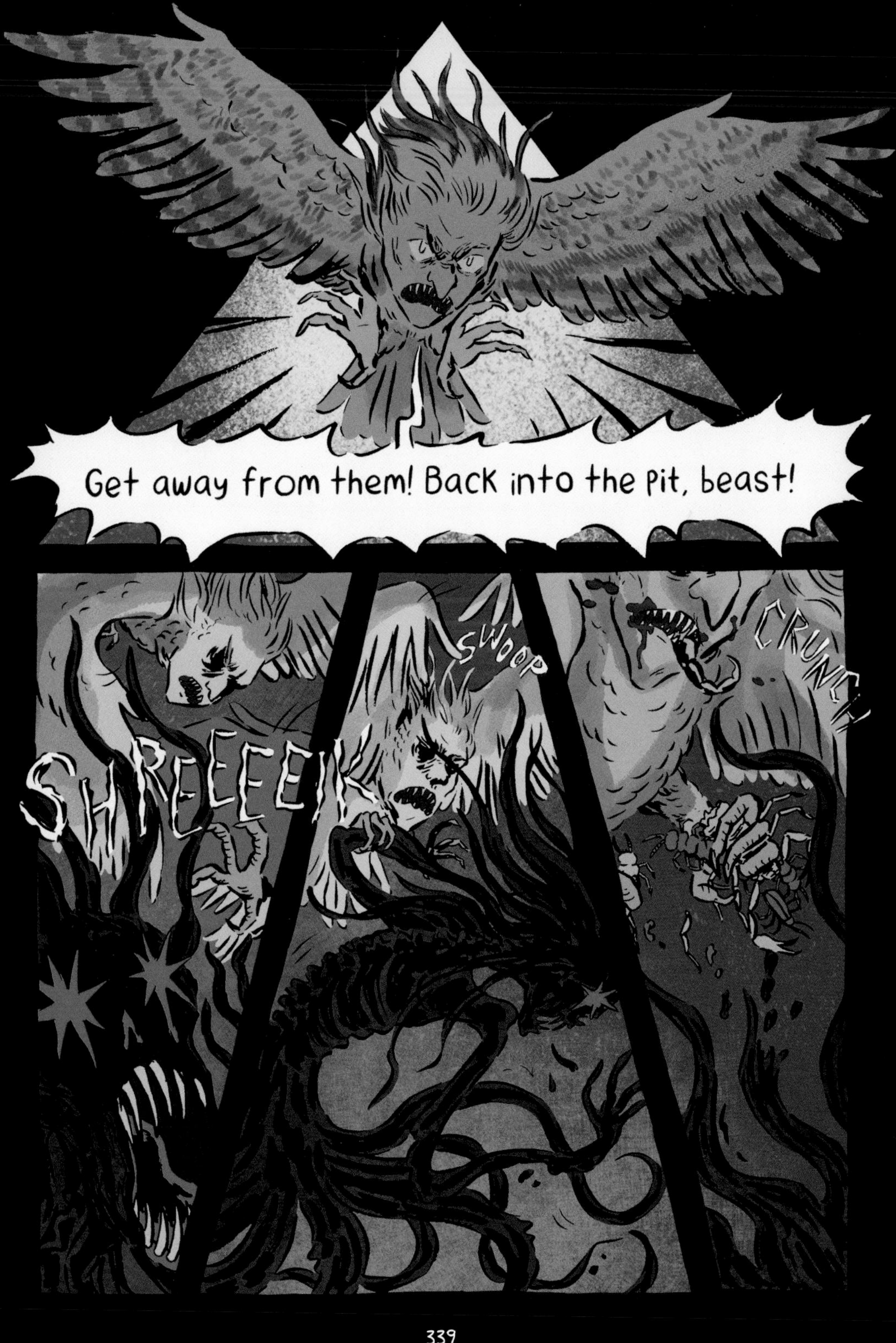
Get away from them! Back into the pit, beast!
SHREEEEK
SWOOP
CRUNCH

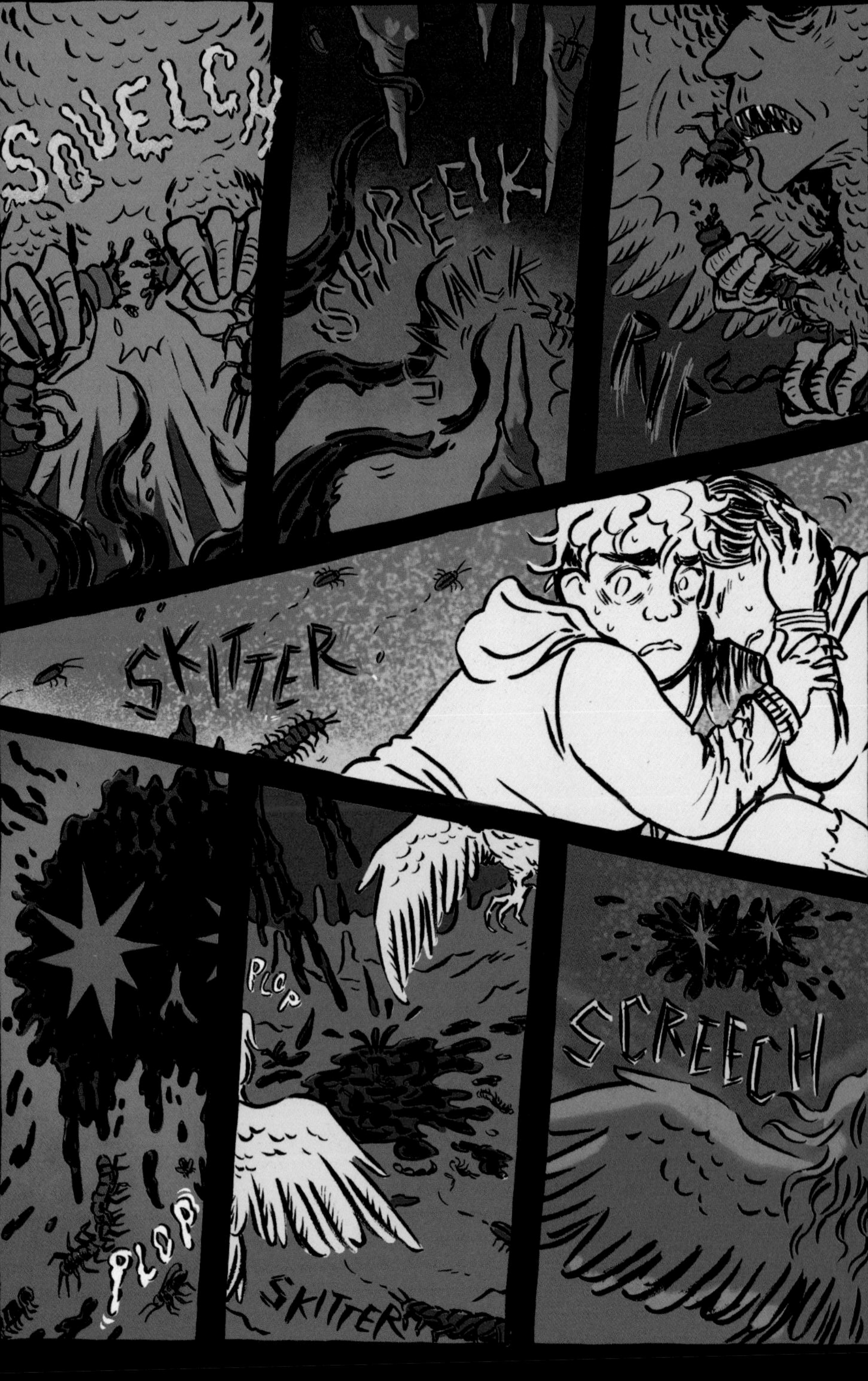
SQUELCH
SHREEIK
SHLACK
RIP
SKITTER
PLOP
PLOP
SCREECH
SKITTER

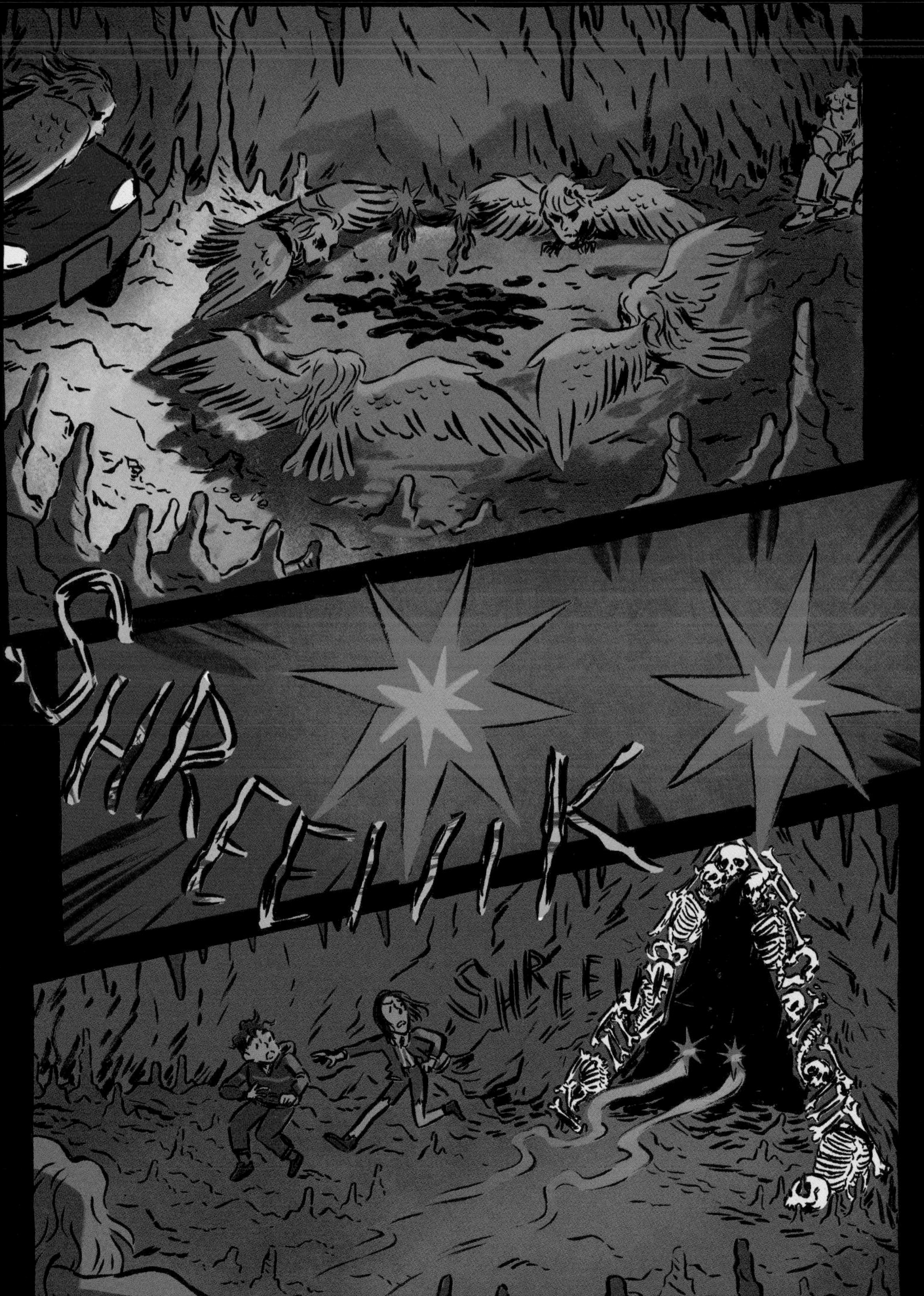
SHREEEEK
SHREE

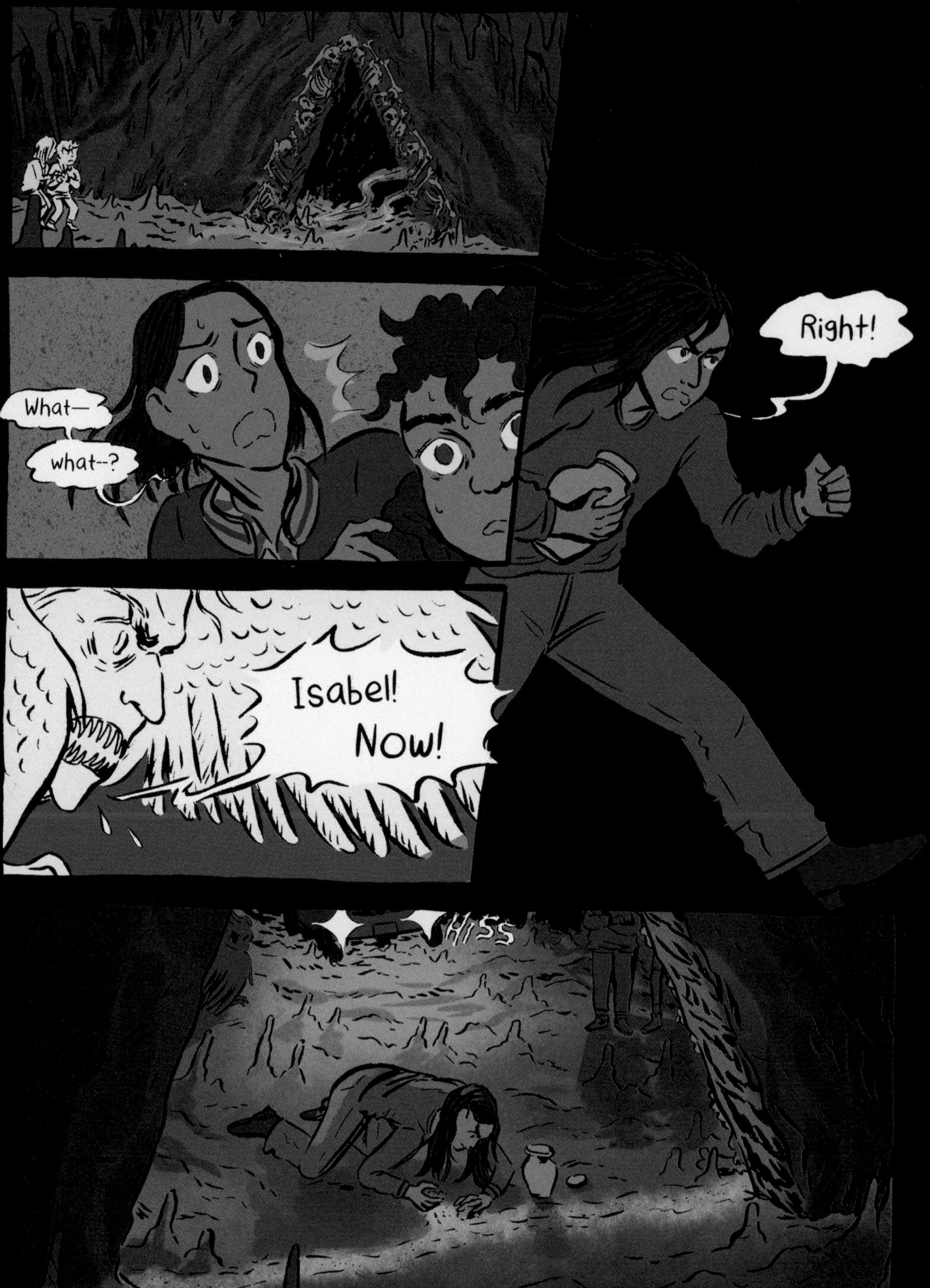
What—
what--?
Right!
Isabel! Now!
HISS

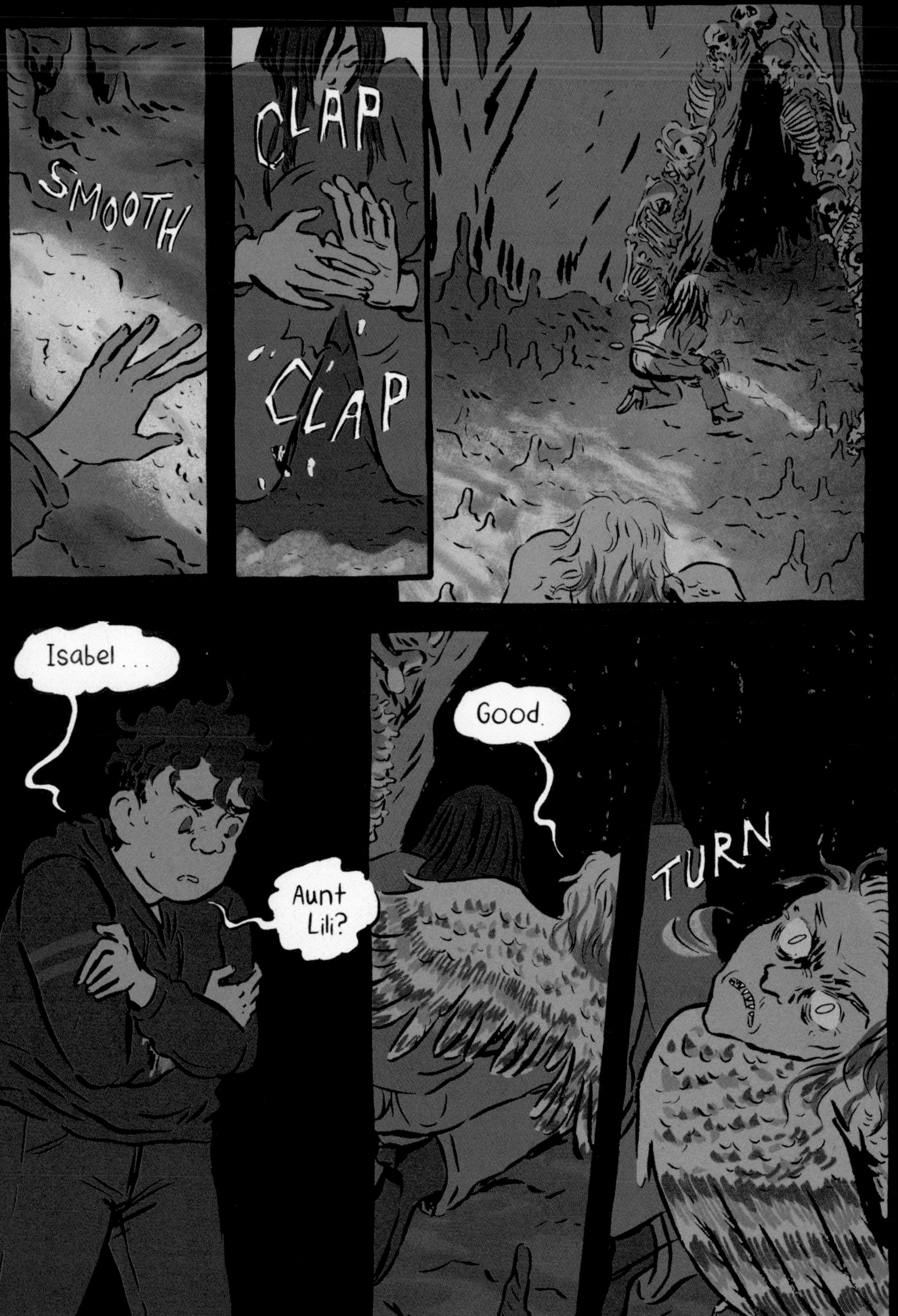
SMOOTH
CLAP
CLAP
Isabel . . .
Aunt Lili?
Good.
TURN

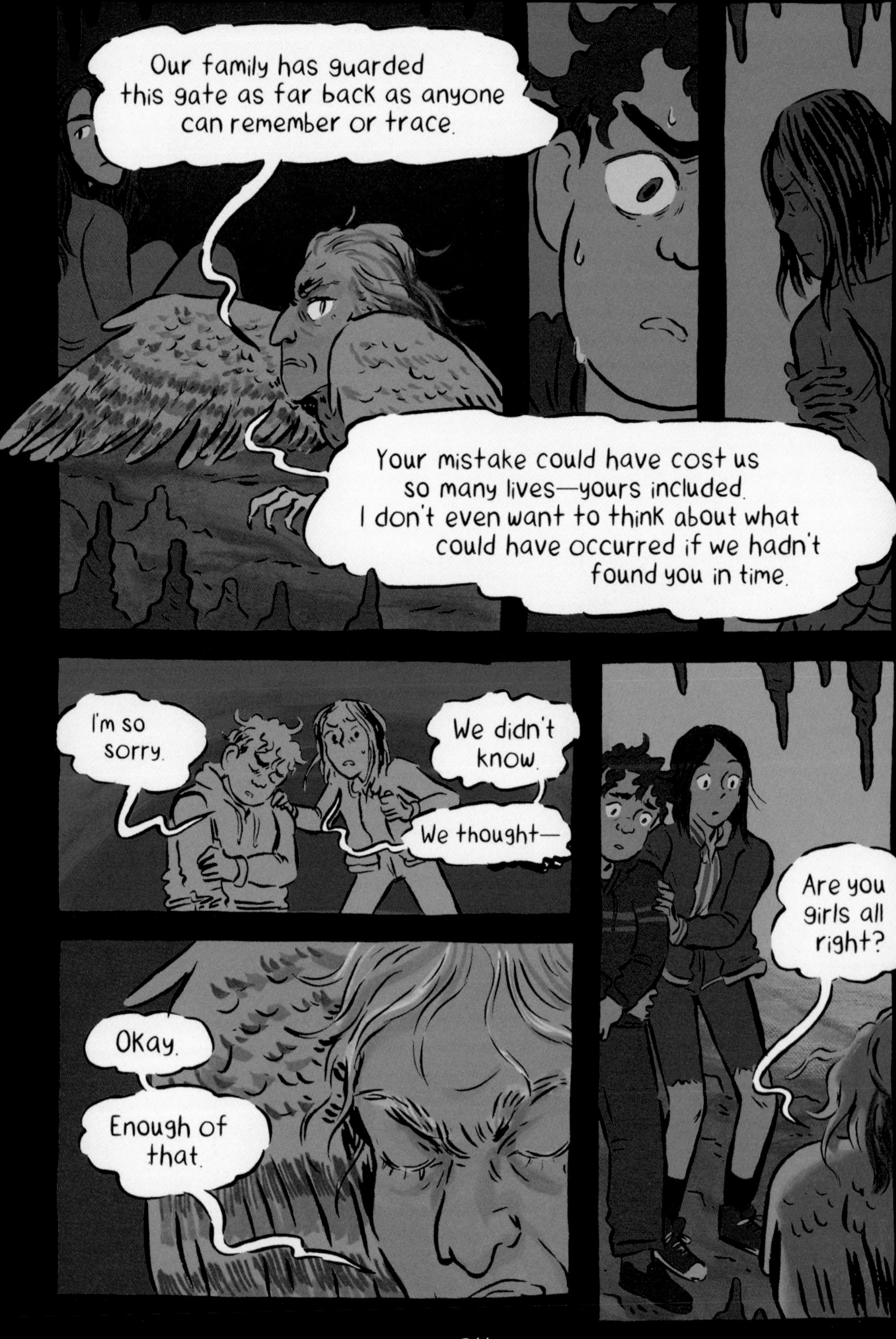
Our family has guarded this gate as far back as anyone can remember or trace.
Your mistake could have cost us so many lives—yours included. I don't even want to think about what could have occurred if we hadn't found you in time.
I'm so sorry.
We didn't know.
We thought—
Okay.
Enough of that.
Are you girls all right?

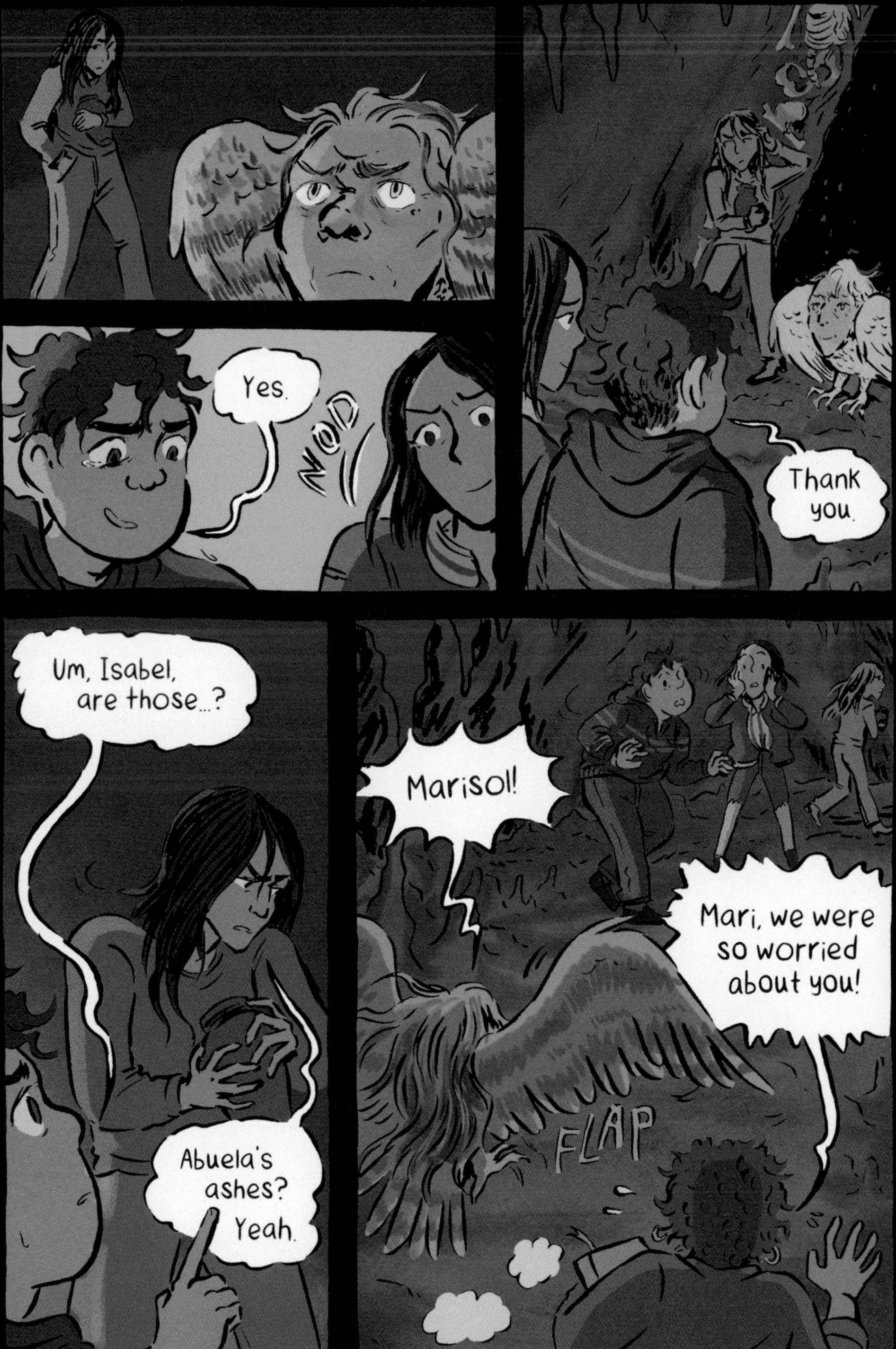
Yes.
NOD
Thank you.
Um, Isabel, are those...?
Abuela's ashes?
Yeah.
Marisol!
Mari, we were so worried about you!
FLAP

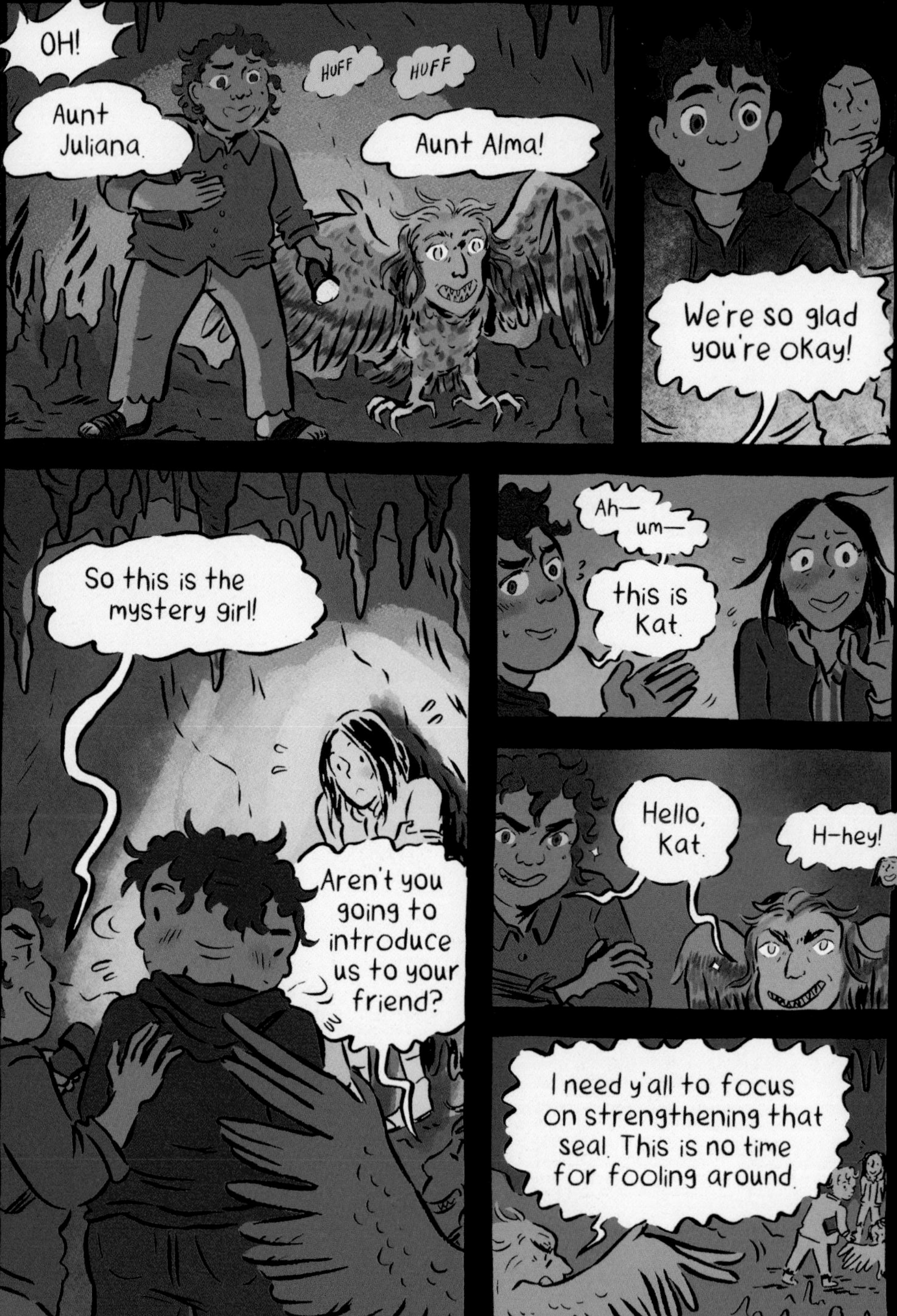
OH!
Aunt Juliana.
HUFF
HUFF
Aunt Alma!
We're so glad you're okay!
So this is the mystery girl!
Aren't you going to introduce us to your friend?
Ah— um—
this is Kat.
Hello, Kat.
H-hey!
I need y'all to focus on strengthening that seal. This is no time for fooling around.

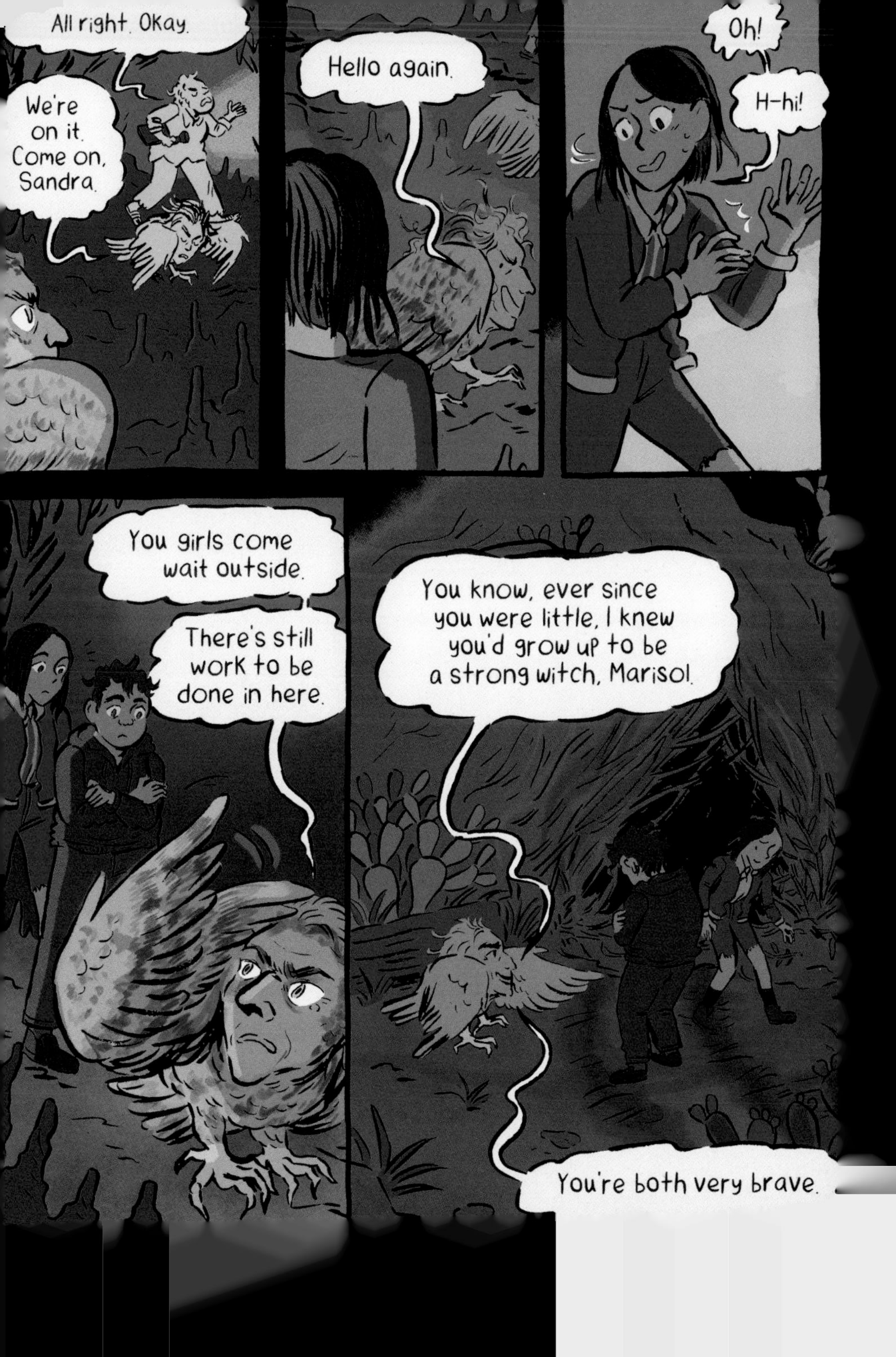

All right. Okay.
We're on it. Come on, Sandra.
Hello again.
Oh!
H-hi!
You girls come wait outside.
There's still work to be done in here.
You know, ever since you were little, I knew you'd grow up to be a strong witch, Marisol.
You're both very brave.

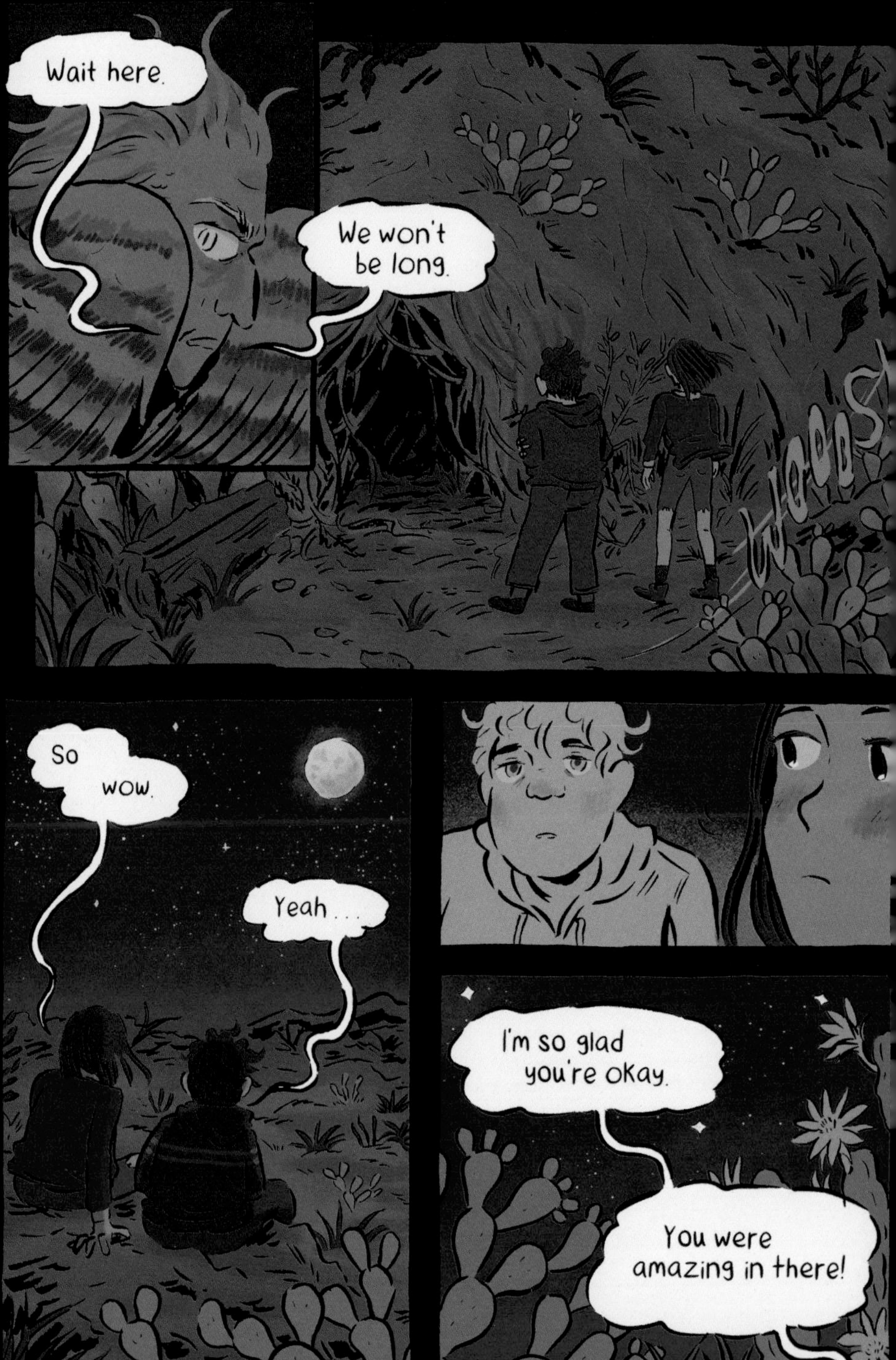
Wait here.
We won't be long.
WOOSH
So wow.
Yeah . . .
I'm so glad you're okay.
You were amazing in there!

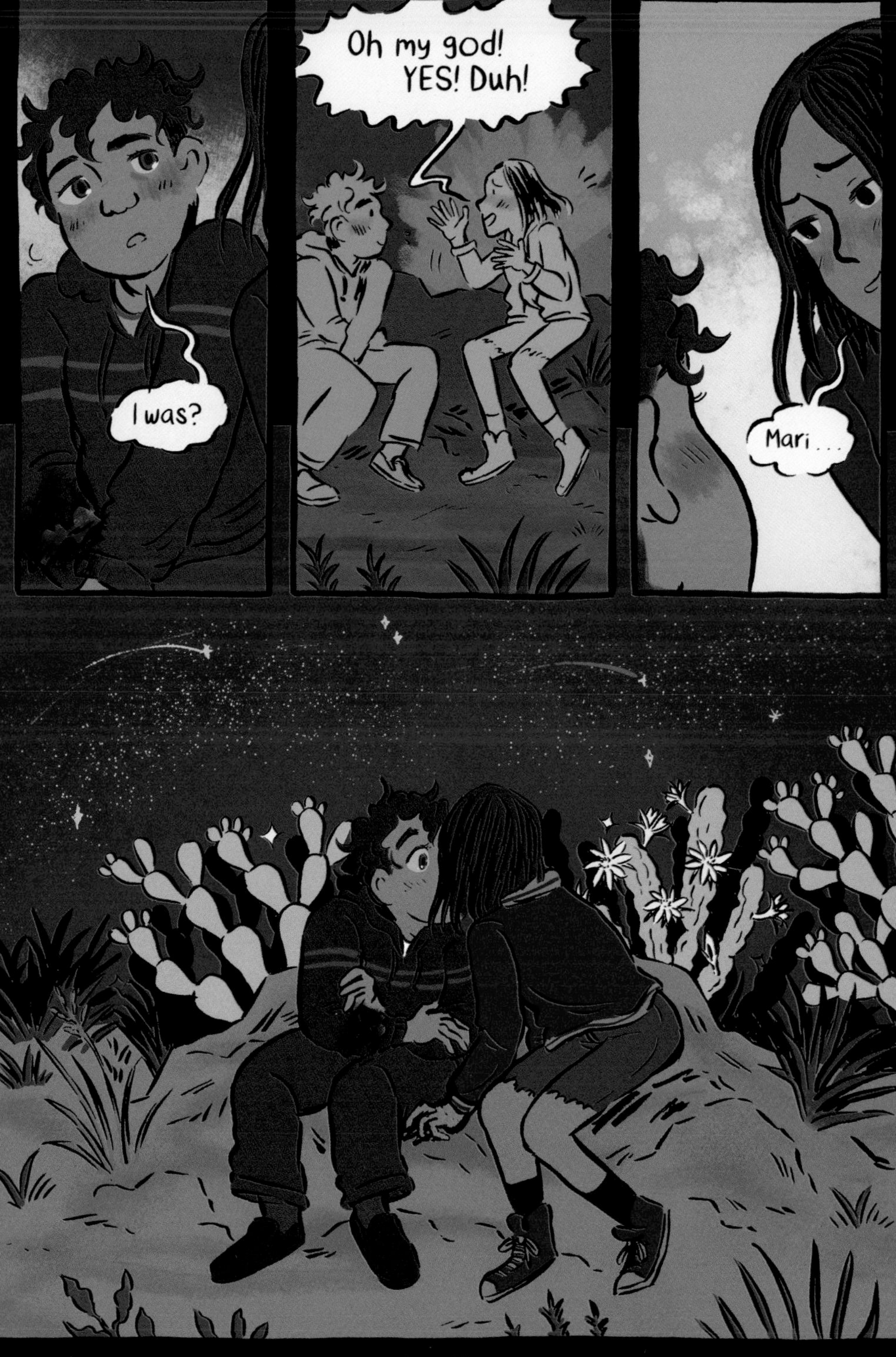
I was?
Oh my god! YES! Duh!
Mari . . .

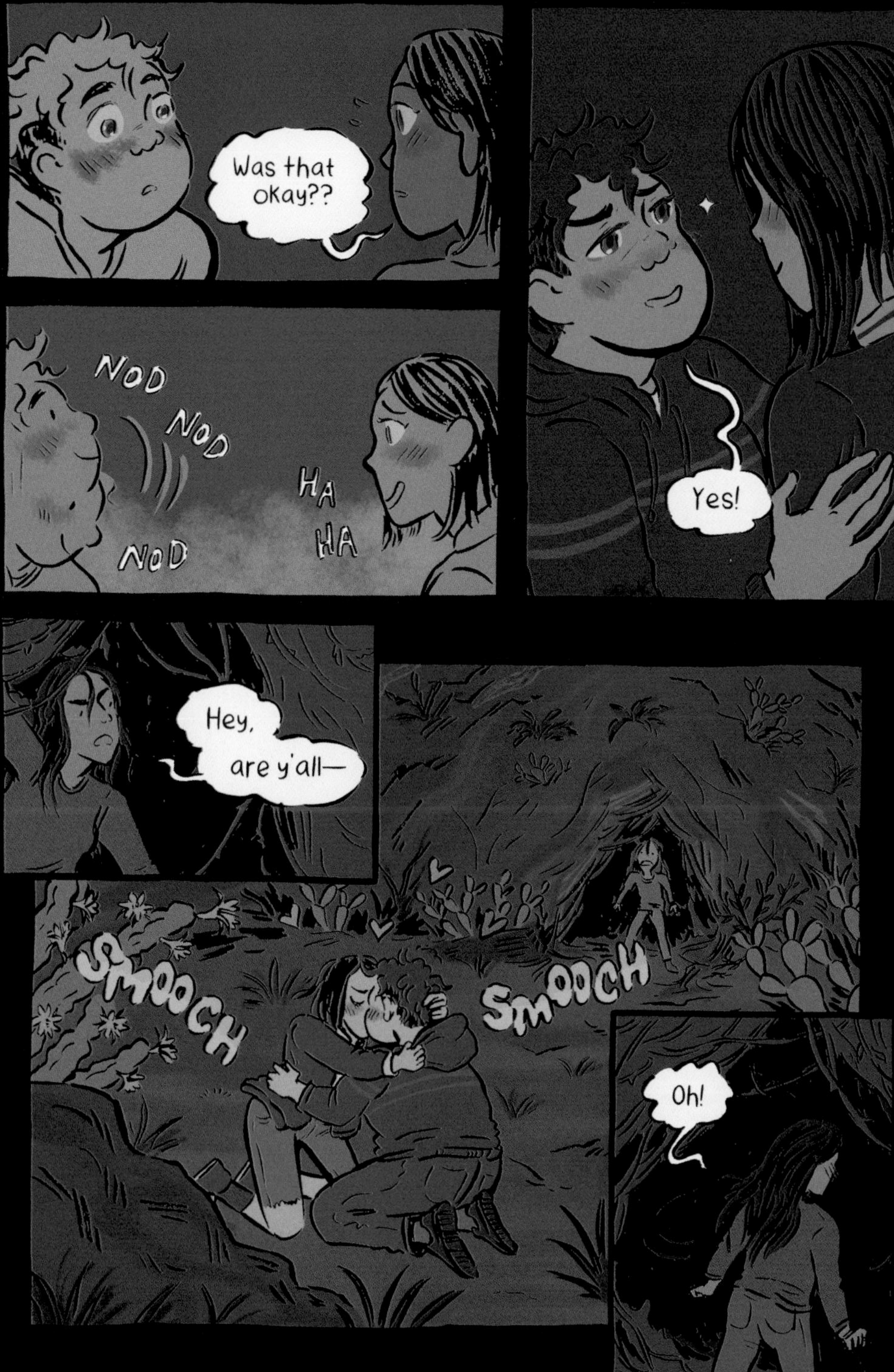
Was that okay??
Yes!
NOD
NOD
NOD
HA
HA
Hey,
are y'all—
SMOOCH
SMOOCH
Oh!

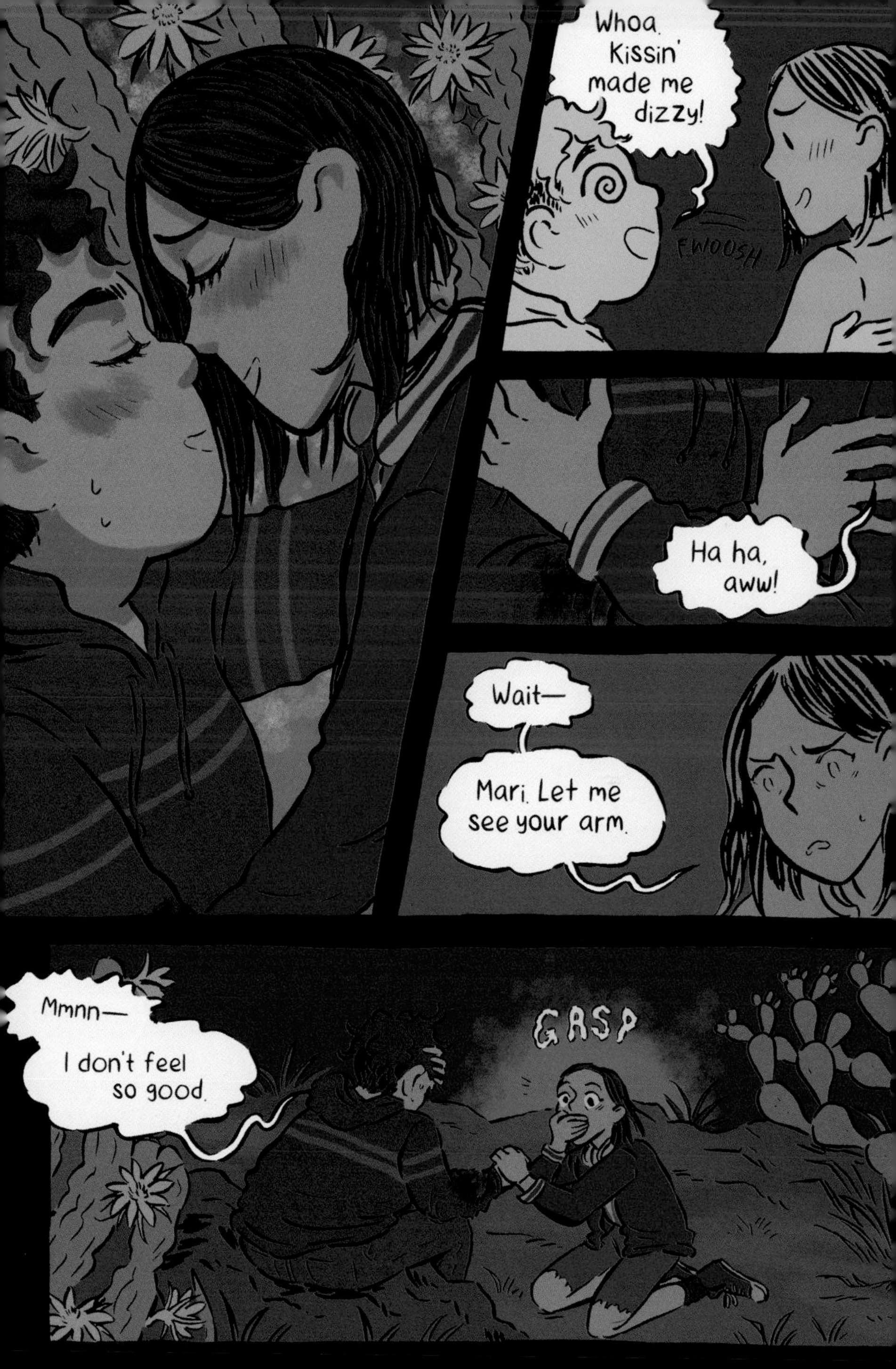
Whoa. Kissin' made me dizzy!
FWOOSH
Ha ha, aww!
Wait—
Mari. Let me see your arm.
Mmnn—
I don't feel so good.
GASP

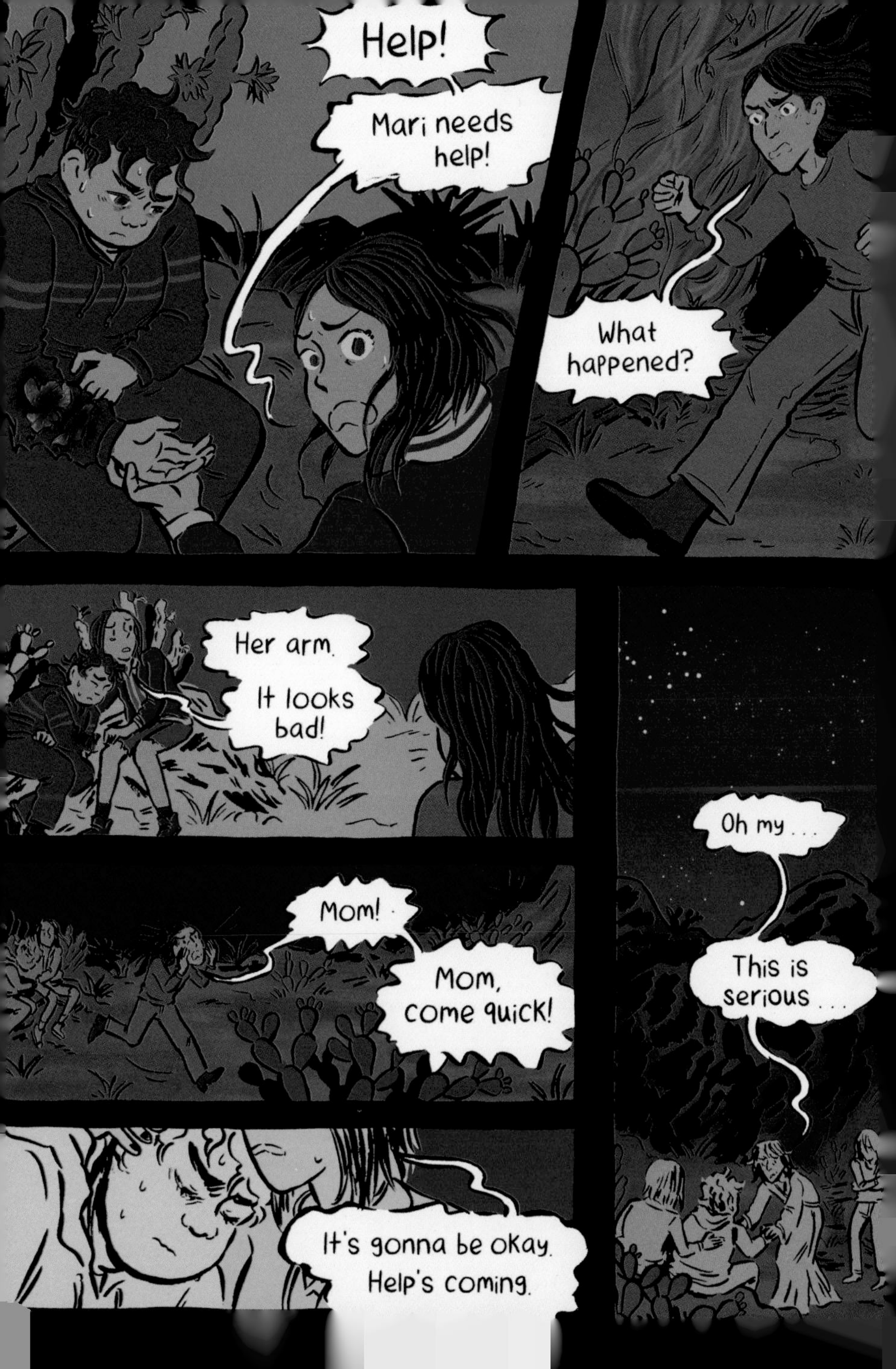
Help!
Mari needs help!
What happened?
Her arm.
It looks bad!
Mom!
Mom, come quick!
It's gonna be okay. Help's coming.
Oh my . . .
This is serious . . .

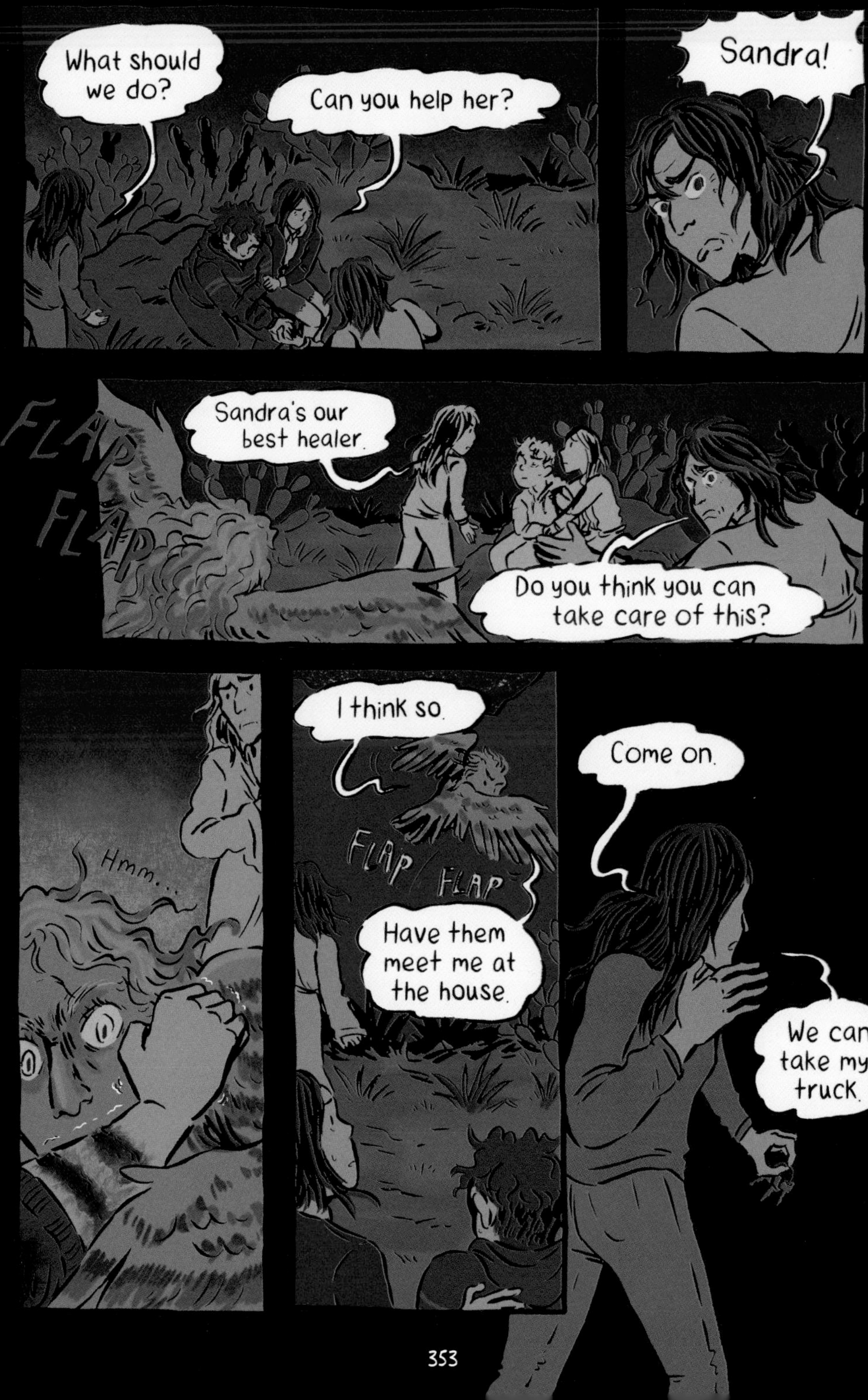
What should we do?
Can you help her?
Sandra!
FLAP FLAP
Sandra's our best healer.
Do you think you can take care of this?
Hmm...
I think so.
FLAP FLAP
Have them meet me at the house.
Come on.
We can take my truck.

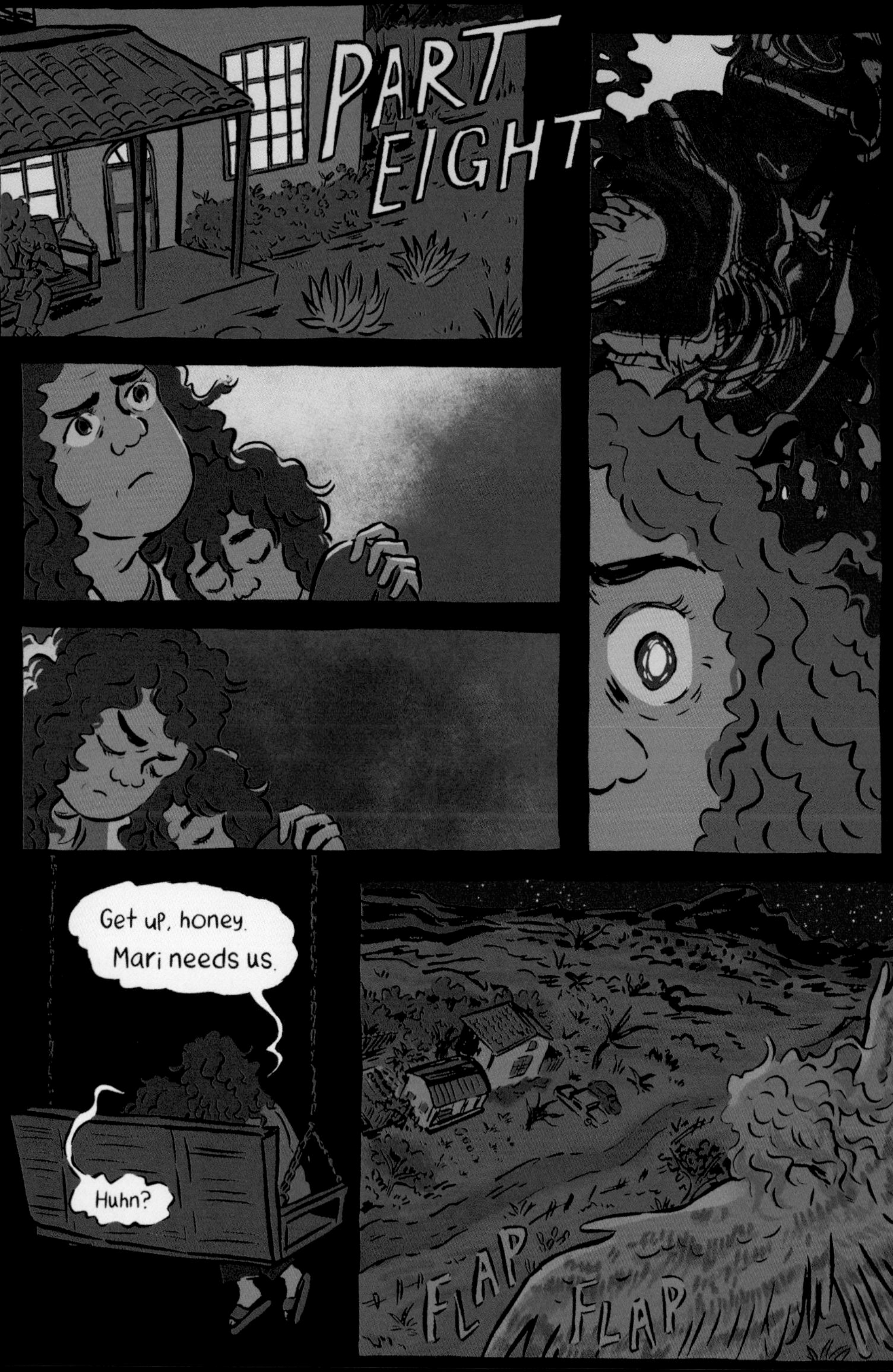
PART EIGHT
Get up, honey. Mari needs us.
Huhn?
FLAP FLAP

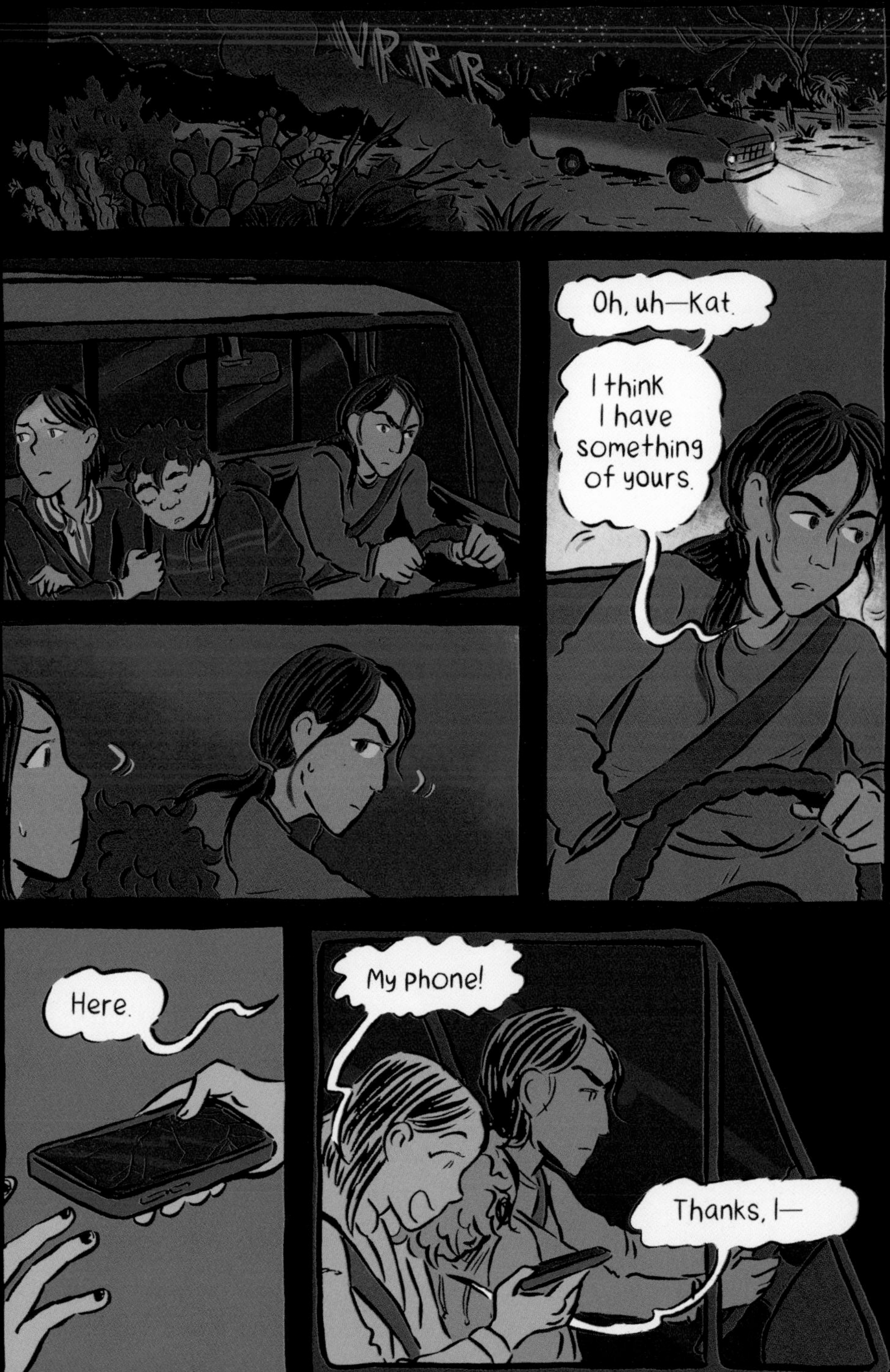
VRRR
Oh, uh—Kat.
I think I have something of yours.
Here.
My phone!
Thanks, I—

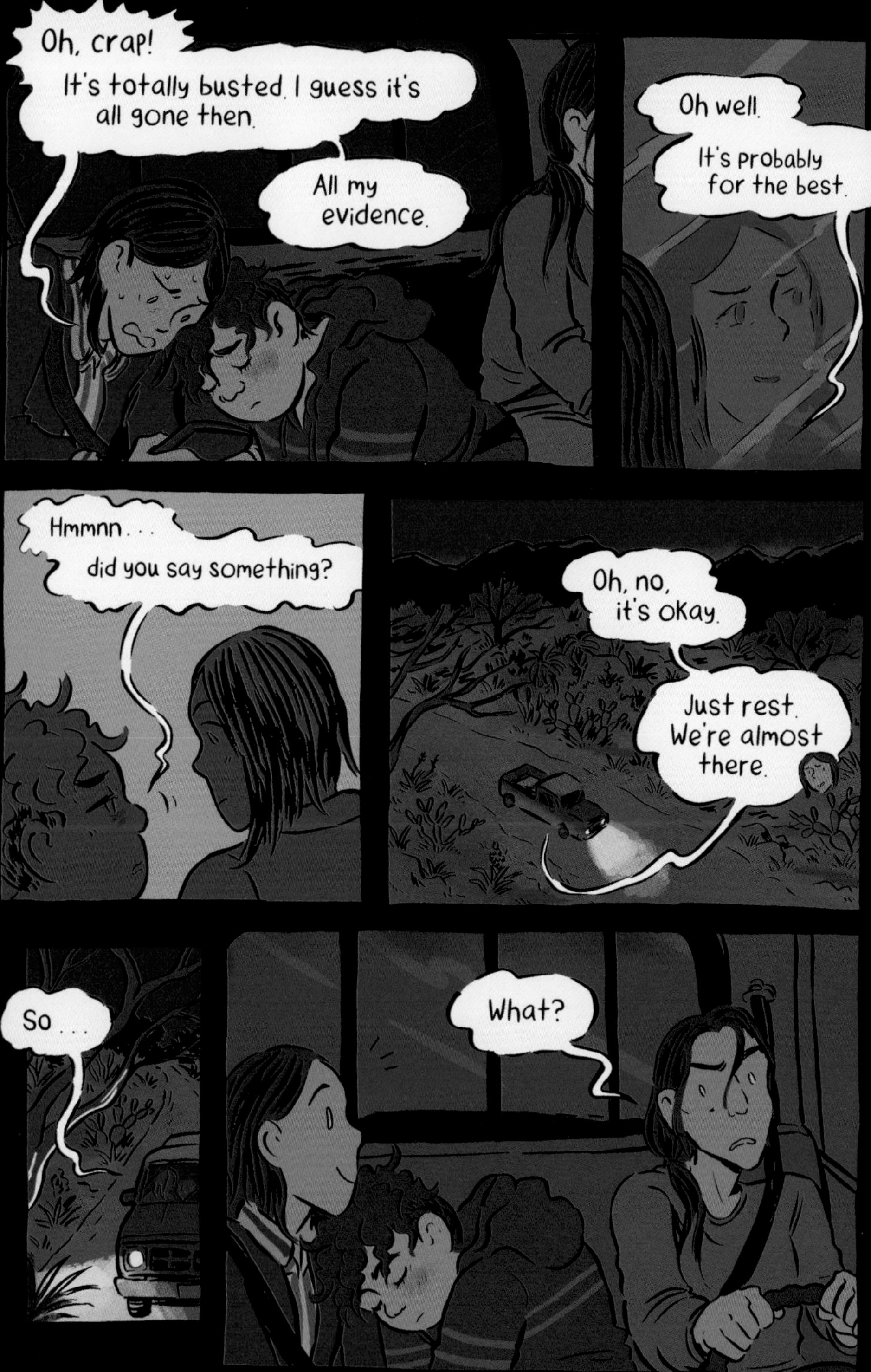
Oh, crap!
It's totally busted. I guess it's all gone then.
All my evidence.
Oh well.
It's probably for the best.
Hmmnn . . .
did you say something?
Oh, no, it's okay.
Just rest. We're almost there.
So . . .
What?

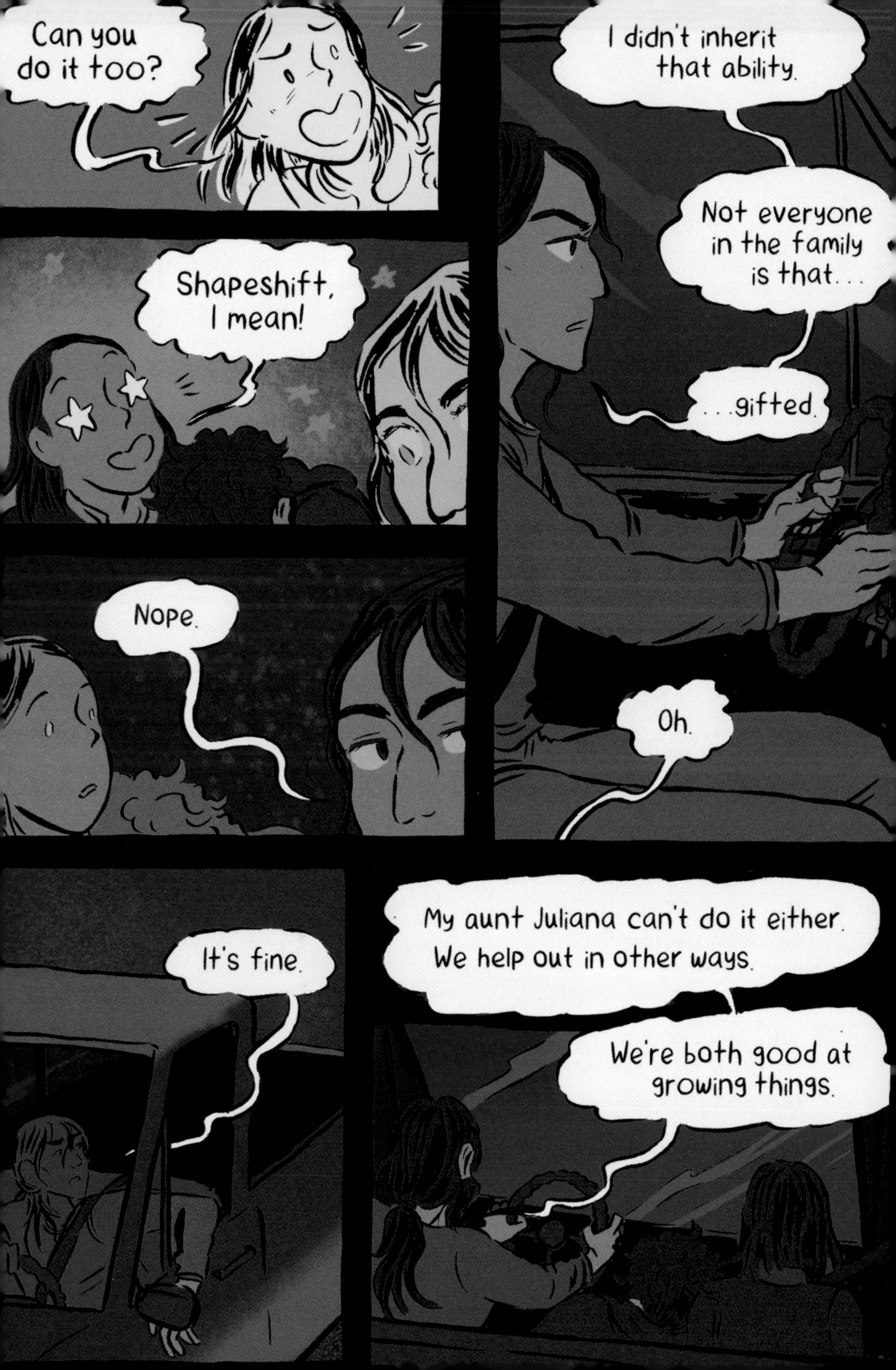
Can you do it too?
Shapeshift, I mean!
Nope.
I didn't inherit that ability.
Not everyone in the family is that. . .
. . .gifted.
Oh.
It's fine.
My aunt Juliana can't do it either. We help out in other ways.
We're both good at growing things.

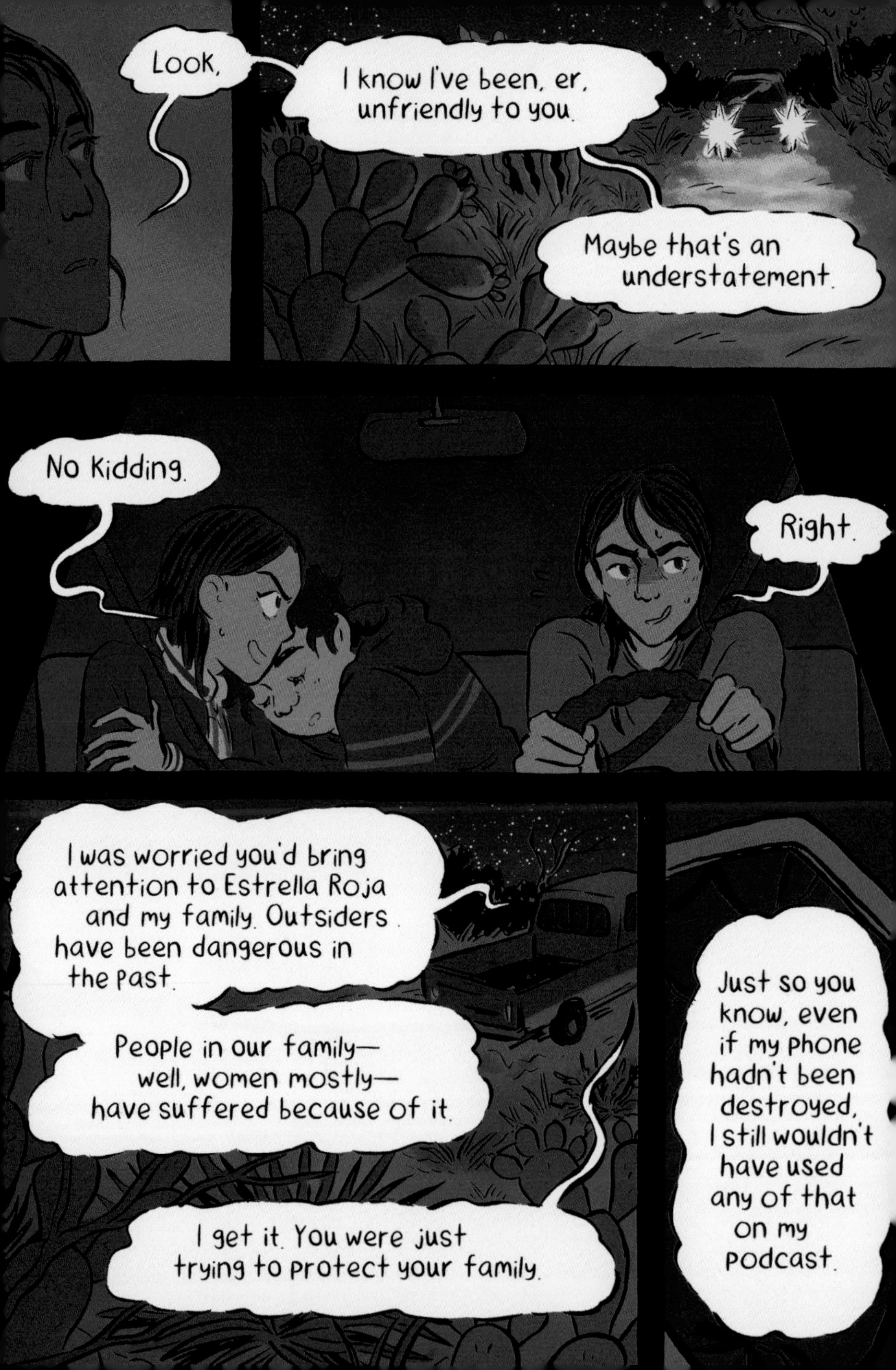
Look,
I know I've been, er, unfriendly to you.
Maybe that's an understatement.
No kidding.
Right.
I was worried you'd bring attention to Estrella Roja and my family. Outsiders have been dangerous in the past.
People in our family— well, women mostly— have suffered because of it.
I get it. You were just trying to protect your family.
Just so you know, even if my phone hadn't been destroyed, I still wouldn't have used any of that on my podcast.

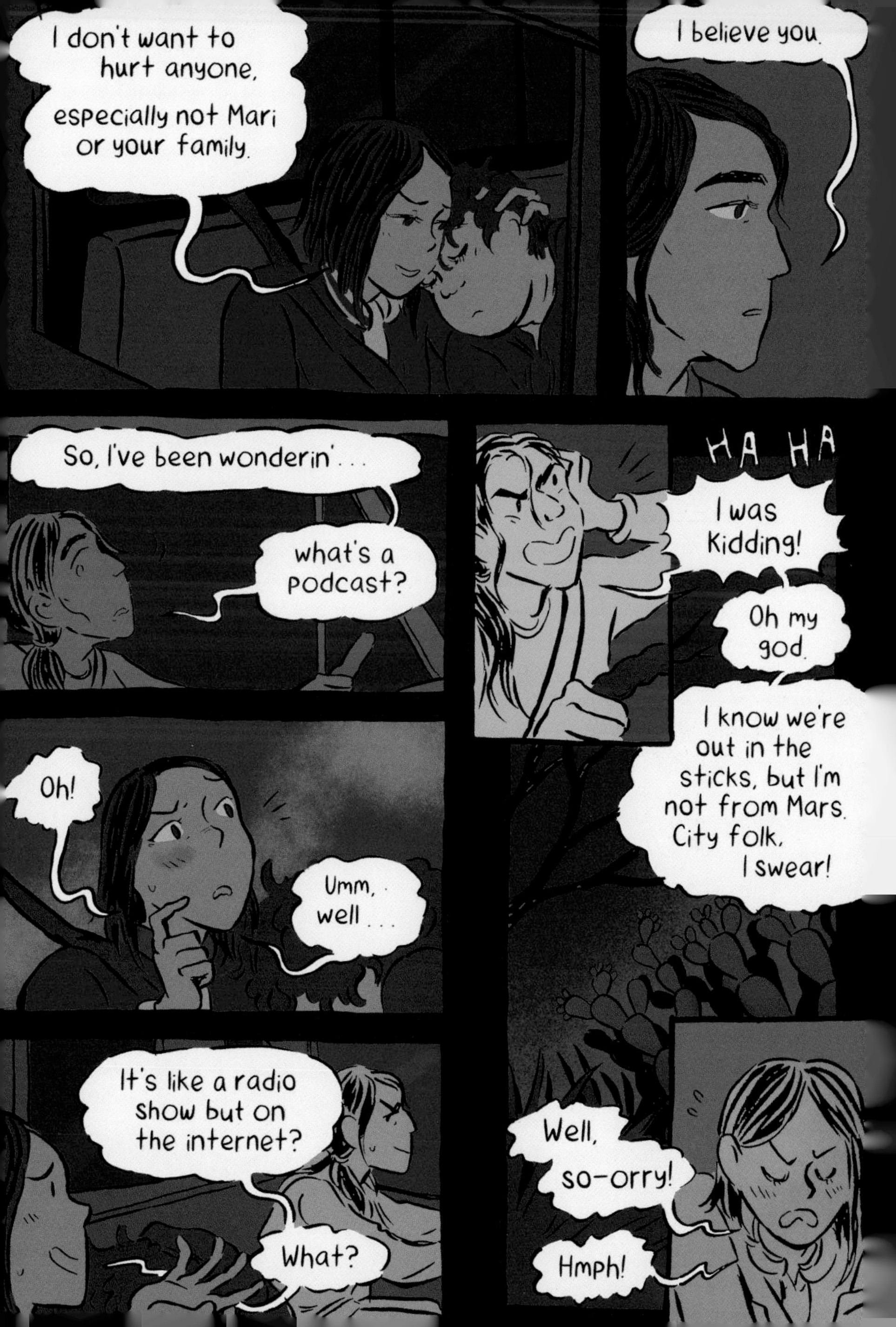
I don't want to hurt anyone, especially not Mari or your family.
I believe you.
So, I've been wonderin'...
what's a podcast?
HA HA
I was kidding!
Oh my god.
I know we're out in the sticks, but I'm not from Mars. City folk, I swear!
Oh!
Umm, well...
It's like a radio show but on the internet?
What?
Well, so-orry!
Hmph!

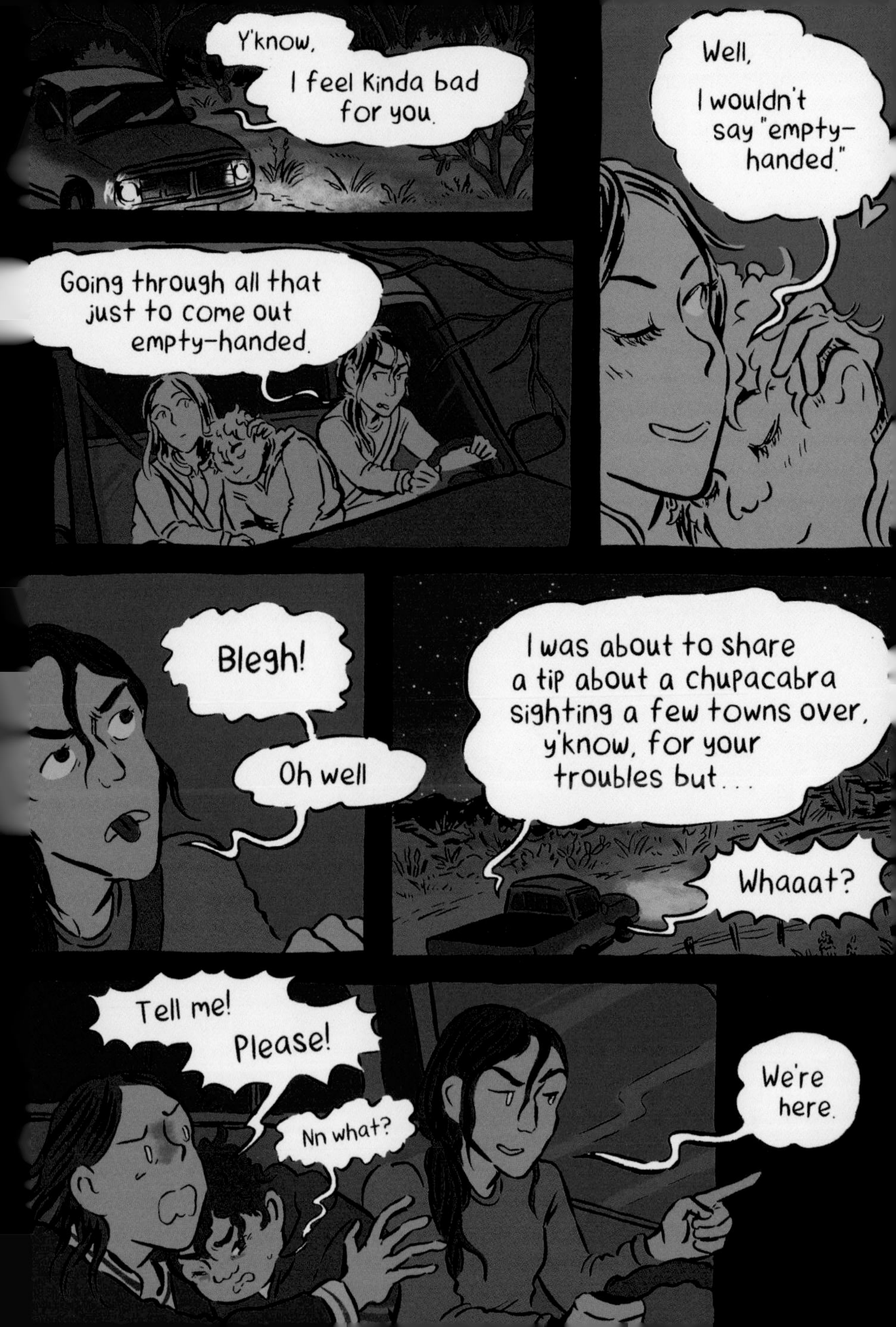
Y'know,
I feel kinda bad for you.
Going through all that just to come out empty-handed.
Well,
I wouldn't say "empty-handed."
Blegh!
Oh well
I was about to share a tip about a chupacabra sighting a few towns over, y'know, for your troubles but...
Whaaat?
Tell me!
Please!
Nn what?
We're here.

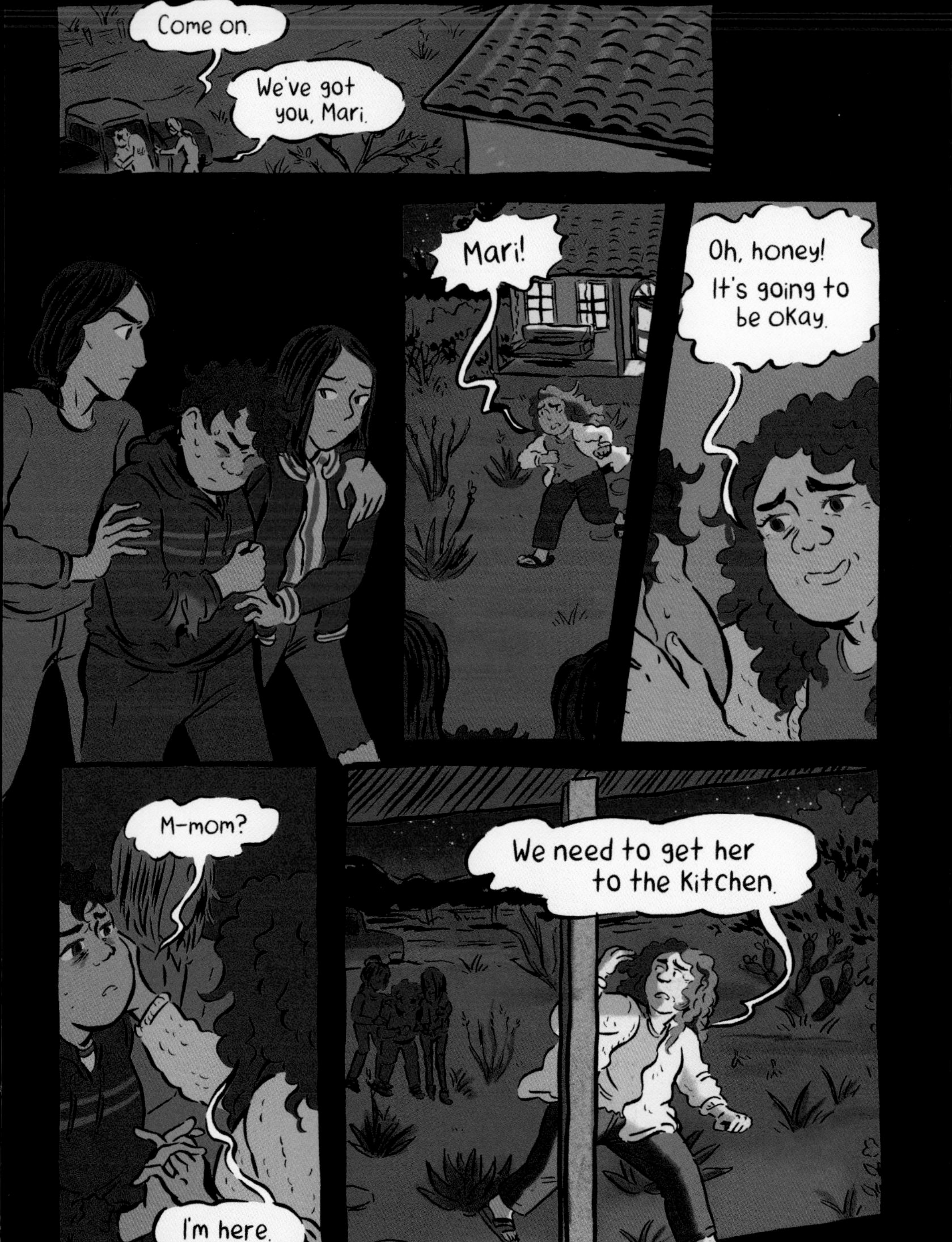
Come on.
We've got you, Mari.
Mari!
Oh, honey!
It's going to be okay.
M-mom?
I'm here.
We need to get her to the kitchen.

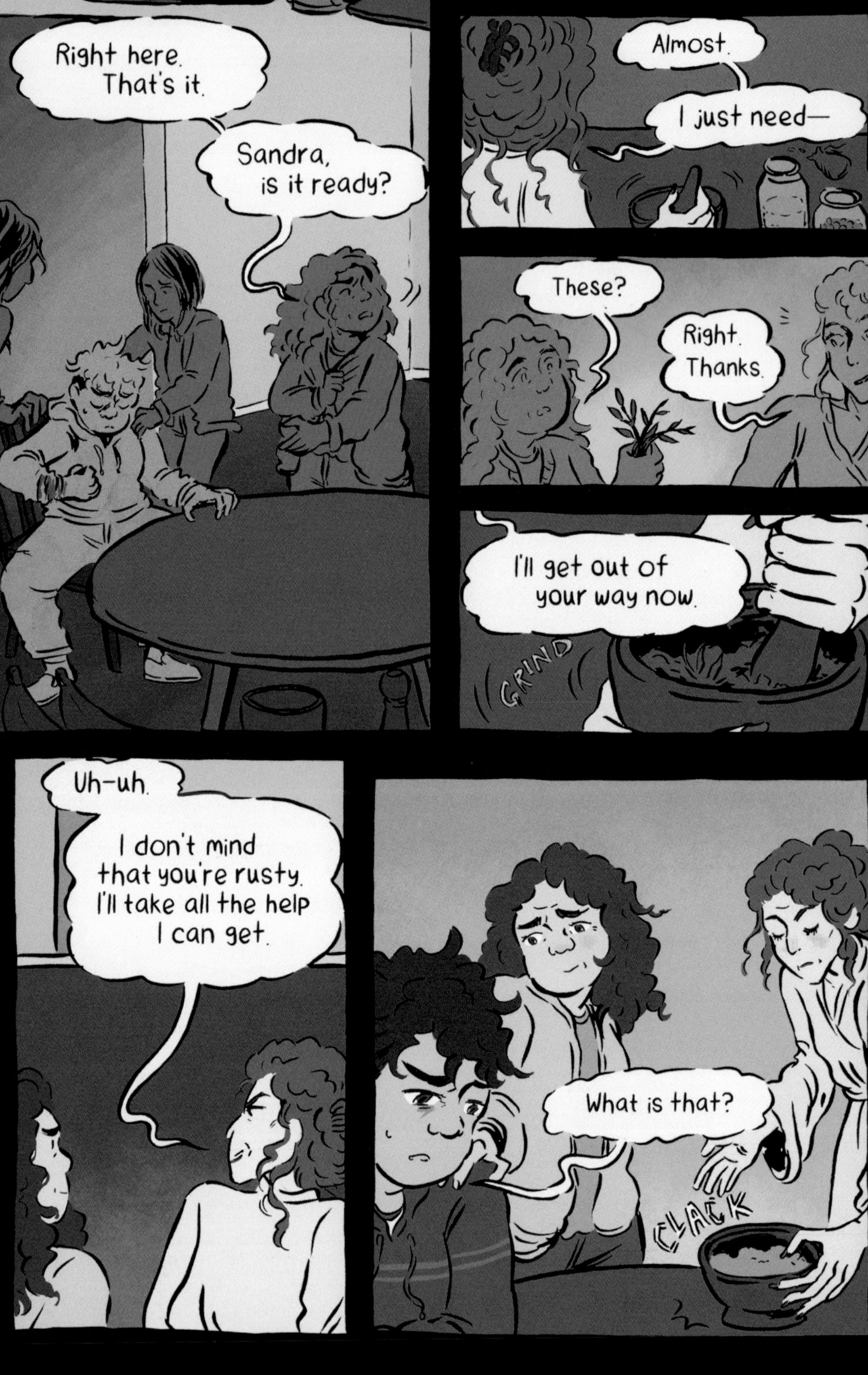
Right here. That's it.
Sandra, is it ready?
Almost.
I just need—
These?
Right. Thanks.
I'll get out of your way now.
GRIND
Uh-uh.
I don't mind that you're rusty. I'll take all the help I can get.
What is that?
CLACK

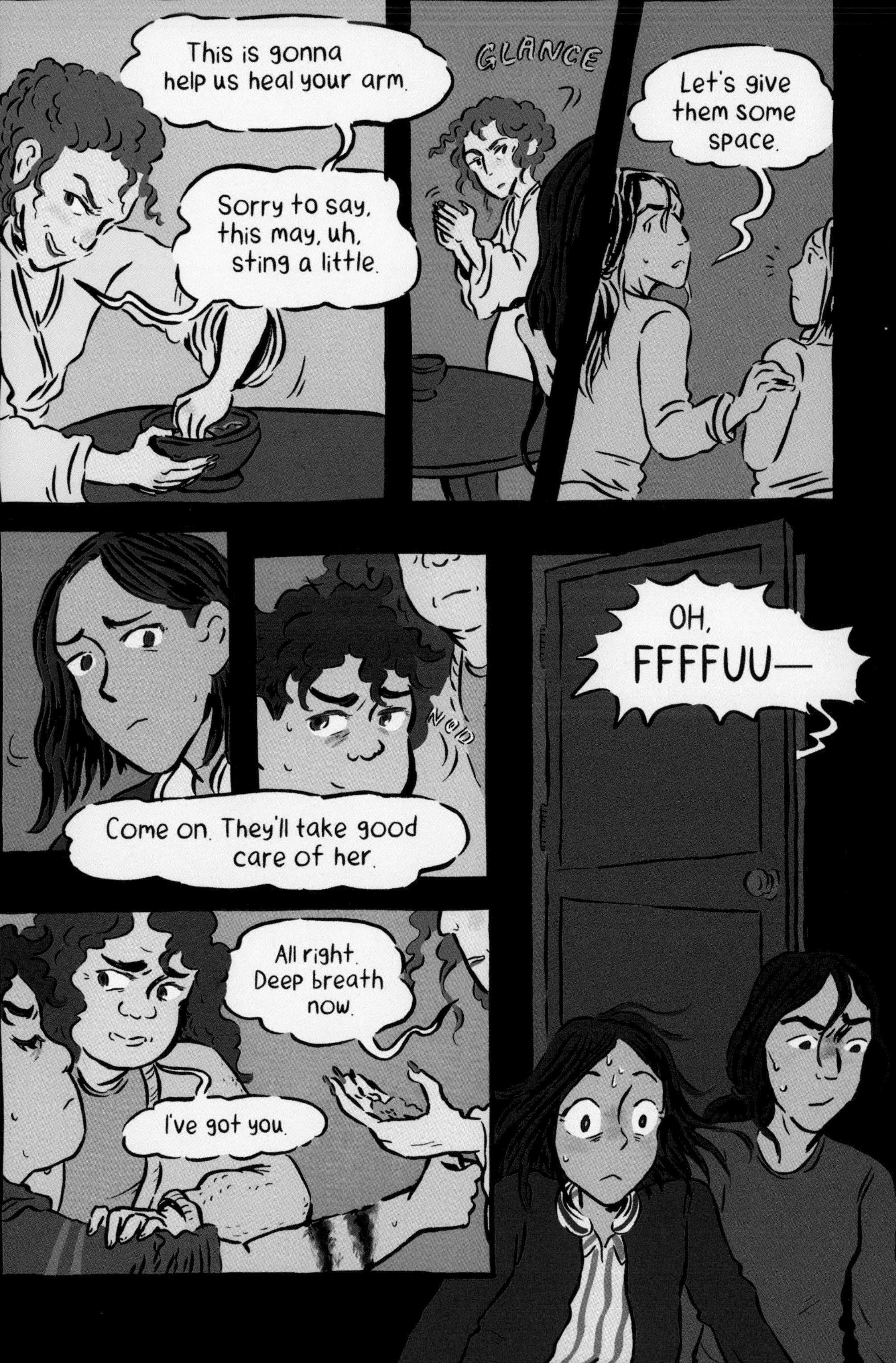
This is gonna help us heal your arm.
Sorry to say, this may, uh, sting a little.
GLANCE
Let's give them some space.
Come on. They'll take good care of her.
NOD
OH, FFFFUU—
All right. Deep breath now.
I've got you.

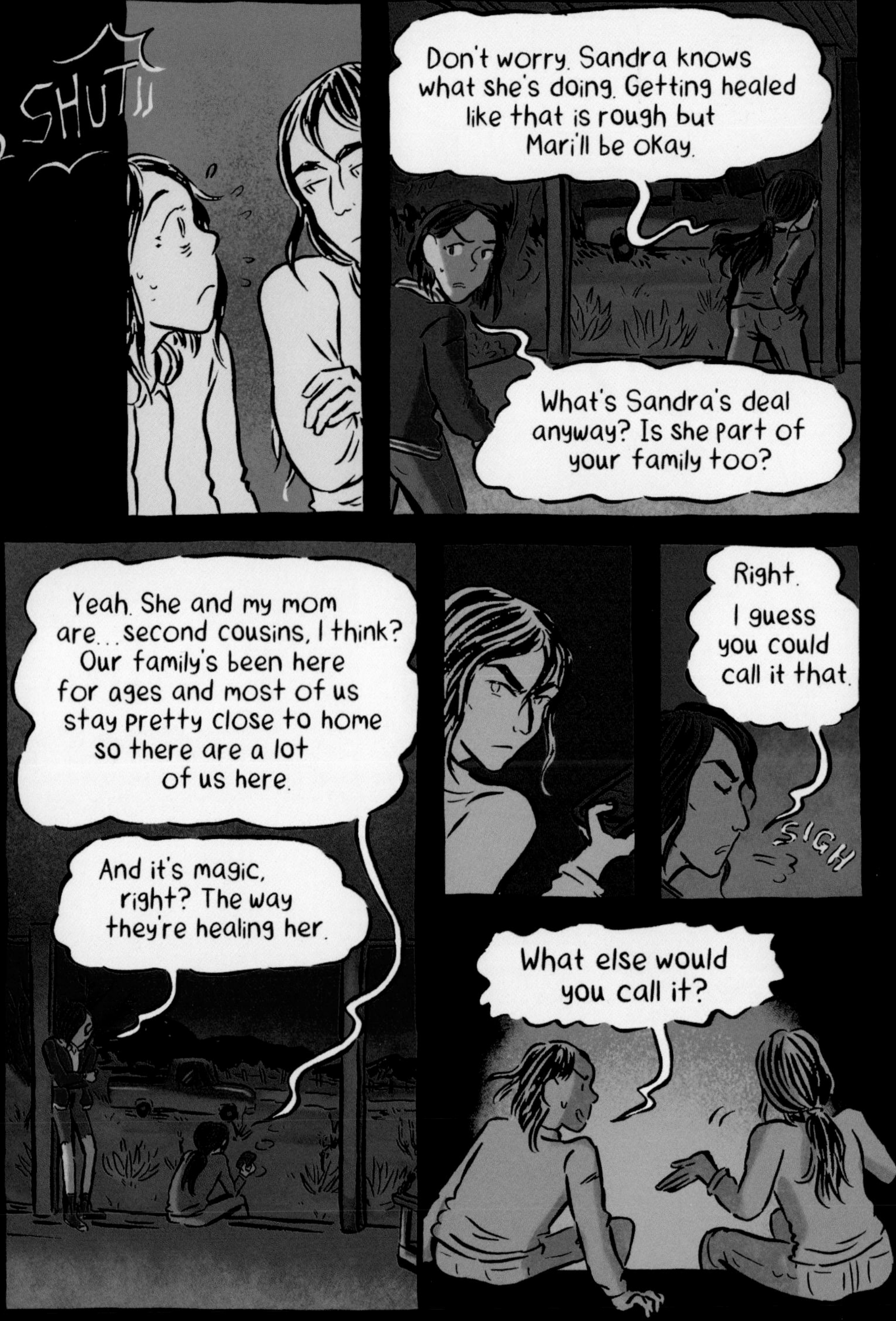
SHUT
Don't worry. Sandra knows what she's doing. Getting healed like that is rough but Mari'll be okay.
What's Sandra's deal anyway? Is she part of your family too?
Yeah. She and my mom are... second cousins, I think? Our family's been here for ages and most of us stay pretty close to home so there are a lot of us here.
Right.
I guess you could call it that.
SIGH
And it's magic, right? The way they're healing her.
What else would you call it?

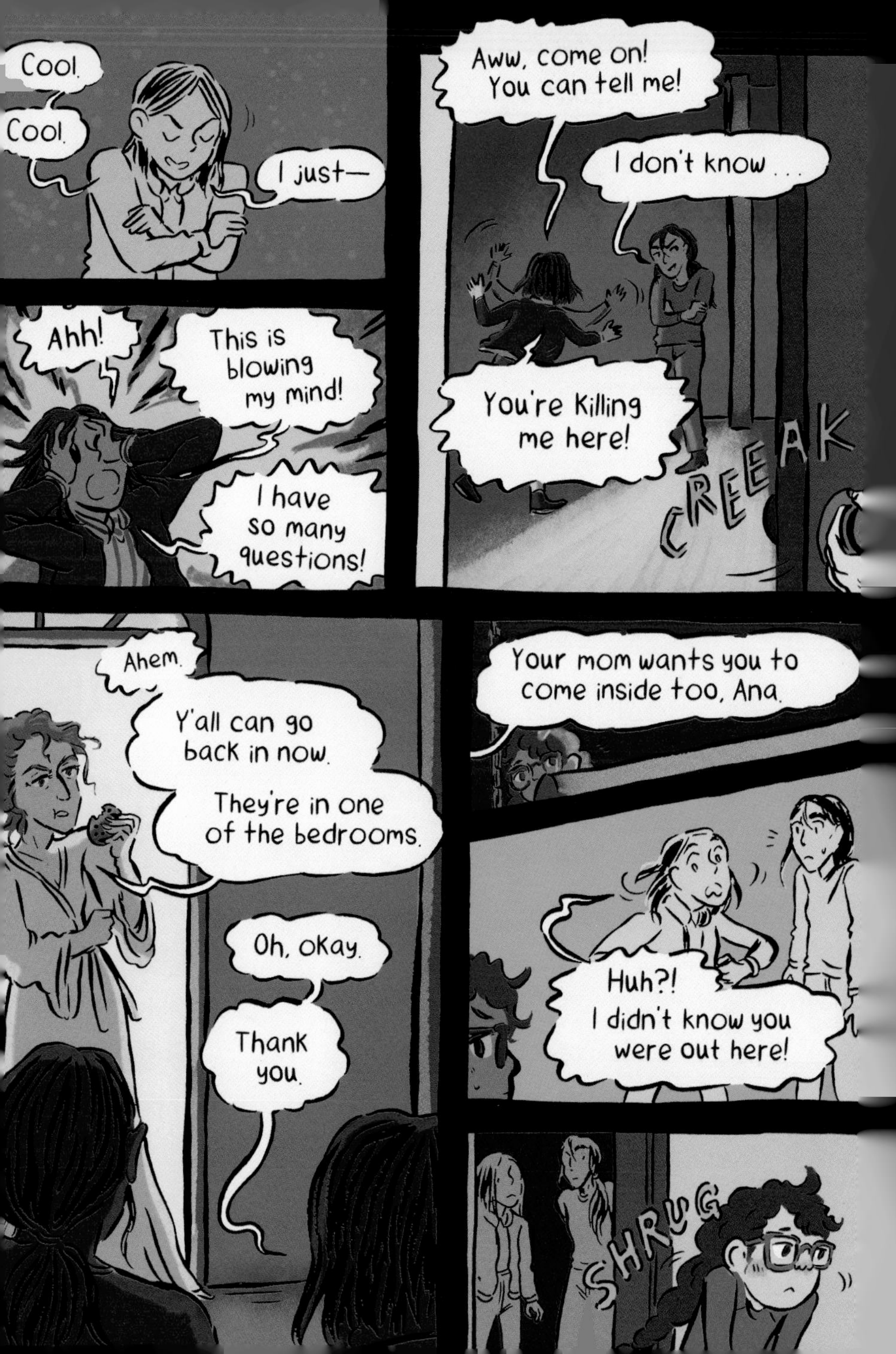
Cool.
Cool.
I just—
Aww, come on! You can tell me!
I don't know . . .
Ahh!
This is blowing my mind!
I have so many questions!
You're Killing me here!
CREEAK
Ahem.
Y'all can go back in now.
They're in one of the bedrooms.
Oh, okay.
Thank you.
Your mom wants you to come inside too, Ana.
Huh?! I didn't know you were out here!
SHRUG

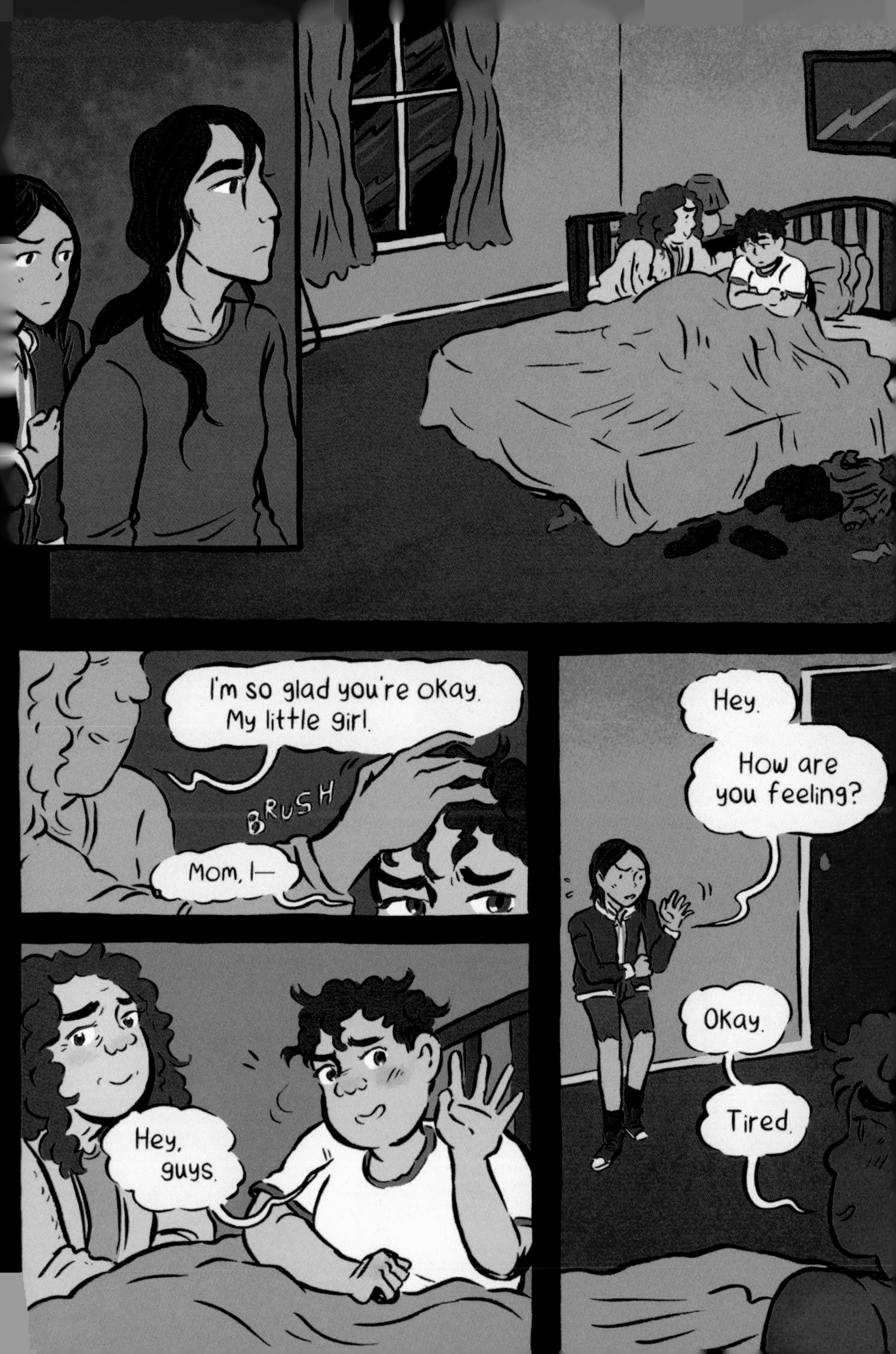
I'm so glad you're okay. My little girl.
BRUSH
Mom, I—
Hey, guys.
Hey.
How are you feeling?
Okay.
Tired.

But my arm doesn't hurt anymore.

Wow! It's pretty much healed!

I don't know if the scar will fully fade.

Oh my god!

It looks—

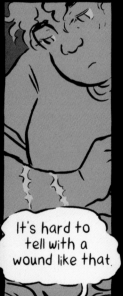
It's hard to tell with a wound like that.

It took a lot from all of us to close it.

Well, I think it looks kinda cool.

Thank you both so much for helping bring my little girl back in one piece.

Mom...

No problem, Aunt Yolanda.

367

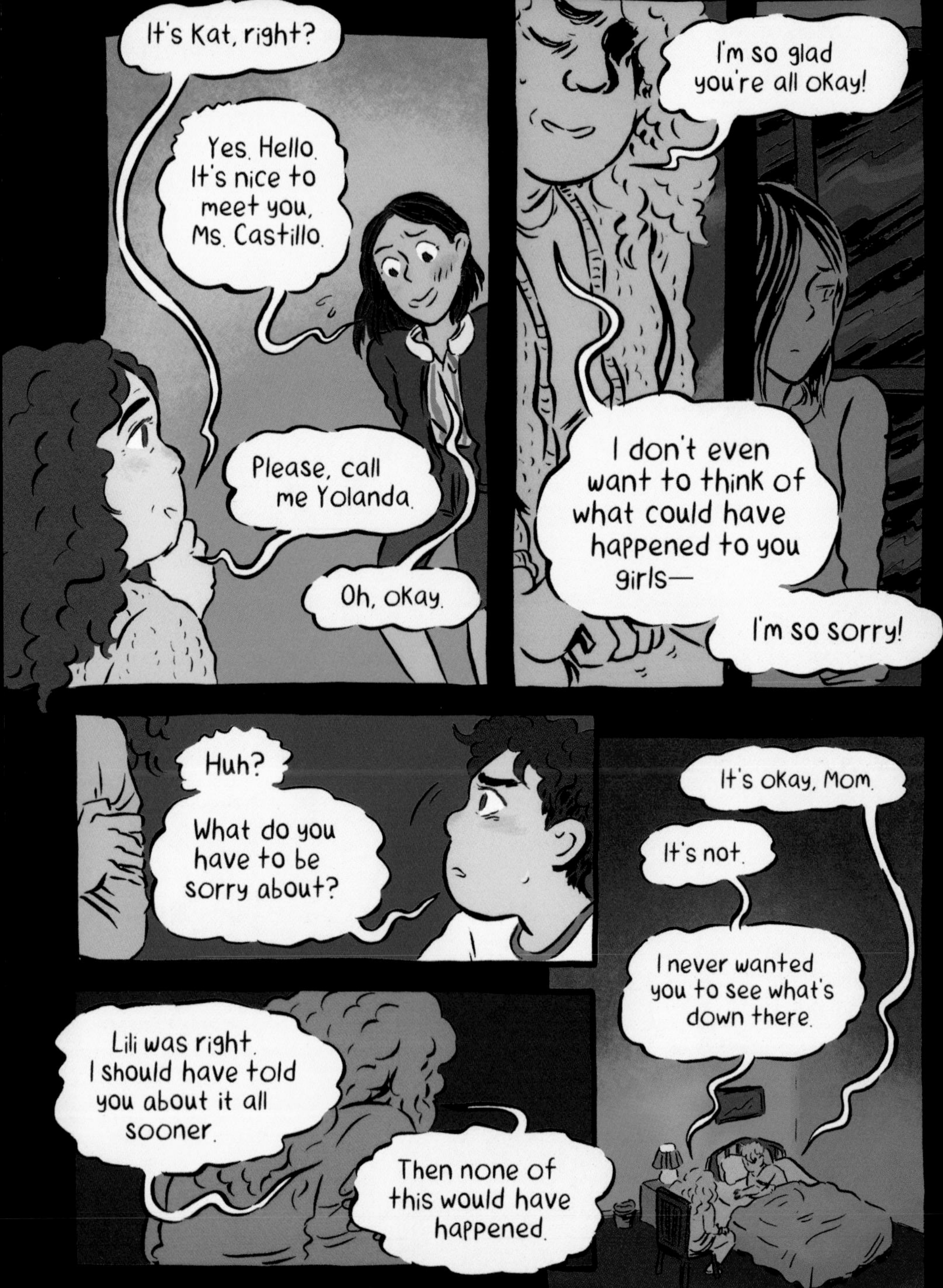
It's Kat, right?
Yes. Hello. It's nice to meet you, Ms. Castillo.
Please, call me Yolanda.
Oh, okay.
I'm so glad you're all okay!
I don't even want to think of what could have happened to you girls—
I'm so sorry!
Huh?
What do you have to be sorry about?
It's okay, Mom.
It's not.
I never wanted you to see what's down there.
Lili was right. I should have told you about it all sooner.
Then none of this would have happened.

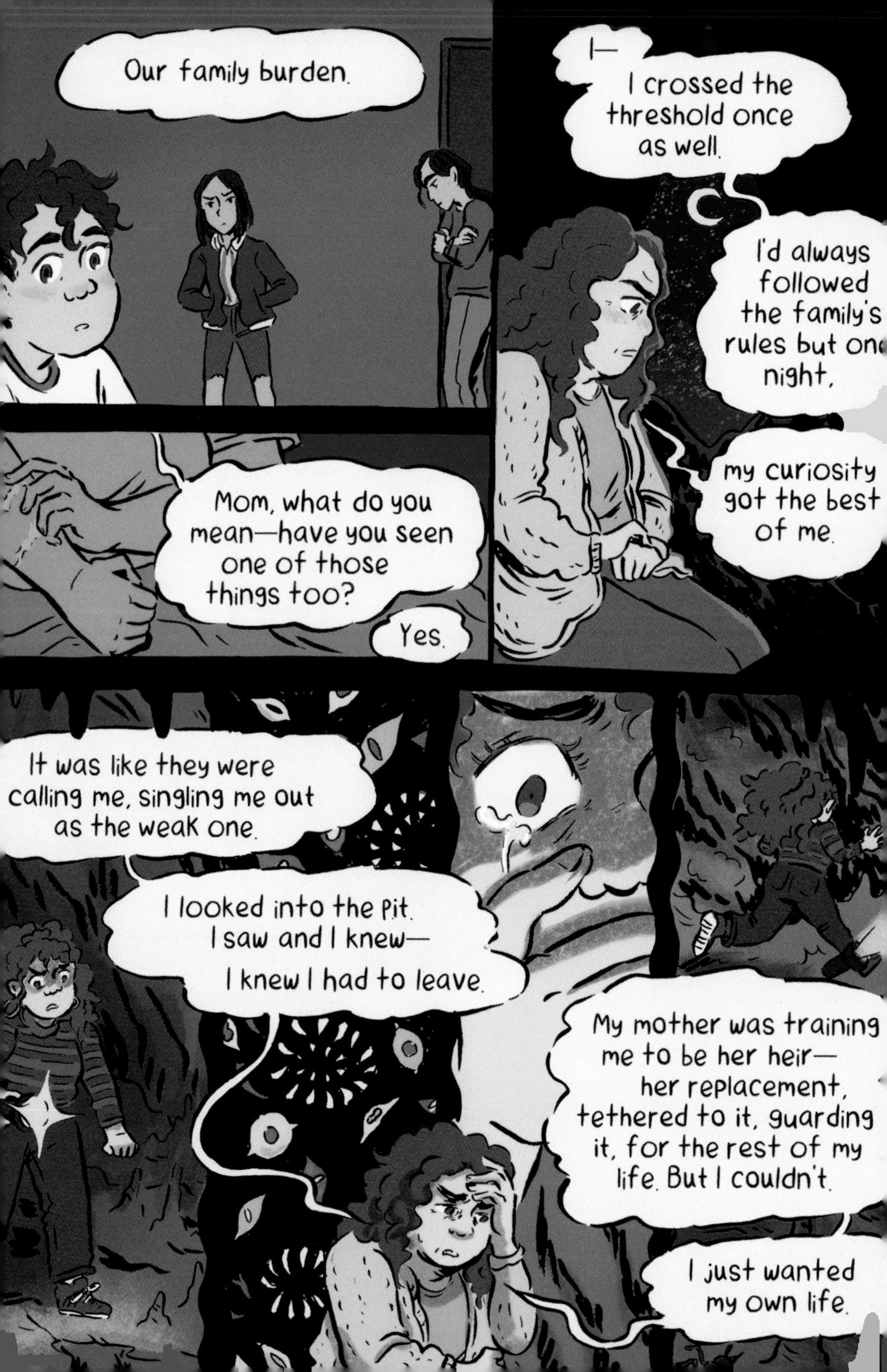
Our family burden.
Mom, what do you mean—have you seen one of those things too?
Yes.
I—
I crossed the threshold once as well.
I'd always followed the family's rules but one night,
my curiosity got the best of me.
It was like they were calling me, singling me out as the weak one.
I looked into the pit. I saw and I knew—
I knew I had to leave.
My mother was training me to be her heir—her replacement, tethered to it, guarding it, for the rest of my life. But I couldn't.
I just wanted my own life.

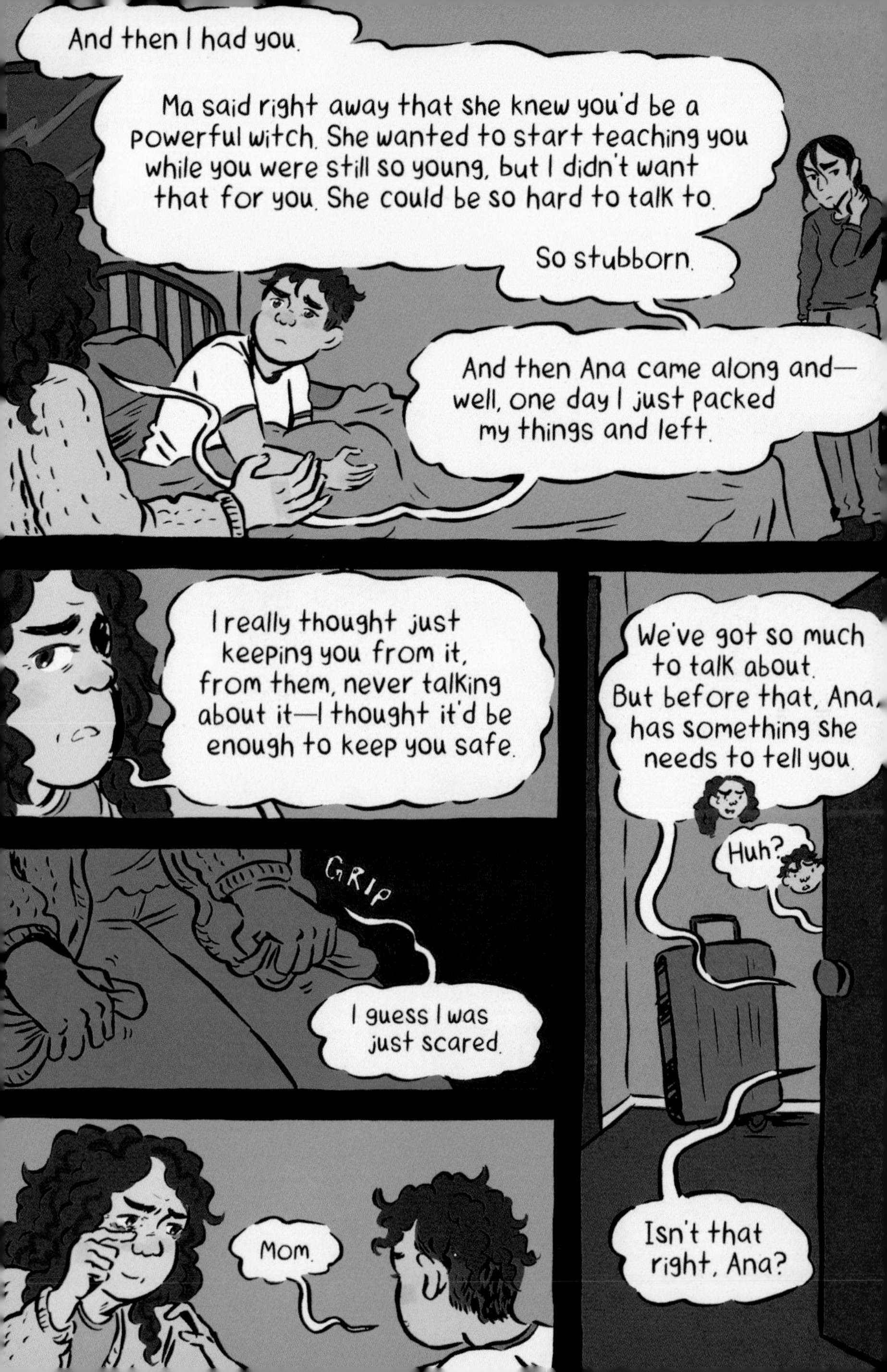
And then I had you.
Ma said right away that she knew you'd be a powerful witch. She wanted to start teaching you while you were still so young, but I didn't want that for you. She could be so hard to talk to.
So stubborn.
And then Ana came along and— well, one day I just packed my things and left.
I really thought just keeping you from it, from them, never talking about it—I thought it'd be enough to keep you safe.
GRIP
I guess I was just scared.
Mom.
We've got so much to talk about. But before that, Ana, has something she needs to tell you.
Huh?
Isn't that right, Ana?

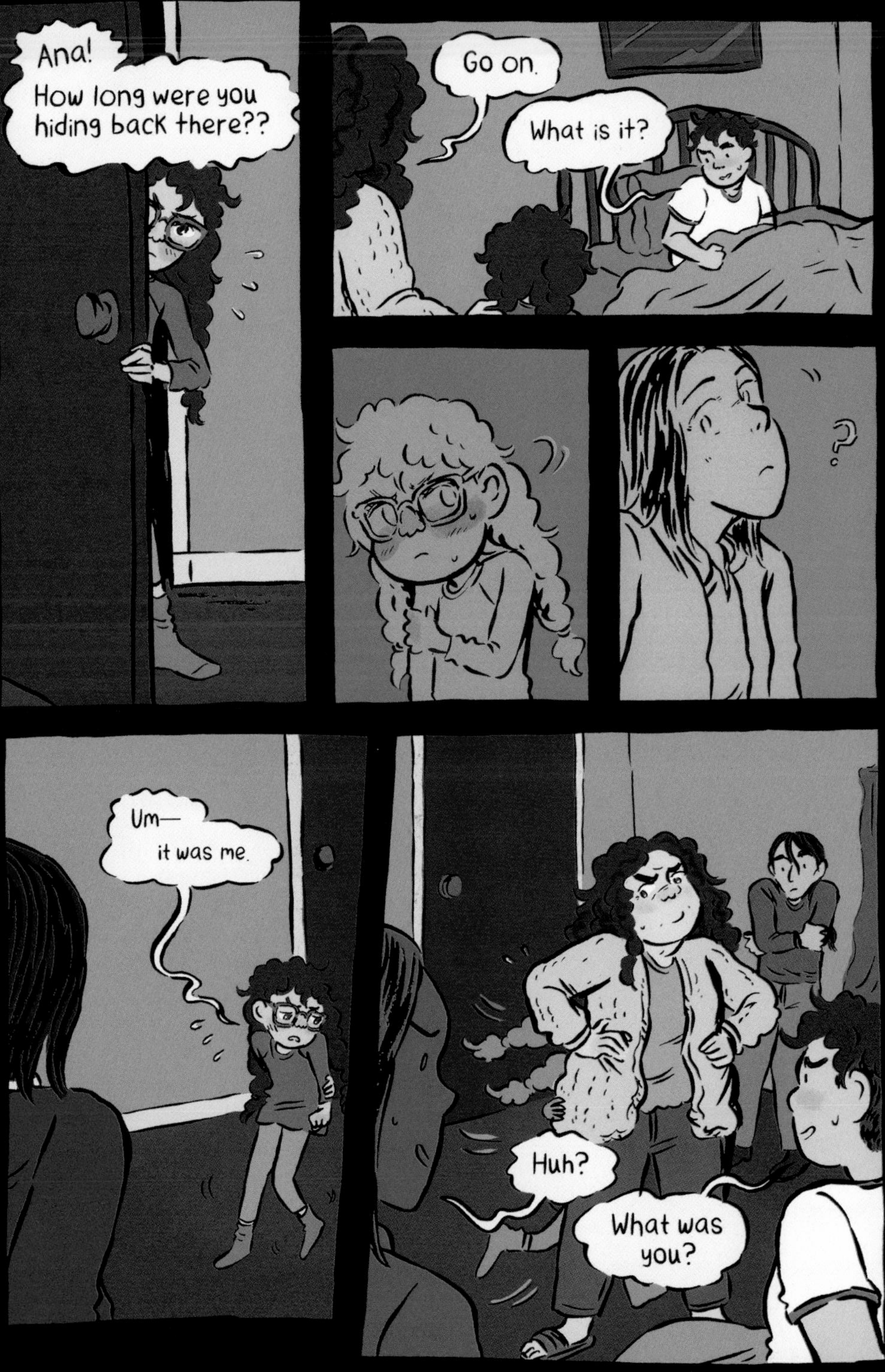
Ana!
How long were you hiding back there??
Go on.
What is it?
Um—
it was me.
Huh?
What was you?

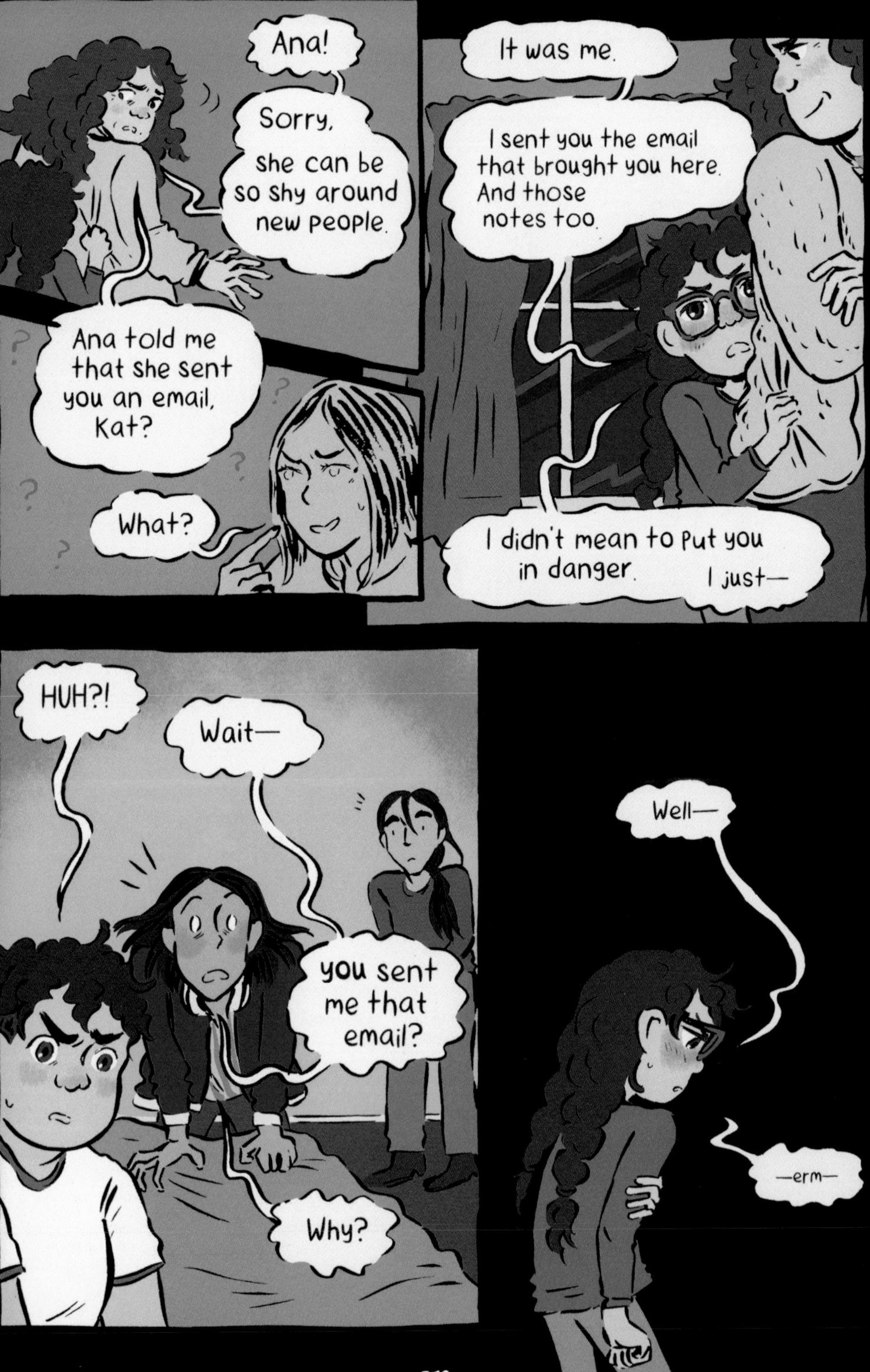

Ana!
Sorry, she can be so shy around new people.
Ana told me that she sent you an email, Kat?
What?
It was me.
I sent you the email that brought you here. And those notes too.
I didn't mean to put you in danger. I just—
HUH?!
Wait—
you sent me that email?
Why?
Well—
—erm—

I listen to your podcast and well . . .
When we got here I noticed all these strange things and everyone was acting so weird around us and—I just had this really odd feeling that something, y'know, paranormal was going on. I've always been interested in that kind of stuff and I just thought that it would be really cool if you and Clem came and checked it out and put it on your show . . .
But I didn't expect you and Mari to meet and, like, fall in love or whatever, and—
Okay, that's enough, sweetie. You're embarrassing the teens.
Oh. Sorry.
Wow, Ana, I had no idea.
Well, you're not always the most observant person.

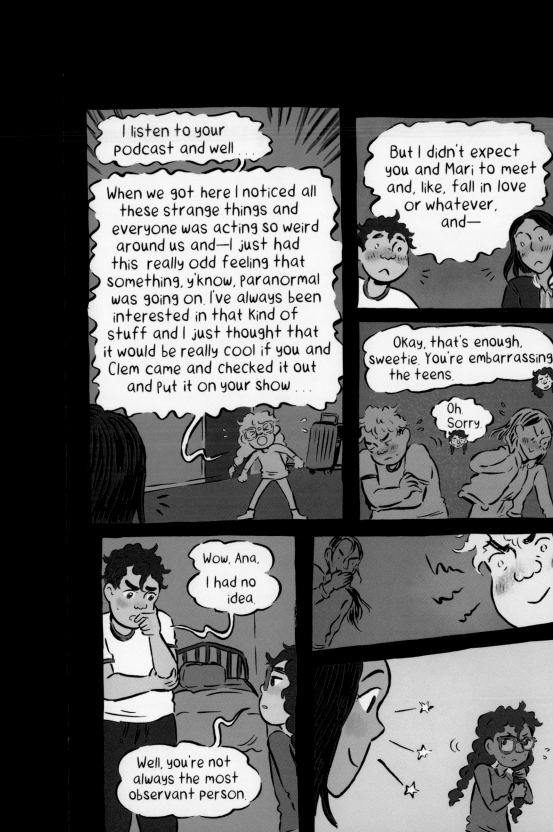

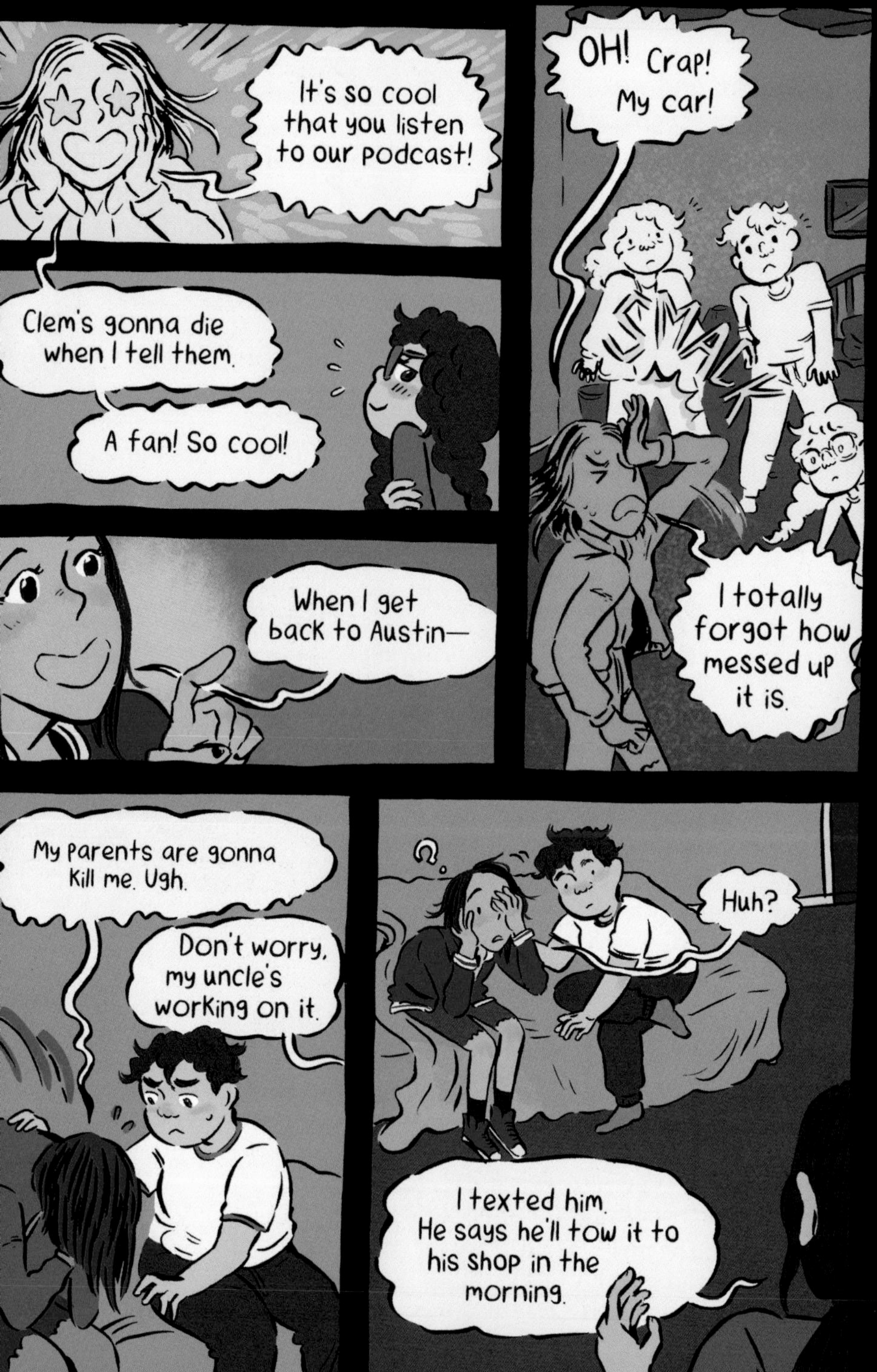
It's so cool that you listen to our podcast!
Clem's gonna die when I tell them.
A fan! So cool!
When I get back to Austin—
OH! Crap! My car!
SMACK
I totally forgot how messed up it is.
My parents are gonna kill me. Ugh.
Don't worry, my uncle's working on it.
Huh?
I texted him. He says he'll tow it to his shop in the morning.

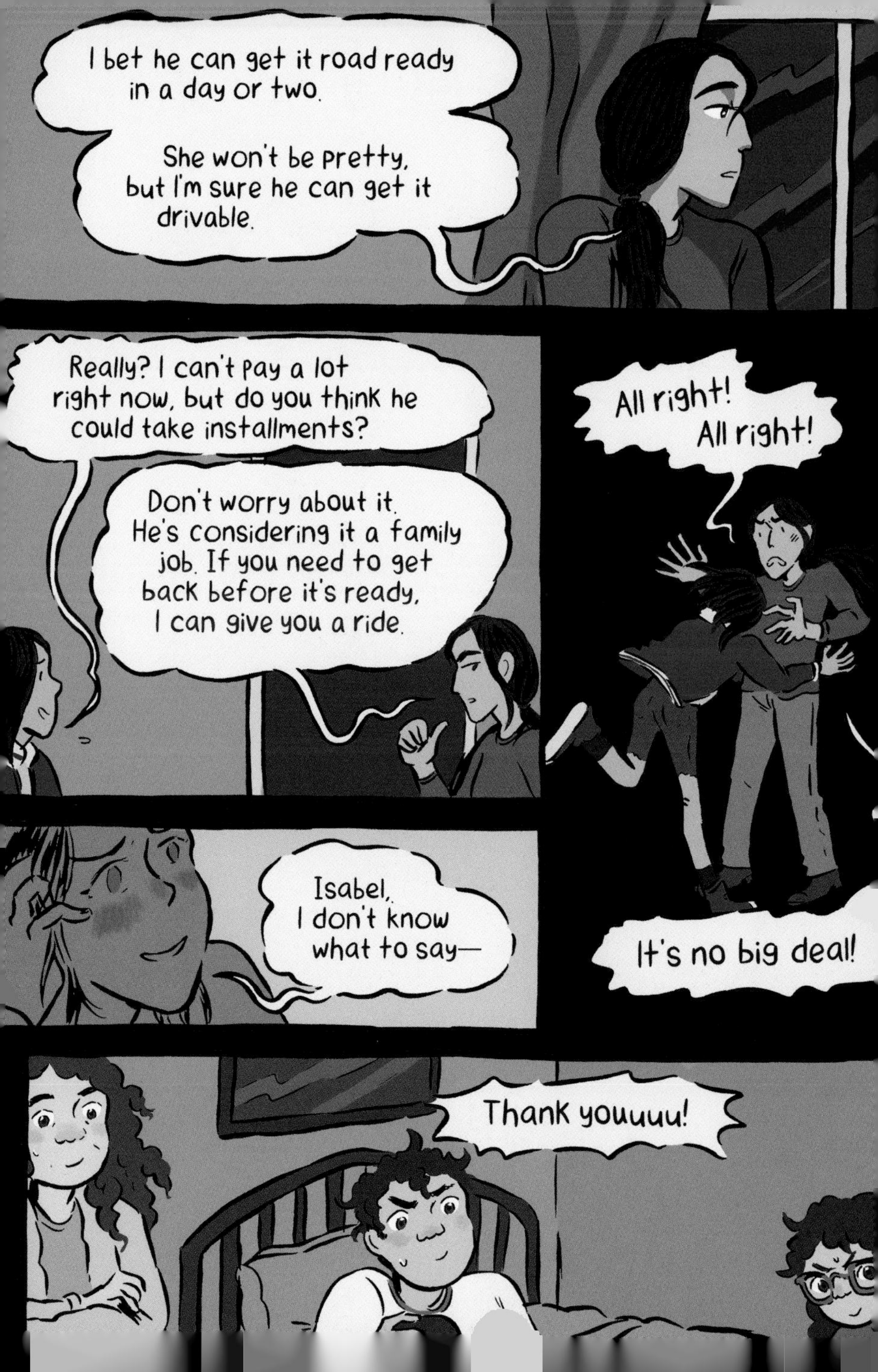
I bet he can get it road ready in a day or two.
She won't be pretty, but I'm sure he can get it drivable.
Really? I can't pay a lot right now, but do you think he could take installments?
Don't worry about it. He's considering it a family job. If you need to get back before it's ready, I can give you a ride.
All right! All right!
Isabel, I don't know what to say—
It's no big deal!
Thank youuuu!

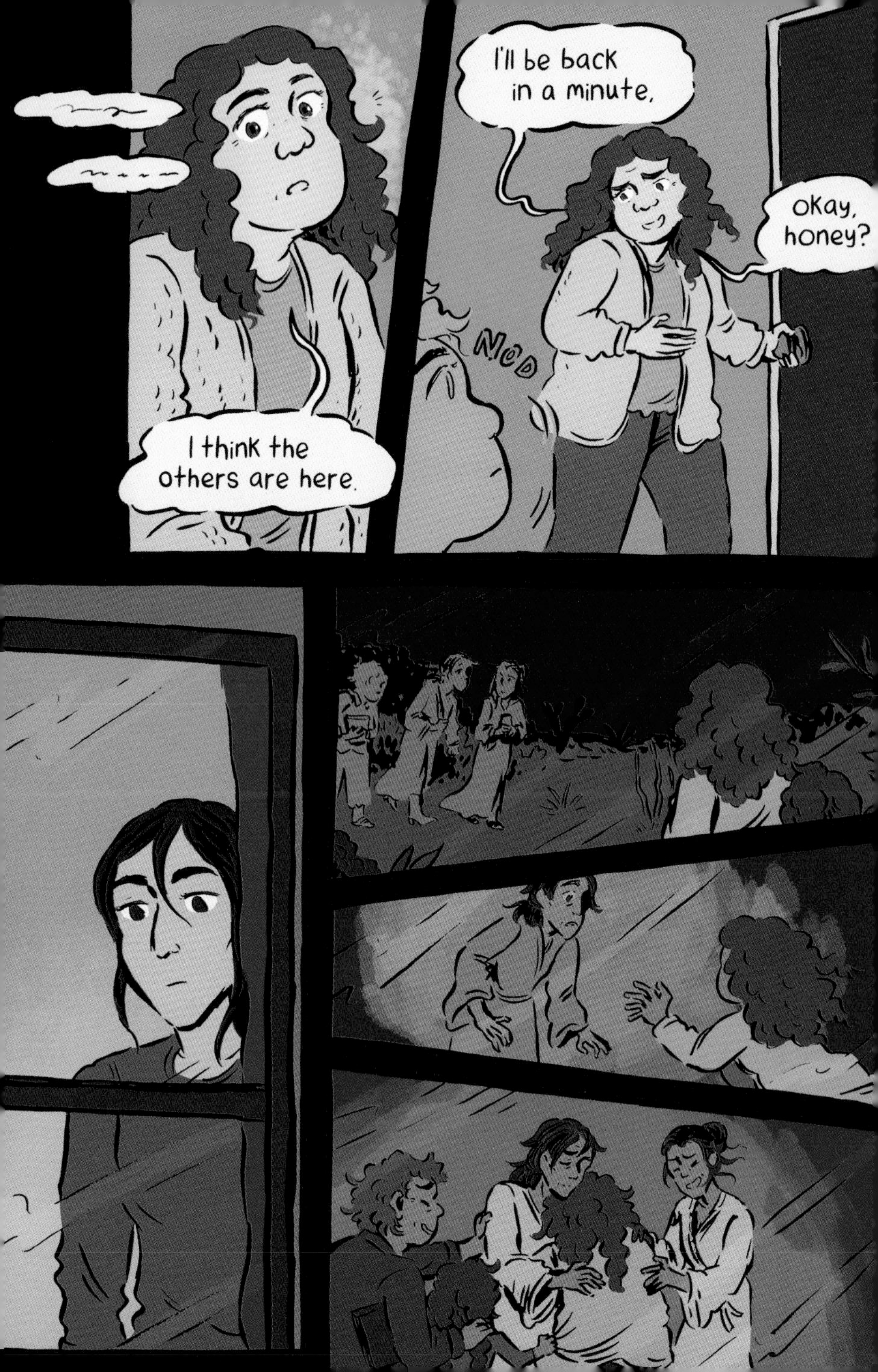
I think the others are here.
I'll be back in a minute,
NOD
Okay, honey?

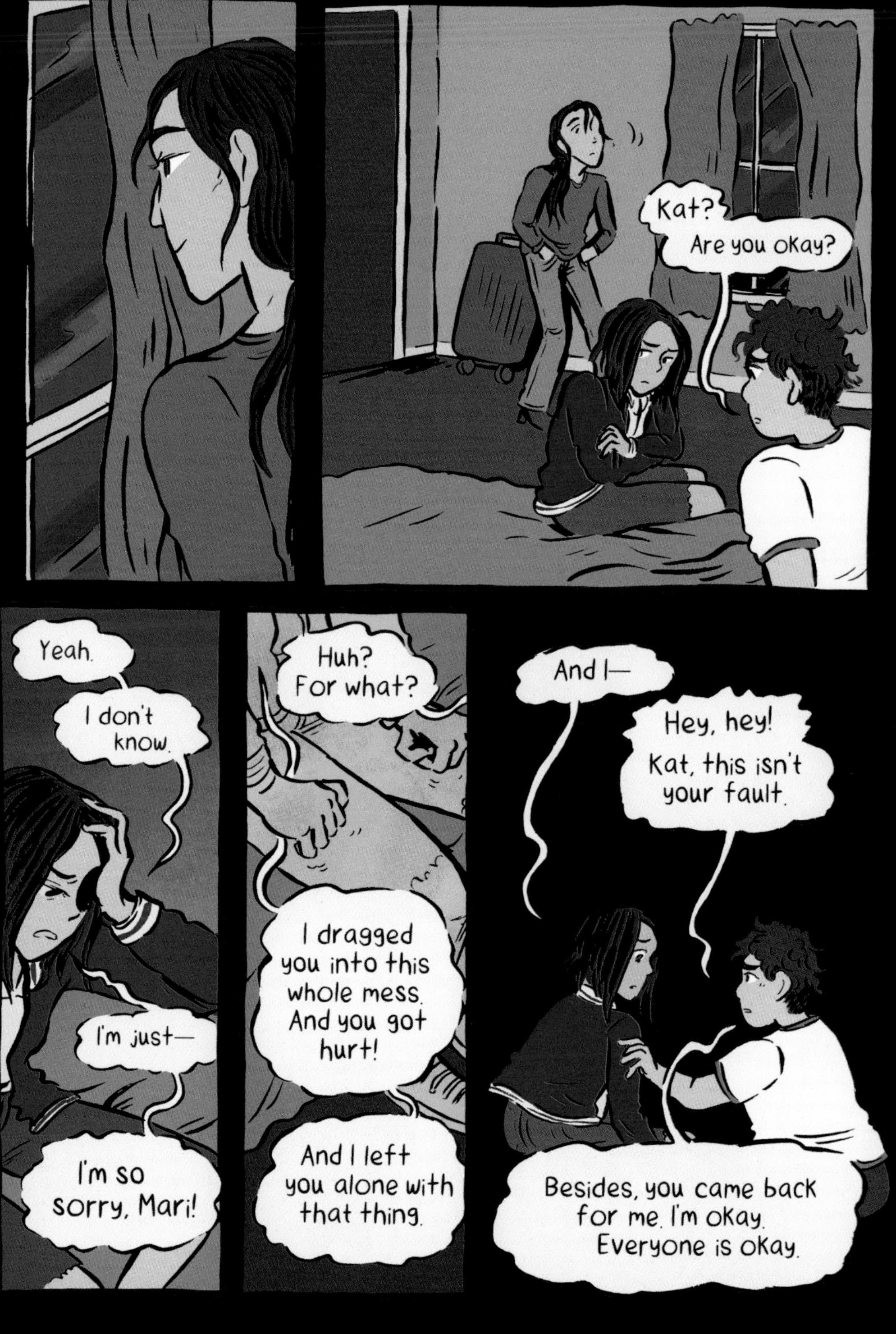

Kat?
Are you okay?
Yeah.
I don't know.
I'm just—
I'm so sorry, Mari!
Huh? For what?
I dragged you into this whole mess. And you got hurt!
And I left you alone with that thing.
And I—
Hey, hey!
Kat, this isn't your fault.
Besides, you came back for me. I'm okay. Everyone is okay.

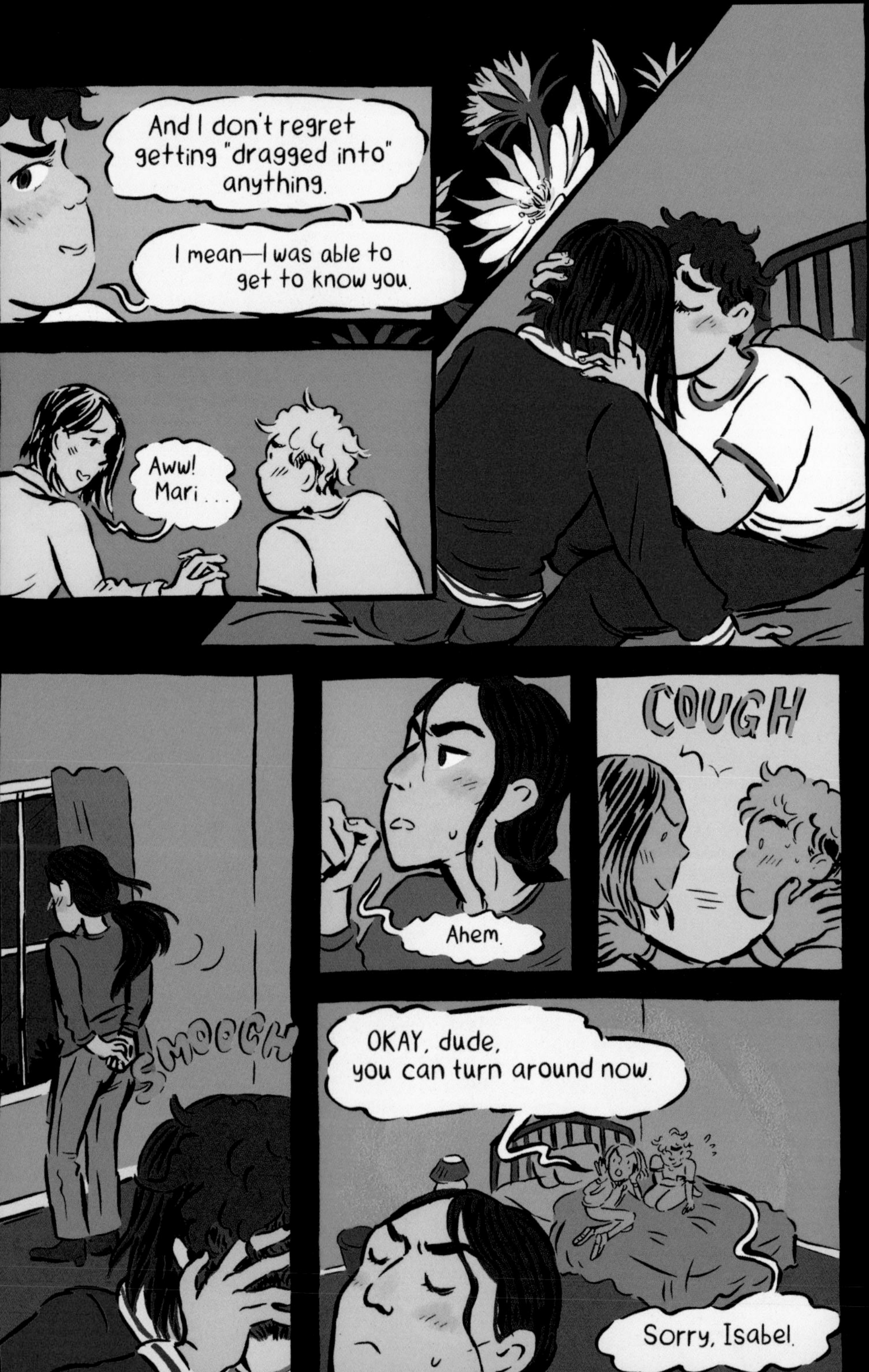
And I don't regret getting "dragged into" anything.
I mean—I was able to get to know you.
Aww! Mari . . .
COUGH
Ahem.
SMOOCH
OKAY, dude, you can turn around now.
Sorry, Isabel.

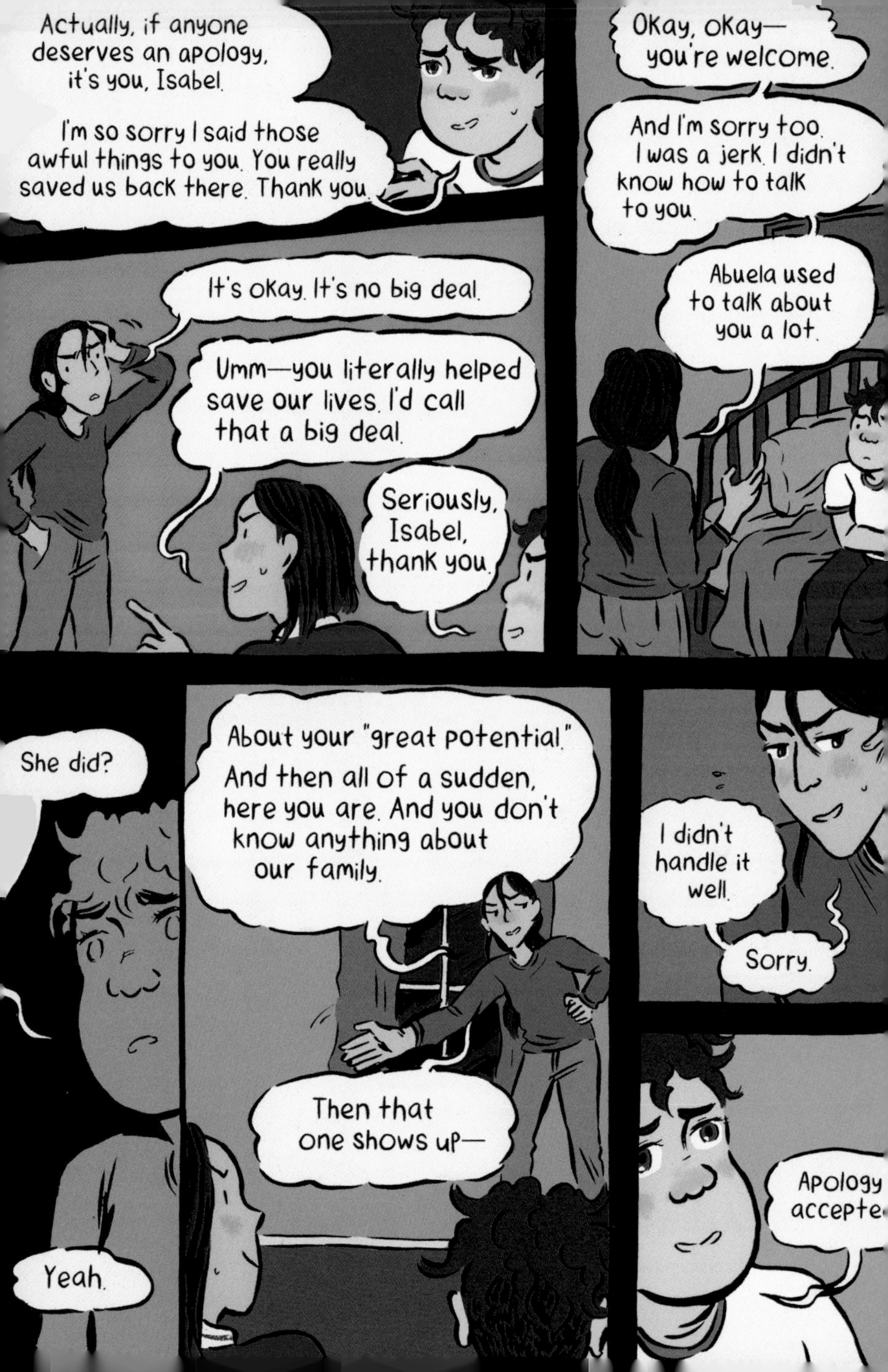
Actually, if anyone deserves an apology, it's you, Isabel.
I'm so sorry I said those awful things to you. You really saved us back there. Thank you.
Okay, okay— you're welcome.
And I'm sorry too. I was a jerk. I didn't know how to talk to you.
It's okay. It's no big deal.
Umm—you literally helped save our lives. I'd call that a big deal.
Seriously, Isabel, thank you.
Abuela used to talk about you a lot.
She did?
Yeah.
About your "great potential."
And then all of a sudden, here you are. And you don't know anything about our family.
Then that one shows up—
I didn't handle it well.
Sorry.
Apology accepte

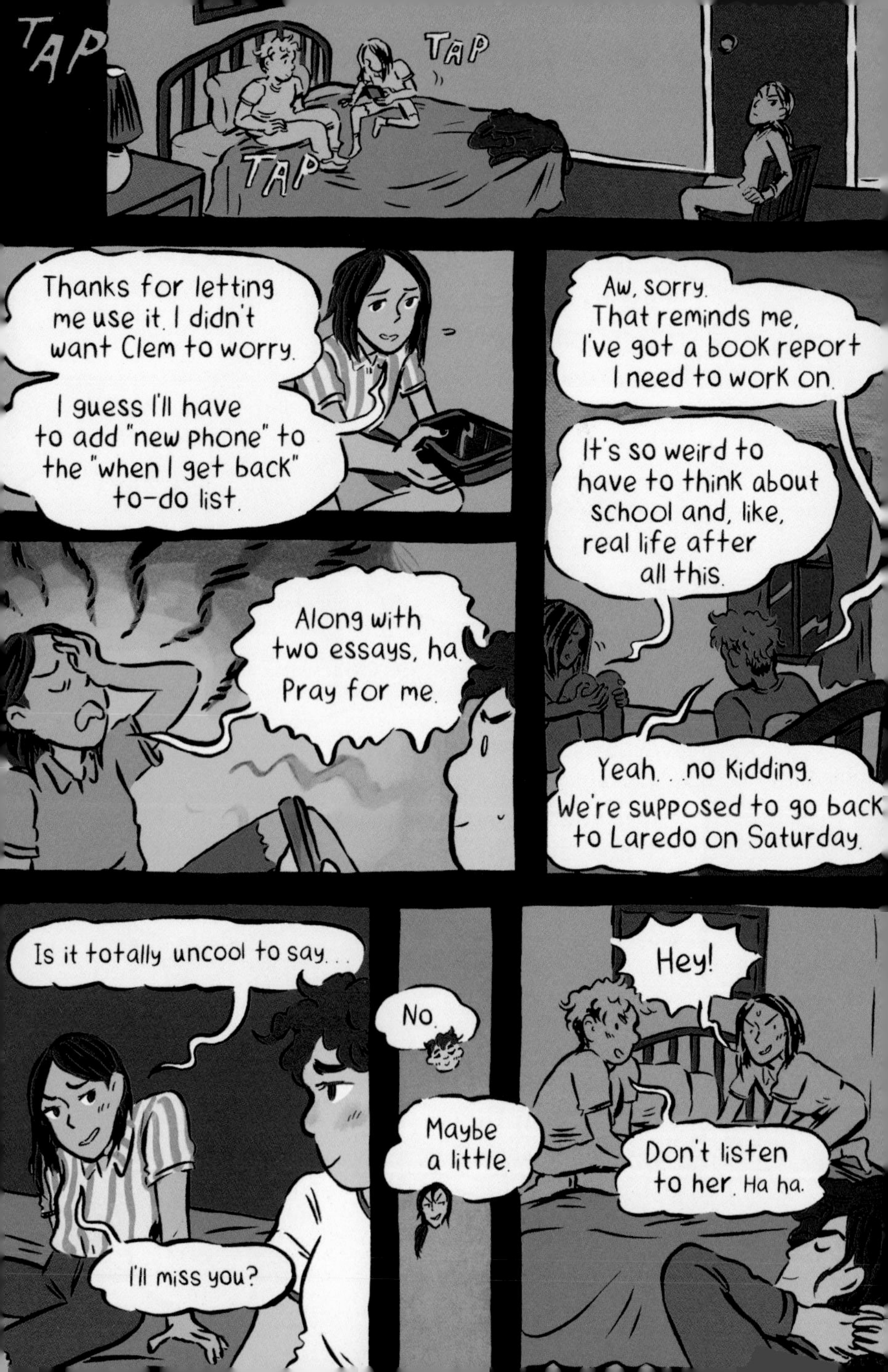
TAP
TAP
TAP
Thanks for letting me use it. I didn't want Clem to worry.
I guess I'll have to add "new phone" to the "when I get back" to-do list.
Aw, sorry. That reminds me, I've got a book report I need to work on.
It's so weird to have to think about school and, like, real life after all this.
Along with two essays, ha. Pray for me.
Yeah. . .no kidding. We're supposed to go back to Laredo on Saturday.
Is it totally uncool to say. . .
I'll miss you?
No.
Maybe a little.
Hey!
Don't listen to her. Ha ha.

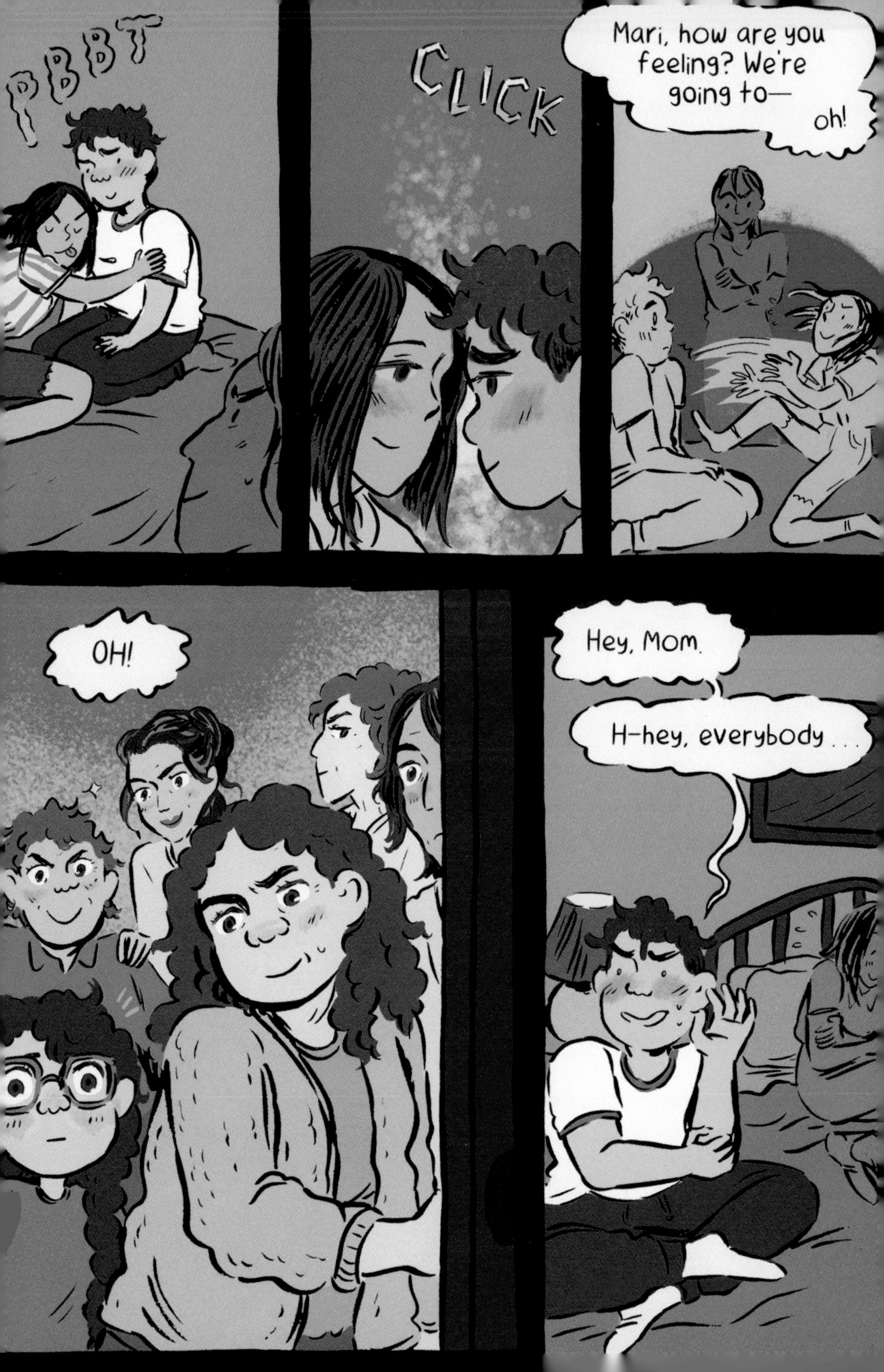
PBBT
CLICK
Mari, how are you feeling? We're going to—
oh!
OH!
Hey, Mom.
H-hey, everybody . . .

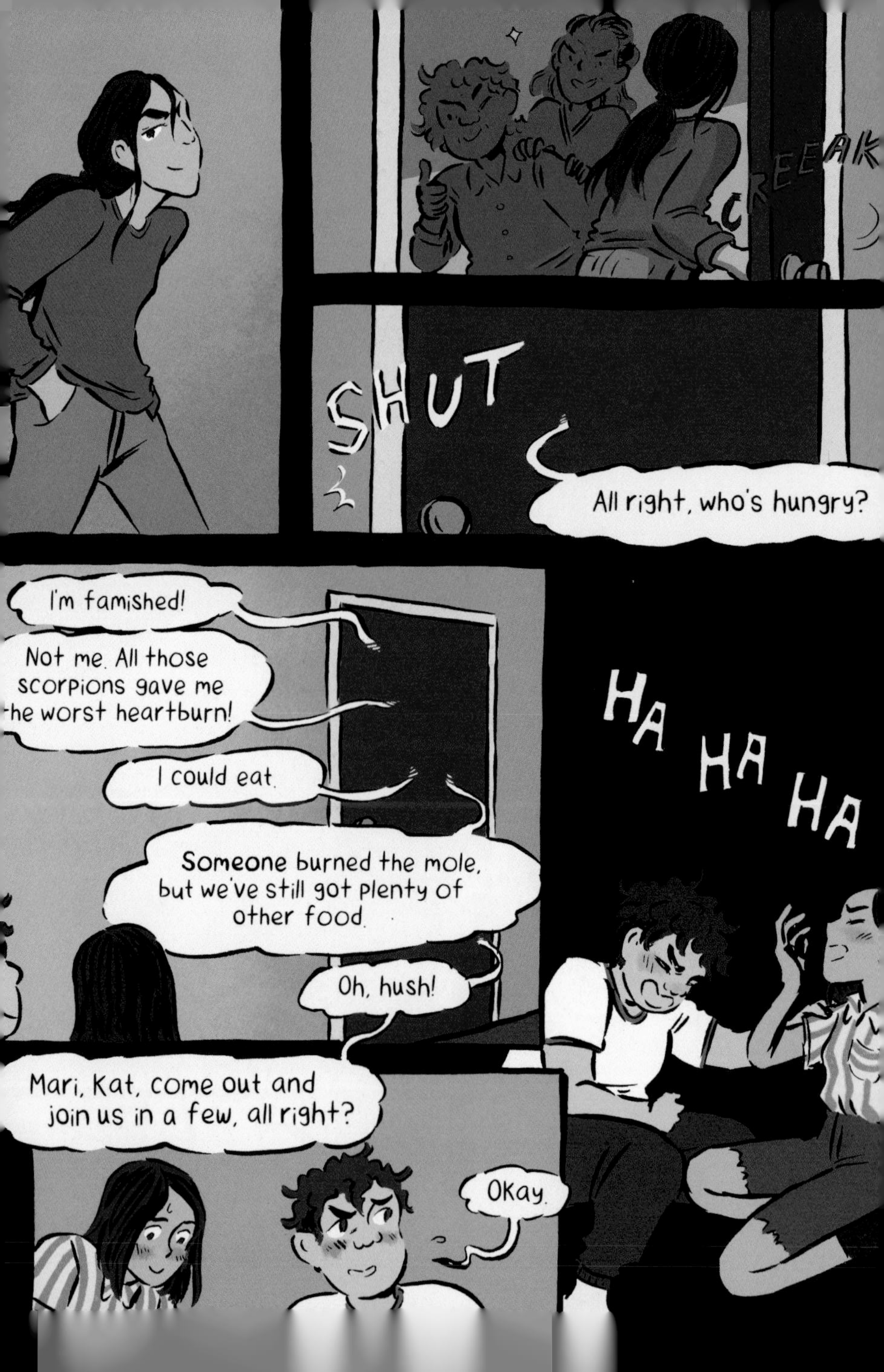
CREEAK
SHUT
All right, who's hungry?
I'm famished!
Not me. All those scorpions gave me the worst heartburn!
I could eat.
Someone burned the mole, but we've still got plenty of other food.
Oh, hush!
HA HA HA HA
Mari, Kat, come out and join us in a few, all right?
Okay.

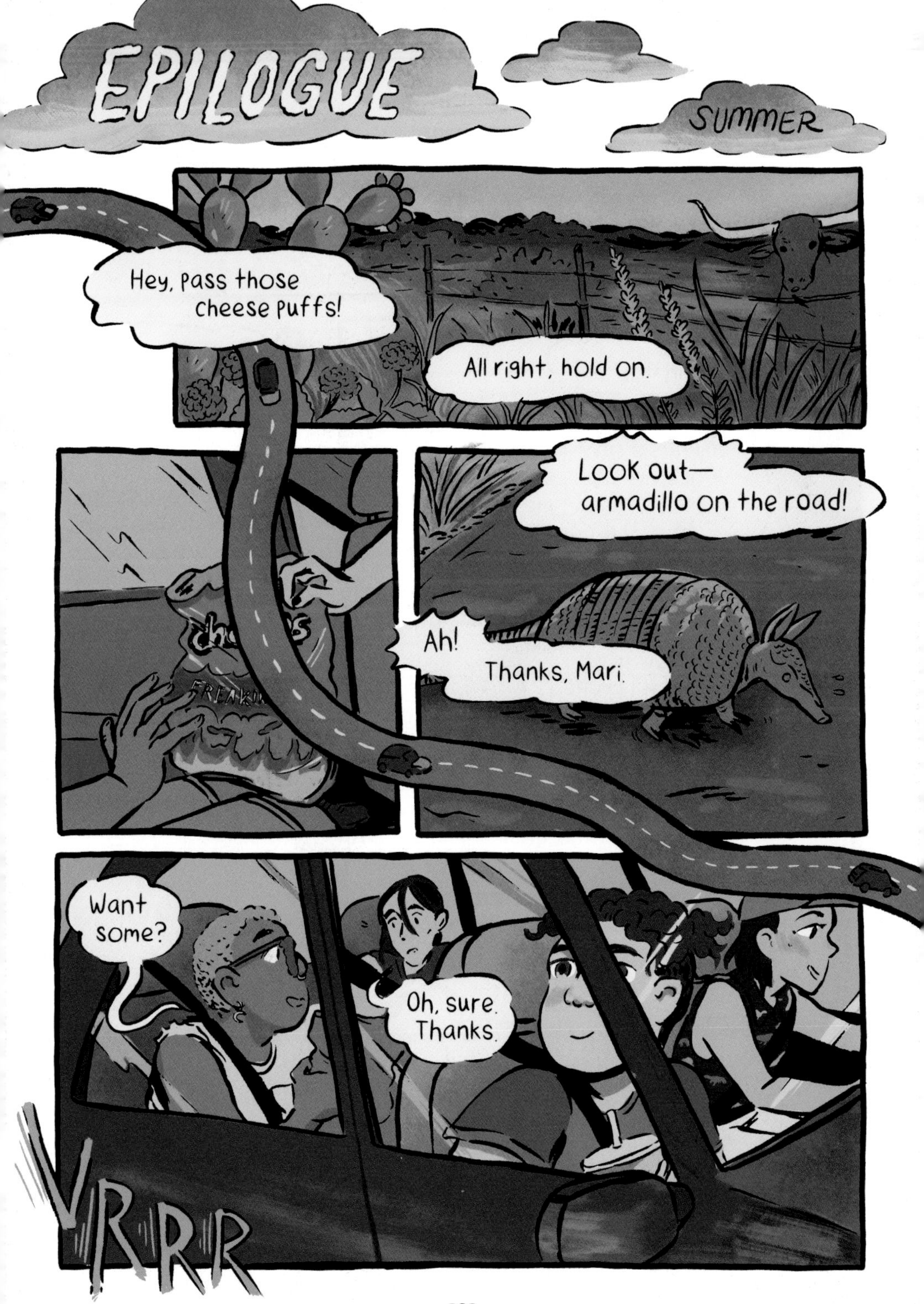
EPILOGUE
SUMMER
Hey, pass those cheese puffs!
All right, hold on.
Look out— armadillo on the road!
Ah!
Thanks, Mari.
Want some?
Oh, sure. Thanks.
VRRR

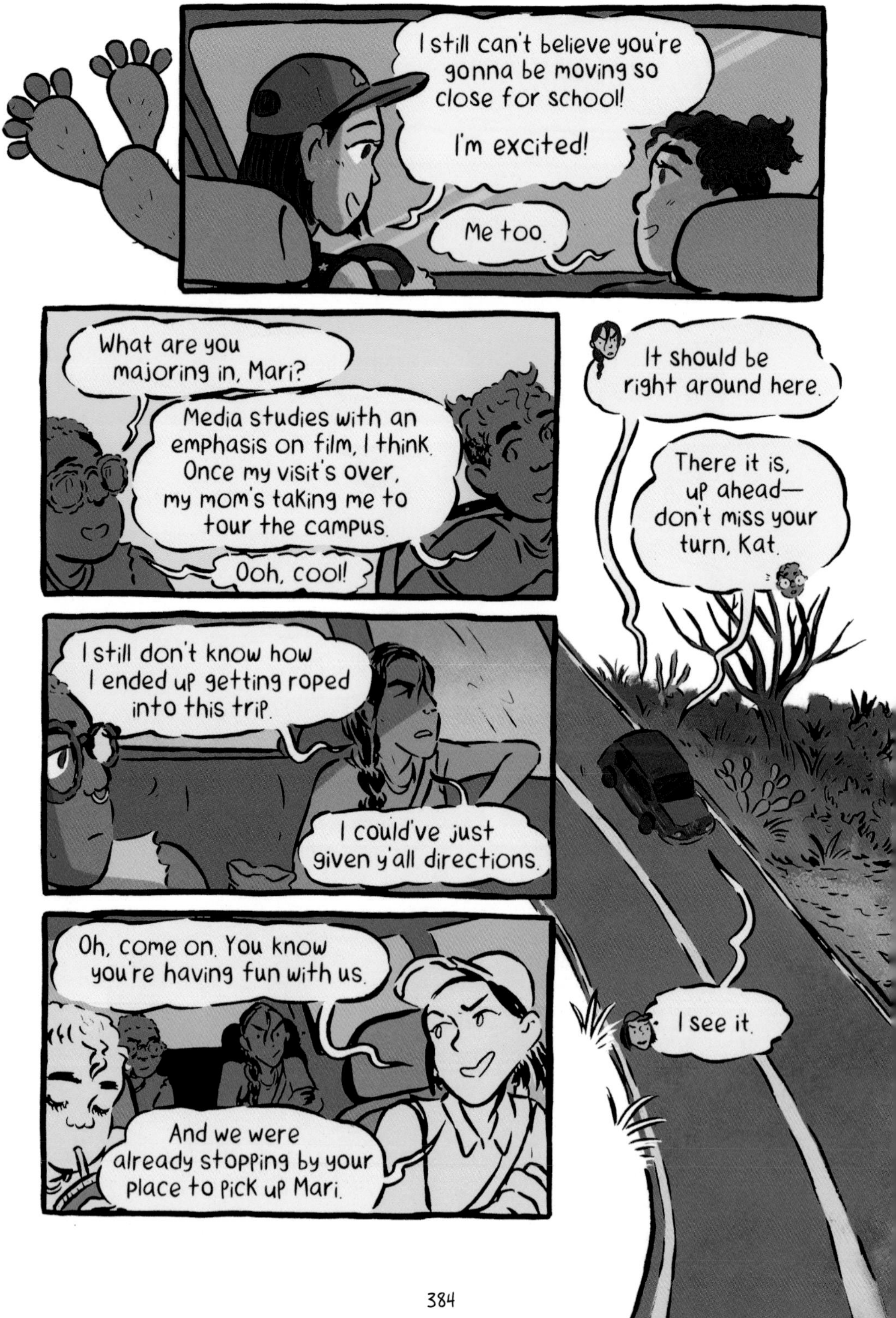
I still can't believe you're gonna be moving so close for school!
I'm excited!
Me too.
What are you majoring in, Mari?
Media studies with an emphasis on film, I think. Once my visit's over, my mom's taking me to tour the campus.
Ooh, cool!
It should be right around here.
There it is, up ahead— don't miss your turn, Kat.
I still don't know how I ended up getting roped into this trip.
I could've just given y'all directions.
Oh, come on. You know you're having fun with us.
And we were already stopping by your place to pick up Mari.
I see it.

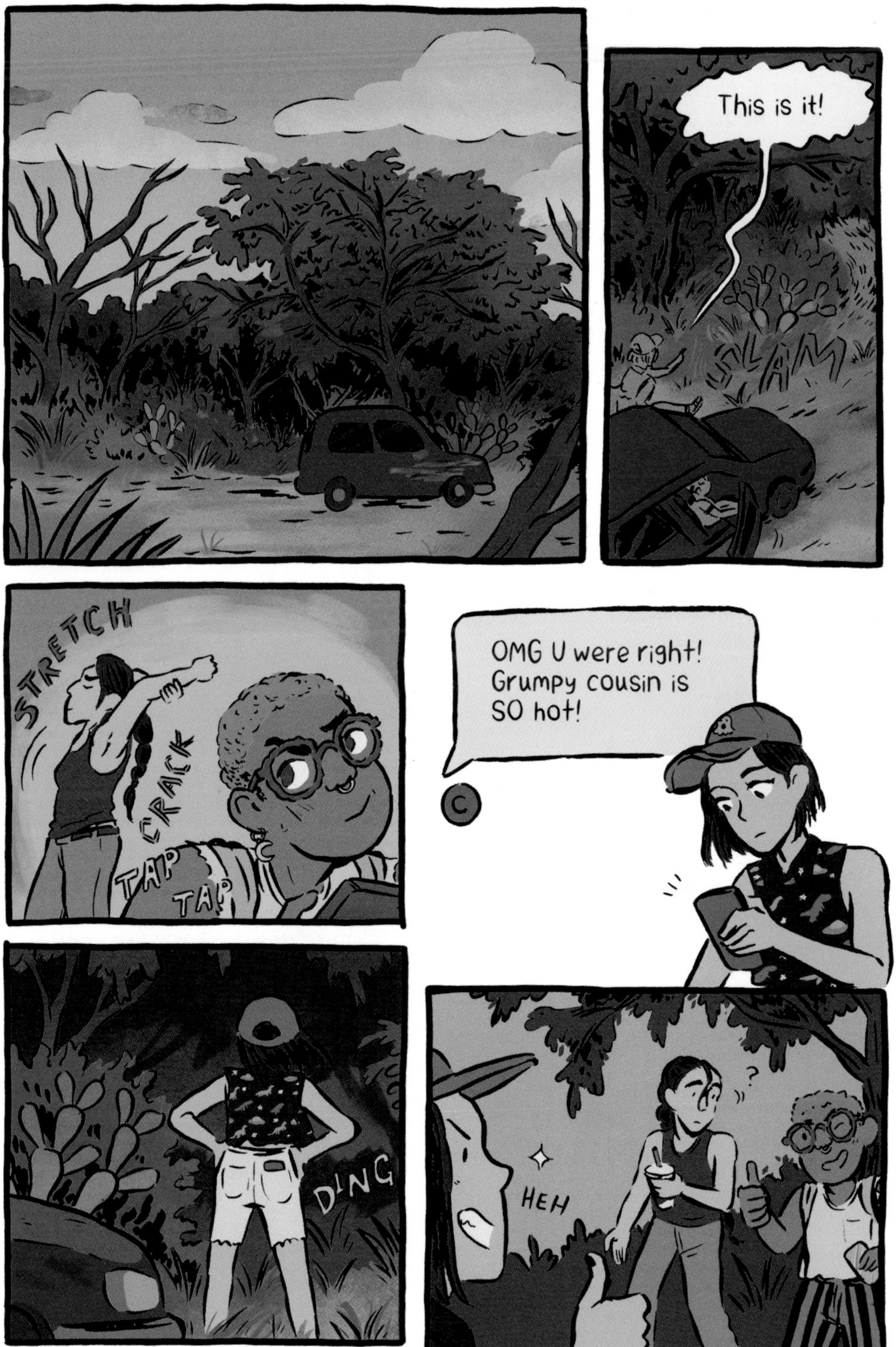
This is it!
SLAM
STRETCH
CRACK
TAP
TAP
OMG U were right!
Grumpy cousin is
SO hot!
DING
HEH
?

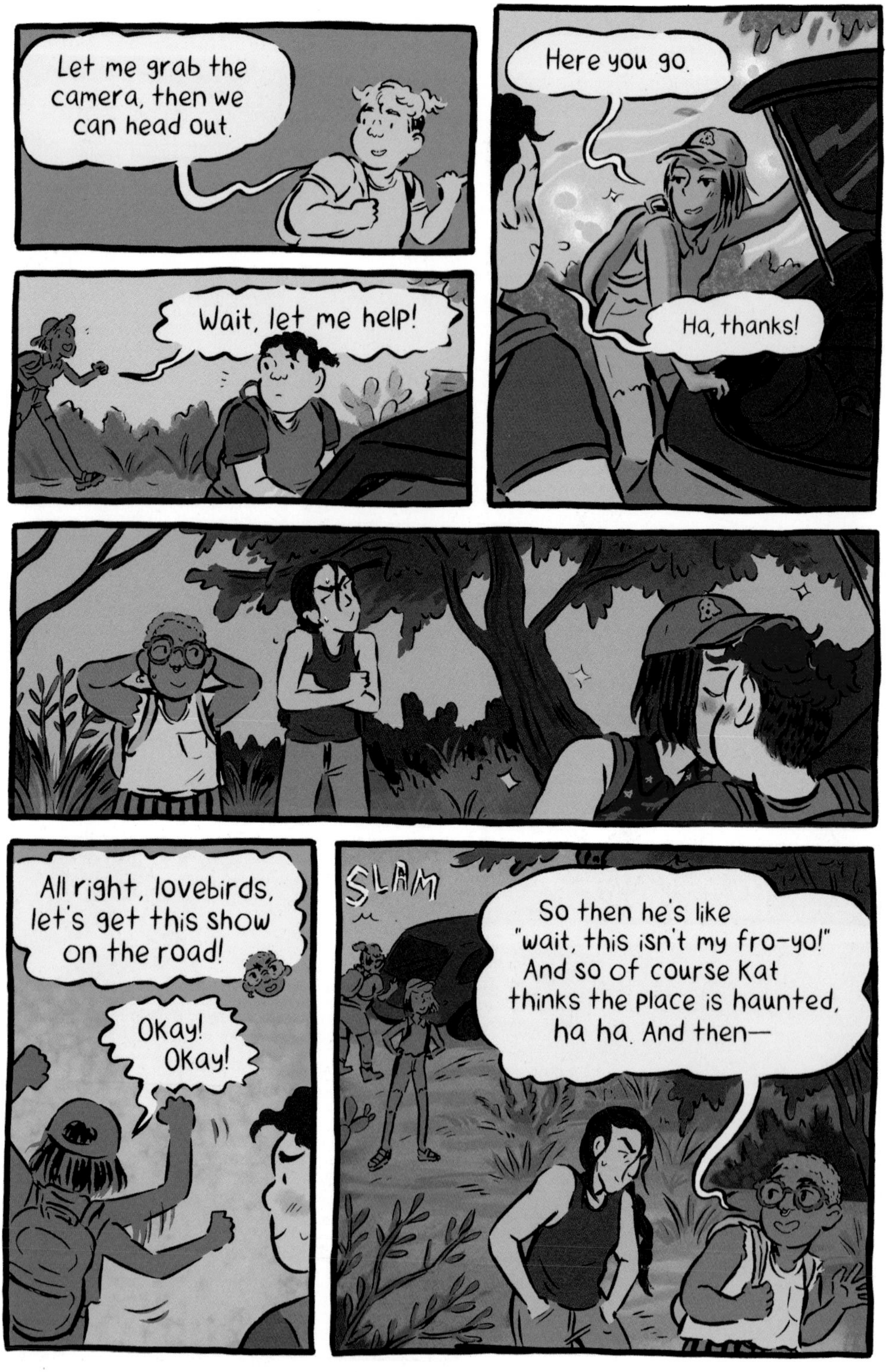

Let me grab the camera, then we can head out.
Here you go.
Wait, let me help!
Ha, thanks!
All right, lovebirds, let's get this show on the road!
Okay! Okay!
SLAM
So then he's like "wait, this isn't my fro-yo!" And so of course Kat thinks the place is haunted, ha ha. And then—

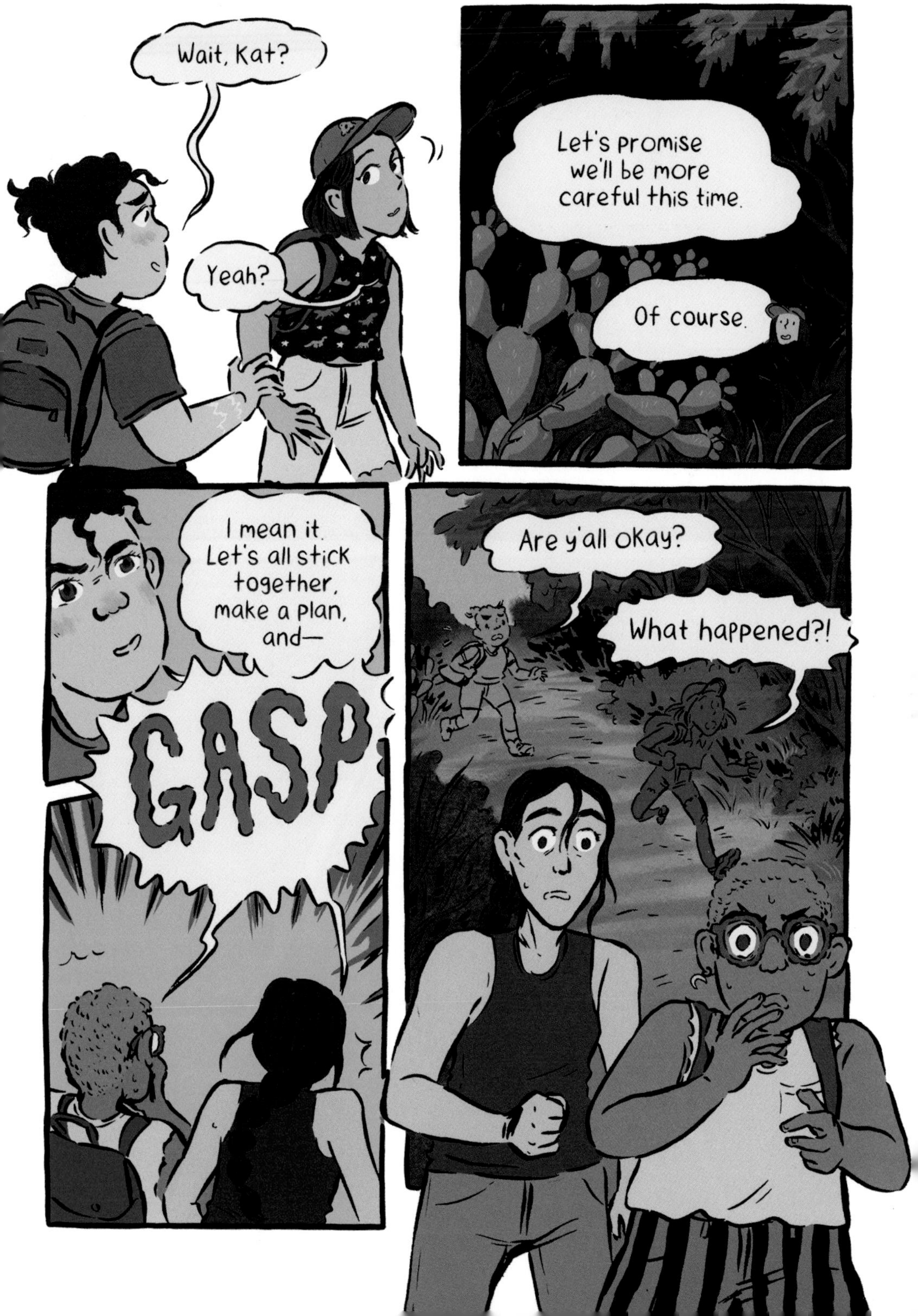
Wait, Kat?
Yeah?
Let's promise we'll be more careful this time.
Of course.
I mean it. Let's all stick together, make a plan, and—
GASP!
Are y'all okay?
What happened?!

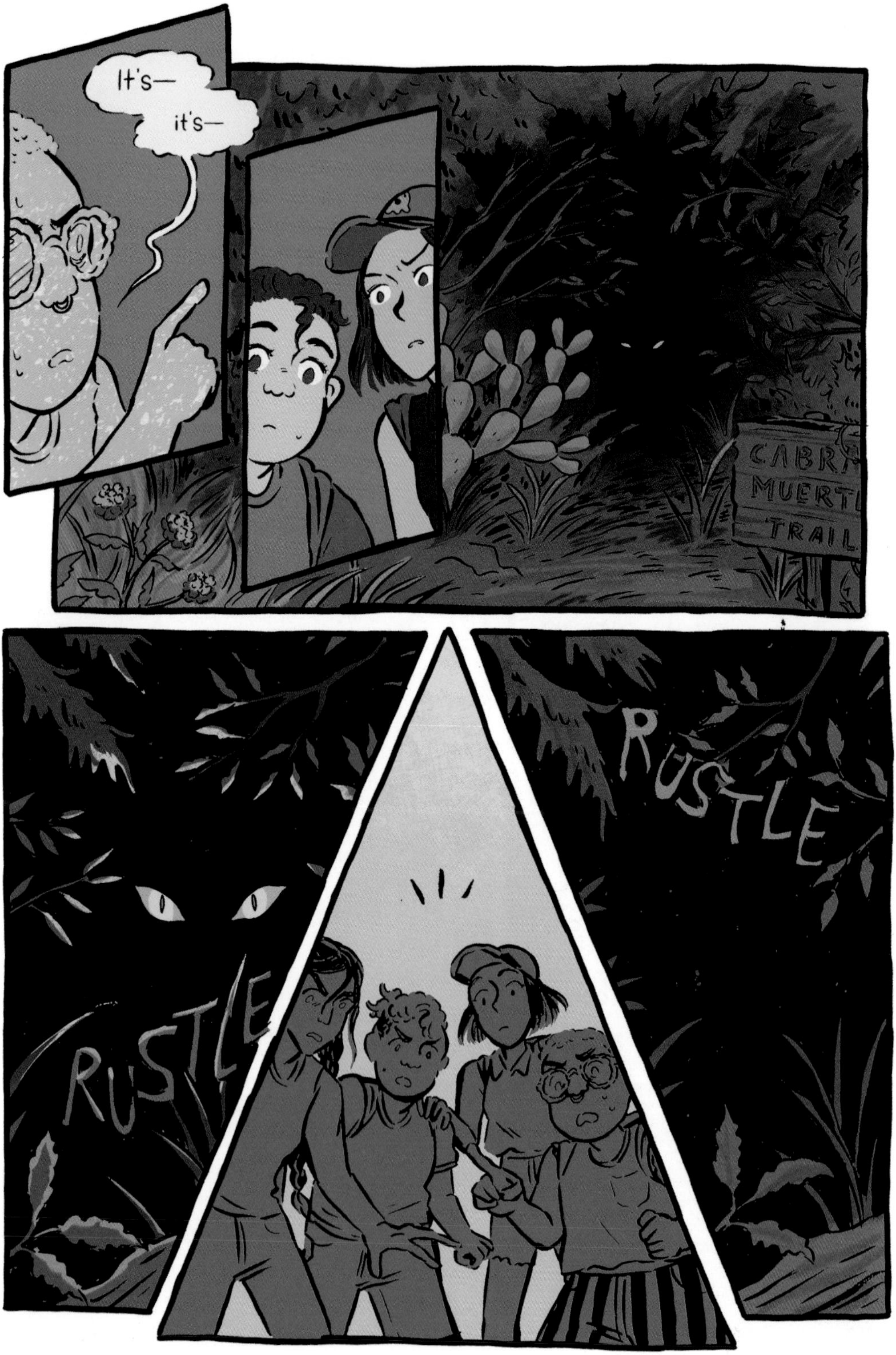
It's—
it's—
CABRA MUERTA TRAIL
RUSTLE
RUSTLE

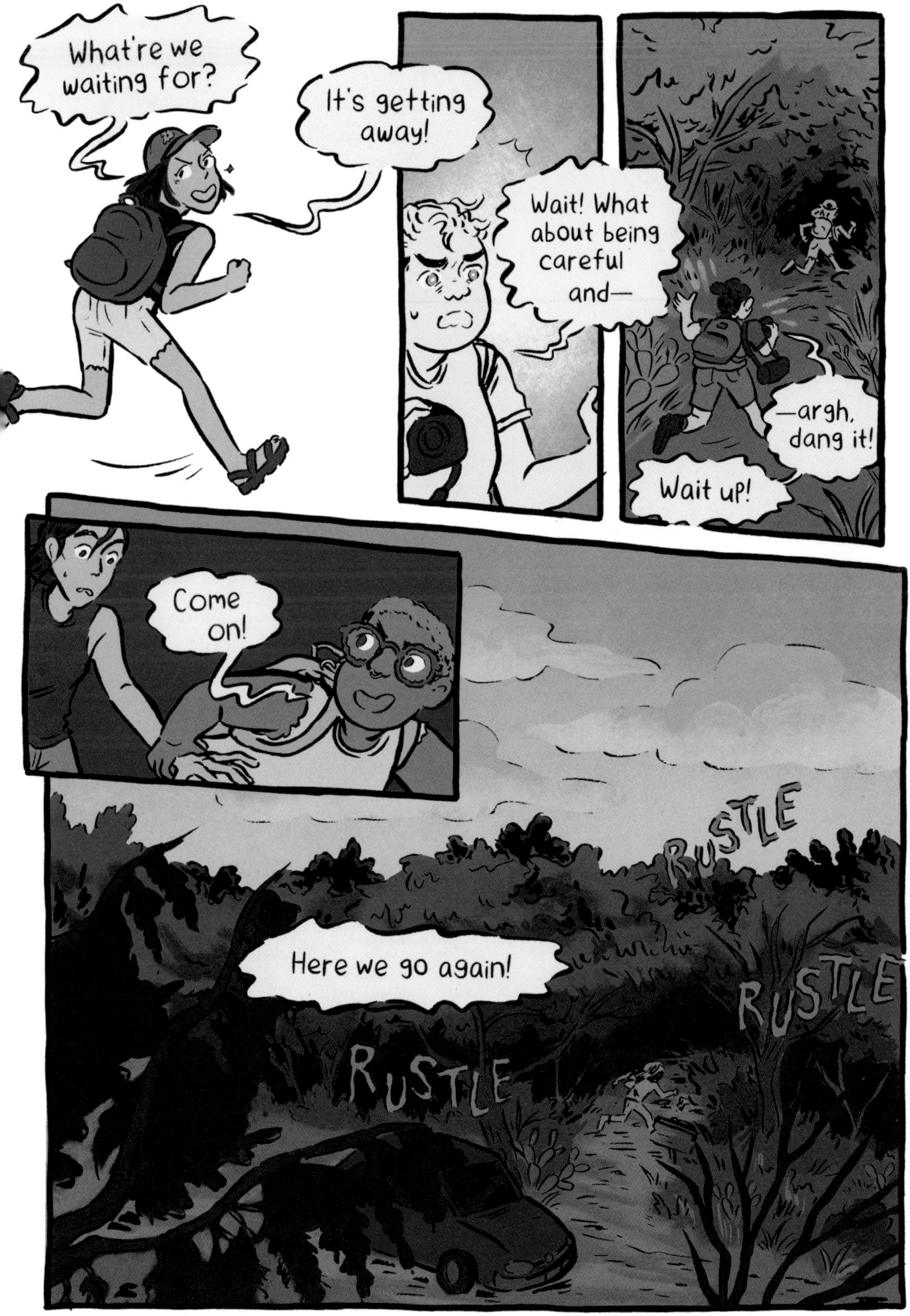
What're we waiting for?
It's getting away!
Wait! What about being careful and—
—argh, dang it!
Wait up!
Come on!
RUSTLE
Here we go again!
RUSTLE
RUSTLE

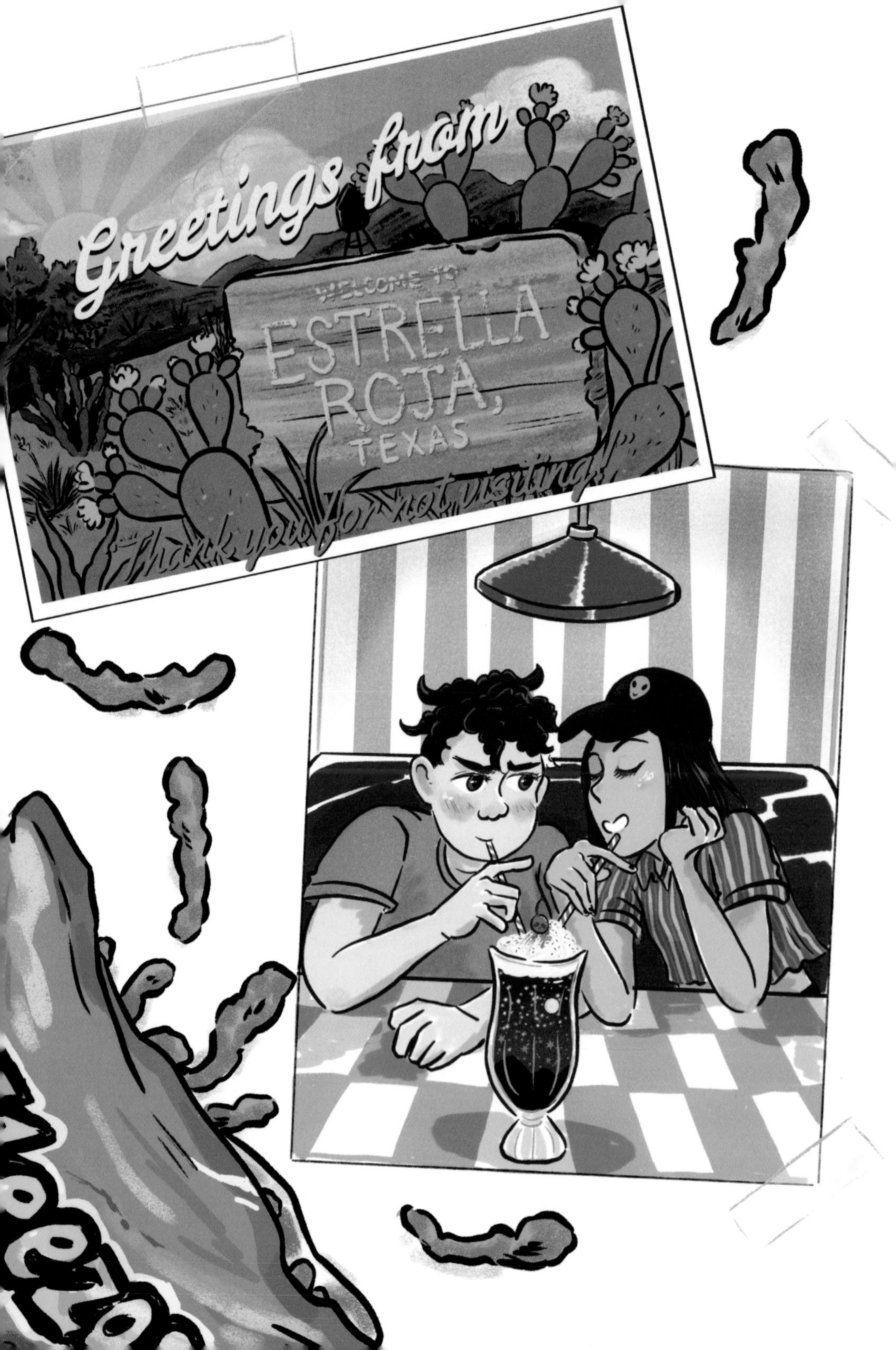
Greetings from
WELCOME TO
ESTRELLA ROJA,
TEXAS
Thank you for not visiting!

Development of The Hills of Estrella Roja

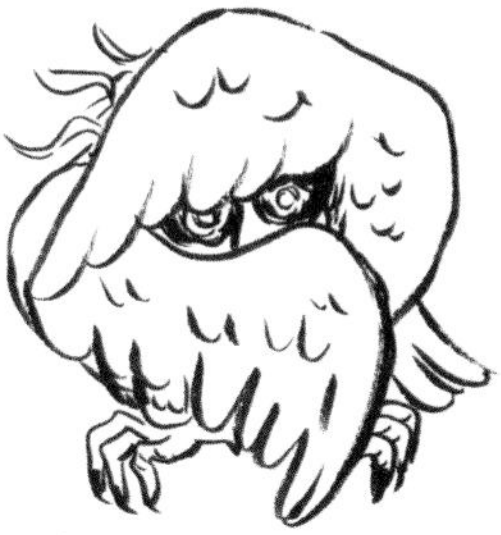

The very first sketch of Kat & Mari— February 2020

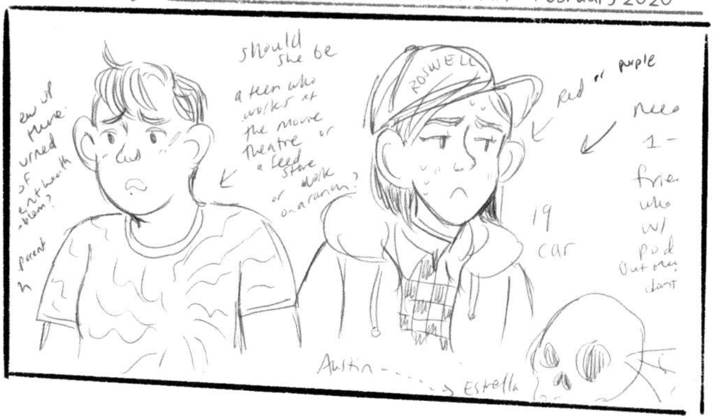
should she be a teen who works at the movie theatre or a feed store or work on a ranch?
ROSWELL
Red or purple
19
car
Austin ----> Estella

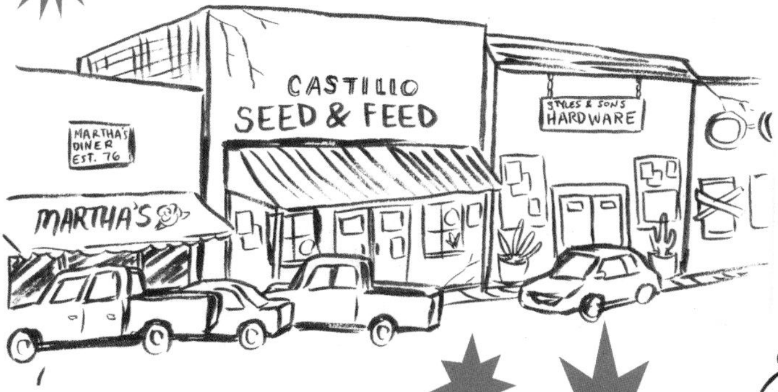
CASTILLO
SEED & FEED
STYLES & SONS
HARDWARE
MARTHA'S DINER EST. 76
MARTHA'S

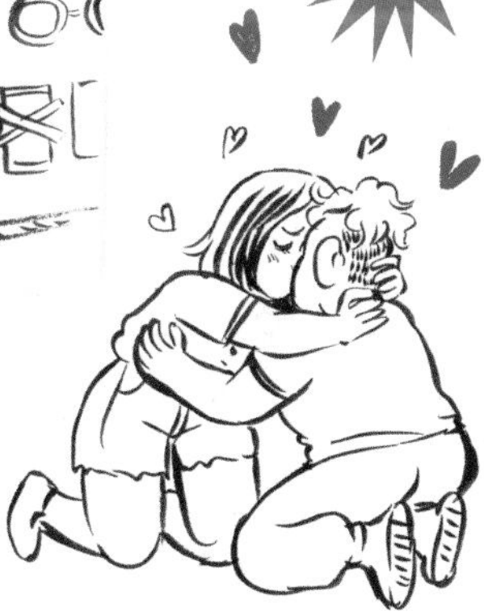

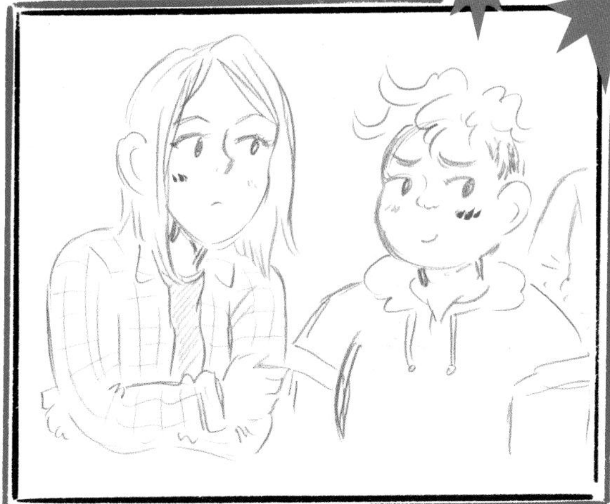

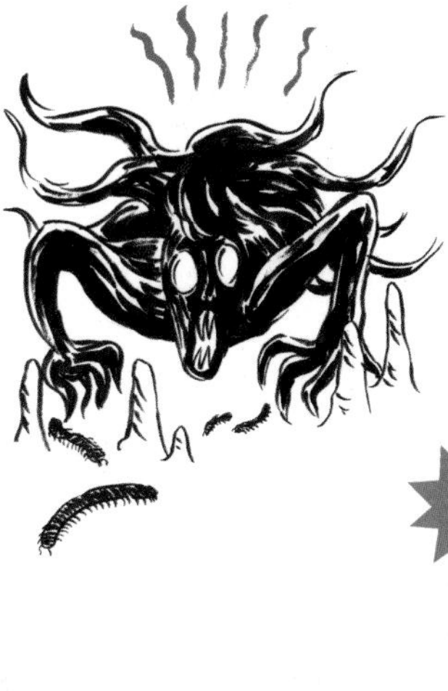

My drawing materials:

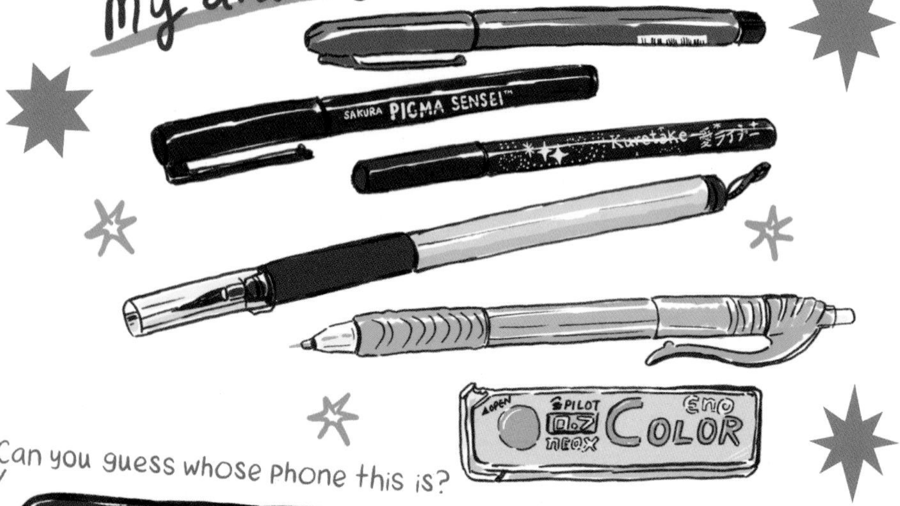
SAKURA PIGMA SENSEI™
Kuretake
OPEN
PILOT 0.7 neox
eno COLOR

Can you guess whose phone this is?

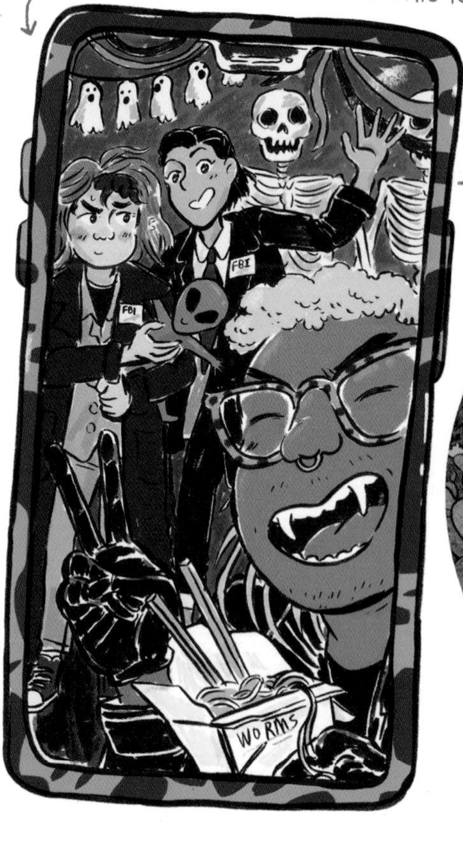
FBI
FBI
WORMS

The Hills of Estrella Roja was drawn traditionally with brush pens on 9 x 12 bristol paper, then the pages were sent over to Nakata Whittle to color.

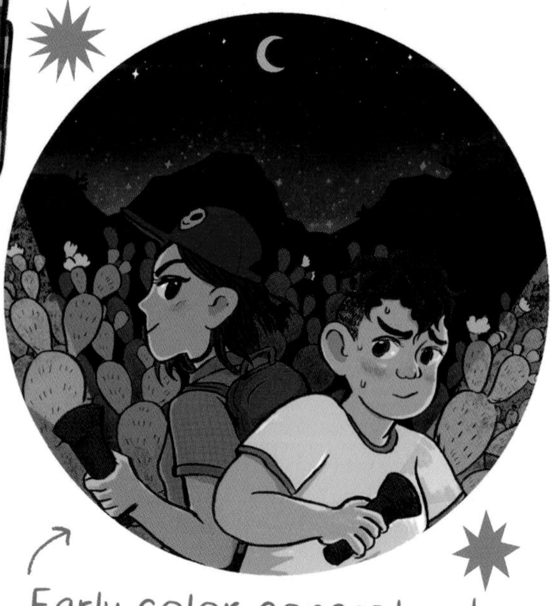

Early color concept art

 # Acknowledgments

Oh my gosh, y'all! So much goes into the creation of a book, and I have so many people to thank! Here goes nothing!

Special thanks to Deanna, Morgan, Steffany, Birdney, Shelby, Max, and Kat. Thanks for being excited about *The Hills of Estrella Roja*, for all your support, and for letting me talk your ears off/send a million process pics and requests for opinions. Kat, thanks for letting me ask you so many questions at the start of this project, and for getting coffee and drawing with me. Your insight was invaluable. Steff, thanks for the special Fridays. Morgan, thanks for crying with excitement when I showed you the cover over brunch—I'll never forget that. Bird, for the goofs, but also the very good process talks. Shelby, for going with me on the retreat where this book first started to come together—you're its official godparent. Max, for the amazing author photo and all the kindness. Deanna, for your constant, unending support.

There are so many more of you—thanks to all my buds who celebrated my book deal, got coffee with me, or just asked me how my first graphic novel was going. I'm truly lucky to have so many amazing folks in my life. I also want to thank all the friends I've made through making comics, posting work online, and going to fests. Thank you to everyone who has made me feel welcome, bought one of my books, or just said something nice and encouraging IRL or online—I couldn't have gotten to this point without y'all.

Thanks to my parents—

Mom, for telling me the creepy story of the lechuza that you learned from your own mother. It clearly stuck with me all these years. Also for my inherited love of horror.

Dad, for filling my life with art from the very beginning, and for that time when you bought me expensive manga supplies on the internet when I was a tween. Also, thank you for the battered copy of *Anatomy for the Artist* that you gave me who knows how long ago—I always pull it out when it's time to draw bones.

Thanks to Cameron and Sarah for giving me a good reason to head out West, where I saw the Marfa lights and had a very creepy owl encounter. Thanks to Lynna and Brad as well for making me feel so welcome on that trip.

An extra special thanks to Chloe for all the pep talks and belief in me and my stories. Thanks for letting me ramble on and on excitedly about early 2000s horror movies that you've never heard of, for celebrating with me, and for always reminding me to take breaks, be kind to myself, and be a human. I sprinkled in a couple of little things just for you in this book—I hope you like them.

Thanks so much to Liz Yerby for organizing an amazing artist retreat in

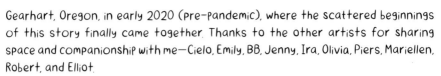

Gearhart, Oregon, in early 2020 (pre-pandemic), where the scattered beginnings of this story finally came together. Thanks to the other artists for sharing space and companionship with me—Cielo, Emily, BB, Jenny, Ira, Olivia, Piers, Mariellen, Robert, and Elliot.

I also want to extend a mountain of gratitude to everyone who's taken a chance on my work before, especially the folks at Pome, where some of my earliest comics found a digital home, and Silver Sprocket, an amazing indie publisher that I've loved making books with.

My final thanks are for the folks who've helped me make *The Hills of Estrella Roja* directly—

Maria Vicente, my wonderful agent—your guidance, insights, and belief in this project have meant the world to me. I couldn't have done it without you! I'm so glad to have you in my corner.

Lily Kessinger, my editor—for being so easy to work with and for your endless enthusiasm. I could tell from the start you really clicked with the story and I knew Kat and Mari would be in good hands.

Thank you so much to my amazing colorist, Nakata Whittle. You're a coloring superstar and a wonderful collaborator, and you really helped bring Estrella Roja to life. I truly appreciate all the time and work you put into this book. Thanks for helping me make my dream come true!

Thank you also to Mary Verhoeven, who was first signed on to be the colorist. Even though it didn't work out because of scheduling, your excitement for the story and support meant a lot to me—and thanks for letting me send you cool pics of cacti!

Thanks to Bones Leopard and the rest of the design team for really rolling with all my ideas and making the book shine. Thank you also to Carolina and Emilia for getting us through the final stretch. A special thank you to all the hardworking folks over at Clarion/Harper that I didn't get to work directly with—I appreciate y'all so much!

And one more! Many, many thanks to you, the reader. Stories are nothing without someone to tell them to. I hope you enjoyed your visit to Estrella Roja.

Until we meet again—